What would *you* sacrifice?

THE MODIFIED

C.A. KUNZ

Cover design by Sarah Hansen
and logo illustration by Nathan Szerdy

For all of our wonderful supporters. We love each and every one of you, and appreciate everything you do for us. We're extremely lucky to have you all in our lives.

First Printing

ISBN-13: 978-1480040311 (pbk)
ISBN-10: 1480040312 (pbk)

C.A. Kunz, LLC
Orlando, Florida

------------ Acknowledgements ------------

First we'd like to thank Robert Kunz, Tim Coleman, Charlie Steffy, Matt Boggs, Andrew Nocar, and Stephen R. Burkett for being our A-list supporters, dedicated readers, much-needed critics, and beta readers. We're truly grateful for all of your assistance throughout this whole process.

A huge thank you should go to Lee Wilson who has been hard at work on a truly awesome companion soundtrack for The Modified. You're an incredibly talented musician and engineer, and we're very lucky to have your help and support on this project.

Tremendous thanks should go to Sarah Hansen for designing an absolutely stunning cover for us. You've seriously given us something very eye catching and stupendous. We can't thank you enough for sharing your talent with us and our book!

Very special thanks to our wonderful editor Hollie Westring. We absolutely love you and all you do to help clean up our writing! You have yet again made one of our books much more polished and refined.

An extremely special shout out goes to all our Paranormal Plumes Society sisters! We can't thank you all enough for your love and support. You are hands down the best group of women we have the privilege of calling friends.

HUGE thanks to all of the super fantastic bloggers that have helped us spread the word about The Modified. These awesome ladies do this because they want to, and not because they're being paid to. Every single one of you has helped us in ways you can't even imagine. We truly appreciate your support and words of encouragement. We can't even begin to thank you enough for all you do:

Mindy (Fangedmom) Janicke from Books Complete Me

Michele Luker from Insane About Books

Megan McDade from Reading Away The Days

Kerry-Ann McDade from Reading a Little Bit of Everything

Becky Paulk from Book Bite Reviews

Alex from Blethering About Books

Katelyn Torrey from Kate's Tales of Books and Bands

Brittni Guillen from Britt Reads Indie

Tess M. Watson from My Pathway to Books

Heather Robbins from SupaGurl Books

Adriane Tait-Boyd from The Indie Bookshelf

Taneesha Freidus from A Diary of A Book Addict

Inga Silberg from Me and Reading

Katrina Whittaker from Page Flipperz

Jackie McPherson from Sated Faery

Tanya Contois from All Things Books

Rachel Marks from Young Adult Novel Reader

Amber and Rosmelie from Me Myshelf and I

Thanks to *you*, our readers, for reading our books. By performing this simple act you are helping us make a lifelong dream come true and you have no idea how much you mean to us.

Finally, we cannot forget to thank all of our wonderful family and friends. Your love and support keep us always moving forward, and for this we are eternally grateful.

Contents

Chapter One
The Draft

"Don't worry, Little Bit. I'll be back before you know it."
Those were the last words my brother said to me before he went
off to war. I never heard his voice again. Though it's been almost
two years since Dylan's passing, the pain I still feel makes it seem
like it only happened yesterday.

As I sit here looking around the large stadium full of
seventeen-year-olds, who like me are waiting to become soldiers,
I witness a mix of emotions. Some are scared, some nervous,
some even seem a little eager. I'm the latter. The war we're all
being forced into is the one that took my older brother from me,
and now I'm being put into the same position he was in when he
turned seventeen.

• • •

1

The Draft

Who knew our first encounter with a life form outside Earth would cause an intergalactic war to break out? We definitely weren't prepared for it, that's for sure. It has the entire world scrambling to find anyone to fight for our unified cause. No one knows exactly why the war even started in the first place, but once it did, we lost a lot of soldiers. So Earth's government, the Allied Federation, decided it'd be a good idea to implement a worldwide military draft for any able seventeen-year-old.

Those damn Bringers have a lot to answer for, and I plan to take the fight directly to them. Of course I'm scared out of my mind, but I have to do this for my family. For our survival. For my little brother, so he doesn't have to make the same sacrifice in three years.

"Are you okay, Kenley?" I hear Joey ask as he places his hand on my knee.

"Yeah, I'm fine. I've just got this weird headache all of a sudden," I reply, looking into his beautiful hazel eyes that have a hint of worry in them. The rubber band holding my long blonde hair up in a ponytail seems to be the cause of my strain, so I take it out, and let my hair fall down around my shoulders. "That feels much better."

He flashes me a smile. "Good to hear."

Joey and Dylan were close friends. No, I take that back, he's actually been more like a brother to us. Due to a lack of a relationship with his parents, he spent many nights over at our house to escape the craziness that was his home life. Joey took Dylan's death just as hard as I did, and we've grown much closer because of it.

Joey's never really cared about school, and his focus has always been on joining the military. At the age of twelve he shaved his bright red curly hair down to just a little fuzz on his head, and has kept the style ever since. Of course his father beat him for doing so, but Joey was always strong and never changed himself to fit what others wanted him to be. I admire him for that.

I, on the other hand, have spent the majority of my life focused on preparing for my future. I was even looking into colleges by the age of eleven. Getting good grades and securing my way into a state university with a full-ride soccer scholarship was at the top of my priority list. Joining the military never even crossed my mind. I especially never thought I'd be drafted into it, since I'm a girl and all. The United States has implemented the draft several times before, but never on a scale like this. I remember how I used to feel in school when we'd talk about past drafts. I didn't quite understand the need for them, but now I do. I may not agree with the overall idea of forcing someone to do something, but I'm ready. I'm ready to fight. Besides, it's not like we have a choice.

"Hey, looks like they're going to start." Joey's voice wades its way into my thoughts.

Since we're sitting in the nosebleed section of the stadium, we can barely make out the faces of the people on the stage. We have to resort to staring at two giant screens that frame either side of it. As a man dressed in a black-and-gold Allied Federation uniform approaches the microphone, his face appears on the screens. He seems cold and stoic.

"Welcome to the state of Maine's Allied Federation draft." He speaks in a rehearsed manner without any emotion in his voice, causing me to shudder. "We appreciate your cooperation during this tough time, and ask that you be patient throughout the assignment process. We will be doing this according to the color associated with your seating section. Line up in front of the stage when your section is called. And again, the Allied Federation thanks you." The man finishes with a salute. As his face leaves the screen, I look down at the ground and see that our section is orange.

"What's your dad doing here?" Joey's excited tone causes me to jerk up and look at the screens again.

"I have no idea," I reply as Joey gives me a confused look.

"He doesn't look very happy," Joey comments as we both stare at his image.

"No, he doesn't."

• • •
4

The Modified

My dad stands there looking a little more ragged than usual, with his face covered in stubble. His hair is longer than it was when I last saw him eight months ago. He came home one day after work, packed a bag, and told us that he had begun working on a top-secret project, and didn't know how long he'd be gone. The phone calls to the house have been sparse and they only came in about once a month, if that. We all miss him terribly, and though he looks worse for wear, I'm so happy to see him. I wonder if he's here because of his project.

My dad taps on the microphone before he begins to speak. "H-hello everyone," he stammers. "My name is Dr. Wyatt Grayson, and I'm the head scientist for the Allied Federation's Research and Development division. I'm here to announce the names of two special draftees who performed exceptionally well in the preliminary evaluations." He pauses and looks bothered by something. He glances over his shoulder and his body language changes. It almost seems like he's trying to convince someone to stop him from saying what he's about to. Sighing, he turns back to the microphone and opens up a piece of paper that he's holding in his hand. "So, without further delay, it's my duty to announce that…Joey Reilly and Kenley Grayson are the top two Maine draftees. If you'd please stand and make your way to the stage, we can continue with the assignments." He stumbles back away from the microphone and hurries off stage.

The Draft

I turn to Joey and his face looks as shocked as I feel. We're both speechless.

"Will Kenley Grayson and Joey Reilly please report to the stage immediately?" another man in a Federation uniform speaks into the microphone. His voice echoes loudly throughout the quiet stadium.

We slowly rise from our seats and begin making our way toward the stage. My feet feel like they're encased in concrete as every step seems to be heavier than the last. I can feel everyone staring at us as we walk by. I look up at the large screens on either side of the stage and there we are, large as life, walking down the stadium stairs. Whispers begin flowing through the crowd as we pass by them, row by row. My stomach sinks and I stop dead in my tracks. I peer up at my face on the screen again, which has been blown up to building size now, and freeze framed on the left side screen, with Joey's face on the right.

Joey takes my hand. "Come on, we're going to do this together, all right?"

I'm finally able to take my focus off the screens and look at him. He stands there anxiously waiting for my reply. I nod and let him lead me to the stage, which feels like it takes an eternity to reach. The man standing at the microphone says something, but it sounds muffled to me as my mind is trying to process what's happening.

The Modified

Standing there on stage, I turn to look out at the thousands in attendance. The bright lights shining in my eyes make it hard to focus on anything.

"Let's have a round of applause for the top two draftees from your state," the man calls out to the crowd. A subdued ovation follows, though I don't really expect anything more than that, given the nature of this whole thing. It's not something really worth celebrating.

"Now, if you two would follow these officers, they'll escort you to the debriefing area." The man gestures to the two armed Federation guards standing off to the side. They make an intimidating pair, each carrying the latest version of plasma rifle, and wearing full helmets so we can't see their faces.

The two guards lead us through one of the back hallways of the stadium. The walls are made of dark grey cement giving the corridor a very cold and confined feeling. As I watch the fluorescent lights overhead reflecting on the shiny red floor, a million questions flood my mind. The biggest one being, where's my dad?

We stop in front of a bright white door at the end of the hall. I look over at Joey and he gives me a reassuring smile while squeezing my hand. I'm so lucky to have him here with me since we've been through so much together. He's definitely my rock.

The Draft

One of the guards sharply raps his knuckles on the door and it opens, revealing my father. Releasing Joey's hand, I throw myself into my dad's arms, and for one split second I feel truly safe.

"Dad! It's so good to see you. We've missed you."

"I've missed you too. You have no idea," he whispers in my ear. Pulling back from me slightly, he looks over my shoulder at Joey. "It's good to see you too, Joey. I wish it was under better circumstances though."

Joey nods. "Yeah, me too."

"So, what's going on here? Why were we singled out like this? They've never done this before, right?" I ask, confused.

"Come into the room so we can talk in private, okay?" he states and then dismisses the guards with a motion of his hand.

My father's weary sigh keeps me from asking more questions as I follow him into the room with Joey right behind me.

We take a seat in the chairs across from my dad who sits behind a large metal desk. "Would either of you like something to drink?" he asks, pointing to a pitcher of ice water and three glasses sitting on the corner of the desk.

Ignoring his failed attempt to stall the conversation I blurt out, "Come on, Dad, why are we here?" While staring intently into his brown eyes, he dodges mine immediately.

The Modified

Combing his hand through his shaggy light brown hair, something he does when he's nervous or upset, he leans back in his chair and shakes his head. "It's not easy for me to tell you this…but you've been handpicked to be a part of a special project."

"A special project? Is this the thing you've been working on?" I ask him directly. He nods slightly and begins to pour himself a drink. I look over at Joey, who shrugs his shoulders, and then I turn back to my father. "What's this project?"

"First, I feel I must point out that once you know the details, you must go through with it. Otherwise, you'll be detained indefinitely. And believe me when I say you don't want that. Nor do I want that for you," he explains and then takes a big swig of his water.

"How would they know you've told us if we don't say anything?" Joey asks.

"The walls have ears, dear boy," is all he says.

"Why is this so secretive?"

"This is the largest undertaking the Federation has ever funded, and unfortunately, that's all I can say until you agree to be a part of it. I don't want to endanger you by telling you too much. Just in case you want to try and back out," he replies.

I sit there, not knowing what to say. I had so many questions before entering this room, and though some were answered, now new ones have taken their places. I pour myself a glass of water and take a sizable gulp as my throat suddenly feels like it's full of sand.

"I can try and convince the Federation to choose two other draftees, but-"

"I want to do it," I blurt out, surprising him.

"I do too. I've always wanted to serve, and if this project will give us a better chance of surviving the war, I want to take the risk," Joey interjects.

My dad seems to be bothered by how quickly we answered his question. His eyes dart back and forth from me to Joey, with a frown fixed on his mouth. "Are you two…absolutely sure?" he struggles to get out. "Because once I tell you about this, there's no turning back." I can see in his eyes he wants us to change our minds.

I look over at Joey, whose eyes give me the answer I need, and then back to my dad. "Yes."

"Well…I can't say that I didn't try. I won't lie to you two, this isn't going to be easy. I honestly can't even imagine you going through with it," he says, sounding concerned.

"More dangerous than fighting in the war?" I ask.

"Unfortunately… yes," he replies bluntly.

The Modified

"Dad, can you please be straight with us? What's this project? I mean, since we've already agreed to it, you've got to tell us now, right?"

My dad lets out a heavy sigh before he begins. "The Federation is choosing five draftees from each of the eight geographical regions in the United States, and then 40 others from each of the five remaining habitable continents as well. They want to modify you through the use of nanotechnology in order to mold you into enhanced soldiers."

"What do you mean 'enhanced soldiers'?" Joey chimes in.

"In a nutshell? Super soldiers. Basically, you'll receive a series of implants, that I've developed, which will modify your biological composition, leaving you with enhanced abilities. You'll be changed forever." He stops, almost seeming like he's mulling something over. I stare at him with anticipation for what he's going to say next, but he dodges it to take another drink of water. After setting down the glass, his focus returns to us. "I know this is going to sound crazy, but the implants are fused with the essence of a Bringer."

"A Bringer!? We're going to have part of those things put inside us? You're right, that is crazy," I reply, completely shocked by what my dad just said. "I won't have any part of those things inside of me! Those things killed Dylan. Does that not bother you at all?"

● ● ●
11

The Draft

"Of course it does, Kenley. And trust me when I say that I hate this as much you do, but the Magnus project is the last hope we have in the war against these creatures. I told you this wouldn't be easy. There's nothing I can do now though. You have to go through with it," my dad says with eyes full of sadness.

"You can't be serious. How is any of this even possible?" I hear Joey ask, but my eyes are still affixed to my father's.

He breaks eye contact with me and looks over at Joey. "We've had some major breakthroughs in bio-modification research, and this project was born because of it. I can assure you that all of this is one hundred percent true. And sadly, you two will see that firsthand very soon."

"I'm so not looking forward to telling Mom about this, especially after all she's been through."

"No. You can't tell her, or anyone else for that matter. This is top secret. If they trace any leak back to you, they'll hunt you down and…well, I'd rather not think about what they'd do to you."

"Got it, don't tell anyone," I reply seriously.

"All we need to tell your mom is that you did well enough in the preliminaries to land you a safe desk job. I hate the fact we have to lie to her, but with what happened to your brother, and me being gone for so long, I don't want to put her through any more stress."

"I hate lying to Mom too," I say and then pause. "I know you guys wanted me to throw the preliminaries so I'd be safe for two years, and then go back to a normal life. But ever since Dylan's death, life has been anything but normal, and I want to fight. There's too much at stake not to," I say, failing to keep the sadness from my voice.

My dad leans forward with his elbows on the desk and his hands clasped. "I knew you wouldn't purposefully fail the tests. To be honest, I wasn't surprised when the Federation wanted you two. You're perfect hosts for the implant." He reclines in the chair and rests his hands on his chest. "You're right though, we did want you to be assigned a desk job, but this is your life, Kenley. I guess I'll have to put my feelings aside. As much as I hate the idea." He wearily pushes himself up from his chair and makes his way to the door. Opening it, "All right, you two. You better get on home. You'll receive your assignment papers through the mail within the next couple of days or so. These papers are very important as they contain the location you'll be meeting with the three other draftees from your region."

As I go to leave the room, my dad grabs me in a hug. I can only remember him hugging me like this one other time. It was right after my brother's funeral. He's holding on to me so tight, it seems like he's afraid that if he lets me go I might disappear.

I hug him back and whisper, "Don't worry, Dad. I'll be fine."

"I know you will. Be safe, and I'll see you soon, okay?" he chokes out.

The drive home with Joey is somewhat quiet. Not because we don't have things to say, we have plenty to talk about, but we just kind of keep to ourselves. We both begin to talk to each other several times, but the conversations kind of just drop off.

Drumming my fingers on the armrest of the car door, I watch the scenery outside fly by. I've always enjoyed gazing into a forest as you drive by it. The blurry pattern the trees make as you look in between them has always fascinated me.

Ahead of us I see a large section of the forest full of charred trees. As we get closer to them, I notice several rows have been leveled, leaving a pathway that leads deep into the woods. A thick smoky haze fills the area.

"Joey, stop the car," I yell out, seeming to startle him. "Do you see that?"

"Yeah, what did that?" he asks, and then pulls the car onto the shoulder of the road.

"I don't know, but it definitely did a number on those trees," I reply while opening the car door. My mouth hangs open with shock as I stand there, scanning the destruction. A path has been cut straight through the trees, ending in a circular section. It looks as if someone took a precision laser and cut them down by hand.

"Are you sure we should just go investigating?" I hear Joey ask through my open car door.

"What if someone needs our help?"

"Out here? In the middle of nowhere?" he asks dryly. "What if it's the Bringers? What would you do then, huh?"

"That's why I have you here to protect me," I joke, but inside a twinge of fear bubbles up at the thought of a Bringer being in the forest.

Joey groans in protest as I move away from the car and close the door. He finally opens his door and glares at me over the top of the car before reluctantly joining me at the edge of the forest. "Just so you know, if we die…I'm going to be really pissed at you," Joey whispers.

I laugh off his comment. "Aren't you the least bit curious about what caused this?"

"Sure, but I can't help thinking of all the movies that have taught me *not* to do this," he replies wryly.

"News flash, this isn't a movie. It's real life, and if it was the Bringers, don't you think we'd already have run into them by now?"

• • •

The Draft

"Fine, we'll go check it out. But I'm definitely still on team 'this is a bad idea,'" Joeys states huffily.

As we make our way down the path, the smell of burnt wood and melted metal assaults our senses. The remnants of the trees crunch under our feet with every step we take. I jump when I see a tree in the distance smash into several others around it, sending them crashing to the ground in front of us.

"Whoa, that was close," I say breathlessly.

"Uh, you think?" Joey replies sarcastically.

Reaching the end of the path, we come upon a crater in the ground with some kind of large shiny object at the center of it. It's still on fire, and black smoke billows from it into the air.

"Is that a wingtip from a spaceship?" Joey points to it.

"Possibly. I think it might be one of ours. It has the logo of the Federation on it," I reply.

"Whatever it is, it definitely did some damage when it crashed here."

"Yeah, you can say that again."

The trees around the edge of the crash site were barely there anymore. Most of them were shadows of their previous selves. I reach out to touch a branch and it crumbles into a pile of ash onto the ground. A gust of wind blows through the area and sweeps the pile of ash up into the air, swirling it around in front of me. It's oddly beautiful.

The Modified

"Could you imagine the whole world ending up like this?" I ask Joey as he stands there continuing to examine the object in the deep craterous hole.

"No, no I can't. These bastards need to be stopped, and we're going to be the ones to do it."

"Agreed."

I grab Joey's hand and pull him in the direction of the car. He pulls me to a stop in order to take one last look at the destruction behind us.

Our attention is drawn to the sound of sirens in the distance. "We better get going. I knew it'd be only a matter of time before the Federation showed up," I say and then tug on Joey's hand.

Standing in front of my house, I hesitate putting the key into the lock on the front door. It feels heavy in my hand as it hovers there just in front of the lock. I know that the moment I open this door, I'll have to lie to my mom, to my little brother, and I dread doing that.

When I finally decide to place the key into the lock, the door suddenly flies open and I see my little brother Gavin standing there, biting his lip. He flings his arms around me and grips me tight in a hug. I've never been happier to see him. Maybe it's because of the finality of my current situation, or the fear that these next couple of days might be the last I get to spend with him.

He backs away and looks up at me with sadness in his eyes. I push back his dirty blond hair that hangs in front of his face to see him more clearly. "Hey, Little Bit," I say with a half-smile, hoping that I sound cheerful.

"Mom's out back if you want to talk to her."

"Thanks. How was school today?"

"It was okay."

"Only okay?" I ask as I put my arm around his shoulder and begin walking with him toward the kitchen. Over the past year he has grown so much, and soon, "Little Bit" will be taller than me.

"You know just as well as I do it's not school anymore. They're training us for the war," he replies, taking a seat at the kitchen table. "I mean, look at these uniforms we have to wear now. They're black and gold. They even say Allied Federation on them."

"It won't be that way for long, we're going to change that," I reply while rubbing his head and messing up his hair.

He pushes my hand away, and his boyish face with his bluish-green eyes that match Dylan's, turns serious. "I don't see how."

"Don't talk like that. This war will end, and things will be back to normal before you know it." I try to reassure him, even though I'm not sure of my own words.

"I hope so," he replies.

I see my mom out in the garden through the kitchen window. She has her light blonde hair pulled up into a ponytail, and her usual navy blue headband is resting atop her head. "Hey, I'm going to go talk to Mom real quick, and let her know I'm home. When I get back we'll play some video games, okay?" My brother nods with a strained smile and leaves the kitchen.

My mom turns to look at me when she hears the back door open and close. At first she smiles at me, but it fades quickly as she goes back to watering her flowers.

"Please tell me they gave you a nice cushy desk job to work at for the next two years," she says as she wipes the sweat from her brow with her gardening glove.

I hesitate to answer. This is a lot harder than I was expecting it to be. I hate that I can't be honest with her. Somewhere, though, I find the strength and reply. "Yep, a real nice cushy one."

"I'm so torn up by this, Kenley. You have no idea. I've been losing sleep for months now, anticipating this very moment…when you'd return with your assignment. I hate the Federation for taking my baby girl away from me," she explains as tears come to her eyes.

I grab her in a hug and she wraps her arms around me tighter than she ever has. I have to do everything in my power not to break down. "Mom, I'm going to be all right. You have nothing to worry about." That lie resonates deep within me and my heart breaks at the thought of possibly never being able to see her again.

She releases the hug and pulls away from me while wiping away her tears. "You've been my saving grace ever since we lost Dylan. It's going to be very tough around here, but at least now I'll be able to get some sleep at night knowing you won't be in harm's way like your brother was," she states, a sad smile returning to her face.

"Here, I got you something." I pull out a small pot of flowers wrapped in a plastic bag from my backpack. "It's some blue poppies for your garden. I had Joey stop by your favorite flower shop in town before he dropped me off."

"Oh, these are lovely, Kenley," she replies, giving me another hug and taking them from my hands. Tears come to her eyes again and it suddenly dawns on me why. "They'll go perfectly with the red ones your brother gave me before he went off to war."

"I'm so sorry, Mom. I didn't even think about that," I reply with sadness in my voice. "I just wanted to get you some of your favorite flowers."

"It's all right, dear. I love them, and I know exactly where I'm going to put these. Right next to your brother's."

• • •

The Modified

"So, have you heard from Dad lately?" I ask, trying to change the subject before I start to cry.

"No, but you know your father's busy with this project of his. He'll call when he has time, dear. I can't wait to tell him the good news about your new assignment, though. I think he'll be relieved to hear you'll be safe for your two-year service with the Federation. Are you hungry? I was planning on making your favorite tonight, eggplant parmesan."

"I'm actually kind of more tired than anything else, but that sounds great, Mom."

"Well you go rest up a bit, and then let's plan on having dinner at around seven?"

"Okay," I reply, trying to keep my emotions at bay. I'm bawling on the inside and it's so difficult not to just burst into tears. I'll be leaving my family soon, and my dad and I are the only ones who know the truth.

After giving my mom another hug, I head up to my bedroom. On my way, I pass by Dylan's old room. The door hasn't been opened for months, and my mom has kept it just as he left it the day he went off to war. I realize the door is slightly ajar and hear noises coming from inside. My heart skips a beat as I push open the door the rest of the way and see Gavin sitting at the edge of Dylan's bed holding something in his hand. I sit down next to him and he doesn't say a word. He just continues to stare at a photo of him, Joey, Dylan, and me. It was taken the day after Dylan's assignment. All of our faces are strained in the picture even though Mom had told us to smile. Tears come to my eyes as I remember back to the day a soldier brought this picture to our front door with a message. A message that would change our lives forever.

"Don't go, Kenley," Gavin whispers.

"I have to," I reply as I wrap my arm around his shoulder, pulling him close. "I'll be okay. You don't have to worry about me or Joey, all right?" I feel him nod into my shoulder and hear him sniffle. Wiping away my own tears, I look into his eyes as he raises his head to me. "Mom says dinner will be ready at seven, so that means we've got an hour to play some games. What do you say?" He nods. "Well, go set it all up and I'll be in soon, okay?"

"Okay," Gavin replies, wiping his eyes and handing me the picture.

I go to put the photo back onto the mirror, but then stop to look at it once more. Tears begin to well up in my eyes again as I look at Dylan's handsome face. He almost looks like he knew this was the last picture he would take with us. "I'll make them pay, Dylan. You have my word."

Chapter Two
The Shrouded Facility

As I pull up to our usual Thursday night hangout, my car's headlights shimmer off the side view mirror of Joey's old red Mustang. The black stripes on the sides of the car have almost all but worn away, and the vehicle is a little beat-up, but he absolutely loves that car. It was what allowed him to get away from his parents.

Thursdays were barhopping nights for his dad, and Joey never wanted to be home when he returned. I'll never forget the first night he came to my bedroom window after his Dad beat the crap out of him. That's actually why we started meeting in this field by Old Man Gary's farm.

The Shrouded Facility

Ever since we were kids, Joey and I have loved looking at the stars, and this field was the perfect place to do that. Before we were old enough to drive, we used to come out here with Dylan. We'd all lie in the back of his truck and stare up into the peaceful night sky. Those were definitely happy times.

"Hey, stranger. I wasn't sure if you'd show up tonight. You know, with us leaving tomorrow and all," I say as I see him shielding his eyes from the brightness of my car's headlights.

"I'd never miss our Thursday nights," he replies with a grin. "Besides, Dad's been in rare form lately, and I didn't want to push my luck." He laughs off his statement, but I know it bothers him. "Hey, what? No pizza this time?"

"Oh crap, I knew there was something I was forgetting."

"You just don't want to go to Jonnie's Pizza Place anymore since you found out that Bobby Fowler has a crush on you," he jokes.

"Not true. Bobby Fowler has a girlfriend."

Joey laughs. "Uh, he's a guy. Just because he has a girlfriend doesn't mean he isn't looking. And word is he's been looking at you a lot lately. And you know how he has a thing for tall, athletic blondes."

"First of all, gross. And for your information, not all men are like that. And second, he's not even my type," I reply with a huff.

The Modified

"Uh-huh," Joey mutters sarcastically as he jumps onto the hood of his car and takes a seat. He taps the space next to him for me to join.

I crawl onto the hood of the car and lay back on the windshield. As I look up into the sky, I take in a deep breath and begin to think about everything that will happen tomorrow. There's a light breeze and I can hear it rustle through the field of long grasses that surrounds us, as they swish and sway. The smell of fresh flowers fills my nose as I take in a deep breath. It's soothing really.

"What's on your mind?" Joey asks me as he settles into a laying position, resting his head on the windshield next to mine.

I let out a little laugh. "Tons," I reply and look over at him with worry in my eyes. He returns my look and grabs for my hand.

"You know what, Kenley? No matter what happens to us, no one can take away the memories and times we've shared. Those are ours, and we will never lose them."

"Wow, you sound final," I state with slight sadness in my voice.

"No, not final. I just want you to know that. Just in case…you know," he says, sending me a little smile while squeezing my hand.

"Please don't say things like that right now, okay? I don't want to even imagine that," I murmur as I turn away to look at the stars again. He just squeezes my hand and lets out a sigh.

"I didn't mean to make you upset. I just wanted you to know that," he says quietly.

"It's okay, Joey. But tonight I just want to live in this moment for a bit and try not to think about what the future holds."

"Got it," he states and turns to gaze toward the stars as well.

I begin to feel bad about how I just handled the last conversation. It eats away at me since I know Joey was just trying to get out what he wanted to say. I was quick with him. He's quite an emotional person and doesn't really have much of an outlet other than talking to me.

"Hey, Joey?" I ask, breaking the silence.

"Yeah?"

"Do you remember the game we used to play with Dylan? He used to drive us out here and we'd sit in the back of his truck while staring up at the sky and play that star game."

"How could I forget? The 'What's Your Star' game, right?"

"Yep."

"Yeah, I remember. You'd pick a star, name it, and then make up a story about it," he replies with a warm laugh, almost like he was remembering back to a particular time.

"Do you want to play? You know, for old times' sake?"

"Sure."

"I'll go first," I say and then scan the sky for a star. The blanket of tiny twinkling lights above our heads is truly breathtaking. There are so many stars in the sky that it almost makes it impossible to choose just one. I finally settle on a large bright one off to our left. It's surrounded by several other stars, but its light is so intense that it shines there like a beacon in the darkness. "That one," I announce as I point to it.

"Good choice. Now, what's its name?" he asks.

"Joey."

"Joey, huh?"

"Yep, I'm dedicating this one to you."

The moment I say that, another star right next to the one I chose begins to shine just as bright.

"Well, I'm choosing that one then," Joey states, pointing to the star next to mine. "That star has your name written all over it."

I laugh and so does he. "What's your star's story?" he asks me.

"Actually, if you don't mind, I have a story for both of them," I reply with a slight smile.

"Oh really? Consider me intrigued," he jokes.

I strengthen my grip on his hand. "The Joey star and Kenley star are best friends, and have been inseparable since they were young. They've been through a lot and have persevered, not allowing their glow to ever be diminished. Joey and Kenley have made a pact that they will always be by each other's sides, and nothing, not even death, will keep them apart. When one of them glows bright, the other one glows just as bright because they support one another, no matter what."

I feel Joey kiss my forehead and lay his head down closer to mine. "Kenley Grayson. You are my best friend in the entire world. You know that, right?"

"Yes, and so are you," I reply as a tear rolls down my cheek. There's a slight pause in our conversation as a silence falls between us.

"Hey, I thought you said you didn't want to get deep and emotional," he says with a laugh.

"I guess I got caught up in the moment."

"Well, that was a great story. Ever thought of becoming a writer?" he jokes.

"Very funny. Let's see you come up with a better one," I giggle, giving him a little love tap on the arm.

"I'm up for the challenge. Here goes nothing," Joey states and I snuggle up close to him as he begins to tell his tale of Joey star and Kenley star.

The Modified

While Joey and I sit in the airport terminal waiting to board our plane, I think about the fact I'm going to fly for the first time in my life. The thought of flying kind of terrifies me, but in the way riding a roller coaster does. The sad truth is I've never left Maine until now. And who knows if I'll ever return after all of this?

As I attempt to find a comfortable sitting position in one of these awkwardly designed airport chairs, I try to push aside the sadness of saying goodbye to my mom and brother earlier that morning. Thinking back to the day when we saw Dylan off, I remember my mom crying a lot, knowing that her son would be on the front lines. She was a wreck the entire time he was gone. There were fewer tears this time, though, mainly because my mom thinks I'm going to be safe behind a desk somewhere. It tears me up inside, but at least she'll have some peace of mind.

I look over at Joey and I'm so glad that I'm not going through this alone. He has his headphones on and seems lost in his own world. I think he might be upset that his parents didn't seem to care about him leaving. He won't admit it though. I wasn't really all that surprised since they've been counting down the days until he was old enough to kick out of their house anyway. Now they have the perfect excuse.

Staring down at the piece of paper in my hand that I received in the mail from the Federation, I sigh. Along with the general admission papers that were inside a shiny oversized black-and-gold folder, there was a handwritten note tucked into a small envelope. The instructions inside told us our plane tickets would be waiting for us at the Portland International Jetport. It also said when we arrive in Washington, D.C., we'd be taken to the Hexagon.

The Hexagon replaced the Pentagon as the headquarters for the World's Department of Defense. Once the Allied Federation was formed, they deemed it necessary to have a centralized area for their base of operations. And since the six habitable continents needed to be represented, they decided to have a six-sided building.

Our plane tickets had Joey and me sitting next to each other, and on the walk over to the terminal, I had begged him for the window seat if he was the one who ended up with it. There's something calming about sitting next to a window in any vehicle.

A row of televisions just above our heads are blaring a commercial about the draft. It's obviously funded by the Federation, and resembles those retro "Uncle Sam Wants You" campaigns the U.S. military used to advertise all the time.

The next segment on the television immediately caught my full attention. An urgent announcement from the World News Network chimes in. It's a report by Julie Chen, one of the network's leading news anchors.

The Modified

"Devastation strikes London. Are the Bringers of Death to blame? Find out in twenty minutes when we bring you updates on this breaking news," Julie states, trying to hold back her apparent excitement.

Hearing them call our seat numbers over the intercom, I tap Joey on the shoulder and remove one of his earphones. "We're up," I tell him with a forced smile. He nods and gathers up his stuff into his backpack.

This is it, I think to myself as we make our way to the tunnel opening that leads up to the plane's entrance. I hand my ticket over to the attendant, take in a deep calming breath, and follow Joey into the tunnel.

As we make our descent, the view of Washington, D.C., through the clouds, is gorgeous. Actually this entire trip has been amazing. I spent most of it staring out the window looking at the wonderful landscapes as we flew over them. I almost forgot the reason we were flying in the first place until I saw several areas that had been devastated by the war.

The seat belt light flashes overhead and we experience some minor turbulence, which jostles me a little. My stomach is a lot less irritated by the descent than it was during take-off. I grip the armrests as more turbulence comes, but thankfully it ends quickly.

The Shrouded Facility

When the plane docks at the Washington National Airport terminal, and the flight attendant gives us the okay to leave our seats, Joey and I grab our backpacks from the overhead compartment and hurry off the plane. We bypass the luggage area since we were traveling light, and at the glass front doors to the airport, we spy a man dressed in a Federation uniform holding a sign with our last names on it. He silently directs us to a large and shiny black Hummer waiting just outside in the loading zone. He says this vehicle will take us to the Hexagon where we'll meet up with the other three regional draftees who are waiting for us. We will then all be taken to the shrouded facility.

"The shrouded facility?" I ask the man. He doesn't answer me, he just points to the open door of the vehicle.

The plush interior of the Hummer was jet black just like the outside. As we begin to drive away, I ask the driver how long it will take for us to get there, but he doesn't respond. I'm beginning to see a pattern.

The drive seems endless. I've never seen so much traffic in my whole life. What's worse is that every time Joey and I begin a conversation, we're shushed by the driver. Not being able to talk makes for a very awkward and silent trip. The driver won't even put on any music. I guess this is life in the military, I better get used to it.

The Modified

We finally arrive at the Hexagon and it's definitely a sight to behold. It towers over us like a giant concrete fortress. As we pull up to the security gate, the driver shows his badge to the guard and he waves us through. We stop in front of a pair of glass double doors, and the driver quickly exits the vehicle. He comes over to my door first, opens it, and waits patiently for me to get out. I say "thank you," but his face remains blank and he doesn't say anything. In fact, he just continues looking straight-ahead as if I'm not there. I shrug at Joey who just decides to exit the car through the same door right after me.

"Head through those doors and down the hall. Your next destination will be the counter at the end," the driver says in a very monotone and robotic way while closing the car door.

"Okay?" was all I got out. I send a confused look to Joey and he returns it. The driver gets into the vehicle and drives off. "What was his deal?" I ask, and Joey does what he does best, and shrugs.

"Did you notice how he moved? Kind of like a robot."

"Yeah, really weird," I reply as I sling my backpack over my shoulder, heading for the entrance.

The doors quietly slide open when we approach them. Ice-cold air meets us as we walk into the building, and I shiver even though I'm wearing a thick jean jacket. A long blinding white hallway that leads to a glass dome enclosed counter lies ahead of

• • •

us. A woman sits behind the counter, typing away at the computer in front of her. As we approach, the lady picks her head up to look at us. Her movements are stiff just like the driver's. Her bleach blonde hair doesn't even move when she raises her head.

"Hello, my name is Ada 38. How may I help you?" she asks in a robotic tone.

"Uh, we're here for the special program," I answer while wondering how odd her name is.

"The Magnus Project, right. Please place all of your belongings into the chute at the end of the counter," she replies.

I look to my left and see a little door with a handle installed into the counter. I grab the handle, pull it open, and look down into the dark hole, which seems to go on forever. "Where does this lead to? Will we get our stuff back?"

"All items will be returned upon exit from the facility," Ada 38 answers with a forced smile. I hesitantly dump my backpack into the chute and step aside so Joey can do the same.

"Now, if you would please take the corridor to my right. You will find your final destination through the last door on your left. It is the only blue door. Thank you for visiting the Hexagon, I hope you have a pleasant stay," Ada 38 says, her hand gesturing toward the hallway, with that same awkward smile plastered across her face.

● ● ●

The Modified

She definitely wasn't lying when she said our door was the only blue door down the hall. Every other door up to this one was blinding white just like the walls.

I suddenly get this feeling like we're the only ones in the building besides Ada 38. There was no writing on any of the doors except for the blue one, which just had one word: *Holding.* I grab the knob, turn it, and push the door open. Joey nudges me forward and I see three teens, who look our age, hanging out in the space. The whole room was the same color as the door, except for the floor, which was made up of large white tiles. As we move forward into the room, the occupants turn to look at us and their eyes widen.

"Don't let the door close," all three of them yell at once. Before we could grab the door, it quickly shuts by itself and we hear it lock.

"Dammit!" the only other girl in the room growls and throws up her arms in frustration. "Way to go, Blondie."

"Wait, we're locked in here?" I ask.

"Yep, you guessed it. You must be Kenley and Joey," a mousy looking guy pipes in. His curly dirty blond hair was a little disheveled and the black wire-framed glasses he wore were resting right at the tip of his nose. "Hi, I'm Geoffrey Milton, and over there, that's Sam Gutierrez," he says as he points to the dark-haired, olive-skinned girl leaning up against the wall. She gives us a half-assed wave and a squinty-eyed sarcastic smile. "Oh, and that's Caleb Walker, over there sitting at the bar." Geoffrey puts his hand up next to his mouth and whispers, "He's a little quiet, so don't expect much out of him." Caleb's back is to us. He raises his right hand and extends his index finger into the air.

I guess that's his attempt at a wave, I laugh to myself.

"Sorry about the whole door thing."

"Oh, don't worry about it. What's a couple more hours of being trapped in here?" Sam asks sarcastically, glaring at us with her bright green eyes.

"Don't mind Sam, she's really harmless," Geoffrey states as Sam scoffs and rolls her eyes.

Sam pushes herself off the wall and plops down on one of the comfy-looking blue leather chairs placed around the room. "So where are you two from?" she asks dryly.

"Maine," Joey and I both say in unison.

"How cute, you guys are like twins," she laughs under her breath as she rolls her eyes again.

"Is there a problem here?" I ask defensively. "Because the last time I checked we're all in the same position, and I don't really appreciate your tone," I continue, looking directly at her. I hear Caleb laugh under his breath, and so does Geoffrey. Sam raises herself from the chair and approaches me with clenched fists. I

* * *

stand my ground and stare directly into her eyes, not backing down. I feel Joey tense up right behind me. She smirks and extends her hand.

"You've got balls, Grayson. I like that," she states.

"Thank you?" I reply as I shake her hand.

Sam laughs and throws her arm around my shoulder, while playfully punching me in the stomach. "I've got a feeling we're going to get along nicely."

"Glad to hear it," I say and flash an unsure look at Joey, who, as usual, just shrugs at me.

"Where are you all from?" Joey asks.

Geoffrey raises his hand. "Pennsylvania."

"New York, baby," Sam says with a wide grin.

For the first time since we stepped into the room Caleb turns around and says, "Tennessee." His eyes are a shocking bright blue, which is a stark contrast to his dark skin tone.

The lone television in the room suddenly turns on and is stuck on what seems to be a test screen with a periodic high-pitch beep. The face of the head general for the Allied Federation, Roman Barclay, flickers onto the screen. He's the youngest head general we've ever had and kind of looks out of place in his uniform. He seems to clean cut to be a general, and his personality is like that of your stereotypical used car salesman.

The Shrouded Facility

His black hair is perfectly slicked back as always, and those piercing green eyes only add to his charming smile.

"If this video is playing, that means everyone is present and accounted for from the Appalachian Mountains region. I'd first like to congratulate you all for being the best and brightest of your entire region. Selection for the Magnus Project is a great honor, and you should feel a sense of pride in the fact you were handpicked for it. You're the last hope for our world, and though that is a huge cross to bear, we know you will succeed. Once again, the Allied Federation thanks you for your service." As the general speaks his last word, the television turns off.

"I've never heard someone so full of shit in my whole life," Sam comments and then laughs.

"I agree, but he sells it well. How else do you think he got where he is today?" I interject.

Sam snorts her reply, "True, true."

The door to the room opens and a Federation guard enters. "Your transport to the Shrouded Facility is ready," the man says, gesturing to the open door. As we head outside, we're greeted by two other guards. They lead us to an elevator with large shiny metal doors. One of the guards presses his palm on a panel at the side of the elevator and a keypad projects out from it. He punches in a code and the keypad sucks back into the panel as the doors to the elevator open. I've only seen technology like that in the movies, but never thought it really existed. My shocked face meets Joey's.

Even though the elevator is enormous, we stay close together as if something bad might happen. The "safety in numbers" thing, I guess. The walls of the elevator are made of frosted glass and are framed in a shiny metal. A white light shines from behind the walls and ceiling. The floor panels light up as we move about the space. I put my hand out to touch one of the walls of the elevator and the light follows my hand around the glass.

"Please don't touch anything," one of the guards snaps at me. I quickly draw my hand back to my side and stare straight-ahead.

It seems like we're in the elevator only a few seconds before the doors open again. It didn't even seem like we moved at all. Before us lies a huge open area with a wide staircase leading up to a platform. The whole area resembles a subway, but with walls made of jagged rocks. It kind of looks like they just hollowed out a cave. As we walk out onto the platform, I notice a shiny metal track suspended from the ceiling over what seems to be a tram tunnel. I glance down the long dark tunnel, first looking right, and then left. Both paths are slightly illuminated, but I can't see down very far in either direction.

"What is this place?" I ask one of the guards standing next to us.

The Shrouded Facility

"This is the Hexagon's light tram platform. This tunnel connects to key destinations throughout the world. It utilizes state of the art suspended tram technology. Your light tram should be arriving shortly to transport you to the Shrouded Facility," he replies in a very cold manner.

"What's this Shrouded Facility everyone keeps talking about?" I ask, but again get no answer. The guard just continues to look forward. *It was worth a shot, I guess,* I think to myself.

We hear a slight buzzing noise coming from down the tunnel and suddenly a huge white vehicle stops right in front of us. The design is something I've never seen before. The whole body shimmers in the lights and looks super polished and smooth. It has a streamlined cylindrical shape, but is rounded off at either end. I notice that the tram is attached at several points to the track overhead.

The double doors on the side of the light tram slide open, which is followed by an odd sounding electronic chime. As we board, the first thing I see is the stark contrast between the floor and the rest of the tram. The floor is a glossy blue surface and the rest of the interior is polished bright white. I almost don't want to touch anything at the risk of getting it dirty.

"Please take a seat," one of the guards says as he steps inside behind us. He performs a similar trick to the one he did with the elevator, and a keypad appears on the interior wall. He puts in a code and proceeds to tell us to buckle up and hang on tight.

"Hey, what about all the stuff we brought with us?" I ask the guard just as he turns to leave.

"You won't need it where you're going," he replies. Once he sees we're all buckled up, he steps out of the tram and the doors close behind him.

I can see into the area at the front of the tram where a driver should be and there is no one. Hopefully it's automatic.

The interior lights slowly dim and we slide back slightly as if it's settling into gear. I hear a noise that sounds somewhat mechanical, which is the best way I can describe it. The next thing I know we launch into high speed. My stomach immediately goes into my throat and all I can get out is a tiny scream. I can hear Sam, who's two seats over from me, yelling to go faster. Joey reaches over and grabs my hand as I tense up even more from the force. My face feels like it's going to peel off.

The tram begins to gradually slow down and I'm able to relax into my seat. "That was kind of cool," Joey states as he pats my hand reassuringly. He knows that I'm not a huge fan of thrill rides.

"Yeah, probably not the way I'd describe that," I joke.

"Oh, come on, Grayson. That was awesome!" Sam cries out.

The Shrouded Facility

I turn to look at Geoffrey, who's sitting right next to me on my left, and he looks ill. I don't think I've seen anyone turn that many shades of green so quickly and then back to pale white. Even paler than normal. "You okay, Geoffrey?"

"Yeah…I'll be fine…just a little motion sickness," he chokes out between gags.

Caleb's just sitting there smiling. I guess he enjoyed the ride.

We begin to slow even more, and it seems like we're getting close to the Shrouded Facility. As I'm gazing out the windows of the tram, I see the tunnel open up into a huge well-lit cave. I notice several other tracks all converging toward one giant area in the distance. Pulling up to the platform, we see a large crowd of teenagers all standing in front of an enormous metal door which is embedded into the rock wall.

The tram comes to a crawl and then stops. I begin to scan the crowd through the window, and my gaze fixes on a single guy. My heart skips a beat. He's unlike any guy I've ever seen. I mean, there have been guys I've had crushes on back home, but there's something so different about him. His sun-kissed skin and beautiful chestnut brown hair takes my breath away. I never thought I'd feel this way, especially not while in my current situation.

Joey catches me staring at something. "What's up?"

I lie and tell him it's nothing.

The Modified

"A boy out there caught your eye, didn't he? Come on, you can tell me," he says with a mischievous grin.

I give him a playful slap on the shoulder. "It's not like that." I laugh because I know I'm lying.

"All right, I believe you," Joey says with an eyebrow raised.

"Ooooh, which one is it?" Sam chimes in. "I bet I can guess."

I look over to Sam. "It's nothing, really."

"Sure it isn't. I got my eye on you, Grayson. Keep those hormones in check, girl. We've got a war to win," she jokes.

My gaze inconspicuously wanders back over to where I saw the guy standing before, but he isn't there anymore.

The tram's doors finally open. We unbuckle our seat belts and head out to join everyone else on the platform.

An unfamiliar male's voice comes over the intercom system. "Welcome, everyone, to the Shrouded Facility. We will begin your processing shortly. We thank you in advance for your patience. When the door opens, we would like all the females to proceed toward the left side entrance, and all the males to proceed toward the right side entrance."

I look around the crowd again to see if I can find the guy from before, but to no avail. I'm still not quite sure why I'm so intrigued by him. Is it wrong to have feelings like this right now?

"Look, the doors are beginning to open," I hear Joey say and then my focus pans over to them. There's a large circle in the

* * *

middle of the door that rotates and then slides upward, disappearing into the frame. The left and right parts of the door slide open quickly after.

As we begin to separate into girls and boys, Joey gives me a hug and whispers into my ear, "See you on the other side, okay? Be strong, Kenley." With that, he moves away from me and into the crowd of males gathering around the right side entrance. I see Geoffrey and Caleb join him as well.

I feel someone put an arm around my shoulder and turn my head to see that it's Sam. "Come on, Grayson, we've got a date with destiny."

"How can you be so calm and cheery about this?" I ask her.

"What? Would you rather me be scared? Life's too short, Grayson. Besides, I've spent plenty of time being all gloom and doom, but now I'm ready to kick some ass. And that makes me happy. We're in a war, if you haven't noticed."

"Oh, I've noticed. Probably more than you think," I murmur. "I've already lost someone to this war."

"Looks like you and I've got a lot more in common than I first thought. I've lost a brother and my dad so far," she replies with a serious face instead of her usual joking one. "But the moment you let that get to you, they've won, and we can't have that now, can we?" she continues and flashes me a smirk.

"You're right."

The Modified

"I'm never wrong," Sam says with a laugh. "Now, like I said, let's go meet our destiny."

Sam and I are two of the last girls to make it through the left side entrance and into the room beyond. The first thing I notice is a pile of clothes to the right of us. There are several lines of girls, all in their underwear, standing in front of more doors. A large sign above the row of doors reads: *Decontamination Zone.*

A few female guards are standing off to our left and one approaches us. "Please strip down and then proceed toward one of the lines. You must be decontaminated prior to receiving your implant," the female guard explains sharply.

Now I know why they split us up, I say to myself.

It's my turn to step into the decontamination chamber. The door slides open and I see a small room ahead of me. A blue scanner grid is stationary in the middle of the space, causing the white walls to have a blue tint to them. As I step into the room, the door slides shut behind me and I begin to feel slightly claustrophobic.

An electronic voice flows into the room. "Please stand still. The decontamination process will commence immediately."

The scanner grid moves back and forth over my body multiple times. It tingles like someone is giving me a light massage with their fingertips.

The Shrouded Facility

The electronic voice comes back into the room. "Decontamination process complete."

The door on the other end of the small room opens, revealing a long and narrow bright white chamber. In front of me is a row of large cylindrical glass tubes, positioned at an angle. They're being held in place by a metal base and a mechanical arm affixed to the top of it that seems to be attached to the wall.

I notice a few of the other girls enter the area and see Sam emerge from the door a few down from mine. The electronic voice filters into the room as the rest of the girls join us in the chamber. "Please proceed to the implant administration conduit directly in front of you."

As I approach the tube, the electronic voice comes through once more. "Please place your hand onto the triangular pad to the right of the implant administration conduit."

I place my hand on the pad and a blue light emanates from it. I feel a prick on all of my fingers and gasp as I pull my hand back quickly. I look at my hand and there are small puncture wounds on each of my fingertips, but they've already begun healing and are not bleeding. I notice a stream of red fluid flowing through the clear hose that's connected from the pad to the base of the tube. I assume it's the blood it just took from me. It mixes quickly with the clear liquid that's collected at the bottom of the tube, turning it a neon blue color.

● ● ●

The Modified

I can't do this. I need to get out of here. This is all too much. I trust my dad, but I'm not ready for this. This is crazy, my inner voice says. My mind begins to ramble with all the worries that I've been holding in. I try to calm myself and not hyperventilate.

"Please enter the implant administration conduit at this time," the electronic voice states. The door to the tube opens and slides upward.

No, I'm not going to do this. I don't care what they do to me, I tell myself.

"Is there a problem with your implant administration conduit? Shall I call a guard over to assist you?" the electronic voice asks. I see a female guard heading my way and I turn to look back at the glass tube in front of me. Taking in a calming breath, I push out all the negative thoughts gathered in my mind. A sense of strength begins to build up inside me.

You have to do this, Kenley. You can't let Dylan down. You can't let your family down. You can't let the world down, I state to myself, trying to muster the courage to proceed.

"Please answer the question: Do you need assistance?"

"No, I'm fine," I reply as I slowly climb up the steps leading to the opening. Raising one leg into it, I grab hold of the handles on the sides and pull myself in the rest of the way. As I settle in and lean against the back of the tube, the cold glass against my skin makes me tremble. The door slides downward and I hear an

• • •
47

electrical locking sound. My heart is pounding so loud that I can hear it echoing within the small confined space. My hands begin to shake and I take a deep breath in an attempt to try and relax. I hear a swooshing sound and feel my feet getting wet. Looking down I see the blue liquid entering the tube through four openings at the bottom. As the liquid creeps up my skin it feels like a million bugs are crawling all over me.

I begin to panic and then I hear the electronic voice again. "Please remain still. Nanobot technology is being administered." I try not to move, but the sensation is almost too much to bear.

The liquid is at my waist now and I wonder how far up it's going to go. I take another deep breath as the liquid reaches my chin. Terror overtakes me as it creeps past my mouth and flows over my nose and ears. I scream, which sounds muffled, as I pound in slow motion on the walls of the tube, trying to break out. In my panic I accidentally swallow a mouthful of the liquid and realize that I can still breathe. *How is this possible? I should be drowning,* I ask myself. A slight calm comes over me as I float there as if in suspended animation. The tingling sensation has stopped and my body almost feels like it's numb. Suddenly, the liquid begins to drain from the tube.

"Nanobot introduction successful. Cleansing process will commence shortly."

The Modified

As I stand there in the empty tube, an immense surge of energy courses through me. Surveying my skin, I see that it's covered in a blue film. I hear the sound of something rushing through the pipe that's connected overhead. A strong blast of warm water hits me like a high-powered shower. Staring at my arms I see the blue film peel away, collect at the bottom, and rush down the drain. The water shuts off and a green light appears at the top of the door.

"Cleansing process is complete. You are now free to exit the implant administration conduit."

The door slides upward and I step out. I shudder in the cold of the room outside. The energetic feeling that I had before disappears and is replaced by nausea. My head begins to pound and my heart feels like it's about to explode out of my chest. I stumble and drop to my knees as I hear a muffled voice call out to me. The blurry outline of someone rushing over fills my vision. The next thing I feel is a strong pressure rising up into my throat and liquid gushing out of my mouth onto the floor. As I stare down at the puddle of neon blue, the whole room fades to black.

Chapter Three
The Escadrille

I slowly open my eyes and scan my surroundings. A headache begins to invade as the blinding white of the room creeps into my pupils. As my haziness dissipates, and I begin to see more clearly, I notice there's a clear glass bubble encasing the bed I'm lying in. When I begin to sit up, the glass dome separates into two pieces at the middle and slides down into the metal frame that surrounds the bed. I look around and I seem to be in a hospital room of some sort, but it doesn't look like any I've ever been in before. The entire room retains the slick polish that everything else at this facility has had, and there are shiny metal objects everywhere that are most likely some kind of advanced medical equipment. I see other cadets in the beds that line the perimeter of the room. They must have passed out like I did.

What I assume is a nurse, approaches me dressed all in white. "Hello, I am Ada 21, your nurse here in the med-wing. I hope you do not mind, but I took the liberty of fitting you with a proper Allied Federation hairstyle, and dressed you in a uniform." Her tone is robotic.

Ada 21? That's the same name of the lady at the front desk, except with a different number. They even look similar except she has brown hair.

"Thank you," I say as I begin to examine the clothes I'm wearing.

I hear the door to the med-wing slide open and turn to see my dad hurrying into the room. He rushes up to my bed, "I came the moment I heard you had complications. Are you okay? What happened?" he asks hurriedly while grabbing me in a hug as he speaks.

"I'm so glad to see you Dad. You can't even begin to know how much," I answer, returning his hug and getting a little teary eyed. "I'm okay. But that was probably the scariest thing I've ever experienced. I don't think there was any way I could've prepared for that."

"I'm so sorry you had to go through that, Kenley. The process is very intense, but full immersion into the Nanobot fluid is the only way to introduce the implant," he explains, pulling back slightly to look me in the eyes.

"Nanobot fluid? There were little robots floating around in that stuff?"

"Correct. The nanobots carried the implant into your body through the pores in your skin."

"Was that why I was able to breathe?"

"No. Actually the liquid has a high concentration of oxygen in it, which makes it breathable. The liquid has properties of water, but is just like breathing air."

"Oh, I see…kind of."

"Listen to me getting all scientific. I'm just so relieved that you're okay."

"Me too," I say, sending him a smile.

"Is there anything that I can be of assistance with?" Ada 21 asks, coming up to the side of my bed.

"I think we're all set here," My dad replies.

As Ada 21 walks away, I turn to my dad and ask, "What's with the nurse having the same name as the lady I met at the front desk at the Hexagon?"

"They're androids," he replies nonchalantly.

"Androids? You mean robots that look like humans?"

"Indeed. Just another wonderful innovation brought to you by the Federation," he jokes. "These are all prototype models though. They're testing them out here before they can be used in combat."

"It's kind of creepy if you ask me."

He just chuckles at my comment. "Well, at any rate, I've got to get back to work. I just wanted to make sure you were all right. I'm glad I got to see you again. I'm sorry I haven't been there more often for you, or anyone for that matter," he says, his voice full of sadness.

"It's okay. We know that you love us, no matter how busy you ever get with work. I'm glad you came by. I definitely feel better now that I've gotten to see you again."

"I love you, Kenley."

"Love you too, Dad," I reply as he kisses my forehead.

After he leaves, Ada 21 walks over again. "Grayson, Kenley, you have a visitor. Would you like for me to allow them in?"

"Yeah, it's okay," I reply.

Joey strolls through the door and the first thing I notice is that his eyes are shockingly blue, almost as if they're electrified. The next thing I see is his uniform. It's a formfitting black-and-red ensemble with white stripes on the sleeves, chest, and legs. Joey's athletic build wears it very well.

"I heard what happened to you," Joey states as he grabs for my hand. "Looks like you weren't the only one that had this reaction though." We both look around the room at the rest of the cadets who are recovering.

"Yeah, that was quite intense, huh?" I ask.

"You could say that," he replies with a slight smile.

"Hey, have you seen your eyes lately? They're like really blue."

"So are yours," he states, pointing at me.

"What?"

"Go look in the mirror," he says, gesturing to the one on the wall opposite my bed.

I stand up, and instantly a wave of dizziness overcomes me. Joey immediately reacts by taking my arm, stabilizing me, and guides me toward to the mirror. My eyes widen as I see that my normal green eyes have turned a shocking blue that match Joey's. Bringing my face close to the mirror, I pull back my eyelid to see my eye more clearly. There are small periodic electrical pulses that flow through my iris that causes me to flinch slightly and let go of my eyelid.

"Pretty cool, huh?" Joey says.

"Yeah."

I examine my hair, which has been pulled back into a tight braided ponytail and looks quite beautiful. *Not too bad for an android*, I think to myself.

The uniform fits snug on me, just like it does Joey, and accents all the right areas of my body. I touch the material and it's super smooth, and seems very breathable. It feels like spandex, but nowhere near as restrictive. I almost feel like I'm not wearing anything at all.

A pair of dog tags hang from my neck, resting against my chest. I examine them and there's an engraving on each one:

Kenley Grayson
Magnus Academy Cadet
1696344-0216

A patch on the sleeve of my shirt catches my eye when I look up at the mirror again. It's a symbol of some sort. A dark grey triangle with light grey points and a light grey infinity triangle in the center of it. There's a deep red M in the top point of the triangle. I assume the M stands for Magnus.

"These uniforms are really cool. Way better than anything we'd have worn if we were in the regular military," Joey comments, smiling at me in the mirror.

I look around and notice the rest of the cadets in the med-wing are stirring in their beds. Most of them prop themselves up and begin to stand, regaining their composure.

A voice comes over the intercom. "All draftees report to the main docking bay for transportation to the Magnus Academy. I repeat, all draftees report to the main docking bay for transportation to the Magnus Academy."

"The Magnus Academy?" I ask, looking questioningly at Joey. He shrugs his shoulders and replies, "Let's go find out."

• • •

The Escadrille

As we exit the med-wing I see the guy I saw back at the entry platform leaning against a wall down the corridor, talking to a group of cadets. He looks in our direction and his eyes meet mine. He sends me a smirk and I dodge it, turning my head toward Joey.

"Hey, so where do you think this main docking bay is?" I ask.

"Uh, probably that way," he answers, pointing down the corridor the guy is hanging out in.

I feel a twinge of nervousness come over me. "What makes you say it's that way?"

"The sign right in front of us that says main docking bay, with an arrow pointing that way," he says with a chuckle.

"Fair enough," I reply, staring down the corridor at the guy again.

A voice comes over the intercom once more. "Will all draftees report to the main docking bay for transportation to the Magnus Academy. The boarding process will begin in five minutes."

I see the guy and the group he's talking to all begin to head down the hallway away from us. I breathe a sigh of relief and make my way down the hall with Joey in tow.

The hallway opens up at the end into a massive industrialized space that resembles an oversized hanger bay for airplanes. There's a moving walkway that leads us out into the area. The walkway is raised high above the ground and there seems to be a sizeable drop from the edge.

As we step onto the walkway and move forward, I look over the side and see several spaceships below us being worked on. I've never seen an entire spaceship this close up before.

"Wow, those things are kick ass. I hope we get to fly in one of them," Joey states excitedly, peering over the edge with me.

I hear someone call out my last name and I turn to see Sam pushing her way through the people behind us to catch up. Geoffrey and Caleb are right behind her.

"You gave us quite a scare back there, Grayson. I wasn't sure you'd make it. You had a wicked reaction to that implant. Glad to see you on your feet though soldier," Sam says after she taps me on the arm.

"Thanks. I'm still a little shook up, but I'll be fine," I reply.

"Apparently this academy we're going to is some kind of training ground. You know, to help us hone our skills as Bio-Mods," Geoffrey chimes in.

"Bio-Mods?" I ask.

"Oh, that's just a little something I came up with. Since we were modified on a biological level with those nanobots, I decided to make up a name for us. Bio-Mods," he replies, seeming proud of himself for coming up with it.

"I like the sound of that," Joey comments.

• • •

"Thanks," Geoffrey replies with a beaming smile.

The moving walkway leads us into a bright white tunnel that's lined with large wide windows trimmed in shiny metal. As we reach the first set of windows, I look out into the area beyond, and a massive spaceship is sitting there like some kind of sleeping giant. The size and scope of it is the most impressive sight I've ever seen. It shimmers in the lights as we pass by it. I can't wait for the next set of windows to come so I get one more look at it. We're all staring at the ship in awe, not saying a word. I notice Joey's mouth is gaped open slightly. Caleb has a huge smile across his face and I see him mouth the word awesome. The ship's stark contrast between shiny dark grey and bright silver across its body make it a sight to behold. Printed in large black lettering on the side of the ship is the word "Escadrille. *"Must be its name, I guess*, I comment to myself.

I finally take my eyes off the ship and look down the moving walkway. I see *that* guy staring at me, with the same smile he gave me back in the hallway. His blue eyes pierce through mine. I blush and immediately return my focus back to the ship. Why is he staring at me? This isn't really the time for this. I glance back over at him, but he's turned his attention away from me. I almost feel disappointed. *Stop it Kenley! This is not what you came here for. Pull yourself together, girl*, I argue with myself.

The Modified

I can see the end of the moving walkway coming up ahead, and the other cadets in front of us begin to step off and walk to the right, out of my view. We empty out into what looks like a futuristic airport loading bridge. You can see the entire docking bay as you walk across the bridge. The walls are made of glass and formed into an archway, leading toward the Escadrille.

As we enter the ship, I notice the interior is massive very spacious. We all look like wide-eyed kids in a toy store while looking around. The cool color pattern on the outside of the ship continues inside with the walls being a combination of shiny dark grey and silver.

We pass through the ship's main bridge and come to the passenger's section. There are rows and rows of oversized plush black leather chairs that are facing each other. We're directed by a voice over the ship's intercom to take a seat and prepare for take-off.

I settle into my seat and immediately look for the seat belt, but there isn't one. "Wait, there aren't any seat belts?" I ask worriedly.

Geoffrey slides into the seat across from me. "It's not like an airplane, Kenley. You don't feel the take-off. If you wanted to, you could walk around the ship during launch," he explains.

"How do you know that?" Joey asks.

"My dad builds ships for the Federation," he replies. "He's taken me on several test flights. This ship is easily the largest one I've ever been on though. I can't wait to see what it can do."

Suddenly, I feel a slight rumbling through the ship. "What was that?" I ask Geoffrey.

"It was probably just us taking off," he replies with a shoulder shrug.

"No way, that was it?" Joey asks surprised.

"Like I said, these spaceships are an entirely different beast than an airplane. It's like when you're on a huge cruise ship and don't feel the waves. Same principle," he explains.

A man's voice comes over the intercom. "We should be arriving at the Magnus Academy in approximately T-minus one hour."

"I think I need to go walk around a bit. I'm getting a little restless," I tell everyone as I stand up from my seat.

"Do you want me to come with?" Joey asks with slight worry in his eyes.

"No, I'll be fine," I reply.

"You sure?" Sam chimes in.

"Yep."

As I begin to walk away from the passengers' section, I notice there are a lot of cadets milling about in the next area. The sign above the room reads: *observation deck*. There's a group huddled around a large window, staring out into space. Very few people have been able to travel up here, and I'm sure for most of us aboard it's our first time. The sight outside the window is truly spectacular and almost surreal.

I see a switch glowing bright green on the wall opposite the window everyone's looking out of. The label just above it says: *window control.* I push it and the metal panel next to the switch slowly slides open, revealing another huge window. The view instantly takes my breath away. The stars look so bright from space. I look to the right and see Earth in the distance. It looks absolutely amazing.

"So beautiful," I hear a male's deep voice say behind me. I spin around and see it's the guy from before. His face is perfection, right down to the chiseled jawline. A grin creeps across his lips as he sees me blush when our eyes meet.

"Yeah…Earth is, beautiful, isn't it?" was all I could say.

"I guess Earth is too," he says and grins wider, his dimples adding an extra touch. My blush deepens and I turn back around to face the window.

So he's one of those line-user types. Is he seriously trying to flirt with me right now? I ask myself.

"Wow, that was pretty bad. Sorry, it sounded much better in my head," he laughs to himself. "I'm not really good at this sort of stuff. I hope I didn't just make you feel uncomfortable."

I turn to face him. "You didn't make me feel uncomfortable. I just don't hear compliments like that very often."

"I find that hard to believe," he states.

I notice his eyes shift from mine and focus on something over my right shoulder. "Look at that," he says, pointing behind me. I turn and see a truly devastating sight. Pieces of spaceships float gracefully just outside the window, littering the area we're traveling through. It almost looks like a ship graveyard. The haunting imagery makes me shiver, and I think of all the lives that must've been lost out here.

In the distance, I see the massive front end of a ship hurling through the rubble, past our position, toward Earth. It bursts into flames as it travels through Earth's atmosphere and crashes right into our planet. I gasp and then a dead silence falls between us as we see the black area around the crash site grow in size, creeping across the surface. We look at each other, exchanging saddened glances, and turn our attention back to the scene in front of us.

"I wonder how many people were there," I say in a reflective tone, pressing my forehead against the glass, still keeping my eyes on Earth.

"I don't know, but I've got a feeling it's only going to get worse," he replies solemnly.

The Modified

"I don't think anyone else saw what just happened," I state looking across the way at the group gathered around the other window.

"Maybe that's a good thing. Maybe not knowing makes you better off."

"I guess," I say distracted, wondering if any of the cadets onboard just lost anyone.

"You know, speaking of not knowing things. It just occurred to me that I don't know your name." His deep voice brought my attention back to him. I think to myself that maybe this isn't the right time to flirt like this, but maybe he's trying to take our minds off what just happened.

"You first."

"Okay. My name's Landon. Landon Shaw."

"Shaw? You wouldn't by any chance be related to Dominic Shaw?" I ask with one eyebrow raised.

"He's my father," he replies hesitantly.

"Huh, the son of war hero Dominic Shaw is standing right here in front of me."

"So…you heard about that, huh?"

"Who hasn't heard of the man who single-handedly led the blitz squad against the Bringers, driving them back to their planet," I answer.

"Yeah, that's him, but I just call him Dad."

I get silent for a minute. He asks if he said something that upset me. I shake my head. "My brother was in your dad's squad when they fought against the Bringers. He was killed in battle. It was his first mission."

"I'm so sorry," he says quietly as he places his hand on my shoulder.

"It's okay. I've had some time to come to terms with it."

"So, I've told you my name, what's yours?" he asks, leaning up against the wall next to me.

"Kenley Grayson."

"Wait, Grayson, like the scientist who created our implants? That Grayson?"

"Yep, the one and only," I joke hollowly.

"It seems like both our dads are important to this war, huh?"

"You could say that." I look at him with questioning eyes and ask, "So, not to be rude or anything, but what made you come over here and talk to me?"

"To be honest, you intrigue me," he replies, returning my stare.

"I intrigue you?"

"Yeah. You didn't seem like most of the girls I run into. You have this...I don't know...'thing' about you that intrigues me."

"I see," I reply and push myself away from the window.

The Modified

"Sorry, that all came out wrong...like I said, I'm kind of terrible at this whole thing," he blurts out.

I giggle. *How could he be bad at this? Has he seen himself in a mirror? He's drop-dead gorgeous. He has to get a lot of practice. There's just no way,* I tell myself.

"Well, I got a giggle, at least that's something," he says and lets out a light laugh while running his hand through his beautiful chestnut brown hair. He must be one of those guys who has no clue they're good-looking.

"If you don't mind me asking, how did the daughter of the lead scientist behind this project end up a part of it? You'd think your father would've done everything in his power to keep you away from all of this."

"Maybe it wasn't his choice," I reply defensively.

"Sorry, didn't mean anything by that. I was just trying to feel you out and get to know you a little better," he explains.

At first I don't say anything as I lean up against the wall next to him. "He did try to stop me from doing this, but I want to fight. Besides, if I didn't go through with this, I'd probably end up no better than my brother did. At least now with this project I might have a fighting chance."

"Fair enough," he replies and lets out a sigh.

The Escadrille

We hear a commotion coming from the group of cadets looking out the opposite window. We rush over to see what all the fuss is about.

"Is that where we're going?" I hear someone in the crowd ask.

In front of us I see a massive dark grey triangular structure floating there. It looks to be about twenty times the size of the ship we're currently on. We seem to be heading straight toward it. "That must be the Magnus Academy," I say under my breath.

A man's voice comes over the intercom. "All cadets, please prepare for departure from the *Escadrille*. We will be arriving at the Magnus Academy shortly."

"Sorry, Landon, I have to go find my friends, see you around."

"I hope so, Ms. Grayson," he says with a cheeky grin.

As I enter back into the passengers' section, I hear my name called and see Joey and Sam frantically waving at me. As I make my way over to them I look back trying to find Landon, but he's lost in the swelling crowd heading toward the exit door of the ship.

The Federation guards on board begin to round us up like cattle and move us closer to the exit hatch. We stand there, waiting for the go-ahead light to appear at the top of it, per the instructions of the voice overhead. The sound of the ship docking with the structure fills the area and we begin to hear this odd whining mechanical noise.

"Don't worry, that's just the passage tunnel connecting to the structure and locking into place," Geoffrey chimes in.

I turn to look at him, the worry slowly draining from my face. "Thanks for that, I was beginning to wonder what the hell that sound was."

"No problem. I thought I'd say something since you seemed a little tense."

"Yeah…just a little," I laugh nervously.

As the light turns green above the exit hatch, its door splits down the middle and both halves slide to either side. Before us lies the passage tunnel, which is made completely out of glass with a shiny metal grated floor.

A voice echoes through the ship again. "We have arrived at the Magnus Academy. Will all cadets please exit the *Escadrille* in an orderly fashion?"

Chapter Four
Magnus Academy

As we come to the end of the tunnel, I immediately recognize one of the people standing in front of us. It's my father again. His eyes scan the crowded corridor and finally find mine. He sends me a strained smile.

A woman with caramel-colored skin dressed in a white lab coat, like my dad's, is standing next to him. Her jet-black hair is pulled up into a tight bun. She's beautiful, almost model-like.

There are two other men standing on the other side of my father. One's dressed in military garb, but it's not from the Allied Federation. It looks like the dark blue uniforms from the U.S. military before all of this happened. He's tall, statuesque, and stands there stiffly with his hands behind his back. He stares at us from under his dark blue beret, with a face that looks chiseled from stone. The other man looks very bookish. He's dressed like a stuffy librarian, but has a youthful energy about him. His wire-framed glasses, which he's constantly adjusting, add to his look.

A door opens behind the small group, and out pours six people who line up on either side of the doorway. There are three men and three women. The three men look like the driver who picked Joey and me up from the airport, except they all have different colored hair. It's the same deal with the women. They all look like the nurse and receptionist, but with different hair colors. Must all be androids.

"Welcome to the Magnus Academy, everyone," my dad announces, looking out at the crowd. "Please proceed to the mess hall for the opening ceremony."

We all begin to file into the facility. As I pass my dad he reaches out and touches my shoulder. He gives me a head nod and I slightly smile back at him before continuing inside.

The area beyond the entrance was unlike anything I've seen before. It looks like a futuristic utopia, a perfect blending of nature and technology. The room had bright white walls, which almost seemed to be illuminated. There is a grand staircase that leads up to a second floor balcony which overlooks where we're standing. The stairs seem to be made up of this bright neon blue light and not metal, wood, or any other solid material. *I've never seen that before*, I think to myself.

Off to the left is a small waterfall surrounded by all kinds of colorful foliage. There are two rows of trees that run up the center of the room, leading to a large fountain. As I pass a tree, I reach out to touch one of the leaves. My hand goes straight through it and the image of the leaf shutters. *What the? Is this all virtual reality?* I ask myself.

"Weird," I hear Joey say beside me as he does the same thing.

Before I have a chance to reply, an Ada android appears beside me and tells us to keep up with the group. Falling back into line we continue toward the mess hall. Upon entering the large space, the first things I notice are the armed guards lined up at the front of the room, right in front of the stage and podium. My eyes grow wide with shock as I recognize the man at the podium. His face was undeniable and one I've seen a thousand times on television. It's the Federation's head general, Roman Barclay.

"Welcome, welcome. Everyone come in and take a seat," he announces with his arms outstretched wide.

Shiny and polished white posts are scattered throughout the area in several rectangular patterns. I'm amazed when suddenly a blue light emanates from the stands, creating tabletops. The smaller white posts that sit next to the four room-length tables begin to project out the same light, forming benches.

I'm wary as I go to sit down. Feeling the blue light that makes up the bench, I find that it's actually solid. *This is crazy,* I think as I take my seat. They seat us by region and continent, so I find myself next to Joey, Sam, Geoffrey, and Caleb. I look down the table a ways and see Landon. He sends me a little wave and I return it with a smile.

"Uh-oh, boy trouble three o'clock," Sam whispers at me jokingly from across the table.

"Shut up," I reply playfully. "It's not like that."

She laughs. "Okay, Grayson. Whatever you say."

I give her a withering stare and her grin grows wider.

We hear the sound of someone tapping on a microphone, so we turn to look at the stage. The general clears his throat and then smiles really big, his pearly whites glistening in the lights overhead.

"I'm sure you all know who I am, so I can probably skip the introduction. This next part, though, I want to emphasize." He pauses and looks seriously out at all of us.

A hologram of a hulking beast projects from the wall behind the general and walks up next to him. Shocked gasps sound throughout the crowd of cadets at the sight of the creature. It stands about seven feet tall, with long muscular arms that hang way below its waist. It almost has a human appearance, except for its face and the fact it's skin is a dark purple color. The creature has two sets of eyes, an almost nonexistent nose, and four mandible-like fangs that encase its mouth.

"This is your enemy…the Bringers. Not many people have seen one of these things and lived to tell about it. This unknown race had been lying dormant for some time now, and their silence since the Shaw Blitz was worrisome. We assumed that they were prepping for something on a large scale. Well, it would seem that the devastation we've suffered from recently was due to falling war debris, and not direct attacks from the Bringers themselves. We've still yet to rule out the possibility that the Bringers were involved in some way though. These 'attacks' may be a part of a much bigger plan of theirs to always keep us on guard. The Bringers have proven in the past to be a malicious, cunning, and unyielding foe, decimating our soldiers without even an afterthought. So we're inclined to believe that their next attack will be an attempt at a crippling blow. That's where all of you come into play. You will help us hit them before they hit us. Every single one of you is an integral part to this war, and the Magnus project. You've committed to the ultimate sacrifice, and there are no words to describe how important you all are to Earth. You are not just representing the Allied Federation here. No, you're representing the entire world…your world. So don't hold back, and make us proud," General Barclay finishes his speech and salutes us as the hologram of the Bringer fades away. We all stand and salute him back. He waves as he leaves the stage and is followed out by his group of armed guards who are dressed in all black, which is slightly different than the rest of the Federation.

The beautiful woman who was standing next to my dad at the entrance, approaches the podium with a clipboard in hand. "Hello, cadets," she begins, "my name is Dr. Sadie Patel. I'm the head of the Fortification Division here at the Magnus Academy. But more on that later." Her British accent is very alluring. "Now, I'm going to call you up in groups of five to receive your Artificial Intelligence partner, or as it is more commonly called, AI. They will act as your guide during your stay here at the academy. Your AI will also monitor your implant and vitals, just to ensure you're acclimating well," she explains and then peers down at her clipboard. "First, we'll begin with North America. We're doing this alphabetically by geographic region, so when you hear yours, please approach the stage. First up is Appalachian Mountains region."

My little section stands and makes our way toward the stage. Five androids are waiting in front of us, holding what look like smooth white strips of hard plastic in their hands. The female android before me smiles awkwardly as I come to stand before her.

"Please present your right arm," the female android says.

I send her a confused look, but still do as she asks. The android holds up the piece of plastic above my arm and then swings it downward. It slaps around my wrist, stinging a little. I flinch in pain. As I examine the piece of plastic that now has become more like a bangle, I can't seem to find any kind of opening or release mechanism. It seems to have sealed itself.

"Please present your right arm once again," the android requests.

I extend it out, wincing in anticipation of more pain, but instead she takes my hand gently and brings my wrist close to her. She smiles awkwardly once more. Bringing her left hand up to the bangle, her index finger opens up and reveals some kind of probe looking thing within. As it touches the band of white plastic, it begins to pulse with a faint blue light and I feel this tingling sensation in my wrist.

"Unification complete," the android tells me.

The bangle begins to pulse again and a little blue hologram projects from it, startling me. The image resembles the nondescript figure of a man. It shutters when it speaks.

"Greetings, Grayson, Kenley. I am called Galileo."

"Hi," I reply hesitantly.

The Modified

"Hi...searching database for *hi*...an informal greeting used in place of greetings like *hello*...adding to vocabulary."

This should be interesting, I think to myself.

"Now, if you five will follow Ada 26, she will give you a brief tour of the facility and then show you to your living quarters," Dr. Patel explains, pointing to an android standing over by the entrance of the mess hall.

While walking through the facility, I find myself faced with technology that I never dreamed could be possible. I'm continuously in awe as we enter each new area.

Ada 26 stops in front of a large window looking into what appears to be a classroom of some sort. Beyond the classroom is another room, but the lights are off and I can't make out what it looks like.

"This is one of the three training classrooms in the facility. All of your Fortification exercises will be discussed and practiced within this room," Ada 26 explains. "Moving along."

"Fortification exercises?" I ask Joey.

"Maybe it has something to do with our implants," he replies.

"Please keep up," we hear Ada 26 call out to us as we lag a little behind, still staring into the training room.

Joey puts his arm around my shoulder and proceeds to act like a robot while whispering mockingly. "Please keep up." We both chuckle and catch up with the rest of the group.

Reaching the second floor balcony, which looks over the entrance to the facility, we peer down the main staircase and see that the stairs are comprised of the same solid blue light that the tabletops and benches are.

The hallway in front of us, across the balcony, has a sign above the entryway that reads: *living quarters*. As we walk down the hallway we pass many doors labeled with a letter followed by a number. The doors are very unique in that they're circular in shape.

"This hall is where you will find your living quarters. Your AI is the key to your room. Each door locks automatically once one enters or exits a room," Ada 26 explains. "Grayson, Kenley. We have reached your quarters. Room number C-15."

"Like the android said earlier, I'm in D-10, okay? So I'm just down the hall if you need me," Joey says with a reassuring smile.

"I'll be fine. No worries," I reply.

"All right, see you soon," Joey says into my ear as he gives me a quick hug.

I watch my group continue down the hall as I stand in front of my door. Looking back at the door, I notice there's no handle. I look down at the band around my wrist and see that it's pulsing with that blue light again. Holding it up to the door, I hear the sound of an electronic lock disengaging. The door rolls to the right, into the wall. *Huh, interesting*, I say to myself.

The room beyond is white like the rest of the facility. There are basics like a bed, a closet, a dresser, a window with blinds, a vanity mirror, and a bathroom. It actually looks like a futuristic version of a college dorm room I visited once.

As I enter, Galileo projects from the bangle. "Welcome to your living quarters. Please let me know if I can be of any assistance," he says in a slightly robotic tone.

"Thanks," I reply.

I sit down on the bed and it's stiff as a board. I bounce up and down, but the bed doesn't move an inch.

"Recalibrating," Galileo says.

The bed becomes softer and feels just like the one I have back home.

"Cool," I say as I plop down onto the bed.

"Grayson, Kenley?" Galileo asks.

"Yes?"

"I must perform a complete vitals scan. It will take approximately two minutes. Could I please have you remain still for the duration of the scan?"

"Sure."

As I lay there I think about home. About how much I miss my mom and little brother. I haven't had much downtime to really just think and reflect.

A tear begins to roll down my cheek as Galileo chimes in. "Scan complete Grayson, Kenley. Implant functioning at optimum level. Vitals are stable."

"Well, that's a relief," I joke hollowly.

"Agreed," Galileo replies seriously. I shake my head and smile.

Pushing myself off the bed, I make my way to the only window in the room. Strangely, I notice tiny slivers of sunshine creeping through the blinds. *How is there sunshine?* I ask myself. When I open the blinds my eyes need a few seconds to take in and process what I'm seeing outside. My heart sinks as I scan the vision before me. A perfect garden lies just outside my window. It's my mom's garden, though off in the distance it begins to fade away like someone forgot to finish a painting. It's the same view I have from my second floor bedroom window at home. I see the red poppies my older brother Dylan gave my mom, but don't see the blue ones I gave her before I left.

"How?" is all I get out at first, but then I breathe and try again, "how is…that outside my window?"

Galileo projects from the bangle and replies, "I re-created it for you."

"What? How do you know about this?" I ask confused.

"The image was stored in your database."

"My database?"

"Searching for alternative word for *database…memory*, the image was stored in your memory," he answers.

I don't respond right away and instead just stare out the window. My eyes become misty as I fight against tears. "Thank you, Galileo," I say softly.

"I detect a slight variation in your vitals. Are you feeling okay? Do you need to lie down?" Galileo asks matter-of-factly.

"No, I just miss home. That's all."

"Portland, Maine, is where you are from. You miss Portland, Maine?"

"Yeah," I answer. "I also miss my brother. I lost him two years ago."

"Grayson, Dylan. Killed in action…I am sorry for your loss," he states.

"You can feel sorry?"

"I do not understand the concept, to feel sorry, but I know by me saying it, your vitals have returned to stable levels."

I laugh to myself and shake my head. "I see, I guess."

"My pleasure," he responds.

Magnus Academy

I hear an electronic clicking sound followed by some quick static that erupts from the speaker above my door. It sounds like the intercoms at my high school.

"Grayson, Kenley. Will you please report to the office of Doctor Grayson, Wyatt? He is expecting you," a monotone female's voice echoes in my room.

Galileo projects out of the band and says, "I can show you the way."

Chapter Five
Becoming Acclimated

I follow Galileo's directions to my dad's office, and after navigating the many corridors of the facility, I finally arrive at his office. There's a sign next to the door that reads:

Dr. Wyatt Grayson
Headmaster at Magnus Academy

"We have arrived, Grayson, Kenley," Galileo announces.

The door to my dad's office is a large metallic oval with a slit down the middle of it. Just as with all the other doors, this one also lacks a handle. Like I did with my room's door, I hold up the bangle to it and hear the familiar electronic unlocking sound before the two oval halves slide apart, revealing the room beyond.

Becoming Acclimated

"Kenley, there you are. Come in, come in," my father says as he rises from behind an oversized desk made up of blue light. "I hope you're settling in all right. I know all of this has been happening so fast," he states, giving me a hug.

Returning his hug I reply, "I'm acclimating, I guess. But Dad this place is amazing. And when were you going to tell me about you being headmaster? Kind of glossed over that one, didn't you?"

"Sorry about that, there was a lot going on and I completely forgot to tell you about the whole headmaster thing. But isn't this place absolutely remarkable? This facility was going to be used to train soldiers in advanced battle tactics, but once the war began, the project was scrapped and has since become home for the Magnus Academy. We've obviously upgraded it a bit," he jokes.

"I'll say. There's stuff here that I never thought I'd ever see."

My dad chuckles. "Well, I'm glad to hear that you're doing okay. How's your implant? Any more nausea from the fluid?"

"Well-"

Galileo's image springs from the band, making me pause. "Implant is functioning at optimal levels," he states before disappearing.

The Modified

"Good to hear," my dad says with a smile. "Seems like your AI is working well. I'd hope so since I designed them," he continues with a laugh.

"It's been interesting to the say the least," I say, glancing down at my wrist, and then back to my father. "Why are we here? What is this place? This is almost too much to process."

"I know, Kenley. That's why I called you here," he replies as he leans up against the desk. "You're a soldier now, Kenley. And as a soldier you must train and hone your skills. That's what this academy is, your training ground. You'll find that you have powers lying dormant inside of you that you can't even imagine. They're just itching to get out."

"You mean the implant?"

"Look at your hands, daughter of mine."

I look down at my hands and they're glowing with a faint blue light. "What's happening?"

"That's only the beginning," he says, clasping his hands around mine. The blue light in my hands fades away. My wary eyes rise to my dad's. "I'm so sorry, Kenley," he says softly and pulls me in for a hug.

So many questions flood my mind, but there's only one that creeps from my lips. "Why did they really pick me, Dad?"

He sighs heavily and replies, "Because I told them to."

I pull back from him slightly. "What? Why?"

Becoming Acclimated

"I had no choice, Kenley. You did so well in your preliminaries, and they were going to put you on the front lines. I couldn't go through that again. At least this way you're here, and your odds of survival have greatly increased," he explains.

"And Joey, what about him?" I ask in a huff.

"I knew you'd need a support base in all of this, so I told them to pick him too."

"I can't believe this. We're here on a lie?" I ask, my voice laced with anger.

"I'm sorry for deceiving you, but I'm not sorry for bringing you here. I hope you understand why I did this. Here you're much safer," he says as he places his hand on my shoulder.

I gently shrug off his hand and back away. "I need time to let this sink in. With everything else going on, this just complicates things even more."

"I understand dear. Just know that I did this for your safety," he states, pushing my chin up and making me look at him.

"I know. I just need time."

"Grayson, Kenley? I sense a slight deviation in your vitals. I suggest removing yourself from the situation that is causing this," Galileo interjects.

"I guess I better go then," I say, making my way toward the door.

• • •

The Modified

"It's probably best you don't tell anyone about this. You don't want to draw any more attention to the fact you're related to the headmaster," my dad says with a worried smile.

"Yeah, no worries about that, Dr. Grayson."

The sound of a familiar song awakens me from my sleep the following morning. It takes me a few moments to gain my composure and fully recognize the tune. I rub my eyes and see the sunshine coming through the window again. The song grows louder and I realize it's coming from my bangle. It's a beautiful song and brings me back to a happier time in my life when my brother was still alive. It was one of our favorites.

"Good to see you are awake, Grayson, Kenley. Sustenance is waiting for you in the mess hall," Galileo states.

"Why did you play that song just now?"

"The song was stored in your memory. I set it as your alarm. Is this okay? I sense a change in your vitals. Does this upset you?" he asks.

"No, it's fine."

"You have forty-five minutes to shower, dress, and arrive at the mess hall. Should I prepare your shower?"

"Sure," I reply with a yawn. I hear the shower turn on in the bathroom.

"Shower is ready. Please proceed into the shower," he says and then disappears.

I look down at the band and wonder if Galileo will *see* me when I undress. "Uh, Galileo?"

"Yes, Grayson, Kenley?"

"First of all, you know you can call me *Kenley*, right? You don't have to be so formal."

"I did not realize I was being formal. I will call you Kenley from here on out," he replies. "Anything else?"

"Yeah, actually there is," I say and think how to ask the question. "Uh, will you be able to *see* me when I'm in the shower?"

"Searching database for response…Kenley, are you uncomfortable with this? You can utilize the privacy cover located in the top dresser drawer, if that will make you more comfortable," he replies.

Opening the drawer I see a round metal casing that looks like it will fit over the bangle. I snap it on and head for the bathroom.

The water is at the perfect temperature. Standing in the shower feels soothing as I watch the water swirl down the drain. It seems to be mixed with a pleasantly smelling bath gel or soap-like substance. As I move my hands around my body, I begin to see bubbles forming all over me. I hear a pleasant chime sound from the showerhead and I see it turn to the right by itself. The water feels different and the soapy substance seems to be gone. It seems like regular water now. When I finish the shower, I look around for a towel to dry off.

I hear Galileo's voice muffled inside the metal casing. "Would you like me to initiate the drying mechanism?"

"Yes, please," I reply.

Several panels on the walls inside the shower shift, revealing metal grates. I'm suddenly blasted with warm air. I can feel the water dripping off me, and at first it's an odd sensation, but I get used to it. The air stops blowing and I feel my skin, it's completely dry and silky smooth.

There's a robe hanging just outside of the shower and I grab for it. It feels like it's made of the same material our uniforms are, and fits a little snug on me. I make my way to the closet and my bangle activates it to slide open. Inside is a row of uniforms, all my size, hanging up on the rack, and also several pairs of black boots on the floor. A little dresser off to the side has two drawers, one contains a bunch of black sports bras and the other contains many pairs of black underwear and socks.

Dressed in my uniform, I look at myself in the full-length mirror. I notice that my hair isn't still in a braid, and I panic. "This is definitely not a military approved hairstyle," I state while combing my hand through it.

Becoming Acclimated

I sigh after trying to fix my hair up into several different styles, but nothing works out.

"Is something wrong, Kenley?" Galileo echoes within the casing.

I apologize for forgetting to remove it and then reply, "I can't seem to get my hair like that android had it."

"You have ten minutes to get to the mess hall. Would you like some assistance?" he asks.

"Well, I think I'd be hopeless without any," I answer.

"Is that a yes?"

I laugh. "Yes."

I hear a soothing electronic sound come from the bangle several times. A couple seconds later there's a knock at my door. I approach the door and it rolls open. A red-haired android is standing there with an awkward smile plastered across her face.

"Greetings, I am Ada 18. I was summoned to braid your hair. Would you like me to braid your hair now?"

"Uh, yes, that would be perfect," I reply. Really? A beauty android?

It only takes Ada 18 a minute to perfectly braid my hair exactly the way the other Ada did. I sit there in front of the vanity mirror admiring her work.

"Thanks, Ada 18," I say with a smile.

"My pleasure, Grayson, Kenley," she says and then leaves abruptly.

"You now have only seven minutes to get to the mess hall," Galileo chimes in.

"Okay, okay, you don't have to be so pushy," I reply. "Oh, and thanks for the hair."

"My pleasure," he answers.

"Hey, I've been meaning to ask why you and all of the androids say *my pleasure*, if you can't actually feel pleasure?" I ask staring at Galileo's hologram.

"We are preprogrammed with common phrases used by humans, but not all. *My pleasure* is a common kind saying, and seems appropriate anytime someone shows gratitude. Why do you ask?"

"Just curious is all," I reply. "Crap, I forgot to brush my teeth. Wait, I didn't see a toothbrush in the bathroom. Galileo, how am I supposed to brush my teeth if there's no toothbrush?"

"There are dissolvable tablets in the bathroom that will assist you with your dental hygiene," he answers. "Check in the mirror cabinet above the sink."

I run into the bathroom and pull open the mirror cabinet. There's a small circular blue tin that's sitting there all alone on the second shelf. Taking it in hand, I open the tin and find

• • •

several flat round tablets. I pick one out and hold it right in front of my face, studying it. "This is it?"

"Yes. Place the tablet in your mouth and it will do the rest," Galileo explains.

Once I pop in the tablet, I immediately feel this strange sensation sweeping across my tongue and throughout my mouth. It feels like I just ate the entire contents of a bag of Pop Rocks and then drank a soda. I open my mouth and see that it's full of a white frothy substance, like I had just brushed my teeth.

"I would suggest you dispose of the excess tablet residue, and then rinse your mouth," Galileo states.

Another knock comes from my door the moment I finish taking a swish of water. As I approach it, the door rolls open and Joey's standing there smiling.

"Well, aren't you a sight for sore eyes," Joey states as his smile turns to an impish grin.

"You're not too shabby yourself," I say jokingly while giving him a love tap on the shoulder.

"Ready to go get some grub?" he asks, putting his arm around me.

"Yep, I was actually just leaving to come get you. Hey, where's the rest of the gang?"

"I think they're already there," he replies.

The Modified

As we walk to the mess hall, it takes every fiber in my body to not tell Joey the truth about why we're here. His constant talk about how cool it is that the two of us were chosen together makes it even harder.

"I wonder what kind of food they serve here," Joey says as we enter the crowded mess hall.

Looking around the room I see all kinds of food on the tables. There's yogurt, cereal, fruit, eggs, bagels, different juices— a whole slew of options.

"Grayson! You've got to check this out," I hear Sam yell out to me as we make our way over to our seating section.

Landon is sitting six people down from Sam and his head pops up when she says my name. Our eyes meet and he mouths *good morning*. I mouth it back to him and smile shyly. *Could he get any cuter? I mean, seriously. He has to have some major flaw*, I tell myself.

"Nothing, huh?" Sam asks, looking at me suspiciously with an eyebrow raised. I roll my eyes and take a seat. Joey nudges me and makes a kissy face, causing everyone in our immediate area to laugh. I shove Joey playfully and my eyes meet Landon's again. He's sitting there, foolishly grinning at me.

"Anyway, like I was saying, you've got to check this out," Sam states and then touches the menu button that is showing on the table. I notice everyone has one in front of them. A hologram of a menu, full of food options, pops up from the table, and Sam begins to flip through it to show me.

"Are you freakin' kidding me? Is that how we order our food?" I ask with wide eyes.

"Yeah, and here's the best part," Geoffrey interjects as he presses on the picture of a bowl of cereal. The menu closes up and shrinks back into the table. A second later a male android is at our table section, setting down a bowl of cereal in front of Geoffrey and then proceeds to pour milk over it.

"That's insane," Joey chimes in and brings up his menu.

I look over and Caleb is sitting there with a smirk on his face while flipping through his menu. *I wonder why he doesn't talk much,* I think to myself.

"So Grayson, how'd you get your hair that way?" Sam asks, flipping my braid.

"I told Galileo and he made it happen. I swear two seconds after I said I needed help, he had an android at my door."

"Too bad my AI isn't as kick ass as yours. I think I got the cheap model or something. I had to put my hair up with this rubber band. I really need a braid. They're harder to grab 'cuz it doesn't swing free while fighting. Can you tell your AI to hook me up?"

"I'm sure if yours can't do it, Galileo would be happy…well, I don't think he knows what happy is, but I think he'd be okay with it," I say as I make my selection from the menu. Moments later, an android with my food places the tray in front of me.

As I finish my oatmeal with blueberries, my bangle begins to ring. It reminds me of the tardy bell we had in high school. I hear the same chime ping from down the table. It's Landon's band. Then I begin to hear more bands ring around the room.

Galileo appears, "Your introductory training session begins in fifteen minutes, Kenley. Please proceed to training room B. Your instructor will be waiting for you."

"See ya, Grayson." Sam nudges my shoulder with hers, while Geoffrey waves sheepishly, and I get a nod from Caleb.

"Good luck," Joey says, placing his hand on my forearm as I get up to leave.

"Thanks," I reply, wishing at least one of them, even Caleb, was coming with me.

Halfway to the door I hear my name being called from behind me. "Hey, Kenley, wait up. Think we could walk to class together?" Landon asks.

How can I deny that face? "Sure, I'd like that."

Both of our bands go off at the same time, interrupting our conversation. "I sense a change in your vitals. Are you okay?" our AIs say in unison. We both laugh nervously. He attempts to cover his bangle while I try to hide mine behind my back.

Becoming Acclimated

"So...I kind of feel we started off on a weird foot," Landon says hesitantly. He pauses. I look at him and smile at his obvious nervousness. "I just don't want you to think I'm some kind of creep because of that atrocious line I used on you when we first met. In retrospect, that probably wasn't one of my finer moments."

I tried, but I couldn't hold back a giggle. "I kind of found it cute. In a bad pick-up line kind way, but still cute nonetheless."

"Really?" he asks, sounding unsure of himself.

"Yeah, just don't do it again though, okay?" I joke.

"Deal," he replies.

As we approach the training room, I see my dad through the large glass window. He's standing at the podium at the front of the class and his name is written really big on the white board behind him. The room doesn't have any desks when we first enter. As if queued, bright white posts slowly rise from holes that appear in the floor, and blue light forms the seat and tabletop of each desk upon each post.

"So, your father's our teacher as well, huh?" Landon asks as we take our seats.

"I guess so," I reply as I flash a confused look at my dad.

"Please, everyone take a seat, and we'll begin shortly," he announces and then sends me his *I'll explain later* look.

The Modified

After the last few cadets filter in and take their seats, my father begins to speak again. "I want you all to look around the room and get to know these faces, because for the next month or so you'll all be training together."

I look around the room and see our group is a mixture of all the continents represented at the academy.

"Now, here at the Magnus Academy there are three divisions that each and every one of you will train in. There's Strike division, which are considered the attack experts. The Tactical division, who are the war strategists, and then there's the Fortification division, who are the main line of defense. All three of these divisions must work together to ensure victory. At the end of the month, you will each be assigned to a division based on which one you excel in most. During the course of your training, you will do things that no other mortal would ever dream of being able to do. For example..." he pauses as he scans the room. "You, in the back row. What's your name?" he asks the girl four seats over from me.

She stands, "Jamie Warren, sir," and finishes with a salute.

My dad chuckles. "At ease, Jamie, this isn't the military," he jokes, causing the whole class to laugh. Jamie smiles and proceeds to relax. "Come on up to the front of the class, I'd like you to demonstrate something for us, please."

Jamie moves quickly to the front.

Becoming Acclimated

"Now, I want you to stand right here and face the class. Then raise your arms straight out in front of you, and clench your fists. A little higher, please, so your arms are at shoulder height. Good. Okay, I want you to concentrate and focus on something that makes you very angry." Jamie's face becomes strained as she concentrates. A hush falls over the class as Jamie's hands begin to glow with a blue light. A little blood begins to trickle down her nose, and I hear a few gasps erupt from the people around me. Her AI chimes in, telling her that her levels have risen significantly.

"Okay, don't overdo it, Jamie. Just relax," my dad says in a soothing voice. "Now open your eyes and look at your hands." Jamie opens her eyes and they fill with surprise.

"I want you all to imagine being able to use this energy, that you see right before your very eyes, in combat. Because over the next month that's exactly what you'll be doing. Thank you, Jamie, you may return to your seat. Oh, and don't worry, with practice the nosebleeds will go away," he explains as he ushers the shocked cadet back to her seat. "So, who else would like to give it a go?" my father asks and then claps his hands together. I see several hands shoot up into the air, mine included.

Chapter Six
Training Ground

I hear a voice and footsteps going back and forth outside my door. Pushing myself off my bed, I make my way toward it. The door rolls open and I'm surprised to see Landon standing there. He looks at me and smiles while combing his hand through his chestnut brown hair. He seems to be at a loss for words.

"Landon, what are you doing here? It's late and we have class tomorrow."

"I know, I know, but some of us are going to the rec hall to unwind and check out what's going on with Earth. I was hoping you'd join me, I mean, us," he rambles.

"Sounds like a plan. I don't think I could sleep right now anyway," I reply with a smile.

Training Ground

When we enter the rec hall, my first thought is that it looks more like a really nice lounge than an actual military recreation hall. There are several large screens affixed to the walls that all tuned into the World News Network. A few tables and chairs that are made up of blue light are scattered about the space, and three large white plastic couches are arranged in the center of the room.

Landon shakes hands with a guy that I recognize as one of the draftees from his region. "Oh, Kenley, this is Bradley Jacobs. Bradley, Kenley Grayson." Bradley nods at me and I nod back. "So, any news about Earth?" Landon asks him.

"It's not good," the guy replies.

"Did something happen?" I ask anxiously.

"South Africa was attacked earlier. They came under heavy artillery fire and were hit by some major spacecraft debris. Everything happened at once. It's all over the news. No one knows why the Bringers concentrated an attack there. They don't expect many survivors out of the areas that were hit," Bradley explains somberly.

"Oh my god," are the only words that escape my mouth while watching the footage playing on the screen behind Bradley. The chatter amongst the rest of the cadets gathered in the rec hall ceases, and a quiet falls over the room as we all just stare at the devastation. "Why is this happening?" I ask, not really expecting an answer.

I feel someone take hold of my hand, it's Landon. His grip is firm and his skin is smooth to the touch. His palms are slightly sweaty. Somehow this simple action calms me.

"I don't know why," is all he says.

The next day Landon walks with me to class again. I want to ask him why he grabbed my hand last night. *Was it because he was sympathizing? Was it a spur-of-the-moment thing? Was it planned? Does he like me? Stop it, Kenley, this is not the time for this*, I argue with myself.

"Here we are, our first official class," Landon states as we reach the door to training room A. The room looks identical to the one we were in yesterday.

We hear a resounding "file in," come from the open door. As we enter the room, I immediately recognize the man standing at the front. He's dressed in the same dark blue military uniform that he wore on the first day we arrived. His penetrating stare makes me feel uncomfortable as he begins to pace back and forth at the front of the class, like a caged animal.

"Line up!" he barks while pointing to the far wall.

I notice there are no desks activated in the room as I rush over to stand against the bright white wall.

Training Ground

The man stops in his tracks and turns to us while putting his hands behind his back and puffing out his chest. "The name's Liam Archer. Commander Archer to you lot. I'm your instructor for Strike division. As you can see there are no desks in this room. You will not be sitting in my class. You will stand. No one in Strike fights sitting down. That's the Tactical Division's job." He pulls out a rectangular device that looks like an electronic tablet, but has a see-through glass screen that's trimmed in shiny metal. I can kind of make out the words through the back of the device and they're a bright neon blue color.

Someone really likes white and blue a lot. I think everything here is either white or blue with shiny metal trim, I joke to myself.

"So if you don't mind…what am I saying? Of course you don't mind. We're just going to jump right in and begin," he barks again as he scrolls through the device in his hand. He pauses and looks up at us. "Grayson, Kenley," he calls out standing right in front of me.

I step forward, "Yes, sir?"

"Where's the salute, soldier?" he yells at me and I swear saliva flew from his mouth toward my face. I raise my hand and give a proper salute. "So, you're the daughter of the headmaster, huh?"

"Yes, sir," I reply.

"Up for a little demonstration, Grayson?" he asks with a smirk.

"Yes, sir."

He hits a button on the device in his hand and a light turns on, revealing another room in the back of the class. Commander Archer points to the open door and says, "After you."

The room is made up of large white square tiles that cover the walls and floor and are trimmed in shiny metal. A large glass window looks into the room from the training room. I see all the other students line up at the window as I move to stand at the center of the room. I'm not really sure what to expect next.

Commander Archer comes up behind me. "Are you ready to begin?"

"Begin what exactly, sir?" I ask confused.

He hits another button on his device and a panel on the floor in front of us rises slightly and slides to the side. What appears to be some kind of robot emerges from the opening. It reminds me of one of a department store mannequin, but this one is all metal. It takes a few steps forward and enters into a combat stance with its hands clenched out in front of it. Totally nervous, my body stiffens as I look over at Commander Archer.

"Well?" he asks.

"Well what, sir?"

"Don't just stand there and look pretty, Grayson. Attack the drone," he orders.

Training Ground

"Aren't you supposed to train us first? This seems a little advanced, sir," I ask hesitantly, hoping he doesn't flip out and yell at me again.

"What better way to learn than to experience it first hand?" he answers smugly.

"With all due respect, sir, I don't feel ready to fight this thing."

"Disappointing, Grayson, truly disappointing," he states shaking his head and crossing his arms. He presses a button on the electronic pad and the drone goes limp. I relax and breathe a heavy sigh of relief.

I turn to make my way back to the training room, but Commander Archer's arm stops me. "I haven't dismissed you, soldier. You said you wanted to train first, well let's train," he says and then presses another button on the touch pad. The drone stands at attention and moves to the center of the room. "I need you right here, soldier," Commander Archer orders me while pointing to the space right in front of him. I take a quick look at Landon and he sends me a look of concern. I turn back and warily make my way over to stand in front of the robot. I would stare into its eyes, but it doesn't have any. Its shiny metal face only shows a distorted reflection of mine.

"Hit it," Commander Archer orders.

"But it's made of metal," I reply.

The Modified

"You know for someone who has superhuman abilities, you sure do give a lot of excuses," he responds smugly. "Hit it!"

I get into a fighting stance and ready myself to throw a punch. Reeling back my arm, I breathe in and then out as I push forward, twisting at my hips to give myself more power. I connect with the drone's face and pain surges through my hand and down my arm. I let out a slight groan as I pull my hand to my chest, cradling it with my other one. There's a slight dent in the drone's face when I stare up at it.

"Again," Commander Archer demands. I give him a look of "are you serious?" and he replies the same, "Again."

Getting back into my stance, I reel back and throw another punch. The pain is even more intense this time. I peel my hand from the drone's face and yell in pain while cradling my hand again. There's blood and a little skin from my knuckles left in the grooves of the dent on the robot's face.

"Harder!" he shouts. I can hear the other cadets chattering amongst themselves as tears begin to well up in my eyes. "I said harder, soldier."

"I can't," I blurt out.

"You can't?" he asks smugly, getting into my face and grabbing a hold of my injured hand. I let out a squeal of pain. "I didn't ask you if you could, Grayson. I gave you an order. Do you really think the Bringers will show you any mercy? Use the pain. Use the fear. Use the anger. They'll keep you alive." He leans in closer to me and whispers so only I can hear. "Your daddy is not always going to be there to save you. You have to fight for yourself, even if that's not how you ended up here." As he backs away from me, my face flushes with anger and I glare at him. "Hit it again," he says forcefully.

My bracelet pulses blue and Galileo projects out. "Your vitals are at high levels, Kenley. I suggest you calm down and rest," he explains.

"Hit the drone!" Commander Archer yells.

"She's had enough," I hear Landon roar as he enters the room.

"Back in line, soldier. I'll decide when she's had enough," he barks at Landon while pointing a finger at him.

I look at Landon and mouth, "I'm okay." He returns the look with one of worry.

"I'm only going to say this one more time, hit the drone, soldier!"

I feel this surge of energy course through my hands and my body. I'm completely blinded by anger as I get into my stance. I notice my hands are glowing bright neon blue and begin to pulse violently.

"Kenley, your vitals have reached critical levels. Risk of overheating is imminent," Galileo chimes in. I ignore him and

The Modified

ready to throw the punch. I release a guttural yell as I propel my fist straight for the drone's chest with all my might. Just before I make contact, my hand stops glowing and then crashes into the cold, hard metal. I hear a crunch but am not sure if it was the sound of the metal, or my bones breaking. My hand goes limp and the intense pain brings me to my knees.

"Kenley!" I hear Landon yell as he rushes over. He crouches down next to me, "Come on, we need to get you to the med-bay."

"That will not be necessary, Shaw," Commander Archer tells Landon calmly.

"What do you mean? She's injured. And all thanks to you I might add," Landon replies defensively.

"You're out of line, soldier," he roars as he grabs Landon by the back of his shirt and pulls him to his feet. "Grayson will be fine. Her hand is already healing."

"What are you talking about?" I ask and then look at my hand. The blood is gone and the gashes on my knuckles are healing up. *I can't believe my hand isn't a bloody mess. I don't even really feel the pain anymore,* I say to myself. I look up at Landon and see that he's just as shocked as I am at the state of my hand.

"The benefits of nanotechnology," Commander Archer states. "Dismissed, Grayson."

Training Ground

Landon helps me to my feet and we both make our way back into the training room. As I peer over my shoulder back at the commander, I see him smirk while hitting a button on his touch pad. The drone stiffens and proceeds to walk back toward the hole it emerged from.

Later that night, sitting on the edge of my bed, I think about what Commander Archer said earlier in class. Looking down at my hand, I still can't believe it's perfectly healed. Not a single scratch or scar left. *What did I get myself into?* I ask myself. A range of emotions wash over me and I break down crying. I feel like an idiot for even shedding a tear, but I can't help it as they begin to flow freely.

"Kenley, I sense a loss of fluid. I do not detect physical stress. Ruling out perspiration by mean of physical activity...scanning database...Kenley, are you crying?" Galileo asks.

"Yes."

"Why?"

"Do you really want to know, or are you just programmed to ask?"

"I am programmed to ask, but there is a true inclination on my part to find out how you really are doing," he replies.

"Well, if you really must know, I'm feeling pretty crappy at the moment."

"Searching database for crappy…slang for *bad*…why do you feel crappy?"

"A lot of reasons. Too many really to talk about," I huff, flopping back onto my bed.

"Care to share? I have been programmed to be a good listener."

I let out a heavy sigh. "I'm not sure that's what I need right now, Galileo."

"Humor me," he says.

How do I even begin to humor an android? I think to myself. "Well…for starters, I'm not even supposed to be here, which was kind of proven today in class. Earth and my family are in danger. And for some reason I decide to start liking a boy during all of this. Oh yeah, and I'm a highly-modified freak of nature," I ramble on, counting off every issue with my fingers.

"It sounds like you have a lot on your mind. Is there anything I can do to help?"

"What exactly could you do? You're just a computer," I reply, feeling bad about what I said the moment the comment leaves my lips.

"I am sorry I cannot be there for you the way you need someone to be," I hear Galileo say, and it almost sounds like his feelings are hurt.

"No, I'm sorry, Galileo. I shouldn't have said that. I'm just venting," I say feeling really guilty.

"Be strong, Kenley. I believe in you. Whatever that is worth," Galileo says, and begins playing the song he has programmed for my alarm.

I smile as I look down at the little blue hologram projecting from my bangle. "Thank you, Galileo."

"My pleasure."

The week in Strike training begins to take a toll on me. I find myself struggling to learn the abilities Commander Archer is teaching us. He still gives me crap about the first day, but that's okay because it just makes me work harder to prove him wrong. It also helps me prove to myself that I do belong here.

Every night I slip out of my room to practice in the gym. No one ever really goes in there at night, so I'm free to practice all I want without being disturbed.

As I reach the gym, I hold my bangle up to the door and it shifts open. I grab a thirty-pound medicine ball from the rack and place it in the middle of the floor. Backing away from it and keeping it always in my sight, I focus on the ball and concentrate. I feel a flicker of energy travel through my fingers. Looking down at my hands, they begin pulsing slightly with the blue light again. Clenching my left hand into a fist transfers the energy that's collected in it to my right hand, which begins to glow even brighter. My focus returns to the ball. I raise my right hand and the ball begins to shake as it slowly drifts into the air, but only barely. My hand begins to tremble and I groan with frustration as the energy becomes too much for me to handle. The ball drops to the ground as the word, "Dammit," escapes harshly from my lips. *I can't do this,* I tell myself.

"You're trying too hard," I hear a familiar voice say behind me. Startled, I turn to see Landon standing in the entryway.

"Easy for you to say. This stuff is coming so naturally to you. But that's to be expected from the son of the great war hero Dominic Shaw," I respond, sounding defeated.

He smiles and walks over to me. "Have you been coming down here every night?"

"Well, when there's a test on Friday, and you're struggling with the material, you take every chance you can to study," I reply. My heart speeds up as he gets closer to me. *Please Galileo, don't say anything,* I think to myself.

"Would you like some help?" Landon asks while placing his hand on my shoulder.

"Uh…sure," I stutter out while gazing into his eyes.

He smirks and spins me around to face the medicine ball. His hands grasp my waist. "Do you trust me, Kenley?" Landon whispers into my ear, sending a warm sensation down my spine. My heart feels like it's about to beat out of my chest.

"Of course I do," I reply softly.

He traces up my back with his fingers and stops at my shoulders. He grips them while applying the slightest amount of pressure. Landon moves his hands along my arms, gently caressing them, and works his way down to my hands. Cupping my hands in his, he brings them out in front of me. I can feel his breath on my neck and I smile. He rests his chin on my shoulder and rubs his cheek against mine. It feels hot and my blush deepens.

"Now, I want you to concentrate on the medicine ball," he whispers. I feel a sudden rush of energy in my hands and look to see both of ours glowing bright blue. "Concentrate, Kenley," he repeats. Landon closes his left hand into a fist over mine, transferring the energy to our right hands. The energy is so bright, it lights up the whole gym in a blue glow. He takes my right hand and begins to raise it into the air. Immediately the ball rises with the motion of our hands. Suddenly, it soars across the room into the wall, and then sits there spinning in the hole it created.

I realize I don't feel Landon holding me anymore. I turn around to find him standing a short distance away with a huge grin on his face.

The Modified

"See, all you needed was a little push. You did that last part all on your own," he says, moving closer to me again.

"Thank you," I say shyly, totally embarrassed by the intense moment we just shared.

"No problem," he replies, pushing the rogue strand of hair from in front of my face and placing it over my ear.

"Landon, what are we-" I begin to ask, but then he puts his finger to my lips and shakes his head. His hand is glowing and I feel the energy as it caresses against my mouth like a cool flame. His blue eyes begin to pulse as he brings his face closer to mine.

"What's going on in here?" A voice asks from the doorway.

All the energy fades from Landon's eyes and hands as we both look over to see Dr. Patel framed by the doorway. I should have recognized the distinct British accent. She stands there with her arms crossed, her head slightly tilted, and an eyebrow raised. She's dressed in workout clothes, which is not surprising since we're in a gym after all.

Dr. Patel's attention moves to the thirty-pound medicine ball that's still spinning in the wall. "Did you do that with your biotics?" she asks with surprise present in her voice.

"Uh, yes, ma'am. We did," I reply, putting a little distance between Landon and myself.

"Fascinating," she remarks, walking over to inspect it closer. "It's still spinning." Turning to look back at us, she smiles. "You two better get back to your quarters. Tonight's a school night, remember?"

"Yes, ma'am," we both say in unison and salute.

"At ease, soldiers," she says with a quick laugh, and we both hurry out of the room.

Approaching Landon's hallway, he stops and grabs my hand. "Well, I guess this is goodnight." I go to say something, but he catches me off guard and silences me with a scorching, mind-numbing kiss. He draws back slowly, "Goodnight, Kenley."

After sending me a quick grin, he turns and begins heading toward his room. I'm left standing here a blushing mess, watching one of the most gorgeous guys I've ever laid eyes on walk away. I feel my cheeks and they're burning up.

"Did that just happen?" I ask under my breath. I head down the opposite hall toward my room with a huge smile etched on my face.

On the day before the Strike final exam I wake up an hour earlier, deciding to do an impromptu training session in the gym before breakfast. While getting dressed I run through all the things we'll be tested on. Out of the three abilities we've learned so far, telekinesis is my strongest one. Of course, I give most credit to the cooperative effort with one Landon Shaw. I notice that I smile every time I think about him or his name.

The Modified

As I go to leave my room, I hear a knock at my door. It slides open when I get close to it. Joey's standing there with a solemn look on his face.

"What's wrong, Joey?"

"Something's happened."

"What?" My voice shakes, dreading to hear the next words out of his mouth.

"California…It was attacked. Most of the state's been leveled. They were showing video up and down the coast on the news," he explains.

"Oh no, Landon. He's from there," I choke out. "I wonder if he knows."

"You should probably go find him," Joey says as he touches my shoulder. He gives me a worried look just before I run out of the room.

I hesitate when I reach Landon's door. I want to knock, but then think of how I'd be feeling if I just found out news like this. *But what if he doesn't know?* I ask myself and then decide to knock anyway. There's rustling on the other side of the door before it opens. Landon is standing there with his back to me. His hands are glowing and there are several holes in the walls. I don't blame him for getting angry. I did the same thing when my brother died. I remember feeling helpless and completely lost. I can't even imagine how I'd feel if I lost most of my family and home.

Training Ground

Landon turns to look at me and his face is tear-stained and his eyes are red and swollen. My heart breaks seeing him like this. I throw my arms around him and he wraps his around me while placing his head on my shoulder. No words are spoken for a few moments, we just hold each other.

"Kenley? You are crying again? Is everything okay?" Galileo asks.

"Sorry Galileo, but this is not a good time," I reply.

"My apologies," he says and sucks back into the band.

"They're all gone." Landon finally speaks.

"I'm so sorry. I don't know what to say," I reply. "Was your Dad there too?"

"No, he's in D.C.," he answers. "I can't believe my home is gone…just like that…everything."

As I squeeze him tighter in a hug I can feel his pain as his chest restricts and he sobs into my shoulder. It's amazing how life can change in the blink of an eye.

"We're going to make them pay, okay?" I say, pulling Landon's face to be in front of mine. We both stare deeply into each other's teary eyes. The only thing I want to do right now is kiss him, in hopes I can ease at least some of his pain.

"I think I'm going to skip breakfast and rest up for class today," Landon says before kissing my cheek. "Thank you." He goes to sit on his bed and I walk over to be by his side.

The Modified

"Would you like some company?" I ask, sitting down next to him.

"Yeah, I'd like that," he replies.

We lay down on his bed and he wraps his arms around me and holds tight. I snuggle up close to him and press my ear to his chest. I drift off to sleep, listening to the beat of his heart.

"Grayson, you're up," Commander Archer announces and then points toward the back room. "Just like everyone else, you'll have four timed tasks to complete. Your overall time will determine your mastery of the skill. Each task will require you to utilize one of the four abilities you've learned in order to complete the task. If you are touched at any point during the task, or perform a different ability that is not the one called for, you will fail, understood?"

"Understood, sir," I reply with a salute.

"Well, get in there then, soldier," Commander Archer orders.

Landon grabs my hand as I go to leave. "Good luck."

I nod to him and head toward the back room. As I enter, I see a giant electronic timer imbedded into the far wall, and there's a switch on the wall to my left that's lit up.

"When you're ready, press the switch on the wall," Commander Archer calls out to me from the training room. The large window that everyone usually lines up in front of to watch is now shielded by a sheet of metal in order to keep the test a secret.

I hit the switch and the timer starts as an electronic voice pipes into the room. "Task is Kinetic Punch. Activating Combat Drone."

A panel in the floor in front of me slides open and a drone rises up from the hole. It goes into a combat stance and readies for my attack. It charges at me and leaps into the air. The drone dive-bombs in my direction and I roll out of the way as it crashes into the ground, causing a dent in the tile on the floor. It recovers and charges me again. The drone reels back to throw a punch, but I counter, throwing a charged kinetic punch straight through its chest. The drone crumples to the floor and the timer stops.

My time shows up yellow and the electronic voice chimes in again. "Satisfactory."

The switch on the wall starts to glow once more. Pushing it, my time starts and the electronic voice comes into the room. "Task is Surge. Activating combat drone."

Another drone emerges from the floor, but this one is surrounded by a wall of blue energy. I concentrate on its barrier with my hands out in front of me, my palms facing the drone. My hands start to glow blue, and the drone's barrier begins to slowly break apart into tiny particles I absorb. With the barrier fully depleted, I release my energy in a wave-like pattern, knocking the drone back against the wall and shattering it into pieces.

The clock stops and turns yellow. "Satisfactory," the electronic voice says.

I press the switch and cue the electronic voice again. "Task is Barrage. Activating Combat Drones."

Wait, combat drones…like multiple? I ask myself.

Three drones emerge from the panels in the floor and all enter into a defensive stance. I drop my hands down to my sides and both immediately ignite with a blue glow. The drone directly in front of me moves first and I dive out of the way as it lunges at me. I flip around and throw a light projectile from my hand right through its chest. As the drone crashes to the floor, I hear the clank of the other two's feet on the tile floor as they move toward me. I spring up and spin to face them. *Wait, there's only one there, where'd the other one go?* I think to myself. I feel two cold arms clasp around me tight, pinning mine to my side, not allowing me to move. I try to break free from its grip, but can't. "Damn," I murmur as a loud buzzer sounds and my time goes red. The electronic voice pipes in as the drone releases me from its grasp. "Unsatisfactory."

The switch on the wall lights up again, but I decide to take a quick breather and regain my composure before starting the next task. I'm feeling pretty low right now after failing the previous one, and the last thing I want to do is rush into the one task that I'm actually okay at. While staring at the switch on the wall, thoughts of me being not good enough begin to enter my mind. I shake off those thoughts, walk over to the switch, and pound it with my fist.

The electronic voice filters into the room. "Task is Telekinesis. Activating combat drone."

Another drone appears in the room along with a metal ball that rolls through an opening in the wall. I immediately concentrate on the ball, channeling all my anger from failing the previous task. Clenching my left hand into a fist I transfer all my energy into my right hand, and then push the ball at the drone. It shoots toward its head and knocks it clean off, causing a firework of sparks to erupt from its neck. My time turns green.

"Excellent," the electronic voice announces.

The door to the exam room slides open and the first person I see is Commander Archer standing in the doorway. "Not bad, Grayson. You probably could've done better, but not too bad at all."

Chapter Seven
Defensive Measures

"So, any word on Landon's return?" Joey asks me as we enter the mess hall.

"Nope, not a word. He just kind of left right after the Strike final and said he was going to see his father in D.C. I'm surprised he was allowed to leave," I reply solemnly.

Joey wraps his arm around my shoulder and gives me a side hug. "I hate seeing you like this—all mopey and stuff. Cheer up, he'll be back soon, don't worry."

"I hope so," I state, looking up into Joey's eyes.

"Well, I don't know about you, but I'm starved. I worked up quite the appetite during my final," Joey says, sitting down at the table.

"Yeah, me too. And if you don't mind, I'd rather not talk about how I did."

"Oh, come on. You couldn't have done that bad," he says with a laugh.

"Let's just say that it wasn't one of my best performances," I say dryly.

"That bad, huh?"

"Yep."

I'm kind of surprised that we're the first two at dinner from our group. Sam's usually the first one here. That girl loves to eat.

I glance over and see Joey flipping through his virtual menu. As I look past it I see Landon's empty seat and wonder how he's doing.

My thoughts are interrupted by Sam plopping down on the seat next to me and brushing my shoulder with hers. "I'm so freakin' hungry," she announces while hitting the menu button on the table in front of her. "Aren't you eating, Grayson?"

"Yeah, just haven't decided on anything yet," I lie, knowing exactly why I haven't picked something.

Geoffrey sits down across from me and Caleb takes the seat next to his. They both stare at me with questioning eyes. Clearly, it's written all over my face that I miss Landon. "So how were all your finals today?" I ask, trying to change the subject and take the focus off me.

The Modified

"I'm not really in the mood to talk about it," Geoffrey states as he keeps his attention on his menu.

"Don't feel bad, Kenley. He won't even tell *me* how he did," Sam chimes in.

Caleb just sits there with a smile on his face and doesn't say anything.

Does he ever talk? I ask myself.

"I think I'm going to head to my room. I had a big lunch earlier and might just turn in early tonight. That Strike final really kicked my butt," I say while standing up.

"You really should eat something," Joey states, looking at me with concern.

"I'm fine, Joey, really. Don't worry. I'm just tired and want to go rest up, okay?" He nods his head, but I can tell that he sees right through me. Joey knows me too well. "Goodnight, guys." I hear everyone say goodnight just before I leave the table.

Walking toward my room, I stop in front of Landon's hallway and stare down at his door. I let out a sigh and continue onward.

My door opens as I approach it and then closes and locks once I'm inside. I proceed to pull out the metal casing for the bangle from the dresser drawer and snap it on. Galileo turns on the shower and I begin to peel off my uniform.

"The water is at your desired temperature," I hear a muffled Galileo say within the casing.

Defensive Measures

"Thanks, Galileo."

Standing in the shower feels wonderful as the warm water just washes over me. I find myself thinking of Landon again and it seems like I can't do anything without him popping into my head. *This is crazy, I've never felt like this before, and I'm not even really sure why I do*, I tell myself.

Leaving the shower, I slip into my robe and head back into my room.

"Galileo?" I ask, taking off the metal casing.

"Yes, Kenley?"

"Can you play that song for me? You know the one that you set as my alarm?"

"Yes, I can play that song for you," he replies and then the song begins flowing from my bangle.

I smile as I look down at the little band of plastic and am immediately brought back to the first night I heard this song. Joey, Dylan, and I were lying out under the stars and it came on over the radio in my brother's truck. Dylan was right in the middle of telling his story about a star, and the song matched the tone of it perfectly. From that night on, it became our song.

A knock at my door takes me away from my musings. I approach the door and it slides open. I'm surprised to see Landon standing there, and when he sees me, a half-smile appears on his mouth. I smile too and want to wrap my arms around him and squeeze tight, but I resist.

"Galileo, you can pause the music for now," I say softly to the bangle. The music stops and I focus back on Landon.

"Hey, what was that song you were just listening to? Sounds familiar," he asks.

"Oh, that? It's just a song I used to listen to a lot when I was younger. Hey, how was your trip?" I ask changing the subject, not wanting to get into the story behind the song.

"Interesting, to say the least. May I come in?" he asks and I don't know what to say. I'm in my robe and a gorgeous boy is asking if he can come into my room.

I hesitate, but then say, "Sure."

He walks into my room, grabs the chair in front of my vanity mirror, spins it around and straddles it with his front facing the back of it. I move to sit on my bed and face him. He's quiet at first and seems like he's contemplating what to say next. He begins to say something a couple times and then stops.

"So…what made your trip interesting?" I ask trying to get anything out of him.

"My mom and little brother are alive," he replies, but sounds oddly less enthusiastic than I would've thought he'd be.

"That's great news, right? I mean, you were worried that they had…well, you know," I state sending him a reassuring smile.

● ● ●
123

He suddenly snaps out of his funk. "Yeah, it's great news. It was good to see them again," he says, sounding a little more upbeat.

It's weird, he still kind of feels disconnected for some reason, I think to myself.

Landon stands and moves over to me. He kisses my cheek softly and turns to walk toward the door. "We'll talk more later, okay?" he says and waits for me to walk over to let him out.

"Yeah, just let me know when," I reply, moving to stand by him and opening the door in the process. He appears so guarded, like something's really bothering him, but he doesn't seem to want to discuss it right now.

"Goodnight, Kenley."

"Goodnight," I say as he leaves my room and the door rolls shut behind him. I lie down on my bed and sigh. I begin to wonder what exactly happened that he can't talk about.

"Galileo, can you please resume playing the song?" I ask and then the song chimes on again as I continue to gaze up at the ceiling.

As we enter our first Fortification class, I smell the faintest hint of lavender in the air. My mom grows lavender in her garden, and I always love helping her tend to it just so I can enjoy the wonderful fragrance. It's so beautiful when it blooms.

The Modified

"Come in, cadets, and take a seat on a floor mat. We'll begin class shortly," Dr. Patel tells us with a huge smile.

Landon picks the mat next to mine.

I laugh. "I find it weird that all of these rooms have desks, but we hardly use them."

"Yeah, that is weird," Landon responds nonchalantly. He's being so hot and cold. I wonder what happened in D.C. that has him acting like this. I wish he would just confide in me.

The last student filters in and Dr. Patel clears her throat. "Welcome to Fortification training. You already know me, so I'll skip over the introductions." She looks down at the electronic pad in her hands and presses the screen. The smell of lavender intensifies as she looks up and smiles at us. "The scent you're all smelling, if you don't already know, is lavender. It's used a lot in aromatherapy for a calming effect. This actually brings me to our first exercise." She sits down on a floor mat at the front of the class in the Lotus position and places her hands on her legs with her palms facing upward. "Now, I want you all to sit as I am, and close your eyes. Concentrate on your breathing and listen to my instruction."

I close my eyes and take in a deep breath, following Dr. Patel's words.

"Your first task is to create a barrier of energy around your person. In order to do so, you must clear your mind and visualize the barrier you require," Dr. Patel explains in a soothing manner. Her voice seems to flow through my head, and as it does the calmer and more focused I become. I feel a sudden burst of energy project from my hands and then it engulfs me. There's this heat that seems to wrap around me like clothes that have just been taken out of the dryer.

I sense a presence in front of me, so I open my eyes and see the distorted face of Dr. Patel through a hazy blue energy field. She startles me and I gasp, causing my barrier to disappear. She continues to stare at me, almost as if I'm a specimen she's studying or something. It's actually kind of creepy to be honest.

"Very interesting," Dr. Patel states, with an intrigued look on her face.

"What is?" I ask confused.

"The speed at which you were able to produce your barrier," she replies. "You were actually the first in the class to do so."

"I was?"

She continues to study me with her eyes. Suddenly something seems to dawn on her and she points at me. "I bet you're a natural protector. You have a true instinct to defend yourself and those around you."

"I do?"

"Indeed," she laughs.

The Modified

Sitting in the mess hall I look down at Landon's seat and it's empty. *He said he'd be right here*, I think to myself. I've been worried about him ever since he got back from D.C. I know there's something wrong with him that he's not telling me. In stereotypical guy fashion though, he acts like he's okay, but you can see in his eyes that he's not.

"So how do you like Fort training?" Joey asks. "At least tell us what you can, since we can't really talk specifics."

Pulling myself away from my thoughts, it takes me a few seconds to process the question, and then I reply. "Apparently, I'm a natural protector. At least according to Dr. Patel. She said I created my barrier quicker than anyone so far."

"Damn, Grayson, I couldn't cast a barrier to save my life last week," Sam chimes in. "I'm Strike all the way, baby."

I laugh slightly. "Don't even get me started on that egotistical jerk, Commander Archer."

"He's a teddy bear compared to how my father was," Sam replies.

"Yeah, mine too," Joey murmurs. I place my arm around his shoulder and give him a comforting look. He smirks back at me.

"How's training going for you, Geoffrey?" I ask him as he flips through the dinner menu hologram.

"I just found out that Geoffrey got all Green during his Tact final. He's a certified whiz kid. Strike on the other hand…not so much," Sam answers for him. He nods, confirming what she just said is true.

"What about you, Caleb?" Joey asks him.

"I received all green in Fort. Actually finished second overall in my class," Caleb replies, shocking everyone with his lengthy response since he usually just keeps it to one-word answers, if he even talks at all. He grins and returns to eating his food.

After dinner I make my way to Landon's room since he never showed up. I knock on his door, but don't hear any movement inside. I knock again, but still nothing. *Where is he?* I ask myself.

"Kenley, I sense you are worried about something. Is there anything I can help you with?" Galileo asks, projecting from my bangle.

"Not unless you've got GPS and can locate people," I respond in a defeated tone.

"GPS? I am sorry, but I am not equipped with such technology."

"That's okay, Galileo. It's not your fault," I reply.

I feel a hand touch my shoulder and I spin around to find Landon standing there. "So, you were worried about me?" he asks.

"You heard that, huh?" I reply and he nods with a smile. "Well, yeah of course I was worried. You never showed for dinner."

"Sorry about that. My dad was on the news talking about California. I didn't really feel like eating afterward," he states, his tone more melancholy with a hint of anger.

"What did he say?" Landon gets quiet as he stares down at the ground.

"Hey, I want to show you something," he says, quickly changing the subject. It's clear he still doesn't want to talk about California or his dad, so I drop the topic.

"What do you want to show me?"

"It's a surprise," he answers, extending his hand for mine. I take it and let him lead me down the hall to the elevators. As we enter the elevator, the floor and walls light up bright white, causing me to squint slightly at first. Landon hits a button on the wall panel that says *observatory*.

The panel flashes red and an electronic voice says, "Password required."

Landon replies, "Kenley," and the panel changes to green.

"Password verified," the electronic voice states as the elevator doors close.

"My name is a password?" I ask looking at Landon with surprise. "Wait, how did you know my name was a password?"

"By accident…don't ask," he laughs nervously.

Only seconds seem to go by and the doors open again, revealing a large triangular-shaped room beyond the elevator. "Top floor, observatory," the electronic voice chimes in.

As we exit the elevator, the walls of the room begin to retract and slide downward as if they're reacting to us entering the area. I stare in awe as I spin around slowly, taking in the sight before me. After the walls completely retract, all that's left between us and outer space is a wall of glass. A blanket of stars completely surrounds us. They're incredibly bright and vibrant, casting a glow over the entire room. I'm completely mesmerized as I continue gazing at the beauty before me. I wish Dylan and Joey could see this.

I feel Landon take my hand into his and squeeze gently as he joins me by my side. A silence falls over us as we just stand there, gazing into space.

"It's hard to believe a war is happening out there amongst such peace and beauty," I say, breaking the silence.

"Yeah, hard to believe, isn't it?" is all Landon says. It seems like he's waiting for something to happen as he stares pensively up at the stars.

"Is this what you wanted to show me?" I ask softly.

"Nope," he replies, still staring up and not breaking his line of sight. "There, that's what I want to show you." Just as those words escape his mouth, I see Earth come into view. "There it is." He squeezes my hand tighter and I look over at him, but he doesn't take his eyes off Earth.

"My father called California a casualty of war…that's it. That's such a bullshit answer," Landon says under his breath. "He didn't say a damn thing about the rest of our family or friends. There was no emotion at all. Nothing but that bullshit answer. Some hero he is, huh?"

"I'm sorry," I say quietly.

"But that's not even it, though. My mom told me my dad had called her and said he missed his family. He told her that he wanted to see them and was sending a plane to bring them to D.C."

"Why would that upset you, though? He missed them," I ask.

"My mom wouldn't leave home to go to Washington, even if it was to see my dad. And as far as my dad missing her, that's a joke. He doesn't care about anyone but himself and his career. I'm glad he made them go because they're still alive, but something's not right. Two days after they arrived in D.C., California was hit. Doesn't that seem strange to you?" he asks.

"How could your dad have known? It would've been impossible for him to know that was going to happen to California, right?"

"Yeah, you're probably right," he responds.

Defensive Measures

Landon goes silent for a moment and then turns to me. His blue eyes start to pulse slightly.

"I miss everyone so much, Kenley. I should've been there with them," he grounds out, clenching his jaw.

"Don't talk like that. You wouldn't have been able to do anything to save them," I say, tearing up at the look of pain on his face.

"I know, but at least I would've been with them."

"No. You were meant to be here. You were meant to live. If you need something to live for, then live to avenge them," I reply.

His eyes return to normal and the anguish leaves his face as I place my hand on his cheek. He brings his hand up and cups it around mine. Landon takes my hand from his cheek and kisses it softly and places it to his chest. He smiles as he stares deeply into my eyes.

"I do have something to live for," he replies and leans in close to me. Our lips touch with the slightest of pressure. He places his hands about my waist and pulls me closer. My hands press on his firm chest and find their way to his gorgeously chiseled chin. I hear Galileo say something followed by Landon's AI, but I am so concentrated on Landon that I can't make out what they're saying. His hands move to my face and I can feel the heat from his power surge through my body. He pulls back slightly, his eyes pulsing again. "I'm so lucky I found you."

The next day in class, I couldn't quit smiling at Landon. I stopped feeling guilty about how I feel about him. These could be our last days alive. Why not spend them happy? The war does still weigh heavily on my mind though, that's for sure. One thing is for certain, I've never felt this way for someone in my whole life. This feeling gives me hope. It gives me strength, and I know Landon feels the same way too.

"Yesterday you all learned how to produce barriers, so today I thought I'd go into a little more of the scientific explanation behind your implants. They're quite fascinating really," Dr. Patel states as she walks around the room. "First of all, it should be noted that your implants are synched with your DNA. That's why your blood was taken before you entered the implant administration conduits. Each implant reacts differently depending on the host who receives it. And since your implants are linked with your DNA, they're also connected with your vitals. Any changes in emotion can activate them. Once you learn how to control your emotions, you'll gain control of your abilities. Speaking of controlling your abilities, let's move on with our second exercise, the multi-barrier," she explains and then sits down in front of us on her floor mat. We again copy her sitting position and close our eyes, waiting for her instruction.

"Let's begin by clearing our minds and focusing on someone in the room to cast a barrier around. We'll practice one barrier at a-"

Dr. Patel suddenly stops talking, which causes me to open my eyes, and I see there are barriers around Landon, her and me. Dr. Patel's surprised look meets mine. As I look around I notice no one else has a barrier around them yet.

"Kenley Grayson, I do believe you have produced three barriers at once," Dr. Patel states in awe as the barrier around her begins to fade away.

"I did?"

"Absolutely remarkable," she says with a huge smile.

I look over at Landon and he grins at me. I return it.

Heading into the Fortification final exam, I feel much more confident than last time. I've definitely proved myself, and Dr. Patel agrees. So maybe I wasn't cut out for Strike, but that doesn't mean I don't deserve to be here.

"Are you ready, Ms. Grayson?" Dr. Patel asks.

"Yes, ma'am," I reply with a salute.

"All right then, head into the test area and press the switch when you want to begin."

The Modified

I nod and enter the room. It is set up exactly like the Strike's test room with a switch on the wall, a large digital timer, and the walls and floor are comprised of big white tiles lined in shiny metal.

I hit the switch, and as the timer starts an electronic voice filters into the room. "Task is Barrier. Activating combat drone."

One of the white tiles in the distance rises slightly and slides to the side. A combat drone emerges from the opening, but this time it has a weapon in its hands. Not just any weapon though, it carries a brand spankin' new shiny plasma rifle. It looks like a newer and sleeker design than any of the rifles I've seen the Federation soldiers carrying. I calm myself, knowing the rifle will be firing fake bullets because that's what Dr. Patel told us.

Taking a defensive stance, I concentrate and focus as I hear the rifle warming up and readying to fire. I hear the bullets begin to rip through the air and my eyes shoot open just in time to see them ricocheting off the barrier I've produced. One by one I see them bounce off in slow motion, causing a ripple effect across the wall of energy upon impact.

The gun ceases fire and I see my time turn green. The electronic voice says, "Excellent."

I hit the switch on the wall again once it begins to glow. "Task is Multiple Barriers. Activating combat drones," the electronic voice announces.

Defensive Measures

A drone appears in front of me with a rifle in hand just like the last one, and another appears next to me without a rifle. *I was wondering how they were going to test this one. All right, bring it!* I tell myself.

I hear the rifle warming up and I concentrate on the robot and myself. I open my eyes and see that there's a barrier around both of us even before the drone begins to fire. As the bullets begin to fly, I feel a slight stress on my barriers. The ripple effect gets larger and I find myself struggling to hold out with every bullet that connects.

The bullet barrage ends and my timer turns green followed by the electronic voice saying, "Excellent."

I wipe away the sweat on my brow from the exertion of the previous task, and take a breather. Then I hit the switch to begin the next one. Again the electronic voice pipes in. "Task is Disarm. Activating combat drone."

The drone that rises up from the ground is not as heavily armed as the previous ones. It only holds a standard issue Federation pistol in its right hand. I immediately cast a barrier around the drone's right hand and pull toward me, causing the gun to fly out and skid along the floor. It immediately whips a rifle from behind its back and takes a few steps forward. I concentrate harder and produce a barrier around the rifle. Pushing off the right, I send it soaring off into the wall.

The Modified

My timer stops and turns green. The electronic voice chimes in and states, "Excellent."

So far I'm three for three. You've got this, Grayson, I think to myself.

The switch glows again and I press it. The timer begins and the electronic voice says, "Task is Restrict. Activating combat drone."

The drone emerges into the room, carrying a rifle identical to the previous ones. I hear the rifle readying to fire, and produce a barrier around the robot. It begins to fire and I hold my focus, ensuring the barrier stays in place. The bullets ricochet around inside the bubble of energy, pounding into the drone many times in the process. After the last shell hits the ground, I release my barrier. The drone collapses to the floor, covered in dents from all the impacts.

My timer turns green and the electronic voice says, "Excellent."

I breathe a sigh of relief when it's all over. I can't believe I just did all of that.

Looking over at Dr. Patel, she gives me two thumbs up.

As I re-enter the training room, I immediately look for Landon's face. He mouths *good job*.

I mouth back *thanks*.

Chapter Eight
Strategic Maneuvers

I'm still surprised every time I enter the library that it's full of books, especially with the advancements in electronic reading. I've loved libraries ever since I was a little girl. It was actually my older brother, Dylan, who sparked my love of reading. I wish he could be here to see all of this. Most libraries back on Earth don't even have a third of the actual books this one has. A lot of people just download them now. It's rare to see people reading a physical copy anymore. And yet here we are on this highly advanced spacecraft with the library full of books.

It's actually a very neat sight to behold. The room is a large three-story cylinder with clear glass comprising the floor on each level, and walls made entirely of antique-looking wooden bookshelves. There are several bookcases randomly placed in the center of each floor as well. As I look up, I can see all the way to the ceiling and people on floors above me seem to just be floating there. The spiral staircase that leads up to each level has the same blue light comprising each step.

Making my way to the top floor, I notice a lone leather chair off to the side sitting on a beautiful ornate rug that's surrounded by stacks of books. There's a man pacing back and forth in front of the chair while reading the book in his hands. He seems to be in deep concentration. He's not wearing a uniform or a lab coat, and then it dawns on me where I've seen him before. He's the bookish-looking guy from the first day. He's dressed in a black button-down shirt with the sleeves slightly rolled up and a nice pair of khaki pants. His tie is loosened and his short brown hair is a little disheveled. *I wonder how long he's been in here,* I think to myself.

Looking closer, I spot the title of the book that's holding his attention. *The Art of War?* Huh? Fitting, I guess.

"Problem?" the man asks, apparently not okay with me staring.

"Oh, no, sorry. I was just curious about the book you were reading. It must be good if it has you that focused," I reply.

He laughs slightly and returns to reading.

"You're head of the Tactical division, right?" I ask.

"It would appear so," he replies, seeming slightly annoyed. I send him a look of confusion as to why he's acting like this.

He abruptly tucks the book under his arm. "Is there something I can help you with? Because as you can see I'm in relax mode, and so far all you've done is cover things that both of us are already aware of."

"I was just going to say that I start tactical training tomorrow and wanted to introduce myself."

"Ms. Grayson, I've already memorized all two hundred and forty students' names and pictures. So no introduction necessary. Now, if you don't mind, I've got some light reading to attend to," he states, gesturing to the pile of books by the chair.

"Sorry, sir. I didn't mean to bother you."

As I turn to leave, his voice stops me. "Oh, Ms. Grayson?"

"Yes, sir?" I reply, facing him.

"Come here," he says pointing to the floor just before him. I walk over to stand right in front of him. "Lesson one. Here in my hand I hold 'The Art of War' by Sun Tzu. A true gem amongst military literature. I've read this book a thousand times and was surprised to find this library didn't have a copy on hand. Good thing I carry my own. It's kind of a security blanket…don't ask. But I digress. I've read this a thousand times, but never have I read it like you're about to right now," he explains and then holds the book out to me. "Go on, take it."

The Modified

"What do you mean?" I ask while grabbing for the book.

"Such a loaded question, Ms. Grayson. Let the answer come to you through action," he replies cryptically with a smirk. "Now, I want you to clear your mind and focus on the book you hold in your hands. Open it up to any page." I do as he says and I start to see the words move around on the page. "I want you to keep concentrating on the book, not allowing anything else into your mind. Now, place your hand onto the page. I want you to visualize the words becoming liquefied, like they're floating around in book. Then imagine your hand is a vacuum, sucking up all those words," he explains.

I feel a sudden surge of power in my hand that runs all the way up to my brain. I see flashes of words, and those words begin to form sentences, and those sentences form paragraphs. I begin to see full pages of writing in my head. The rush is intense. When it's all finished, the book in my head closes and I can read the title, *The Art of War* by Sun Tzu.

Letting out a gasp, my eyes shoot open and I drop the book onto the floor. A headache begins to invade and I touch just below my nose to find it's bleeding. "What the hell just happened?"

"You just dropped my one hundred and fifty dollar book on the floor, that's what just happened," he replies flippantly, picking up the book and dusting it off.

● ● ●

"I meant with me. What happened to me just now?"

"Good to know where your priorities lie, Ms. Grayson," he states and I glare at him. "Relax, Ms. Grayson. It's called perception. Just another one of the wonderful abilities which have been bestowed upon you."

"Perception?"

"Oh, sorry, explanation, right? Well in short, you just read this whole book in a matter of seconds and stored it away in that little head of yours. You know, in the ninety percent of your brain you don't use. Congratulations, you're now using forty percent of your brain," he states sarcastically.

"Wait you're telling me that whole book is in my head now?" I ask and he nods. "So how do I access the information?"

"Well that's lesson two and it's a little advanced for someone who hasn't even started the training yet," he states and then shoos me away. "See you in class tomorrow, Ms. Grayson."

I turn back to face him just as I step onto the stairs. "Yeah, see you tomorrow, Mr....?"

"Doctor. The name's Dr. Harvey Wilhelm."

As I make my way downstairs I bump into Joey on the second floor. "I just had an interesting experience with Dr. Wilhelm," I state, walking up to him.

"Oh, that guy. Yeah, he's a piece of work. I could never tell if he was being serious or sarcastic," Joey replies.

"He showed me how to use perception," I whisper so no one else could hear me.

"Wait, he taught you that out of class?" Joey asks.

"Yeah," I whisper back.

"It's pretty cool, huh? I wasn't really good at it at first, and I'm still practicing," he replies, holding up the book in his hands. "But we could get in trouble for talking about it until we're assigned to our divisions."

"Yeah, I know. There can't be any cheating," I say while rolling my eyes. Joey laughs.

I get serious. "Hey, how are you doing, really? We haven't gotten to chat for a while now."

He smiles. "Kenley, we see each other and talk all the time."

"I know we do, but not like we used to back home."

"Well, things haven't really been conducive to that. It's been a little crazy around here, you know?"

"A little? I think this place would qualify as more than that."

Joey chuckles. "You know what I mean."

"Yeah, I do. I just don't want things to change between us. You're my best friend, a brother. We're in this together, remember?" I pause for a moment and then grin. "I love you, Joey Reilly."

Strategic Maneuvers

"I love you too, Kenley Grayson," he says seriously, placing his hands on my shoulders and looking directly into my eyes. "I also think you're being overemotional," he jokes.

I give him a light tap on the chest. "Maybe so, but you can't blame a girl for worrying, can you?"

I can always count on Joey to make a serious situation into a joke. He's always been like that. I think it's kind of a defense mechanism. He's always trying to avoid serious situations when words are involved, but if those situations call for physical action, he's right there in the thick of it. Dylan had to save his ass many times growing up. Trouble always seemed to find Joey, and he rarely ever used his words.

I shoot up in bed, startled and breathing heavily. A loud bang in the distance makes me focus. I go to step out of bed and my whole room shakes, causing me to stumble and fall to the floor. Several louder bangs sound in the distance. I try to stand, but fall to my knees again as it feels like an earthquake just ran through my room.

"Kenley, your heartbeat is irregularly fast, and your blood pressure is high. Is something wrong?" Galileo asks popping out from my bangle.

"I'm okay, but something's happening in the facility Galileo-" I begin to reply and then another loud bang echoes throughout the hall outside, shaking my room and sending me crashing into my door, which doesn't open when I get close to it. Regaining my composure, I look up above the door and there's a red light on. "Why didn't the door open, Galileo?"

"I am not sure, Kenley. It seems to not be responding to my interface. One moment…I will perform a scan of the facilities' energy outputs," he responds and retracts into the band. The band begins to pulse neon blue while he's performing the scan. "Scan complete…it would appear that the emergency shield generator has been activated. The facility is on reserve energy, which would explain the door's malfunction. All doors must be opened manually during this time," Galileo explains.

Several more loud bangs resonate through the facility, but this time I hit the ground and ride out the tremors that follow.

"Why would the emergency shield generator be on, Galileo?"

"The emergency shield generator only activates in the instance of an attack from an outside force on the facility," he replies.

I hear scurrying outside. The next thing I know my door is being rolled open. I see Landon and Joey pushing the door aside, together. There's a group of people behind them, but I can't make them out in the dark.

"Kenley?" I hear Landon and Joey call out into the room.

"Yeah, I'm here."

Strategic Maneuvers

"We need to get to the mess hall," Landon announces as he pulls me to my feet.

"What? Why? What's going on?" I ask, my head still a little dizzy from being tossed around the room like a rag doll.

"We don't know what's going on. Your dad told all of us to head for the mess hall," Joey pipes in breathlessly.

I see Sam in the doorway over Landon's shoulder looking concerned, which is so unlike her. Caleb is standing next to her, looking worried as well, with Geoffrey cowering behind him.

"Let's go then," I say and push out of the room with everyone else, joining the crowd of cadets hurrying through the halls.

All of the hallways are lit up with red swirling emergency lights. There's an electronic voice that's sounding throughout the facility. "Magnus Academy is in emergency lockdown mode. Excess power is being utilized by the emergency shield generator." The message is on repeat and echoes throughout every area we travel through.

A couple more loud bangs sound around us as we approach the entrance to the mess hall. The aftershock rocks us off balance, causing me to crash into Landon and Sam. Steadying ourselves, we make our way into the mess hall and find everyone gathered there. My dad and the heads of each division are on the stage, trying their best to calm the crowd. We feel a few more quakes, but they fizzle out before causing any damage.

We hear a microphone chime on and my dad's voice follows. "Can I please have your attention?" The crowd quiets and we all look toward the stage. "I know you're all probably startled and confused by what's happening. Just know that you're safe and main power should be returning to the facility shortly."

"What's going on?" I hear someone yell from the crowd, followed by a rumble amongst the gathered group.

"The emergency shield generator was activated around the facility, which is why we lost centralized power," he answers.

"Why?" I hear someone else ask.

"We were attacked by the Bringers," my father responds and then unrest rolls throughout the crowd. "I need for everyone to calm down. Our gun turrets have warded off the enemy fleet and the Allied Federation is on their way to assess the damages. We're in the clear and power should be returning momentarily." His calming voice seems to put everyone at ease.

As the lights flicker back on, a female electronic voice chimes in. "Shield integrity at eighty-five percent. Centralized power restored. Threat neutralized. Shield generator repair required."

"Now, training sessions will go on as scheduled tomorrow. This attack only serves to prove what we're doing here has them threatened. I know you all are probably a little shaken, but we must press on," my dad says into the microphone. "So please return to your rooms, and try to get some rest."

When the students begin to filter out of the mess hall, I make my way against the crowd toward the stage where my father is. I tell the rest of my group to stay put and wait for me. I call out to my dad and he smiles, gesturing for me to come closer. He exits off the stage and joins me on the ground.

"How did the Bringers find us? I thought this facility was cloaked?" I ask in a whisper.

"I have my suspicions about that," he replies, placing his hand on my shoulder and guiding me off to the side for more privacy. "I believe the Bringers picked up on the energy you all were producing by activating your implants. You have to realize that you have the essence of this species coursing through your veins. With your implants activated, it must've been like a beacon set off for them," he explains in a whisper.

"Did you guys expect this attack then?"

"Sort of, which is why we took such drastic measures to improve the defense capabilities of the Magnus."

"Will they be back?"

"Unlikely. They know we're heavily fortified now, and besides, the Allied Federation will be patrolling the perimeter of the facility from here on out. So no worries," he says with a smile.

The Modified

I hear Dr. Patel call out to my father and he turns to look at her.

"I have to go deal with some issues. Sorry we can't talk more about this right now," he says looking back at me.

"It's okay, you deal with what you got to deal with, and we'll talk later."

"Deal," he replies and gives me a quick hug.

As my dad leaves I look over to my group that's gathered by the entrance of the mess hall. I try to organize my thoughts as I make my way over to them in order to tell them what my father had said. It's weird, but even after what my dad told me, I don't feel any more at ease, or safe for some reason.

For the first time since our introduction session, I find myself actually sitting down in one of the desks inside a training room. They're not as comfortable as I remembered them being though. We've been waiting here for a little while now, and I'm surprised that Dr. Wilhelm is late to class since I pictured him as the "always on time" type.

Everyone still seems to be on edge from the attack on the facility yesterday, me included. I've begun to notice an increased presence of Federation guards patrolling the facility. My dad continues to tell everyone that it's routine procedure, and will only last until the shield generators are at full capacity. I'm not so sure though.

I look around the room and my eyes stop on Landon. He seems to have been staring at me this entire time.

"What's up?" I ask, seeming to break into his thoughts.

He snaps out of his daze. "Just thinking," he replies.

"About what?" I inquire, leaning in closer to him, giving him all my attention.

He leans in too, almost like he's about to tell me a secret. "About all the Federation guards who have been stationed at the facility. I know that we were attacked, but what good are they going to do from the inside?"

"I know, right? It's also weird how they walk around here and seem more like robots than the androids do."

I notice everyone's attention focuses on the door and I turn to see Dr. Wilhelm strolling into the classroom. "Morning, cadets, I hope you weren't waiting too long," he announces dryly. He sets his briefcase down on the desk at the front of the room and turns to us. He points at me almost immediately when he faces the class. I look from side to side to make sure that he was pointing at me. His eyes never leave my position. "Ms. Grayson, thanks for volunteering. Please come forward."

The Modified

Standing from my desk, I hesitantly make my way to the front, wondering the entire time what Dr. Wilhelm has in store for me. He takes my hand and spins me around to face everyone.

"Remember when you asked me in the library how to retrieve the information in your brain after utilizing the perception ability?" he asks and I nod slightly. "Well, I'm about to show you." Dr. Wilhelm moves to be in front of me. "I want you to close your eyes and clear your mind until all you see is white. Now, try and visualize the cover of the novel *The Art of War* right in the center of the white space. Grab hold of the book in your mind and begin flipping through the pages."

As he talks me through this exercise, I visualize everything he's saying. I see the cover, myself grabbing the book and flipping through the pages—all of it. My eyes open abruptly and a rush of information floods my head as I remember the entire novel. Dr. Wilhelm asks me to recite a line from page 29 and I do. He doesn't even have to check the line in the copy of the book he holds in his hand, because he's memorized it. He nods when I'm correct.

"Very good, Ms. Grayson," he comments. "Just remember that when you use perception again, you will erase the previous thing stored in your mind. That is all. You may take your seat."

Strategic Maneuvers

A knock comes from my door, and I spring from my bed to open it. Landon is standing there as it slides open.

"Hey, what are you doing here? You should be studying for our Tact final tomorrow," I say, but he doesn't say anything back, he just stands there grinning at me with his gorgeous lips. The image of Landon shutters and I hear "crap" from down the hall. The image fully disappears as I see Landon approaching from around the corner of the wall in front of me.

"I can't believe you just used your decoy ability on me," I state playfully.

He laughs. "Well, I had to practice somehow, didn't I?" Landon jokes while placing his hands about my waist and pulling me close.

"Landon, I've got to-"

He places his thumb over my mouth and runs it from my upper to lower lip. "I know, I know, you need to study, right?" he says softly, cutting me off.

I bring my hand up to touch his face and it goes straight through his image. I hear "crap" from around the corner in front of me again and I glare in that direction. I swat through the image of Landon and it dissipates.

Storming over to the wall that Landon is hiding behind, "I can't believe you. Seriously? You didn't have to do that a second time. That wasn't fair," I whine and slap his shoulder.

The Modified

He just stands there, grinning foolishly. "Okay, okay, I'm sorry I did that," he chuckles. "But you have to admit that I did pretty well, huh? Huh?"

"Go study, please," I reply dryly, not acknowledging the fact that he did do well because he fooled me twice.

I turn to walk away, but I feel Landon grab me by my waist and pull me toward him. He presses his firm chest against my back and for a moment I forget that I'm annoyed with him. He whispers "okay" closely to my ear and releases me. Landon smiles when I turn to look at him. Blowing me a kiss, he starts to walk away. I hear him say "goodnight" and wave as he continues to move down the hall.

"Goodnight, Landon," I call out and hear him laugh. Shaking my head, I return to my room with a huge grin on my face.

The Tactical final is definitely set up different from our previous ones. Since each ability is pretty much non-combative in nature, none of the tasks involve combat drones.

The first task has the whole class of cadets using perception. Dr. Wilhelm walks around every desk and places a copy of *Generation Kill* by Evan Wright in front of us. He then instructs us to "read" it and answer a multiple choice question test. Our success rate is dependent on how fast we're able to answer the questions.

Strategic Maneuvers

I focus on the book in front of me and put my hand on top of it. Visualizing the words from each page sucking up into my hand, I see the cover of the book as it closes in my head, and now have the entire novel stored away in my memory.

A multiple choice question test projects from my desk and I blow through it quickly. My desk turns green in color instead of the blue it was before, and the word *Excellent* appears on it. The test kind of reminded me of the ones I used to take in A.P. English class back in high school, except for the whole question-projecting-from-the-desk part.

The second task begins and a map projects from the desk in front of me. "Use your scan ability to find the most direct route from your current position on the map, indicated by the flashing X, to your enemies' position, indicated by the flashing O."

I focus on the map and feel my eyes begin to pulse with energy. Taking in a full scan of the entire map, I begin to trace my path with my finger, leaving a neon blue line where it travels. My map flashes red when I make a wrong decision in direction and makes me start over.

"Crap," I mutter out loud accidentally. I look around and a few people are staring at me, including Dr. Wilhelm. Focusing back on the map, I attempt to trace the path again. Reaching my goal, the map turns yellow and the word *Satisfactory* shows on my desktop.

The Modified

Dr. Wilhelm instructs us to stand from our desks and pushes a button on his touchpad, causing them to suck back into the floor. "Task three is Decoy. I want you to project a copy of yourself and hold it for as long as you can within five minutes."

I look over at Landon and he already has his copy projecting in front of him. *Of course he already has his, he's had lots of practice*, I joke with myself.

Concentrating, I project my "twin" in front of me. She looks like an exact copy of me, other than the fact that her image shutters every few seconds. A timer projects from my bangle and I look down at it to see that I've held my decoy for just over a minute. Her image begins to shutter more frequently until it becomes too much for me to hold on to. I release the image and it fades away. Letting out a sigh of exhaustion, I look down at my time and it's just over three minutes.

Galileo projects from the bangle. "You did well, Kenley. That was satisfactory," he tells me.

"Thanks, Galileo."

"You've all done well up to this point," Dr. Wilhelm states as he moves to the front of the class. "We only have one more task, and that's Optics."

We all file into the test area at the back of the training room and wait for further instruction. Dr. Wilhelm hits a button on his data pad and suddenly the room elongates and stretches about triple its current size. He calls us up one at a time to stand on a bright blue light line that forms on the floor and stare straight ahead. It's my turn and I toe the line while facing forward.

"Use your optics ability to properly recognize an enemy from an innocent," Dr. Wilhelm states, pressing another button on his data pad and starting the timer on the wall next to us.

Without my optics activated, I can barely see the end of the room. I focus and my eyes begin to pulse. Now everything has a blue tint to it. Images in the distance begin to pop into my field of view and I can clearly make out the far wall of the room.

After successfully naming all five images either friend or foe, my time turns green and an electronic voice filters into the room. "Excellent."

"Good job, Ms. Grayson. You did much better than I was expecting you to," Dr. Wilhelm states with a smirk.

"Thanks?" I say, giving him a confused look.

"That was a compliment, Ms. Grayson. Don't get used to it though. I'm not usually one for giving them." He laughs at his own comment.

Chapter Nine
Division Assignment

Finally, the day of the division assignments arrives. After about a month of grueling training, we're about to find out which division we're going to be assigned to. Based on our times during finals, most of us already know which one we'll end up in, but today makes that assumption real.

As I'm about to leave my room to meet up with everyone, Galileo projects from my bangle, but he doesn't say anything. "Yes, Galileo?" I ask looking at his hologram.

"Kenley…I just wanted to say that…I am proud of you."

"Thanks, Galileo."

"You have more than proven that you belong here. I am honored to be your AI."

Division Assignment

"Hey, that sounds like inflection in your voice, Galileo. Are you showing emotion?"

"The possibility in there does lie…scanning database…All systems seem to be operating at maximum capacity. No sign of change present," he responds.

"Never mind, there's the Galileo I know," I giggle.

Sitting in the mess hall, we all patiently wait for the ceremony to begin. Federation soldiers file into the hall and line up at the front of the stage with guns by their sides. The Federation's pledge song begins playing in the room, which means only one thing, that General Roman Barclay is gracing us with his presence. As he makes his way across the stage, we stand and salute.

General Barclay flashes us a huge grin. "At ease, soldiers," he says into the microphone. We all take our seats. "To say that the Allied Federation is proud of you would be a huge understatement. You have all exceeded our expectations and then some." He pauses for a moment and his face becomes serious before he continues. "As you all are well aware of by the recent attack on the facility, the Bringers are becoming increasingly hostile. South Africa, California, sections of Canada, the southern part of Texas, parts of Asia, Europe—they've all seen devastation recently at the hands of these monsters. Our situation is becoming more dire, and this project is looking more and more like our last hope in the fight against this evil. Now, I know it may be overwhelming to think that you're all that stands between mankind and its extinction, but I want you to use that feeling. Use that fear, strength, and emotion to defeat your enemy."

This guy sounds just like Commander Archer, not surprising though, I think to myself.

"I've decided that since the importance of this project has risen significantly, I will be staying aboard with my command to monitor your exit exam personally," the general states.

I turn to Joey and mouth *Exit exam?* He shrugs, looking just as confused as I feel.

"Now, onto the division assignments," he announces.

Ten large flag holograms project above our heads. There are five flags on either side of the mess hall. The flags sway like there's a nonexistent breeze. On each flag there's an identical picture of a triangle with three stars in the center of it.

"First division up is Strike," General Barclay announces.

Joey and Landon's bands begin to pulse and then their AIs project out. I notice Sam's does the same thing, and so does many of the other cadets around me. I hear Joey and Sam's AIs congratulate them for making Strike division.

Division Assignment

"Congratulations, Strike division. All one hundred and seventy of you." General Barclay grins with what I assume is pride. A subdued applause follows.

The ten flags ruffle in the wind and the symbol changes on them. It's now a triangle with three bold lines running vertically down them. "Next up is Fortification division."

My bangle begins to glow and I see that Caleb's is as well. He smirks at me and I return it. Galileo projects out, and instead of congratulating me he says, "Well, this was a no-brainer," followed by an electronic chuckle.

"Hush, Galileo," I joke, joining in with his laughter. I stifle my laugh with my hand as I notice the room gets quiet. The general congratulates the fifty members of the Fortification division, which is followed up by another round of subdued applause.

The flags change once more. The symbol is now a triangle with three diamonds spanning the shape. "The third and final division is Tactical," General Barclay states.

Geoffrey is the only band that pulses in our immediate area. Sam smacks him on the back to congratulate him and he sends her a half-smile.

Immediately following the assignments, a disembodied voice enters the room through the speakers surrounding us. It's followed by the holographic image of the world's president walking across the stage with his arms outstretched wide toward us.

"Hello, cadets," he announces with a huge smile. "I apologize for not being able to be there with you in person today, but I want to congratulate all of you on a job well done. You were all handpicked as being the best, and I am glad to be informed that our choices were correct. I feel I know each and every one of you, and though you are young, you have handled yourselves like adults. I know all your parents would be proud if they knew of your accomplishments."

"I guess he doesn't know me as well as he thinks he does," Joey says under his breath. I nudge him and send him an empathetic smile.

"Each and every one of you is special, and I know you will utilize your talents to defend us against these creatures. As I'm sure you're all well aware of by now, your job is far from over. And with the recent Bringer activity, I'd say it's only the beginning. I only wish that we could disclose to the world what is going to transpire. But the few of us who do know will be rooting for you through it all. Keep up the good work, soldiers, and know that the world and I thank you." His hologram fades away when he finishes his speech.

"Damn, didn't that just bring tears to your eyes?" Joey comments sarcastically.

"Yeah, I know I got a little teary eyed," Sam comments sarcastically.

"Let's all hear it for the world's president," General Barclay declares as he makes his way back toward the microphone while clapping his hands enthusiastically.

"He does know that the president was a hologram, right? Not to mention that he's gone now? What a dipshit," Sam whispers to our section of the table. We all chuckle and then bring our focus back to the stage as General Barclay clears his throat.

"As the president said, you all are very special. And I hope to come to know you better in the days to come. Keep up the good work, and I will be watching you. Cadets, dismissed."

We all stand and hold our salute until he leaves.

"Well, that was a bunch of bull. The only truth that came out of either of their mouths was that our asses are going to be on the line. I hate politics," Sam murmurs.

As we go to leave the mess hall, I notice most of the cadets seem to be less enthusiastic. There was more of a celebratory mood in the room before the presentation, but now the tension in the area seems almost palpable. You can actually see the pressure of everything that they feel now right there on their faces.

The Modified

Staring out my window, I see the garden Galileo creates for me every day. I find it strange that I only see the flowers my brother Dylan gave my mother, and not the ones I gave her before I left. If this was created using my memory, shouldn't my last memory of the garden be after I saw her plant the blue poppies?

"Hey, Galileo?"

"Yes, Kenley?"

"Am I able to go down there?" I ask, looking longingly out at the garden.

"Where would you like to go?"

"The garden outside my window," I reply.

"Of course you can. I can guide you there, if you like?"

"I'd like that."

Following Galileo's directions, I exit the facility through a hatch that leads into the garden below my window. The vision before me immediately brings me back home. It literally feels like I just stepped out into my back yard. I almost expect to see my mom tending to the lavender bushes. A light breeze blows through the garden and everything sways in the wind. I reach out my hand and let it travel over the hedges and then the flowers as I pass by them. My hand stops over the red poppies. I crouch down to touch the flowers, but my hand goes straight through them. The image shutters and I sigh, wishing I were touching the real thing.

"Hope you don't mind, but I followed you out here." I hear a low sexy voice behind me. I turn and grin, seeing Landon standing there.

"Of course I don't mind."

"So what is this place? There's nothing like this anywhere else at the facility."

"Galileo recreated this from my memory. It's my mom's garden back home," I answer.

"Your AI did this?" Landon asks staring intently at his hand passing through a bed of flowers.

"Yeah, doesn't your AI do things like this for you?"

"Not exactly, no. Mostly it just talks about my vitals," Landon replies, coming to stand right in front of me. "It's beautiful," he continues as he places his hand to my cheek.

"So why did you follow me out here, huh?" I inquire with an impish grin.

He laughs. "I was intrigued. Plus, you looked like you were sneaking around. So naturally I thought I'd see what you were up to."

"Ahh, I see."

"When we're back on Earth I'd like to see this in person. If you'll have me over, of course," he says with a slight smile.

"I'd like that," I reply, gazing into his eyes.

"So, you say your AI created this for you, huh?" Landon asks as he begins to walk around, perusing the garden again.

"Yep, every day when I wake up."

"It's kind of cool how it looks like an unfinished painting. Like the artist just gave up or something," he comments while making his way to the edge of the garden where the green grass stops suddenly. He lets out a little laugh as he reaches out and touches the white interior wall of the structure.

"Funny, I actually thought that same thing after I first saw it," I reply, joining him by the wall.

"Did you ever think in a million years that you'd be doing this? That the whole world would be depending on you?" he asks suddenly, kind of catching me off guard.

I think for a moment and then respond. "No…to be honest, I wasn't even supposed to be here."

"What do you mean by that?" he asks, turning to look at me.

"I'm not really supposed to talk about it. I'm not even sure why I mentioned it in the first place," I reply sheepishly, looking away from him.

"You can talk to me, Kenley. I won't tell anyone, I promise," he says, pulling my chin lightly to face him.

"My dad…kind of pulled some strings to get me in here. I didn't know about that little fact until I got here, though." As I continue to speak, surprise registers on Landon's face. "For a while I felt like a fake and that I didn't belong here or something. And Strike training didn't help much in that department either."

Landon places his hand about my cheek. "Kenley, it doesn't matter how you got here. You've proven yourself time and time again. You've got nothing to be ashamed of. Besides, if you never would've come, we wouldn't be sharing this moment right here," he says with a grin as he looks deeply into my eyes.

"I know, and believe me I've thought a lot about this. After making Fort division, I realized I belonged here. I finally felt a part of this place. And I have you to thank for a good deal of that."

No more words are spoken as Landon leans in and kisses me. It feels like the area around us disappears and we're just floating in space. In this moment I feel so much joy. I'm the luckiest girl in the galaxy.

After finishing breakfast in the mess hall, I make my way with Caleb to our very first Fort training session after division assignments. Caleb continues to be a guy of few words as we walk together. He only says like three words the whole time, and they're all one word answers to questions I ask.

Entering the training room, I take a seat on the mat next to Caleb's. Dr. Patel is standing at the front of the room with her chest pushed out and face full of pride as she smiles at us. When the last cadet takes his (or her) seat, she clears her throat.

"The Magnus Academy Exit Exam is a true test for you and your implant," Dr. Patel says seriously as she paces back and forth in front of us, her hands crossed behind her back. "You will be paired up with two other random cadets and made to work together in order to overcome certain obstacles that mimic actual battlefield scenarios." She stops, looks at us, and then takes in a deep breath, seeming like she's gathering her thoughts, before continuing. "You all have performed exceptionally well up to this point, so I have no worries about your performance during the exam. I know you will make me proud, but most of all, I know you will prove to yourself that there are no limits to what you can do." She smiles as she scans the room. "Over the next week, we will train and hone your skills as Fortification division cadets, in order to prepare you for what you're sure to face within the exam. Any questions?"

I look around and see no one raising his or her hand. There was this one question bubbling up inside me that I tried fighting to ask. It's actually been eating away at me ever since I heard about the exam. Giving in, I raise my hand.

"Yes, Ms. Grayson?" Dr. Patel asks.

"Whose idea was it to put us through this exam? It seems like it was added on at the last minute," I ask.

● ● ●
167

Division Assignment

"You're right in assuming that, Ms. Grayson. It was actually the brainchild of General Barclay. He requested we train you to participate in this exit exam," she answers.

"Does anyone find it weird that we're being forced into an exam because of orders from General Barclay?" I ask the small group at the table during dinner.

"Yeah, it is. Must be because of some power trip he's on or something," Joey comments.

"It's a load of bull, in my opinion. But if that's what the Federation wants to do, and test me, then bring it on," Sam interjects while pausing every few words to take a bite of her food.

I feel a hand on my shoulder and look up to see Landon hovering there just behind me. "Want to go for a walk?" he asks and I notice that the smile on his mouth doesn't quite make it to his eyes.

"Sure," I reply and excuse myself from the table.

"So this exit exam seems like a big deal, huh?" I ask as we stroll through one of the many corridors outside the mess hall.

"Yeah," is all he says as he grabs my hand.

I come to a stop and wait for him to turn and look at me. "Are you okay?"

The Modified

"Of course I am, what makes you think I'm not?" he replies, but I can tell there's something up.

"All right, enough of avoiding the issue. Spill it. What's on your mind?" I ask, trying to stare him directly in his eyes, which he successfully dodges.

"Uh…well-" he begins to say, but then hesitates.

I pull his face to mine and stare him directly in the eyes. "If something is bothering you, Landon, please tell me. Let me know what's going on in that head of yours."

A smirk crawls across his lips and he lets out a laugh under his breath. He then sighs, his face becoming more serious as he starts to speak. "This exam means we're getting closer to the end of our stay here. Which also means that we're closer to us being split up. I've lost a lot of people in my life because of this war, and I just can't imagine my life without you," he says softly.

I begin to say something, but then pause, trying to gather my words. *Damn, what a great time to be speechless, Kenley,* I tell myself. Biting my lip, my eyes dart to the floor and then back to Landon's face to find it full of concern.

"I'm sorry, I know that was a lot for you to take in and process," he states. "I'm just worried about tomorrow, that's all."

"Me too." I say, and then think that's the dumbest short answer I could've given. I want to just tell him how I really feel too, but for some reason I'm finding it difficult to do.

● ● ●
169

Division Assignment

"Hey, what do you say we go play some games in the rec hall?" he asks, changing the subject.

"I'd like that."

Chapter Ten
Final Assessment

I stand in front of a giant metal door that's traced in blue light, waiting for the exit exam to begin. I have no idea who the other two are in my group, or even what the test actually entails. All I know is that just beyond this door I'll truly be pushed to my limits.

"Kenley?" Galileo calls my name as he projects from my bangle.

"Can't this wait? I'm about to start my test," I reply.

"This actually pertains to that subject. During your exit exam, I will be deactivated so that no communication can happen between us," Galileo explains.

"Deactivated? Like on purpose? What for?"

Final Assessment

"This is an exam, and having me activated could possibly give you an advantage," he replies matter-of-factly. "As soon as you enter the examination area, I will deactivate."

I stare down at the band of plastic and become a little emotional seeing the little hologram shutter as it speaks. I usually don't want Galileo interfering too much with things, but the thought of him being deactivated makes me sad, like saying goodbye to a good friend.

"Kenley, I sense that you are feeling depressed. Is it because of me?"

"Of course, silly. You're not going to be in there with me."

"Cheer up, Kenley. I shall return the moment you are finished with your exam," he replies.

Is it just me, or did his voice sound warm and fuzzy? I ask myself.

"Kenley?" Galileo asks again.

"Yeah?"

"Good luck."

I smile down at the hologram, just before it goes back into the bangle.

Turning my focus back to the door, I see there are three circular lights on above it. One of them goes out, followed by an electronic sound, leaving two still lit up: I assume it's a countdown for the door to open.

The Modified

My heartbeat quickens and my palms become hot and sweaty. I take in a deep calming breath as the second light goes out. An even louder chime follows. I look from side to side nervously, as I think about what lies beyond the door. The third light fades away and a loud prolonged buzzer sounds. The door slowly slides open to the side. I look into the room and all the walls are black and the floor is made up of large white tiles just like in the training rooms. The space is enormous.

I see two other doors open up into the room, one is far in the distance in front of me, and the other is far off to my left. I use my optics ability in order to see who comes through them, and smile when I see Landon emerge through the door to my left. I wave to him. He sends me a smile and a wave back. I want to run over and hug him, but I see a red light line creating a box around me on the ground, and I'm pretty sure I'm not supposed to cross it. The same red light box appears to surround Landon as well.

Looking across the room, I see Geoffrey standing there. He seems to be more nervous than I am, so I wave to him in hopes it will reassure him. He waves back and seems to be a little more at ease than before.

An electronic voice filters into the room. "Please stand on your activation panel to commence with the exam."

Final Assessment

I look in front of me and one of the large panels on the floor is pulsing bright blue. As I step on it, the panel turns solid blue and stops pulsing. I look over at Landon and Geoffrey as they do the same.

A pleasant electronic chime sounds throughout the area. Suddenly, white walls shoot out of the floor and begin to connect and arrange themselves. They form a room around me without any sign of an exit, except the closed door behind me.

The electronic voice pipes in again. "Milton, Geoffrey, please proceed into the exam. Your first task is to reach Grayson, Kenley. Your time begins now."

After a few seconds pass, the voice says, "Initializing Tactical assessment."

As the voice fades away, a shiny white post emerges from the floor to my right. At the top of the post seems to be some kind of switch, but it's not lit up. I stand there waiting for something to happen, anything. The only activity in my enclosed area is the bright blue lines that pulse across the walls in a zigzag pattern. It's actually kind of hypnotic.

Several minutes pass and suddenly the wall in front of me begins to slide open. Geoffrey is standing there, hunched over slightly, and breathing heavily. His hands are glowing and I notice sweat on his forehead and his cheeks are flush as he looks up at me with his electric blue eyes.

The Modified

"What happened out there?" I ask as he begins to make his way over to me.

"A lot," he replies, trying to catch his breath.

The electronic voice flows into the area. "Phase one complete. To begin phase two, Grayson, Kenley, you must activate the switch in your area."

The switch on the post begins to glow as I look over at it. I turn to Geoffrey to make sure he's okay to continue and he nods. His cheeks are still flushed.

As I hit the switch, a melodic chime sounds throughout the room. "Milton, Geoffrey, Grayson, Kenley, please proceed into the exam area. Your second task is to reach, Shaw, Landon."

As we step out into the hall beyond the room we're in, the wall we entered through closes up behind us. The first thing I notice is that the same blue zigzag line pattern is coursing through these walls as well. Since all the walls are bright white, the lines of light actually show where walls stop and transition into the next corridors.

"Initiating fortification assessment."

Geoffrey and I begin to move forward cautiously. There are two corridors ahead of us and Geoffrey grabs my arm and tells me to stop. His eyes start to pulse as they begin to roll back into his head. He must be using *scan* to see where we need to go next.

Final Assessment

"That way," he says, pointing to the left hallway. "We need to stay alert, I sense movement ahead."

I nod to him and both of our hands begin to glow as we move forward. Peering around the corner into the next hallway, I don't see any sign of movement. I take a deep breath and hesitantly step out around the corner with Geoffrey following at my side. The familiar hum of a rifle warming up sounds in front of us as a combat drone pops out from behind the corner in the distance. A barrage of bullets flies in our direction. I immediately throw up two barriers, one around me and the other over Geoffrey. We stand there watching each bullet ricochet off the walls of energy, with each bullet seeming like it's hitting harder than the last.

The drone ceases fire and creates a barrier around itself in the process. I dig down deep and concentrate on the drone's barrier. As the energy enters my hands, ours disappear, leaving us vulnerable. The rifle begins to hum again and I release a shockwave of energy from my hands. It knocks the drone against the far wall, shattering its body into several pieces.

We seem to be in the clear while making our way down the hallway. Geoffrey moves ahead of me and uses his *scan* ability again.

The Modified

"There's more movement ahead. Seems like there are three signatures in the next area, but I can't tell what they are," he explains as his eyes return to normal.

"All right, let me take a look," I say, moving up to the corner that leads into the next corridor. I peek around and see three short walls, standing about four feet tall, and staggered in a left-and-right pattern down the hall. There's no sign of movement again. I go to step out into the open and I feel Geoffrey grab my arm, pulling me back behind the wall.

"Allow me," he says with an impish grin.

Geoffrey concentrates, and suddenly a copy of him projects out right in front of me.

"Of course. We can use decoy to draw out the enemy," I whisper and then concentrate as well. I open my eyes and see an exact copy of myself standing in front of me.

We send both of our decoys out into the hall and within seconds we begin to hear gunfire. I look around the corner and see both our decoys crouched behind the low-lying walls. Two combat drones are moving in on their position and the gun turret on the wall is focused on them as well.

"You stay put and keep control of your decoy. I'm going to create a distraction," I say to Geoffrey and he nods.

"Be careful, Kenley. The bullets may be rubber, but they still hurt like hell," he states.

Final Assessment

"Will do," I reply with a smile. "Okay, so you send your decoy forward the moment I step around the corner, and then I'll do the same."

"Got it."

"Ready?" I ask and he nods again.

I whip around the corner and our decoys run toward the drones. They begin to take heavy damage and I see their images start to shutter and fade away just before I dive behind the first low wall on the left. With the fire still concentrated on the decoys, I'm able to cast barriers around both drones, restricting their movements. As they continue to fire, the bullets ricochet around inside the barriers, incapacitating them. They collapse to the floor just as the turret downs both of our decoys.

As I go to move behind the next low wall, the turret hones in on my position and begins to fire. The bullets fly right by my face and I duck back against the wall I was just hiding behind. The turret ceases fire and I turn to see Geoffrey running up to the wall adjacent to mine.

"What the hell are you doing?" I yell at him as he slides behind the wall, barely dodging the flurry of bullets directed at him. He winks at me and points back to the hall he just ran from. I see Geoffrey kneeling there giving me the okay sign. I smile and shake my head. *How was he able to produce another decoy so quickly?* I think to myself.

The Modified

Out of the corner of my eye I see Geoffrey's "twin" dash out from behind the wall and begin to take a barrage of bullets to the chest. This is my chance. I pop out from behind the wall and focus on the turret. It begins to glow bright blue. The turret starts to vibrate as I clasp my hand shut into a fist. I move my hand to the left and the turret rips from the wall it's mounted to and hovers there, waiting for my next move. I slam my fist downward and the turret crashes to the ground in a crumpled pile of metal.

Geoffrey's decoy fades away as he joins me by my side.

"Nice work, Milton."

"Not too bad yourself, Grayson," he replies with a grin.

We cautiously continue down the corridor. As we make our way through the maze toward Landon, we're surprised we haven't encountered any more resistance.

Reaching a dead end, I turn to Geoffrey and ask, "What now?"

"The hall leading up to your position came to a dead end too. When I touched the wall, it opened. Maybe you have to do the same," he explains.

"All right, here goes nothing," I say and extend my hand to touch the wall. My hand begins to glow and then we hear the sound of an electronic lock disengage. The wall slides to the side and as my eyes meet Landon's, a smile forms on his mouth. I smile too and run up to him, enveloping him in a hug.

"I was beginning to worry. Sounds like you guys had fun out there," Landon says, returning my hug.

The electronic voice sounds again. "Phase two complete. To begin phase three Shaw, Landon, you must activate the switch in your area." The light from the switch on the post to my right catches my eye when it pulses on. Landon looks over at it too. He gives me a reassuring look as he pulls away and walks over to the switch. As he presses it, an electronic chime echoes throughout the room.

"Milton, Geoffrey, Grayson, Kenley, Shaw, Landon, please proceed into the exam area. Your third task is to reach the exit."

The three of us enter the maze and the wall closes up behind us, sealing us in. The walls begin to shift and the hallway directly in front of us disappears. The only directions we have to choose from are the corridor to our left, or the corridor to our right. I notice that the zigzag lines of light coursing through the walls are now bright neon red instead of the blue like before.

"Initiating Strike Assessment," the electronic voice states.

I look at Landon and ask if he's ready, he nods. I do the same to Geoffrey with the same result. "Which way should we head, Geoffrey?" I ask. His eyes and hands begin to glow as he concentrates.

The Modified

"Left," he answers.

"Left it is then," Landon interjects.

As we begin to move down the left hallway, the electronic voice filters into the room and we come to a halt. "Initiating deployment of advanced combat soldiers." A few low-lying walls rise up from the floor in front of us after the announcement.

"Advanced combat soldiers?" I ask, turning to look at Landon. I see a little red dot of light on his chest and follow the source to the corner up ahead. The moment I hear the charge up sound of a rifle, I shove Landon against the wall out of the way of the red light. A sharp sting courses through my arm and I let out a cry of pain. Looking down, I see a large red circle on my forearm where the rubber bullet struck me. My hand begins to glow and I feel a surge of power rush into my fingertips. Anger bubbles up in me and makes me forget the pain from the bullet. I clench both hands into fists and throw them down to my sides, as I turn to stare at the three heavily armed Bringers rushing into the hallway. The anger suddenly leaves me as I'm faced down with these creatures. One of them lets out an ear-piercing screech as it points at us. I feel like I'm frozen in place, just staring at the very things that killed my brother. Landon's voice causes me to snap out of my trance.

"Kenley, get down!" Landon yells at me as he and Geoffrey take point behind the low walls in front of us.

Final Assessment

I look down at my chest and there are three red dots resting just by my heart. Hearing the hum of the rifles, I throw up a barrier and just watch as every bullet bounces off. With each bullet, the anger inside me surges until I can't stand it anymore.

I throw open my hands and clutch my left one into a tight fist, sending the glow to my right hand, making it brighter. Rearing back, I let out a yell as I launch a projectile of energy from my hand in the direction of one of the Bringers encroaching on our position. It pierces through my barrier, causing it to break apart and shower down to the ground. The projectile blows right through the Bringer's chest, sending an explosion of black cubes out of its back and leaving a large gaping hole. The creature collapses to the floor and shatters into hundreds of cubes upon impact. As the bullets begin to fly at me again, I duck behind the low-lying wall where Landon is. "That was intense," I state while trying to catch my breath.

"That was freakin' awesome," Geoffrey calls out to me. "My turn," he says and quickly projects his decoy to draw their fire.

Landon grabs my hand and I can tell he's saying thank you with his eyes. He smiles and kisses me. I forget for a split second that we're in the heat of battle, but the bullets hitting the wall behind us makes me snap out of it.

I peek over the wall and notice that two more Bringers are posting up at the corner leading into the next hallway. With the two directly in front of us distracted, I'm able to cast a barrier over both of them. They cease fire and Landon hurdles over the wall he's hiding behind and dashes up to their position with both hands glowing. He clenches his fists and his hands ignite. Leaping into the air, he comes down onto the creatures and rips through the barriers with both fists, causing them to shatter like glass. His fists penetrate both Bringers, and they crumble into a pile of shiny black cubes. He ducks down behind another wall when the Bringers up ahead open fire.

I wait for a break and leap over the wall I'm posted up behind and dive behind the next one. All three of us look at each other and then nod, knowing what one another is thinking. We each project a decoy, sending them out into the fray. As the Bringers begin to fire, we jump over the walls and huddle behind our "twins," using them as shields from the bullets. My decoy's image begins to shutter and I decide to throw a barrier over Landon, Geoffrey, and myself. As the three decoys fade, all that's between us and the flurry of bullets are my barriers. I stay behind, concentrating on keeping our defenses active. The amount of energy I'm expending takes a toll on me as my hands and arms begin to tremble. I dig down deep and keep the barriers strong enough to withstand the bullet barrage. Beads of sweat dribble down my forehead, but I hold my ground knowing that

• • •

183

Final Assessment

I'm the only thing between those bullets and the people I care for.

I see Landon and Geoffrey push through and lunge at the creatures. Landon punches through his own barrier, breaking it apart, and while using full force, smashes in the Bringer's face. It shatters from head to toe under the pressure of the punch just as Geoffrey dispatches the other one with a barrage blast from his hand.

After feeling drained of energy, I release the barrier around me and hunch over while clutching my knees. My breathing is a little labored, but I pull myself together and wipe away the sweat pouring down my face. Landon and Geoffrey look back at me as I make my way over to stand with them.

"I'm not sure how much more of this I can take," I murmur, feeling an ache all over my body.

"We're almost to the end, I think," Geoffrey states while using his scan ability. "There are only a few more rooms until the exit."

"You can do this, Kenley. We can do this…together," Landon says, reaching his hand out to me.

"Yeah, what he said," Geoffrey jokes, extending his hand toward me as well.

The Modified

I reach out and grab both of their hands. "All right, let's do this." They both smile at me and we move ahead into the next hallway.

It's quiet and all I can hear is our breathing echoing off the walls. I expect to hear the heating up of rifles at every turn we make. For this being the last part of the test, we sure haven't run into anything else for a good stretch of the maze.

Just before we round the corner to the next area, Geoffrey tells us to be still. We all stop immediately in our tracks and wait for his go-ahead. He stands there, his eyes and hands glowing as he uses his ability. "There's something big ahead of us, and a few smaller signatures in the next hall. The small things are probably gun turrets, but I've got no idea what that other thing is," he explains as his eyes return to a normal blue color and his hands stop glowing.

Landon tells us to stay put and he'll check out the next area. Geoffrey and I nod, but follow closely behind him just in case he needs assistance. Landon holds up his hand in a fist, signaling us to stop. He peers around the corner and then moves back to our position to give us a report of what he saw.

"There's five turrets in the next hall. They seem to be guarding a room at the end of it. I bet that's where the exit is," Landon explains.

"Yeah, and that big thing is probably in there too," I chime in.

"Let's just stick with the strategy we've been using and down these turrets. Then we'll regroup for the big bastard in the next area, okay?" Landon says, looking seriously at us.

"That thing is giving off a lot of energy. So we need to keep our wits about us out there," Geoffrey interjects.

"Don't worry. We'll deal with that *after* we take these turrets out," Landon reiterates. Geoffrey and I nod. I place an arm around Geoffrey because he seems nervous.

"It's going to be all right. Let's just stick to what we've been doing so far, and we'll be fine," I say reassuringly, trying to calm him.

"I hope so," Geoffrey replies with a strained smile.

We creep up to the end of the wall with Landon in front. He stops and peeks around the corner. "There's a low-lying wall in the middle of the next hall. We just need to make it there, and then we can take out those turrets. They're too far away right now for any of our powers to have an effect," he states looking back at us. "Barriers up, everyone. This is going to get serious."

I focus and throw a barrier up around myself.

"All right, move out," Landon says.

The three of us come around the corner and are immediately fired upon by all five turrets. As the bullets bounce off my barrier, everything seems to be going by in slow motion. Every shell gracefully deflects off the bubble of neon blue and falls to the floor. The sound of the shells hitting the ground is oddly comforting since that means one hasn't passed through my barrier yet. Landon makes it to the wall first and I'm almost there when I hear a groan of pain behind me right on my heels. Looking back, I see Geoffrey on the ground. I feel every syllable of his name scream out from my throat as I stop and begin running back toward him. Immediately, I cast a barrier around him, weakening my own in the process. I hear Landon cry out to me, but I must see if Geoffrey is okay. I begin to feel every bullet as they continuously pound into my barrier.

Geoffrey's lying there on the ground with his eyes squeezed shut and his hands holding his chest. I see several shells around him on the ground.

"Geoffrey, are you okay?" I ask him as I kneel down by his side.

"Yeah…just got the wind…knocked out of me," he replies.

"You need to get up. We have to make it to the wall and then you can rest, all right?" I say as I begin to help him stand. He throws his arm around my shoulder and I lead us toward the wall. Our barriers fuse together, creating one large one. Though our barrier feels stronger now, the constant barrage of bullets almost becomes too much to bear. I feel like I'm losing control when all of a sudden I feel a surge of energy course through it. It almost feels stronger somehow. I look ahead of me and see Landon focusing on us, his eyes and hands glowing. He must be helping us keep our barrier up.

When we reach the wall, I let Geoffrey down gently to rest behind it. As I plop down, my barrier fades away. I take a deep breath in, preparing myself for yet another onslaught when we try to take out those turrets. Looking over at Geoffrey, he seems to be recovering and is in the process of catching his breath.

"Are you okay, Geoffrey?" I hear Landon ask him over my shoulder.

Geoffrey nods. "So what's our next plan of attack?"

"You sure you're okay to continue right now?" I ask him with worry present in my voice.

"Yeah…I feel like a million bucks," he jokes, and then laughs slightly while clutching his chest. "Just tell me what I have to do, and I'll do it."

"Can you muster a decoy?" Landon asks him.

In a matter of seconds Geoffrey's "twin" was kneeling next to him. "I think so," he laughs.

"Good, now when Geoffrey sends his decoy out there to distract the turrets, Kenley, you and I will throw barriers over them. And the ones that don't disable themselves we'll hit with barrage, okay?" Landon explains.

The Modified

"Got it," I reply and then I look over to Geoffrey, who gestures in agreement.

"Ready? Go!" Landon says forcefully.

I watch as Geoffrey's decoy leaps over the wall and instantly we hear gunfire. Landon and I peer over and cast our barriers as planned. As their bullets bounce off our energy fields and pound back into them, three of the turrets go limp and begin to spark. We see that our barriers failed to reach the two farthest targets.

Landon and I both look at each other and then at the two remaining turrets that seem to be out of our power's reach.

"Kenley, remember what we did with that medicine ball?"

"How could I forget?"

He grins. "Well, we're going to do the same thing here. Give me your hands and we'll combine our power into a stronger barrage attack, okay?"

"Got it," I reply and Landon moves behind me, grabbing my hands. I can feel his strength as he presses up against my back. His muscles constrict as his arms and chest touch me. A tingle surges through my body as his power melds with mine. He's so strong. We concentrate and the light around our hands intensifies and envelops both of us.

"On the count of three," Landon whispers in my ear. "One...two...three!"

Final Assessment

Two large electrified projectiles shoot from our hands, barreling through the air toward the turrets. They pierce through them, causing an explosion. When the smoke clears, a pile of twisted broken metal is all that's left of them.

"Got 'em," Geoffrey says triumphantly.

I look at Landon over my shoulder and smile as he lightly squeezes me in a hug.

"Can you do a scan of the area ahead, Geoffrey?" I ask, joining him on the ground behind the wall.

"Sure thing," he answers as he stumbles to his feet and supports himself on the low wall. His eyes and hands start to glow. He slowly drops back down beside us and his eyes return to normal. His face is not reassuring at all.

"Well?" Landon asks impatiently.

Geoffrey turns to look at us and his expression fills me with concern. "What is it, Geoffrey?"

"Whatever it is, it's through those doors. And it's huge," he replies.

I look over at Landon and his face reflects the concern I'm feeling right now. I push through my emotions and dig down deep to find the strength to continue. "I think we should keep moving. We have to, it's not like we have a choice." Both Landon and Geoffrey stand up and turn to face the door with me.

The Modified

"All right, let's do this," Geoffrey declares.

Landon reaches his hand down to mine, I take it and he pulls me to my feet. "Whatever is behind that door, we can take it out," Landon states forcefully.

I nod, and proceed to climb over the low wall, followed by Landon and Geoffrey.

Standing in front of the large metal door at the end of the hall I feel this sudden rush of dread, but then I push it aside. We all assume we have to touch the door like we had to with the walls before. We reach out our hands and place our palms on the door. A harsh electronic tone assaults our ears and the door slowly begins to slide open.

The room beyond is pitch black. There's no light to speak of. I go to step inside and the floor suddenly illuminates row by row, tile by tile, almost in a wave pattern. Several low walls pop up around the area and a bright red barrier shimmers on in the very center of the room. The floor begins to open up within the barrier and a large machine looking thing rises up from the hole. It looks inactive. The big bold black lettering on the side of it reads: H.E.R.C.

"What the hell is it?" I ask out loud.

"A HERC...highly evolved robotic combatant. That's a HERC!" Geoffrey exclaims. "My dad told me about those things. They're supposed to be modeled after the tank-like vehicles the

Bringers use in battle. He wasn't supposed to tell me about this stuff, but he did anyway."

"Whatever it is, we need to either take it out, or get by it to the exit over there," Landon states, pointing to the open door just behind the HERC.

Just as he says those words, two red lights beam from the front of the HERC directly at us. The front begins to shift, followed by the rest of it, filling the room with the sound of twisting metal. A head forms, followed by a body and then eight legs sprout from its sides, slamming to the ground with great force. Standing before us is this giant spider-like robot. Its body is more rectangular-shaped, though.

A loud ear-piercing electronic shriek sounds from the large beast in front of us as it rears back, causing us to clasp our ears. It lowers itself close to the ground, almost like it's getting ready to pounce. The barrier around it disappears and I notice the wall of energy moves to block our exit from the area.

"Looks like we're going to have to fight this thing," Landon calls out.

Suddenly the HERC leaps over at us. I stand there in shock, watching as this giant machine hurls toward me. At the last second I snap out of it and join Landon and Geoffrey as they jump out of the way. The HERC crashes into the ground, cracking the floor around it.

The Modified

We spring to our feet. "Barrage!" Landon yells. We all focus and start hurling light projectiles toward the robot. Every hit pushes it back slightly, but ends up only stalling the machine instead of destroying it. The HERC shakes off the barrage and charges at us. I throw up a barrier and slide underneath it as Landon and Geoffrey roll out of the way. The HERC connects with my barrier and is flipped up into the air by the energy field. It lands on its back as it comes crashing down. It struggles to turn itself over, but eventually does. The HERC rears back, bucking its legs toward us like a horse does when it's agitated. I notice a diamond shape on its stomach glowing bright red.

"Maybe we need to hit that," I yell, pointing to the diamond.

"Let's give it a shot," Landon replies and Geoffrey nods.

We stand there waiting for the HERC to make its next move. I hear this shifting mechanical noise sounding from the HERC and notice its front two legs have formed themselves into an angled upright position, framing its head, and pointing straight at us. The tips of them begin to glow bright red.

"Everyone get behind a wall now!" I shout as I dive behind the closest one. I hear the impact of whatever it fired at us on the wall I'm crouched behind. *Damn, how are we going to take this thing out when it has that much firepower?* I ask myself.

As an idea hits me I look over at Landon and then to Geoffrey. "Landon, Geoffrey! Produce your decoys, I've got a plan!" I yell as more projectiles crash into the wall I'm posted up against.

"Kenley, don't do anything stupid. We don't need you getting yourself hurt," Landon yells worriedly.

"Yeah, Kenley, you don't have to be a hero, all right?" Geoffrey calls out.

"Don't worry guys. Just trust me, okay?"

"Okay," they both cry out almost in unison.

"Wait for my signal," I state as I wait for the HERC to fire at us again. The moment it does, I signal for Geoffrey and Landon to project their decoys. I cast a barrier over myself and then spin out from behind the wall. I see the HERC in the distance preparing for all of us running toward it. It seems confused as to whom to shoot at first as its focus darts back and forth between us. *I can't believe I'm doing this right now, holy crap!* I yell to myself.

The left leg fires first and completely decimates Geoffrey's decoy. Then it fires the next shot at me. I roll out of the way, but keep my barrier up. Landon's decoy distracts it as it charges up again. I sprint toward the HERC and proceed to slide under it, but remove my barrier at the last moment so not to knock the HERC over. It stumbles back slightly while I'm underneath it, and I charge my barrage attach. I see out of the corner of my eye Landon's decoy get destroyed by its next round of blasts. *I have to do this now!* I tell myself and release all the energy I've built up in my hands right into the red glowing diamond. The projectile pierces right through it, leaving a large hole in its metal abdomen. The red light flickers and fades away as the HERC slowly begins to crumble down onto its legs. I roll out from under it and instantly begin to hear the cheers from Landon and Geoffrey.

"You kicked that thing's ass!" Geoffrey yells as he runs up to me, wrapping me in a hug.

Landon smiles really big as he comes in for a hug too. "You were amazing, Kenley," he whispers in my ear and then kisses my forehead.

I can hardly express how I feel because I'm so overcome by emotion at what I just did, and by Landon's kiss.

A loud melodic chime sounds throughout the room as the barrier blocking the exit fades away. Blue light arrows begin to illuminate on the floor, pointing toward the exit. We join hands, and make our way toward it. We did it. We passed our test together as a team, and it feels good.

Chapter Eleven
The Magnus Ball

Who knew I could accomplish so much? Yes, I had help from my implant, but I still passed. Me…Kenley Grayson. Would Dylan be proud?

"Earth to Kenley." Joey's voice interrupts my ponderings about what we all just went through. "Hey dork, wake up. Dr. Patel's about to make an announcement," Joey whispers in my ear. "So, were you thinking about a certain someone who's been staring at you for the past five minutes?"

"No," I say, looking down the table and catching Landon's smirk. "I was thinking about the exam…and wondering what Dylan would think about all of this."

The Modified

Joey's mischievous grin turns solemn. "Sorry, Kenley." His blue eyes show his sadness.

"It's okay."

"All right, cadets," Dr. Patel begins, "as of right now, and until after this evening, you are to act like you're not in the military. Just forget for a moment that you're soldiers. Treat tonight almost like shore leave, because we're going to have a dance. A celebration, really." Her smile encompasses the room. "Now off to your quarters to get ready. Oh, and just so you know, we may have a few surprises in store for you back in your rooms."

"A dance? Really? Damn, I wonder what they'll think of next." Sam's voice is filled with sarcasm.

"I think it'll be fun," I reply, and then see Geoffrey shake his head. Caleb looks completely bored, and Joey's grinning as he sees Landon approaching our little group.

"So, is everyone looking forward to tonight?" Landon's deep voice makes me weak in the knees.

"Kenley is. She loooves to dance," Joey teases while draping his arm around my shoulder. Landon's eyes narrow and his smile seems a little forced.

"I do love to dance. It's not a crime, you know. Now let me go so I can get to my room…you know, like we were all directed to do."

"Okay, let's all follow orders everyone and go find out what surprises await us." Joey winks at me and then takes off. We all stand there watching him leave.

"I still don't feel up to par after the exam. I may sit this one out, guys," Geoffrey moans, and then lets out a squeak as Sam grabs his arm, pulling him behind her out of the room. Caleb follows quietly after.

"So you love to dance, huh?" Landon's smile is warm again, his eyes meeting mine.

"Yeah, kind of-"

I pause as he leans down pressing his lips to mine, so brief, as if in a blink of an eye. As he lifts his head, my eyes dart left and right to find thankfully the room is empty.

"Kenley, I don't know why, but when I'm near you…I feel the need to touch you."

My tongue seems to be stuck. "I've noticed."

Landon's infectious laugh fills the empty room, and I blush as he takes my arm to escort me out the door.

"Galileo, are you there?"

"Yes, Kenley…just silent. I am pondering the reaction your body has to Shaw, Landon."

"Well-" A loud knock sounds at my door, delaying my answer.

The Modified

"Enter," Galileo announces and the door opens revealing two Ada androids carrying various bags and boxes.

"We are here to help you get ready, Grayson, Kenley." They both say in unison.

"Ready? What's all this?" I ask, watching the two as they proceed to place everything in their hands on the bed.

"Your clothes, shoes, and makeup for the Magnus Ball of course. This is all a special gift to you from the Allied Federation," the androids reply again in sync.

"Wow, look at that dress. It's beautiful!" I say gushing at the long delicate purple creation being hung up on a hanger outside my closet. It's a very simple gown with thin straps. The material feels soft as it slides over my hand. The identical duo begins to pull out beautiful dainty underwear and a pair of shoes from the bags that match the dress perfectly.

"We are ready to begin, Grayson, Kenley. Please take a seat in the chair," the androids say, standing beside the only chair in the room, waiting patiently.

"That is my cue to leave, I will be back later," Galileo states and fades into my bangle.

"Okay, ladies, do your best." I giggle as they both look perplexed by my statement. "Oh, I mean, you can start."

"Done." The duo's monotone voices make me jump.

"Thank you," I reply, hesitant to look in the full-length mirror. As if they can read my mind, each of them grab an arm and put me in front of the dreaded mirror. Standing there looking at my reflection, my mouth hangs open. *Is that me?* I ask myself. Blinking, I see the image doing the same. Wow, where's the old Kenley?

"Kenley, are you okay? Your heart rate is high, and your body is trembling slightly." Galileo's image comes into view. "Kenley, you look very acceptable. Different may be a more appropriate word."

"I know, Galileo. I feel like I'm a princess or something. You know, like Cinderella?"

"I do not know this Cinderella. Let me check my database. You two may leave," I hear him say to the two Ada androids that are waiting to be dismissed. I barely notice them exit as I'm still fixated on my reflection.

"It's a fairy tale, Galileo."

"A fairy tale? Ah, okay now I have found it. But you are not a servant, your father is alive, and you have a mother not a stepmother."

Hearing poor Galileo's confusion brings my full attention back to him. "No, I don't mean it literally, silly. I just feel so different. Like how she must've felt dressed up to go to the ball."

The Modified

"I will have to take your word for it, as I still cannot see the similarities."

"It's okay, Galileo."

I take one last look at my reflection. My blonde hair is pulled up into a bun and is wrapped in a purple metal spiral that matches the color of my dress. My makeup is stunning and goes perfectly with my skin tone. Tiny purple stars outline the sides of my eyes and follow down to the middle of my cheeks. They shimmer when the light hits them. And finally, my dress—it fits like it was made specifically for me. The material hugs my curves and then plunges like a purple waterfall to the tops of my feet. My shoes have a small heel, making a soft tapping noise as I make my way across the room to sit back in the chair.

"Kenley, it is time for you to attend the festivities. You do not want to be late," Galileo speaks loudly as if I'm deaf.

"No need to yell, I'm going. I just need a minute."

"I never yell, you did not respond the first time I informed you."

"Sorry, Galileo. I'm just a little preoccupied…nervous, really. What will people say when they see me? I mean, I look so different."

"You look fine." Another knock comes at the door. "Now, who is that?" he asks.

"It's probably Joey," I reply moving to open it.

"Hey Jo-" I stop, surprised to see Landon standing there looking so…unbelievably handsome in his black tux.

"Sorry, but it's not Joey. Just me. Is he taking you to the dance?" His smile doesn't quite reach his eyes.

"No, I was kind of hoping-" I begin to say and then pause, gazing at him. He's so gorgeous.

"May I?" Landon asks, returning my gaze.

"What?"

"Take you?" He reaches out for my hand as he asks.

"Yes," I reply quickly.

"You look amazing, by the way." Landon's sexy smile makes my knees start to quiver. Good thing I'm wearing a long dress.

"You clean up pretty well yourself," I reply, looking him up and down.

"Well, Ms. Grayson, it'll be my pleasure to be your escort for the evening. We're civilians right now, and tonight we'll pretend there's no war. And we'll just have fun."

"Sounds like a plan, Mr. Shaw. By the way, do you know how to dance?"

"This may shock you, but I do dance. And even if I didn't, I'd fake it so nobody would have the chance to take you away from me tonight."

I'm thankful we're walking down the corridor and not face-to-face because of the major blush I have going on. And what a time for my hair to be up. I guarantee it would hide my face perfectly right now if it were down.

When we reach the mess hall, both of us stop at the entrance. We're in awe at the transformation our eating area has undergone. It looks so surreal. Our usual tables are missing, and instead, spread out around the outer edges of the room are intimate white stands which are topped with a solid surface of shimmering blue energy. They're surrounded by highly polished white stools. But the most amazing sight in the room is the dance floor. The transparent floor has soft blue lights shining from below it, and when someone walks over the tiles the soft lights turn into a pulsating vivid blue.

"Kenley, look up," Landon whispers in my ear. Following his lead I raise my eyes. My thought of the dance floor as being the most amazing thing quickly changes once I look up. The ceiling looks nonexistent. In its place, a beautiful starry night sky covers the span of the room as a huge bright moon shines in the opposite corner of where we're standing.

"Wow, I wonder how they did that," I say in total astonishment.

"I don't know, but it's pretty awesome."

"Well, don't just stand there blocking the entrance, move it, soldiers." Sam's quip is startling, and we quickly comply. "Where's the grub?" she asks, looking around.

"Don't you think this is amazing? Oh, Sam, you look so beautiful." She pushes past us, ignoring my compliment.

"She cleans up well too," Landon says, raising his voice and then chuckles as we see her back stiffen at his comment.

"Hey, this is cool. If I didn't know better, I'd think this wasn't the mess hall." Joey's teasing voice comes from behind us. "Is that Sam? Wow, that red dress and her dark hair, who knew she was such a hottie," he adds.

"So, are you into girls now, Joey?" I ask jokingly, knowing very well the answer to my own question.

"No, but I can appreciate beauty, can't I?" He pauses, turning to look at me. "Well, Landon's quite the lucky guy, huh? Look at you, you're stunning." Joey's grin is infectious as he takes my hand and spins me around to get a better look at my dress. "I only wish Dylan could be here to see his sister all grown up," he says and kisses my cheek.

"Thanks, Joey. Me too," I say with a slight smile.

"Treat her well, Landon. You've got precious cargo here," Joey states, giving Landon a little slap to the side of his shoulder. He moves ahead and leaves us standing in the doorway.

"He's g-?" Landon begins to ask as he turns to look at me.

"Yep. His parents practically disowned him when they found out he was gay. His father thought he could beat 'the disease,' as he called it, out of him. Joey came to our house late one night, beaten up pretty badly. We immediately took him in and let him stay with us for a while. His parents didn't even seem to care that he didn't come home for a week. Just like that he went from being a friend, to being a member of our family."

"Huh."

"You don't have an issue with that do you?" I ask, looking at Landon questioningly.

"No, not at all. I actually thought… I mean, you and him were-"

"Oh, no. Joey's like a brother to me. When we lost Dylan, Joey became a rock for my little brother and me," I say, trying to keep the tears at bay, but one escapes, sliding down my cheek where Landon's finger catches it. "Hey," I say taking in a deep breath, "you said you can dance, right? Well, I want to see."

"Don't worry, we'll dance. Just waiting for the right moment," he says wiggling his eyebrows and making me giggle. "I'm really glad I don't have to fight Joey for you. I would've, but I'm glad I don't have too."

"You would have, huh?"

"In a heartbeat," he replies with his mouth close to mine. I can feel every syllable that leaves lips.

As if on cue a slow song begins to play and Landon grabs my hand, pulling me onto the dance floor. I feel like I'm in a dream that I definitely don't want to wake up from. This evening is so perfect. Everyone seems to be having a good time and the only bad part is that tomorrow reality will set in again.

Looking around I notice Sam dancing with a tall hot guy from Russia. I think his name is Ivan. Geoffrey is smiling, sitting at one of the tables and eating the delicious food from the buffet with Mara, a fellow Tactical member. They seem to be having a deep conversation even though Geoffrey's grinning constantly.

I scan the room and find Joey talking to Alex, a dark-haired Irish guy. Joey seems relaxed and laughs at something Alex is telling him. The one person I can't find is Caleb, and wonder if he decided he's too cool to be here.

Landon didn't lie about being able to dance, and after about an hour, I'm dragging him off the floor toward the refreshments. My stomach is starting to protest at its lack of sustenance.

"I'm starved, Landon."

"Me too," he replies in a voice that makes me turn around and look at him. He licks his lips as he watches my mouth and I feel like he's not talking about food.

"For food, silly," I say poking his chest.

He grabs my hand and pulls me close, his eyes suddenly serious as his lips come close to mine. I shut my eyes anticipating the kiss and then nothing. I blink and open my eyes, realizing he's let me go, and all I can see is his retreating back moving toward the buffet. *Oh, Mr. Shaw, you're going to get it now*, I think to myself.

The tables are filled with such an array of mouthwatering food. I find it hard to choose. With my plate finally piled high, I make my way to a vacant table in the corner. I feel eyes staring at me and find Landon with two plates in his hands making his way toward me. I sit down and place my napkin on my lap and start to eat, not waiting for him.

"This food's amazing. There's stuff on those tables I haven't eaten in years. Fresh tomatoes, oh how I've missed you." Landon then bites into one, and I try not to look as he slowly savors the flavor. My heart starts to speed up a little as I sneak a peek after hearing his groan of satisfaction.

"Kenley, are you feeling all right?" Galileo's voice startles me as he glows from my bangle.

"Yeah, she's fine, Galileo," Landon answers before I can even get my thoughts together to reply.

"But her heart rate is up, and that usually doesn't happen when she eats," Galileo responds. Could I possibly be any more embarrassed than I feel right now? I think not!

"I'm fine, Galileo. I just ate something that was a little too spicy for my taste," I say before I take a long swig of water, trying to convince him, Landon, and myself of the obvious lie.

The Magnus Ball

The only spicy thing in this room is the guy sitting across from me, and right now he could be the death of me.

Landon sends me a lazy, sexy smile as he leans back in his chair, obviously not believing my lie. I savagely attack my chicken breast with a knife and fork while ignoring him. He finally gives up and starts to eat again. If the music wasn't playing, the silence between us would be deafening.

"Hey, you two, what's up?" Joey's voice pierces through the music.

"Duh, we're stuffing our faces," I say before I think, and now I'm even more miffed at Landon for making me take it out on Joey.

"Hey, I just asked a question." Joey looks at me puzzled, and then looks at Landon who is smiling while chewing something he just put in his mouth.

"Let's dance," I say grabbing Joey's hand and drag him out onto the dance floor, feeling Landon's eyes following us.

"Okay, spill. What's got your panties all in a twist?" Joey asks pulling me close as a slow song starts.

"Insufferable men, that's what," I say, and then step on his toe when he chuckles.

"You have a crush on him, don't you?"

"I do not. Okay, maybe I do. And the worst part is, I think he knows it. What's happening to me? We're at war! We're soldiers, and here I am crushing on some guy from California. Am I nuts?"

"No, you're just human. I like Landon. You know I have that sense about people, and he's a good guy. Have a little fun, who knows what will happen soon."

"I so love you, Joey! Now what about you and the eye candy you were with just a little while ago?"

"Oh, Alex? We were just chatting. I kind of dig his accent," he replies with a slight laugh. "He's really nice, though. Kind of reminds me of a boy I knew in high school. Anyway, back to you. Are you going to let yourself have a little fun, or what?"

"Or what, Kenley? Do you mind, Joey? I think this is our dance." Landon takes my hand and pulls me in his arms. I hear Joey laugh and see him making goo-goo eyes at me as he walks away.

The music is slow and we move together as if we're one person. The dance floor feels crowded, but I'm not paying attention to our surroundings. My only focus is on Landon's arms around me.

"Let's get out of here," Landon whispers in my ear, and pulls me through a side doorway into a darkened corridor. My heartbeat speeds up as Landon gently pushes me against the wall and moves in close. His lips touch mine and his hands roam up and down my back sending shivers of delight where they touch. I clutch onto him as he pushes his way into my mouth and the kiss deepens. Everything disappears except for this delicious feeling of warmth and our dual heartbeats moving at warp speed.

"Kenley, you're driving me crazy. I've never felt this way about anyone before. I feel like I'm losing my mind," he says breathlessly, close to my ear.

"Kenley? Landon?" Both our AIs respond together.

"Not now," Landon tells the two images, and after a few seconds they disappear back into our bands. "I'm sorry if this is all too much for you."

My throat is dry, and my brain is trying to comprehend what Landon is saying. I want him to grab me again and kiss me forever, but I realize he's looking at me waiting for me to say something.

"Landon, I'm not sure what to say. I feel something strong between us too, but can't decide if it's just because of what we've gone through together," I reply and then pause. "I think this is real, but there's just so much going on, it's hard to know for sure. Did any of that make sense?"

"Perfect sense," Landon's says softly before his lips find mine again, and then nothing else seems to matter in this moment.

Outside of my door in the dimly lit hallway, Landon traps me between the wall and his body. I hear the door slide open as he proceeds to gently kiss me, and then pull away while resting his forehead on mine.

"Do you want to come in?" *Kenley, what the heck are you saying? Are you nuts? You know what will happen and how much trouble you guys will get into.* My inner voice speaks up.

"I want to so badly, but I can't… because I think I'm in love with you," Landon quietly whispers.

He swiftly kisses me, and then to my amazement leaves me standing at the door. I watch as he turns the corner and disappears.

Entering my room I walk over to the sink and look in the mirror. My eyes are glowing and my lips are slightly swollen. My perfect bun is now in disarray.

"He thinks he loves me," I say out loud. I really like Landon, but I think I'm scared of getting close to him because I don't want to lose him. I've already lost one person I care about to this war.

I jump as Galileo projects from my bangle. "What is love? And why might Shaw, Landon love you?" he asks, making me chuckle.

How do I explain love to a computer? I ask myself.

"Love is a feeling…an emotion that one feels for another…oh, Galileo, I don't know how to describe love," I respond still completely overwhelmed and at a loss for words. "All I know is that Landon told me he thinks he loves me."

"I know, I heard. I realize now that it is normal for your heart to move faster when you are in the presence of Shaw, Landon. I will not interrupt you again. One more question?"

"Okay, let's hear it?"

"Why did Shaw, Landon not want to come into your room?"

"Because…because he knew what would probably happen. He respects me enough to wait until it's the right time."

"What would have happened?" Galileo's monotone voice asks.

"You said only one more question, so I can't answer that," I joke with him. "I'm going to take a shower."

I open my top drawer, pull out the metal casing, and place it on over my bangle. I want no more interruptions to my thoughts for the rest of the night.

Chapter Twelve
The Fortification Division

I hear the song that wakes me up every morning and let out a little groan. "Kenley, it's time to 'rise and shine.' Your shower is ready when you are," Galileo's voice interrupts the dream I'm trying to fight to stay in. This is definitely one of those I just want to spend a little extra time with.

"Two more minutes," I grumble and turn over, stuffing my arm and the bangle under the pillow. I hear Galileo mumbling and try to return to my dream, but I'm awake now and it's hopeless.

"Kenley, that was not necessary," Galileo sounds indignant as I pull my arm out from beneath the pillow and he projects out.

"Galileo," I whine, "you interrupted the best dream I've ever had."

"And that was?"

I feel the blush creeping into my cheeks as I recall it. Instead of answering him, I jump out of bed and reach for the metal casing.

"Kenley, I am waiting for your answer," he says just before I cover him up.

"Whoa, so not a convo intended for your ears," I mumble as I undress and jump in the shower, still blushing.

Standing in the steamy hot shower, I begin to remember the best part of my dream. Landon and I were on an isolated tropical beach that was covered with blinding white sand. His perfectly chiseled body was wearing only a pair of trunks that left nothing to the imagination. I scrunch my nose as I remember that I was in the skimpiest bikini I've ever seen. We emerged hand in hand out of the sparkling blue ocean and I watched as beads of water ran down from Landon's beautiful chestnut brown hair onto his chest. I followed the flowing water as it touched every inch of his body. My knees turned to rubber when he smirked at me after catching me staring at him. He swept me up in his arms and carried me the rest of the way toward a huge blue sand umbrella. He laid me gently on a fluffy soft blanket that was sprawled out underneath it. My mouth watered as he followed me down and his upper body covered mine. It was then that I realized I had somehow lost my bikini top. I become a mass of sensation as I think back to how I felt as my bare skin touched his. Then Galileo's voice sounded in my ear, totally ruining it. I wonder how I can face Landon without blushing now, especially after vividly remembering that dream.

I hear the muffled voice of Galileo underneath the casing. Removing it, "Sorry, what did you say, Galileo?"

"I said that you have only five minutes to get down to the mess hall for breakfast."

"Oh crap," I reply and rush from the bathroom to get dressed, my skin still tingling from thinking about my dream.

I barely make it to the cafeteria in time to eat some fruit and an omelet. I try to act normal, but Joey and Sam seem to be fixated on me. I ignore their stares and shovel in my food.

"So did you enjoy the dance last night?" Sam asks, with a sly grin.

"Yeah, Kenley you just up and disappeared. What was up with that?" Joey gives me a playful nudge with his shoulder.

I ignore their comments and continue eating, hoping to keep my embarrassment in check. I look down the table and meet Landon's shocking blue eyes. He sends me a mouth-watering smile that makes me drop my forkful of food, and I feel my face heating up. *Damn, fair skin!* I yell to myself. I turn away, letting my hair fall over my face and then realize my hair is not in a braid. I was so distracted that I forgot to have an Ada do my hair.

"It is time for all cadets to report to their designated training areas." A robotic voice fills the room through the intercoms. I quickly grab my tray and make my way to the exit, dumping my uneaten food and leaving the room before any more questions. I feel bad about Landon, but I need to get my composure before he sees how much he affects me. I make a quick stop at my room and have Galileo call for an Ada, and then hurry to my Fortification training room.

I'm the last one to step foot into Dr. Patel's room and all eyes dart to me as I enter. I look around and it seems like everyone's paired up except for Caleb. I smile and wave as I walk over to him, but he seems less enthusiastic about the pairing. At first he acts like he's bored, but then an hour into the class he changes.

Caleb grabs a colorfully striped medicine ball with his telekinesis and makes it float in the air. It spins so fast that it begins to look less like a ball and more like a rainbow blur. A tap on his shoulder from Dr. Patel sends the ball flying across the room, sending people diving for the ground.

The Modified

I hold back a giggle as Caleb walks over to me and whispers in my ear. "Top that, Grayson." I open my mouth to give him a snarky reply and then see him grinning at me mischievously.

"Caleb, where did that come from? This playful side of you?"

"I've always been fun, I just chose when and if I let it out."

"I like *this* Caleb," I say and watch his face change, gone is the grin. Before I can say anything, two androids enter with trays of sandwiches and drinks. I regret that I won't see my friends at lunch, but I feel a reprieve from having to see Landon before I can get my emotions under control.

This session has been intense, and I'm totally exhausted by the time Dr. Patel announces the end of training. I go to leave the room and find my exit blocked by our instructor.

"Ms. Grayson, are you okay? You seem a little distracted today?"

"Yes, ma'am. I just had a hard time sleeping last night. I'll do better tomorrow, promise."

"Good to hear, because you're one of the best, and I need my best cadets always on their toes."

"Got it. I won't let you down, Dr. Patel."

"Warm milk," she says as I move past her to the door.

"Warm milk?" I ask, turning to face her.

"Yes, it always helps me sleep," she replies with a smile.

The Fortification Division

Warm milk? As if that will help me sleep, I think as I enter the mess hall for dinner. Looking at our table section, I realize I'm the last one to arrive again. Thankfully, everyone's occupied with eating.

"Is that steak?" I ask, sitting down and pressing the menu button on the table in front of me.

"Yeah, and it's delicious. I can't remember the last time I ate steak and it was so tender. It's literally melting in my mouth." Caleb's voice is full of pleasure and we all stare in surprise at the expression of pure joy on his face.

"I thought there was a shortage of beef in the world," I state confused.

"I guess the Federation has its connections. And I'm glad too," Caleb replies with a crazy grin.

"I guess we've found Caleb's Achilles heel…a good steak," Joey chimes in.

"Man, Caleb, what's got into you? You're like all happy and shit. Like a freakin' bundle of joy," Sam asks jokingly when the laughter dies down.

"I don't know what you mean. I'm always the life of the party, right, Kenley?" Caleb responds with a wickedly handsome smirk.

Everyone's attention turns to me. "Caleb was quite the rebel today during training. He got a little carried away and caused a ball to spin out of control, almost wiping out half the class. And he so got busted by Dr. Patel."

"So you got in trouble, huh, Caleb?" Joey quips. "And here I thought you'd be teacher's pet."

"Nope, that honor goes to your girl, Kenley." Caleb stuffs another piece of steak into his mouth.

Geoffrey sits with his mouth hanging open watching Caleb as if he has sprung horns suddenly. Sam shakes her head and dives into her steak. I look down the table at Landon and give him a quick smile, still embarrassed about my crazy dream. *Wake up, Kenley. It was only a dream. Yeah…but it felt so real,* the irritated voice in my head yells.

"So now that we know Caleb has finally woken up and decided to be human. Kenley is Dr. Patel's little lab rat, and Joey and I had a bitchin' day, what about you, Geoffrey?" Sam asks, looking pointedly at him.

"Oh um, me? Yes, well…I reviewed and revised some battle plans. It was all done digitally on a simulator. Mara and I worked together and-"

"Mara, huh? Is that the hot little number with the glasses you were in a deep convo with at the dance last night?" Sam asks slyly.

"Why yes, she's very nice and we have the same IQ. And she didn't mention she was hot at the dance, in fact we didn't dance, so why would she have been hot? I mean the temperature is kept at a comfortable level in all the rooms," Geoffrey rambles, completely missing the point of what Sam was trying to say.

"Can someone explain to him, please?" Sam begs, rolling her eyes.

"Geoffrey, Sam means that Mara's hot, good-looking, nice to look at, Wake up and notice," Joey says and nudges Geoffrey who turns bright red when he realizes what Sam meant.

"I...err...guess. I hadn't really paid much attention. She's nice and super intelligent."

"Well damn, I give up." Sam shoves a piece of steak in her mouth and chews vigorously.

The rest of us dig into our food and I feel more relaxed than I have all day.

"That was just what I needed. I'm so stuffed that I think I need a nap now," Joey quips.

"I heard you got quite a workout today," I say to Joey as we exit the cafeteria.

"Yeah, I was paired up with your boy, Landon. He's one tough SOB."

"Hey, I was paired up with Johnston, and I can't believe he's in Strike. What a wuss. He refuses to hit a girl," Sam's disgusted voice chimes in.

The Modified

"So, I'm a tough SOB, huh? I'm flattered Joey, and you're not too shabby yourself." I jump a little when I hear Landon's voice right behind me. I can feel his breath, he's that close.

"Thanks, Shaw. Of course, I wasn't using my full potential," Joey replies, pushing out his chest and grinning like a fool. "I didn't want to hurt you too much."

"Of course you didn't," Landon says while slapping Joey on the back, and then moves to my left side. "If you don't mind I'd like a word with Kenley. If that's all right with you guys?"

"Yeah, sure. Come on guys, let's give them some alone time," Joey says and then winks at me. He laughs as I send him a withering stare and then drapes his arms lazily around the shoulders of Geoffrey and Sam. "You too, Caleb. Keep up."

"Hey, I'm coming, wait up," Caleb calls out from behind us.

"Come on slow poke," Joey says over his shoulder as he begins to walk away with Geoffrey and Sam.

"Come back and say that to my face, Joey. I dare you," Caleb jokes while quickening his pace to catch up to the laughing group ahead of him.

"Caleb's something else. He's suddenly a man of many words, what the heck happened?" Landon asks while taking my hand and guiding me through the corridor opposite the one our group just disappeared down.

• • •

"Yeah, I couldn't believe how he was during our session, he's always so quiet. And did you hear poor Geoffrey, I think Mara likes him, and he doesn't have a clue."

"Do you?" Landon asks as he pulls me into a little alcove in the deserted hallway.

"Do I what?"

"Have a clue that I have strong feelings for you, or are you scared about what I said last night?" Landon pushes his hand through his hair, looking perplexed.

"No, not scared, just confused. I mean, we've only known each other for a little while and you tell me…that." I bite my lip nervously, not able to say the words I want to.

"It isn't a line, Kenley. From the first time I saw you in the crowded tram station, I knew I wanted to meet you. I felt this connection that made me want to push my way through the mass of bodies just to talk to you. I know you probably think I'm crazy or something. And I am crazy…for you." Landon's eyes meet mine and I realize I feel the same way. There is a connection between us. Is it love? Maybe, but I'm not sure. All I know is that I'm happy whenever Landon is around, and I don't want to lose that feeling.

I lean in and pull his head down so my lips meet his, and softly kiss him. His arms slide around my waist, pulling me close, and he nudges my mouth open and slips in his tongue. His mouth engulfs mine and my body begins tingling from head to toe.

He gently pulls away and looks into my eyes. "Yes, I feel it too," I say as I reach up to pull him to me again.

"I think we need to find another spot. How about we go up to a special place on the seventh floor?" His voice is husky with emotion.

"A special place, huh?"

"Yeah, you'll like it. Trust me. I've been meaning to take you there for a while now."

Landon takes my hand and we quickly make our way to a bank of elevators down another deserted hallway. We stand in front of the first elevator and it swishes open. We enter and the doors close behind us. Landon presses one of the many buttons and says, "Kenley," after the electronic voice asks for a password.

Seconds later the doors open up to a sight that is truly remarkable. Vibrant plants and full-size trees fill the area inside. The area is unbelievably huge and slightly humid. Gone is the air-conditioned feeling the others floors have. Small colorful birds and giant butterflies share the air space. Landon takes my hand and we walk down one of the cobblestone paths lined with tropical looking plants and flowers of every color.

"Oh, Landon, it's beautiful. How do you think they recreated all of this?"

"Look at that, it's a toucan. It doesn't even look real, but it just blinked." Landon squeezes my hand as we both take in the lush scenery surrounding us. "I don't know how they did this, but it's incredible. Look, there are even bumblebees, they haven't been on Earth for years."

I reach out to touch a giant plant leaf and watch as a monarch butterfly gracefully lands on my finger. We both instantly hold our breath not wanting to scare it away. After a few seconds it takes off and flies high up to the clear dome ceiling above.

"I wonder why this place is such a secret. It's so wonderful. Everyone should have a chance to see this," Landon comments.

"Maybe it's an experiment or something."

"Well, if it is an experiment, it's an unbelievable one. I've already seen several birds and insects that I know have been extinct for years," he replies.

"Shush, I hear voices," I whisper, whipping my head around to face Landon. He points to a bush behind us and quietly pulls me to duck behind it as the voices grow louder. Through little holes in the shrubbery, I can see a pair of military boots and a pair of men's dress shoes.

"Is this it?" a familiar voice I recognize as General Barclay asks.

The Modified

"Yes sir, everything's there in those files. It's exactly what you asked for," Dr. Wilhelm says.

I see Landon's confused face when he hears Dr. Wilhelm's voice.

"Very well, I'll let my superiors know. Harvey, you've performed your job well, and you'll be compensated justly."

"Thank you, General. I'm honored you asked for my help. It was my pleasure to aid the Federation."

"Yes, indeed. This experiment will be revolutionary. Not to mention the progress you've made with this place," the general states while pointing to the green jungle surrounding us.

"Yes, this has been quite the unique project. I do hope we'll be able to utilize what we've learned from it one day." Dr. Wilhelm beams at the compliment.

"Yes, well, I have to go and notify my superiors of your excellent work here. This is a great place indeed." The general shakes Dr. Wilhelm's hand and then makes a hasty exit toward the elevator. Landon and I see the doctor bend down, pull a weed out of the grass, and then he too follows the general out.

"What do you think that was all about?" I ask Landon, wondering why the two men had to meet in a place probably the majority didn't know existed.

"I don't know, but I get this feeling we weren't supposed to hear that."

· · ·

The Fortification Division

A noise from my arm has me realizing that I forgot to take the casing off Galileo again. I quickly remove it and he instantly pops out.

"Kenley, I wish you would not do that so often. If you want me not to talk, all you have to do is ask. Now, I have a message from your father. He wants you to report to his office ASAP."

"Sorry, Galileo," I reply, but he's already returned to the bangle.

"I'll walk with you to your dad's office," Landon says, grabbing my hand and leading me back to the elevators.

"Do you think Galileo sounded miffed at me just then?" I ask as we wait for our ride down.

"Yeah, he did seem a little put out, but he's a computer. They don't have feelings, remember?"

"I know, but-" The elevator arrives and interrupts me. As we ride down in silence, I contemplate what just happened.

Landon leaves me at the door to my dad's office with a quick kiss, and tells me he's going to wait in the mess hall.

When I approach the door, it doesn't open. "Hey, Dad, it's me," I announce, knocking on the door. I hear him say "sorry" and then it slides open. The first thing I notice is that his hair is messier than usual, like he's been running his fingers through it all day. His face is void of a smile, and in its place is an intense frown. He's sitting at his desk, studying something in front of him very intently. I shudder, thinking about what could be wrong.

"Ah, Kenley, there you are," he says, raising his head to look at me.

"Dad, are you okay?" He stands up from his desk chair and comes around to give me a hug. "Please tell me what's going on." The butterflies in my stomach increase because he's still hugging me and not answering me.

"Kenley, I want to tell you something. It may all be in my head, but you have to listen, okay? Sit down," he says as he releases me and guides me to a chair. "Now, where do I begin?" He runs his fingers through his hair before sitting in the chair opposite me. Leaning forward, he stares at me with his hands trembling a little. "Kenley, I need you to look at this map of the facility." He presses a button on his watch and a screen projects up from his desk.

"We're here, and these items over here are escape pods, which are utilized in case of an emergency evacuation. You need to memorize where they're located, because you might have to use them in the coming days.

"What makes you think that?" I ask, nervous to hear his reply.

"I know this may sound crazy, but I want you to promise me that you'll use the pods if things change around here, okay? Don't wait for me to tell you to leave. Go with your gut feeling if the time comes. Now promise," he says, his voice suddenly demanding.

"I promise, but-"

"No more questions. It's probably nothing. I'm most likely just overreacting. Now, run along, and I'll see you later, okay?" He rises from his chair and pulls me up from mine. I'm feeling unsure of what to say next as he hugs me tight and lets me go, shooing me out of his office. Before I can turn around to say anything, he shuts the door behind me.

"What the heck just happened?" I say out loud.

Making my way to the mess hall, I begin going over the confusing conversation I just had with my dad, and try to make sense of it. A body blocks my way and I look up to find Landon, grinning at me. One glance at my face and his grin disappears, replaced by a look of uncertainty.

"Kenley, what's wrong?" He grabs my hand and pulls me in to an empty room, sensing we need privacy.

"I just had the weirdest talk with my dad. He showed me a map of the Academy, and the location of the escape pods."

"Why?" Landon's arms are around me and he's looking intently into my eyes.

The Modified

"Your guess is as good as mine. He didn't say outright, but he told me to memorize the locations. He said he had a feeling something isn't right, whatever that means."

"I think we need to go and find these pods," Landon says firmly.

"I think you're right. Just us though. If we bring the others with us it'll draw more attention, and I don't think that's a good idea right now."

"You're right. Listen, it's probably your dad being cautious. But we should go take a look, just in case." Landon gives me a quick kiss and we make our way down the many corridors to locate the pods.

Chapter Thirteen
The Takeover

I open my eyes and instantly a feeling of grogginess hits me. I feel my head as I slouch up in bed. I'm finding it hard to focus, and it feels like I've slept for like twelve hours. I feel rested, but almost too much. Everything seems to be stagnant and very quiet. My ears pop from the pressure of the silence. There seems to be no activity outside my door, and I begin to feel like something's wrong. Maybe it's just my dad getting into my head with what he said yesterday.

"Galileo, what's going on? Why didn't you wake me up?" I ask, but there's no response. "Galileo?" I ask my bangle again with the same result. Tapping on it, I call out to him again. It just lies there on my wrist looking like a hard piece of cheap plastic. There's no pulsing light or activity.

"What the hell's going on?" I murmur with confusion as I stare at the bangle and then at the door.

The ground is freezing cold as my feet touch down on it. *That's odd, why isn't the floor heated like usual?* I ask myself. I approach the door and put my hand on it, but it doesn't open. There's no chime, or light, or anything. I tap on my band again and look at the door. Strangely there are no emergency lights on either.

I try knocking on the door, but there doesn't seem to be anyone outside to hear me. I listen for any sign of movement, but there's nothing, not even the light sound of shuffling around. "Am I dreaming this?" I ask myself out loud and pinch my arm. As I feel the sting of the pinch on my skin, I know I'm not dreaming.

Nothing in my room works. I try to open the closet door with my bangle, but it doesn't open. I have to pull on the handle and open it manually. I go into the shower and try to turn it on, but it just sputters out when I press on the manual touch pad just below the showerhead. This can't be good. Maybe this is what my dad was warning me about.

I start to feel claustrophobic inside the room, and my mind begins to reel with all the possible causes for what's going on. My thoughts immediately take a turn for the worse as I wonder if everyone else is okay.

A loud prolonged beep echoes in the room and is followed by the crackle of the speaker that's just above the door.

"Good afternoon, cadets," a familiar male's voice comes through. "This is General Roman Barclay speaking. Now, you're probably all wondering why the electronics have been disabled in the facility, especially your personal AIs. The answer is simple, and will be explained in due time. So, if you would all please report to the mess hall, the Allied Federation has prepared a little presentation for you." The speaker crackles off and my door slides open.

I begin to hear people moving about in the halls and I decide to peek out to see if everyone is complying with the orders. Joey and the rest of the group are hurrying toward my room, but I don't see Landon. Once I step outside, the door closes and locks behind me. "Dammit," I curse under my breath as I kick the door.

"That won't do any good. They've locked us all out of our rooms," Joey comments as he reaches me.

"Kind of figured that, but thought I'd try anyway," I reply.

"What the hell's going on?" Sam asks in a frustrated tone. "Our AIs aren't working, and this dipshit of a general wants us to go to the mess hall? Something doesn't seem right about this."

The Modified

"Geoffrey, you're right near Landon's room. Did you see him?" I ask, concerned.

"He was being corralled toward the mess hall by some Federation guards. We all had to push our way through the crowd to get to your room. He tried, but they overtook him," he answers.

"Hey you!" We hear in the distance. "Report to the mess hall immediately, or you will be detained!" I look and see a few heavily armed Federation guards approaching us.

As I walk by them toward the mess hall, I notice one of the guard's helmet shields is pulled back and he glares at me. I send him an equally harsh look. He grabs my arm and pulls me close to him. "You better wipe that smug look off your face, soldier, or I'll do it for you," he says forcefully.

"Take your hands off of her, asshole!" Joey interjects. Before I can say anything, the guard standing beside the one who has a grip on me clocks Joey right in the face with the butt of his rifle. As Joey lies on the floor, the guard straddles over him and begins taunting him, adding insult to injury.

"Joey!" I cry out as I see blood running down from his nose.

Sam shoves the guard off Joey and stands toe to toe with him. I can see her trying to muster some power, but her hands fail to glow and so do her eyes. "What the hell? What's going on with my implant?"

The Takeover

"Fall back in line!" the guard says to Sam and pushes her back. Her eyes fill with anger, but she's powerless to fight back, so she just stands there, pissed off.

I turn back to the guard to tell him to let me go, but he doesn't. I grab his hand with mine and try to break his grip, but to no avail.

He smirks at me. "Now be a good little girl and report to the mess hall," he says coldly as he pushes me back. I just glare at him as I walk away and the rest of my group follows behind me.

The mess hall is somber as we enter. The walls are lined with armed guards and the cadets are all sitting quietly around the tables. I gasp when I see all of the androids standing hunched over in front of the stage, seeming to be deactivated. All of the Adas and Adams are lined up and motionless. It's actually quite sad-looking, especially since I just saw them moving around yesterday.

We're shoved farther into the room and toward our table by the guards behind us. They close the double doors leading into the mess hall once we're all in. I see Landon and he sends me a concerned look.

All of the guards suddenly slam down one foot and salute as the general walks onto the stage. He has this air about him, like how someone looks after successfully pulling off a plan. His smug grin sickens me and as he approaches the microphone, I can hear the laugh that he lets out under his breath.

"Well, aren't you all just a sight for sore eyes," he begins and then pauses as he scans the crowd. "You've all made Earth very proud of you, you know that? Earth and the Allied Federation." The general snatches the microphone from the stand and proceeds to walk to the front of the stage. "You've all done so well with your training. But you see, there's just one more part that still needs to be addressed. And it involves us controlling every…little…movement…you make."

The crowd erupts in chatter, and the noise in the mess hall gets to be at deafening level. The general gives a signal and suddenly the guards around the perimeter begin to fire into the air. I clutch my ears trying to block out the sound from the gunfire echoing loudly off the walls. The room goes silent as we hear the last shell hit ground.

"Now that you've all got that out of your system, maybe we can continue," the general says snidely. "So, to explain how all of this is going to work, I'm going to bring out three people you know very well."

All three of our professors are dragged onto the stage by several guards. Their hands are restrained behind their backs. I quickly scan the stage in search of my dad, but don't see him.

The Takeover

Where's my dad? Intense worry sets in, and I feel I'm about to burst into a fit of rage at the sight before me.

"As you may have already noticed, your AI bracelets have been deactivated. Actually, to put it more precisely, we've made it to where you're AI bands are restricting your implant's activity altogether. Just in case any of you tried to do anything you might regret later."

The moment the general finishes that sentence, a few of the cadets rush the stage. "Like you idiots," he states while pointing to the group of cadets. Gunfire rings out in the room and I see the small group fly back after being hit by what seem to be electrified bullets. They writhe around on the ground, as a visible electrical current restricts their movements. A few guards collect them from the floor and drag them out of the mess hall.

"I hope we don't have a repeat performance lined up." The general pauses while scanning the room with questioning eyes. "Good, then shall I continue?" he asks while looking around the room as if waiting for everyone to nod. "Like I was saying, your implants are useless to you right now, and you have one very important person to thank for that," the general states and then gestures toward Dr. Wilhelm.

Confusion spreads through me and I can't believe for a second that Dr. Wilhelm would do something like this. Yeah, he's a sarcastic jerk, but I wouldn't take him for a traitor, though.

The Modified

Dr. Wilhelm wrestles free from the grip of the guard who's holding him. "That's a lie, you bastard! I had no idea you were going to do something like this. You were supposed to give that information to the Federation and not manipulate it like this. You used me," he yells out.

The general shakes his head, draws out a gun from underneath his jacket, and points it at Dr. Wilhelm. "And what makes you think this isn't a direct order from the Allied Federation?" he asks.

"What the hell are you doing, General?" Commander Archer asks forcefully, also breaking free from the grip of the guard who's holding him. "Have you gone absolutely insane?"

I hear the general laugh slightly as he turns the gun toward Commander Archer. "You know what I've always admired about you, Archer? You're incredibly dimwitted and so by the book that you practically jump at the chance to follow orders, and never see what's going on right in front of your face."

"What? Are you going to shoot me?" Commander Archer grounds out through clenched teeth.

"Well, actually, that's exactly what I'm going to do. Sorry, but we can't have any loose ends, you understand, right?" the general states and pulls the trigger. The shot rings out and screams can be heard throughout the crowd. We all watch as Dr. Wilhelm falls to the ground with a sickening thud after jumping in front of Commander Archer just as the shot was fired. He lies lifeless on the floor, blood trickling from his chest and soaking his white button-down shirt where the bullet entered. Commander Archer stands there looking down sadly at Dr. Wilhelm and then raises his angry eyes to the general.

I cover my mouth and a tear forms in my eye, but just stays there and doesn't fall. "No," I whisper and hear it echo in my hand. I begin to hear sobbing around me, but can't tell who it is. I can't believe what I just saw. I've never seen someone killed in front of me before, especially not someone I know. This image will be forever burned into my memory. As the sadness leaves me, anger fills that void and I glare at the general who's standing there proud of his cowardly act.

"I guess this is your lucky day, Commander. I only needed one person to take the fall for this, and since Harvey volunteered…" the general explains slyly. Commander Archer makes a move toward the general, who points the gun in Archer's face and waves it from side to side. The general then motions the gun in the direction of Dr. Patel, ushering Commander Archer to join her. The commander glares at him and moves to be next to Dr. Patel, but never takes his eyes off the general. "I've got major plans for the two of you. Take them away." After some struggle and resistance from Commander

Archer, he and Dr. Patel are ushered off stage and all we're left with is the damn general.

I find myself so worked up and filled with anger. I feel I'm going to regret what I'm about to say, but can't hold my words back any longer. "What the hell have you done with my dad?" I yell at the top of my lungs. Everyone turns to look at me, but I don't care, I want an answer.

"Ah, Ms. Grayson. Your dad is fine, don't you worry your pretty little head over that. You won't remember him shortly anyway, so what's the point," he responds smugly.

My face becomes flush with rage and I clench my teeth. I want to punch a hole through his skull, but can't. I've never hated anyone in my whole life like I hate this man standing in front of us right now. I feel a hand on mine and look over to see that it's Joey. He sends me a calming look and shakes his head.

"Calm down, you don't think straight when you're angry," he whispers.

I nod and my anger subsides slightly, but only slightly.

"Guards, will you see that all the cadets make it safely back to their quarters?" the general asks and the guards begin filing us out of the mess hall. "Oh, and one more thing." We all stop and turn to look at the stage. "We'll be calling you, one by one to implement the final phase of your modification. Do try and be prompt once you're called." The general's face becomes softer and friendlier, as if a second personality has taken over. "And remember, this is all for the common good. The Allied Federation thanks you for your sacrifice," he finishes with a sinister grin.

As we're leaving the mess hall, I hear a commotion behind me. Just when I turn to see what's going on, I come face-to-face with Landon. He immediately kisses me as he grabs hold of me tightly.

He pulls away. "I just clocked two guards to get to you. I had to kiss you once more in hopes that whatever happens, I never forget you," he says seriously, gazing into my eyes. His eyes, I notice, are full of worry and I almost tear up at the thought of forgetting him. Suddenly he's ripped away from me. I see two guards dragging him off, with him struggling, trying to reach me again.

I try to push through the crowd that's being corralled in my direction, but it's no use. I scream out his name, tears streaking down my cheeks. I hear Landon call out to me and see him pulled around the corner into the hallway in the distance. "Where are you taking him?" I yell down the hall.

I feel someone grab my arm, and I turn to see that it's Sam. "Do you want to get yourself killed, Grayson?" she asks me.

"I've got to get to him. I can't lose him, I just can't," I reply teary eyed.

The Modified

"We'll think of a way, okay? But now's not the time."

I just nod to her as I wipe away my tears. There are several armed guards making their way toward us and I grab Sam's hand and join the motion of the crowd heading for the living quarters.

By the time we reach my room, the crowd has thinned out. A guard grabs my arm and forcefully shoves me through my open door and closes it behind me. I throw myself at the door just as it shuts and bang on it in frustration. My head hits the door and rests there as I think about everyone I love who are on the other side of it. I pound on it again as I begin to slide down to my knees, fully giving in to my tears now. Please don't tell me this is it. Please don't tell me this is how everything's going to end? It can't be.

As I pace around my room nervously, I listen to the names of each cadet as they're called out through the intercom. I wonder to myself what's going to happen to them. There doesn't seem to be any kind of order to how they're calling out the names, they seem to be random. Every time a name is called out, I pray that it's not one of my close friends.

There's a pause in the names being called and I relax, plopping down onto my bed, which feels rock hard and not soft like it usually is. I stare down reflectively at the band of shiny white plastic around my wrist and long to hear that little voice I was so used to. That little stuttering blue hologram, I miss him.

A sudden crash into my door startles me and turns my attention to it. There seems to be one heck of a commotion happening on the other side. Pushing myself away from my bed, I make my way over to the door, just as another loud crash sounds outside. I flinch at the sharp noise and stare at the door questioningly. What a great time for my powers not to be working.

The door slowly begins to slide open and a cloud of smoke fills my vision so I can't see into the hallway beyond. Two bodies come flying out from the smoke and land at my feet with a thud. They're Federation guards. I get into a defensive stance as I peer into the haze before me and ready for something to attack.

"Kenley? Are you in there?" I hear a familiar voice call out.

"Galileo? Is that you!?"

"Yes, indeed," a disembodied voice says.

I see the silhouette of a body begin to emerge from the smoke and am shocked to see an Adam android standing in front of me.

"That's you, Galileo?" I ask hesitantly.

"Yes, Kenley. It is me," he says and then smiles.

"How did you get into that body?"

The Modified

"Your father put me in here. He told me to find and protect you. Like I would do anything other than that," he laughs slightly while grinning at me.

I rush over and wrap my arms around him. "It's so good to see you, Galileo," I cry into his shoulder.

He pats my head while holding on to me. "I agree, Kenley. It is good to see you as well." He pulls back slightly and looks me directly in the eyes. "We have to get you out of here to safety, okay? I can never disobey an order."

"But we have to save people, Galileo. My friends, my dad."

"Your father has already been taken away by the Allied Federation. And I regret to say that it is futile to try and save anyone else on board. I must get you, and only you, to safety," he replies matter-of-factly.

"No! I won't leave without them. We have to at least try," I say forcefully.

"That is not my order, I cannot comply with that."

"You're my AI, right? Then I order you to help me get my friends out of here."

"If we leave now, our probability of getting you out safely has a ninety-two percent success rate. Our probability decreases five percent every minute we waste," he replies.

● ● ●

The Takeover

"Well, if your order is to get me out of here safe, you have no choice but to help me rescue my friends, because that's what I plan to do."

"If these friends mean that much to you, Kenley, I will assist you in your efforts. But just know that my sole purpose now for being here is to get you to safety."

"Thank you, Galileo," I reply and hug him again.

"My pleasure, Kenley."

Chapter Fourteen
Breakout

The hall outside my room is quiet. Strangely, there are no guards patrolling around.

"Shaw, Landon, was in the research lab when I took over this body. We should start there," Galileo states.

"Wait, Landon was in there, but you didn't think to help him? Were any of my other friends in there too?" I ask harshly.

"My orders were to get you out of here. Not Shaw, Landon. And no, I did not see anyone else you knew closely."

"Whatever, let's just get there, okay?" I reply as I turn to walk away.

"Kenley, I must inform you that there is a chance, Shaw, Landon…may not be himself anymore," I hear Galileo say and then turn back to face him.

"What do you mean by that?"

"It is the last step of the modification procedure. Complete control of mind and body by the Allied Federation."

"Then it looks like we don't have any time to waste. Let's go already," I reply impatiently.

As I begin to walk away again, I feel Galileo grab my arm.

"What now, Galileo?"

"Here, this will help," he says softly as he brings his hand toward my bangle. Galileo extends his index finger out and it begins transforming into what looks like a probe or something. He presses it to the band and penetrates it, causing a neon blue glow to emit from the opening. The band separates into two halves and falls to ground.

A surge of power rushes through me and I feel ten times stronger than I did with the bangle on. My hands ignite in a blue glow and I smile at Galileo.

"Thanks," I say to him.

"Remember to not over exert yourself, Kenley. I am not there monitoring your implant anymore, use it wisely," he explains with a serious face. I nod and follow him as he pushes forward to the research lab.

The Modified

We meet no resistance in our travels and I begin to feel confused. "Where are all the guards? You'd think this place would be crawling with them," I whisper.

"I took them all out on my way to you," Galileo replies. "I made sure to do it quietly as to not arouse suspicion. This Adam body your father gave me has great defense mechanisms set in place." He lets out a tiny laugh under his breath and I almost feel like he's becoming more aware of himself.

"Good to know, because I have a feeling we'll need to utilize some of those soon."

"Indeed."

The door to the research lab seems to be heavily fortified by two guards standing there equipped with large shiny plasma rifles. We duck behind a wall as we see a third guard emerge from inside.

"Those Allied Federation guards were not there when I left earlier," Galileo states.

"What should we do?"

"It would be best not to cause a commotion."

As I peek back around the wall to look at the guards again, I hear a voice come over one of their hand transmitters. As the guard responds, it's clear to me that we don't have much time and they've found evidence of Galileo's handiwork on his way to reach me. Without thinking, I move around the corner, hands glowing, and throw up three barriers around the guards. Two of them begin to fire and are taken down by their own electrified bullets ricocheting around inside the barrier. The last guard is unarmed and stands there defenseless. I hold my barrier around him as I approach. I can't see his face, but I'm sure he's terrified. He puts up his hands in surrender and I have a choice to make. I reach the edge of the force field and I stare at him, contemplating what to do.

"To some, it is a sign of cowardice to kill an unarmed man." I hear Galileo say as he approaches us.

I rear back and my hand begins to glow even a brighter blue. I lean forward and throw the punch, breaking through the wall of energy. At the last moment, I ease off my power and my hand stops glowing. It connects with the guard's chin, which is exposed beneath his helmet's face shield, and he falls to the ground.

"I was never going to kill him, Galileo. If I did, then I'd be no better than he is," I reply, looking down at the unconscious man in front of me. "We need to get moving, we don't have much time."

"Agreed," Galileo answers.

Once we enter the research lab, the lights begin to flicker on and reveal a large space full of scientific-looking equipment and seven large glass tubes that look eerily like the ones where we received our implants. Five have green lights on above them and two have red.

I continue looking around the lab and see several androids, dressed in lab coats, but they are deactivated and hunched over the tabletops they're standing in front of. It's eerie seeing them lying there motionless with their eyes still open, but no sign of activity in them.

"Do not open any of the conduits with a green light above them, Kenley. Those cadets have already been processed," Galileo states and it almost sounds like there's sadness in his voice.

Scanning the tubes, I stop on one that has a red light over it and hurry over when I realize that Landon is propped up inside of it. He's lying there only in his boxers and seems to be in a deep sleep. I try to open the door, but it won't budge. A keypad appears on the front of the tube, asking me to input a code.

"I need a code, Galileo. Do you know it?" I ask over my shoulder hurriedly at him.

"Let me see," he replies, moving to stand next to me in front of the tube. He scans the keypad and presses his hand to it. The numbers begin punching in automatically and once the last number chimes, the keypad turns green. The door slides open and Landon falls into my arms. I cradle him to the ground. He breathes in deeply as his eyes shoot open.

Breakout

When he realizes that it's me in front of him, he grabs me tightly. "You have no idea how glad I am to see you," he whispers into my ear.

"Me too," I choke out.

I just live in this moment for a while and let him hold me. I feel safe in his arms and just want to be there forever. It isn't until Galileo taps me on the shoulder and presents Landon's uniform that I let go of him.

While Landon gets dressed, I walk over to the tubes again. All of the cadets inside are lying there motionless, just as Landon was, and my heart begins to break. The red light that was on above the tube next to the one Landon was in is now green. I recognize the girl inside as Jamie Warren. She was the girl my dad called up during the first day of training. I put my hand up to the glass and it starts to glow. I want to just punch through and pull her out to safety.

"Kenley, it is too late for her now," I hear Galileo comment behind me. I turn to look at him and feel my eyes stop glowing. Returning my focus back to Jamie, I jump back as I see her eyes are now open and staring at me. She slowly places her hand up to the glass in front of mine, and it begins to glow neon red. I pull my hand back quickly as her eyes begin to glow the same color as her hands. My hands stop glowing and almost like a hunter losing track of its prey, Jamie relaxes and closes her eyes while leaning to rest against the back of the tube.

"It's almost like my implant was causing her to react," I state, backing away from the row of tubes. I stumble into Landon's strong arms and he props me up. I turn to face him and give him a wan smile just before he kisses me.

"Thanks for saving my ass for a second time," he says quietly, close to my lips after we kiss.

"I hate to be the bearer of bad news, but I do believe we should know the meaning of haste and be on our way," Galileo states.

"Are you going to be okay to fight?" I ask Landon with worried eyes.

He shows me that he no longer has the bangle on his wrist and his eyes begin to glow. I guess Galileo did the same trick on his bangle that he did on mine. "To protect you, I'm ready for anything," he replies with slight force and all seriousness. I place my hand on his cheek and caress it softly. He sneaks a quick kiss on to my palm as it passes his chin.

Over Landon's shoulder I see Galileo motioning for us to follow him. I look back once more at the tubes that house the "processed" soldiers, and can't help but feel mournful. I mouth *I'm sorry* toward them just before leaving the lab.

"We have to find a way to release the rest of the cadets," I say to Galileo as we reach outside.

"Your father has an emergency override switch in his office. But if it is triggered, an alarm will sound, and the Allied Federation will be alerted," he explains.

"Will it open all the doors in the facility?" Landon asks.

"Yes, it will."

"I don't see any other choice, do you?" I ask both of them.

Landon shakes his head. "They all deserve a chance to get away. The rest of them shouldn't have to end up like those cadets in the lab."

"I agree with Landon. Let's head to my dad's office," I tell Galileo.

"No, Kenley. You go rescue your friends and then get to the escape pods. I will go to your father's office and push the switch. You will need to be there to protect the ones you love," Galileo replies with a smile.

"Will you be okay?" I ask worriedly. "You have to promise me that you'll make it to the escape pods too."

"I will be there. I have to keep my promise to your father," he states seriously. "Now go, we don't have much time."

I give Galileo a hug and whisper in his ear, "Be careful."

"Don't worry, Little Bit, I will be," he whispers back.

● ● ●

The Modified

Pulling away from him, I look at him questioningly. No one has ever called me 'Little Bit' other than Dylan. Why would he call me that?

I feel Landon grab my hand and pull me toward him. "Come on, we've got to get to the others," he states.

I watch as Galileo runs down the hall toward my dad's office and disappears around the corner into the next hallway.

"Kenley, we have to go," Landon says again while tugging on my hand. I let him lead me down the hall toward the living quarters.

When we reach the corridor that goes to my room, we see two guards standing in my doorway, examining the two guards on the floor from earlier. My hands begin to glow and I focus, using my scan ability. They're the only ones I detect in the area.

"Let's take them out quick and quiet," I whisper, turning to look at Landon.

He nods his head and we rush up to the intersecting hallway just before my room. I hide behind the wall on the left side and Landon hides behind the one on the right. I give him the okay signal after checking again if we're open for an attack.

My heartbeat picks up the moment I see Landon dart out from behind the wall. I pivot around the corner as well and focus my attention on their guns. My hands begin to glow, and as they move to point their weapons at Landon, the guns start to glow blue as well. I pull my hands to me and both of their guns fly from their grip down the hall in my direction. I see Landon's hands ignite as he continues to rush the guards. He throws two kinetic punches, sending the guards crashing against the back wall of my room.

"Not exactly what I'd call quiet, but at least they're down," I comment as I approach Landon.

"Yeah, sorry about that. I'm still not used to being free of the AI band yet."

"I feel we're going to need every ounce of power we've got, because something tells me this is just the start of our fight off this facility," I say, turning to look at him seriously.

Suddenly, an alarm sounds throughout the area and I see all of the doors to the rooms lining the hall we're in roll open.

"Sounds like Galileo made it to the switch," I say feeling relieved. That feeling quickly leaves me as I realize that Federation guards will be swarming us any second now.

"Hurry, we need to get to everyone," Landon yells as we begin seeing cadets leave their rooms.

"Get to the escape pods on the lower level of the facility!" I yell to everyone in a panic.

I hear the buzzing of assault rifles charging up and I leap into my room, dragging Landon with me as a flurry of bullets pound into the walls around us. I look back out into the hall and see a few cadets downed by the stun bullets. Jumping to my feet, I position myself up behind the wall next to my door and peer out into the hall. Landon follows and pins himself up on the other side of the doorway.

A group of guards with guns at the ready are encroaching on our position. I notice the cadets in the hallway to our left are huddled there waiting nervously.

"Double surge?" I ask, looking over at Landon.

"Double surge," he replies.

I cast a barrier over Landon and me the moment we whip out around the wall and into the corridor. We're faced down by the guards ahead of us, and as they begin to fire, we stop dead in our tracks and focus our energy. As the bullets deflect off my barrier, I feel the power in my hands grow stronger and they almost feel like they're on fire.

Several more guards come up behind the group already positioned in the hall.

"Ready, Landon?" I ask him as I place my hand on the side of my barrier that's touching his.

"Ready, Kenley," he replies while doing the same thing and places his hand on the side of his barrier that's touching mine.

Our barriers converge into one large force field and I feel my power increase even more. This is such an intense sensation, and

Breakout

I almost feel connected with Landon on a deeper level than I've ever been.

Another round of bullets is fired in our direction, but ricochet off, causing slight ripples in our barrier. It begins to expand and I start to see cracks forming in the barrier under the pressure. Suddenly it shatters, sending a huge shockwave of energy down the hall. I watch as the wave rips through the corridor, pulling up the ground, scorching the walls, and leaving a pathway of destruction in its wake while sending the group of guards soaring down the hall.

We stand there staring at the devastation we just caused.

"Wow, what a rush," Landon comments as he looks over at me with a little grin on his face.

"Yeah…you could say that again," I reply, returning his grin.

I notice the crowd of cadets emerge from behind the wall they were posted up behind. "Now's your chance, guys! Get to the escape pods," I call out. I notice a few of the cadets help the ones who were shot earlier to their feet and escort them.

I hear the familiar crackle of the speakers followed by the general's voice. "What do you expect to accomplish by doing this, Kenley? Don't you realize that your actions so far have been futile? Can't you see what we're doing here is for the common good?" he states and I see one of the cameras on the wall focusing on us. I clench my hands with anger, glaring up at the camera. I hurl a projectile toward it, causing the camera to explode into a shower of mangled metal.

"All right, have it your way then," the general says and I can almost hear his smirk. "Attention, guards. If you see one Kenley Grayson or Landon Shaw, feel free to use lethal force if necessary."

"Screw you, asshole!" I yell at the speaker as if the general can hear me.

"Come on, we have to get going," I hear Landon say as I continue staring up at the destroyed camera. The anger leaves me and I focus on him.

"Right," is all I can get out before I feel Landon grab my hand and pull me down the hall.

The alarm continues to sound throughout the facility as we hurry toward Joey's room since he's the closest. His room is empty.

"Joey!" I yell at the top of my lungs, hoping to hear a response. "Joey!" My heart sinks at the thought of losing my best friend. My mind can't even comprehend the idea as I become overwhelmed with emotion.

"Maybe he went to get the others," Landon states as he places his hand on my shoulder.

"Maybe-" I begin to say sadly, and then see Joey running down the hall toward us with the rest of our group with him. A smile of relief shows on my face and I hope the vision before me is not a dream. I run up and wrap my arms around him.

"I'm so glad you're okay," I choke out as he squeezes me back.

"Me too," he says softly into my ear.

"Okay, we can save the mushy stuff for later, but now we have to get the hell out of here," Sam interjects.

"Yeah, like now," Caleb says.

"Kenley and I will lead the way since we have our powers back," Landon explains. "Try not to split up and keep behind us, okay?" Everyone nods with serious faces.

"Hey, how the hell did you two get your powers back?" Sam asks harshly.

"Galileo," Landon and I reply almost in unison.

"Right on," she replies.

We join the rest of the cadets running toward the escape pods, meeting little resistance along the way. Coming to the intersection with a hall in front of us and one to either side, I stop and try to remember which way is the best route. A small group of cadets join just behind us.

"Mara!" Geoffrey calls out and I see him run up to her. She smiles at him and gives him a hug.

"The right hall…that's the quickest way," I hear Landon call out.

The Modified

"Yeah, that's the way we went earl-" I start to say and then see bullets zip past my face, hitting a couple of the cadets standing just behind me. I throw up a barrier, blocking any further gunfire. I look back and see a girl and two guys on the floor just writhing around in pain. As blood pools up in their wounds, I realize the general was serious about the use of lethal force.

I yell out "No!" as I launch a projectile in the direction of the group of guards in front of us who are encroaching on our position. There's no time to see where it hits as I dive toward the right hall and post up against the wall, avoiding further gunfire. I take in a deep breath, looking over at Landon, who's sitting next to me. Gunfire continues to ring out into the intersection and I stare at the cadets on the ground. I'm overcome with a sense of guilt for what happened to them.

"We can't help them," Landon says, noticing my change in mood.

"I know," I reply and then turn to look at him. His face suddenly fills with worry. "What is it?" I ask, not knowing if I want the answer. All he does is point to the hallway across from us. There's Joey, Caleb, and a few of the other cadets huddled behind the wall, dodging the incoming fire.

"We must've gotten split up when they began firing," Landon says to me.

• • •
259

"Joey, Caleb, you and the rest of the cadets have to get to the escape pods!" I yell over the sporadic gunfire.

"Got it!" they answer.

"You guys better be there when we get there!" I tell them.

"We will be, Kenley. Don't worry!"

I smile at him and he returns it. "Go now!" I cry out to him and signal to the hall behind them. He nods and corrals the cadets together before heading out.

Looking around the corner I throw another projectile down the hall, but duck back behind the wall before it hits. Turning to look at Landon I notice that Sam, Geoffrey, and Mara are behind him on the wall.

I grab Landon's hand. "Let's go," I say confidently, but am still thinking about Joey and Caleb, hoping they make it.

At the end of the hall we come to a door that says stairwell access. I hear the humming of a rifle readying to fire behind us and spin around to see a few guards at the end of the hall, guns aimed in our direction.

"Move!" I yell to everyone while pointing to the stairwell. As the bullets start to fly, I throw up a barrier, protecting everyone from the barrage. Keeping my barrier up, I follow closely behind the rest of my group, but always keeping an eye on the guards in front of me. I look back at the stairwell to see that everyone's made it out safely and then I see Landon hurrying back to my position. He throws a projectile down the corridor causing the guards to duck behind the wall. I release my barrier into a wave of energy down the hall, giving us a little time to flee down the stairs.

We meet up with the group a few levels down and continue on our way through the labyrinth of halls that lead to the escape pods. With every step we take, my heartbeat quickens, wondering if we'll encounter any more guards.

I see the open door ahead of us at the end of the hall and remember it from Landon's and my search earlier. There's a sign above the door that reads: *Evacuation site.*

Going through the door, we enter into a huge room that stretches out for quite a distance. The first thing I notice is there's no Joey. No Caleb. No other cadets.

"Where are they? They said they'd be here," I state forcefully with a hint of sadness in my voice.

"They'll get here, Kenley," I hear Landon say behind me in a reassuring tone.

There are numerous hatch-like doors that line the one wall of the room, each one leading to an escape pod. There's a number above each one, and I notice a couple have already been dispatched. Maybe Joey and Caleb have already gotten out.

"Everyone, get into pod twenty-one," I call out while pointing to it. They all do as I say and head over to the pod and get in. "If you have to leave, leave. Don't hang back for us, okay?" I call out to Sam.

She steps back out and looks at me. "You guys better get your asses in here as soon as possible. Because we're not leaving without you, understand?" she says in a very serious tone.

I nod and smile slightly before turning back to Landon. He takes my face in his hands. "You should go. I'll wait for the others."

"No, I won't leave you here. You and I are the only ones that have powers right now. We need to stick together," I reply looking seriously into his eyes.

"But-"

Landon's interrupted by the sound of an explosion within the other hall leading into our area. As I stare in horror waiting to see if anyone emerges from the opening, seconds seem like an eternity. My heart sinks and my stomach churns as I stand there helpless. I go to move forward, but Landon grabs my hand and pulls me back to stand next him. His hands are glowing and so are his eyes. I feel his strength growing as he just stares at the doorway, anticipating an attack.

My worst fears are realized as I see Joey come stumbling out from the hall into the room. He's grabbing his side and seems like he can barely walk.

The Modified

"Joey!" I yell as I see him rest up against the wall and slide down it to the ground. Letting go of Landon's hand, I begin to run over to Joey. I hear Landon call my name, but my want to save my best friend outweighs my own safety.

I see Joey push himself off the wall to stand when he sees me rushing over. He takes a few steps and I can hear "Kenley!" leave his mouth. I slide to a halt as I see a large group of soldiers pour out of the doorway behind him. They begin to open fire and I clench my eyes shut while throwing up a barrier. As my eyes shoot open the scene before me plays out in slow motion. I stand there mortified, watching Joey being shot multiple times, his body reacting to every impact. I immediately go into shock, and can't believe what I'm seeing is real. *My barrier failed to protect him*, is all I can think as he drops to his knees and reaches his hand out to me. Tears come to my eyes as I shout out his name. I feel the pain from my heart caress my lips as I cry out to him.

My body surges with anger and I feel like I've caught fire. The heat is so intense. As sweat drips down my face, my barrier begins to pulse violently. I grind my teeth and stare down the group of soldiers moving toward me cautiously. Letting out a scream of anguish, I release all of the power I've built up into a barrage of light projectiles. Explosion after explosion sound in the distance as each projectile hits the ground decimating the group in front of me.

● ● ●
263

Breakout

I feel suddenly dizzy as a wave of nausea washes over me. I stumble backward and feel someone cradle me to the ground. Through the blur, I can make out a familiar face, it's an Adam android.

"I have got you, Kenley," is all I hear Galileo say before my vision is consumed by darkness.

Chapter Fifteen
Safe Haven

"Galileo, are you sure she's okay?" I hear Landon's worried voice fade in and out nearby.

"Yes, Kenley just overheated her implant, causing her body to shut down. Hence, the fainting spell. Kenley can you open your eyes?" Galileo's voice seems to be right above me.

I feel exhausted and my body aches with even the slightest movement. My head throbs with a serious migraine as I struggle to open my eyes, but they feel like they weigh a ton. My mouth is dry, and as I lick my lips I hear a few sighs of relief.

"Kenley, please open your eyes?" Landon's voice pleads.

I try again and tiny slivers of light enter my eyes as they open slowly. Through the haziness, I make out Landon and Galileo hovering over me. Landon smiles and I crack one too as I feel someone rubbing my head. I see Galileo grin and then leave my side.

"You scared me, Kenley. Don't ever do that again, okay?" Landon leans down and wraps me up in a hug. He lays me back down and begins to caress my face with the back of his hand.

I lick my lips again and attempt to speak. "Landon...what happened? Where...are we? My tongue sticks to the roof of my mouth because it's so dry. Landon seems to read my mind and props me up while putting a cup up to my lips. The cool liquid feels heavenly as it enters my mouth and slides down my parched throat.

"We're in an escape pod. You fainted. You've been out for a few hours, though to me, it seemed like a lifetime. I thought I lost you." Landon's voice breaks a little, and his beautiful blue eyes become misty with tears.

My heart trembles when I hear the intense feelings in his voice. Raising my hand to his face, I stroke his cheek. I realize he must be feeling how I felt when Galileo and I rescued him from the lab. There's no doubt in my mind now that I love him, and he definitely feels the same way.

Landon helps me sit up, and I see Geoffrey, Mara, Sam, and five others, whose names seem to escape me at the moment.

The Modified

They all smile weakly at me while resting in the blue seats attached to the walls of the escape pod.

"Welcome back, Grayson. It's about time too. I don't think I could've stood much more of Shaw's moping," Sam quips, but I see sadness reflected in her eyes.

"Are we the only ones who got out?" I ask and panic at the small number of people I see.

I notice everyone's face becomes somber after I ask the question. Geoffrey and Sam dodge my eyes, refusing to look at me and I wonder why. Galileo's voice draws my attention to the front area of the pod. "No, other pods were dispatched when ours did," Galileo replies, positioned in front of a panel with a slew of buttons lit up like a Christmas tree.

I breathe a sigh of relief, but then it hits me why everyone is acting the way they are. I'm struck with the last vision I saw of Joey being gunned down right in front of me. "Joey!?" I yell as the scene plays out vividly in my head. Tears begin to stream down my face as Landon takes me in his arms. Intense emotions fill my every being, and in this moment I feel lost and utterly devastated. This was my all fault, and I'll have to live with that image in my head forever.

"He didn't make it," I hear Landon answer solemnly. "We tried to get to him, but we were overrun by Federation guards."

"He's gone because of me," I wail into his shoulder.

"That's not true. You did everything you could, Kenley," Landon says softly next to my ear.

"Then why isn't he here with us? Why didn't my barrier protect him? I failed him."

"Stop it, you didn't fail anyone. You tried, I saw you. It was the general that did this, not you. Don't blame yourself, okay?" Landon explains with slight force, pulling my face to be in front of his.

I go quiet for a few moments, not saying anything, as I stare back at Landon. He moves his thumbs just below my eyes and wipes away the tears rolling down. His face is the only thing I'm focusing on and I let out a huff. "Well, I guess I didn't try hard enough," I reply and hang my head low, breaking eye contact. I feel Landon kiss my forehead and move to sit next to me with his arm around my shoulder.

"We will arrive at our touch down destination soon." Galileo announces. I lean back against the wall and Landon reaches across my lap, taking my hand. His light touch puts me slightly at ease.

The last hour seems to have flown by even though we've all been silent since my breakdown. Poor Geoffrey still looks like he's in shock, as does Mara who's sitting next to him. Sam's frown lines are still present and she seems to be in deep thought.

The Modified

I catch her glancing over at me every once in a while, but neither of us smile when our eyes meet.

I feel numb as I keep replaying my last vision of Joey. I feel so helpless. Looking over at Landon, he smiles at me while rubbing my arm, seeming happy just to be able to touch me again. A strained smile appears on my face as I go to rest my head on his chest and try to ward off the tears that threaten to spill out.

A thought about my dad enters my mind, and I remember Galileo telling me that the Federation had taken him. I hope he's okay…wherever he is.

"Hey, where are we going, Galileo?" I hear Landon ask and feel the reverberations from his voice through his chest.

"Somewhere safe. Coordinates Dr. Grayson, Wyatt gave to me."

Landon sighs as he returns his attention back to me and begins stroking his hand through my hair. I snuggle up closer to him after seeing Joey's face in my mind once more.

"Are you feeling any better?" Landon whispers.

"Kind of," I reply quickly, not really wanting to talk right now.

"We're going to make it through this," Landon says kissing my head again. "You should try to relax, and maybe get some rest." Some of my numbness fades away and I begin to feel so grateful that Landon's still with me. I lay my head back onto his chest and close my eyes, hoping that when I wake up, everything will have just been a bad dream.

"Attention, everyone. I need you all to report to the nearest seat and buckle up. We are in for a rough landing," Galileo's voice echoes within the pod, waking me up. My head is leaning on Landon's shoulder and I wonder how long I've be asleep. Everyone's awake and adjusting their seat belts while preparing for our descent. Landon helps me settle into mine, giving me a quick kiss along the way.

We begin to feel the harsh turbulence and my stomach sinks to my feet because of the pressure. I feel like I'm on one of those drop rides at the carnival, only it feels a hundred times worse. The whole pod begins to shake and I find it hard to focus on anything, so I close my eyes, waiting for it to all be over. Suddenly, we crash into something and I feel the pod spin in all different directions. I can't even tell which way is up anymore. As we come to an abrupt stop, I feel my body suddenly jerked forward and then pushed back with great force. The sensation is very jarring, even with my seat belt strapped tight.

"We have landed. Please wait for the hatch to fully open before you alight from the craft." Galileo's voice fills the cabin.

The Modified

As the hatch slowly raises open, we undo our seat belts and stand. Looking outside through the hatch, we see a dismal scene awaiting us. Black clouds fill the sky, threatening to pour down on us as we stare out at the desolate wasteland. My hopes are immediately dashed, and the thought of being safe fades away.

Galileo leaves his seat and moves toward the hatch. We hear a loud engine noise sounding just outside. From behind Galileo, we see an old dark green military-style jeep pull up beside us, followed by a large green truck. The jeep idles and a man jumps out dressed in battle fatigues that I remember seeing in our history books. He's tall, and even though he's wearing a jacket, I can tell he's all muscle. His hair is covered by a tattered black ball cap, and his face is rugged, complete with a large scar that runs down the left side of it. Despite this, he's oddly handsome.

Galileo moves down the ramp and, to my surprise, shakes hands with the stranger.

"So the worst has happened, huh? I'm not really surprised since the Federation was involved. Where's the doc?" the man asks Galileo, and glances over his shoulder at me.

"He's not with us."

"Who the hell's that?" Sam whispers in my ear.

I shrug my shoulders and resume listening to Galileo talking to the stranger.

"How many got out?" the man asks.

"Five pods were dispatched successfully, I lost track of the others. We have eleven in our group including myself. All are Modified," Galileo replies.

"Well, let's hope the others show up soon. We've got to get going. It's not safe to be out in the open for very long."

"Good idea." Galileo turns around and motions for us to exit the escape pod.

I notice the back of the truck outside is covered with a heavy-duty green cloth. Several people with guns in hand step down and out from the open flaps at the back. Their faces seem friendly, but I wonder if they're really on our side. As I move down off the ramp, Galileo stops me with a hand.

"Kenley Grayson, I want to introduce you to Young, Malcolm. He is the contact your father set up many months ago."

"You're Grayson's kid? He never mentioned you to me."

"Funny, my dad never mentioned you either," I reply bothered by the smirk on his face as he glances from me to Landon, who's holding my hand.

"Well, I guess that makes us even. We should probably get everyone else on the truck. But you, Ms. Grayson," he says pointing to me, "you and Galileo will ride with me."

The Modified

I feel Landon tense up beside me and I squeeze his hand while looking over at him. I shake my head and then let go, following Galileo over to the jeep as it begins to drizzle.

Landon makes his way with the others to the truck and looks back at me. I give him a slight smile and then watch as the truck takes off with us following behind it.

"So, your dad didn't tell you about us, huh?" Malcolm asks, turning in his seat to look at me. I semi-ignore him since I don't really want to discuss anything right now. The driver keeps looking straight ahead making sure the jeep stays on the bumpy road. The rain seems to be increasing and several drops of rain land on my forearm, but thankfully the jeep has a roof, otherwise we'd be soaked by now. I stare out at the scenery around us and it's bleak. There are no trees, no grass—just wet, scorched earth.

"Did you hear me, Grayson?" I hear Malcolm asks.

"Sorry, where are we?"

"We're in England. So I guess your dad didn't tell you much, did he?" Malcolm's piercing light blue eyes meet mine.

"Not really. My dad said he had a bad feeling, and that if anything happened we were to get to the escape pods. That's it"

"Just like him, vague and all. Well, I guess we'll have to have a chat real soon, but unfortunately this is not the time or place," Malcolm says as we pass through a broken chain-link fence that has a huge sign partially attached. It reads: *R.A.F. Lakenheath.*

Safe Haven

I can't believe it. RAF Lakenheath! Why would my dad send us here to this place that impacted our life so much two years ago? This place is where the Shaw Blitz occurred. The awful day my brother was killed in the first large scale battle of this war. Tears well up in my eyes remembering the pain and sorrow our family suffered back then. My mom constantly crying, my dad's eyes red and swollen on a daily basis, and me comforting Gavin, holding him for hours in my arms until he cried himself to sleep. Our lives did go on, but everything changed that day. Now two years later I'm in the area where my brother drew his last breath. *Dad, why did you send us here?* I ask myself.

We travel in silence following the truck until we reach a dilapidated, airplane hangar. When I was little, my dad had taken me to an air base once, and I remember being amazed at how big the structures were that housed the planes.

The truck stops and I peer out the open window at the ground surrounding it. There's a big red circle painted on the platform it seems to be parked on. I hear a mechanical sound and suddenly it begins to lower into the ground until the truck disappears.

"Neat, huh?" Malcolm comments, turning his head and flashing me a smile.

"Unexpected is more like it," I reply.

• • •

The Modified

"It's our turn now," he states while facing forward as the driver pulls the jeep into the red circle. I hear the sounds of the platform shifting and grinding as we slowly begin to move downward. Lights track up the sides of the shaft as we descend and cast an eerie bluish-green glow into the jeep.

The elevator dumps us out into a massive area lit up with numerous floodlights, leaving no dark corner. A variety of military vehicles fills one end of the area and at the opposite end are four large tunnel entrances. I see the others getting out of the truck as we pull up and park next to them. Landon is the first to reach me, taking my hand before looking at Malcolm with questioning eyes. Sam, Geoffrey, Mara and the rest of the cadets move in behind us.

"This is our staging area. It's been quiet for several weeks, since Bringer activity has lessened for now, but we're always prepared. My driver, Rodney, will show you around and take you to the living quarters. I'll meet up with you all at dinner," Malcolm says hurriedly, and then abruptly leaves down the first tunnel on our left following the larger green truck as it pulls away.

"Right, as the boss said, follow me and try to keep up." Rodney sounds irked as he moves toward the second tunnel entrance. Galileo takes the lead and we pull up the rear.

Safe Haven

The walls of the tunnel are comprised of carved rock—all different shades of grey. As we make our way down the tunnel, I feel a chill from the damp coldness of the confined space, and wonder how far underground we are. The lightweight material of our uniforms does absolutely nothing to fend off the cold.

Landon hasn't said a word. In fact nobody's talking. The only noise I hear is our boots hitting the concrete floor.

"Hey, Rodney?" I ask breaking the silence.

"Yes, soldier?" he replies sharply.

"Who are you guys?"

I hear him laugh slightly. "We call ourselves the Defects."

"The Defects?"

"Our group is comprised of soldiers who have all turned their backs on the Allied Federation."

"I can see why you all did," I state dryly. "I know why I hate them, but what did they do to piss you guys off?"

"Sorry soldier, but that information is classified. No offense," he answers.

"None taken," I say, knowing that once a soldier says it's classified, there's no use pushing the issue. They won't talk.

We finally reach the end of the tunnel only to find a round chamber with three tunnels leading from it. We take the middle one and soon meet a large number of people, all dressed in fatigues, who immediately stop what they're doing and stare at us as we pass by.

Rodney keeps moving forward until we reach a long corridor made of some kind of shiny metal. At the end is a massive white dome-shaped room with a series of numbered doors lining the walls.

"Rooms one thru five are yours. Each room," Rodney begins to say as he takes a key card and pushes it into a slot in the door, "has two beds and a full bath. You'll have to pair up. Galileo, your recharge station has been prepared for you."

"Thank you," Galileo replies.

"No problem. Oh, and here are the rest of the room keys," he states handing them out. "I've got duties to attend to, so rest up and someone will come get you for chow time." Rodney looks down at his watch. "You've got two hours." Without another word he spins on his heel and leaves.

"Mr. Personality, he's not," Sam says loudly and chuckles.

"Kenley and I'll take this room," Landon says, removing the key from the door and then faces the others.

Sam smiles broadly and grabs Mara while waving the key card around in her hands. "We'll take the one next to the love birds. Come on, Mara, home sweet home," Sam says as she ushers Mara into their room.

Safe Haven

Landon gently guides me into ours and I miss seeing the others pairing up. He closes the door and lets out a heavy sigh.

"Sorry I didn't ask you first about the room, Kenley. I saw Lakenheath on the sign and knew you'd probably be upset. So I wanted to make sure you're okay. Besides, I can't let you out of my sight. I almost lost you today. I'm sorry I didn't ask if this was okay." He looks at me, his eyes pleading with me.

"I can't believe my dad sent us here. All those feelings from two years ago slammed into me the moment I saw that sign. I thought I had moved passed all of this, but now I'm not sure. And now I've lost Joey too. I feel so hopeless."

Landon pulls me into his arms and rests my head on his chest. I instantly feel the warmth from his body seeping into mine. No words are said as we stand there holding each other and it seems like time is standing still.

A sharp knock at the door interrupts our peace. Landon reluctantly releases me and opens the door. Galileo is standing there with a duffel bag in hand and presents it to us.

"Here is your bag, Kenley" he says as Landon grabs a hold of it.

"My bag? I didn't have one," I reply.

"It was prepared for you before the incident at the Magnus Academy. Doctor Grayson, Wyatt thought of every contingency."

The Modified

"Sounds like my dad, always prepared. What's in it?" I ask.

"Just some necessities. A care package of sorts," he answers.

"Thanks," I say, taking the bag as Landon passes it to me.

"Oh, and Young, Malcolm would like to see you in his office, Kenley. I can take you there. It will be like old times," he states with a smile.

"Did he by any chance say what this is about?"

"Not at all, he just told me to come get you," he answers.

I follow Galileo out of the room after saying bye to Landon and leaving my bag on the bed. Galileo takes my arm as we walk and pulls it around his, so that they're linked. "You know, I miss our little walks together. With our arms like this it almost feels like I am there on your wrist again," he laughs.

"I've so missed you Galileo. I'm really glad to see you. I can't thank you enough for helping us escape, you were so brave."

"I was only following orders, Kenley. Though I guess that's not completely true. There was this feeling inside of me that made me want to do everything in my power to keep you safe. It was an odd sensation that I could not explain. That same feeling is present right now," he states as he pats my hand resting in the crook of his elbow.

"Maybe you're evolving. Becoming more aware of yourself and the world around you."

"Maybe, but I am not quite sure yet," he says hesitantly. "Kenley?"

"Yes, Galileo?"

"I wanted to tell you how sorry I was to see you lose Reilly, Joey. I had this feeling come over me when I saw him on the ground, not moving as we carried you away. He was a good friend to you, and I know he will be greatly missed," he states, seeming to get a little choked up.

"Thank you for that, Galileo. Joey was a great friend…family to me really. And you're right, I do miss him very much," I reply, my eyes becoming misty. I wipe away the stray tear that creeps down my cheek as Galileo comes to a halt in front of a large green door.

"We have arrived at Young, Malcolm's office. He is waiting for you inside," Galileo says, motioning toward the door with his hand.

"Thanks," I reply, giving him a hug.

"I am feeling that warm and fuzzy feeling, Kenley. This must mean we are friends," Galileo says, returning my hug.

"Of course we are, silly," I reply.

Opening the door to Malcolm's office, I'm immediately surprised to find the room in complete disarray with stacks of papers, all various heights, scattered around the space.

The Modified

"Excuse the mess, I've been doing some research and got a little carried away," Malcolm laughs as he welcomes me in.

"What kind of research?" I ask confused, still scanning the amount of papers and folders littering the room.

"Well…I'm working on a plan of sorts for our group to strike a crippling blow to the Federation. And in the process, rescue your father," he replies.

"Wait, you have a plan to help my dad? What is it? I want to help," I state and feel my hands begin to glow.

"Easy, Kenley. We'll get to that. You've got to be careful with how much you use those things. You don't want the same result you had back on the Magnus," Malcolm cautions.

My hands return to normal and I calm myself. "Can I help in any way?"

"Later, Kenley. Right now, I just want to see how you're holding up. Being the daughter of Dr. Grayson means that your safety is just as important to me as his is."

"How are you so close to my dad?"

"I was your dad's head of security during his work on the Magnus project. Before I defected from the Allied Federation, I told your father that I'd be there if he ever needed anything. I owed him a lot, and now I'm repaying my debt. That's why he sent you all here. So I could keep you, and as many of the cadets I can, safe," Malcolm explains.

"What exactly did my dad do for you?"

"Sorry, but that's between me and your father. I'll have him tell you once we rescue him, how does that sound?" he replies.

"Sounds like I don't really have a choice," I state, crossing my arms in front of my chest.

"Pretty much," he jokes followed by a laugh under his breath. "For what it's worth, I'm glad you're doing all right. We'll be heading to dinner in about an hour or so. If you want to go rest up or something, now would probably be the best time to."

"Yeah, I think I'll go rest a bit before eating," I reply and go to exit the room.

Just as I turn the handle and begin to open the door, I hear Malcolm's voice sound behind me. "Your dad's a great man. But I bet you already knew that, huh?"

"Yeah, I did. But it's nice to hear that other people think so too," I reply and turn to see Malcolm smile at my comment.

As I walk back to my room, my mind begins to reel with thoughts about my dad, and what he must've done for Malcolm. I sigh as I push open the door leading into my room. Landon leaps to his feet from the bed when he sees me enter. His face is relieved, but there seems to be a hint of concern in his eyes.

"So, what did Malcolm have to say?" he asks, moving closer to me.

"Not much. But he's working on a plan to rescue my father. So, I guess that's something, right?"

"Yeah. Hey, you look exhausted. Maybe you should go lie down and rest?" Landon says as he places his hands about my hips.

"Yeah, I'm pretty freakin' tired. Will you come lay down with me?" I ask, hoping he will.

Without a word, Landon takes my hand and leads me to the bed. He lies down, pulling me to rest beside him. His arms encompass me as he kisses me gently. His deep blue eyes meet mine and as he pulls me close, I can feel his heart beating rapidly. Closing my eyes, I rest my head on his chest and fall asleep to the sound.

A loud banging rips me from my deep sleep and I jerk my head up, bumping into something solid. "Ow." Landon's voice fills my ears, as I realize I hit his chin with my head.

"I'm so sorry. Are you okay?"

"It takes more than a little bump like that to bring me down," he jokes, massaging his jaw.

"Hey, you two get your butts in gear, it's time for dinner," Sam calls from outside the door.

"Our own wake-up call…how special." Landon grins as he wraps his arms around me.

283

Safe Haven

We reluctantly roll out of bed and meet everyone outside, both of us ignoring Sam's smirk. We all follow down a metal-walled corridor, and eventually after many winding passages, we end up in a large room with delicious smells emanating from it, making my stomach growl.

I'm surprised at the number of people sitting around the tables filling the room. They all stop eating and stare as Galileo leads us up to Malcolm's table. There are a handful of people sitting at his table, but one really stands out. She's beautiful. Her hair is a vibrant red, and her skin is porcelain white. Her radiant smile is directed at Malcolm, who seems to be hanging on every word as she talks. She raises her striking blue eyes and catches me staring at her. A frown line shows up on her forehead as she sweeps our group with a questioning glare. Malcolm turns to look at us after noticing her focus shift to our presence and then whispers something to her. The woman rises from her seat and attempts a smile as we approach the table.

"Ahh, here they are now, our refugees," Malcolm announces. "Everyone, this lovely lady next to me is Elizabeth," he continues, putting a name to the redhead.

"So nice to meet you. Please have a seat. I'm sure you're all hungry after your long trip." Elizabeth's smile looks so genuine, but as I look at her eyes they seem wary and suspicious.

• • •

The Modified

We take our seats at the large round table, and I find myself seated next to Elizabeth. Several women bearing trays of food stop at our table and place plates in front of us. My stomach decides to growl so loud that I turn red from embarrassment. Elizabeth lets out a slight giggle. I grab my napkin-wrapped silverware, unwrap it, and watch out of the corner of my eye as she does the same.

"Kenley...may I call you Kenley?" Even though she's sitting next to me I jump a little at her sudden and abrupt question.

"Yes," I get out, suddenly tongue-tied.

"Malcolm tells me that your father is a prisoner of the Federation. I know you must be worried, but we both agree that he's still alive. He's a vital part of their plan," she says it so breezily like as if she were discussing the weather.

"I really hope you're right. But for how long? Can we discuss the plan to rescue him now?" I ask, my hunger forgotten at the thought of my dad suffering at the hands of the Federation.

"We'll be discussing that later. You need to eat and regain your strength first," Malcolm interjects, pointing to my plate.

Landon reaches for my hand that's lying on my lap and gently squeezes it. I turn to him and smile. *Malcolm's right. I need to take care of myself so I can help find my dad*, I tell myself.

"Oh, and please do forgive the fact we haven't removed any of your bangles," Elizabeth states, looking around at all of the other cadets, since Landon and I already have ours off. "It's not that we don't trust you…it's more because your implants can be affected by emotion, and since you've been under a lot of stress, we wanted to wait until you were more relaxed, and settled," she continues explaining casually.

I glance around at our group, and none of them seem to be bothered by what Elizabeth just said. Not even Sam, who I thought would be the first to speak up. I also notice that no one has started eating yet. Malcolm and Elizabeth pick up their forks and everybody else follows their lead. Every once in a while I look over at Elizabeth and see her studying us as we all eat. There's definitely something off about her.

"Come on," Landon says, pulling me along a corridor with a metal door at the end.

"Where are we going? Better yet, are we supposed to be here?" I ask, anticipating someone catching us at any moment.

"Don't worry, I got permission. And Galileo told me where we'd be safe to travel. I think we both need some fresh air. Besides, Malcolm says it's safe since there's been no Bringer attack for a couple of weeks now. He also gave me this little device just in case we run into any trouble. Malcolm said just press this button and we'll be surrounded by soldiers." Landon finally takes a breath as he punches in the code on the data pad to the left of the door.

The first thing I notice as the door opens is the rain has stopped. There are a few steps leading up to ground level in front of us. At the top of the stairs, we see a wide low-lying wall positioned in front of a dilapidated building. Landon pulls me over to the one of windows on the building and we peer inside. There are tables and chairs strewn about an area that resembles a cafeteria.

"Malcolm said this used to be a part of a boarding school, and this building was called the Dayroom. See those buildings over there?" He points to the right, "Those were dorms the students lived in. He said these buildings are all that's left of this air base."

"It's crazy to think that this place was once full of people. Now look at it…doesn't really give much hope for the future, huh?" I ask, looking around at the barren wasteland that surrounds us. "I wonder what it looked like when my brother was here?"

"Hey, I got an idea," Landon says, changing the subject. He clearly knows that all of this is bothering me.

Landon jumps up onto the wide low-lying wall, and then pulls me up to join him. The full moon that hangs overhead casts everything in a soft glow. Landon shrugs out of the raincoat he was given and places it down on the wall. He gestures to the makeshift blanket and I slip out of my raincoat as well. Adding my coat to his, making the "blanket" bigger, I lie down and Landon comes to my side while taking hold of my hand. He leans over and kisses me gently at first, and then when I grab him and pull him closer, he deepens the kiss. We finally separate, both of us a little breathless. He returns to his position next to me, and I listen as his breathing returns to normal.

"Landon?"

"Yeah?"

"Do you think we're safe here?"

"Yes. I don't think your father would've sent us here otherwise," Landon replies, stroking his fingertips through my hair.

"I just wish Malcolm would've given us more information. I get the feeling he's keeping a lot from us."

"He's a military man, Kenley. He's that kind of guy that only lets you know what he wants you to know. We'll find out everything in time, don't worry," Landon explains.

"I hope so."

"For now, let's just live in this moment," he says while giving me a light squeeze.

We both lay there looking up at the stars with the raincoats acting as a barrier between the wall's damp, cold surface and us.

The Modified

The stars in the sky are so vibrant and plentiful since there aren't any major city lights to keep them from our view. It reminds me of the view from Old Man Gary's farm. I can almost hear the wind sweeping through the long grasses. I long for the smell of flowers instead of the rain soaked air I'm currently breathing in. The memory of Joey and me playing the star game seeps into my mind and I become overcome with emotion. The starry sky becomes blurred as tears fill my eyes.

"Hey…Landon?"

"Yeah?"

"Want to play a game?"

Landon releases a content sign as he takes a hold of my hand. "I'd love to."

----------------- **About the Authors** -----------------

Carol and **Adam Kunz** make up the mom and son author duo, **C.A. Kunz**. They thoroughly enjoy writing about things that go bump in the night and action-packed dystopian romances while drinking massive amounts of English breakfast tea and Starbucks coffee. The author pair currently reside forty-five minutes away from each other in the sunny state of Florida. If you would like to find out more about this duo, **The Modified**, or **THE CHILDE** series, please visit the links below:

Author Website- http://www.cakunz.blogspot.com
Facebook Author Page- http://www.facebook.com/cakunz11

23019753R00177

Made in the USA
Charleston, SC
08 October 2013

Federal Tax Policy

Federal Tax Policy

JOSEPH A. PECHMAN

REVISED EDITION

 New York W · W · NORTON & COMPANY · INC ·

Studies of Government Finance

THE BROOKINGS INSTITUTION

THE BROOKINGS INSTITUTION is an independent organization devoted to nonpartisan research, education, and publication in economics, government, foreign policy, and the social sciences generally. Its principal purposes are to aid in the development of sound public policies and to promote public understanding of issues of national importance.

The Institution was founded on December 8, 1927, to merge the activities of the Institute for Government Research, founded in 1916, the Institute of Economics, founded in 1922, and the Robert Brookings Graduate School of Economics and Government, founded in 1924.

The general administration of the Institution is the responsibility of a Board of Trustees charged with maintaining the independence of the staff and fostering the most favorable conditions for creative research and education. The immediate direction of the policies, program, and staff of the Institution is vested in the President, assisted by an advisory committee of the officers and staff.

In publishing a study, the Institution presents it as a competent treatment of a subject worthy of public consideration. The interpretations and conclusions in such publications are those of the author or authors and do not necessarily reflect the views of the other staff members, officers, or trustees of the Brookings Institution.

Foreword

THE FEDERAL GOVERNMENT enacted six major tax laws during the 1960s. Some of them were primarily for the purpose of raising or lowering revenues in the interest of stabilization policy; others were intended to improve the structure of the tax system and to promote economic objectives; still others combined the stabilization and structural objectives. All of these tax bills were controversial; each was considered and debated at length by the public and the Congress. Despite all this legislative activity, however, many people believe that the nation's tax system continues to be in need of substantial change.

The purpose of this volume is to explain the intricacies of the tax system so that the interested citizen may better understand and contribute to the public discussion and to the resolution of the main issues. This revision of the first edition (1966) reflects the tax developments that took place between 1966 and mid-1970. It emphasizes the newer issues, including the effects of the Tax Reform Act of 1969 on the income tax structure, reform of the estate and gift tax, family assistance, and revenue sharing.

The reader should be reminded that this book is one economist's interpretation of professional opinion in this difficult and controversial sector of public policy. Conflicting points of view are presented, but their proponents will not necessarily agree with the author's interpretation and evaluation. Moreover, in the interest of brevity, the discussion sometimes omits details that others might regard as important. For further information and different points of view, the reader should refer to the extensive literature cited in the bibliographical notes.

The volume is part of the Brookings series of Studies of Government Finance, a program of research and education in taxation and government expenditures at the federal, state, and local levels, supported by the Ford Foundation, sponsored by the National Committee on Government Finance, and now completed after ten years of activity. It is one of three books in the series designed to give the public an overview of a major field of government financial policy. The others are *Federal Budget Policy*, by David J. Ott and Attiat F. Ott, and *Financing State and Local Governments*, by James A. Maxwell.

Joseph A. Pechman is Director of Economic Studies at the Brookings Institution and Executive Director of Studies of Government Finance. He wishes to acknowledge once again his debt of gratitude for the assistance he received on the first edition from Charles B. Saunders, Jr., who edited it, and from Andrew T. Williams, who was his research assistant. He also wishes to repeat his acknowledgement of the constructive review and comments on the original manuscript by Boris Bittker, L. Laszlo Ecker-Racz, Richard Goode, Arnold C. Harberger, and Richard Slitor. In preparing the revised edition he received valuable suggestions from John F. Manley on the tax legislative process, Gerald R. Jantscher on estate and gift taxes, and Charles F. Conlon on state income and sales tax coordination. Anne Haaga Hammett and John Yinger provided research assistance in updating and revising the manuscript, and Mr. Yinger programmed the calculations of the effects of the various special provisions on effective rates of the individual income tax presented in Chapter 4. Evelyn P. Fisher reviewed the manuscripts of both editions for accuracy and consistency. The revised edition was edited by Virginia C. Haaga and indexed by Meyer Zaner. Fred Powell prepared the figures.

The views expressed in this study are the author's and are not presented as those of the National Committee on Government Finance or its Advisory Committee, or the trustees, officers, or other staff members of the Brookings Institution or the Ford Foundation.

November 1970   KERMIT GORDON
Washington, D.C.   *President*

Contents

3. The Tax Legislative Process *continued*

4. The Individual Income Tax   52

5. The Corporation Income Tax   105

Text Tables

Figures

Appendix Tables

CHAPTER ONE

Introduction

FEDERAL, STATE, AND LOCAL government receipts now amount to almost one-third of the gross national product. They come from a variety of taxes, as well as from fees, charges, and other miscellaneous sources. The taxes cover almost the entire spectrum: income taxes, general and selective consumption taxes, payroll taxes, estate and gift taxes, and property taxes.

Despite the large amount of money collected—$277 billion in fiscal year 1969—U.S. taxes are by no means the heaviest in the world. Most advanced European countries impose relatively higher taxes. In 1966, for example, taxes ranged between 35 and 40 percent of the gross national product in Austria, France, Germany, the Netherlands, and Norway, as compared with 28 percent in the United States (Appendix Table C-4).

Features of the U.S. Tax System

The most distinctive feature of the U.S. tax system is that it places great weight on the individual and corporation income taxes. These account for about 50 percent of the total revenues (including receipts from social insurance taxes) of all levels of government. At the federal level, they account for over 65 percent (Appendix Table C-5).

A second distinction is that it is a federal system (Figure 1-1). The

1

FIGURE 1-1. Receipts of Federal and State and Local Governments, 1929–69

Billions of dollars (ratio scale)

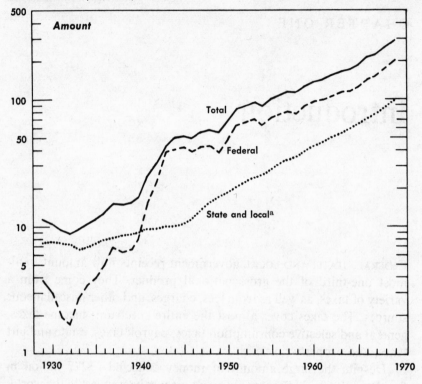

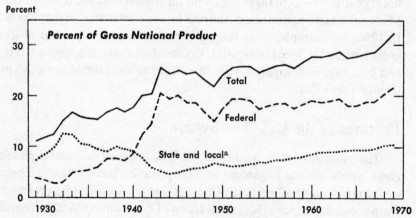

Source: Appendix Table C-2. Receipts are on a national income accounts basis.
a State and local receipts have been adjusted to exclude federal grants-in-aid.

national and state governments have independent taxing powers, while the local governments derive their taxing powers from the state governments. There is duplication among the tax sources of the three governmental levels, especially between the federal government and state governments, but the tax structures differ markedly. The federal government relies primarily on income taxes, the states on consumption taxes, and the localities on real property taxes (Table 1-1).

Two-thirds of all taxes are collected by the federal government, but state and local taxes have been rising at a much more rapid rate during the past two decades. This reflects the rapid growth in demand for the public services that are operated and administered primarily by state and local governments. All governments finance most of their revenue needs from their own taxes. However, there is a well developed system of intergovernmental assistance, which transfers funds from higher to lower levels of government. Intergovernmental transfers have risen rapidly in recent years.

The broad outlines of the tax system have remained the same since World War II, when the federal government greatly expanded the coverage of the individual income tax and substantially increased corporation tax rates. Nevertheless, the structure has not been static—during the past ten years, great changes have occurred at all levels of government. Federal income tax rates have been reduced substantially; increases in the personal exemption and the adoption of a low-income allowance have eliminated from the income tax rolls virtually all individuals and families who are officially classified as poor; depreciation allowances have been liberalized, and an investment credit was in effect between 1962 and 1969; practically all selective excise taxes other than the taxes on liquor and tobacco and highway and airway user taxes have been reduced or eliminated; payroll tax rates have been raised; and numerous revisions have been made in the income tax bases. At the state and local levels, tax rates have been rising steadily. Traditional opposition to state income and sales taxes has broken down; two-thirds of the states now have both. To alleviate the burden of the sales tax on the poor, the idea of a tax credit for state sales taxes against state income taxes (with refunds to those not subject to income tax) has begun to take hold. State and local governments have also been improving administration of the property tax, which continues to be the major revenue source for local governments.

TABLE 1-1. Federal, State, and Local Taxes and Other Revenues, by Major Source, Fiscal Year 1969

Major source	Revenues[a] Amount (billions of dollars)	Revenues[a] Percentage of total
Federal		
Individual income	86.0	44.9
Corporation income	38.9	20.3
Excises	15.2	7.9
Estate and gift	3.5	1.8
Payroll	44.2	23.1
Other	3.5	1.8
Total	191.3	100.0
State		
Individual income	7.6	16.7
Corporation income	3.3	7.3
Sales and excises	21.5	47.1
Estate and gift	1.0	2.2
Property	1.0	2.2
Other	11.2	24.5
Total	45.7	100.0
Local		
Property	29.7	73.7
Individual income	1.3	3.1
Sales and excises	2.3	5.8
Other	7.0	17.4
Total	40.3	100.0
State and local		
Individual income	8.9	10.4
Corporation income	3.3	3.9
Sales and excises	23.8	27.7
Estate and gift	1.0	1.2
Property	30.7	35.7
Other	18.2	21.2
Total	86.0	100.0
All levels		
Individual income	94.9	34.2
Corporation income	42.3	15.2
Sales and excises	39.0	14.1
Estate and gift	4.5	1.6
Payroll	44.2	15.9
Property	30.7	11.1
Other	21.8	7.8
Total	277.3	100.0

Sources: Worksheets of the U.S. Department of Commerce, Office of Business Economics. Figures are rounded and do not necessarily add to totals.

[a] Revenues are defined as receipts in the national income accounts less contributions for social insurance other than federal payroll taxes.

These developments foreshadow continued change and evolution in the years ahead. Tax rates will be raised or lowered as domestic and international circumstances require. Reforms in federal individual and corporation income taxes will continue to be made. Consideration is being given to methods of further alleviating the tax burden on low incomes and to integrating payroll taxes with the individual income tax. New interest is being shown in the federal estate and gift taxes. State and local finance will continue to be a major concern of policy at all levels of government.

The purpose of this book is to explain these and other emerging issues in federal taxation and to discuss alternative solutions. Chapter 2 examines the relation between taxation and economic growth and stability and between tax policy and overall economic policy. Chapter 3 describes the tax legislative process, discusses its weaknesses, and suggests ways to improve it. Chapters 4 through 8 are devoted to the major federal tax categories: the individual income tax, the corporation income tax, consumption taxes, payroll taxes, and estate and gift taxes. Each chapter describes the basic features of the tax under review, recent changes in the law, and the problems yet unsolved. Chapter 9 analyzes the issues in state-local taxation that are relevant to federal policy.

Goals of Taxation

Taxation—the means by which a government implements decisions to transfer resources from the private to the public sector—is a major instrument of social and economic policy. It has two goals: to distribute the cost of government fairly by income classes (vertical equity) and among people in approximately the same economic circumstances (horizontal equity); and to promote economic growth, stability, and efficiency. From these standpoints, the U.S. tax system is both a source of satisfaction and an object of criticism. The federal part of the system is progressive, thus placing a proportionately greater burden on those who have greater ability to pay. It is also responsive to changes in business activity, and therefore it has an automatic stabilizing effect on private incomes and spending. The state-local part of the system is neither progressive nor responsive to changes in income, and is responsible for the many fiscal crises that have occurred at the state-local level throughout the country.

Some criticize the U.S. tax system as being too progressive; others say it is not progressive enough. But there is a consensus in favor of at least *some* progression in the overall tax burden. Some believe that special provisions go too far toward promoting economic incentives; others believe that these provisions do not go far enough. Nonetheless, tax policy is generally regarded as a legitimate and useful device for promoting economic growth and stability, provided the particular measures chosen are effective means of accomplishing their objectives. Within these broad areas of agreement, there is considerable controversy regarding the relative emphasis to be placed on equity and economic objectives.

These issues involve difficult, technical questions of law, accounting, and economics. They are often obscured by misunderstanding, lack of information, and even misrepresentation. Yet they have important implications for the welfare of every citizen and for the vitality of the economy. This volume attempts to provide factual and analytical information that will help the reader make up his own mind. It was prepared in the belief that tax policy is too important to be left solely to the experts, and that taxation can and should be understood by the interested citizen.

CHAPTER TWO

Taxes and Economic Policy

DURING MOST OF THE NATION'S HISTORY, federal budget policy was based on the rule that tax receipts should be roughly equal to annual government expenditures. Declining receipts during a business contraction called for an increase in taxes or a reduction in expenditures, while surpluses that developed during periods of prosperity called for lowered tax rates or increased expenditures. This policy reduced private incomes when they were already falling and raised them when they were rising. By aggravating fluctuations in purchasing power, the policy of annually balanced budgets accentuated economic instability.

In the 1930s, new concepts of budget policy emerged that emphasized the relationship of the federal budget to the performance of the economy. Adjustments in federal expenditures and taxes were to be made to reduce unemployment or to check inflation. Budget surpluses were to be used to restrain private spending during prosperity, deficits to stimulate spending during recessions. But variations in government expenditures were expected to play a more active role than tax rate variations in counteracting fluctuations in private demand.

The view today is that private demand can be stimulated or restrained by tax as well as expenditure changes. Higher taxes and lower government expenditures help to fight inflation by restraining private demand; lower taxes and higher expenditures help to fight recession

7

by stimulating private demand. Fiscal policy was actively used in the decade of the 1960s to promote economic stability, with results that exceeded expectations on some occasions (for example, when taxes were cut in 1964) and fell below expectations on others (for example, when the Vietnam war surtax was imposed in 1968).

The purpose of this chapter is to explain how the fiscal actions of the government, including changes in expenditures and taxes, affect the level of economic activity and the rate of economic growth. Major emphasis will be placed on taxes because the major focus of this volume is on taxation. But changes in government spending cannot be ignored, as the rapid increase in expenditures for the Vietnam war clearly showed in the latter part of the 1960s. That experience also demonstrated that the growth and stability of the economy depend not only on fiscal decisions, but on many other government decisions —particularly those concerning monetary policy—which are outside the scope of this volume.

Fiscal economics is based on national income analysis as it has developed over the past thirty-five years. The essence of this analysis is that the level of expenditures depends on total output or gross national product (GNP), which in turn depends on the total spending of consumers, business, and government. At any given time, there is a level of output that is consistent with full employment of the nation's supply of labor (except for seasonal, and a small amount of frictional, unemployment). This level is called *potential* or *full employment GNP* (Figure 2-1). The major objectives of fiscal policy are to stabilize the economy at full employment, maintain price stability, and promote economic growth and efficiency.

Stabilization Policy

The federal government exerts great influence on total spending, and hence on output, through its expenditure and tax policies. It alters total spending directly by varying its own spending, or indirectly by raising or lowering taxes. If expenditures are increased or taxes lowered, the spending of higher incomes by the recipients requires additional output, which in turn generates still more income and spending; and the cycle repeats itself. The cumulative increase in GNP is, therefore, a multiple of the initial increase in government expenditures or reduction in taxes. Correspondingly, reductions in

FIGURE 2-1. Gross National Product, Actual and Potential, and Unemployment Rate, 1955–70

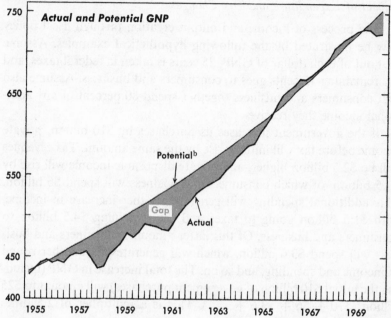

Billions of 1958 dollars (ratio scale)[a]

Actual and Potential GNP

Potential[b]

Gap

Actual

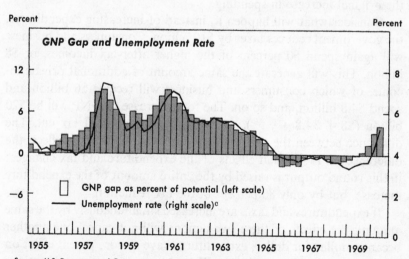

Percent

Percent

GNP Gap and Unemployment Rate

□ GNP gap as percent of potential (left scale)
— Unemployment rate (right scale)[c]

Sources: U.S. Department of Commerce and Council of Economic Advisers.
a Seasonally adjusted annual rates.
b Trend line of 3½ percent through middle of 1955 to 1962 IV, 3¾ percent from 1962 IV to 1965 IV, 4 percent from 1965 IV to 1969 IV, and 4.3 percent from 1969 IV to 1970 II.
c Unemployment as percentage of civilian labor force; seasonally adjusted.

expenditures or increases in taxes reduce GNP by a multiple of the initial action.

Impact of Expenditure and Tax Changes

The process of income and output creation through fiscal policy may be illustrated by the following hypothetical examples. Assume that out of each dollar of GNP, 25 cents is taken in federal taxes, and the remaining 75 cents goes to consumers and business. Assume also that consumers and business together spend 80 percent of any additional income they receive.

If the government increases its purchases by $10 billion, private income before tax will initially rise by the same amount. Tax revenues will be $2.5 billion higher, and private disposable income will rise by $7.5 billion, of which consumers and business will spend $6 billion. This additional spending will generate another increase in income, with $1.5 billion going to taxes and the remaining $4.5 billion to consumers and business. Of this latter amount, consumers and business will spend $3.6 billion, which will generate still another round of income and spending, and so on. The total increase in GNP (including the initial $10 billion of government purchases) will amount to $25 billion ($10 + $6 + $3.6 + . . .). This is a multiplier of 2.5 times the original increase in spending.

Consider what will happen if, instead of increasing expenditures, the government reduces taxes by $10 billion. Consumers and business will again spend 80 percent of the higher after-tax incomes, or $8 billion. This will generate the same amount of additional private income, of which consumers and business will receive $6 billion and spend $4.8 billion, and so on. The total increase in GNP will be $20 billion ($8 + $4.8 + . . .), or two times the original tax cut. The difference between the multipliers in the two illustrations reflects the differences in first-round effects of the expenditure and tax changes: in this round output is raised by the entire amount of the expenditure increase, but by only 80 percent of the tax reduction.

If expenditures and taxes are increased simultaneously by the same amount, the effects of these two actions will not cancel one another because, dollar for dollar, expenditures have a more potent effect on the economy than do tax changes. For example, given the assumptions in the previous illustrations, if a tax increase of $10 billion were enacted together with a $10 billion increase in government spending, the former would reduce GNP by $20 billion, while the latter would stimulate a $25 billion increase, leaving a net increase of $5 billion. In other words, an increase in expenditures that is fully financed by an increase in taxes will on balance increase the GNP. (This theorem assumes that the change in spending resulting from an increase or decrease in private disposable income will be the same regardless of the source of the income change and that investment and other economic behavior will not be influenced by the government's action. The multipliers used are illustrative only; estimates of the multipliers vary greatly.)

The effect of changes in government expenditures and taxes on the size of the government's deficit depends on the increase in GNP generated by the fiscal stimulus and on tax rates. In the previous examples, federal taxes were assumed to account for about 25 percent of an increment to GNP. Thus, the increase in GNP would raise tax receipts by $6.25 billion if expenditures were increased by $10 billion (0.25 × $25), causing an increase in deficit (or a reduction in surplus) of $3.75 billion. If taxes were reduced by $10 billion, the increase in GNP would raise tax receipts by $5 billion (0.25 × $20), causing a $5 billion increase in the deficit. If expenditures and taxes were raised simultaneously by $10 billion, the increase in GNP would raise tax receipts by $1.25 billion (0.25 × $5) and *reduce* the deficit (or increase the surplus) by that amount.

Monetary policy also plays an important role in stabilization policy. Suppose the federal government increases expenditures or reduces taxes. As GNP increases, individuals and business firms will need additional cash to conduct their business affairs. If the money supply fails to increase, the greater demand for cash will drive up interest rates. The higher interest rates will tend to reduce residential construction, business investment, and state-local construction, thus offsetting at least some of the effect of the initial increase in spending. Fiscal policy thus requires an accommodating monetary policy if it is to be fully effective, but the precise combination of monetary and fiscal measures necessary to obtain any desired response is not known.

Built-in Stabilizers

In addition to discretionary changes in taxes and expenditures (that is, deliberate government actions to vary taxes or the rate of expenditures), the fiscal system itself contributes to stabilization by generating automatic tax and expenditure adjustments that cushion the effect of changes in GNP. These *built-in stabilizers* moderate the fall in private income and spending when GNP declines and restrain private income and spending when GNP rises. They are automatic in the sense that they respond to changes in GNP without any action on the part of the government.

The two major groups of built-in fiscal stabilizers are: (1) taxes, in particular the federal individual income tax; and (2) transfers, such as unemployment compensation and welfare payments.

Among taxes, the federal individual income tax is the leading stabilizer. When incomes fall, many individuals who were formerly taxable drop below the taxable level; others are pushed down into lower tax brackets. Conversely, when incomes rise, individuals who were formerly not taxed become taxable, and others are pushed into higher tax brackets. Under the 1964 act rates, federal individual income tax receipts (excluding the Vietnam war surcharge) automatically increased or decreased by about 14 or 15 percent for every 10 percent increase or decrease in personal income. Since consumption depends on disposable personal income, automatic changes in receipts from the individual income tax tend to keep consumption more stable than it otherwise would be.

Variations in receipts from the corporation income tax are proportionately larger than variations in individual income tax receipts, because profits fluctuate widely over a business cycle. The variation in corporate profits is a major nonfiscal stabilizer in the economic system. When economic activity slows down, profits fall in absolute terms and as a percentage of GNP, thus absorbing much of the impact of the reduction in incomes. During a cyclical recovery, profits rise much faster than do other kinds of income. Corporation taxes vary almost directly with profits, and they assist corporations to absorb the impact of declining incomes during the downswing. During the upswing, rising tax liabilities tend to restrain the growth of corporation incomes. The effect of variations in corporation tax liabilities on dividends is relatively small because corporate managers try to keep dividends in line with long-term earnings. Fluctuations in investment are probably reduced to some extent, but the precise effect is unknown.

On the expenditure side, the major built-in stabilizer is unemployment compensation. Insured workers who become unemployed are entitled to benefits for up to twenty-six weeks in most states. Benefits for an additional thirteen weeks are paid throughout the nation when the national unemployment rate is 4½ percent for three consecutive months, and in any state when the state unemployment rate increases by 20 percent over the average of the two preceding years and is at least 4 percent. These payments help to maintain consumption as output and employment fall, even though the recipients are not participating in production. As incomes go up and employment increases, unemployment compensation declines. Other transfer payments (old-age insurance, public assistance, and the like) also tend to vary inversely with changes in GNP.

It is possible to calculate the effect of built-in stabilizers on the federal surplus, as distinct from the discretionary actions of the government. Because of the built-in stabilizers, the actual surplus or deficit reflects the prevailing levels of income and employment, as well as the government's fiscal policy. Figure 2-2 shows how the effect

FIGURE 2-2. Effect of Level of Activity on Federal Surplus or Deficit

Surplus or deficit (billions of dollars)ᵃ

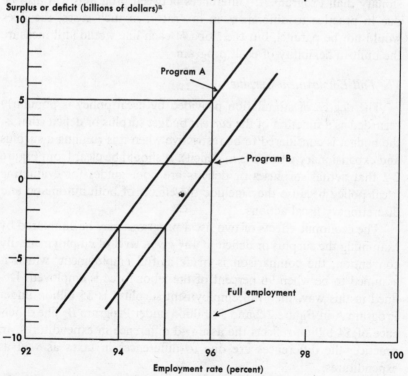

Source: Adapted from *Economic Report of the President*, January 1962, p. 79.
ᵃ National income accounts basis.

of the built-in stabilizers may be separated from the discretionary changes.

Each line in the figure shows the surplus or deficit that would be realized at various levels of employment under two different budget programs, A and B. For simplicity, it is assumed that the tax system is the same, but that expenditures are $4 billion higher under Program B. (The surplus is, therefore, $4 billion lower, or the deficit is $4 billion higher.) The lines slope upward, indicating that as employment and income increase, the deficits become smaller or the surpluses larger. The effect of the built-in stabilizers is given by the slope of each line: the greater the slope, the larger the impact of the built-in stabilizers on the surplus or deficit. As is shown in Figure 2-2, both programs have the same built-in stability features because the tax systems are identical. However, an actual deficit of $3 billion is realized when employment is at 94 percent of the labor force under Program A and 95 percent under Program B. Clearly, Program B is more expansionary than Program A. Differences between programs will also be due in practice to differences in tax rates; in such cases, the lines would not be parallel, but the slope of each line would still measure the built-in flexibility of each program.

The Full Employment Surplus

The degree of stimulation provided by fiscal policy is popularly regarded as a function of the *current* budget surplus or deficit (that is, the budget is considered to be restrictive when it is running a surplus and expansionary when it is in deficit). It should be clear from Figure 2-2 that actual surpluses or deficits are poor guides for evaluating fiscal policy because they include the effects of both automatic and discretionary fiscal actions.

The economic effects of two fiscal programs may be compared by examining the surplus or deficit at any given level of employment. By convention, the comparison is made at full employment, which is assumed to be when 96 percent of the labor force is employed. Defined in this way, the "full employment surplus" is $5 billion under Program A in Figure 2-2 and $1 billion under Program B. The difference of $4 billion reflects the assumed difference in expenditures. In practice, the differences are due to differences in taxes as well as expenditures.

There are two types of budget statements in current use—the

official *unified budget* and the *national income accounts budget*. The full employment surplus is usually computed on a national income accounts basis, but it can be adjusted to the definitions in the unified budget (see page 16).

The budget program that is appropriate at a given time depends upon the strength of private demand for consumption and investment goods. When private demand is high, a large full employment surplus is called for; when private demand is weak, a small full employment surplus, or even a full employment deficit, is required. Efforts to achieve a larger surplus or a lower deficit than is consistent with full employment would depress employment and incomes. If the budget called for too small a full employment surplus, total demand would be too high, and prices would rise.

Another characteristic of the full employment surplus is its tendency to increase with the passage of time and the growth of the economy. With the growth of the labor force, the stock of capital, and productivity, potential federal receipts also rise. At current tax rates and assuming full employment, federal receipts increase by about $18 billion a year. Thus, the full employment surplus will creep up by about $18 billion each year, or about 1.6 percent of potential GNP in 1971, unless the government takes steps to prevent it.

This upward creep in the full employment surplus has been called the *fiscal dividend* or the *fiscal drag*. It is identified as a *dividend* when used to describe the elbow room available in the federal budget to finance higher federal expenditures without raising tax rates. During the early 1960s, the fiscal dividend was large enough to finance tax rate reductions as well as expenditure increases. More recently, with continued high commitments for defense, the fiscal dividend has not been adequate to provide fully for urgently needed domestic social programs.

The automatic increase in federal receipts that accompanies economic growth is also called the *fiscal drag* because it acts as a retarding influence on the economy unless it is offset by rising expenditures or tax reductions. This terminology was in vogue in the early 1960s, when government expenditures were not rising fast enough to absorb the automatic growth in tax receipts.

According to current estimates, the federal budget would have been in surplus in every quarter between mid-1955 and mid-1965, had full employment been maintained (Figure 2-4). However, the actual

The Two Budgets

The official budget statement of the federal government is the *unified budget*, which is an instrument of management and control of federal activities financed with federally owned funds. This budget includes cash flows to and from the public resulting from all federal fiscal activity, including the trust funds, and the net lending of government-owned enterprises. Thus, the unified budget provides a comprehensive picture of the financial impact of federal programs, but it does not measure their contribution to the current income and output of the nation. For this purpose, economists make use of the statement of receipts and expenditures in the official national income accounts, often called the *national income accounts budget.*

Like the unified budget, the national income accounts budget includes the activities of trust funds and excludes purely intragovernmental transactions (for example, interest on federal bonds owned by federal agencies) which do not affect the general public. However, there are significant differences between the two in timing and coverage. The national income accounts budget includes receipts and expenditures when they have their impact on private incomes, which is not necessarily when the federal government receives cash or pays it out. This adjustment involves putting receipts (except those from personal taxes) on an accrual basis and counting expenditures when goods are delivered rather than when payment is made. The adjustment for coverage excludes purely financial transactions because these represent an exchange of assets or claims and not a direct addition to income or production.

There are substantial differences in the size of surpluses or deficits between the two accounts, and even in their movements (Figure 2-3). In recent years, the national income accounts budget has shown the smaller deficit (or larger surpluses).

FIGURE 2-3. Federal Deficits and Surpluses, Two Budget Concepts, Fiscal Years 1954–70

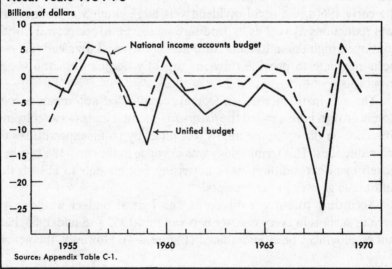

Source: Appendix Table C-1.

FIGURE 2-4. Full Employment Surplus as a Percentage of Potential Gross National Product, National Income Accounts Basis, 1955–70

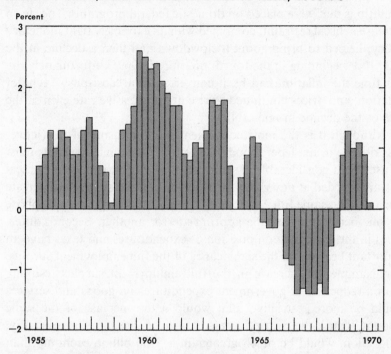

Sources: Arthur M. Okun and Nancy H. Teeters, "The Full Employment Surplus Revisited," in *Brookings Papers on Economic Activity* (1:1970), pp. 104–05; Teeters, "Budgetary Outlook at Mid-Year 1970," in *Brookings Papers on Economic Activity* (2:1970), p. 304 (adjusted to exclude the corporate financial adjustment).

budget showed a deficit during most of the period, reflecting the disappointing performance of the economy. It was only after the full employment surplus was sharply reduced in 1964 to stimulate the economy that employment began to move toward 96 percent of the labor force, which is regarded by most people as the minimum acceptable level. This experience illustrates the principle that planning for a budget surplus, without regard to the strength of private demand, may produce unsatisfactory rates of employment and output and create budget deficits besides.

The rapid build-up of military expenditures for the Vietnam war quickly wiped out the full employment surplus beginning in mid-1965, the deficit on a full employment basis averaging 0.5 percent of potential GNP in 1966, 1.4 percent in 1967, and 0.9 percent in 1968. This was the period when prices rose at an unacceptably rapid rate. The full employment budget was restored to a surplus position in early 1969, reflecting the effect of the Vietnam war surtax and the strict limitations that were placed on domestic federal programs. The sharp increase in fiscal restraint, combined with an extremely tight monetary policy, helped to bring about a slowdown and then a decline in the real GNP beginning in the fourth quarter of 1969. Unfortunately, by this time the inflation had been converted to a "cost-push" type of inflation, and prices continued to rise at an excessive rate even in the face of the decline in real GNP.

Although it is the most convenient single measure of restrictiveness or ease in the federal budget, the full employment surplus must be used with considerable care. In the first place, the degree of fiscal restraint needed at any given time depends on the strength of private demand. The same full employment surplus that may be appropriate for one period may not be appropriate for another. Second, differences in the level and composition of expenditures and taxes have an important bearing on the significance of the full employment surplus. For example, an increase in the full employment surplus resulting from a reduction in government expenditures on goods and services would be more restrictive than would a tax increase of the same amount. Third, the restrictiveness of a given *amount* of surplus, say, $10 billion, would be much greater in a $750 billion economy than in a $1,000 billion economy. In making comparisons over time, the full employment surplus should be expressed as a percentage of potential GNP (see Figure 2-4). Finally, there is no simple way to adjust the full employment surplus for the effect of price increases. Most calculations of the full employment surplus remove the effect of the built-in response of the federal budget to a business recession, but do not remove the built-in response of the budget to inflation. For these reasons, the meaning of the full employment surplus is likely to be unambiguous only during relatively short periods when changes in expenditures and taxes, and in the rate of growth of prices, are relatively small. Analysis of the fiscal impact of the budget over long periods requires more detailed information than the full employment surplus provides by itself.

Expenditure versus Tax Adjustments to Promote Stability

Both expenditure and tax rate changes can be used for stabilization purposes. While it is true that expenditure changes have somewhat larger multiplier effects, they are not necessarily preferable to changes in tax rates. In the first place, government expenditures should be determined on the basis of long-run national needs and not of short-run cyclical considerations. The controlling principle is that government outlays should not exceed the level where the benefit to the nation's citizens of an additional dollar of expenditures would be the same in public and private use. It is hardly likely that this point would shift sharply in one direction or the other during such short periods as a business contraction or even during an inflation. Second, considerations of economic efficiency argue against large short-run variations in expenditures. For example, it would be wasteful to slow down construction of a road or hydroelectric facility, once construction has begun, in the interest of reducing aggregate spending. Third, there may be a long time lag between a decision to undertake an expenditure and its effect on output and employment. When recessions are relatively brief—as they have been since the end of World War II—the impact of a decision to make an expenditure change often is not felt until recovery is under way. However, during periods of rapidly rising defense expenditures, such as occurred during the Korean and Vietnam wars, a slowing down or deferment of some government programs usually becomes necessary to keep total demand from outstripping the productive potential of the economy.

Among the various taxes, the individual income tax is the best suited for stabilization purposes. Under the withholding system for wages and salaries, changes in tax rates can be made effective in a matter of days and can also be terminated quickly. In most cases, the effect of a tax change on a worker's take-home pay is indistinguishable from the effect of a change in his gross weekly wage. Corporation income tax changes are not likely to have significant effects on investment if it is known, or expected, that they will be of short duration. Consumption tax changes may have a perverse effect in the short run; the expectation of a reduction may delay spending, and the expectation of an increase may accelerate spending. Nevertheless, once they become effective, consumption tax changes are at least as powerful as income tax changes in stimulating or restraining consumer demand.

Some economists believe that consumption depends on income that is expected to be received regularly and is not much affected by temporary or transitory changes in income. On this hypothesis, temporary income tax changes would have relatively little impact on consumption. Most economists believe that a temporary income tax change would have some effect on consumer spending, although they agree that it would be less powerful than a permanent tax change. Income tax changes also operate with a lag, because consumers do not alter their consumption immediately in response to changes in disposable income.

Tax changes are often assumed to have the largest effect on consumption if they are confined to the lower income classes. This view presupposes that poor people spend proportionately more out of any additional dollars they may receive than do the rich. There is no evidence, however, to confirm or deny this assumption. For policy purposes, it is probably satisfactory to assume that the incremental consumption rate is fairly high throughout most of the income distribution. This would suggest that, if the distribution of the tax burden is considered equitable by the large majority of taxpayers, tax rates could be moved up or down uniformly for stabilization purposes under a simple formula, such as an equal percentage change for all taxpayers.

Tax rate changes are sometimes criticized on the ground that they are too small to exert a significant economic effect. With sixty-five million taxpayers, a $13 billion individual income tax cut would be equivalent to an average increase in take-home pay of only $4 a week per taxpayer, a negligible amount in comparison with the total GNP of $1,000 billion. The comparison is erroneous, however, because it compares weekly and annual income flows. A $13 billion tax cut would amount to more than 1 percent of the GNP, whether expressed on a weekly, monthly, or annual basis. Because tax changes have a multiplier effect, a tax cut of this magnitude would provide a substantial stimulus to the economy. The deviation from full employment GNP, which tax cuts are intended to narrow, is usually less than 5 percent.

Tax adjustments can be used to restrain as well as to stimulate demand and are therefore important policy instruments for counteracting inflation. It may be impractical, if not impossible, to cut back government expenditures when inflation threatens. About half of federal expenditures are for defense, foreign aid, education, and research and development, which should not be altered for short-run reasons. Much of the remainder of the federal budget provides assistance to low-income persons, who are particularly hard-pressed during an inflation. Moreover, the inflationary pressures may have been due to an increase in government spending for defense or war purposes. In these circumstances, tax increases must be used to withdraw excess purchasing power from the income stream.

The time required for the legislative process to be completed is the major obstacle to prompt use of tax changes for stabilization purposes. Congressional consideration of major tax legislation may take as long as eighteen months. Proposals have been made to give the President authority to make temporary changes in individual income tax rates, or to speed up congressional procedures for action on presidential recommendations. However, Congress has not seriously considered such plans (see pages 49–50).

Automatic Budget Rules

It is now widely understood that following a policy of annually balanced budgets would accentuate business fluctuations. But many people continue to believe that it is unwise to rely exclusively on discretion to guide budget decisions. Discretionary policy depends heavily on forecasting techniques that are still subject to error. There is also a fear that removing budgetary restraint would lead to excessive federal expenditures. To avoid these pitfalls, attempts have been made to formulate rules that would reduce the element of judgment in budget decisions without impairing economic growth and stability.

The best known plan is the *stabilizing budget policy* of the Committee for Economic Development (CED), a nonprofit organization of influential businessmen and educators. Under this policy, tax rates would be set to balance the budget or yield a small surplus at full employment. Tax rates would remain unchanged until there was a major change in the level of expenditures. Reliance would be placed on the built-in stabilizers to moderate fluctuations in private demand.

The CED plan would operate successfully, however, only if full employment could be achieved with a balance or a small surplus in the federal budget. Moreover, the CED plan does not offer a systematic method for raising additional revenues if federal expenditures should rise by more than the amount of the automatic growth in tax receipts, or of lowering taxes if federal expenditures should rise by less than the amount of the automatic growth in tax receipts. With federal expenditure needs rising rapidly and recession still a considerable threat to economic stability, it would be both hazardous and unwise to keep tax rates unchanged for long periods.

A second type of plan—which would aim at helping to solve the fiscal drag problem—would provide for individual income tax rates to be reduced each year by a given amount, say 1 percentage point (which would reduce income tax receipts by about $4 billion a year at 1971 income levels), with the $14 billion remaining from the fiscal dividend of approximately $18 billion to be used for increasing federal expenditures. Presumably, the plan would begin with a surplus or deficit consistent with full employment. The difficulty with this approach is that it would freeze the allocation of increased federal receipts between tax reduction and increased expenditures. Periods when it would have been desirable to cut tax rates by a fixed amount or a fixed percentage each year have been rare in the nation's history.

A third approach to an automatic budget policy would be to build into the budget a formula that would trigger upward or downward changes in tax rates when certain predetermined economic indices are reached. For example, legislation might provide for a 1 percentage point reduction in income tax rates for every increase of 0.5 percent in unemployment above 4.5 percent of the labor force, or an increase of 1 percentage point for every rise of 2 points in a general price index, such as the consumer or the wholesale price index. While this type of formula would add to the effectiveness of the built-in stabilizers if the changes were correctly timed, no one index or set of indices could be used with confidence to signal an economic movement justifying tax action.

It is evident that budget policy cannot be based on a rigid set of rules. Nevertheless, the search for budget rules has greatly improved public understanding of the elements of fiscal policy. Great emphasis is placed on the automatic stabilizers for their cushioning effect on private disposable incomes and spending. Recognition of the capacity of the federal tax system to generate rising revenues has alerted policymakers to the need for making positive decisions to determine the relative social priorities of public and private expenditures, so that the appropriate amounts can be allocated to tax reduction and to higher government expenditures. Unfortunately, the political advantages of an immediate tax reduction tend to be more attractive than the long-run benefits of new or improved government programs. Thus, the Tax Reform Act of 1969 included net tax reductions, phased in over a period of years, which amount to $8 billion a year (at 1975 income levels), even though the remaining fiscal dividend was acknowledged to be inadequate to finance urgently needed federal programs.

Policies to Promote Economic Growth

Fiscal policies are useful in promoting long-run economic growth as well as short-run stability. The objective of growth policy is to provide relatively full employment for the labor force and industrial capacity, at stable prices. Growth may be disappointing for two reasons: the resources of the economy may not be employed up to their full potential because the economy is in recession or is being artificially held down to combat inflationary pressures, or the rate of growth of potential output at full employment may be too low. The policies required under these circumstances differ, although they are often confused.

Achieving Full Employment and Stable Prices

The major contribution that fiscal policy can make to economic growth is to help keep total demand roughly in line with the productive potential of the economy. An economy operating at less than full employment is one in which potential GNP is larger than the total of actual spending by consumers, business, and government. The remedy for this deficiency is to increase private or public spending through fiscal and monetary stimulation. Conversely, when total demand exceeds the capacity of the economy to produce goods and services, the remedy is to curtail private or public spending through fiscal and monetary restraint.

Although the basic principles of stabilization policy are clear, they have been difficult to apply in practice. Failure to absorb the normal growth in revenues will produce successively higher full employment surpluses, which may hold actual output below the economic potential of the economy. The high levels of unemployment and the large gap between potential and actual GNP in the late 1950s and early 1960s (see Figure 2-1) were caused largely by excessively restrictive fiscal policies that arose in this way. On the other hand, too large a growth in government expenditures relative to normal revenue growth may produce excess demand, which in turn leads to rising prices. The inflation that began in mid-1965 was triggered by the large rise in Vietnam war expenditures, which were superimposed on an economy already operating at close to full employment. A 10 percent surtax on individual and corporation income taxes was enacted in the summer of 1968, but this was about three years after the decision to escalate the war had been made.

It now seems clear that it will always be difficult to maintain full employment in a modern industrial economy and keep price increases within acceptable limits. Since the end of World War II, prices have shown a tendency to rise in the United States, even when total spending has been below potential GNP. Many economists believe that this dilemma can be resolved only by supplementing fiscal and monetary policies with some form of wage-price or "incomes" policy to keep wage increases roughly in line with the average growth in productivity of the economy as a whole, and to prevent price increases that are not justified by cost increases. Under such a policy, prices would decline in industries with above-average productivity increases and rise in industries with less-than-average productivity increases, but the average of all prices would be stable. These principles were established by the Council of Economic Advisers in 1962 as voluntary "guideposts" for wage and price behavior. The guideposts had the strong backing of Presidents Kennedy and Johnson and appeared to have some effect in restraining wage and price increases (a judgment that some professional economists dispute) until mid-1965, when the rapid build-up of military expenditures for the Vietnam war upset the balance between supply and demand. No country has yet devised a workable incomes policy under conditions of full employment, and the search continues.

Experience has shown that the major effect of inflation on growth is felt when the attempt is made to restore balance in the economy. Inflation distorts the distribution of the national income among different groups. Each group tries to protect itself against erosion of its share through wage or price increases or government transfer payments. Such pressures continue to be felt long after excess demand has been removed by fiscal and monetary restraint. Thus, without an effective incomes policy, it may be possible to halt inflation only at the cost of high unemployment and slow growth for relatively long periods. It is, of course, much less costly in social and economic terms to avoid inflation in the first place.

Raising the Growth Rate

If full employment is maintained, the rate of economic growth will depend on the ability of the economy to raise the rate of growth of potential output. The factors affecting potential output are the size of the labor force, the length of the average workweek and workyear, and productivity (output per man-hour). Productivity depends on the size of the capital stock, the quality of human resources, the attitudes and skills of management, the efficiency of resource use, and the amount of technological progress. Most of these factors are influenced to some extent by government expenditure and tax policy, but the influence is most direct and quantitatively most important with respect to the rate of national investment in both physical and human resources.

To increase the rate of growth, the rate of national investment must be raised to a permanently higher level and held there for a long period of time. The federal government can contribute toward increasing the investment rate through fiscal policy in three ways: (1) it can adopt a policy of budget surpluses when the economy is operating at full employment; (2) it can increase investment in physical and human capital directly through its own expenditures; and (3) it can adopt tax measures that provide incentives for private saving and investment.

SAVING THROUGH BUDGET SURPLUSES. The key to an understanding of growth policy is the relation between saving and investment. As measured statistically, national saving is the difference between national output and the amounts spent by consumers and government; private investment is also that part of the national product that is not consumed or used for government purposes. Thus, national saving is equal to private investment. In effect, through saving, the nation sets aside the resources needed for private investment purposes; otherwise the resources would be used to produce goods and services for consumers and government.

When the federal government runs a budget surplus, it adds its own saving to that generated by the private economy. When the budget is in deficit, national saving is reduced. Since increased saving and investment are needed to raise the growth rate, the federal government can stimulate a higher growth rate by running budget surpluses at full employment. Moreover, the larger the surplus at full employment, the larger the potential contribution to growth.

This growth strategy can be implemented only if there is sufficient investment demand in the private economy to use up the saving generated in the federal budget. If private demand for investment is too low, the federal surplus will generate unemployment rather than more growth. In other words, the full employment surplus must be just large enough to offset the deficiency in private saving. If there is more than enough private saving for the existing investment demand, the budget should be in deficit even at full employment.

An important ingredient of any strategy to increase the rate of private investment is monetary policy. Easy money provides ready access to credit and lowers the cost of borrowing for investment purposes by reducing interest rates. Tight money restrains the growth of credit and raises interest rates. Therefore, the best policy to promote private investment would combine a budget surplus with easy money. In implementing such a policy, it is important to avoid taxes that impair investment incentives.

In practice, the extent of monetary ease that a nation can afford is limited by balance-of-payments considerations. If interest rates are driven down too far, private capital will leave the country to take advantage of higher interest rates abroad. In extreme cases, the outflow of funds may require devaluation of the nation's currency to restore international equilibrium. When interest rates must be kept up for balance-of-payments reasons, fiscal policy must be easier (that is, the surplus must be lower or the deficit higher) to prevent a drop in demand and employment.

INCREASING INVESTMENT DIRECTLY. It is not generally realized that investment is undertaken by government as well as by private firms. Outlays for education, training of manpower, health, research and development, roads, and other public facilities are essential elements of national investment. Such outlays are not substitutable for private investment, or vice versa. Education and research expenditures are perhaps the most important components of national investment, yet most of these expenditures are paid for by government (primarily state and local in the case of education, and primarily federal in the case of research). There is no basis for prejudging how total investment should be distributed between the public and private sectors, and it is important to avoid doctrinaire positions about one or the other. Both types of investment contribute to the nation's economic growth.

Public investment is financed directly by government through the tax system. If private demand is strong, the appropriate policy for growth would be to raise enough tax revenues to pay for needed government investment as well as to leave an additional margin of saving for private investment.

INCREASING SAVING AND INVESTMENT INCENTIVES. Given the aggregate level of taxation, the tax structure can be an important independent factor in determining the growth potential of the economy. The tax structure may encourage consumption or saving, help to raise or lower private investment in general or in particular industries, stimulate or restrain the outflow of investment funds to foreign countries, and subsidize or discourage particular expenditures by individuals and business firms. Most tax systems, including that of the United States, have numerous features specifically intended to promote saving and investment. For example, the federal income taxes provide liberal depreciation allowances, full offsets for business losses against other income over a period of nine years, averaging of individual income for tax purposes over a period of five years, and preferential treatment of capital gains. A 7 percent credit against corporation and individual income taxes was used to stimulate investment between 1962 and 1969. These and other provisions will be discussed in later chapters.

The "Debt Burden"

Effective use of fiscal policy to promote the full employment and growth objectives is hindered by public concern over the growth of the national debt. There is widespread fear that a long succession of annual deficits and a resulting rise in the national debt will impose dangerously heavy burdens on later generations. There is also concern about the economic burden of interest payments.

Growth of the national debt can impose a burden on future generations if it interferes with private capital formation. In this respect, there is a difference between debt created under conditions of excessive unemployment and debt created under conditions of full employment.

In a situation of substantial unemployment, an increase in the public debt can finance deficits that government uses to purchase goods and services directly or to provide transfer payments. Since there are unemployed resources, the goods and services acquired by government or by the recipients of transfer payments do not take the place of goods and services that might otherwise have been produced. If accompanied by the appropriate monetary policy, the debt increase can be absorbed without impeding the flow of funds into private capital formation. In fact, private investment will rise as a result of the stimulus that arises from a higher level of economic activity. The community is better off when the expenditures are made; and later generations will also benefit to the extent that the expenditures increase private and public investment in human or physical capital that will yield future services.

The situation is more complicated if the economy is at full employment. In this setting an increase in government expenditures that leads to a deficit (or reduces a surplus) in the federal budget cannot increase total output. This means either that prices will rise or that offsetting tax increases or monetary restraint will be required. If inflation is to be avoided, the necessary restraint must reduce consumption or investment. If the impact is on consumption, taxpayers will have in effect exchanged a collective good or service for current consumption. If the impact is on private or public investment, later generations will be worse off to the extent that the rate of growth of productive capacity has been reduced.

Since the federal government usually runs surpluses when the economy is at full employment (see Figure 2-4), there is little likelihood that the federal debt added in peacetime will be burdensome in an economic sense. Deficits incurred to restore or maintain full employment raise output and employment and actually increase the resources available to current and later generations.

The existence of the national debt does mean that interest must be paid to holders of the debt, and tax rates are therefore higher than they would be without the debt. The transfer of interest from general taxpayers to bondholders is a burden on the economy if the taxes levied to pay interest on the debt reduce saving or lower economic efficiency. (If the government debt is paid back by a per capita tax—which has no effect on economic incentives—and the market for bonds is competitive, the debt is exactly equivalent to the tax receipts and therefore does not impose a burden on future generations.) In any case, the debt burden in the United States must be small because net interest payments represent a relatively small proportion of federal expenditures (6 percent in 1969). Moreover, the ratio of net federal debt to the gross national product has been declining since the end of World War II (Figure 2-5), and interest payments on the

FIGURE 2-5. Relation of Net Federal Debt and Net Interest on Debt to the Gross National Product, Fiscal Years 1942–69[a]

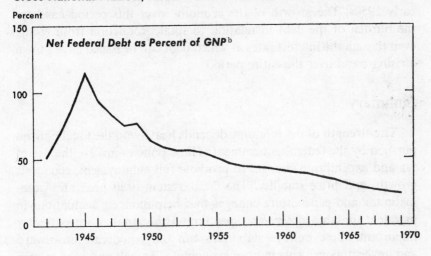

Percent

Net Federal Debt as Percent of GNP[b]

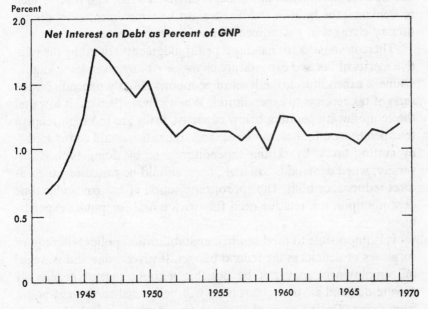

Percent

Net Interest on Debt as Percent of GNP

Sources: Net federal debt: *Economic Report of the President*, February 1970, p. 255. Net interest: 1946–69: Interest payments to the public shown in *The Budget of the United States Government*, various years, or supplied (for 1967–69) by the U.S. Bureau of the Budget, less Federal Reserve bank earnings on U.S. government securities by fiscal years (supplied by Board of Governors of the Federal Reserve System); 1942–45: Estimated from data in *Federal Reserve Bulletins*. Gross national product: *Survey of Current Business*, July 1970, pp. 8, 17; *The Budget of the United States Government, Fiscal Year 1971*, p. 593; and *The Budget of the United States Government, Fiscal Year 1969*, p. 544.

[a] Net federal debt is debt held outside U.S. government investment accounts and Federal Reserve banks. Interest on net federal debt is total interest payments to the public less interest earned by Federal Reserve banks.

[b] Net federal debt at the end of calendar years divided by fiscal year gross national product.

net debt, which fell markedly in the early postwar years, have amounted to only slightly more than 1 percent of GNP since the early 1950s. The growth of the economy over this period has kept the burden of the debt in relation to total production from rising, even though the interest rates at which debt can be issued have shown a rising trend over the entire period.

Summary

The strength of the economy depends heavily on the fiscal policies pursued by the federal government. These policies involve the use of tax and expenditure changes to promote full employment, economic growth, and price stability. The fiscal system itself generates automatic tax and expenditure changes that help dampen fluctuations in private disposable income and spending. Although they are extremely important, these built-in stabilizers can only moderate downward and upward movements in business activity. To halt and reverse such movements, the built-in stabilizers must be supplemented by discretionary changes in government expenditures or tax rates.

There is no basis for making a priori judgments regarding the relative merits of tax and expenditure changes. At any given level of government expenditures, the level of economic activity depends on the *ratio* of tax receipts to expenditures. When private demand is low and the economy is operating below capacity, taxes are too high relative to expenditures. In these circumstances, the ratio should be reduced— by cutting taxes, by raising expenditures, or by doing both. Conversely, when demand is too high, taxes should be raised or expenditures reduced, or both. The appropriate action at any particular time depends upon the relative need for private and for public expenditures.

It is impossible to predict whether stabilization policy will require surpluses or deficits in the federal budget. If private demand is weak, full employment may not be possible without federal deficits. If private demand is strong, surpluses will be needed to prevent prices from rising. On the basis of the past record, there is little reason to expect that the U.S. economy will need the stimulus of sustained deficits to remain at full employment.

The first step toward a policy to promote economic growth is to maintain full employment of resources. This requires avoidance of both inflation and recession. Inflation cannot be halted without interrupting the growth of the economy, sometimes for long periods. Recession not only wastes human and physical resources but also leaves a legacy of inadequate investment, which retards the growth of productivity.

After full employment has been achieved, the growth rate can be increased only by raising the rate of growth of potential output. This will require more saving and more investment. The best strategy for increasing saving and investment would be to combine a large budget surplus with an easy money policy. The surplus will increase national saving, while easy money will increase private investment by making credit more readily available and by reducing interest rates. Saving and investment incentives may also be improved through higher depreciation allowances, investment credits, and other structural tax provisions.

CHAPTER THREE

The Tax Legislative Process

THE PROCESS OF DECISION MAKING in tax policy is one of the most interesting, puzzling, and controversial features of the federal legislative process. It can be speedy and effective, or slow and ponderous. A small army of people participates, but only a few key figures are familiar to the public. The process has been criticized by many, but attempts to alter it even in minor respects have been unavailing.

Basic to an understanding of how the process works is the stipulation in Article I, Section 8, of the Constitution that "Congress shall have power to lay and collect taxes." Congress has always guarded its taxing power jealously. Presidents can recommend changes, but only Congress has the power to translate these recommendations into law. Practically every major presidential tax proposal is thoroughly revised by Congress, and not a few are rejected outright.

A tax law is always a compromise among the views of powerful individuals and groups. The President, the secretary of the treasury, and members of the two congressional tax committees—the House Committee on Ways and Means and the Senate Committee on Finance—are subject to great pressures from the numerous political, economic, and social groups affected by the bill or attempting to have it changed to their advantage. Substantial delays in enactment of tax legislation occur when the participants have difficulty finding a formula to reconcile major opposing interests.

The tax legislative machinery is backed by competent staffs of experts in both the legislative and executive branches of the federal government. Taxation is one of five major policy areas deemed important enough to warrant a joint congressional committee (atomic energy, defense production, economic policy, and reduction of nonessential federal expenditures are the other four). Established in 1926, the Joint Committee on Internal Revenue Taxation consists of five ranking members each from the House Ways and Means Committee and from the Senate Finance Committee, with three from the majority party and two from the minority party. Its official functions are to review large refunds proposed by the commissioner of internal revenue and to make studies for the two tax committees. The joint committee itself does not participate in the legislative process. In practice, however, its major function is to provide a technical staff of about fifteen lawyers and economists to prepare tax legislation for the committees. Additional help is provided by the committees themselves and by the legislative counsels of the House and Senate, who do the actual drafting. Treasury experts are also available for assistance during the legislative process. Through long and intimate association, the committees have learned to rely on the various staffs for background information needed to help formulate a consensus and to assist in translating committee decisions into legislative language.

The present tax structure is an outgrowth of legislation dating back to the beginning of the republic. The laws were first assembled and codified in the *Internal Revenue Code of 1939*, which was completely revised and superseded by the *Internal Revenue Code of 1954*. Changes in the tax laws have since been enacted as amendments to the 1954 code.

The code is a technical and complex legal document. Many of its sections reflect years of study and analysis by government and nongovernment tax experts. Few people have mastered its technicalities and nuances. Nevertheless, it is the vehicle through which the federal government now collects $200 billion of internal revenues annually. It is also the basis upon which each year over 100 million tax returns are filed, 50 million refunds are paid, 2.5 million delinquent notices are served to taxpayers, and more than 500 people are convicted of tax crimes.

Between 1948 and 1969 Congress enacted thirteen major tax bills and dozens of lesser bills. Each bill required months of preparation before the President made his recommendation, and from one to eighteen months before it was passed by the Congress. The two tax committees listened to hundreds of witnesses presenting thousands of pages of testimony. The final bills ranged in size from a few pages to 984 pages in 1954, when the code was recodified. Six of the major bills increased taxes on balance, six reduced them, and tax liabilities were not changed in one; the amounts involved ranged from a net increase of $10.2 billion in 1968 to a net reduction of $11.4 billion in 1964 (Table 3-1).

The tax system cannot be understood without an appreciation of the personalities, pressures, forces, and conflicts involved in making the many difficult decisions that shape a tax bill. This chapter describes the manner in which Congress considers and enacts tax legislation, and also describes some of the key people in the process. It will be concerned only with tax legislation; tax administration and enforcement, which are extremely important in the overall tax process from the standpoint of the individual taxpayer, fall outside the scope of this volume.

Executive Preparation of a Tax Bill

The Treasury Department has primary responsibility for the vast amount of work that goes into preparation of the President's tax recommendations. The work is supervised by the assistant secretary for tax policy (or occasionally by the under secretary). He has at his disposal two staffs: an Office of Tax Analysis, consisting of twenty-five to thirty economists and statisticians who provide the economic analysis of tax problems, estimates of the revenue effects of tax changes, and revenue projections for the budget; and an Office of the Tax Legislative Counsel, consisting of about twenty tax attorneys and an expert in accounting, who are responsible for legal and accounting analyses of tax problems, drafting of tax legislation, and review and approval of tax regulations. The assistant secretary calls on the technical, legal, and statistical facilities of the Internal Revenue Service for assistance as needed. He may also seek advice or assistance from consultants in academic, business, and professional fields, or in other government agencies.

It is difficult to pinpoint how and when the decision is made to study a particular tax or set of taxes. The impetus often comes from outside groups and experts after considerable public discussion, agitation, and pressure. Occasionally the congressional committees request assurances that certain matters will be taken up in the next tax bill. Or the President, after formal or informal consultation with his

TABLE 3-1. Legislative History of Major Federal Tax Bills Enacted, and Revenue Gain or Loss, 1948–69

Title of act	Date of President's message	Date of House passage	Date of Senate passage	Date of enactment	Time between initiation and enactment (months)	Full-year revenue gain (+) or loss (−) (billions of dollars)
Revenue Act of 1948	a	2/2/48	3/22/48	4/2/48[b]	3[c]	−5.0
Revenue Act of 1950	1/23/50	6/29/50	9/1/50	9/23/50	8	+4.6
Excess Profits Tax Act of 1950	d	12/5/50	12/20/50	1/3/51	3	+3.3
Revenue Act of 1951	2/2/51	6/22/51	9/28/51	10/20/51	8	+5.7
Internal Revenue Code of 1954	1/21/54[e]	3/18/54	7/2/54	8/16/54	7	+1.4
Excise Tax Reduction Act of 1954	a	3/10/54	3/25/54	3/31/54	2[c]	−1.0
Federal-Aid Highway Act of 1956	2/22/55	4/27/56	5/29/56	6/29/56	16	+2.5
Revenue Act of 1962	4/20/61[f]	3/29/62	9/6/62	10/16/62	18	−0.2[g]
Revenue Act of 1964	1/24/63	9/25/63	2/7/64	2/26/64	13	−11.4
Excise Tax Reduction Act of 1965	5/17/65[f]	6/2/65	6/15/65	6/21/65	1	−4.7
Tax Adjustment Act of 1966	1/24/66[e]	2/23/66	3/9/66	3/15/66	2	h
Revenue and Expenditure Control Act of 1968	8/3/67	2/29/68	4/2/68	6/28/68	11	+10.2
Tax Reform Act of 1969	4/21/69	8/7/69	12/11/69	12/30/69	8	−2.5

Sources: *Congressional Record, Congressional Quarterly, Annual Reports of the Secretary of the Treasury.*
a Not recommended by the President.
b Passed by Congress over President's veto.
c Time elapsed from date of first consideration by House Ways and Means Committee.
d Revenue Act of 1950 directed the House and Senate tax committees to report to their respective houses an excess profits tax bill retroactive to July 1 or Oct. 1, 1950. No special message by President.
e Recommended by President in his Budget Message.
f Recommended initially in the Budget Message transmitted in January of the year indicated.
g Net after offsetting revenue increases of about $800 million.
h Bill introduced graduated withholding for individual income tax purposes and accelerated corporation income tax payments, but did not alter tax liabilities.

advisers, may signal a new departure in tax policy in a speech or news conference. For example, the first official word that President Kennedy was considering a large tax reduction came in a news conference on June 7, 1962.

Studies of possible tax legislation are constantly in progress at the Treasury. Intensive work on a particular measure may begin after a decision is made by the President on the advice of responsible officials in his administration. The Council of Economic Advisers and the Office of Management and Budget (formerly the Bureau of the Budget) are equal partners in making decisions on fiscal policy, and they participate in decisions on major features of the tax bill. Decisions on technical tax questions in proposed legislation are usually made within the Treasury (subject, of course, to the approval of the President).

Materials prepared within the Treasury on the various aspects of the tax program include economic, legal, and accounting memoranda discussing each problem from almost every angle. The analysis reviews the history of the problem, evaluates its impact on particular groups and industries and on the economy as a whole, and presents the equity, economic, revenue, and administrative arguments for and against alternative solutions. Lawyers, accountants, economists, and statisticians participate in this evaluation. Task forces, committees, or informal working groups consisting of representatives of the Treasury and other federal agencies may be organized to consider alternative solutions. Most of the work is done within the executive branch, frequently in cooperation with the staff of the Joint Committee on Internal Revenue Taxation, which plays a crucial role in the tax legislative process. Discussions are also held by senior staff members of the Treasury with industry and labor representatives, officials of business corporations, professional groups, the academic community, and other knowledgeable individuals.

Work on a major tax bill begins months before the administration's recommendations are transmitted to the Congress; in some cases, the lead time may be as much as a year or longer. The information amassed during these months of research and analysis is funneled through the assistant secretary for tax policy. He may initiate new studies, suggest other approaches, and ask for still more information. He also consults the various experts individually or in groups to narrow the range of alternatives. The secretary of the treasury keeps in touch with the work at all stages and makes the final decision on the program that is submitted to the President, often after consulting other government officials and members of the White House staff.

In a typical year the main features of the tax bill are completed by mid-December. At this time, the President reviews the proposal and approves or modifies it. Final revenue figures are estimated by the Treasury on the basis of an economic projection prepared by the Council of Economic Advisers in consultation with other federal agencies. Drafts of sections to be included in the budget message and the economic report are prepared, and a start is made on the materials to be submitted for congressional consideration.

The President sometimes mentions the broad outlines of his tax program in the State of the Union message. Further elaboration is given in the budget message, which must be transmitted fifteen days after Congress convenes, and the broad economic justification is presented in the economic report, which is due on or before January 20. (In practice, there is some slippage in these dates, and with the consent of Congress the messages may be transmitted one or two weeks after they are legally due.) When the program covers a broad field or is particularly complicated, or when the President wishes to emphasize the importance of his recommendations, he transmits a special tax message to Congress, usually at the end of January or in February; occasionally, when circumstances require new tax legislation, a special tax message is transmitted later in the year.

Disclosure of a major tax program signals the beginning of public debate. Representatives of business, farm, labor, and other groups begin to make pronouncements about the wisdom of the program. National organizations like the Committee for Economic Development, the U.S. Chamber of Commerce, the National Association of Manufacturers, the AFL-CIO, the major international labor unions, trade associations, and citizens committees scrutinize the program carefully from the standpoint of their own interests and what they regard as the public interest. Newspapers, periodicals, radio, and television discuss major aspects of the program.

By the time the House Ways and Means Committee opens public hearings on the bill (usually in February or March), the lines of support and opposition are drawn. At this point Congress takes over.

The Bill in Congress

Article I, Section 7, of the Constitution states that "All bills for raising revenue shall originate in the House of Representatives." Accordingly, a tax bill begins its legislative history in the House and is transmitted to the Senate after the House has completed action. Otherwise, the Senate is an equal partner in the tax legislative process and frequently makes extensive and fundamental changes in the House version.

The Ways and Means Committee

The tax legislative process begins in the Committee on Ways and Means of the House of Representatives. The committee consists of twenty-five members, most of them relatively senior, divided between majority and minority parties in approximate proportion to their representation in the House. It has responsibility for revenue, debt, customs, trade, and social security legislation. The Democrats on it select the Democratic membership of other committees—a role that makes it the most powerful committee in the House.

The committee begins its study by scheduling public hearings for persons who request an opportunity to testify. The Ways and Means Committee room, which seats more than a thousand people, is usually filled to capacity for the first witness, the secretary of the treasury. His testimony typically begins with a long, carefully prepared statement, which gives the full rationale for the administration's position. For example, Secretary Dillon's presentation on the 1964 bill in January 1963 lasted two days and totaled 643 closely printed pages, including a main oral statement of 31 pages and 612 pages of supplementary tables, legal and technical explanations, and memoranda of analysis.

The secretary ordinarily reads his statement without interruption. The chairman then opens the interrogation and turns the questioning over to each member of the committee, alternating between majority and minority party members in order of seniority. Committee members may take this opportunity to make a public record of the positions they expect to take. Sympathetic members ask questions to buttress the administration's position or to help prepare the way for suitable compromises on difficult issues; those who are opposed attempt to trap the secretary into making untenable, erroneous, and inconsistent statements so as to discredit the tax proposals. Key committee members have a detailed knowledge of the tax law and the intricacies of the new tax bill. The secretary, in turn, is usually well briefed and handles most of the questions himself, turning to an associate for assistance only in connection with technical matters. Occasionally, he handles a question by promising a written reply to be included in the printed record.

After the secretary's testimony, the committee may hear witnesses from other executive agencies. For example, in 1963, the secretaries of commerce and labor and the director of the bureau of the budget appeared before the committee. Testimony is then heard from bankers, businessmen, lawyers, economists, and others representing the interests of private groups (and sometimes of individual clients). Except when the administration's witnesses testify, the broader "public interest" is seldom represented. On rare occasions unaffiliated individuals and representatives of public-spirited organizations take the trouble to appear. In a few instances the committee has invited professional economists to testify as experts, but this is not general practice.

Meanwhile, the committee members are besieged in private by large numbers of people seeking changes in the bill. Through these contacts, the committee evaluates the strength of the forces aligned for and against the bill.

The hearings continue until all interested parties have testified. The length of the hearings depends on the importance of the bill, the controversy it has aroused, and the positions of the committee chairman and ranking members. If there is considerable opposition, the hearings may continue for months. For example, twelve days of hearings were held in 1964 by the Ways and Means Committee on what eventually became the Excise Tax Reduction Act of 1965, while the hearings on the controversial Tax Reform Act of 1969 lasted about seven weeks.

After concluding the hearings, the committee goes into executive session. These sessions are conducted in an informal, seminar-type atmosphere. Members of the committee discuss the bill freely, calling on the staffs of the Joint Internal Revenue Committee and the Treasury for information, advice, and assistance as needed. Each proposal is carefully explained by Treasury officials and staff members, and the relevant information and opinions assembled during the hearings are summarized. Votes are taken only after members are satisfied that they have all the information needed to make up their minds.

Several people play a major role in the process of negotiation and compromise that takes place in executive sessions. The most important figure is the chairman of the Ways and Means Committee, who is not only the presiding officer but also the chief moderator. The ranking spokesman for the minority also exercises substantial influence, particularly if he can persuade a few members of the majority to side with him. The chief of staff of the Joint Internal Revenue Committee supervises the large secretariat that assists the Ways and Means Committee in its deliberations. He attends all sessions, joins in negotiations on the bill, and helps shape the compromise proposed by the chairman and other committee members. The assistant secretary of the treasury acts as chief negotiator for the administration (under instructions from the President and the secretary of the treasury). The secretary often participates in the executive sessions when key issues are discussed.

As tentative decisions are reached, they are translated into legislative language. Preparation of the legislative draft is the responsibility of the legislative counsel of the House of Representatives, but the staffs of the Joint Internal Revenue Committee and the Treasury are regularly called on for assistance. The drafting process is usually slow and time-consuming in the attempt to make the intent of the committee explicit and the provisions of the bill as unambiguous as possible. Considering the pressure under which the draftsmen operate and the complexity of the material, remarkably few errors are made in the process, which is generally completed for quick final action by the committee shortly after the last tentative decision has been made.

At this time, work begins on the committee's report under the direction of the chief of staff of the Joint Internal Revenue Committee. The report, frequently several hundred pages in length, contains a detailed statement of the committee's rationale for recommending the bill, estimates of its effect on revenues, and a section-by-section analysis of its provisions. It also contains the minority views of committee members who disapprove of the bill. As the only written record of the reasons for the committee's actions, the report serves to inform members of the House and provides a basis for later interpretation of the legislation by the Internal Revenue Service and the courts.

When the report is completed, the Ways and Means Committee approves it and instructs the chairman to send the bill to the House.

House Approval

According to the rules of the House of Representatives, revenue legislation is "privileged" business, which obtains priority consideration on the floor. In practice, however, the approval of the Rules Committee is always sought before the bill is placed on the calendar for floor action. This is done so that the tax bill can be debated under a "closed rule," which requires the House to accept or reject the entire bill except for amendments approved by the Ways and Means Committee.

Because it is conducted under a closed rule, debate on the tax bill in the House is brief, lasting usually only two or three days. The Ways and Means Committee chairman acts as floor manager and chief proponent. Other members of the majority are assigned to defend particular aspects of the bill. The opposition, usually led by the ranking minority member of the committee, may attack the bill with vigor and predict great harm to the nation if it is enacted. But the chairman and ranking minority member of the committee work closely together on every bill and often join in pushing a tax bill through the House.

At the end of the debate, a motion is presented to recommit the bill to the Ways and Means Committee with instructions to report it back with one or more specified amendments. This motion, which provides the test vote on the most controversial aspects of the bill, enables its opponents to obtain a vote on a modified version without having to reject the bill altogether. Then there is a final vote on the bill itself. Only on rare occasions has a major tax bill reported by the Ways and Means Committee been rejected by the House.

The Senate Finance Committee

After House passage, the bill is sent to the Senate, where it is immediately referred to the Committee on Finance. This committee of seventeen senior and influential senators has jurisdiction over tax, trade, and social security legislation, veterans' affairs, and other financial matters. Its organization and operations are similar to those of the Ways and Means Committee.

The Finance Committee begins by holding public hearings, and the secretary of the treasury is again the first witness. His appearance here is no less an ordeal than his appearance before the Ways and Means Committee. He may largely repeat his arguments, although focusing his testimony on the House version of the bill. He may ask the committee to modify or reject certain provisions that are unacceptable to the administration; or he may accept the House modifications with only a slight demurrer. The secretary is followed by much the same parade of witnesses that appeared before the Ways and Means Committee, in many instances repeating their earlier statements.

In executive session, most of the cast of characters that assisted on the House side now appear on the Senate side. The Finance Committee usually starts with the first section of the bill and considers amendments proposed by the members in order. On rare occasions the committee approves a substantially unamended version of the bill, but typically the bill is changed in significant respects before it is reported to the Senate. For example, the Senate Finance Committee report on the 1969 tax bill listed over forty major amendments to the House bill and reduced the revenue gained from tax reform by $250 million a year.

When the Finance Committee has agreed on a bill, the staff prepares the committee report, which covers the same ground as the Ways and Means Committee report (often in identical language) and explains the reasons for the Finance Committee amendments.

The Senate Debate

Unlike the House, the Senate places no limit on debate or amendments. Many amendments are offered on the floor. Some of them are intended to change the entire character of the bill, and some are completely unrelated to the subject matter of the bill. Administration officers are usually very active at this stage. The President's aides and Senate leaders of his party work together to defeat amendments that are unacceptable to the administration or to restore provisions deleted by the Finance Committee.

Senate discussion of a tax bill is longer and more colorful than that in the House. Individual senators take the occasion not only to make a record but also to try to persuade their colleagues. The debate usually concerns features of the bill that directly affect the pocketbooks of particular groups and individuals and is often highly technical. The debates on many of the postwar tax bills (for example, on the 1951, 1962, 1964, and 1969 acts) rank among the most informed discussions held on the Senate floor.

Most of the amendments proposed on the floor are opposed by the administration or the Finance Committee and are rejected; but the Senate has been known to act against the wishes of both the administration and the committee majority. On the other hand, the Senate debate is the only stage in the entire legislative process when the administration may successfully exercise pressure against the wishes of the powerful committee chairman and ranking committee members. Such pressure, of course, is used sparingly and only when needed on major issues.

After the bill has been debated and amended to the satisfaction of the Senate, it is brought to a vote. If it fails to pass, the legislation is abandoned. If the Senate passes the House bill without amendments, it is sent directly to the President. If the Senate amends the bill—and this is the rule rather than the exception—further congressional action is necessary. (During the thirteen days of Senate debate on the Tax Reform Act of 1969, 111 amendments were proposed, of which over 70 were accepted and made part of the Senate version of the bill.) The House generally adopts a motion to disagree with the Senate amendments, thus calling for appointment of a conference committee to adjust the differences between the two versions.

The Bill in Conference

The Committee of Conference is appointed by the speaker of the House and the president of the Senate. Both usually appoint three from the majority and two from the minority. On occasion, there is a difference in the number of conferees from the two chambers, but this has no bearing on the final decision reached by the committee, since each chamber votes as a unit with a majority controlling each group. The members of the committee are normally the senior members of the two tax committees, unless they elect not to serve.

Conferences may last from a day or two to a week or more, depending on the number of amendments, differences between the two versions, and the complexity of the bill under consideration. Joint Committee and Treasury staff members are often called upon to explain the issues, evaluate the feasibility of suggested compromises, and provide revenue estimates. The bill remains in conference until all differences between the House and Senate versions have been reconciled. High officials of the administration, including the secretary of the treasury and the President, follow the deliberations of the committee carefully and may intervene (directly or through subordinates) with individual conferees to obtain support for the administration's position.

The conference report merely lists the amendments accepted by each house and is highly technical. Floor statements explaining how the two bills were reconciled provide the essential information necessary for interpreting the legislation.

After approval of the conference report by both houses, the bill is sent to the White House.

Presidential Action

As in the case of all legislation, the President has ten days to consider the bill. During this period, the various government departments analyze the bill and submit their views in the form of written memoranda to the Office of Management and Budget. The major issues are then summarized by the office, and the President makes his final decision, often after hours of consultation and soul-searching with key officials and White House staff members.

By the time the bill reaches the President's desk, administration forces in Congress have tried every legislative device to modify it to meet his requirements. For this reason, the President rarely vetoes a tax bill, even though very few of them satisfy him in every detail. In the past thirty years, only two important bills—the Revenue Act of 1943 and the Revenue Act of 1948—have been vetoed, the former by President Roosevelt and the latter on three occasions in 1947 and 1948 by President Truman. Congress passed both bills over the President's veto by the necessary two-thirds majority. (The 1943 veto led to the temporary resignation of Senator Alben Barkley from his position as majority leader.) Since 1948, the President has signed every major tax bill that has passed both houses.

The President usually issues a statement when he has acted on the bill. If he has approved it, the statement is brief and usually expresses pleasure over its enactment. Occasionally he takes exception to some of its provisions, even though he has signed it. If he has vetoed the bill, he issues a longer statement or message explaining why it is unacceptable.

A tax bill may provide that the rates take effect within a few days after its final approval. For example, the lower withholding rates provided by the 1964 act became effective eight days after the President signed it. Some of the excise tax reductions of 1965 were put into effect the day following enactment. Some tax bills have been retroactive, reducing or increasing tax liabilities from the beginning of the calendar year, fiscal year, or quarter in which the bill was finally approved. Others have taken effect at the end of the year.

After the President has signed the bill, the Treasury issues regulations to explain its interpretation of the new law, and the Internal Revenue Service prepares to administer it by issuing new tax forms, advice to taxpayers, revised instructions to withholding agents, and so on. The issuance of regulations may itself be a lengthy process, sometimes requiring over a year if the legislation is particularly complex. Long before these tasks have been completed, a new tax bill may be under way, and the same harassed officials who are responsible for implementing the old law begin the new tax legislative cycle.

Improving the Process

The tax legislative process has been examined by numerous congressional committees, political scientists, students of taxation, citizen and professional committees, and other groups. Opinion is generally critical: the process is said to be unnecessarily influenced by special interest groups who do not speak in the national interest; it does not give Congress an opportunity to make decisions on the government's overall fiscal policy or to weigh the needs for public services against tax costs; and its slowness restricts the possibilities of prompt tax action for stabilization or other reasons. Each of these criticisms has some validity, but practical solutions are hard to devise.

Representation of the Public Interest

Individuals who appear before the two tax committees hardly represent a cross section of opinion on tax matters. The committees generally permit anyone to testify and rarely invite expert testimony, except from administration officials. The result is that, day after day, the committees are subject to a drumfire of complaints against the tax system, arguments why special tax advantages should not be eliminated, and reasons why additional preferences are needed.

In such an atmosphere, the secretary of the treasury assumes the role of defender of the national interest. He spends much of his time fighting off new tax advantages and is only moderately successful in eliminating old ones. Whether taxes are to be raised or lowered, most of the witnesses find good reasons for favoring the groups or individuals they represent. The secretary takes a broader, national view and tries to strike a balance among competing claims. Since the stakes are high and there are no generally accepted criteria for evaluating questions of tax policy, his decisions may be regarded as arbitrary or contrary to the public interest by some groups and be vigorously opposed in open hearings or in behind-the-scenes lobbying. Occasionally, he is supported by some of the national citizens' organizations, but testimony from them—although more frequent in recent years—is still the exception rather than the rule.

Fortunately, the committee members are not neophytes in the legislative process. Most of them have the capacity to detect a self-serving witness. Furthermore, they have an excellent opportunity to check the merits of the public testimony in executive session with the staffs of the Joint Internal Revenue Committee and the Treasury. When the hearings are particularly long and involved, the staffs prepare confidential summaries of the pros and cons of the various positions. Through such methods, individual committee members familiarize themselves with the major issues and evaluate the mass of information hurled at them.

It would be helpful, nevertheless, to give the public, congressmen, and committee members easier access to impartial analysis and expert opinion on tax matters. Two things can be done to improve consideration of tax legislation in committee without altering the present balance of power.

First, the Joint Internal Revenue Committee or the two separate committees might organize special subcommittees to provide background materials *before* a tax issue is put on the legislative calendar. Subcommittees are used sporadically now and generally only on highly technical subjects. It should be possible to divide the entire field of taxation among several subcommittees that would be responsible for continually reviewing the subjects assigned to them and for soliciting new ideas. Their procedures might follow the pattern set by the Ways and Means Committee's famous 1959 *Tax Revision Compendium*, a three-volume collection of articles by leading tax experts, which has greatly influenced all tax legislation since its publication.

Second, the method of scheduling the open hearings held by the tax committees could be revamped. Most witnesses now simply read prepared statements and depart without any interrogation by committee members. The committee chairman already has the authority (which, in practice, is exercised by the committee counsel) to invite testimony from selected experts when it becomes evident that some points of view will not be represented. More regular use should be made of this authority to invite individuals or panels of experts to testify on the economic and technical aspects of tax legislation. To speed the hearings, the chairmen should limit the number of witnesses representing one point of view. This would not preclude the filing of statements by others for publication in the official record of the hearings.

Consideration of Overall Fiscal Policies

Legislative control over the fiscal policies of the federal government is now divided between the appropriations committees and the tax committees. The result is that Congress cannot make decisions about the size of the budget in relation to total taxes collected. Nor can it decide whether economic conditions warrant a surplus or a deficit, or how large the surplus or deficit should be.

Some have argued that this fractionation of the expenditure-tax process encourages higher expenditures, since no one committee must face up to the need for balancing benefits against costs. In fact, however, the process has probably been too restrictive in recent years. Congress has been slow to accept the principle that a major objective of fiscal policy should be to promote full employment, although a good deal of progress has been made since the enactment of the Revenue Act of 1964 (see Chapter 2). The appropriations committees, which act through a large number of subcommittees working on individual agency appropriations, view their roles as primarily that of watchdogs over the efficiency of government operations, rather than of general policy makers; and the tax committees are conservative about changing the level of taxes either upward or downward. The disappointing performance of the economy in the late 1950s is now widely acknowledged to have been in large part the result of overly restrictive fiscal (and monetary) policies. Similarly, the tax reductions made by the Congress in 1969, to take effect over the next several years, put a tight limit on government expenditures at a time when there was an urgent need for federal spending on domestic social and economic programs.

Fiscal policy planning and guidance by the President are undertaken primarily through his annual budget messages and economic reports. These are reviewed and considered by the Joint Economic Committee, which was created by the Employment Act of 1946. Its hearings, which are usually brief but structured to bring out opposing views, and its report on the President's economic report, have improved public and congressional understanding of economic policy problems. However, the Joint Economic Committee does not have authority to propose or initiate legislation.

It has been suggested from time to time that a joint committee on the budget should be created to give Congress a greater role in fiscal policy planning. This was tried in 1947 and 1948 (the Joint Committee on the Legislative Budget), but the results were disappointing. The committee did not have enough information to make judgments regarding overall fiscal policy, and its recommendations were not binding on the appropriations and tax committees. As a result, the committee resolutions were political in nature and served little purpose. The effort was abandoned after both houses ignored the resolutions.

The Revenue and Expenditure Control Act of 1968 imposed a limit on some government expenditures at the insistence of the chairman of the Ways and Means Committee, who viewed the growth of government expenditures with alarm. Whether this attempt to legislate the level of total expenditures in a tax bill did very much good is still the subject of debate. But it is clear that control of expenditures can hardly be exercised in a responsible manner through the tax process.

Since the appropriations and tax committees cannot be expected to give up any of their authority, hope for improving consideration of overall fiscal policy must lie in better liaison with the Joint Economic Committee. After twenty-five years of effective operation, this committee now commands considerable respect from members of Congress and the public. To make its influence felt more directly on actual legislation, the Joint Economic Committee should make frequent public reports on fiscal developments, evaluate their impact on the economy, and recommend specific legislative changes for action by the appropriations and tax committees. (Reports on budget developments are made sporadically, usually at the request of the chairmen, by the Joint Internal Revenue Committee and the Joint Committee on Reduction of Nonessential Federal Expenditures, which, after twenty-nine years of obscurity, published a "budget scorekeeping report" in 1970.) Closer cooperation between the staffs of the Joint Internal Revenue Committee and the Joint Economic Committee would be desirable, perhaps through special task forces to consider problems of national interest and through participation of key staff members in the executive sessions of other committees operating in the economic field.

Accelerating Tax Action

The most serious drawback of the tax legislative process is that it cannot be used to raise or lower taxes quickly. The President does not have a practical method for obtaining immediate congressional consideration of a new tax proposal, since tradition dictates that all tax changes must be carefully considered by the Ways and Means Committee and the Finance Committee. The delay in enactment of the Vietnam war surtax prevented timely action to control the inflation that was already under way. To combat recessions, exclusive reliance has been placed on expenditure changes, which have two shortcomings. They create inefficiencies in the conduct of government programs that should not be turned on and off for short-run economic reasons. They also tend to have a delayed impact on the economy because of the long lead time generally required to put them into effect.

Many tax experts and national citizens' organizations have recommended that the President be authorized to make temporary increases or reductions in tax rates. This approach would emphasize changes that are neutral in their impact on the existing tax structure, as opposed to changes that would alter the distribution of the tax burden. More fundamental reforms would be reserved for long-run revisions of the tax structure, which necessarily involve lengthy and searching debate.

In general, the proposals would permit the President to make a uniform change—up or down—in individual income tax rates of a maximum percent or a maximum number of percentage points for a period of six months, with the authority to renew the change for additional six-month periods as conditions required. The change would take effect thirty or sixty days after submission to Congress, unless it were rejected by a joint resolution. President Kennedy made such a recommendation (but limited it to changes in a downward direction) in 1962 and 1963, and President Johnson renewed it in 1964; but the tax committees have shown no interest in this approach and have not even brought it up for discussion.

President Johnson modified the proposal in his 1965 economic report to allay suspicion that he sought to preempt congressional authority over tax rates. He suggested that Congress merely alter its procedures to permit rapid action on temporary income tax cuts proposed by the President to combat recession. (Tax increases were not mentioned.) Because of congressional sensitivity, the President did not fill in the details, preferring to have Congress make the decision. After Congress acted swiftly on excise tax legislation in 1965, President Johnson modified his position still further. His 1966 economic report simply stressed the need for background studies to establish guidelines for temporary tax changes.

As a result of the long delays on the tax proposals made by Presidents Johnson and Nixon during the Vietnam war, experts believe that the only practical way to speed congressional action on changes in tax rates is for the President to establish the practice of formally recommending at the beginning of each year a positive or negative surtax (of the type enacted during the Vietnam war) or no tax change at all. If the Congress acted promptly on this recommendation, other tax changes would be needed during the year only in wartime or other emergencies. Adoption of this practice would go a long way toward increasing the speed and flexibility of the tax legislative process.

Summary

The tax legislative process begins in the Treasury and other federal agencies where tax problems are analyzed and solutions are proposed for the President's consideration. The President transmits his recommendations to the Congress, where they are carefully reviewed by the two powerful tax committees, are revised to compromise the conflicts of major opposing interests, and are sent in turn to the House and Senate floors for approval. Differences between the two bills are settled by a conference committee; the revised version is returned to both houses for approval; and the bill becomes law when the President signs it or when Congress passes it over his veto.

The tax legislative process is unique in several respects. The work concerns a highly complex set of laws, yet all the decisions are made (as they should be) through the political process. Key roles are played by the President, the secretary of the treasury and his assistant secretary for tax policy, the chairmen of the two tax committees, and the chief of staff of the Joint Internal Revenue Committee. Behind the scenes, competent staffs in both the executive and legislative branches help move the tax bill through its various stages. For all these people, a tax bill is a grueling experience, demanding physical stamina as well as political acumen.

Reform of the tax process is needed: (1) to give better representation to the public interest in the open hearings conducted by the Ways and Means Committee and the Finance Committee; (2) to increase attention to overall fiscal policies by the appropriations and tax committees and both houses of Congress; and (3) to accelerate congressional action on tax changes to combat inflation or recession. Suggestions for implementing these objectives have frequently been made, but Congress has not given them serious consideration.

Some believe that the federal tax legislative process impedes progress toward a better tax system, but this is probably an unfair assessment of the work of the congressional tax committees and an unrealistic appraisal of the balance of forces for and against tax reform. While many questionable provisions have crept into the U.S. tax laws, erosion of the tax base has been halted in recent years, and some steps have been taken to reverse it. Moreover, the overall distribution of federal taxes continues to be progressive despite the strong interests arrayed against progression and equitable taxation. More progress will be made along these lines only when sufficient political power is mobilized to persuade the tax committees, and the Congress as a whole, that tax reform has widespread and determined popular support.

CHAPTER FOUR

The Individual Income Tax

ANY SURVEY OF TAX SOURCES should begin with the nation's fairest
and most productive source of revenue, the individual income tax.
All advanced industrial countries levy a direct tax on individual incomes, but nowhere is this tax as important as in the United States.
In recent years, 45 percent of federal budget receipts have come from
this source.

The individual income tax is uniquely suited for raising revenue
in a democratic country where the distribution of income, and therefore of ability to pay, is unequal. Theoreticians may disagree about
the meaningfulness of the term "ability to pay," but the close association between a man's income and his taxpaying ability is commonly
accepted. There is also general acceptance of the idea that the income
tax should be progressive.

The individual income tax has still another attractive feature. Income alone does not determine a man's ability to pay; his family
responsibilities are also important. A single person may be able to get
along on an income of $4,000 a year, but a married man with two
children would have great difficulty in making ends meet on that
income. The individual income tax takes such differences into account
by allowing personal exemptions and deductions, which are subtracted from an individual's total income to arrive at his income subject to tax.

For almost thirty years after its adoption in 1913, the individual income tax applied mainly to a small number of high income people. Exemptions were high by today's standards, and few incomes were large enough to be subject to tax at the lowest rate, let alone the higher graduated rates. In the national effort to raise needed revenue during World War II, exemptions were drastically reduced. They were raised again in 1946, 1948, and 1970 and are scheduled to rise further in 1971, 1972, and 1973, but have remained low by prewar standards. Tax rates were also raised in wartime and have remained much higher than in earlier years. At the same time, personal incomes have continued to increase with the growth of the economy (and with the inflation associated with World War II, the Korean war, and the Vietnam war.) The combination of lower exemptions, higher rates, and higher incomes increased the yield of the individual income tax manyfold. In 1939, tax liabilities were about $1 billion; in 1970, they were more than $90 billion.

This tremendous expansion would not have been possible without ready compliance with income tax laws and effective administration. In many countries where compliance is poor and administration is weak, there is great reluctance to rely heavily on the income tax. In this country, the record of compliance is good—although it can still be improved—and practical methods have been developed for administering a mass income tax, at a cost of only about ½ of 1 percent of the tax collected. In the late 1930s, many people—even highly placed officials of the Bureau of Internal Revenue—doubted that an income tax covering almost everyone could be administered effectively. Although some problems remain, in an advanced country the administrative feasibility of an individual income tax of almost universal coverage is no longer questioned.

There are good economic reasons for using the income tax as a major source of revenue. The automatic flexibility of the tax promotes economic stability, and the progressive rates reduce excessive concentration of economic power and control. Some believe that the income tax is needed also to moderate the growth of private savings of high income people, which is likely to hold down private demand for goods and services. Others believe that a high income tax impairs work and investment incentives and, therefore, reduces the nation's economic growth. These are difficult questions, which will be discussed later. Nonetheless, it is correct to say that the modern individual income tax, if carefully designed and well administered, is a powerful and essential economic instrument for a modern industrial economy.

Structure of the Federal Income Tax

The basic structure of the federal income tax is simple. The taxpayer adds up his income from all taxable sources, subtracts certain allowable deductions and exemptions for himself, his wife, his children, and other dependents, and then applies the tax rates to the remainder. But this procedure has many pitfalls for the taxpayer, and difficult questions of tax policy arise at almost every stage. Therefore, it is important to understand the main features of the income tax structure.

Adjusted Gross Income and Taxable Income

The two major concepts of income that appear on the tax return are: adjusted gross income and taxable income.

Adjusted gross income is the closest approach in tax law to what an economist might call "total income." But it departs from an economic definition of income in important respects. It is the total income from all taxable sources, less certain expenses incurred in earning that income. In general, only *money* income is treated as taxable, but many items of money income are excluded. These exclusions include one-half of realized capital gains on assets held for six months or more, interest on state and local government bonds, all transfer payments (for example, social security benefits and unemployment compensation), fringe benefits received by employees from their employers (the most important of these are contributions to pension plans), and income on savings through life insurance. The emphasis on money income means that automatically unrealized capital gains and such imputed income as the rental value of owner-occupied homes are excluded.

Adjusted gross income is used on the tax return in two ways. First, it is the income concept built into the simplified tax table, which is used for determining tax on more than 25 million returns. Second, it provides the basis for placing limits on some of the personal deductions that are subtracted in computing taxable income.

Taxable income is computed by making two sets of deductions from adjusted gross income. The first are those personal expenditures that are allowed as deductions by law—charitable contributions, interest paid, state-local income, general sales, property, and gasoline taxes, medical and dental expenses above 3 percent of adjusted gross income, and casualty and theft losses above $100 for each loss. In lieu of these deductions, the taxpayer may use the *standard deduction*, which was 10 percent of adjusted gross income (up to a maximum of $1,000) for the period 1944–69 and will be gradually increased to 15 percent (up to a maximum of $2,000) by 1973. A minimum standard deduction of $200, plus $100 for each exemption, which was in effect from 1964 through 1969, has been replaced by a "low-income allowance," which began at $1,100 in 1970 and is reduced to $1,050 in 1971 and $1,000 in 1972 and thereafter.

When the standard deduction was first adopted in 1944, it was used by over 80 percent of the persons filing returns. As incomes have risen and deductible expenditures have increased, the percentage using the standard deduction has declined. In 1968, the standard deduction was still being used on 41.7 million returns, or 56.5 percent of the 73.7 million filed (Appendix Table C-6). But the amount of the standard deduction was small compared to the itemized deductions, which have increased with the growth of home ownership, state-local taxes, and use of consumer credit, as well as the normal increase in expenditures that occurs as incomes rise. Total deductions reported on all 1968 returns amounted to $91.3 billion; of this amount, $69.2 billion were itemized deductions, and $22.1 billion were standard deductions.

The second set of deductions provides an allowance for personal exemptions. The exemptions for the taxpayer, his wife, and other dependents are on a per capita basis at the rate of $625 per person in 1970, $650 in 1971, $700 in 1972, and $750 in 1973 and later years. The law also gives one additional exemption each to a taxpayer and his wife if they are over 65 years of age, and still another exemption to the blind.

Figure 4-1 traces the changes in the tax base (that is, taxable income) since the beginning of World War II. In 1939, only $7.2 billion, or about 10 percent of personal income, was subject to tax; by 1968, it had risen to $352.7 billion, or 51 percent of personal income. This spectacular increase was caused by the two factors mentioned earlier—the substantial reductions in exemptions and the upward shifts in incomes. The rise has been interrupted only when nontaxable

FIGURE 4-1. Ratio of Taxable Individual Income to Personal Income, 1939–68

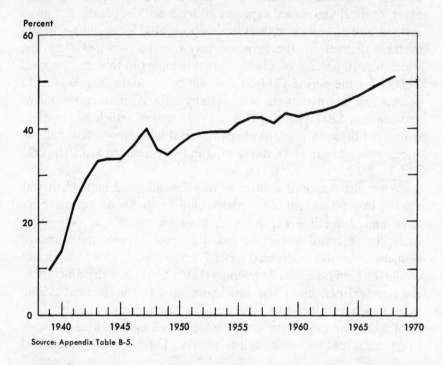

Source: Appendix Table B-5.

military pay was very large (1945), when exemptions were increased (1948), and when nontaxable transfer payments increased during recession years (1949, 1954, 1958, and 1960).

Between 1948 and 1968, when the definition of the tax base remained virtually unchanged (except for changes in 1964, which were roughly offsetting), 57.9 percent of the increase in personal income went into the tax base, 13.4 percent represented differences in definition between personal income and adjusted gross income, 3.8 percent either was not reported on tax returns or was received by persons who were not taxable, 10.8 percent was accounted for by exemptions and another 14.1 percent by deductions (Table 4-1). Stated somewhat differently, about $5.8 billion out of every $10 billion increase in personal income went into the tax base.

Tax Rates

The tax rates are graduated by a bracket system (Table 4-2). Other methods of graduation have been used elsewhere, but this

TABLE 4-1. Comparison of Increases in Personal Income and the Federal Individual Income Tax Base, 1948–68[a]

Derivation of the tax base	Increase, 1948–68 (billions of dollars)	Percentage distribution
Personal income	478.5	100.0
Conceptual differences between adjusted gross income and personal income[b]	64.0	13.4
Adjusted gross income not reported on tax returns or reported by individuals who were not taxable	18.3	3.8
Personal exemptions on taxable returns	51.8	10.8
Personal deductions on taxable returns	67.3	14.1
Taxable income (tax base)	277.1[c]	57.9

Source: Appendix Tables B-2 and B-4. Figures are rounded and do not necessarily add to totals.
[a] No adjustment has been made for the relatively small impact of the Revenue Act of 1964 on the tax base.
[b] For details, see Appendix Table B-1.
[c] Does not include $800 million of taxable income on nontaxable returns.

seems to be the most practical. Under this system, the income scale is divided into segments, or brackets, and rates are applied only to the income in each bracket. Rates increase by no more than 5 percentage points from one bracket to the next, in order to avoid large and abrupt increases in tax rates as incomes rise.

There are now four separate rate schedules for different categories of taxpayers. The basic rates, which apply to married taxpayers filing separate returns, range from 14 percent on the first $500 of taxable income to 70 percent on the amount of taxable income above $100,-000. For married couples filing joint returns, the tax rates are applied to half the taxable income of the couple, and the result is multiplied by two. As Table 4-2 shows, this income-splitting feature doubles the width of the brackets for married couples. Single persons have a special rate schedule which insures that their tax is never more than 120 percent of the tax imposed on joint returns with the same total taxable income. Single persons who are heads of households also use a special rate schedule, with rates that are about half way between the rates for single persons and the rates for joint returns.

Although the rates are graduated up to $100,000 of taxable income, much of the tax base is concentrated in the lowest brackets. In 1967, 76 percent of taxable income was subject to the 14–19 percent rates in the first six brackets, and only 3 percent was taxed at rates of 50 percent or more (Appendix Table B-6).

TABLE 4-2. Federal Individual Income Tax Rates, 1971

	Tax rates (percentages)			
Taxable income (dollars)	Married couples (separate returns)	Single persons	Heads of households	Married couples (joint returns)
0– 500	14	14	14	14
500– 1,000	15	15	14	14
1,000– 1,500	16	16	16	15
1,500– 2,000	17	17	16	15
2,000– 3,000	19	19	18	16
3,000– 4,000	19	19	18	17
4,000– 6,000	22	21	19	19
6,000– 8,000	25	24	22	19
8,000– 10,000	28	25	23	22
10,000– 12,000	32	27	25	22
12,000– 14,000	36	29	27	25
14,000– 16,000	39	31	28	25
16,000– 18,000	42	34	31	28
18,000– 20,000	45	36	32	28
20,000– 22,000	48	38	35	32
22,000– 24,000	50	40	36	32
24,000– 26,000	50	40	38	36
26,000– 28,000	53	45	41	36
28,000– 32,000	53	45	42	39
32,000– 36,000	55	50	45	42
36,000– 38,000	55	50	48	45
38,000– 40,000	58	55	51	45
40,000– 44,000	58	55	52	48
44,000– 50,000	60	60	55	50
50,000– 52,000	62	62	56	50
52,000– 60,000	62	62	58	53
60,000– 64,000	64	64	58	53
64,000– 70,000	64	64	59	55
70,000– 76,000	66	66	61	55
76,000– 80,000	66	66	62	58
80,000– 88,000	68	68	63	58
88,000– 90,000	68	68	64	60
90,000–100,000	69	69	64	60
100,000–120,000	70	70	66	62
120,000–140,000	70	70	67	64
140,000–160,000	70	70	68	66
160,000–180,000	70	70	69	68
180,000–200,000	70	70	70	69
Over 200,000	70	70	70	70

Source: Internal Revenue Code.

In addition to the new rate schedule for single persons, the 1969 act introduced two additional features into the income tax. First, the tax rate on earned income (salaries and professional and self-employment income) was limited to a maximum marginal rate of 50 percent beginning in 1972 (60 percent in 1971). In effect, the provision slices off the rate schedule for earned incomes at 50 percent. Second, certain "tax preferences" were made subject to a new, separate minimum tax of 10 percent. The base of the minimum tax is computed by subtracting from the total of the statutory tax preferences a $30,000 exemption and the regular income tax for the year.

Methods of Tax Payment

Between 1913 and 1942, federal income taxes were paid in quarterly installments during the year following receipt of income. When the coverage of the income tax was extended to the majority of income recipients during World War II, it was realized that the old system could not operate successfully. Low-income people tend to use their income as it becomes available. Their future incomes are uncertain, and it is difficult to budget taxes that do not fall due at the time when the income is received. If income stops because of unemployment or sickness, an income tax debt accrued in the prior year may become a serious burden. Even high-income taxpayers find it easier to meet tax payments currently than a year later, particularly when incomes fluctuate. Synchronization of tax payments with receipt of income is also desirable from an economic standpoint to maximize the stabilizing effect of the income tax.

The current payment system, introduced in 1943, is based on the principle that taxes become due when incomes are earned, rather than in the following year when tax returns are filed. In practice, the system has been fully current for most wage and salary earners because their taxes are withheld by their employers. Persons who receive other types of income estimate their tax and pay it in quarterly installments during the year when it is received.

WITHHOLDING. Withholding for income tax purposes applies to all employees, except farm workers and domestic servants, at rates ranging from 21 percent of wages and salaries over $92 a month to 30 percent in the top brackets. (Beginning in 1973 the top withholding rate will be reduced to 27 percent.) Employees with additional income that is not subject to withholding may elect to have an extra amount withheld from their wages or salaries in order to reduce or avoid the quarterly installment payments. Withholding is also available for pensions and annuities at the request of the recipient.

The amounts withheld by the employer are remitted to the government quarterly if they total less than $100 a month. Employers withholding between $100 and $2,500 are required to deposit the tax withheld in an authorized bank within fifteen days after the end of each month. Employers withholding more than $2,500 a month are required to make deposits of the amounts withheld twice each month.

The withholding system is the backbone of the individual income tax. In recent years, it has collected about four-fifths of total individual income tax liabilities each year. In 1968, the latest year for which data are available, the total tax liability amounted to $78.3 billion. Withholding brought in $62.7 billion; payments of estimated tax, $15.8 billion; and final payments on April 15 of the following year, $10.4 billion. These payments exceeded the total tax due by $11.0 billion, which was refunded to the taxpayers (Appendix Table C-7).

DECLARATION OF ESTIMATED TAX. Since withholding applies only to wages and salaries and the rate cuts off at 30 percent (27 percent by 1973) rather than 70 percent, millions of taxpayers do not have their taxes fully withheld; and no tax at all is withheld from nonwage sources. The declaration system was devised to take up the slack.

A declaration is required of all persons who have estimated tax payments of $40 or more and who have relatively large incomes (more than $200 of nonwage income or a gross wage income of more than $10,000 if they are married and filing joint returns or are heads of households, and of more than $5,000 if they are married and filing separate returns or are single). Declarations are filed on or before April 15, and the estimated tax that is not withheld is payable in installments on April 15, June 15, and September 15 of the current year and January 15 of the following year (January 31 if paid with a final tax return). These requirements were set so that persons whose income is not subject to withholding—farmers, businessmen, and recipients of property income—will pay their tax currently, and so that wage and salary earners in the higher brackets will pay on a current basis the part of their tax that is not withheld. Farmers and fishermen may file their declarations on January 15 of the following year or omit them entirely if they file their final returns by March 1.

Taxpayers who do not pay as much as 80 percent of their final tax through withholding and declaration (66⅔ percent in the case of farmers and fishermen) must pay a charge of 6 percent a year for the amount falling short of 80 percent. However, no charge is made for any installment if the tax paid by the date of the installment is based on (a) the previous year's tax; (b) the previous year's income with the current year's rates and exemptions; or (c) 90 percent of the tax on the actual income received before the installment date.

As a result of these liberal provisions, the sums collected through declarations of estimated tax have been relatively small. Whereas taxes withheld increased from $9.6 billion to $62.7 billion between 1944 and 1968, declaration payments increased from $5.5 billion to only $15.8 billion during the same period (Appendix Table C-7).

Final Tax Reconciliation

The reconciliation between an individual's final tax liability and his prepayments is made on the final tax return, which is filed not later than April 15. If the taxpayer owes more tax, he sends a check for the balance due to the Internal Revenue Service along with his return; if too much tax has been withheld, the excess is refunded or credited to the next year's tax if the taxpayer so requests.

Few returns have identical prepayments and final liabilities. In 1968, only 2.8 million out of a total of 73.7 million returns showed prepayments exactly equal to final liabilities (including returns of taxpayers who file but are not subject to any tax). Of the remaining 70.9 million, 50.6 million received a refund check (or chose to credit the overpayment against the estimated tax for the following year or to invest the overpayment in federal savings bonds), and 20.3 million had a balance of tax due (Appendix Table C-8).

Refunds greatly outnumbered balances of tax due for several reasons: (1) Withholding is based on the assumption that the employee works regularly (part-time or full-time), and thus the total amount of his exemptions for the year is apportioned equally among his pay periods; but employment is often irregular because of seasonality, changes of jobs, illness, and the like. (2) Employees may claim fewer exemptions for withholding purposes than they are entitled to.

(3) The withholding tables allow only for the standard deduction, whereas many employees—particularly those who own homes—have large deductions, which they itemize when filing their returns. To moderate overwithholding on this score, the Tax Adjustment Act of 1966 permitted those who have large itemized deductions to claim additional exemptions for withholding purposes.

When the current payment system was adopted, great concern was expressed that overwithholding might be resented by taxpayers. Since the end of World War II, the number of returns with overpayments has never fallen below 30 million in any one year and reached 51 million in 1968 (Appendix Table C-8). Nevertheless, there have been few complaints. Apparently, people would rather receive a check from the government than pay a tax bill, particularly since most of the refunds are mailed within two months after the tax return is filed.

Possible Modification of the Current Payment System

Proposals have been made to expand the withholding system to include incomes other than wages and salaries. On several occasions Congress has rejected plans for withholding on interest and dividends at a flat rate. A withholding system without exemptions was considered too burdensome on the aged and other nontaxable persons; and corporations, banks, and other financial institutions paying interest and dividends argued that it would be too costly to administer a plan involving exemption certificates. In 1962, Congress compromised the issue by requiring payers of interest and dividends to send an information return (with a copy to the government) to all recipients receiving $10 or more of interest or dividends per year. Interest and dividend reporting has greatly improved, but interest underreporting is still large. Although it was anticipated that present procedures would be evaluated after a few years of experience, no interest has been shown either by the executive branch or by Congress in remedying the situation.

Economic Effects

Three issues are of particular importance in appraising the economic effects of the individual income tax: its role as a stabilizer of consumption expenditures, its effect on saving, and its impact on work and investment incentives.

Role as Stabilizer

Stability of yield was once regarded as a major criterion of a good tax. Today there is general agreement that properly timed changes in tax yields can help increase demand during recessions and restrain the growth of demand during periods of expansion. The progressive individual income tax has the virtue that its yield automatically rises and falls more than in proportion to changes in personal income. Moreover, the system of paying taxes currently has greatly accelerated the reaction of income tax revenues to changes in income. An important by-product of current payment is that changes in tax rates have an almost immediate effect on the disposable income of most taxpayers. These features have made the personal income tax extremely useful for promoting economic stabilization and growth.

The automatic response of the individual income tax—its *built-in flexibility*—can be explained by the following example. Suppose a taxpayer with a wife and two children earns $10,000 a year when he is employed and uses the standard deduction. His taxable income is $5,500 ($10,000 less $1,500 for the standard deduction and $3,000 for the personal exemptions), and the tax under 1973 rates and exemptions is $905. The following table shows what the effect on his taxable income and tax would be if his income dropped to $8,000:

Adjusted gross income	$10,000	$8,000
Less exemptions	3,000	3,000
Less standard deduction	1,500	1,200
Taxable income	5,500	3,800
Tax	905	586
Disposable income	9,095	7,414

Whereas adjusted gross income declined by only 20 percent, taxable income declined 31 percent (from $5,500 to $3,800), and the tax declined 35 percent.

Such examples are multiplied millions of times during a recession, while the opposite occurs during boom periods. Those with lower or higher incomes find that their tax is reduced or increased proportionately more than their income. As a result, disposable income is more stable than it would be in the absence of the tax. (In the above example, disposable income declined only $1,681 while income before tax declined $2,000.) Since disposable income is the major determinant of consumption, expenditures by consumers are also more stable than they would be in the absence of the tax.

Individual income tax rate changes are also used to restrain or stimulate the economy. The Revenue Act of 1964 reduced tax receipts by $11.4 billion, of which the individual income tax reduction accounted for $9.2 billion. The Vietnam war surtax, which was enacted in 1968 to reduce inflationary pressures, increased tax receipts by a total of $10.2 billion, including $6.8 billion of individual income tax. The tax cut was designed to raise the level of expenditures by consumers and businessmen and thus to stimulate a higher rate of economic growth. Consumer expenditures had already increased in anticipation of the tax cut when it went into effect for withholding purposes early in March 1964; in the succeeding year, they rose $28 billion. While the increase in consumption cannot be attributed wholly to the tax cut, this was undoubtedly the most important factor. However, the Vietnam war surtax did not have a major effect on spending, because monetary policy was relaxed prematurely and because expectations of inflation were more pervasive than had been anticipated. Those who believe that consumption is determined largely by what individuals regard as their "permanent" income argue that the surtax was not effective because it was a temporary tax change. Nevertheless, most people are persuaded that income tax changes can have a significant effect in helping to regulate the rate of growth of private demand, but that the effect is greater for permanent than for temporary changes.

Countercyclical changes in tax rates seem to be rare in most countries, partly because there are long delays in recognizing significant changes in economic conditions and partly because the legislative process is too slow. However, as was indicated in Chapter 3, it should be possible to devise procedures for varying tax rates quickly in response to changes in the level of economic activity.

Effect on Saving and Consumption

The individual income tax applies to the entire income of an individual whether it is spent or saved. Some have argued that the income tax is unfair to those who save because it applies both to the income that gives rise to the saving and to the income produced by the saving. But almost all economists now agree that, on equity grounds, this double taxation argument does not have much merit.

At any particular point in time, an individual has the option to make a new decision to spend or save from the income that is left to him after tax. If he decides to save the income, he does not necessarily incur a new tax. It is only if the saving is invested in an income-producing asset that new income is generated, and this new income is subject to additional tax.

The individual income tax is often contrasted with a general consumption or expenditure tax, which is an alternative method of taxing individuals in accordance with "ability to pay." In the case of the income tax, the measure of ability to pay is income; in the case of the expenditure tax, the measure is consumption. The tax on consumption may also be levied at progressive rates (but the rates must be greater than 100 percent to equal the impact of the progressive income tax in the higher brackets).

Consumption taxes can be avoided simply by reducing one's consumption. This means that an expenditure tax encourages saving more than does an equal-yield income tax that is distributed in the same proportions by income classes. In practice, where the income tax is paid by the large mass of the people, much of the tax yield comes from income classes where there is little room in family budgets for increasing saving in response to tax incentives. As a consequence, the differential effect on total consumption and saving between an income tax and an equal-yield expenditure tax is likely to be small in this country.

Economics alone does not provide a basis for deciding whether the income tax is more or less "equitable" than an expenditure tax. The income tax reduces the gain made when an individual saves rather than consumes part of his income, while an expenditure tax makes future consumption relatively as attractive as present consumption. Under the income tax, the interest reward for saving and investing is reduced by the tax; under the expenditure tax, the net reward is always equal to the market rate of interest regardless of the tax rate.

While this subject has not been widely discussed in the United States, the continued heavy reliance on the income tax suggests that it is probably more acceptable on equity grounds than an expenditure tax. An expenditure tax was recommended by the Treasury during World War II, but it was rejected by the Congress primarily because of its novelty and complexity.

Graduated expenditure taxes are often proposed as a method of avoiding or correcting the defects of the income tax base, particularly in the top brackets, where the preferential treatment of capital gains, tax-exempt interest, depletion allowances (see Chapter 5), and other favorable provisions permit the accumulation of large fortunes with little or no payment of income tax. An expenditure tax would reach such incomes when they are spent without resort to regressive taxation. Despite this advantage, the expenditure tax has not been widely used. It is more difficult to administer and also raises more serious problems of compliance for the taxpayer. Although it is difficult to imagine total replacement of the income tax by an expenditure tax, the latter might be a useful supplement if and when it became necessary to discourage consumption.

Work and Investment Incentives

The individual income tax affects economic incentives in two different directions. On the one hand, it reduces the financial rewards of greater effort and risk-taking and thus tends to discourage these activities. On the other hand, it may provide a greater incentive to obtain more income because it cuts down on the income left over for spending. There is no basis for deciding which effect is more important on an a priori basis.

Taxation is only one of many factors affecting work and investment incentives. This makes it extremely difficult to interpret the available statistical evidence or the results of direct interviews with taxpayers. The evidence suggests that income taxation does not significantly reduce the amount of labor supplied by workers and managers. Work habits are not easily changed, and there is little scope in a modern industrial society for most people to vary their hours of work or the intensity of their efforts in response to changes in tax rates. Nearly all people who are asked about income taxation grumble about it, but relatively few say that they work fewer hours or exert less than their best efforts to avoid tax. The maximum 50 percent marginal rate for earned income, which was enacted in 1969, was justified on incentive grounds, but there is no evidence that it will have a significant impact.

As for risk-taking, the problem is much more complicated. In the first place, the tax rates on capital gains are much lower than those on ordinary incomes. Numerous studies have demonstrated that the opportunity to earn income in the form of capital gains stimulates investment and risk-taking. Second, taxpayers may offset business losses against ordinary income not only for the current year but also for three prior years and five succeeding years; capital losses may similarly be offset against capital gains, and half of these losses (up to $1,000 a year) may be offset against ordinary income for an indefinite period. Such offsets greatly diminish the consequences of loss by the investor. Third, much of the nation's investment is undertaken by large corporations. These firms are generally permitted to retain earnings after payment of tax at the corporation rate, which is more moderate than the rates applying to investors in the top personal income tax brackets. Finally, the law provides incentives to invest through generous depreciation allowances. In any case, experience suggests that the major stimulus to investment comes from a healthy and prosperous economy.

The discussion in the next section will indicate that much can be done to improve the structure of the income tax. But there is little basis for the assertions made from time to time that the income tax has had an adverse effect on the economy.

Structural Problems

The personal income tax is determined by the definition of income, allowable deductions, personal exemptions, and tax rates. These elements can be combined in various ways to produce a given amount of revenue. In recent years, there has been increasing recognition that the definition of taxable income under the United States tax law is deficient. Many of the exclusions and deductions are not essential for effective personal income taxation and have cut into the income tax base unnecessarily. This process of "erosion" has been halted in recent years, but only limited progress has been made in reversing it.

Erosion of the income tax base makes higher tax rates necessary. It puts a premium on earning and disposing of incomes in forms that receive preferential treatment, thus often distorting the allocation of resources. Erosion also violates the principle that taxpayers with equal incomes should pay the same tax. These departures from horizontal equity, which often seem arbitrary, contribute to taxpayer dissatisfaction and create pressures for the enactment of additional special benefits—pressures that legislators find difficult to resist. Most of the special provisions in the tax law serve the same ends as direct government expenditures but are not explicitly included in the federal budget. For this reason they have been called "tax expenditures." (See Appendix Tables C-14 and C-15.)

Figure 4-2 shows the practical effect of erosion. If the total income reported by taxpayers were subject to the nominal tax rates without any exemptions, deductions, or other special provisions, effective tax rates would begin at 14 percent and rise to almost 70 percent in the very highest brackets. But nobody pays these rates on his entire income. The effect of all the special provisions rises from 12 to 15 percent of total income below $15,000 to a maximum of 35 percent above $1,000,000. Thus, after allowing for the special provisions, the *maximum average effective rate* for any income class is about 34 percent. Exemptions are most important in the lowest income classes, and deductions in the top classes; when taken together the effect of these provisions declines somewhat as income rises. Three sets of provisions —those relating to capital gains, the preference items, and the maximum tax on earned income—reduce taxes primarily for those in the top brackets, although only the first has a significant effect. Income splitting, which aids all classes above $5,000, gives its largest benefits to persons with incomes between $25,000 and $150,000. The effective rates shown in Figure 4-2 are average rates, and there are wide variations in taxes paid at all income levels.

A personal income tax conforming strictly to the principle of horizontal equity is easily described, but difficult to implement. This tax would include in the tax base all income from whatever source derived, permit deductions for expenses of earning income, and also make an allowance for the taxpayer and his dependents through the personal exemptions. "Income" is defined by economists as consumption plus tax payments plus (or minus) the net increase (or decrease) in the value of assets during the taxable period. In practice, this definition is usually modified to exclude gifts and inheritances, which are subject to separate taxes, and, for practical reasons, to include capital gains only when realized or when transferred to others through gifts and bequests. In the discussion that follows, this comprehensive definition of income will be used as a basis for evaluating the major features of the income tax and the more important proposals for reform.

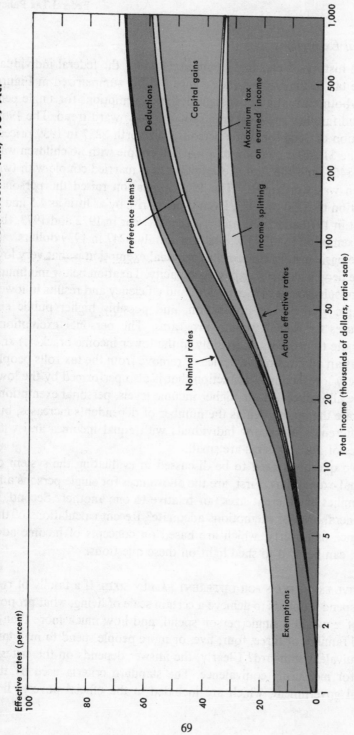

FIGURE 4-2. Influence of Various Provisions on Effective Rates of Federal Individual Income Tax, 1969 Act[a]

Effective rates (percent)

Total income (thousands of dollars, ratio scale)

Exemptions

Nominal rates

Preference items[b]

Deductions

Capital gains

Actual effective rates

Income splitting

Maximum tax
on earned income

Source: Appendix Table C-11.
[a] Rates, exemptions, and other provisions of the Tax Reform Act of 1969 scheduled to apply to calendar year 1973 incomes.
[b] Preference items as defined by the Tax Reform Act of 1969, except excluded net long-term capital gains.

Personal Exemptions

The history of personal exemptions under the federal individual income tax in the United States since 1913 is summarized in Figure 4-3. In both current and constant dollars, exemptions for single persons and families show an unmistakable downward trend. The 1969 exemption of $600 for single persons was worth $227 in 1939 prices, while the $1,200 exemption of a married couple with no children was worth $455, and the $2,400 exemption of a married couple with two children was worth $910. The 1969 legislation raised the personal exemption to $750 by 1973. Even if prices rise by as little as 4.5 and 4 percent in 1970 and 1971, and 3 percent a year in 1972 and 1973, the $750 exemption for 1973 will be worth only $247 in 1939 dollars.

The basic justification for the personal exemption is that very low income people have no taxpaying capacity. Taxation below minimum levels of subsistence reduces health and efficiency and results in lower economic vitality, less production, and possibly higher public expenditures for social welfare programs. The personal exemptions contribute to progression (mainly in the lower income brackets) and serve as an administrative device to remove from the tax rolls people with very low incomes, a function that is also performed by the low-income allowance. At the higher income levels, personal exemptions moderate the tax burden as the number of dependents increases, but the differences in tax for individuals with equal incomes and with families of different sizes are small.

Two questions need to be discussed in evaluating the system of personal exemptions. First, are the allowances for single persons and for families of different sizes fair relative to one another? Second, is the general level of exemptions adequate? Recent calculations of the incidence of poverty, which are based on concepts of income adequacy, can be used to shed light on these questions.

RELATIVE EXEMPTIONS FOR DIFFERENT FAMILY SIZES. If a family of two must spend x dollars to achieve a certain scale of living, what proportion of x would a single person spend, and how much more than x would families of three, four, five, or more people spend to maintain an equivalent standard? Clearly, the answer depends on the criteria used for measuring equivalence. The standard criteria used by the federal government, which are included in the official poverty line

FIGURE 4-3. History of Federal Individual Income Tax Exemptions in Current and 1939 Prices, Actual 1913–69; Projected 1970–73[a]

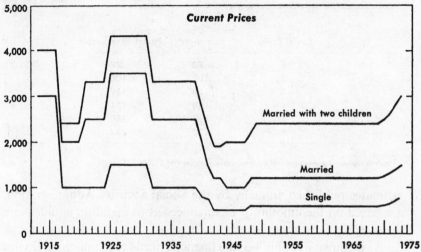

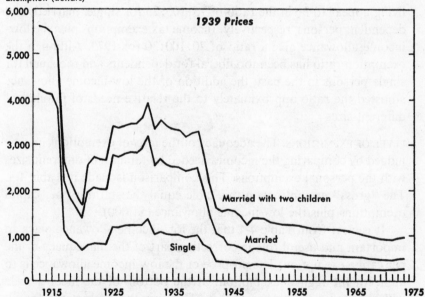

Sources: Derived from data in Appendix Table A-1 and U.S. Department of Labor, Bureau of Labor Statistics, consumer price index, all items, series A. The consumer price index is projected to increase 4.5 percent in 1970, 4 percent in 1971, and 3 percent in 1972 and 1973.

[a] For 1944–45, exemptions shown are for surtax purposes only.

TABLE 4-3. Indexes of Federal Individual Income Tax Exemptions and Estimated Poverty-Level Budgets for Families of Various Sizes, 1973

(Two-person family = 100)

Size of family	Index	
	Exemptions[a]	Poverty-level budget
1	70	78
2	100	100
3	130	119
4	160	151
5	190	180
6	220	202

Source. Table 4-4.

[a] Includes personal exemptions and the low-income allowance of $1,000.

estimates published annually by the Social Security Administration, are based on the amount of income needed to maintain an adequate diet.

As is shown in Table 4-3, the financial needs of a household do not increase in proportion to the number of people in the household. The relative incomes that would provide roughly equivalent standards of living appear to be in the ratio of 75:100:25 for single, married, and dependent persons, respectively. Income tax exemptions plus the low-income allowance give a ratio of 70:100:30 for 1973. Although the exemption ratio has been too liberal for dependents and too small for single persons in the past, the addition of the low-income allowance adjusted the ratio approximately to the relative needs of families of different sizes.

LEVEL OF EXEMPTIONS. The adequacy of the *level* of exemptions may be judged by comparing the incomes needed by families of different sizes with the personal exemptions. This comparison is made in Table 4-4. The "gross" exemptions in this table equal the statutory per capita exemptions plus the low-income allowance ($1,000).

It is clear from Table 4-4 that the low-income allowance plays an important and useful role in correcting part of the inadequacy of the per capita exemption. The purpose of the low-income allowance is to augment the regular exemptions at the bottom of the income scale without incurring the heavy cost of raising the exemptions for all taxpayers. Thus, a single person is not required to pay tax until his income exceeds $1,750 as compared with $750 without the allowance.

TABLE 4-4. Comparison of Federal Individual Income Tax Exemptions with Estimated Poverty-Level Budgets for Families of Various Sizes, 1973

(In dollars)

Size of family	Exemptions[a]	Poverty-level budget[b]	Difference
1	1,750	2,210	−460
2	2,500	2,840	−340
3	3,250	3,390	−140
4	4,000	4,290	−290
5	4,750	5,120	−370
6	5,500	5,740	−240

Sources: Exemptions: Appendix Table A-1. Poverty levels: based on data in *Family Assistance Act of 1970*, Report of the Committee on Ways and Means on H.R. 16311, 91 Cong. 2 sess. (1970), p. 26.

　a Includes personal exemptions and the low-income allowance of $1,000.

　b Poverty-level budgets for 1969 were adjusted for projected increases in the consumer price index of 4.5 percent in 1970, 4.0 percent in 1971, and 3.0 percent in 1972 and 1973.

A married couple with two children, not taxed without the low-income allowance until their income reached at least $3,000, is exempt up to $4,000. The exemption system would thus be grossly inadequate without the low-income allowance. As is indicated in Table 4-4, the exemptions and the low-income allowance will probably be moderately lower than the poverty lines in 1973 and will become even more inadequate unless inflation is halted.

VARIABLE EXEMPTIONS. Since costs are relatively higher for the principal income recipient in the family than for dependents, a return to the pre-World War II variable exemption system is often suggested. For example, one combination might be $800, $1,600, and $400 exemptions for single persons, married couples, and dependents, respectively.

　　Two considerations argue against abandoning the per capita exemption system. First, the per capita system commends itself as both fair and simple to many people. Although the bare physical needs of children may be provided for at less cost than those of adults, the obligation of parents to their children goes beyond mere physical maintenance, and a per capita exemption recognizes this obligation. Others believe that tax policy should provide liberal protection for those with children as a matter of social policy. In Great Britain and Canada, where the dependent exemption is lower than the exemptions for the taxpayer and his wife, this protection is given in the form of a family allowance, which is paid as a direct subsidy to those with children.

Second, abandonment of the per capita exemption would complicate administration and compliance. The withholding tax tables and the simplified tax table would become more cumbersome and unwieldy. Employers would have to keep track of their employees' marital status as well as the number of exemptions. Thus, the simplicity of the present system argues against departing from the per capita exemption, while the budget figures argue for higher exemptions for taxpayers and their wives than for dependents.

COST OF EXEMPTION INCREASES. Policymakers have been hesitant to raise the per capita exemption because the cost is relatively high. The increase from $600 to $750 enacted in 1969 is expected to reduce 1973 revenues by over $8 billion. By contrast, a reduction of only one percentage point in all tax rates would cost over $5 billion.

An alternative method of reducing the tax burden of low-income persons, also included in the 1969 legislation, is to increase the minimum standard deduction. This change was designed to help those who were in greatest need without incurring heavy revenue losses. The low-income allowance of $1,000 (which replaced the minimum standard deduction) raised the effective exemption to $1,750 for a single person, $2,500 for married couples without children, and $4,000 for married couples with two children. The cost of this reform will be over $2 billion by 1973, and, as already indicated, it will go far to correct the inadequacy of the $750 exemption.

TAX CREDITS IN LIEU OF EXEMPTIONS. Allowances for taxpayers and dependents have always been given in the form of exemptions under the federal income tax. An alternative method, now used in several states, is to convert the allowance to a tax credit computed by multiplying the value of the exemption by the first bracket rate. Thus, with the present 14 percent first bracket rate, the $750 exemption would be converted to a credit of $105. The credit would increase the tax liabilities of single persons with taxable incomes of more than $500 and married couples with taxable incomes of more than $1,000. It would also narrow the tax differentials among families of different sizes at all income levels.

The tax credit limits the tax value of the exemption to the same dollar amount for all taxpayers. Carried to the extreme, the logic of the tax credit would lead to an exemption that vanished at some point on the income scale. A vanishing exemption is often supported on the ground that exemptions are not justified for individuals with very large incomes, since expenditures for children are not a hardship at these levels. However, in recent years, few people have seriously recommended converting the exemption to a credit, primarily because it is considered undesirable to adopt a measure that would bear more heavily on those with family responsibilities and with relatively modest means.

The Negative Income Tax

Raising the exemptions or lowering the bottom bracket tax rates would do little to alleviate the economic hardship of low-income families. In the first place, to the extent that poor families pay any income tax at all, the amount is small; even full relief from income taxation would not help much. Second, families with incomes below the present gross exemption levels cannot be helped at all by income tax reduction.

The traditional method of helping poverty-stricken families has been through public welfare and other direct transfer payments (for example, old-age assistance, aid to families with dependent children, medical assistance for the aged, aid to the blind and disabled persons, and general relief). Most of these programs reach specific categories of poor persons; except for general relief, which is inadequate almost everywhere, they provide no assistance to families headed by able-bodied workers who, for reasons of background, training, or temperament, do not participate effectively in the modern industrial economy.

Considerable thought has been given in recent years to the relationship between the welfare system and the income tax system. The two developed side by side in response to different pressures, but it has become recognized increasingly that one may be regarded as an extension of the other. Direct assistance to low-income persons is an extension of progression into the lowest brackets, with negative rather than positive rates. Once this relationship has been understood, it is only a natural step to consider the adoption of a negative income tax.

A negative income tax would provide assistance to families on the basis of the deficiency in income below certain minimum standards, without inquiring into the reason for the deficiency. The various welfare programs conducted by government and private nonprofit agencies do not reach all of the poor. The negative income tax is regarded by many as a way to supplement these welfare programs rather than replace them. Experts point out, however, that a comprehensive negative income tax could be used to replace the categorical welfare payments.

BASIC FEATURES. The negative income tax would involve the same computations of taxable income as does the positive income tax. An individual would add up all his income and subtract his exemptions and deductions. If the result were negative, he would be entitled to a payment *from* the government. The amount of the payment would be computed by applying a new set of tax rates to the negative taxable income. The rates might begin with the first bracket rate of 14 percent and increase as the amount of negative taxable income increased. But there is no necessary relationship between the first bracket rates of the positive and negative parts of the income tax. The rates on negative incomes could begin with, say, 30 percent and go as high as 70, 80, or even 100 percent. However, most negative income tax plans provide for only one tax rate.

A negative income tax with only one rate would involve a fixed relationship among three variables—the basic allowance (A), the breakeven level (B), and the tax rate (t) on the family's income—and it is impossible to change one variable without affecting at least one of the other two. The relationship is that the basic allowance is the product of the tax rate and the breakeven level (or $A = tB$). Thus, if the breakeven level is $4,000 and the tax rate is 50 percent, the basic allowance is $2,000. Conversely, in order to have a basic allowance of $3,000 and keep the breakeven level at $4,000, the tax rate must be 75 percent. Examples of consistent As, Bs, and ts are shown in Table 4-5; there are, of course, many other possibilities.

TABLE 4-5. Illustrative Basic Allowances, Tax Rates, and Breakeven Levels under a Negative Income Tax Plan

Basic allowance (A) (dollars)	Tax rate (t) (percent)	Breakeven level (B) (dollars)
1,000	33⅓	3,000
1,500	50	3,000
2,000	66⅔	3,000
2,000	50	4,000
2,500	50	5,000
3,000	75	4,000
3,000	100	3,000

Because of these relationships, the negative income tax can be thought of in two ways. It can be regarded as providing a basic allowance to all persons, together with a special tax rate on the incomes of those who accept the allowance. Or, it can be regarded as a payment that reduces the gap between income and the breakeven level by the same tax rate. The equivalence between these two approaches may be illustrated with the first combination of A, t, and B in Table 4-5. According to the first approach, a family with an income of $1,500 would receive a basic allowance of $1,000 and would pay a tax of $500 on its income, which would leave it with a disposable income of $2,000. According to the second, the family would receive a payment of $500 —33⅓ percent of the difference between the $3,000 breakeven level and its income of $1,500—leaving it with the same disposable income of $2,000.

The last entry in Table 4-5 shows a basic allowance equal to the breakeven level. This occurs whenever the income recipient must give up one dollar of his allowance for every dollar of income he may receive: in other words, when the tax rate is 100 percent. The welfare system in the United States had this feature until the Social Security amendments of 1967 required the states to permit recipients to keep some part of whatever they might earn. (This provision became fully operative in mid-1969.)

It might also be noted that there is essentially no difference between a negative income tax and a guaranteed minimum income plan. Under the negative income tax, individuals would receive the basic allowance if they had no other income, and in this sense the basic allowance is a guaranteed minimum. Some guaranteed minimum income plans would impose a tax rate of 100 percent on any income the family might receive, but this is not an essential feature of such plans.

RELATION TO THE POSITIVE INCOME TAX. So long as the breakeven levels are no higher than the levels at which the positive income tax begins to apply, the negative income tax can be operated quite independently. However, if the negative income tax is to provide more than a pittance as a basic allowance, the breakeven levels may be higher than the levels at which the positive tax takes effect. For example, with a basic allowance of $2,500 and a tax rate of 50 percent, the breakeven level would be $5,000 (see Table 4-5). The personal exemption and the low-income allowance for a family of four in 1973 amounts to only $4,000.

Thus, the two systems would overlap in the range between $4,000 and $5,000.

The answer to this problem would be to give the family the option of choosing the system under which its disposable income is higher. In the above example, it is obvious that all families with incomes of $5,000 or less would choose the negative income tax. Some families with incomes above $5,000 would also choose the negative income tax, because the switch from the negative to the positive income tax precisely at $5,000 would raise the tax rate on an additional dollar of income above 100 percent. At $5,001, the positive tax for a family of four (at 1973 rates and exemptions) would be $140, leaving the family with a disposable income of $4,861 instead of the $5,000 it would have had without the additional dollar of income. Paradoxically, the option of paying the higher negative income tax rate would yield a family of four a higher disposable income until its income exceeded $5,400 in this example (see Figure 4-4). The exact location of this "tax break-even point" need not concern the individual taxpayer because the final tax return would provide a reconciliation between the positive and negative income tax.

THE FAMILY ASSISTANCE PLAN. In 1969, the Nixon administration proposed a family assistance plan to guarantee a small annual income to poor families with children. Such families would receive an allowance of $500 for the first two members of the family and $300 for each additional member. Benefits would be reduced by fifty cents for each dollar earned after the first $720. To be eligible for the plan, nonworking members of the family, except for mothers with children under six years of age, would be required to register for training or employment at a public employment office. Single persons and married couples without children would not be eligible. The net additional cost of the plan above expenditures under the current law was estimated at about $4 billion a year.

The negative income tax is a novel idea for welfare and tax experts, as well as for the American public. The family assistance plan goes only part way toward an effective, comprehensive negative income tax. It is, nevertheless, a good first step.

Personal Deductions

Personal deductions itemized on taxable returns in 1968 amounted to $65.9 billion. Of this total, about $25.0 billion would have been deductible through the standard deduction in any event. The tax

FIGURE 4-4. Illustration of a Negative Income Tax Plan for a Four-Person Family with a $2,500 Basic Allowance and a 50 Percent Tax Rate

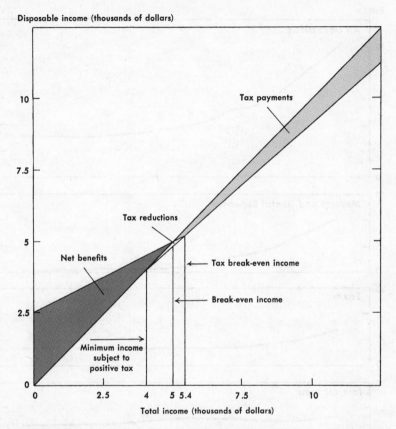

Disposable income (thousands of dollars)

Total income (thousands of dollars)

Source: Adapted from James Tobin, Joseph A. Pechman, and Peter M. Mieszkowski, "Is a Negative Income Tax Practical?" *Yale Law Journal*, Vol. 77 (November 1967), p. 7. (Brookings Reprint 142.)

savings from the additional $40.8 billion of itemized deductions amounted to $9.6 billion.

The relative importance of the itemized deductions at different income levels is shown in Figure 4-5. Because taxpayers had the alternative of taking the 10 percent standard deduction, it is not surprising to find that, at low income levels, those who itemize their deductions subtract much more than 10 percent on the average. Deductions account for a decreasing percentage of income as incomes rise to $100,000, but increase in the highest brackets. In 1968, they averaged 18 percent of adjusted gross income on taxable returns with

FIGURE 4-5. Itemized Deductions as a Percentage of Adjusted Gross Income, Taxable and Nontaxable Federal Individual Returns, 1968

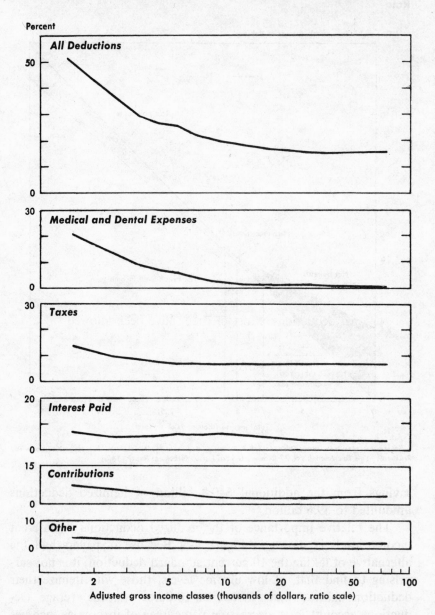

Source: U.S. Treasury Department, Internal Revenue Service, *Preliminary Report, Statistics of Income—1968, Individual Income Tax Returns* (1970), p. 31.

itemized deductions. They were even more important for nontaxable returns, where they accounted for over half of adjusted gross income (Appendix Table C-12).

The largest deductions at most income levels are interest and taxes, but medical deductions—which are subject to a 3 percent floor except for one-half of health insurance premiums up to $150—are heaviest in the lowest income classes. Interest is particularly important for those with incomes between $5,000 and $20,000, because of the high incidence of mortgage-financed home ownership.

There is very little variation among income groups in the average ratio of standard *plus* itemized deductions to income, except at the very highest levels. In 1968, the standard and itemized deductions combined amounted to 16.3 percent of adjusted gross income on taxable returns below $5,000; 15.7 percent on those between $5,000 and $10,000; 15.2 percent between $10,000 and $25,000; 14.8 percent between $25,000 and $100,000; and 18.7 percent over $100,000. The rise at the top is due to an increase in the ratio of contributions to income, reflecting the importance of philanthropy among the wealthy and the incentive for giftmaking provided by the tax deduction.

There is no recorded explanation of the justification for many of the personal deductions. Most of them have been allowed since the beginning of the income tax. Given the definition of "income" stated earlier, deductions would be allowed only for expenditures that are essential to earn income. An exception to this rule might be made for unusual personal expenditures that create hardships when incomes are low; but to avoid subsidizing personal consumption, the personal expense deductions should be kept to a minimum. The current tax law departs from these criteria to a substantial degree.

PURPOSES OF THE PERSONAL DEDUCTIONS. There are four major groups of itemized deductions under present law. The first is for large, unusual, and necessary personal expenditures. Deductions for extraordinary medical expenses are the best examples of this group. Such expenses are often involuntary and unpredictable and may exhaust a large proportion of the taxpayer's total income in a particular year. When a serious illness strikes a member of a family, its ability to pay taxes is clearly lower than that of another family with the same income whose members are healthy. For these reasons, taxpayers are permitted to deduct medical expenses in excess of 3 percent of their income, with generous maximum limitations. Other deductions for large, involuntary, and unpredictable costs are those for noninsured losses due to thefts, fires, storms, or other casualties. Since 1964, these deductions have been limited to the amount of loss from each casualty that exceeds $100.

The second group of deductions in effect subsidizes particular groups of taxpayers. Thus, deductions for taxes paid on owner-occupied residences and for interest on home mortgages help the homeowner. Since the rental value of an owner-occupied house is not included in the owner's income, the deduction of expenses—including interest and taxes—connected with the home is not warranted. In addition to the direct benefit from the deductions and the exclusion from taxable income of the rental value of their homes, homeowners also derive an indirect benefit by being able to utilize other itemized deductions. Tenants with low and middle incomes rarely accumulate deductions aggregating more than the standard deduction. The result is that homeowners are the primary beneficiaries of the remaining deductions. Moreover, when a new deduction is introduced, home-owners who already itemize ordinarily receive the full benefit. Other taxpayers must first sacrifice the standard deduction before receiving some value from the new deduction.

Another deduction of the subsidy type is for contributions to religious, educational, and other nonprofit organizations, which may be deducted up to 50 percent of a taxpayer's adjusted gross income (20 percent for foundations and other organizations that are not regarded as "public" charities). Some question the incentive effect of this deduction. Others have argued that private philanthropy should not be encouraged at the expense of the federal treasury, since, in effect, it permits individuals to divert tax funds to certain kinds of organizations. However, most people believe that the activities of these organizations are generally socially desirable.

The deduction for interest is justifiable where the interest is paid in connection with a loan used to produce taxable income. The interest payment is in effect a negative income, which should be offset against the positive income produced by the asset purchased with the loan proceeds. Alternatively, an individual may prefer to borrow money and pay interest rather than sell an asset; in such cases, the interest deduction is also required to measure the individual's true net property income. However, a substantial proportion of the interest deducted on tax returns is for loans on homes and consumer durables or for other purposes that do not produce taxable income.

The third group of deductions is for income, property, gasoline, and sales taxes paid to state and local governments. A deduction for income taxes reduces the combined impact of federal, state, and local income taxes; it is also an effective way of moderating interstate tax differentials in the higher income brackets. For example, if an income were subject to the highest state rate of 14.6 percent and also to the 70 percent rate for federal tax purposes, the combined marginal rates would be 84.6 percent. By allowing taxpayers to deduct the state tax on their federal returns, the maximum combined rate is reduced to 74.4 percent. If the state also permits a deduction for federal taxes, the maximum combined rate is 71.5 percent.

At one time, federal excises and all the minor state and local taxes were allowed as deductions, but these were gradually eliminated. The deductions for general sales and property taxes survived because it was felt that some federal relief for these taxes was needed to encourage state and local governments to raise needed revenue, without coercing them to use a particular source. The deduction for gasoline taxes was retained for the same reasons, but here the rationale is strained.

The fourth group contains the only theoretically necessary deductions, namely, those that make allowances for expenses of earning income. These deductions are required to correct the deficiencies of the adjusted gross income concept. To avoid complicating the tax return, expenses incurred in earning nonbusiness incomes (that is, wages and salaries, interest, and dividends) are generally not allowed as deductions in arriving at adjusted gross income. This deficiency is corrected by permitting taxpayers to deduct some of these expenses in arriving at taxable income. Examples of these deductions are fees for investment counselors, rentals of safe deposit boxes used to store income producing securities, custodian fees, work clothing, and union dues. Moving expenses and nonreimbursed travel expenses of employees are deductible in arriving at adjusted gross income.

The deduction for child care, which was enacted in 1954 and liberalized in 1964, permits all employed single persons and married couples (with both husband and wife employed) having incomes of less than $6,000 to deduct up to $600 for the cost of the care of one child while they are at work, and $900 for two or more children.

Congress justified this deduction on the ground that child care expenditures must be incurred by many taxpayers to earn a livelihood and are comparable to ordinary business expenses.

POSSIBLE REVISIONS OF THE PERSONAL DEDUCTIONS. Revision of the personal deductions should begin with those that subsidize personal expenditures, which account for the major share of itemized deductions on taxable returns (Appendix Table C-12). They include the deductions for charitable contributions, interest on personal loans, and state and local taxes other than income and sales taxes.

Among these deductions, only charitable contributions seem to have such overwhelming social priority under present institutional arrangements as to warrant the use of tax incentives. However, the deduction for contributions probably has little effect on charitable giving by the lower and middle income classes, since the income tax advantage is relatively small at these levels. If an income tax deduction is deemed necessary to encourage large contributions, it might be better to give the deduction only when the contribution is larger than some average amount. For example, the deduction might be allowed for the amount of contributions in excess of, say, 2 or 3 percent of adjusted gross income, with the total deduction limited to the present 50 percent of adjusted gross income. This revision was recommended by the Treasury in 1969, but was not accepted by the Congress because of the strong opposition of tax-exempt organizations.

With respect to the provision permitting medical expenses above 3 percent of income to be deducted, surveys indicate that 3 percent of income is about the median expenditure of families with incomes below $10,000. However, the median is only an arbitrary dividing line between "usual" and "extraordinary." The lower limit could be restored to 5 percent for all taxpayers without violating its basic rationale. This would permit medical deductions on about 30 percent of all tax returns with itemized deductions.

The interest deduction presents a special difficulty because interest is paid on both business and personal debts, and it is difficult to distinguish between the two. Clearly, the deduction should be allowed for interest on a loan made to the owner of a grocery store to carry inventories, while interest on a loan to purchase a consumer durable hardly merits a deduction. The inventory loan produces taxable income, while the consumer durable goods loan generates income in the form of services which do not enter into the tax base. However, it is often difficult to identify the purpose of loans because owners of unincorporated enterprises take out personal loans to finance their business activities, and vice versa.

The best way to handle this difficulty would be to permit deductions (with carryover privileges) for interest paid up to the amount of property and business income reported by the taxpayers, on the ground that interest paid must be subtracted to obtain *net* income from these sources. This test would exclude about three-fourths of the interest now deducted.

The 1969 act adopted a weak variant of this approach by allowing a taxpayer to deduct interest paid to purchase investment assets up to $25,000, plus his net investment income (dividends, interest, long-term capital gains, and so forth), plus one-half the amount of such interest in excess of net investment income. Any interest disallowed in one year may be carried over to offset investment income and capital gains in subsequent years. Capital gains that are used to offset investment interest are treated as ordinary income for purposes of the alternative capital gains tax, the capital gains exclusion, and the minimum tax on income from preference sources. The provision, which becomes effective in 1972, will yield only $20 million a year—a tiny fraction of the $3 billion to $4 billion revenue loss from all interest deductions in excess of property income.

Among the deductible taxes, gasoline taxes are least justified as a deduction. The federal deduction in effect places part of the burden of user charges levied for automobile use on the general taxpayer. This is unfair as between users and nonusers of automobiles and also among people with different incomes. The deduction of property taxes on owner-occupied houses discriminates against renters, and this might also be eliminated in the interest of equity. This would leave deductions for state and local income and sales taxes, which can be justified as a way of encouraging the use of general taxes for state-local purposes.

It may be concluded that the itemized deductions allowed are too generous and that substantial increases in revenues might be gained by trimming them to the most essential items. But this is not all. If the itemized deductions were curtailed, it would be possible also to reduce the standard deduction. To an important degree, the standard deduction violates the rationale of the itemized deductions since it tends to reduce differentiation in tax liabilities. The existence of both standard and itemized deductions suggests that there is some ambivalence towards many of the personal deductions.

Under the circumstances, interest has been expressed recently in alternative approaches that would not involve direct repeal or modification of the questionable deductions. One possibility would be to eliminate the standard deduction and convert it to a floor on itemized deductions. Taxpayers might be permitted to deduct only the amount of their itemized deductions exceeding, say, 10 percent of their adjusted gross income. The attractive feature of this approach is that it would greatly increase the yield of the present tax rates and thus permit substantial reductions in these rates without increasing the overall burden of the income tax. A variant of this proposal was recommended by the Treasury in 1963, but it was virtually disregarded by the congressional tax-writing committees.

Another approach is to increase the standard deduction so that fewer persons will be encouraged to itemize personal deductions. The proposals call for increasing the rate of the standard deduction and raising the ceiling. The main objection to this is that it corrects one inequity by further reducing the tax base. Nevertheless, when Congress was in a tax-cutting mood in 1969, it raised the standard deduction from 10 to 15 percent and doubled the ceiling to $2,000. This action will reduce revenues by more than $2 billion a year when it becomes fully effective in 1973.

On balance, equity would be better served by pruning the unnecessary itemized deductions and using the revenues to reduce tax rates. Although it recognizes the inequity of the present system, Congress hesitates to remedy the situation directly for fear of alienating the large groups of taxpayers who benefit from the deductions. The only progress in recent years was made in 1964, when deductions for numerous state-local taxes and casualty losses of less than $100 were eliminated.

The Family

During most of the history of the income tax, differentiation for family responsibilities was made among taxpayers through the personal exemptions. More recently, there has been a trend toward differing tax rates to provide additional differentiation, particularly in the middle and higher tax brackets. In the United States and West Germany this has been accomplished by adoption of the principle of "income splitting" between husband and wife. In France, income splitting is permitted among all family members. Other countries achieve a similar objective by providing separate rate schedules for families of different size.

The adoption of income splitting in the United States arose out of the historical accident that eight states had community property laws, which treated income as if divided equally between husband and wife. By virtue of several Supreme Court decisions, married couples residing in these eight states had been splitting their incomes and filing separate federal returns. Shortly after World War II, a number of other states enacted community property laws for the express purpose of obtaining the same advantage for their residents, and other states were threatening to follow suit. In an effort to restore geographic tax equality and to prevent wholesale disruption of local property laws and procedures, the Congress universalized income splitting in 1948.

The effect of income splitting is to reduce progression for married couples. The tax rates nominally begin at 14, 15, 16, and 17 percent on the first four $500 segments of taxable incomes and rise to 70 percent on the portion of taxable incomes above $100,000. A married couple with taxable income of $2,000 splits this income and applies the first two rates to each half; without income splitting, the first four rates would apply to this income. Thus, whereas the nominal rate brackets cover taxable incomes up to $100,000, the actual rates for married couples extend to $200,000 (Table 4-2). The tax advantage rises from $5 for married couples with taxable income of $1,000 to $14,510 for couples with taxable incomes of $200,000 or more. In percentage terms, the tax advantage reaches a maximum of almost 30 percent at the $28,000 level (Figure 4-6).

The classic argument in favor of income splitting is that husbands and wives usually share their combined income equally. The largest portion of the family budget goes for consumption, and savings are ordinarily set aside for the children or for the enjoyment of all members of the family. Two conclusions follow from this view. First, married couples with the same combined income should pay the same tax irrespective of the legal division of income between them; second, the tax liabilities of married couples should be computed as if they were two single persons with their total income divided equally between them. The first conclusion is now firmly rooted in our tax law

FIGURE 4-6. Federal Tax Saving for Married Couples Filing Joint Returns, Heads of Households, and Single Persons, as a Percentage of the Basic Rate Schedule[a] Tax, by Taxable Income, 1971 Rates

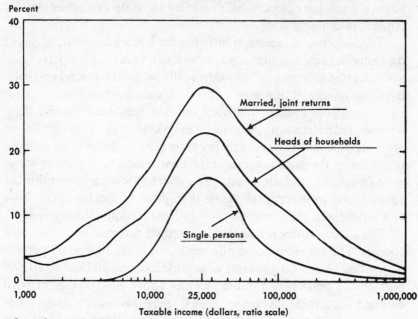

Source: Computed from Table 4-2.
[a] Married, separate returns.

and seems to be almost universally accepted. It is the second conclusion on which opinions still differ.

The case for the sharing argument is most applicable to the economic circumstances of taxpayers in the lower income classes, where incomes are used almost entirely for the consumption of the family unit. At the top of the income scale, the major rationale of income taxation is to cut down on the economic power of the family unit, and the use made of income in these levels for family purposes is irrelevant for this purpose. Obviously, these objectives cannot be reconciled if income splitting is extended to all income brackets.

The practical effect of income splitting is to produce large differences in the tax burdens of single persons and married couples, differences which depend on the *rate of graduation* and not on the level of rates. Such differences are difficult to rationalize on any theoretical grounds. Moreover, it is difficult to justify treating single persons with families more harshly than married persons in similar circumstances. As a remedy, widows and widowers are permitted to continue to split their incomes for two years after the death of the spouse, and half the advantage of joint returns is given (through a separate rate schedule) to single persons who maintain a household for children or other dependents or who maintain a separate household for their parents. This is, of course, a makeshift arrangement which hardly deals with the problem satisfactorily. For example, a single taxpayer who supports an aunt in a different household receives no income splitting benefit; if he supports an aged mother, he receives these benefits. Pressures on the Congress to treat single persons more liberally—by liberalizing the head-of-household provision, increasing their exemptions, and other devices—resulted in the adoption of a new rate schedule for single persons under the 1969 act. In this schedule, the single persons' rates never exceed by more than 20 percent the rates for married couples filing joint returns. In keeping with prior practice, the rate schedule for heads of households is half way between the single-person and joint-return rate schedules.

One of the major reasons for acceptance of the consequences of income splitting may well be the fact that personal exemptions do not provide enough differentiation among taxpayers in the middle and top brackets. Single persons, it is felt, should be taxed more heavily than married couples because they do not bear the costs and responsibilities of raising children. But income splitting for husband and wife clearly does not differentiate among taxpayers in this respect since the benefit is the same whether or not there are children.

The source of the difficulty in the income-splitting approach is that differentiation among families by size is made through the rate structure rather than through the personal exemptions. It would be possible to differentiate among taxpayer units by varying the personal exemptions with the size of income as well as the number of persons in the unit, with both a minimum and a maximum. This procedure could be used to achieve almost any desired degree of differentiation among families, while avoiding most of the problems and anomalies produced by income splitting.

Despite the theoretical objections to income splitting, the provision seems to be fairly popular in the United States. Under these circumstances, Congress has not considered alternative methods of allowing for marital status and family size.

The Aged

A graduated tax on income, after allowances for personal exemptions and extraordinary medical expenses, automatically allows for special circumstances of the taxpayer. Beyond this, the federal income tax has been particularly solicitous of the special circumstances of the aged. Taxpayers over 65 years of age have an additional personal exemption, pay no tax on their social security or railroad retirement pensions, and receive a 15 percent tax credit on other retirement income, less any earned income, up to a maximum of $1,524 ($2,286 on joint returns with only one earner and $3,048 with two earners). Until the end of 1966, they were also allowed to deduct all of their medical and dental expenses, instead of only the excess over 3 percent allowed other taxpayers. The latter benefit was eliminated when the federal program of hospital and medical insurance for the aged was enacted.

The exemptions for age and blindness, which will amount to over $5 billion on taxable returns when the $750 exemption becomes effective, were justified on the ground that these taxpayers have less ability to pay than do other members of the community. The aged and the blind are in fact concentrated at the lower end of the income distribution. However, the personal exemptions, the low-income allowance, and the graduated income tax rates were specifically designed to differentiate among the taxpaying abilities of individuals with different incomes. The aged and the blind would have a valid claim for an additional exemption if it could be shown that they are required to spend more out of a given income than are other taxpayers. There are no data on the expenditures of the blind, but the available evidence indicates that a family headed by an individual over 65 years of age actually spends less than a family headed by a young person in the same income group. It has also been argued that the aged find it difficult to obtain employment and, therefore, have less resilience to financial reverses than do other taxpayers. However, many other groups of taxpayers are handicapped in one way or another (for example, by physical or mental disabilities or lack of opportunity to receive training), and it would be impractical to take account of all these individual differences under an income tax.

The omission of social security and railroad retirement benefits from the tax base dates from the 1930s, when incomes were so low that it did not matter whether these payments were subject to tax or not. As incomes grew and social security was extended to almost the entire population, it became clear that the tax exemption for these benefits is extremely generous. Contributions by employees do not account for more than 10 to 20 percent of their benefits at the present time and will account for much less than 50 percent even when the systems mature. By contrast, up to 1954, recipients of pensions from other publicly administered retirement programs and from industrial pension plans were fully taxable on the portion of their benefits that exceeded their contributions. This discrimination was deeply resented by the recipients of taxable pensions. As a result, a credit against tax of 20 percent of the first $1,200 of retirement income (other than social security and railroad retirement benefits) was enacted in 1954. The maximum income subject to the credit was raised to $1,524 in 1962, and the credit was lowered to 15 percent in 1965.

Aside from the fact that special relief of this sort is questionable, the objections to these provisions are that it gives more tax advantage to aged persons the higher their income and discriminates against those who continue to work. In principle, it would be fairer to remove the additional exemption for age and make all retirement income taxable (with an allowance, of course, for the portion contributed by the employee, on which tax was paid when earned). The additional revenue could be used to good advantage to raise social security benefits for all aged persons. However, these suggestions appear to be politically impractical at this time.

As a substitute, in 1963, President Kennedy proposed replacing the extra exemption for the aged and the retirement income credit with a credit of $300 against tax at all levels. To avoid double benefits the credit would have been offset by an amount equal to the taxpayer's bracket rate times one-half the social security and railroad retirement benefits (the portion presumed to be attributable to the employer's contribution). These changes would have reduced the taxes of persons over 65 by more than $300 million on balance.

These proposals were eliminated from the 1964 tax bill, despite the fact that the administration would have accepted a substantial net tax reduction in the interest of reform in this area. A number of interested groups complained that a few elderly persons would be subject to somewhat higher taxes even taking into account the rate reductions; and this was obviously intolerable in an atmosphere of tax reduction. Although the final bill reduced the retirement income credit from 20 to 15 percent (to keep it at the average rate applicable to the first $2,000 of taxable income), it retained all the special provisions for the aged and made three additional concessions: (1) capital gains attributable to the first $20,000 of sales price on the sale of a personal residence by an individual aged 65 years or over were given a one-time exemption from tax; (2) the limit on income subject to retirement credit on joint returns was raised 50 percent, from $1,524 to $2,286, for married couples if both are over 65 and only one of them works (to allow for the 50 percent supplementary social security payment received by a husband on behalf of his wife) and was raised to $3,048 for aged couples both of whom work; and (3) the cost of all medicine and drugs purchased by persons over 65 was made fully deductible. (Other taxpayers may deduct only the excess over 1 percent of income.)

Earned Income

Personal exemptions for the taxpayer and his dependents and deductions for business and certain personal expenses are the only adjustments now made under the federal income tax in deriving the taxable income of an individual from his total income. One further adjustment was made in the United States in the years 1924–31 and 1934–43, and is still made in the United Kingdom and other countries. This is an allowance for incomes earned from work rather than through property ownership. The earned income allowance is justified by those who support it on the ground that earned incomes are not on a par with unearned incomes. It is also urged as a method of increasing work and management incentives.

THE EARNED INCOME ALLOWANCE. In the United States, the earned income allowance was granted in the form of a deduction that ranged from 10 percent to 25 percent of earned net income. In some years, the deduction was allowed for normal tax purposes only; in others, it was allowed for both normal tax and surtax. In all years, a certain minimum amount of income ($3,000 or $5,000) was presumed to be earned, whether it actually was earned or not, and the deduction was limited to a maximum ranging from $10,000 to $30,000. The tax value of the deduction was always small. It was never worth more than $496 for a family of two (in the period 1928–31); immediately before it was eliminated in 1944 as part of the wartime simplification program, the maximum value was $84. One state—Massachusetts—taxes investment income at a higher rate than earned income.

The equity argument in favor of an earned income allowance is that one person with a given amount of income that is earned has less ability to pay than does another who has the same amount of income, but which is unearned. Several reasons are cited to support this view. First, recipients of earned income do not have the benefit of an allowance for depreciation, and yet their productive capacities decline as they grow older and are ultimately exhausted. Second, expenses of earning an income are not taken into account fully by the individual income tax deductions. It was only recently (in 1964) that the law permitted a deduction for nonreimbursed moving expenses in connection with a new job. But such outlays as commuting expenses, the additional cost of lunches and other meals away from home, office clothing, and laundry and dry cleaning, make the costs of generating earned income higher than the costs of generating the same amount of income from property. Third, earning an income involves psychic costs and the sacrifice of leisure, warranting special income tax relief.

While these arguments appear to have some merit, there are good counterarguments. An earned income allowance is at best only a rough method of correcting for the alleged inequities. To the extent that there are inequities, they should be corrected directly through adjustments either in the structure of the income tax or in other government programs. For example, the depreciation argument is essentially a question involving old age insurance; if retirement benefits are inadequate, the best method of providing more adequate benefits is to increase them. If there are special costs involved in earning incomes, income tax deductions should be liberalized. Finally, as to the view that recipients of earned income have greater psychic costs, it can be argued that the accumulation of capital which produces unearned incomes also involves costs and sacrifices.

On balance, the case for an earned income allowance does not seem overwhelming. Where it has been employed, the allowance has been given to all people with incomes below a certain level and denied to those with incomes above a certain level, whether the income was earned or not. This means that, in practice, there was only a rough differentiation between earned and unearned incomes. There is also no basis for calculating the earned income element of the incomes of self-employed persons (for example, farmers and professional persons); in practice, this separation is made on the basis of an arbitrary formula. Moreover, a substantial earned income credit could be very expensive. For example, if the rate of tax on all earned incomes were reduced by 10 percent below the ordinary rates, the annual cost would be more than $7 billion. Further, an earned income credit is not simple, and it would complicate the tax return form.

MAXIMUM TAX RATE ON EARNED INCOME. The 1969 legislation took a new approach to increasing work incentives by placing a maximum marginal tax rate of 50 percent on earned income beginning in 1972 (60 percent in 1971). Such income includes wages and salaries, professional fees, and self-employment income. (Where capital is a material income-producing factor, not more than 30 percent of the net profits of a business is considered to be earned income.)

The effect of this provision will be to give significant tax reductions to business managers, highly paid lawyers, physicians, and other professionals, and successful businessmen who prefer to operate as sole proprietors rather than through the corporate form. The action was justified on the ground that it would substantially reduce the incentive to seek out tax avoidance schemes and would permit diversion of effort from tax planning into normal business operations. Since most tax preferences apply to unearned income, it is hard to see how the tax reduction on earned income will materially affect the search for tax avoidance schemes. Nor is the provision likely to have a measurable impact on the work actually performed by those who benefit from it. When it becomes fully effective in 1972, the 50 percent maximum tax rate will cost an estimated $170 million a year.

DEDUCTION FOR SAVINGS OF SELF-EMPLOYED. The law also permits self-employed persons to deduct all savings set aside for a retirement plan up to 10 percent of their earned income or $2,500, whichever is less. This provision was adopted because it was felt that self-employed persons find it difficult to accumulate tax-free savings for purposes of retirement. By contrast, wage earners and salaried employees do not pay tax on the amounts contributed to qualified pension plans in their behalf by the employers. The savings deduction for the self-employed was intended as an analogous provision for them, since they cannot participate in such plans.

When originally proposed, the plan did not have an upper limit to the allowable deduction for these contributions, and it also granted capital gains treatment to withdrawals from the retirement funds in which the savings were invested. As a result, it was regarded as a device to avoid taxes rather than to correct an inequity. These defects were corrected before the legislation was enacted. Although an increasing number of taxpayers have made use of this provision, there is no longer much concern about its abuse. In 1968, 244,070 individuals reported $374.6 million for this deduction.

ALLOWANCE FOR WORKING WIVES. Wholly apart from the treatment of earned income generally is the difficult question of taxing the incomes of working wives. A special exemption is given to working wives under the British income tax system. In the United States, except for an allowance of up to $15 against the normal tax in 1944 and 1945, a working wife credit or deduction has never been granted.

Working wife allowances are supported partly on incentive grounds and partly on equity grounds. The incentive argument is that, if the husband already earns income, the wife's earnings are taxable beginning at the first dollar. The higher the income of the husband, the higher is the marginal rate of tax on the additional income from the wife's employment. This high rate plus the additional costs of operating the household may deter some wives from seeking employment.

The equity argument is that the ability to pay taxes is not commensurate with the actual earnings of the working wife. The services that a wife performs at home (for example, housework, care of children) are ordinarily performed by domestic servants if she obtains gainful employment; moreover, clothing, laundry bills, and food are usually more expensive if the wife works and the family purchases are, in general, less efficient. It is not fair to tax all the additional earnings of the wife since they are partly absorbed in meeting these extra expenses.

A deduction for working wives that would be generous enough to encourage many to enter the labor market would be fairly costly. For example, if a deduction were allowed for 25 percent of the earned income of women with family responsibilities, revenues would probably be reduced by more than $2.5 billion annually. Most of this benefit would go to women who are already at work, so that there would be little incentive effect to compensate for the major part of the revenue loss. A relatively small deduction—say, 10 percent of earned income with a limit of perhaps $2,000—would cost more than $1 billion a year.

Capital Gains and Losses

An economic definition of income would include all capital gains in taxable income as they accrue each year. This would be impractical for three reasons: first, the value of many kinds of property cannot be estimated with sufficient accuracy to provide a basis for taxation; second, most people would regard it as unfair to be required to pay on income that had not actually been realized; and third, taxation of accruals might force liquidation of assets to pay the tax. Thus, capital gains are included in taxable income only when they are realized.

The United States has taxed the capital gains of individuals since it first taxed income, but this has not been the practice in many other countries. Realized capital gains were originally taxed as ordinary income, but since the Revenue Act of 1921 they have been subject to preferentially low rates. The provisions applying to such gains changed frequently during the 1920s and 1930s, but were stabilized beginning in 1942. In general, half of the capital gains on assets held for periods longer than six months are included in taxable income, and the amount of tax on such gains is limited to a maximum of 25 percent. The 1969 act left all of the old provisions intact, but added a new maximum rate for long-term gains of more than $50,000 of 29½ percent in 1970, 32½ percent in 1971, and 35 percent thereafter, and included in the base of the 10 percent minimum tax the half of the capital gains that are excluded from taxable income. Gains on the sale of owner-occupied houses are exempt if they are applied to the purchase of a new home within 12 months (18 months if newly built). For persons over 65, such gains are entirely exempt up to $20,000 of the sales price.

The treatment of capital gains is a compromise among conflicting objectives. From the standpoint of equity, it is well established that capital gains should be taken into account in determining personal tax liability. Moreover, preferential treatment of capital gains encourages the conversion of ordinary income into capital gains. Preferential legislation and business manipulation of this sort distort patterns of investment and discredit income taxation. The low capital gains rates are now provided for patent royalties, coal and iron ore royalties, income from livestock, income from the sale of unharvested crops, and real estate investments. The amount of ordinary income thus converted into capital gains is unknown, but a great deal of effort goes into this activity.

In addition to the overwhelming rate advantage, the law permits capital gains to escape income tax completely if they are passed from one generation to another through bequests. In the case of gifts, the gain is taxed only if the assets are later sold by the recipient. The result is that increases in the value of securities and real estate held in wealthy families may never be subject to income tax. Suppose a stock is now selling for $100 per share. An investor who bought 100,000 shares at $50 per share has a capital gain of $5,000,000. If he sold the stock (in a year in which his ordinary income is equal to the sum of his exemptions and deductions), under the 1969 law he would pay a capital gains tax of about $1,721,000 and a minimum tax of about $75,000, making a total tax of $1,796,000, or almost 36 percent of the total gain. If he bequeathed the stock to his children, no tax would ever be paid on the $5,000,000 gain. In its punitive mood against foundations in 1969, Congress removed this tax advantage for gifts or bequests to private foundations. In such cases, the donor is subject to the capital gains tax on the amount of the unrealized capital gains included in the gift or bequest.

On the other hand, bunching of capital gains in years of realization requires some moderation of the rates or some provision to average them over a period of years. Full taxation of capital gains is also criticized because it might have a substantial "locking-in" effect on investors and reduce the mobility of capital. It is also argued that preferential treatment of capital gains helps to stimulate a higher rate of economic growth by increasing the attractiveness of investment generally, and of risky investments in particular.

The "bunching problem" that would arise with full taxation of capital gains could easily be handled either by prorating capital gains over the length of time the asset was held or by extending the present general averaging system to the full amount of capital gains. (It now applies only to the portion of long-term gains that is included in taxable income.) However, unless the marginal rates were reduced drastically, the tax might still discourage the transfer of assets. Part of the difficulty is that adherence to the realization principle permits capital gains to be transferred tax free either by gift or at death. The solution to this problem is to treat capital gains as if they were constructively realized at gift or at death, with an averaging provision to allow for spreading of the gains over a period of years. (This method was proposed by President Kennedy in 1963 and by President Johnson's Treasury Department in early 1969, but has not been approved by Congress.) Under such a system, the only advantage tax-payers would have from postponing the realization of capital gains would be the accumulation of interest on the tax postponed. Unless the assets were held for many years, this advantage would be small compared to the advantage of the tax exemption accorded to gains transferred at death; in any event the net advantage is small because the interest on the tax postponed would be subject to income tax when the assets are transferred. Under these circumstances, the incentive to hold gains indefinitely for tax reasons alone would be greatly reduced.

In the quest to reconcile equity and economic objectives in the taxation of capital gains, tax experts differ as to the best approach. A sizable number believe that realized capital gains and those transferred by gift or at death should be taxed in full, with a provision for averaging either over the period during which the asset was held or over an arbitrary but lengthy period. Some believe that present arrangements may be the best that can be devised, while others insist that the capital gains rates are still too high. Most experts agree that there is little justification for granting preferential treatment to income that is not a genuine capital gain.

The preferential rates apply to capital gains on assets that have been held for six months or longer. This "holding period" has been criticized as being both too long and too short. Investor groups urge that the holding period be reduced to three months, and some even recommend that it be eliminated entirely, maintaining that the resulting additional security transactions would increase capital gains tax revenues. On the other hand, in an annual income tax, there is no logical equity reason for reducing the tax rate on incomes earned in less than a year. There has been disagreement on this point since the six-month holding period was enacted in 1942.

In principle, capital losses should be deductible in full against either capital gains or ordinary income. However, when gains and losses are recognized only upon realization, taxpayers can easily time their sales so as to take losses promptly when they occur and to postpone gains for as long a period as possible. There is no effective method of avoiding this type of asymmetry under our system of capital gains taxation. The stopgap used in the United States is to limit the deduction of losses. From 1942 through 1963, individuals were allowed to offset their capital losses against capital gains plus $1,000 of ordinary income in the year of realization and in the five subsequent years. In 1964, the loss offset up to $1,000 of ordinary income was extended to an indefinite period. In computing the offset, long-term losses were taken into account in full between 1952 and 1969; prior to 1952 and after 1969, only 50 percent of the long-term loss may be offset against ordinary income up to the $1,000 limit.

The annual limit on the amount of the offset is perhaps most harmful to small investors, who are less likely than those in the higher brackets to have gains from which to subtract their losses. The only solution to this problem is a pragmatic one that is reasonably liberal for the small investor without opening the door to widespread abuse of the provision and large revenue losses.

State and Local Government Bond Interest

Interest received from state and local government bonds has been exempt from income tax ever since its enactment in 1913. The tax exemption has been criticized by secretaries of the treasury, tax experts, and others who believe that it is inequitable, reduces risk investment by high bracket taxpayers, and costs an excessive amount to the federal government. Interest rates on state-local bonds have increased as state-local debt has risen in recent years, and the relative advantage of the exemption to the top income classes has greatly increased. Proponents of the exemption argue that its elimination would make state-local borrowing costs prohibitive and that it would be unwise to impair the borrowing ability of these units of government in view of their mounting needs. Bills to remove the exemption have reached a vote in Congress six times, but each time they have been defeated.

By discriminating between income from municipals and from other securities, and by giving an advantage to investors in the high income brackets, the exemption violates the generally accepted principles that an income tax should apply equally to equal incomes and should be progressive. It also reduces investment in productive enterprises by diverting risk or venture capital from the private sector. It distorts the allocation of resources within the private sector, and between the public and private sectors when state and local governments issue tax-exempt securities to finance such "business" enterprises as public utilities and housing developments, or to subsidize the growth of local industry. (Even many who favor the exemption agree that the use of so-called industrial development bonds to build tax-exempt facilities for private firms should be halted.) Interest on such bonds was made subject to tax in 1968 if the value of the amount issued for a single project exceeds $1 million.

Further, the exemption is an inefficient type of subsidy. Empirical studies suggest that the saving in interest payments by state and local governments is little more than half the revenue loss to the federal government. There are less costly ways to assist or subsidize capital outlays by state and local governments. There are also more equitable methods, since governmental units benefit more from the exemption to the extent that they issue more debt, rather than on the basis of need.

Interest costs of state and local governments would rise if the exemption were removed. Municipals are more difficult to market than are corporates and other securities. Many issues are too small to appeal to large institutional buyers. Moreover, a lack of information about the finances of small units of local government discourages some investors. Thus, if the municipals were fully taxable, they would have to bear higher interest rates than do corporate bonds of comparable quality. This would probably discourage borrowing in some localities and thus reduce capital expenditures for public purposes. If total outlays were to rise in some areas, state and local taxes would ultimately be increased to meet higher interest charges. Since local taxes tend to be regressive, a greater burden might fall on the lower-income groups. It has also been argued that the heavier financial burden on state and local governments, added to existing unmet needs for public facilities, would intensify pressure for federal aid, bring greater federal participation in local affairs, and further reduce the fiscal independence of states and localities.

Because opponents of the exemption concede that some desirable investment in social capital might be curtailed if the localities had to pay higher interest charges, they have often coupled suggestions for abolishing the exemption with proposals to provide alternative federal subsidies. These have generally taken one of two forms: (1) subsidies tied to state and local borrowing (for example, the payment of a portion of the interest on state-local debt by the federal government) as a quid pro quo for giving up the exemption, or (2) subsidies tied to capital outlays rather than borrowing and thus not allocated strictly according to exemption benefits lost. In 1969, the House bill provided that state and local governments could voluntarily relinquish the tax-exemption privilege with respect to any specific bond issue and the Treasury would pay up to 40 percent of the interest on the issue, depending on the value of the tax exemption in the market. The provision was strongly opposed by representatives of state and local governments and was dropped in the Senate version of the bill.

Proposals to remove the exemption have usually been limited to new issues only. This approach reflects the belief that taxing outstanding securities would be a breach of faith by the federal government, causing capital losses and the inequitable application of taxes to holders of existing securities.

Some lawyers have argued that taxing state-local bond interest is unconstitutional, whether the proposal is to apply the tax to new issues only or to existing ones as well. The majority opinion seems to be that there is no constitutional bar to taxing state-local bond interest if Congress wants to do so.

The major problem is political. If the tax exemption is replaced by a generous subsidy, many people fear that there will be an unhealthy increase in federal control over state and local fiscal affairs. Even the possibility of more federal control is often sufficient argument for some to oppose removal of the exemption. In this view, inefficiencies or tax inequities arising from the exemption are trivial compared to the dangers of more centralization of fiscal activity and possible disruption of the usual credit channels used by the state and local governments. Others argue that efficiency and tax equity are important enough to justify exploring the possibility of substituting for the tax exemption an alternative formula that would not involve greater federal control.

These differing views are irreconcilable, and it seems clear that modification of the exemption would not stand a chance of being adopted unless an alternative method of compensation for state and local governments could be devised that would not involve any federal participation, let alone interference, in the purposes for which state-local borrowing is undertaken.

Income Averaging

The use of an annual accounting period, combined with progressive income taxes, results in a heavier tax burden on fluctuating incomes than on an equal amount of income distributed evenly over the years. For example, a single taxpayer who has a taxable income of $25,000 in each of two successive years pays a total tax of $14,380 (1971 rates) in the two years. If he received $50,000 one year and nothing the next, his tax would be $20,190.

This type of discrimination is hard to defend on either equity or economic grounds. Taxpayers usually do not and cannot arrange their business and personal affairs to conform with the calendar. Annual income fluctuations are frequently beyond the control of the taxpayer, yet he is taxed as if twelve months were a suitable horizon for decision making. In addition, in the absence of averaging, there are great pressures for moderating the impact of the graduated rates on fluctuating incomes by lowering the rates applicable to them. As already indicated, reduced rates on capital gains have been justified on this basis although the rate reductions for such gains more than compensated for the lack of averaging.

There is general agreement on the need for averaging, but the roadblock has always been the administrative problem. Keeping an accurate account for a number of years is difficult for the government as well as for the taxpayer. It was felt, therefore, that it would be desirable to start modestly.

A start was made under the Revenue Act of 1964, which permitted averaging income over a five-year period if the income in the current year exceeded the average of that of the four prior years by one-third and if this excess was more than $3,000. The provision was made available to taxpayers who had been at least 50 percent self-supporting for the four prior years. The averaging technique is (a) to compute a tentative tax on one-fifth of the "averageable income" and (b) to multiply the tentative tax by five. The 1969 act increased the amount of income that can be averaged by permitting averaging if the current year's income exceeds the average of the four prior years by 20 percent and this excess is over $3,000. The 1969 act also permitted for the first time the averaging of the portion of capital gains included in taxable income.

The restriction of averaging to those who have an *increase* in income eliminated from the averaging system the millions of persons who have a sharp reduction in income at retirement. It would be desirable to provide averaging for those who have reductions in income if a suitable way to avoid including retired persons in the averaging system can be devised. The present provision is nevertheless a step in the right direction.

Minimum Tax and Allocation of Deductions

The introduction of the minimum tax in the Tax Reform Act of 1969 was an attempt to obtain some tax contribution from wealthy individuals who had previously escaped income taxation on all or most of their income. The tax is levied at a 10 percent rate on a selected list of preference incomes to the extent that income from all the items exceeds (1) a $30,000 exemption and (2) the regular income tax for the year. The most important preference incomes in the minimum tax base for individuals are the 50 percent of long-term capital gains excluded from taxable income, depletion deductions in excess of the amount that would be allowed on the basis of cost, accelerated depreciation on real property, and the value of a stock option given to an employee at the time the option is exercised. The minimum tax is expected to yield $285 million a year from individuals (at 1969 income levels).

The minimum tax may be criticized on three grounds. First, the application of a low flat rate of tax violates the principle of progression. Since the tax applies only to wealthy people, the preference incomes would be taxed at or near the top bracket rates if they were included in the regular income tax base. Second, the list of preferences is not comprehensive. The most important preferences not included in the minimum tax base are tax-exempt interest and personal deductions. Third, the generous exemption and the deduction for the regular income tax paid restricts the applicability of the minimum tax to a small number of taxpayers.

Another method of cutting down the benefits of tax-exempt income would be to allocate personal deductions proportionately between the individual's taxable and nontaxable sources and to permit a deduction only for the amount allocated to the taxable sources. This proposal is based on the reasonable assumption that personal outlays—whether deductible or not—come out of the taxpayer's total income, rather than out of his taxable income alone. The House version of the 1969 act included this provision, but it was eliminated by the Senate, largely because of the opposition of representatives of tax-exempt institutions and of state and local governments, who generally disapprove any proposal that would reduce the tax advantages of the charitable contribution deduction and of state-local securities.

Although allocation of deductions was rejected, the enactment of the minimum tax reflects an awareness on the part of Congress of the growing public resentment toward unwarranted tax privileges. Although it is a weak compromise, the minimum tax is the first break in the long struggle to achieve a comprehensive income tax base. Mere publication of the amount of the tax preferences reported on tax returns will dramatize the inequities of the present tax structure. Enlargement of the base and eventual unification of the minimum tax with the regular income tax should be high on the agenda for income tax revision in the years ahead.

Summary

The individual income tax—the most important tax in the federal tax structure—is widely regarded as the fairest source of government revenues. Its yield expands or contracts more rapidly than personal income during a business cycle, thus imparting built-in flexibility to the revenue side of the federal budget. The tax is less burdensome on consumption and more burdensome on saving than a consumption or expenditure tax of equal yield would be. Its potential effect on work and investment incentives is unclear. There is no evidence to support the contention that the income tax significantly retards growth. The nation has grown at a satisfactory rate during most of the period since the income tax was enacted.

Many unsettled problems remain regarding some of the major features of the individual income tax. These include the treatment of the family, the aged, earned income, special deductions for personal expenditures, capital gains and losses, tax-exempt interest, the appropriate length of the tax accounting period, and the minimum tax. Even in its present form, however, the individual income tax continues to be the best tax ever devised. Further improvement through broadening the tax base and lowering the tax rates would pay handsome dividends in still greater equity and better economic performance.

CHAPTER FIVE

The Corporation Income Tax

THE CORPORATION INCOME TAX was enacted in 1909, four years before the introduction of the individual income tax. To avoid a constitutional issue, Congress levied the tax as an excise on the privilege of doing business as a corporation. The law was challenged, but the Supreme Court upheld the authority of the federal government to impose such a tax and ruled that the privilege of doing corporate business could be measured by the corporation's profits.

Since 1909, the corporation income tax has been a mainstay of the federal tax system. It produced more revenue than the individual income tax in seventeen of the twenty-eight years prior to 1941, when the latter was greatly expanded as a source of wartime revenue. From 1941 through 1967, corporation income tax revenues were second only to those of the individual income tax, but they were overtaken by payroll taxes in 1968. In fiscal year 1970, the corporation income tax accounted for about 17 percent of federal receipts. Like the individual income tax, a tax on corporation profits is likely to be a major federal revenue source for a long time to come.

A special tax on the corporate form of doing business is considered appropriate because corporations enjoy special privileges and benefits. These include perpetual life, limited liability of shareholders, liquidity of ownership through marketability of shares, growth through retention of earnings, and possibilities of intercorporate affiliations. More-

over, the modern corporation—particularly the large "public" corporation in which management and ownership are separated—generates
income that nobody may claim for personal use. The growth of the
corporate sector could not have taken place if the corporation had
not been endowed with these valuable privileges. The Supreme Court's
acceptance of the constitutionality of the corporation income tax was
based on the view that the corporation owes its life, rights, and power
to the government.

Whether or not this basic rationale is accepted, the corporation
income tax is needed to safeguard the individual income tax. If corporate incomes were not subject to tax, individuals could avoid the
individual income tax by accumulating income in corporations. Short
of taxing shareholders on their shares of corporate incomes whether
or not the incomes are distributed (a method that is attractive to tax
theorists, but not to businessmen and tax practitioners), the most
practical way to protect the individual income tax is to impose a separate tax on corporate incomes. The existence of two separate taxes
side by side creates other problems; these will be discussed at some
length in this chapter.

Despite its prominence in the federal revenue system, the corporation income tax is the subject of considerable controversy. In the first
place, there is probably less agreement about who really pays the
corporation income tax than there is about any other tax. Some believe that the tax is borne by the corporations and, hence, by their
stockholders. Others argue that the tax is passed on to consumers
through higher prices. Still others suggest that the tax may be shifted
back to the workers in lower wages. A substantial number believe
that it is borne by all three groups—stockholders, consumers, and
wage earners—in varying proportions. This uncertainty regarding the
incidence of the tax makes strange bedfellows of individuals holding
diametrically opposed views and often puts them in inconsistent
positions. Some staunch opponents of a sales tax vigorously support
the corporation income tax even though they believe it is shifted to
the consumer, while many who believe that the corporation tax is
"just another cost" (and is, therefore, shifted) demand reduction of
the corporation income tax and substitution of some form of consumption tax for all or part of it.

Second, the proper relation between individual and corporation
income taxes has never been settled. At various times, dividends have

been allowed as a credit or deduction in computing the tax on individual income. Today, individuals are allowed a $100 exclusion for dividends, which is intended to relieve the small shareholder from paying both individual and corporation income taxes on his dividends. The present situation is makeshift and satisfies few people.

A third set of issues has to do with the impact of the corporation tax on the corporate sector and on the economy in general. It has been argued that the tax curtails business investment and thus reduces the nation's growth rate. Since interest paid is deductible in computing taxable corporation profits, while dividends paid are not, the tax is said to favor debt over equity financing. Some question the desirability of a tax that discourages the corporate form of business. Others believe, however, that alternative tax sources yielding the same revenue would be much more harmful to the economy.

Characteristics of the Tax

Since the corporation income tax is a tax on business, many of the refinements required in the computation of taxable income of individuals do not arise. For example, the deductions allowed under the corporation income tax, with the exception of that for charitable contributions, are confined to expenses incurred in doing business. State-local bond interest is exempt from the corporation income tax as well as from the individual income tax, and capital gains and losses receive special treatment. Corporations are also required to pay taxes in quarterly installments as profits are earned during the year.

The Tax Base

The corporation income tax is a complicated instrument because it must be applied to a wide variety of organizations doing business in the corporate form or in a form that closely resembles a corporation. The major features will be discussed in a later section of the chapter; but at this point, a number of the significant provisions may be noted.

1. As in the case of individuals, capital gains realized on assets held more than six months are taxed at a lower rate than that applying to ordinary income. However, the maximum tax rate on corporate capital gains is 30 percent, instead of the 35 percent maximum that applies to capital gains of individuals. The treatment of capital losses is also different. Whereas individuals may deduct half of net capital

losses up to $1,000 from ordinary income, corporations are allowed
to offset capital losses only against capital gains. The remaining capital losses may be carried back for three years and forward for five
years to be offset against capital gains.

2. Net operating losses may be carried back and offset against
taxable income of the three preceding years. If the income in these
years is not sufficient, the remaining losses may be carried forward
for five years. In effect, this provides a nine-year period for offsetting
losses against gains.

3. Generous provision is made for recovery of capital. In the case
of plant and equipment, the original cost may be amortized over the
useful life of the asset. Formerly, the law in effect limited the rate of
amortization for most corporations to the straight-line method (that
is, the cost was allocated evenly over the life of the asset). New methods adopted in 1954 permit a faster rate of depreciation in the early
years. Service lives were shortened in 1962. In addition to depreciation, an investment credit of 7 percent against tax liability was
allowed between 1962 and 1969 for purchases of new equipment.
(Buildings were not entitled to the credit.) For minerals and gas and
oil, the law allows deductions for the costs of exploration, discovery,
and depletion, which often exceed the cost of the mine or oil or gas
fields.

4. All current outlays for research and development may be deducted in full in the year they are made. Taxpayers may elect to cap-
italize such expenditures and, if regular depreciation cannot be used
because the useful life cannot be determined, the expenditures may
be written off over a period of five years.

The provisions for net operating losses, recovery of capital, and
research and development expenses (items 2, 3, and 4 above) are also
available to individuals and partnerships under the individual income
tax.

5. Intercorporate dividends paid by one corporation to another
are subject to tax at a relatively low rate. Corporations are allowed to
deduct 85 percent of the dividends they receive from other domestic
corporations. This means that intercorporate dividends are subject
to an extra tax of 7.2 percent (the regular 48 percent rate multiplied
by 15 percent). The tax on intercorporate dividends is waived, however, if the two corporations are members of a group of affiliated
corporations. These provisions encourage the use of consolidated

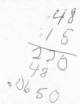

returns on the presumption that only in this way can the true net income of the affiliated group be determined.

6. Corporations are subject to U.S. tax on foreign as well as domestic income. Income received from foreign branches is included in the corporation's tax return in the year it is earned. If the corporation operates through a subsidiary, foreign earnings are subject to tax when they are distributed to the U.S. parent corporation as dividends. However, credit against the domestic tax is allowed for foreign income taxes paid on earnings and dividends received from abroad. A rate reduction in the corporation income tax of 14 percentage points is in effect granted to domestic trade corporations conducting 95 percent of their business outside the United States, but in the western hemisphere.

7. Corporations with no more than ten shareholders may elect to be treated as partnerships for tax purposes. Such shareholders are subject to individual income tax on the entire earnings of the corporation, whether or not distributed, and may deduct any losses from other personal incomes. In 1967, 200,784 small corporations reporting profits of $2.5 billion and deficits of $632 million elected this treatment.

8. Religious, educational, and charitable organizations, trade associations, labor unions, and fraternal organizations are exempt from the corporation income tax, but the corporation income tax does apply to the "unrelated business income" of these organizations. Private foundations are subject to a special tax of 4 percent on their investment incomes. Cooperatives are subject to special provisions designed to tax their earnings at least once under the individual or corporation income tax, but the revenue collected from them is small. Investment funds that distribute at least 90 percent of their dividends and realized capital gains to their shareholders are not taxable. Mutual financial institutions, including savings and loan associations, mutual savings banks, and insurance companies, are taxed, but they are permitted to accumulate substantial tax-free reserves because of their fiduciary character.

Tax Rates

Since corporations do not have "ability to pay" in the same sense that individuals do, the corporation income tax is levied at a flat rate on most corporate incomes. A lower rate is applied to the first $25,000 as a concession to small businesses; the remainder is taxed at one rate. Today, the corporate tax consists of a 22 percent normal tax and a 26 percent surtax, with an exemption of $25,000 for the surtax only. Thus, the combined rates are 22 percent on the first $25,000 and 48 percent on the excess over $25,000. Roughly 95 percent of corporate taxable income is subject to the 48 percent rate (Appendix Table B-9).

The 1969 legislation imposed a 10 percent minimum tax on the preference items of corporations as well as individuals. The most important of these items for corporations are: interest payments in excess of investment income, $\frac{18}{48}$ of long-term capital gains (that is, the proportion of gains that is not subject to the full corporation tax), accelerated depreciation on real property in excess of straight-line depreciation, depletion in excess of adjusted basis depletion, and bad debt deductions of financial institutions in excess of loss experience. The minimum tax is applied to the total amount of the preferences above an exemption of $30,000 plus the regular income tax paid.

Tax Payment

The provision for paying taxes currently applied only to individuals when it was enacted during World War II. Corporations continued to pay their tax, as they had from the beginning, in four installments in the year following the tax year. This state of affairs continued until 1950, when payments were gradually shifted over a period of five years to two installments to be paid in the first six months of the year following the tax year (Appendix Table C-16).

Further acceleration of corporation tax payments was legislated in 1954. After another transition period of five years, corporations were required to pay half of their estimated tax over $100,000 in September and December of the tax year, and the remaining liability in two installments in March and June of the following year.

Further steps to place corporations on a current payment basis were taken in 1964 and 1966. After an additional transition period of four years (originally seven years under the 1964 legislation), corporations paid their estimated tax (in excess of $100,000) in four installments in the current year. Since 1967, large corporations and individuals filing declarations of estimated tax have paid tax on the same time schedule. The 1968 act extended the current payment system to all corporate tax liabilities, to be fully effective in 1977.

Shifting and Incidence of the Tax

There is no more controversial issue in taxation than the question: *Who bears the corporation income tax?* On this question, economists and businessmen alike differ among themselves. The following quotations are representative of these divergent views:

> The initial or short-run incidence of the corporate income tax seems to be largely on corporations and their stockholders. . . . There seems to be little foundation for the belief that a large part of the corporate tax comes out of wages or is passed on to consumers in the same way that a selective excise [tax] tends to be shifted to buyers. (Richard Goode, *The Corporation Income Tax*, John Wiley, 1951, pp. 71–72.)

> . . . the corporation profits tax is almost entirely shifted; the government simply uses the corporation as a tax collector. (Kenneth E. Boulding, *The Organizational Revolution*, Harper and Brothers, 1953, p. 277.)

> Corporate taxes are simply costs, and the method of their assessment does not change this fact. Costs must be paid by the public in prices, and corporate taxes are thus, in effect, concealed sales taxes. (Enders M. Voorhees, chairman of Finance Committee, U.S. Steel Corporation, address before the Controllers' Institute of America, New York, Sept. 21, 1943.)

> The observation is frequently made that because in the long run the [corporate] tax tends to be included in the price of the product, it is to this extent borne by consumers. This observation misconstrues the nature of the tax. Fundamentally, it is a tax on a factor of production: corporate equity capital. (Arnold C. Harberger, "The Corporation Income Tax: An Empirical Appraisal," *Tax Revision Compendium*, House Ways and Means Committee, Vol. 1, 1959, p. 241.)

> . . . an increase in the [corporate] tax is shifted fully through short-run adjustments to prevent a decline in the net rate of return [on corporate investment], and . . . these adjustments are maintained subsequently. (Marian Krzyzaniak and Richard A. Musgrave, *The Shifting of the Corporation Income Tax*, Johns Hopkins Press, 1963, p. 65.)

Unfortunately, economics has not yet provided a scientific basis for accepting or rejecting one side or the other. This section presents the logic of each view and summarizes the evidence.

The Shifting Mechanism

One reason for the sharply divergent views is that the opponents frequently do not refer to the same type of shifting. It is important to distinguish between short- and long-run shifting and the mechanisms through which they operate. The "short run" is defined by economists as a period that is too short for firms to adjust their capital to changing demand and supply conditions. The "long run" is a period in which capital can be adjusted.

SHORT RUN. The classical view in economics is that the corporation income tax cannot be shifted in the short run. The argument is as follows: all business firms, whether they are competitive or monopolistic, seek to maximize net profits. This maximum occurs when output and prices are set at the point where the cost of producing an additional unit is exactly equal to the additional revenue obtained from the sale of that unit. In the short run, a corporation income tax should make no difference in this decision. The output and price that maximized the firm's profits before the tax will continue to maximize profits after the tax is imposed. (This follows from simple arithmetic. If a series of figures is reduced by the same percentage, the figure that was highest before will still be the highest after the percentage reduction is made.)

The argument against this view is that today's markets are characterized neither by perfect competition nor by monopoly; instead, they show considerable imperfection and mutual interdependence or oligopoly. In such markets, business firms may set their prices at the level that covers their full costs *plus* a margin for profits. Alternatively, the firms are described as aiming at an after-tax target rate of return on invested capital. Under the cost-plus behavior, the firm treats the tax as an element of cost and raises its price to recover the tax. Similarly, if the firm's objective is the after-tax target rate of return, imposition of a tax or an increase in the tax rate—by reducing the rate of return on invested capital—will have to be accounted for in making output and price decisions. To preserve the target rate of return, the tax must be shifted forward to consumers or backward to the workers, or be shifted partly forward and partly backward.

It is also argued that the economists' models are irrelevant in most markets where one or a few large firms exercise a substantial degree of leadership. In such markets, efficient producers raise their prices to recover the tax, and the tax merely forms an "umbrella" that permits less efficient or marginal producers to survive.

When business managers are asked about their pricing policies, they often say that they shift the corporation income tax. However, there is little evidence to support this position. Economists have debated whether firms actually behave in this way, but they have not reached a consensus.

Even if this behavior on the part of business firms is accepted, some doubts must be expressed about their ability to shift fully the corporation income tax in the short run. In the first place, the tax depends on the outcome of business operations during an entire year. The businessman can only guess the ratio of the tax to his gross receipts, and it is hard to conceive of his setting a price that would recover the precise amount of tax he will eventually pay. (If shifting were possible, there would be some instances of firms shifting more than 100 percent of the tax, but few economists believe that overshifting does in fact occur.)

Second, the businessman knows that if he should attempt to recover the corporation income tax through higher prices (or lower wages), other firms would not necessarily do the same. Some firms make no profit and thus pay no tax; among other firms, the ratio of tax to gross receipts differs. In multiproduct firms, the producer has very little basis for judging the ratio of tax to gross receipts for each product. All these possibilities increase the uncertainty of response by other firms and make the attempt to shift part or all of the corporation income tax hazardous.

LONG RUN. Unless it is shifted in the short run to consumers or wage earners, or both, the corporation income tax influences investment in the long run by reducing the rate of return on corporate equity. The tax may discourage the use of capital altogether or encourage investment in debt-intensive industries (for example, real estate) and unincorporated enterprises. The result is a smaller supply of corporate products, unless the reduction in equity investment is offset by an increase in borrowing.

The incidence of the corporation income tax depends on whether the tax is or is not shifted in the short run. Short-run shifting means that net after-tax rates of return are maintained at the levels prevailing before the tax; the burden of the tax falls on consumers or wage earners. If the tax is not shifted in the short run, net after-tax rates of re-

turn are depressed, and the amount of corporate investment is reduced. After-tax rates of return tend to be equalized with those in the
noncorporate sector, but in the process, corporate capital and output
will have been permanently reduced. Thus, in the absence of short-run
shifting, the burden of the tax falls on the owners of capital.

The Evidence

The evidence on the incidence of the corporation income tax is
inconclusive. The data do not permit a clear determination of the
factors affecting price and wage decisions: different authors examining the same set of facts have come to diametrically opposite conclusions.

With respect to the long run, there is evidence first that unincorporated business has not grown at the expense of incorporated business.
Corporations accounted for 58 percent of the national income originating in the business sector in 1929, 61 percent in 1948, and 68 percent in 1969 (Figure 5-1). Much of the increase comes from the rela-

FIGURE 5-1. Percentage of Business Income Originating in the Corporate Sector, 1929–69[a]

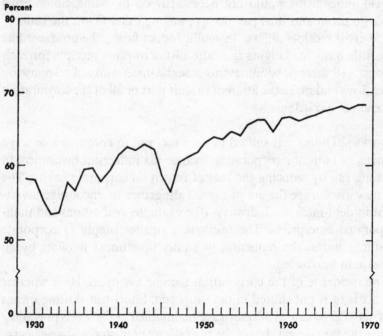

Source: Appendix Table C-17.
[a] Business income is national income originating in business enterprises.

tive decline of industries, particularly farming, in which corporations are not important; but, even in the rest of the economy, there is no indication of a shift away from the corporate form of organization. The advantages of doing business in the corporate form far outweigh whatever deterrent effects the corporation tax might have on corporate investment.

Beyond this, the data are conflicting. On the one hand, rates of return reported by corporations after tax were slightly higher in the 1950s and 1960s than in the late 1920s, when the corporation income tax was much lower. After-tax rates of return on equity capital in manufacturing were 7.8 percent in 1927–29, 8.8 percent in 1953–56, 6.9 percent in 1957–61, and 9.6 percent in 1964–67. On total capital (equity plus debt), the returns were 7.8 percent, 8.0 percent, 6.5 percent, and 8.7 percent, respectively (Table 5-1). Before-tax rates of return were 70 to 100 percent higher in the 1960s than in the late 1920s.

On the other hand, the share of property income before tax (profits, interest, and capital consumption allowances) in corporate gross product changed little over the same period (Figure 5-2). Thus, corporations have been able to increase their before-tax profits enough to avoid a reduction in the after-tax return, without increasing their share of income in the corporate sector. These observations suggest that corporations have not increased rates of return before tax by marking up prices or by lowering wages, but by making more efficient use of their capital. However, what might have occurred in the absence of the tax is unknown, and thus its long-run effect remains unclear.

TABLE 5-1. Rates of Return and Debt-Capital Ratio, Manufacturing Corporations, Selected Years, 1927–67

(In percentages)

Item	1927–29	1936–39	1953–56	1957–61	1964–67
Return on equity[a]					
Before tax	8.8	7.8	18.4	14.1	17.8
After tax	7.8	6.4	8.8	6.9	9.6
Return on total capital[ab]					
Before tax	8.7	7.3	15.6	12.2	14.9
After tax	7.8	6.2	8.0	6.5	8.7
Ratio of debt to total capital[c]	15.2	15.0	19.0	20.5	25.1
General corporation tax rate[d]	12.2	17.0	52.0	52.0	48.5

Source: Appendix Tables A-3 and C-18.
[a] Equity and debt capital are averages of book values for the beginning and end of the year.
[b] Profits plus interest paid as a percentage of total capital.
[c] End of year.
[d] Statutory rate of federal corporation income tax applicable to large corporations (average of annual figures).

FIGURE 5-2. Property Income Share in Corporate Gross Product Less Indirect Taxes, 1922–29 and 1948–69[a]

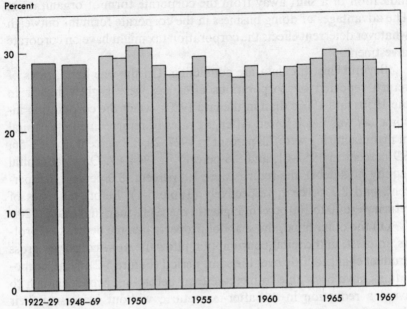

Sources: 1922–29: Worksheets of U.S. Department of Commerce, Office of Business Economics; 1948–69: Appendix Table C-17.

[a] Property income includes corporate profits before tax and inventory valuation adjustment, net interest, and corporate capital consumption allowances.

Economic Issues

The corporation income tax has been subject to a continuous barrage of criticism on economic grounds. The most critical issues have been its effect on: (1) investment and saving; (2) equity and debt finance; (3) resource allocation; (4) built-in flexibility of the tax system; and (5) the balance of payments. The charges and countercharges reflect different assumptions as to who bears the tax and the inherent difficulty of separating the effect of taxation from other factors.

Investment and Saving

The corporation income tax may affect investment in either of two ways: through investment incentives or through the availability of funds for investment.

INVESTMENT INCENTIVES. New investments will be undertaken by corporations if they promise to yield a satisfactory rate of return *after tax*. The higher the corporation tax, the higher the pre-tax rate of return must be to preserve the after-tax return. To remain equally attractive, an investment that promised a 10 percent return in the absence of the tax must yield a pre-tax rate of return of 19.2 percent with a tax rate of 48 percent. If 10 percent after tax is required to induce investments, corporations will defer the construction of new facilities and the purchase of new equipment unless there are projects that yield 19.2 percent or more before tax. This is the process, discussed earlier, through which the tax exercises its effect on investment; it depends crucially on the assumption that the corporation income tax is not shifted in the short run.

Is it possible to detect any reduction in the rate of investment that can be attributed to the high corporation income tax? The answer is no, for two reasons. First, high tax rates were introduced during World War II, when wartime demands and support by government helped maintain investment at a high level. In the immediate postwar period, the rate of investment was extremely high because of the huge backlog of demand. Investment demand receded in the late 1950s, but this is attributed primarily to the slowdown in the rate of economic growth. The ratio of investment to the gross national product rose during the recovery of the early 1960s and stayed at high levels in the latter half of the decade.

Second, although the corporation tax rate has remained at a high level in the last two decades, part of its adverse effect on investment has been cushioned by substantial increases in investment allowances. Whereas straight-line depreciation was the rule before World War II, regulations since 1954 have allowed more liberal depreciation methods. In addition, as was noted above, a 7 percent tax credit was allowed for investment in plant and equipment between 1962 and 1969. The effect of these changes may be illustrated by the following figures: in 1954, the corporation tax amounted to 32.8 percent of corporation profits before tax and capital consumption allowances; it was reduced to 30.5 percent in 1959 and 27.7 percent in 1963 (Table 5-2). This five-point reduction in the effective rate occurred during a period when the general corporation income tax rate remained at 52 percent. The effective rate declined to 26 percent in 1965–67, when the corporation

TABLE 5-2. Comparison of the General Corporation Income Tax Rate and Effective Rate of Federal Taxes on Corporation Profits before Tax and before Capital Consumption Allowances, 1946–69

Year	General corporation tax rate (percentages)	Corporation profits before tax and capital consumption allowances[a] (billions of dollars)	Federal corporation taxes	
			Amount (billions of dollars)	Percentage of profits before tax and allowances
1946	38	28.9	8.6	29.8
1947	38	36.6	10.7	29.2
1948	38	41.4	11.8	28.5
1949	38	36.0	9.8	27.2
1950	42	50.4	17.0	33.7
1951	50.75	53.1	21.5	40.5
1952	52	49.3	18.5	37.5
1953	52	52.7	19.5	37.0
1954	52	51.9	17.0	32.8
1955	52	64.4	20.6	32.0
1956	52	65.9	20.6	31.3
1957	52	66.1	20.2	30.6
1958	52	61.6	18.0	29.2
1959	52	73.8	22.5	30.5
1960	52	72.7	21.7	29.8
1961	52	74.2	21.8	29.4
1962	52	82.9	22.7	27.4
1963	52	88.7	24.6	27.7
1964	50	97.6	26.4	27.0
1965	48	110.9	29.3	26.4
1966	48	120.5	32.1	26.6
1967	48	119.2	30.7	25.8
1968	52.8	131.3	37.5	28.6
1969	52.8	136.6	39.2	28.7

Sources: Tax rates: Appendix Table A-3; other data: 1946–63, U.S. Department of Commerce, Office of Business Economics, *The National Income and Product Accounts of the United States, 1929–1965: Statistical Tables* (1966), pp. 22, 53; 1964–69, *Survey of Current Business,* July 1968, pp. 24, 31; July 1970, pp. 22, 29.
a Excludes corporation profits and capital consumption allowances originating in the rest of the world.

income tax rate was reduced to 48 percent, and rose to 29 percent in 1968–69, when the Vietnam war surtax was in effect.

AVAILABILITY OF FUNDS. All other things being equal, the corporation income tax may be expected to reduce the amount of corporate funds available for investment, but other factors have been operating to maintain internal corporate funds at a high level. The rise in the corporation tax has been accompanied by a much larger rise in high-bracket individual income tax rates. Recent studies indicate that these high individual rates and the preferential rate on capital gains have stimulated a higher rate of corporation retentions (that is, lower dividend pay-out rates) than in earlier years. In addition, the generous depreciation allowances enacted in recent years have enabled corporations to set aside large amounts for investment purposes.

Since the end of World War II, dividends have represented 25 percent on an average of the cash flow of corporations (Appendix Table C-17). This is considerably lower than the rate in the late 1920s. As a result of the lower dividend rates and higher depreciation allowances, gross corporate saving has more than kept pace with the growth of the economy. From 1929 to 1969, gross national product increased 803 percent, while gross corporate saving increased 810 percent. During the large upswing in investment in the first half of the 1960s, internal sources of funds generally exceeded plant and equipment expenditures of corporations in each year; in the latter half of the decade, internal funds were insufficient to finance all corporate investment, but this was due to the high level of investment demand (Appendix Table C-19). There is no evidence in the figures that the supply of corporate funds has been impaired by the corporation income tax.

Equity and Debt Finance

Corporations are allowed to deduct from taxable income interest payments on borrowed capital, but there is no corresponding deduction for dividends that are paid out to stockholders in return for the use of their funds as equity capital. At the present 48 percent tax rate, a corporation must earn $1.92 before tax to be able to pay $1 in dividend, but it needs to earn only $1 to pay $1 of interest. This asymmetry makes the cost of equity more "expensive" to the corporation than is an equal amount of borrowed capital.

Large corporations borrow long-term capital funds at interest rates ranging from 6 to 10 percent. With stocks selling at ten to twenty times net earnings, corporate earnings *after* tax on equity capital range between 5 and 10 percent. Under these conditions, the earnings rate before tax (at the rate of 1.92:1) must range between 9.6 and 19.2 percent to prevent equity financing from reducing the rate of return. It is in this sense that equity capital costs more than borrowed capital.

Financial experts discourage large amounts of debt financing by corporations. Debt makes good business sense if there is a safe margin for paying fixed interest charges. However, business firms may be tightly squeezed when business falls off, and the margin will evaporate rapidly. At such times, defaults on interest and principal payments and bankruptcies begin to occur. Even though borrowed capital may increase returns to stockholders, corporations try to finance a major share of their capital requirements through equity capital (mainly retained earnings) to avoid these risks.

The available data suggest that these reasons for caution have tended to restrain the use of borrowed capital despite its lesser cost. However, the ratio of debt to total capital rose gradually after World War II and then increased rapidly during the investment boom of the 1960s. The ratio for manufacturing corporations was about 15 percent in 1927–29, 20–21 percent from 1957 to 1961, and 25 percent in the years 1964–67 (Table 5-1).

Resource Allocation

If the corporation income tax is not shifted in the short run, it becomes in effect a special tax on corporate capital. This does not necessarily mean that the tax permanently reduces rates of return on capital in the corporate sector. Capital may flow out of the taxed sector into the untaxed sectors, and rates of return will tend to be equalized. In the process, the allocation of capital between corporate and noncorporate business will be altered from the pattern that would have prevailed in the absence of the tax.

How much capital, if any, has left the corporate sector as a result of the corporation income tax is not known. It is possible that the corporate form of doing business is so advantageous for nontax reasons that, for the most part, capital remains in the corporate sector despite the tax. Moreover, the preferential treatment of capital gains under the individual income tax provides an offsetting incentive to invest in the securities of corporations that retain earnings for reinvestment in the business. These earnings show up as increases in the price of common stock rather than as regular income. In any case, the corporate sector has been getting larger, both relatively and absolutely, for several decades (Figure 5-1 and Appendix Table C-17). The discouragement of investment in the corporate form induced by the tax system, if any, must have been relatively small.

Distortions may also take place if the tax is shifted in the short run. If prices increase in response to an increase in the tax, they rise in proportion to the use of corporate equity capital in the various industries. Consumers will buy less of the goods and services produced in industries using a great deal of corporate capital, because the prices of these products have risen most, and will buy more of the goods and services produced in industries with less corporate capital. Within the corporate sector, profits will fall in the "capital intensive" industries as a result of the decline in sales and will rise in the "labor intensive" industries. In the end, not only will less capital be attracted to the corporate sector, but less will be attracted to the capital intensive industries in that sector, and the economy will suffer a loss in efficiency as a result. The quantitative effect of this process is heavily dependent, of course, on the degree to which the noncorporate form of doing business can be substituted for the corporate form and production can be transferred from capital intensive to labor intensive industries. As in the nonshifting case, even a shifted corporate tax would tend to distort the composition of output, but in the aggregate this effect also is probably small.

Built-in Flexibility

Receipts from the corporation income tax are volatile over the business cycle because corporate profits rise and fall relatively more than do other incomes. However, this characteristic does not necessarily qualify the tax as an effective built-in stabilizer. To qualify, a tax must automatically moderate the changes in consumer disposable income or reduce fluctuations in investment. When profits fall, dividends tend to be maintained, but this appears to be due largely to the dividend policy of corporations rather than to the reduction in tax paid by corporations. Similarly, corporate investments are determined largely by current and prospective sales volume and rates of return, although the reduced tax liability may have an effect through its impact on cash flow. Thus, the corporation income tax is not regarded as one of the significant built-in stabilizers, despite the fact that it contributes heavily to the large swings in federal surpluses and deficits during business cycles.

The more important stabilizing feature of the corporate sector is the policy of cutting into saving when economic activity declines, rather than reducing dividends. A reduction in retained corporate earnings prevents a corresponding decline in disposable personal income, thus maintaining spending on the part of consumers. Quantitatively, corporate saving is second only to the federal tax structure as a built-in stabilizer. In three of the recessions following World War II, undistributed profits of corporations declined about as much as federal receipts (Table 5-3). Largely because of these two factors, disposable personal income declined less than the gross national product in the 1948–49 recession and actually rose in the 1953–54, 1957–58, and 1960–61 recessions.

TABLE 5-3. Changes in Gross National Product, Federal Receipts, Federal Corporation Income Tax, Undistributed Corporate Profits, and Disposable Personal Income in Four Postwar Recessions

(In billions of dollars)

Prerecession Recession peak[a] trough[a]	Gross national product	Federal receipts	Federal corporation tax	Undistributed corporate profits	Disposable personal income
IV 1948– II 1949	−8.7	−3.6	−2.2	−4.3	−5.9
II 1953– II 1954	−7.1	−9.0	−4.6	−1.7	+1.3
III 1957– I 1958	−11.6	−6.3	−4.2	−5.5	+0.6
II 1960–IV 1960	−1.4	−2.5	−2.7	−3.5	+1.3

Source: U.S. Department of Commerce, *The National Income and Product Accounts of the United States, 1929–1965*, Tables 1.1, 1.14, 2.1, 3.2.
[a] Gross national product peaks and troughs.

Balance of Payments

The corporation income tax has figured prominently in recent discussions of ways to improve the U.S. balance of payments. France, Germany, and several other countries have a general broad-based commodity tax, which is rebated on exports. Hence, firms in these countries can sell goods abroad at prices below those charged their domestic customers. Imports are subject to a compensating tax. American exporters, on the other hand, are not subject to a federal consumption tax; they receive no refund for taxes on exports and cannot cut their prices in foreign markets. It has been contended that the United States should, for competitive reasons, reduce the corporation income tax, enact a value added tax (see Chapter 6) as a substitute, and rebate the value added tax on exports.

A major question surrounding this issue relates to the effects of the two taxes on prices. If the corporation income tax is not shifted, substitution of a value added tax with a rebate for exports would accomplish little. The value added tax would raise prices on all goods and services, while the rebate would return export prices to their former level. Trade in commodities produced by U.S. firms would not change because their prices in international markets would remain unchanged. On the other hand, if the corporation tax is shifted, the switch to a value added tax would keep domestic prices the same as before, but export prices would decline by the amount of the rebate. Prices of U.S. goods in foreign markets would be lower, and the trade balance would improve (if the demand for goods produced in the United States were price elastic; that is, if foreign consumers actually increased their total expenditures on U.S. goods as prices were reduced).

To the extent that the corporation income tax is not shifted in the form of higher prices, it reduces the rate of return to investment in this country. Removal of the corporation income tax and substitution of a value added tax that would bear more or less equally on all factors of production would raise the net yield to capital. This would encourage investment in the United States and might in the long run provide balance-of-payments relief by attracting capital from abroad and discouraging the outflow of capital from the United States.

Since views on corporation tax shifting are divided, no consensus has been reached on these matters. Some improvement in the balance of payments may be expected, on either trade or capital account, but the improvement would probably be small. In 1966, the ratio of corporation taxes to the gross national product was from 1 to 3 percentage points higher in the United States than in other major industrial countries (Appendix Table C-4). This spread has probably not changed significantly in the intervening years. Thus, even if the United States greatly reduced its corporation income tax, its export prices would probably not decline very much relative to the export prices of its foreign competitors. Under the circumstances, the balance-of-payments effect cannot be regarded as a major consideration in deciding whether a shift should be made from the corporation income tax to an indirect tax.

Structural Problems

The structural problems under the corporation income tax are highly technical and therefore rarely understood by the average taxpayer. The major issues are: (1) allowances for capital consumption;

(2) depletion and other allowances for the minerals industries; (3) multiple incorporations to secure multiple surtax exemptions; (4) financial institutions; (5) tax-exempt organizations; (6) real estate firms; and (7) foreign income. (The first, second, sixth, and seventh issues also apply to individual income taxation, but they are treated here because their revenue and economic implications are much more important in the corporation income tax.) The purpose of this discussion is to show how these technical issues affect particular firms and industries, the economy as a whole, and the equity and yield of the corporation income tax.

Capital Consumption Allowances

The law has always permitted "a reasonable allowance for the exhaustion, wear and tear" of capital as a deduction for depreciation. Such a deduction is necessary to avoid taxing capital rather than income. In addition, liberalized capital consumption allowances are proposed as devices to stimulate investment.

DEPRECIATION. The annual deduction for depreciation is determined by spreading the cost of the depreciable asset over its "service life." Prior to 1954, the law and regulations were relatively strict, requiring fairly exact estimates of the period of use. Asset costs were amortized primarily by the "straight-line" method, which assumes a uniform amount of depreciation each year. The declining-balance method at 1.5 times the straight-line rate, while not specifically authorized by statute, was also permitted but seldom used. In 1954, the law was amended to permit the use of the declining-balance method with an annual depreciation rate twice the straight-line rate or the sum-of-years-digits method.

The differences among the three methods are illustrated for a $1,000 asset with a service life of ten years in Table 5-4. The straight-line method provides a uniform annual depreciation deduction of $100 a year. The declining-balance method permits the taxpayer to use a *rate* of depreciation and to apply this rate to the undepreciated amount each year. In the first year, the double declining-balance method provides a 20 percent allowance, or $200, leaving $800 undepreciated. In the second year, the 20 percent is applied to $800, giving an allowance of $160, and so on. (The taxpayer is permitted to switch to straight-line depreciation at any time; as is shown in the

TABLE 5-4. Comparison of Three Methods of Depreciation for a Ten-Year, $1,000 Asset

(In dollars)

| | Depreciation | | |
| | Straight-line | Double declining-balance | Sum-of-years-digits |
Year			
1	100	200	182
2	100	160	164
3	100	128	145
4	100	102	127
5	100	82	109
6	100	66	91
7	100	65.5	73
8	100	65.5	55
9	100	65.5	36
10	100	65.5	18
Total	1,000	1,000	1,000
Present value at 6 percent:			
Depreciation allowances	736	787	800
Tax value of depreciation allowances[a]	353	378	384

[a] At a tax rate of 48 percent.

example, this is profitable beginning in the seventh year.) Under the sum-of-years-digits method, the fraction allowed as depreciation each year is computed by dividing the number of years still remaining by the sum of years in the useful life. With a ten-year asset, the sum of the years is 55 ($10 + 9 + 8 \ldots + 2 + 1$), so that the depreciation allowance is $\frac{10}{55}$ in the first year, $\frac{9}{55}$ in the second year, and so on until it reaches $\frac{1}{55}$ in the tenth year.

As Table 5-4 shows, the two accelerated depreciation methods concentrate a larger percentage of the deductions in the early years. Under straight-line depreciation, half the original cost of a ten-year asset is written off in the first five years, as compared with 67 percent under the double declining-balance method and 73 percent under the sum-of-years-digits method. A useful way of comparing the value of the three methods is shown in the last line of the table. At a corporation income tax rate of 48 percent, the present value at the time of investment of the tax savings from the depreciation deductions (assuming a 6 percent interest rate) is $353 under straight-line depreciation, and $384 under sum-of-years-digits depreciation.

There seems to be some resistance to changing depreciation methods, but the inertia has been gradually overcome as management became more aware of the tax advantages. The proportion of corporations using the accelerated methods increased from 13 percent in 1954 to 30 percent in 1960, while the proportion of the amount of depreciation computed under the accelerated methods increased from 7 percent to 39 percent. This trend toward increasing use of the accelerated method doubtless continued in the 1960s.

SERVICE LIVES. Suggested useful lives were first published by the Bureau of Internal Revenue in 1931. These were incorporated in 1942 in *Bulletin F*, a small pamphlet originally issued in 1920 with narrative material on useful lives. Useful lives for about 5,000 separate items were first published in 1942. *Bulletin F* remained substantially unchanged until 1962, when the Internal Revenue Service issued a new set of depreciation rules, Revenue Procedure 62-21, in a pamphlet entitled *Depreciation Guidelines and Rules*. The new procedure assigned guideline lives to much broader classes of facilities, numbering less than one hundred. These new guidelines reduced the write-off period in manufacturing industries by about 15 percent below those used earlier.

A second innovation made in the 1962 revenue procedure was a set of rules governing the determination of depreciation allowances, which is called the "reserve ratio test." This test permits taxpayers to gear depreciation allowances to actual experience in replacing facilities. (The reserve ratio is the ratio of depreciation actually taken to the cost of the asset or group of assets in a depreciation account.) Taxpayers who replace assets more frequently than is implied by the guideline lives find that their reserve ratios are lower than the ratio computed by the Internal Revenue Service. In such cases, they are allowed to shorten the service lives of their assets. On the other hand, taxpayers who use assets for periods longer than those implied by the guideline lives would be required to lengthen service lives.

To give taxpayers enough time to conform with the reserve ratio test, all firms were considered to have met the test for the first three years. They were also given a period of years equal to the guideline life to bring their reserve ratios down to the appropriate range or to show that the ratios were moving toward that range. Nevertheless, it became clear that many taxpayers would not be able to meet the reserve ratio test within the three years, and the Treasury liberalized its regulations in 1965 so that taxpayers who were progressing toward the guidelines were considered to have met the test.

Many taxpayers believe that the reserve ratio test is inequitable and unworkable; they urge that the guideline lives be permitted without requiring use of the test. On the other hand, the test protects both the equity and the yield of the corporation income tax, and only a few taxpayers have had difficulty complying with the 1965 regulations. If the repeal of the investment credit creates strong support for further liberalization of depreciation allowances, revision or repeal of the reserve ratio test may be considered by the tax legislative committee.

INVESTMENT CREDIT. The investment credit, which was in effect between January 1, 1962, and April 18, 1969 (except for a temporary five-month suspension), was a major innovation in tax policy. Under this provision, business firms were permitted to deduct as a credit against their tax 7 percent of the amount of new investment with service lives of eight years or more (3 percent for utilities). One-third of the full credit was allowed for assets with service lives of four to six years and two-thirds for those with service lives of six to eight years. Qualified investments included all tangible personal property and excluded all buildings except research and storage facilities. The credit was allowed in full for firms with tax liabilities up to $25,000 and up to 50 percent of the tax above $25,000 (25 percent from 1962 to 1966).

The 1962 law required deduction of the credit from the cost of the asset before computing depreciation for tax purposes. However, this requirement complicated accounting for the credit, and it was eliminated in the 1964 act. Thus, taxpayers had the benefit of the full credit plus the liberalized depreciation allowances adopted in 1954, 1962, and 1965. At 1969 profit and investment levels, the revenue cost of the credit was estimated to be about $2.5 billion.

The effect of an investment credit is similar to that of an increase in the depreciation allowances above 100 percent of the cost of the asset. For corporations subject to the 48 percent rate, the same results could have been achieved by allowing the taxpayer to deduct an additional 14.8 percent in the first year. However, a credit has two virtues. First, it is simpler to understand and does not interfere with depreciation accounting. Second, it provides the same credit for all taxpayers regardless of their marginal rate. (It will be recalled that individuals are subject to rates up to 70 percent; and, in addition, small corporations are subject only to the normal tax rate of 22 percent if they have incomes below $25,000.)

Even though the credit appeared small, it provided a sizable incentive for new investment (assuming that the corporation income tax is not shifted into higher prices). In effect, the credit reduced the cost of the asset and hence increased the rate of return. For example, for an investment yielding 10 percent after straight-line depreciation and after the 48 percent corporation income tax, the credit increases the rate of return to 11.5 percent for an asset with a ten-year life, 11.2 percent for a fifteen-year life, and 11.0 percent for a twenty-year life. To increase the rates of return by equivalent amounts would require rate reductions of 8.8, 7.3, and 6.3 percentage points, respectively.

COMBINED EFFECT OF INCREASED CAPITAL CONSUMPTION ALLOWANCES. It has already been noted that the liberalization of capital consumption allowances beginning in 1954 reduced the effective rate of corporation income tax, even though the tax rate remained constant through 1963 (Table 5-2). Another measure of the benefits provided by the various provisions is given in Figure 5-3, which shows their effects on after-tax rates of return for assets with ten-, fifteen-, and twenty-year service lives, assuming that the assets yield 10 percent on a straight-line depreciation basis.

The combined effect is dramatic in all three cases. The rate of return is increased by double declining-balance depreciation and a 7 percent investment credit to 12.5 percent for a ten-year asset, 12 percent for a fifteen-year asset, and 11.7 percent for a twenty-year asset. The investment credit accounts for about 60 percent of the increase in rates of return.

When it was first introduced, there was substantial resistance on equity grounds to liberalization of capital consumption allowances. But the attitude toward liberalization changed in the early 1960s, when the government began using its fiscal powers aggressively to promote a rapid rate of economic growth. The widespread use of these methods in other countries also made them more acceptable in the United States. Today, except for the disagreement on the merits of the reserve ratio test, depreciation allowances no longer provoke much controversy in this country.

FIGURE 5-3. Effect of 7 Percent Investment Credit and Double Declining-Balance Depreciation on Rate of Return of Ten-, Fifteen-, and Twenty-Year Assets Yielding 10 Percent with Straight-Line Depreciation[a]

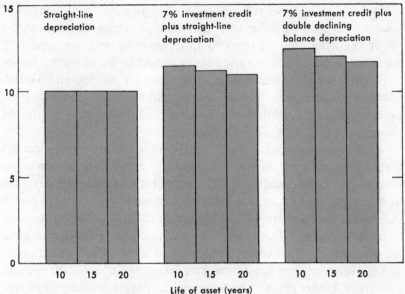

Rate of return (percent)

Straight-line depreciation

7% investment credit plus straight-line depreciation

7% investment credit plus double declining balance depreciation

Life of asset (years)

[a] Assuming a constant stream of annual receipts during life of the asset.

The investment credit also encountered resistance before it was finally enacted—even from businessmen who were to benefit from the new provision. While many still oppose the credit on equity grounds, few deny its effectiveness as a method of stimulating investment incentives. The credit was originally enacted as a permanent feature of the tax system, but the rate of the credit could be raised or lowered as a stabilization measure. The investment credit was suspended during the period October 10, 1966, through March 9, 1967, to counteract the inflationary pressures that developed during the early stages of the Vietnam war. Later, as inflation continued at a high rate, the credit was permanently repealed as of April 19, 1969.

Allowances for the Minerals Industries

In computing their taxable income, firms engaged in extracting oil and gas and other minerals from the ground are entitled to a "depletion" allowance for exhaustion of the mineral deposit, just as other firms are entitled to a depreciation allowance for wear and tear on the capital they use.

Although there is little distinction in theory between depletion and depreciation, there are substantial differences in practice. First, it is difficult to estimate what proportion of a mineral deposit has been used up. Second, the value of a mineral deposit may be substantially larger than the amount invested in discovering and developing it. Some argue that depletion allowances should be based on the higher "discovery value" of the deposit, rather than on the amount invested. Others argue that there is no reason to treat minerals differently from other investments and that only the original investment in producing the mine or oil field should be amortized.

Present allowances for the minerals industries are more generous than depreciation allowances. Allowances in excess of depletion based on costs were first granted for 1918 in the form of *discovery depletion* to stimulate exploration for war purposes and to reduce taxes of small-scale prospectors who often made discoveries after years of fruitless searching. (The 1918 act was not actually passed until after the war was over.) Discovery value proved to be difficult to estimate, and in 1926 Congress substituted *percentage depletion* for oil and gas properties. Under percentage depletion, taxpayers deduct a fixed percentage of receipts from sales as a depletion allowance, regardless of the amount invested. The deduction for gas and oil, which was 27.5 percent during the period 1926–69, is now set at 22 percent. Beginning in 1932, the same method was extended to other products taken from the ground, at percentages currently ranging from 22 percent for sulfur, uranium, and other rare metals to 5 percent for gravel, sand, peat, clay used in the manufacture of tile, and pumice. The deduction for percentage depletion cannot reduce the net income from the property (computed without regard to the depletion allowance) by more than 50 percent.

In addition to depletion, an immediate write-off is permitted for certain capital costs incurred in exploration and development without limit for oil and gas. This treatment of expenses does not reduce percentage depletion, so a double deduction is allowed for the same capital investment. Studies made over the years by the Treasury Department indicate that the annual depletion deductions greatly exceed the deduction computed on the basis of the original investment (after allowance for depreciation). The tax benefits of these special provisions are now in excess of $1.2 billion a year.

This special treatment is justified by its proponents on several grounds: there are unusual risks in oil and gas exploration and development; national defense requires continuous exploration and development; the allowances are needed to finance new discoveries; and the present provisions serve as a strong impetus for taxpayers who discover new sources of oil and gas to operate these properties rather than to sell them for the preferential capital gains rates.

On the other hand, the risks in these industries could be satisfactorily handled by the general deductibility of losses; the industries involved are no more strategic from a national defense standpoint than are many other industries; and the large revenue cost of the benefits requires the imposition of higher tax rates than would otherwise be necessary to raise a given amount of revenue, thus penalizing other taxpayers. Moreover, the provisions lead to overinvestment in the favored industries and hence seriously distort the allocation of resources. The policy of allowing percentage depletion on foreign oil is particularly irrational since the major economic justification of the allowance has been the need for stimulating the domestic industry.

The allowances for oil and gas and other minerals have been the subject of acrimonious debate for many years. In 1950, President Truman recommended the reduction of percentage depletion to a maximum of 15 percent. However, Congress took no action and in later years extended percentage depletion to other minerals and also raised the percentage depletion rates. Bills were introduced frequently to curtail the allowances, but only minor changes were made until 1969, when the depletion allowance for oil and gas was reduced from 27.5 percent to 22 percent for taxable years beginning after October 9, 1969, and "excess" depletion was made subject to the minimum tax beginning in 1970.

Multiple Surtax Exemptions

The $25,000 surtax exemption, which was intended to help small corporations, provided a strong monetary incentive for larger business firms to form multiple corporations. With a surtax rate of 26 percent, each additional corporation reduced the annual tax liability by $6,500 ($25,000 × 0.26). Thus, a firm with a net profit of $1,000,000 paid a tax of $473,500 if it was a single corporation, but only $220,000 if it operated through forty corporations, each having a $25,000 profit. Since incorporation is relatively inexpensive, many firms took the opportunity to spin off a large number of subsidiaries. In some instances, several hundred corporations were involved, and the tax savings were large.

There are valid business reasons for incorporating different units of a business enterprise, but this hardly justified treating each unit for tax purposes as if it were an independent small business. Moreover, the income tax rules often provided an incentive for uneconomic corporate arrangements and discriminated against firms and industries in which multiple corporations are impractical. Chain stores, personal finance companies, movies, and other businesses involving separate outlets were particularly easy to break up into separate corporations. As a consequence, the reduced rate for the first $25,000 of profits conveyed unintended benefits to many medium-sized and large businesses.

The Treasury Department attempted to prevent such abuse on a number of occasions. In 1963, it proposed that corporations subject to 80 percent common ownership and control be limited to a single surtax exemption. Controlled corporations were to be defined as corporations that are 80 percent owned by the same corporate parent (parent-subsidiary type) or by five or fewer individuals or corporations (brother-sister type). The proposal was watered down under the Revenue Act of 1964. First, the definition of controlled corporations of the brother-sister type was restricted to corporations that are 80 percent owned by one person instead of five. Second, a controlled group of corporations was permitted to continue claiming separate surtax exemptions by paying an additional tax of 6 percent on the first $25,000 of corporate income. This removed only 23 percent ($\frac{6}{26}$) of the advantage of the surtax exemption and was therefore less effective in discouraging multiple corporations. The Tax Reform Act of 1969 eliminated 100 percent of the advantage of the multiple surtax exemption for affiliated groups and broadened the definition of brother-sister type affiliations to include corporations owned by as many as five persons. Affiliated groups of corporations are now limited to one surtax exemption and are not taxed on intergroup dividends. The new arrangement is phased in over a five-year period for groups that were committed to the multiple exemption in 1969. These amendments should go a long way toward curbing abuses in this area.

The 1964 act also eliminated the 2 percent penalty tax previously paid by a group of affiliated corporations for the privilege of filing a consolidated return. Consolidated reporting of income results in a more meaningful and fair representation of taxable income than does unconsolidated reporting. Consolidation also has the advantage of providing offsets for losses of one corporation against the gains of other members of the group and of eliminating the tax on intercompany dividends (15 percent of which are included in taxable income). Now that the rules against multiple corporations have been tightened to prevent abuses of the surtax exemption, the dividend tax could be eliminated entirely.

Financial Institutions

Financial institutions have always presented a difficult problem for income taxation because many of them are organized on a mutual basis. At one time, mutuals were completely exempt from tax on the theory that they belonged to their members and were not corporations in any ordinary sense. But with the growth in numbers and size of mutuals, it became increasingly evident that the mutual status was not sufficient reason for exempting them from taxation. Attempts have recently been made to tax financial institutions—whether they organize as mutuals or not—like other corporations, but many observers feel that they are still not paying their fair share of the tax burden. Since the problems depend on the type of business conducted, it is necessary to discuss separately: (a) the thrift institutions (savings banks and building and loan associations), (b) life insurance companies, (c) fire and casualty insurance companies, and (d) commercial banks.

THRIFT INSTITUTIONS. Savings banks and building and loan associations were made subject to the corporation income tax by the Revenue Act of 1951, which required them to pay the regular corporation income tax rate on retained earnings over and above allocations to reserves. Payments of interest to depositors were allowed as a deductible expense, as in the case of ordinary commercial banks. However, the law permitted thrift institutions to build a reserve for bad debts of up to 12 percent of their deposits, while the regulations permitted commercial banks to set aside a reserve of three times their annual loss experience over a twenty-year period (or less than 3 percent on the average). With steady growth in deposits, the amounts covered by the 12 percent ceiling increased steadily, and the result was that savings banks and building and loan associations paid very little tax.

The ineffectiveness of the 1951 law was remedied by a 1962 amendment providing, in effect, that thrift institutions may add to their
reserves for bad debts an amount equal to 60 percent of their taxable
income (or an amount equal to actual loss experience). While this
fell short of full taxation, the tax paid by savings and loan associations and mutual savings banks increased from $6.4 million in 1960
to $96 million in 1967. The 1969 act gradually lowered the deduction
for additions to reserves from a maximum of 60 percent to 40 percent
of taxable income over the period 1970 to 1979. When fully effective,
the 40 percent rule is expected to increase revenues by $120 million a
year.

LIFE INSURANCE COMPANIES. The problem in life insurance company
taxation also concerns the method of computing appropriate reserves.
The intention of the law is to exempt that part of their income deemed
necessary to meet contractual obligations to policyholders. Methods
of achieving this objective have been considered periodically by
Congress over the past fifty years.

Initially, life insurance companies were taxed as ordinary corporations, but this method was abandoned because of the administrative
difficulties of establishing deductions for additions to reserves. Beginning in 1921, a deduction of a specified percentage of legal reserves
(4 percent from 1921 to 1931 and 3.75 percent from 1932 to 1941) was
permitted. Because of this high allowance, insurance companies paid
practically no tax during the 1930s, and the law was again amended
in 1942. This time they were allowed a tax credit for the amount
presumed to be needed to meet policy commitments. The credit was
a flat percentage of net investment income, determined by the secretary of the treasury on the basis of a formula that yielded high reserve
figures for the industry when interest rates declined during the war.
As a result, the life insurance companies paid virtually no tax.

A new formula for taxing the industry was enacted as stopgap
legislation in 1951. Life insurance companies were subjected to a tax
of 6.5 percent on their net investment income (3.75 percent on the first
$200,000) in lieu of the regular corporation income tax. This rate was
equivalent to the 52 percent tax, on the assumption that the industry
required 87.5 percent of its investment income for policy reserves.

The present method of taxing life insurance companies was enacted in 1959, effective with respect to 1958 incomes. The theory was

that life insurance companies should be taxed not only on their net investment income but also on the "underwriting" profits resulting from the fact that the life expectancy tables upon which premiums are based usually understate actual life expectancies. To reach such profits, the 1959 law required companies to report premium as well as investment income and allowed deductions for benefit payments, insurance losses, and other ordinary business expenses. Additions to reserves were also allowed, but were to be computed on the basis of each company's needs and experience.

The 1959 law had a number of technical provisions that did not become fully applicable until 1961. Tax payments of life insurance companies rose from $294 million in 1957, the year before the 1959 law became effective, to $529 million in 1960. Most of this increase was due to the change in the method of taxation, which, now correct in principle, has been stable for over a decade. Tax payments by this industry rose to almost $1 billion in 1967, reflecting the tremendous growth in life insurance in this country.

FIRE AND CASUALTY INSURANCE COMPANIES. Stock companies selling fire and casualty insurance have long been taxed on both their investment and underwriting profits (as life insurance companies have been taxed beginning in 1958). However, between 1942 and 1962, mutual fire and casualty insurance companies paid tax under special formulas that excluded underwriting profits. In 1963, underwriting profits were included in the formula for these companies, but they were allowed to set up a deferred income account which, in effect, permanently defers one-eighth of their underwriting gains from taxation and, in addition, defers taxation of another large portion of their underwriting gains for five years.

COMMERCIAL BANKS. Commercial banks are regarded as ordinary business corporations for tax purposes and are subject to tax on their profits, after allowing for payment of interest on their deposits. One peculiarity in their taxation in the past was the treatment of capital gains and losses. Long-term capital gains of commercial banks were taxed at a maximum rate of 25 percent, as were the gains of ordinary business corporations. However, capital losses of commercial banks were deductible in full not only against capital gains but also against ordinary income. This treatment was justified on the grounds that dealings in securities are part of normal business operations in commercial banking and losses should therefore be treated as ordinary losses. By this reasoning, capital gains from the sale of bonds should have been regarded as ordinary income and subjected to the ordinary corporation income tax rate. The 1969 legislation finally corrected this asymmetrical treatment by treating such gains as ordinary income.

Commercial banks were also allowed to maintain a reserve for bad debts that was about three times their actual loss experience. Prior to 1969, the allowable reserve was set by regulation at 2.4 percent of their outstanding loans. The 1969 law reduced this percentage to 1.8 in 1970–75, 1.2 in 1976–81, and 0.6 in 1982–87. Beginning in 1988, the actual loss experience for the current and the preceding five years will be the only criterion.

Tax-Exempt Organizations

The federal tax law exempts a variety of nonprofit organizations, including religious, charitable, educational, and fraternal organizations. Favorable tax treatment for these organizations dates from a time when the federal government assumed little responsibility for relief and welfare activities and the value of the tax exemption was relatively small. Today, the federal government has substantial responsibilities for public assistance and welfare activities, while the revenue loss from the exemptions has become significant.

The tax status of these organizations might never have been altered had they remained small and not entered into business and public affairs. In recent years, numerous complaints have been made against tax-exempt organizations for unfair competition and for involvement in public activities that seem to be political in nature to those who disapprove of them. As a result, the permissible activities of private foundations have been spelled out in some detail in the Internal Revenue Code, and the business income of all exempt organizations has been made taxable under the corporation income tax, even though they are still "exempt" under the Internal Revenue Code. The special taxes apply to (a) unrelated business income, (b) rental income from "lease-back" arrangements, (c) investment income of private foundations, and (d) the income of cooperatives.

UNRELATED BUSINESS INCOME. The major change in the tax status of exempt organizations was made in 1950, when Congress decided to tax their "unrelated business income." This is defined as income from a business that is not substantially related to the exercise of charitable, educational, or other exempt purposes. Unrelated business income is subject to the regular corporation income tax rates; the Tax Reform Act of 1969 eliminated the original exemption of $1,000 and extended coverage to all exempt organizations except for government agencies (other than publicly supported colleges and universities).

LEASE-BACK ARRANGEMENTS. Exempt organizations often purchased property from private business firms with borrowed funds and then leased the property back to the same firms. In some cases, the original owners were given lower rentals or were paid a higher price for the property than going market rates. Even where the transaction was at arm's-length, the exempt organization was trading on its tax exemption to accumulate property. To solve these problems, the 1950 legislation defined unrelated business income to include rental income from leased property owned by tax-exempt organizations to the extent that the ownership is financed by borrowed funds. The 1969 legislation extended the definition still further to include rental income for property held less than five years. These changes permit tax-exempt organizations to use their funds for investment in real estate, but make it difficult to use their exemption as a means of acquiring property.

PRIVATE FOUNDATIONS. Private foundations are defined as tax-exempt organizations other than (a) religious, charitable, and educational institutions and (b) organizations that derive more than one-third of their income from contributions and less than one-third from investment income. These foundations were made subject to a new tax on investment income and to a variety of restrictions under the 1969 legislation; the tax is 4 percent of net investment income. The 1969 act also requires foundations to distribute all their income each year or 6 percent of their assets, whichever is greater; prohibits financial or "self-dealing" transactions between a foundation and persons with a direct or indirect interest in the foundation ("disqualified persons") or government officials; and limits the amount of stock a foundation and disqualified persons can hold in any business enterprise. These provisions are phased in gradually over a period of years and are supported by a variety of sanctions for noncompliance.

COOPERATIVES. Farm, irrigation, and telephone cooperatives and like organizations are exempt from income tax. Other nonfinancial cooperatives are taxable. However, all cooperatives are allowed to deduct from their income amounts paid as "patronage dividends" to their patrons on the ground that they represent readjustments in prices initially charged patrons.

Originally, patronage dividends were deductible even if distributed in noncash form ("written notices of allocation"). The deductibility of noncash patronage dividends enabled cooperatives to expand from earnings not taxed at the cooperative level. Furthermore, such dividends often were not taxable to patrons until redeemed at some future date because the written allocations had no fair market value.

The law was revised beginning with the income year 1963. Earnings of taxable cooperatives distributed as written notices of allocation cannot now be deducted by the cooperatives unless at least 20 percent of the face amount of the allocation is in cash. Deductibility of noncash allocations is limited further to those which: (1) the patron, at his option, can redeem in cash for the face amount within ninety days of the payment thereof; or (2) the patron has consented to include at face value in his income in accordance with the federal income tax laws. Thus, taxable cooperatives may, in effect, retain 80 percent of their earnings by the use of noncash patronage dividends. At the same time, noncash dividends currently are taxable to patrons to the extent that the dividends are related to transactions entered into for business purposes. Dividends on purchases for personal consumption are not required to be included in a patron's income.

Real Estate

When accelerated depreciation allowances were introduced in 1954, they were applied to real estate with little thought as to the consequences. As a result, investors in real estate were able to offset their ordinary income with depreciation and interest paid on the debt financing of their property. When the property was sold, this income was converted to capital gains and was taxed at the lower capital gains rates. Since these provisions applied to used as well as to new property, rapid turnover was encouraged, and property investment was distorted.

In response to the large revenue loss through such real estate tax shelters, President Kennedy recommended in 1961 that gains from the sale of real estate be treated as ordinary income to the extent of prior depreciation allowances. Congress was unable to agree on the appropriate legislation, however, and it was not until 1964 that action was taken. Under the Revenue Act of 1964, gains from buildings held for one year or less were treated as ordinary income up to the amount of prior depreciation. For buildings held from thirteen to twenty months, gains were treated as ordinary income up to 100 percent of the excess of actual depreciation over straight-line depreciation. This percentage was decreased by 1 point for each month beyond twenty, so that gains from the sale of a building held for ten years or more were taxed strictly as capital gains.

This limited recapture decreased, but did not eliminate, the advantage of the real estate tax shelter. The Tax Reform Act of 1969 attempted to deal with these problems in several ways. First, it eliminated the use of the most rapid depreciation methods for real estate, except in the case of residential rental property. Second, it called for the complete recapture of all excess depreciation over straight-line for property held more than twenty months. This new provision does not apply to new residential *rental* property, for which recapture is decreased by 1 percent a month after one hundred months. Finally, it provides a special tax advantage to rehabilitation expenditures for low-income housing during the period 1970–74 in the form of five-year depreciation.

Foreign Income

Before 1962, the income earned by foreign subsidiaries of U.S. corporations was subject to tax when it was "repatriated" through the payment of dividends to the parent corporation. To avoid double taxation, the parent was allowed a credit against the U.S. tax for any tax paid on these dividends to a foreign government. Income of foreign branches was (and still is) included in the taxable income of the parent, but credit was also allowed for any foreign tax paid on this income.

The deferment of tax on income of foreign subsidiaries was at one time considered to be a desirable feature of the tax system because it encouraged foreign investment by U.S. firms. Attitudes toward this policy changed in the 1950s and early 1960s as a result of two developments. First, the United States encountered a serious balance-of-payments problem, which was aggravated by private capital outflows. Second, some U.S. corporations were using the deferral privilege as a method of tax avoidance. This was done by establishing "tax haven" subsidiaries in countries with little or no tax on foreign income and using these subsidiaries as base companies for accumulating earnings from foreign operations.

To solve both problems, President Kennedy in 1961 recommended elimination of the deferral of taxes on earnings of U.S.-owned foreign subsidiaries, except for those in underdeveloped countries. The deferral provision had originally been designed to achieve *foreign neutrality* in the taxation of U.S. companies doing business abroad (that is, to permit their foreign income to be taxed at the rates applicable abroad). In view of the changed balance-of-payments circumstances, the government argued that it was time to give priority to *domestic neutrality* (that is, to eliminate the tax as a factor in the choice between domestic and foreign investment).

The business community launched a successful campaign to convince Congress that complete elimination of deferral was too extreme. Congress agreed, but was annoyed by the factual evidence that some foreign subsidiaries were able to avoid paying taxes in any country through the use of tax havens. In the end, the Revenue Act of 1962 provided for new ways of dealing specifically with tax havens for business operations in developed countries, but left the basic deferral provisions unchanged. The technique was to single out certain tax avoidance transactions of tax haven corporations for inclusion in the taxable income of the parent corporation in the year in which income is earned.

As time has passed, the disagreement over the deferral provision has almost been forgotten. But experts do disagree over whether the 1962 amendments solved the problems of the tax havens. Some argue that the 1962 provisions are too weak; others believe they are complicated and unnecessary.

Integration of the Corporation and Individual Income Taxes

Taxation of corporate earnings under two taxes continues to be controversial. Some people regard double taxation as inequitable and urge its elimination or moderation on this ground alone. Others believe that taxation of the corporation as a separate entity is justified. Whether something needs to be done about double taxation depends in part on an evaluation of the economic issues discussed earlier.

With respect to the equity issue, few people realize that the problem is tricky.

The Additional Burden on Dividends

Assuming that all, or a significant portion, of the corporation tax rests on the stockholder, the effect of the tax is to impose the heaviest burden on dividends received by persons in the lowest income classes. This can be seen by examining the illustrative calculations in Table 5-5, which show the total and additional tax burden (ignoring the effect of the present $100 exclusion) on stockholders who receive $52 of dividends under present tax rates. Given the present rate of 48 percent, the corporation income before tax from which $52 of dividends were paid must have amounted to $100. If this $100 had been subject to individual income tax rates only, the tax on these dividends would go from zero at the bottom of the income scale to a maximum of 70 percent at the top. With the corporation tax, the combined individual and corporation income tax increases from $48 for those subject to a zero rate to $84.40 for those subject to a 70 percent rate (Table 5-5, column 6).

TABLE 5-5. Additional Burden on Dividends of the Corporation Income Tax on $100 of Corporation Income[a]

(In dollars)

Marginal individual income tax rate (percentages) (1)	Corporate income before tax (2)	Corporate tax at 48 percent (3)	Dividends received by stock-holders (4)	Stockholder's individual income tax (5)	Total tax burden[b] (6)	Additional burden of the corporate tax (7)
0	100	48	52	0	48.00	48.00
10	100	48	52	5.20	53.20	43.20
20	100	48	52	10.40	58.40	38.40
30	100	48	52	15.60	63.60	33.60
40	100	48	52	20.80	68.80	28.80
50	100	48	52	26.00	74.00	24.00
60	100	48	52	31.20	79.20	19.20
70	100	48	52	36.40	84.40	14.40

Column (3) = 0.48 × Column (2).
Column (4) = Column (2) − Column (3).
Column (5) = Column (4) × Column (1).
Column (6) = Column (3) + Column (5).
Column (7) = Column (6) − [Column (1) × Column (2)].
[a] Assumes that corporation income after tax is devoted entirely to the payment of dividends.
[b] Does not take into account the effect of the exclusion of the first $100 of dividends from the individual income tax base.

However, the *additional* burden resulting from the corporation tax falls as income rises. For example, the taxpayer subject to a zero individual rate would have paid no tax on the $52 of dividends; the additional burden of the corporation income tax in this case is the full $48 tax. By contrast, a taxpayer subject to the 70 percent rate pays an individual income tax of $36.40 on the dividend, and the total tax burden on the original $100 of corporate earnings is $84.40. But since he would have to pay $70 under the individual income tax in any case, the additional burden to him is only $14.40 (Table 5-5, column 7).

The test of an equitable method of moderating or eliminating the "double tax" on dividends is whether the method removes a uniform portion of the additional burden shown in Table 5-5. If the percentgae removed is the same for all individual income tax rate brackets, the method deals evenly at all levels. Deviations from a constant percentage indicate the income classes favored or penalized by the method.

Methods of Integration

Four basic methods of integrating the corporation and individual income tax have been used at various times in different countries: (1) a dividend received credit for individuals; (2) a deduction for dividends paid by the corporation in computing the corporation income tax; (3) a method that considers all or a portion of the corporation income tax to be withholding on dividends at the source; and (4) an exclusion for all or a portion of the dividends received from the individual income tax base. A fifth method would be to treat all corporations like partnerships and tax their income to the stockholders whether or not it is distributed. Of these methods, only (2) and (3) and the partnership plan would remove the same proportion of the additional burden of the corporation tax at all individual income levels. The analysis assumes that there is no shifting of the corporation income tax.

THE DIVIDEND RECEIVED CREDIT. Under this method, dividend recipients are allowed to deduct a percentage of their dividends as a credit against their individual income tax. Between 1954 and 1963, U.S. taxpayers were allowed a credit of 4 percent for dividends in excess of a $50 exclusion ($100 for joint returns).

Although the credit grants the same relief on a dollar of dividends at all income levels, it removes an increasing proportion of the additional burden of the corporation tax as incomes rise. For those subject to a zero rate, the credit is worthless. For a taxpayer subject to a 10 percent rate, the 4 percent credit would remove 4.8 percent of the additional burden, while for a taxpayer subject to the maximum 70 percent rate, the credit would remove 14.4 percent (Table 5-6). This pattern of relief led to its repeal.

TABLE 5-6. Portion of the Additional Burden of the Corporation Income Tax Removed by the 4 Percent Dividend Received Credit

Marginal individual income tax rate (percentages) (1)	Additional burden resulting from corporate tax (dollars) (2)	Dividend received credit (dollars) (3)	Percentage of additional burden removed by the dividend credit (4)
0	48.00	0	0
10	43.20	2.08	4.8
20	38.40	2.08	5.4
30	33.60	2.08	6.2
40	28.80	2.08	7.2
50	24.00	2.08	8.7
60	19.20	2.08	10.8
70	14.40	2.08	14.4

Column (2) = Column (7) of Table 5-5.
Column (3) = 4 percent of $52.
Column (4) = Column (3) ÷ Column (2).

THE DIVIDEND PAID DEDUCTION. This is the simplest method of dealing with the double taxation problem; it was used in the United States in 1936 and 1937. Corporations deduct from their taxable income all or a portion of the dividends they pay out, and the corporation tax applies to the remainder. Table 5-7 shows the relief that would be granted under this method assuming that the corporation were allowed a deduction of 11.74 percent of dividends paid. As is shown in column 6, the relief would be exactly 6.5 percent of the additional tax imposed by the corporation income tax at all income levels.

Aside from granting the same proportionate relief at all income levels, the dividend paid credit has the merit of treating dividends more like interest. (If a full deduction were allowed, the treatment

TABLE 5-7. Portion of the Additional Burden of the Corporation Income Tax Removed by the Dividend Paid Deduction

(Assuming a deduction by the corporation of 11.74 percent of dividends paid)

Marginal individual income tax rate (percentages) (1)	Additional burden resulting from corporate tax (dollars) (2)	Reduced corporate tax (paid to stockholders as additional dividends) (3)	Tax on additional dividends (4)	Net benefit (5)	Percentage of additional burden removed by dividend paid deduction (6)
0	48.00	3.12	0	3.12	6.5
10	43.20	3.12	0.31	2.81	6.5
20	38.40	3.12	0.62	2.50	6.5
30	33.60	3.12	0.94	2.18	6.5
40	28.80	3.12	1.25	1.87	6.5
50	24.00	3.12	1.56	1.56	6.5
60	19.20	3.12	1.87	1.25	6.5
70	14.40	3.12	2.18	0.94	6.5

The column header "Tax benefit of dividend paid deduction (dollars)" spans columns (3), (4), and (5).

Column (2) = Column (7) of Table 5-5.
Column (3) = Amount of additional dividends corporations could pay out with an 11.74 percent dividend paid deduction. This percentage was used to remove exactly 6.5 percent of the additional burden of the corporate tax (as shown in Column 6).
Column (4) = Column (1) × Column (3).
Column (5) = Column (3) − Column (4).
Column (6) = Column (5) ÷ Column (2).

would be identical.) This would reduce the discrimination against equity financing by corporations. Nevertheless, the dividend paid credit is rarely proposed seriously because its use during the 1930s raised a storm of protest. Corporations complained that it reduced their ability to save and invest at a time when the market for corporate equities was almost dried up. The method is also criticized on the ground that it discourages internal financing by corporations and might reduce total saving and investment. On the other hand, some believe it unwise to permit corporations to avoid the capital markets for financing their investment programs. Forcing them "to stand the test of the market place" might exercise a desirable restraint on bigness and also give the investor-owner more control over the disposition of his funds.

THE WITHHOLDING METHOD. Under this method, all or a portion of the individual income tax is regarded as having been paid at the source (through the corporation tax). For example, if 6 percent of the dividend received is regarded as having been withheld, a shareholder receiving a $52 dividend would include $3.12 (0.06 × 52) in his income and then take the $3.12 as a credit against his tax. In this illustration, the portion of the additional burden of the corporation income tax removed is also exactly 6.5 percent at all income levels (Table 5-8).

The withholding method achieves the same result as the dividend paid deduction for corporations, but is less likely to discourage corporate saving. This advantage frequently makes the withholding method more attractive, even though it is more difficult to understand and would also complicate the individual income tax return. The withholding method was a basic part of the British tax structure from 1803 until 1965, when a separate corporation income tax was enacted for the first time.

TABLE 5-8. Portion of the Additional Burden of the Corporation Income Tax Removed by the Withholding Method

(Assuming 6 percent of dividends received regarded as withheld)

Marginal individual income tax rate (percentages) (1)	Additional burden resulting from corporate tax (dollars) (2)	Withholding credit (dollars)			Percentage of additional burden removed by the dividend credit (6)
		Amount withheld at source (3)	Tax on amount withheld (4)	Net credit (5)	
0	48.00	3.12	0	3.12	6.5
10	43.20	3.12	0.31	2.81	6.5
20	38.40	3.12	0.62	2.50	6.5
30	33.60	3.12	0.94	2.18	6.5
40	28.80	3.12	1.25	1.87	6.5
50	24.00	3.12	1.56	1.56	6.5
60	19.20	3.12	1.87	1.25	6.5
70	14.40	3.12	2.18	0.94	6.5

Column (2) = Column (7) of Table 5-5.
Column (3) = 6 percent of $52.
Column (4) = Column (1) × Column (3).
Column (5) = Column (3) − Column (4).
Column (6) = Column (5) ÷ Column (2).

THE DIVIDEND EXCLUSION. This method, adopted in the United States in 1954, permits the individual income taxpayer to exclude all or a portion of his dividends from his taxable income. In 1964, the maximum exclusion was raised from $50 to $100 ($200 on joint returns). Like the dividend received credit, the exclusion grants an increasing amount of relief on a dollar of dividends as incomes rise. Accordingly, it cannot remove the same proportion of the additional tax burden at all levels of income.

THE PARTNERSHIP METHOD. The most radical solution to the double taxation problem is to regard the income of corporations as belonging to their stockholders in the year in which it is earned. The corporation income tax would be abolished, and stockholders would pay individual income tax on their prorated share of the earnings of corporations in which they held stock. Tax would be payable by individuals on corporate earnings whether they were distributed or not.

This method would automatically apply the correct individual income tax rates to all corporate earnings, but it is impractical for the United States. Many stockholders would not have funds to pay tax on earnings they did not receive. This would force them to liquidate security holdings or apply pressure on corporations to distribute a much larger portion of their retained earnings. In either case, it would be bad public policy: in the former, because it would discourage stock ownership among people with modest means; in the latter, because it would greatly reduce corporate saving.

Treatment approximating this method is available under present law for closely held corporations with no more than ten shareholders. These corporations operate substantially like partnerships and can arrange to distribute enough earnings to the partners to avoid forced liquidations. Moreover, the decision to be treated like a corporation for tax purposes is made only if it is advantageous to the shareholders. Most experts agree that it is not practical to extend the partnership method to large, publicly held corporations with complex capital structures, frequent changes in ownership, and thousands or millions of stockholders.

In 1966, the Canadian Royal Commission on Taxation devised a new procedure that would approximate the effect of the partnership method and avoid its liquidity problems. Under this procedure, corporations would be permitted to allocate all or a portion of their undistributed earnings to their shareholders. The corporation income tax would be converted to a withholding tax for the individual income tax, and the withholding rate would be set at the top-bracket individual income tax rate. Shareholders would include the allocated dividends as well as cash dividends in their taxable income and would deduct the amount of tax withheld as a credit against their income tax. The only difference between this procedure and the original partnership method is that the allocation of earnings by corporations to shareholders would not be mandatory. But, since shareholders would be denied immediate credit for the withheld tax, the pressure on corporate managements to allocate all undistributed earnings would probably be irresistible. The commission's proposal has merit (if a separate corporate tax is considered inappropriate), but it was not adopted by the Canadian government and has not been seriously considered elsewhere.

The Value Added Tax as a Replacement for the Corporation Tax

Another method of dealing with double taxation that has been proposed with increasing frequency is to replace the corporation income tax with a value added tax. This tax is imposed at a flat rate on the "value added" by each firm (computed by subtracting from gross receipts the value of purchases from other firms). Assuming the same yield, a value added tax would reduce the tax burden of firms and industries relying heavily on capital and increase it on those relying heavily on labor. The value added tax has been supported recently by those who see in it a method of increasing the after-tax rate of return on U.S. capital, and thus helping the balance of payments by encouraging U.S. firms to keep more capital at home and by attracting capital from abroad.

The value added tax will be discussed in the next chapter. Here it should be noted that use of this tax in place of the corporation income tax would raise difficult equity problems. Repeal of the corporation income tax would probably increase stock prices and generate large capital gains. It would also stimulate additional retention of corporate earnings and thus enable shareholders to avoid the individual income tax. Since a departure of this sort would change the complexion of the federal tax system, it should not be adopted without fundamental revisions (particularly in capital gains taxation) to prevent windfall gains to the minority of taxpayers who have large stockholdings.

Summary

The corporation income tax ranks third in the federal tax system despite continued criticism. It produces a large amount of revenue that would be hard to replace with any other tax and protects the equity and yield of the individual income tax. Without it, a substantial part of the individual income tax would be permanently lost from the tax base through retention of earnings by corporations.

The arguments that are made against the corporation income tax are largely economic. The tax may: reduce the saving capacity of corporations and their incentives to invest; encourage debt financing by discriminating against equity financing, thus exposing many corporations to unnecessary risks; protect marginal producers by keeping up the prices of more efficient producers; and distort the allocation of resources, both as between the corporate and noncorporate sectors and as between capital and labor intensive industries. However, there is no evidence in the available data that high corporation tax rates have impaired the growth of the corporate sector.

Numerous changes have been made in the structure of the corporation income tax since the end of World War II. Foremost among these have been the liberalization of depreciation and a seven-year experiment with the investment credit to encourage investment. Revisions have also been made to prevent tax avoidance by tax-exempt organizations, financial institutions, real estate firms, and cooperatives. The tax advantage of multiple incorporation has been eliminated, and a minimum tax now applies to income items that receive special treatment. Nevertheless, some difficult problems remain. The reserve-ratio test for depreciation allowances has not yet been carefully reviewed by the congressional tax committees. The treatment of oil and gas and other minerals industries is still a major issue. There is also some question whether the problem of tax treatment of foreign income has been permanently solved.

The most difficult issue concerns the so-called double taxation of dividends. Even if it were agreed that something needs to be done about double taxation, there is no easy solution. Among the various alternatives, the theoretically correct methods are the partnership method, deduction of dividends from the corporation tax base, and the withholding method. But the partnership method is impractical; the dividend deduction would tend to discourage corporate saving; and the withholding method is difficult to understand.

CHAPTER SIX

Consumption Taxes

CONSUMPTION TAXES are not very popular in the United States. It is true that general sales taxes are used by state and local governments (see Chapter 9), but even when they are taken into account, consumption taxes are less important here than anywhere else in the world. In fiscal year 1970, excise taxes accounted for only about 8 percent of federal budget receipts.

Types of Consumption Taxes

There is a bewildering variety of consumption taxes. An *expenditure* tax is levied on the total consumption expenditure of the individual; a *sales* tax is levied on the sales of goods and services; and a *value added* tax is levied on the difference between a firm's sales and its purchases. Expenditure taxes may be proportional or progressive; sales and value added taxes are imposed at a uniform rate on all commodities or at differing rates on various groups of commodities. Expenditure taxes are collected from the consumer, while sales and value added taxes are collected from the seller. Sales taxes are in widespread use throughout the world; the value added tax, now used in many Western European countries, is gaining popularity; the expenditure tax has been used—without much success—only in India and Ceylon.

The sales tax can be a single-stage or a multistage tax. Canada

149

levies its sales tax at the manufacturers' level, Great Britain at the wholesale level, and U.S. state and local governments at the retail level. Italy levies a *turnover* tax, which derives its name from the fact that the tax is levied every time a commodity "turns over" from one firm to another. The value added tax is also a multistage tax, but it is figured on the *net* value added by each firm.

A common form of consumption tax is the *excise* tax on the sale of a particular commodity or group of commodities. Excise taxes are levied almost everywhere on alcoholic beverages and tobacco products, but they apply to many other products as well. They are also employed as "user charges" to collect part or all of the cost of government services enjoyed by specific groups of taxpayers. Thus, gasoline taxes and taxes on automobiles and automotive products are used to pay for highway construction and maintenance. Appendix Table A-5 summarizes the major excises imposed by the federal government since 1913.

Customs duties, which are levied on imports, are used in this country primarily to protect domestic industries against foreign competition. The policy of the United States government is to reduce trade barriers in the interest of promoting world trade, but the size and pace of the reductions depend on international negotiations, which are complicated and time-consuming. The negotiations are concerned with the role of customs duties in the nation's foreign economic policy, rather than with their role as taxes to produce revenue. Customs duties, therefore, are not discussed in this book.

The major issue regarding consumption taxes in this country is equity. Because the poor consume more of their income than do the rich, the burden of a flat rate sales tax falls as incomes rise. The sales tax also bears more heavily on families that have larger expenditures relative to their incomes, such as families with a large number of children or those that are just beginning a household. Some excise taxes may be progressive, but they are usually levied on mass consumption items and tend to be regressive on balance.

Sales and excise taxes are also criticized on economic grounds. Consumption taxes are never levied at a uniform rate on all goods and services; and thus they interfere with the freedom of choice of consumers and misallocate the nation's resources (except, as will be noted below, when they are employed as user charges or to discourage consumption of items, such as narcotics, that lead to increased social costs). They rank low as automatic stabilizers, because they respond no more than in proportion to changes in income. Moreover, purchasers may be charged more than the amount of the tax through *pyramiding* when successive markups are applied to the same goods as they move through the channels of production and distribution. On the other hand, sales and excise taxes are often supported for their relative stability of yield, a characteristic which commends itself for financing state-local government activities, but not federal.

Because of the equity and economic shortcomings of sales and excise taxes, other forms of consumption taxation have been proposed as substitutes. Some economists have been partial to a graduated expenditure tax, but this tax is generally regarded as too difficult to administer. Value added taxation, on the other hand, is beginning to spread, particularly among countries that have relied heavily on turnover taxes and have come to recognize their economic deficiencies.

In this country, the allocation between the federal and state-local governments of consumption taxes as a source of revenue has been stabilized and is not a major issue. Federal consumption taxes are restricted to selective excises, while the state and local governments levy general sales taxes as well as excises. In 1965, all but a few major federal excise taxes were eliminated. Substitution of a value added tax for part or all of the corporation income tax has been suggested, but Congress has not shown interest in such a trade. Forty-five states and many local governments levy retail sales taxes, and the trend is toward greater use of this tax at the state and local levels.

Issues in Excise Taxation

The imposition of heavy taxes on particular commodities substantially alters the results of the market mechanism. Such interference should be avoided, but there are circumstances under which excise taxes are useful and even necessary.

Economic Effects of Excise Taxes

The immediate effect of an excise tax is to raise the price of the taxed commodity. The consumer's response will be to consume less of the taxed commodity and to purchase other commodities or to save more. The burden of the tax is thus borne in part by consumers and in part by producers (and distributors) of the taxed commodity. If demand is relatively inelastic (that is, if the consumer does not reduce his consumption of the particular item very much as its price increases), most of the burden is borne by the consumer. On the other hand, if supply is relatively inelastic (if the producer does not or cannot reduce his production as price declines), the burden is borne mainly by the producer.

In general, the objective of excise taxation is to place the burden of the tax on consumers; and most excise revenues are derived from taxes imposed on articles for which the demand is relatively inelastic. For example, taxes on alcohol, tobacco, and gasoline accounted for almost two-thirds of federal excise revenues in 1969 (Table 6-1). Furthermore, supply is generally so highly elastic in the taxed industries that, even where demand is relatively elastic, very little of the burden of consumer taxes is borne by the producers.

BURDEN OF EXCISES. The effects of excise taxes on the allocation of economic resources depend on the sensitivity of consumption to a rise in price. If consumption is not reduced much by the increased price, the consumer responds by cutting his consumption of other

TABLE 6-1. Federal Excise Tax Revenue by Major Sources, Fiscal Year 1969

(Dollar amounts in millions)

Major source	Amount	Percentage of total
Alcohol	$ 4,482	29.4
Tobacco	2,136	14.0
Highway and automobile taxes		
Gasoline	3,053	20.1
Automobiles, trucks, buses, and trailers	2,464	16.2
Tires, inner tubes, and tread rubber	582	3.8
Other[a]	426	2.8
Telephone and teletype services	1,304	8.6
Air transportation	222	1.5
Interest equalization tax	109	0.7
Other[b]	443	2.9
Total	$15,222	100.0

Source: *The Budget of the United States Government, Fiscal Year 1971*, pp. 551–53. Refunds were distributed proportionately among the items, except for alcohol and tobacco, for which the specific amount of refund was available. Figures are rounded and do not necessarily add to totals.
  [a] Includes diesel fuel, lubricating oils, and use tax on certain vehicles.
  [b] Includes (1) taxes on firearms, shells, and cartridges, fishing equipment, documents, wagering, sugar, gaming devices, foreign insurance policies, and "other," and (2) undistributed excise tax collections.

commodities as well as the taxed commodity. The effect is much like that of an income tax, which reduces disposable income and causes the consumer to reduce consumption of a wide range of commodities. There is little incentive for labor and capital to move out of the taxed industry, and the allocation of resources elsewhere in the economy is not altered significantly.

When consumption is fairly sensitive to price, however, production and employment in the industry producing the taxed commodity declines. Demand for other products increases at the expense of the taxed industry, and over time the labor and capital will move to other industries (assuming that full employment is maintained). In this case, the tax substantially alters the pattern of production and consumption in the private economy. It also may create hardship for the employees and owners of capital in the industries affected.

Thus, an excise tax imposes a burden on the economy because consumers are not as well off as they would have been if the same revenue had been raised by another tax that did not change patterns of consumption. The loss due to this distortion is called the *excess consumer burden* of the excise tax. The amount of the excess burden is the difference between (a) the value placed by consumers on the consumption they give up and (b) the yield of the tax. Excess burden is, in other words, the loss in economic efficiency caused by the imposition of the tax.

This analysis holds only in a world in which the allocation of resources before imposition of the commodity tax is optimum. In the real world there are substantial departures from the conditions necessary for this optimum for reasons other than taxes, and there is no a priori basis for making the judgment that a new excise tax necessarily involves a loss in consumer welfare. Consumers may value the newly taxed commodity less highly than other commodities that they consume in its place after the tax is imposed, particularly if the new tax causes consumers to shift their consumption to commodities that are already heavily taxed.

Nevertheless, the case for selective excise taxes is weak. Conceivably there are excise taxes that would not reduce consumer welfare, but there is no basis for making such a selection. Excise taxes should be avoided unless there is a compelling reason for altering the allocation of resources and for discriminating among individuals and families on the basis of their consumption preferences.

EXCISE TAXES IN WARTIME. One situation in which the government has a definite interest in changing the pattern of resource use is in wartime or in a similar national emergency. Many materials that are in short supply are needed for production in war industries. In extreme cases, as in the two World Wars, the government is forced to replace the market mechanism with direct rationing and to halt production of items that conflict with the war effort. During a more limited emergency, such as the Korean war, it may not be necessary to take such drastic steps. In the latter situation, excise taxes may be helpful both as a rationing device and as a selective way of reducing consumer demand. By increasing the prices of the taxed commodities, the government can reduce demand and divert it to other commodities that are in more plentiful supply, or to saving.

Excises are among the first taxes to be increased in a national emergency. Criticism of this practice is usually based on the fact that the taxes chosen are hard to justify on economic and equity grounds. Further, the rationale of discouraging consumption on a selective basis is quickly forgotten once excises are imposed and the revenue objective becomes paramount. Even in wartime, the use of excise taxes as a major source of revenue should be avoided, first, because there are better ways to raise general revenues and, second, because the wartime taxes are apt to linger on—and do considerable damage—for many years. For example, the excises levied by the federal government on many electric, gas, and oil appliances in 1941 were not repealed until 1965.

USER CHARGES. Selective excise taxes may be used to good advantage to obtain payments from individuals who benefit from particular public services. When public programs lower the cost of a particular activity, that activity is artificially stimulated, and too many resources may be used in its performance. An excise tax, or some other means of charging for the service, is needed to maintain economic efficiency.

Despite the sound theoretical justification for such "user charge" excise taxes, they are not employed nearly enough for this purpose at any level of government in the United States. Specific excise taxes are allocated to the federal Highway Trust Fund, which was established in 1956 to finance the interstate highway system, and to the Airport and Airway Trust Fund, established in 1970 to finance airport and airway development. However, the last four presidents have recommended the adoption of a wide range of special taxes as user charges, including payments for the use of federal air and inland waterway transportation facilities, recreation facilities, and many other federally financed benefits. The pollution of water and air by private individuals and businesses imposes heavy costs on society, which should not be borne by the general taxpayer. User charges to pay for these benefits and costs would ease the burden of other taxes, promote equity, and improve economic efficiency. But successive administrations have had little success in persuading Congress to accept this approach. User charges are strongly resisted by the groups that would be required to pay, and past experience suggests that this resistance is politically potent and difficult to overcome.

SUMPTUARY AND REGULATORY TAXES. Excises on commodities or services that are considered socially or morally undesirable are known as *sumptuary* taxes. The best examples are the excises on liquor and tobacco. The rationale for sumptuary taxes is that the use of some articles for consumption creates additional costs to society that are not borne by the producers and are not reflected in the prices they charge. For example, mass consumption of liquor involves costs in the form of loss of working time, accidents, broken homes, and increased delinquency; and consumption of cigarettes has been shown to be associated with higher frequencies of a wide range of illnesses. An excise tax raises prices on such commodities to a level that more nearly reflects total social costs as well as private costs.

In some cases, the costs imposed by certain items are so great that society prohibits their consumption entirely. This is true, for example, of narcotics and gambling. The federal government prohibits the sale of narcotics except under very strict rules, while most states either outlaw or regulate gambling. Taxes are imposed on these items largely to aid in regulation and law enforcement.

In a democratic society, complete prohibition of the use of any commodity or service requires virtually unanimous agreement that its consumption is harmful or immoral. Where this unanimity does not exist, the majority expresses its view by levying a heavy tax that will discourage consumption without eliminating it entirely. Those who place a high value on the consumption of such items are allowed to purchase them but at a higher price. This explains why gambling is illegal in some states and is subject to regulation and to special taxes in others. Similarly, since opinion on the harmful effects of alcoholic beverages and cigarettes is not unanimous, purchases of these items are permitted but are heavily taxed by the federal and state governments and even by some local governments. The main effects of these taxes as levied in the United States are to tax smokers and drinkers heavily without curtailing their consumption very much and to introduce an element of regressivity into the system.

Another type of regulatory tax, introduced in the United States in 1964, is the interest equalization tax. This excise applies to purchases by U.S. residents of foreign securities issued in industrial countries (except for new Canadian bond issues and limited Japanese bond issues), and to loans abroad with maturities of one year or more. The tax is levied on common stock at a rate of 11.25 percent and on foreign bonds and loans at rates that increase the cost to foreigners of borrowing U.S. funds by roughly three-fourths of a percentage point. The purpose of this discriminatory tax is to improve the U.S. balance of payments by discouraging the flow of capital abroad. The tax was first applied at higher rates to purchases made after July 18, 1963; the current rates apply to purchases made after April 4, 1969. The tax is now scheduled to expire on March 31, 1971.

Equity Considerations

Excise taxes rank low in terms of equity on a number of grounds. First, consumers probably bear the major burden of the excise taxes that have been levied in the United States. How this burden is distributed depends on what proportion of income is allocated to consumption of the taxed items at the various income levels. For example, excise taxes on beer and cigarettes are highly regressive, while those on furs and some consumer durables are progressive. On balance, the post-World War II excise tax structure was regressive throughout the income scale (Table 6-2).

Second, excise taxes are unfair as among different people with the same incomes. Families whose preferences for the taxed commodities are high are taxed much more heavily than those who prefer to spend their incomes in other ways. This violation of horizontal equity is not justified unless there are overriding social reasons for discouraging the use of particular goods or services. However, where there are special costs or benefits associated with the production or distribution of a particular commodity that are not borne or paid for by the in-

TABLE 6-2. Effective Rates of Federal Excise Taxes, 1954, and of a Hypothetical General Retail Sales Tax, 1965

Income class (dollars)	Federal excise taxes 1954[a] (percentages)	2 percent retail sales tax, 1965[b] (percentages)	
		Including food	Excluding food
0– 1,000	} 5.0	2.12	1.39
1,000– 2,000		1.50	0.91
2,000– 3,000	4.5	1.41	0.92
3,000– 4,000	4.1	1.32	0.89
4,000– 5,000	3.9	1.35	0.95
5,000– 6,000	} 3.6	1.30	0.92
6,000– 7,500		1.28	0.92
7,500–10,000	3.3	1.24	0.92
10,000–15,000	} 1.9	1.17	0.91
15,000 and over		0.92	0.73
All classes	3.4	—	—

Sources: Federal excise taxes: Richard A. Musgrave, "The Incidence of the Tax Structure and Its Effects on Consumption," *Federal Tax Policy for Economic Growth and Stability,* Papers Submitted by Panelists Appearing before the Subcommittee on Tax Policy, Joint Committee on the Economic Report, 84 Cong. 1 sess. (1955), p. 98; retail sales tax: Advisory Commission on Intergovernmental Relations, *Fiscal Balance in the American Federal System* (1967), Vol. 1, p. 125.

[a] Effective rates are based on money income, including transfer payments and capital gains, plus retained corporate earnings and unshifted portion of the corporation profits tax attributed to individual stockholders.

[b] Effective rate on income after taxes.

dividuals and firms creating the costs or receiving the benefits, the imposition of a selective excise tax improves equity and the allocation of resources.

Third, while most of the pre-1965 excise taxes were levied on goods and services used by consumers, some applied to items that were used primarily or exclusively by business (such as business and store machines, lubricating oils, long-distance telephone services, and trucks). Taxes levied on such items enter into business costs and are generally reflected in higher prices for consumer goods. Since low-income persons spend a larger proportion of their income than those in the higher income classes, taxes that enter into business costs are by nature regressive. Furthermore, they often create unfair competitive situations by discriminating against firms that use the taxed commodity or service and distort the choice of production methods. The classic example of a bad excise tax is the one on freight, since it discriminates against firms that are distant from their markets. The freight tax was eliminated in 1958.

The Excise Tax Reduction Act of 1965 eliminated most federal excises, except for a few regulatory taxes and highway taxes that recover the costs of services or facilities directly benefiting individuals and business firms. The act reduced the tax on passenger cars in stages from 10 percent to 1 percent on January 1, 1969. It also provided that the 10 percent telephone tax be reduced in stages until it was completely eliminated by January 1, 1969. However, the scheduled reductions were postponed in 1966, 1968, and 1969; both taxes are scheduled to be eliminated on January 1, 1974.

A General Consumption Tax?

The major drawback of selective excise taxes is that they are not neutral; that is, they discriminate among different items of consumption. A broadly based tax is much more appropriate for taxing consumption. The three broadly based taxes mentioned most often are the general sales tax, the value added tax, and the expenditure tax.

The General Sales Tax

Sales taxation has been used extensively throughout the world, and there is almost no limit to the variations in the structure of these taxes. On the whole, experience suggests that a single-stage tax is preferable to a multistage or turnover tax and that the scope of the tax should be as broad as possible. Among single-stage taxes, the retail sales tax is preferable on economic and equity grounds, but it is somewhat more costly to administer than either a manufacturers' or a wholesalers' tax.

SINGLE-STAGE VERSUS MULTISTAGE TAXES. The advantage of a multistage tax is that any particular revenue goal can be realized at the lowest possible rate. This makes the turnover tax politically attractive, but it is highly objectionable on other grounds. A turnover tax levied at a uniform rate results in widely varying total rates of tax on different goods, depending on the complexity of the production and distribution channels. This means that the total tax burden differs among commodities, much as it does under a selective excise tax system. Moreover, the multistage tax provides a strong incentive for firms to merge with their suppliers and contributes to greater concentration in industry and trade.

Even the uniform rate turns out to be a will-o'-the-wisp whenever the turnover tax is tried. The discriminatory effects of the uniform rate soon become very serious, and the government finds it difficult to resist pressures to moderate the tax load where it is demonstrably out of line. Once introduced, modifications of the uniform rate proliferate, and the tax becomes a maze of complications and irrational distinctions. Thus, a tax that was originally intended to be relatively simple turns out to be an administrative monstrosity and highly inequitable.

WHOLESALERS' AND MANUFACTURERS' SALES TAXES. Administrative complications are reduced if the tax is levied at the wholesale or manufacturing level. The number of firms is smaller, their average size is larger, and their records are more adequate. These advantages are offset, however, by the difficulty of identifying taxable transactions and of determining the price on which the tax is based.

The most troublesome feature of the wholesalers' tax involves the determination of wholesale values when manufacturers sell directly to retailers. To avoid discrimination among industries with differing degrees of integration, these manufacturers' prices are usually raised to include a normal wholesale markup. The adjustment goes the other way in the case of the manufacturers' tax: the price charged by a manufacturer to a retailer must be lowered to eliminate the value of the wholesale services.

Both taxes are subject to the criticism that the rate tends to pyramid as goods move to the retail level. Thus, a 10 percent manufacturers' tax may become a 20 percent tax at the retail level, after the wholesaler and retailer have applied their customary markups. There is less pyramiding under a wholesalers' tax, but the problem is by no means avoided. In time, competition tends to wipe out the effect of pyramiding, but the adjustment process may be slow.

On balance, there is little to choose between the wholesalers' and the manufacturers' tax. The wholesalers' tax is more practical when the wholesale and retail stages are fairly distinct; on the other hand, complications arise if there is a substantial degree of integration between manufacturers and retailers. The manufacturers' tax is more practical when there is either a high degree of integration in most consumer lines or none at all; the mixed situation raises the most difficulties.

RETAIL SALES TAX. A retail sales tax is intended to apply uniformly to most goods and services purchased by individual consumers and is basically much less complicated than a wholesalers' or manufacturers' tax. However, retail sales taxes are rarely completely general, although they are usually imposed on a broad base. It is difficult to reach many consumer services, although it is possible to include such services as admissions, repairs, laundry, and dry cleaning. The retail sales tax does not apply to housing—the largest service in most consumer budgets—but housing is subject to the property tax. Many state sales taxes in the United States exempt food and other commodities that are regarded as necessities.

Although the retail sales tax often falls short of complete generality, it is in many ways better than the taxes levied at earlier stages of the production or distribution process. Its most important advantage is that there is little or no pyramiding. For goods purchased by consumers, wholesale and retail markups are not inflated by the tax since it applies only to the final price. An attempt is sometimes made to exempt from the retail sales tax investment goods purchased by business firms, but taxes on business purchases often run as high as one-fifth of sales tax receipts, making such exemptions expensive. These taxes enter into business costs and are probably pyramided, but the extent of pyramiding must be only a small fraction of that which occurs under a manufacturers' or wholesalers' sales tax.

The broader base of the retail sales tax means that lower rates can be used than with other single-stage taxes to yield a given amount of revenue. And this difference in rates is not small, since prices may be 50 or 100 percent higher at the retail level. Thus, a retail tax of 5 percent may yield the same revenue as a manufacturers' tax of 7.5 or 10 percent.

On administrative grounds, the retail sales tax has both advantages and disadvantages. It is more difficult to deal with the large number of small retailers than with the less numerous and more sophisticated manufacturers or wholesalers. On the other hand, the problems of defining a transaction and of determining the base of the tax are more easily handled at the retail level, although even there the problems are not insignificant. The state governments have had retail sales taxes for many years, and most of them have learned that they are not easy to administer and enforce.

The introduction of a retail sales tax by the federal government would involve duplication of existing state and local taxes. The state and local governments would interpret this as unwarranted interference with their freedom of action with regard to the rates and coverage of their own taxes. At the minimum, some effort would have to be made to coordinate the definition of the tax bases and perhaps also to administer collection of the taxes on a cooperative or joint basis.

The strongest objection to a retail tax, which also applies to wholesale and manufacturing taxes, is its regressivity. Estimates indicate that in 1965 a 2 percent sales tax on all tangible commodities, including food, amounted to 2.1 percent of income for families below the $1,000 level and 0.9 percent for those above $15,000 (Table 6-2). These figures, based on income and consumption in a one-year period, may overstate the regressivity of the sales tax, since persons temporarily in the lower-income classes do not reduce their consumption by the entire amount of the reduction in their incomes, and those temporarily in higher classes do not raise their consumption by the entire increase in their incomes. Some economists have suggested that the burden of the sales tax should be measured against income over a longer time period. On this basis, a retail sales tax might be proportional, but it is unlikely that it would turn out to be progressive in any significant degree, regardless of the time period used.

Many units of government have exempted food and certain other items of consumption from the sales tax to alleviate its burden on the poor. These exemptions moderate, but do not eliminate, the regressivity of the tax (Table 6-2). As an alternative, experts have long suggested refunding the estimated tax paid by individuals with low incomes. This suggestion was ignored until 1963, when Indiana introduced a retail sales tax and adopted a small tax credit against the income tax as a relief measure for the sales tax paid by low-income recipients. Since then, Colorado, Hawaii, Idaho, Massachusetts, Nebraska, and Vermont have adopted the same device, and other states are considering it.

The Value Added Tax

The value added tax, first proposed in 1918 by a German industrial executive, was discussed sporadically for another three decades before it was actually put to use. A modified version was adopted in 1953 by the state of Michigan and repealed in 1967; in 1954, the central government of France imposed such a tax, and Belgium, Denmark, Germany, Netherlands, Norway, and Sweden have since followed suit. Other countries are now considering it as a substitute for other forms of consumption taxes. Some have advocated the inclusion of a value added tax in the federal tax system to provide a revenue source that could be raised or lowered in the interest of stabilization.

FORMS OF VALUE ADDED TAXATION. Conceptually, the value added tax is a general tax on the national income. For any given firm, value added is the difference between receipts from sales and the amounts paid for materials, supplies, and services purchased from other firms. The total of the value added by all firms in the economy is equal to total wages, salaries, interest, rents, and profits and is therefore the same as the national income.

In practice, there are two types of value added taxes that differ only in the way outlays for investment purposes are treated. The first type permits business firms to subtract purchases of capital goods in computing the tax base. Total value added is thus equal to total retail sales of final consumer goods. With the second type, purchases of capital goods are not deducted; instead, firms are permitted to deduct an allowance for depreciation over the useful life of the asset. Thus, only the second type is equivalent to a tax on the national income; the first, which is proposed most often, is a general consumption tax.

There are two methods of computing the allowance to be made for purchases from other firms. Under the "tax credit" method, the tax rate is applied to the total sales of the firm, and the tax paid on goods purchased is then deducted. Where this method is used, the tax on all goods shipped must be shown separately on each invoice. Under the second, so-called "calculation," method purchases are subtracted from sales, and the tax rate is then applied to the net figure. Both approaches have the same result, but some administrators believe that the tax credit method is easier to control, because it automatically provides an accounting of the tax to be remitted on exports (the standard practice to avoid putting domestic firms at a competitive disadvantage in foreign markets) and solves some of the problems raised by the inclusion or exclusion of various items, such as charitable contributions, that are troublesome under the calculation method.

ECONOMIC EFFECTS OF THE VALUE ADDED TAX. The value added tax reduces or eliminates the pyramiding that would occur under the turnover tax or the manufacturers' and wholesalers' sales taxes. Since a firm receives credit for the tax paid by its suppliers, it is not likely to apply a markup to its purchases in computing the price to be charged. For example, suppose a retailer who pays $52.50 for an item (including $2.50 tax) wants to apply a markup of 100 percent. Under the tax credit method, he charges his customer $105 ($100 plus $5 tax) and takes a credit of $2.50 in computing the amount to be paid to the government, leaving a net tax of $2.50. If the calculation method is used, the retailer deducts from the $100 the $50 paid to his supplier and then applies a tax rate of 5 percent to the remainder to obtain the same $2.50 net tax. The customer pays the same total price of $105, which consists of the $100 price net of tax, the $2.50 tax paid by the supplier, and the $2.50 tax paid by the retailer.

The base of the consumption-type value added tax is the same as that of a retail sales tax and is confined to consumption goods. On the other hand, the income-type value added tax is equivalent to a proportional income tax. Whether the patterns of distribution of the burden of the income-type and consumption-type value added taxes are the same is in dispute, reflecting a difference of opinion as to the impact of a proportional income tax and a general tax on consumption. The income-type value added tax is paid on capital goods at the time the purchase is made, and the tax is presumably recovered as it is depreciated. Under the consumption-type value added tax, purchases of capital goods are free of tax. Thus, at any given time, the income-type value added tax imposes an extra tax on net investment. Some argue that prepayment of the tax under the income-type tax reduces the return on capital; others believe that it is reflected in higher prices for final consumption goods and has no effect on the rate of return. The difference is not likely to be significant, however.

THE VALUE ADDED TAX VERSUS THE RETAIL SALES TAX. The consumption-type value added tax and the retail sales tax are similar on both economic and equity grounds. Both are, for all practical purposes, taxes on general consumption. The retail sales tax involves fewer administrative problems because the determination of tax liability is less complicated and the number of taxpayers is smaller. But in practice retail sales taxes always exclude many items of consumption, while a value added tax could probably be levied on a more general basis.

The Expenditure Tax

The expenditure tax has long been discussed in the economic literature but was not seriously considered until the U.S. Treasury Department recommended it during World War II. It was also advocated by a minority of the British Royal Commission on the Taxation of Profits and Income in 1955. Although neither recommendation was adopted, the tax has since come to be regarded as a respectable possibility.

Unlike the consumption taxes already discussed, the expenditure tax is levied on the individual consumer rather than on the seller of goods and services. In practice, there is little difference in the method of administration between the expenditure tax and the individual income tax. The individual taxpayer submits a form at the end of the year estimating the amount of his expenditures. Deductions for selected expenditures may be allowed, as well as personal exemptions. The rates may be proportional or graduated; usually, however, it is suggested that the expenditure tax be graduated.

Expenditure taxation is proposed either to replace or to supplement the income tax. It is supported strongly by those who believe that the income tax has an adverse effect on incentives to save and invest (see Chapter 4). It is also supported as a useful supplement to income taxation when capital gains and other income either are not taxed or are taxed at a preferential rate. While capital gains are not reached by the expenditure tax as such, the tax does apply to consumption that is financed out of capital gains.

Some believe that the income tax is inequitable because it taxes income when it is saved and then again when the savings earn additional income. It is now generally agreed that this double taxation argument is sterile. Both the expenditure tax and the income tax may be progressive and redistributional in effect. If one considers that income is the better measure of ability to pay, the expenditure tax is inferior. If expenditures are considered the better measure, the income tax is inferior.

The expenditure tax is not more widespread than it is primarily because of difficulties of compliance and administration. It is impractical to ask taxpayers to estimate their expenditures directly, since almost no one keeps adequate expenditure records. Thus, expenditures must be estimated by subtracting income that is saved from total income received during the year. This requires the taxpayer to provide balance sheet information (to estimate saving) as well as an income statement. Some proponents of the expenditure tax have pointed out that the requirement to supply balance sheet information should be regarded as a major advantage and not as a disadvantage of the expenditure tax, since the information would be helpful in administering the income tax. However, it is generally agreed that the administrative and compliance problems of an expenditure tax are formidable and that it would be very difficult for most countries to enforce such a tax with the present state of administrative know-how.

Consumption versus Income Taxes

Until recently, the major argument for adoption of a general consumption tax by the federal government was the arbitrariness of the excise tax system. Except for sumptuary and benefit taxes, the excises that were in effect between 1944 and 1965 could hardly be defended on rational grounds. If revenues from consumption taxes were needed permanently, it would have been better to replace the miscellaneous excises with a general low-rate tax on consumer goods.

This argument was eliminated by enactment of the Excise Tax Reduction Act of 1965. It can be said that, for all practical purposes, the federal government has reduced consumption taxation to a minimum. The appeal of a general consumption tax must now rest on the substantive ground that it would be better national policy to replace part of the income tax with a general consumption tax.

Heavier reliance on a general consumption tax by the federal government is opposed for several reasons:

First, the shift from income taxes to a consumption tax would impair the built-in flexibility of the tax system. The automatic reductions in income tax revenues during the postwar recessions were of major importance in moderating the declines in disposable income and contributed to the brevity and mildness of the recessions. Although the United States has avoided a downturn that has been officially labeled a recession for more than ten years, the business cycle has not been eliminated. Maintenance of built-in flexibility is good insurance against the possibility of a serious business contraction in the future.

Second, a general consumption tax would bring the federal government into an area that is now the most important source of state revenue and is also becoming important at the local level. Federal use of this tax source would almost surely restrict its use by the state and local governments, which would impair their fiscal capacities at a time when they face large financial responsibilities.

Third, because of the opposition of the state and local governments, any general consumption tax enacted by the federal government might be a tax at the manufacturers' or at the wholesalers' level. As has been seen, such taxes tend to be pyramided through conventional markups and thus to burden the consumer by more than the amount of revenue collected. Moreover, experience in other countries has shown that it is hard to define the tax base so as to avoid serious inequities.

Fourth, taking federal, state, and local taxes together, the tax load on low-income recipients is already heavy. The increases in state-local revenues in the years immediately ahead will come largely from taxes that are most burdensome on low-income groups. Additional consumption taxes at the federal level would make the combined structure even more regressive. Such a policy would be particularly inappropriate at a time when the federal government is trying to moderate the impact of poverty in the United States.

On the other hand, several arguments are advanced in support of greater use of consumption taxes by the federal government:

First, even though income tax rates were reduced in 1964, they are still too high, particularly for individuals with high incomes. These high rates may reduce incentives and the willingness and capacity to save.

Second, built-in flexibility does not require that all elements of the federal tax system be highly sensitive to changes in income. Furthermore, a large automatic growth in tax receipts has the undesirable side effect of promoting higher federal expenditures. If these revenues were not so easily obtained, federal expenditures might be much lower.

Third, the federal government need not impair the fiscal capacities of the state and local governments in order to build up its own consumption tax revenue. If a value added tax were adopted, the federal government would not encroach on state-local revenue. Since practically all business enterprises already file income tax returns, the administrative and compliance problems of a value added tax should not be insurmountable.

Fourth, adoption of a general consumption tax in lieu of part of the corporation income tax would improve the U.S. balance-of-payments position. This substitution would improve either the trade surplus, if the corporation income tax is shifted to the consumer in the form of higher prices, or the capital account, if the tax is borne by the owners of capital (see Chapter 5). Even a modest improvement in the nation's balance of payments would be a contribution, since the problem has not been easy to solve.

While there are a number of important peripheral considerations, the major issue in the income tax versus consumption tax controversy concerns the degree of progression. Proponents of a general consumption tax rarely recommend a graduated expenditure tax as an alternative to income taxation. Their concern is to reduce progression, and they propose a flat rate sales or value added tax as a way to accomplish this objective. On the other hand, those who oppose a general consumption tax either defend the present degree of progression or believe it is inadequate. Most of them would support a graduated expenditure tax if a new consumption tax were necessary, but would oppose the adoption of a sales or value added tax.

Summary

The federal government has relied exclusively on selected excises for consumption tax revenues. These taxes were increased during every major war and were subsequently de-emphasized as the need for revenue declined. The cycle lasted somewhat longer during and after World War II, but the last vestige of the wartime excises was eliminated by the 1965 Excise Tax Reduction Act. When this law becomes fully effective (scheduled for January 1, 1974, by the Tax Reform Act of 1969), the only excise taxes remaining in the federal revenue system will be the sumptuary taxes on alcohol and tobacco, the benefit taxes for highways, airways, and some recreational activities, and certain regulatory taxes.

Sumptuary taxes help to offset the additional cost imposed on society by the consumption of certain commodities; taxes imposed on those who benefit from particular government services are needed to prevent excessive use of such services; special charges would be helpful to discourage private activities that lead to pollution; and regulatory taxes are used primarily to assist law enforcement rather than to raise revenues. Otherwise, excise taxes are bad taxes: they discriminate arbitrarily against the consumption of the taxed commodities and distort the allocation of resources in the economy.

If consumption taxes are needed for revenue purposes, economic and equity considerations suggest that a general consumption tax would be more appropriate than a series of selective excise taxes. A general tax does not discriminate against particular forms of consumption and therefore produces less distortion in the economy.

Among general consumption taxes, manufacturers' and wholesalers' sales taxes are probably easiest to administer, but they are pyramided through the markup of prices as goods go through production and distribution channels. Retail sales taxes and the value added tax involve much less pyramiding, if any. All these taxes are regressive or, at best, proportional. Progression can be achieved by adopting a credit for sales taxes paid against the individual income tax, or by taxing consumption through a graduated expenditure tax. The expenditure tax has a number of attractive features, but it is generally regarded as too difficult to administer.

Consumption taxes are more burdensome on the low-income classes than are income taxes, and they have less built-in flexibility. Adoption of a general consumption tax by the federal government would also interfere with a revenue source that has become a mainstay of state and some local tax systems. However, consumption taxes are vigorously supported by those who believe that the federal tax system is too progressive and that income taxation has impaired economic incentives. More recently, some have been supporting the adoption of a value added tax as a replacement for part of the corporation income tax to help improve the U.S. balance of payments.

CHAPTER SEVEN

Payroll Taxes

TAXES ON PAYROLLS, first introduced into the federal revenue system by the Social Security Act of 1935, have grown markedly during the past three decades. They rank second in order of importance, accounting for about 23 percent of federal budget receipts in fiscal year 1970 (Figure 7-1). Payroll tax receipts will continue to increase in the 1970s and 1980s, as scheduled rate increases go into effect. Unlike income, excise, estate, and gift taxes, payroll taxes are "earmarked"—through trust funds—to finance the nation's social insurance programs.

Development of Payroll Taxes

Most countries levy special taxes on payrolls (or income) to finance social insurance. When the United States passed its Social Security Act, twenty-eight countries had well developed national retirement systems. The depression of the 1930s demonstrated that the state and local governments and private industry did not have the capacity to develop and finance a stable and adequate retirement program for the general population.

The 1935 act established two social insurance programs: a federal system of old-age benefits (now OASDHI, commonly called "social security") and a federal-state system of unemployment compensation. The first is financed by equal payroll taxes collected from employees

169

FIGURE 7-1. Payroll Taxes as a Percentage of Gross National Product, Federal Budget Receipts, and Individual Income Tax Receipts, Fiscal Years 1954–70

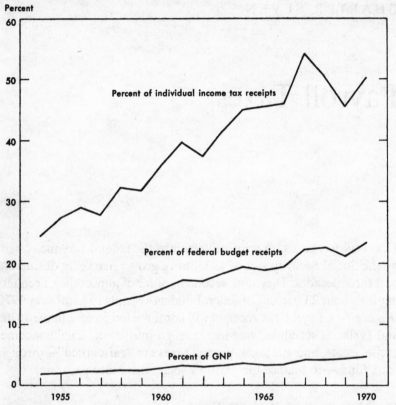

Sources: Gross national product: *The Budget of the United States Government, Fiscal Year 1971*, p. 593, and *Survey of Current Business*, Vol. 50 (September 1970), p. S-1; other data: Appendix Table C-3.

and employers; the second is financed mainly by payroll taxes on employers (a few states tax both employers and employees). The major characteristics of these programs are summarized in Table 7-1.

The original programs have undergone considerable change in coverage, benefits, and tax rates. Old-age benefits were supplemented by survivors' benefits in 1939, disability benefits in 1957, and hospital and medical benefits for persons 65 and over in 1966. The tax rate, initially 1 percent each on employers and employees for wages and salaries up to $3,000 annually, is now (1970) 4.8 percent on each and is scheduled to rise to 5.9 percent by 1987. Effective January 1, 1968, the top limit on earnings subject to tax was raised to $7,800. Self-employed persons with net earnings in excess of $400 per year were

TABLE 7-1. Major Characteristics of the Social Insurance Programs as of July 1, 1970

Program	Contribution rates Employee	Contribution rates Employer	Maximum earnings subject to tax	Eligibility requirements for benefits	Benefits
Old-age, survivors, and disability insurance	4.2%[a]	4.2%[a]	$7,800 per yr.	OASI: 1½ to 10 years of coverage; age 62 and over for men and women workers and wives; age 60 for widows[b]	Individual: Maximum $250.70 per month[c] Individual: Minimum $64.00 per month[b] Family: Maximum $434.40 per month[c] Family: Minimum $96.00 per month[b]
				Disability: Insured status for OASI and recent employment; 6 months' waiting period following total disability	Same as OASI
Hospital	0.6%[d]	0.6%[d]	$7,800 per yr.	Over 65 years of age[e]	60 days (with $52 deductible) plus 30 days at $11 per day; also post-hospital services,[f] and a lifetime reserve of 60 days with a $20 daily coinsurance
Medical (voluntary)	$5.30 per month premium[g]	—	—	Over 65 years of age	$50 deductible and 20% coinsurance[h]
Unemployment compensation	—	3.2%[i]	$3,000[j] per yr.	Typically one year of covered employment	Typically 50% of weekly wage: from 9 to 39 weeks, depending on state laws
Railroad retirement	9.55%[k]	9.55%[k]	$650 per mo.	10 years of coverage, age 65 and over[l]	Individual: Maximum $613 per month[m] Individual: Minimum $67 per month[n] Family: Maximum $728 per month[m] Family: Minimum $100 per month[n]
Railroad unemployment compensation	—	4%[o]	$400 per mo.	Compensation of at least $1,000 in base year[p]	Typically 60% of daily pay for last employment in base year up to 130 days[p]

[a] Increases to 4.6 percent in 1971–72, 5.0 percent in 1973 and after.

[b] Permanently reduced benefits payable for retirement between ages 62 and 65, or between 60 and 62 for widows. Minimum benefits are before the reduction for early retirement.

[c] Generally not payable for many years to come. Maximum payable to a worker who retires at age 65 in 1970 is $195; to a family, $361.60.

[d] Increases to 0.65 percent in 1973–75, 0.7 in 1976–79, 0.8 in 1980–86, 0.9 in 1987 and after.

[e] Shorter work requirements than under OASI until 1974; after 1974, same as OASI.

[f] Post-hospital services include care in a nursing home (cost of first 20 days and excess over $6.50 a day for next 80) under a registered professional nurse, or care in a private home (for 100 visits) if only intermittent nursing is needed.

[g] In December of each year the secretary of health, education, and welfare determines the premiums necessary to collect one-half the projected expense of the program, and premiums are adjusted accordingly.

[h] Includes most physician and related services.

[i] In most states rates are reduced on basis of experience rating.

[j] $4,200 beginning January 1, 1972.

[k] Increases in steps in accordance with OASDHI increases to 10.65 percent in 1987 and after.

[l] Benefits payable at age 60 with 30 years of service (benefits are reduced for males), or at age 62 with 10 years of service (benefits are reduced for both males and females). Survivors and disability insurance also available to railroad employees.

[m] Not payable to workers who retire before 2008. Maximum payable in 1970 to a retired worker at age 65 is $429.79; to a family, $545.29. Temporary 15 percent increase provided in the 1970 amendments to the Railroad Retirement Act not included.

[n] Temporary 15 percent increase provided in the 1970 amendments to the Railroad Retirement Act not included.

[o] Statutory rates vary from 1.5 to 4 percent depending on balance in trust fund.

[p] Base year is calendar year preceding the beginning of the benefit year which runs from July 1 to the following June 30.

added to the social security system in 1951, with a tax rate 1.5 times the rate applying to employees. For the self-employed, a maximum of 7.9 percent is scheduled to be reached in 1987. This rate includes the tax for hospital protection, which is the same as for employees.

The federal unemployment compensation tax rate started at 1 percent of payrolls of employers of eight or more persons; in 1972, it will reach a maximum of 3.2 percent for employers of one or more persons on wages and salaries up to $4,200 (lower rates are permitted in most states, depending on the stability of the employer's past record of employment).

Railroad workers are covered, though at higher rates, for both retirement and unemployment under their own systems. As under social security, employer and employee each pay half of the railroad retirement insurance tax; and, as under the federal-state system, the employer pays all of the railroad unemployment insurance tax.

The employee share of payroll taxes is withheld at the source by employers, but these taxes differ from the pattern established by the individual income tax in other respects. In the first place, they are levied at a flat rate on gross wages and salaries up to a certain maximum amount each year, with no exemptions or deductions. Second, the employee—even though he is liable for half the OASDHI tax— does not file a return. The reporting of earnings, which provide the basis for calculating benefits, is handled entirely by the employer. Taxes are paid by the self-employed on an estimated basis quarterly.

The federal old-age, survivors, disability, and health programs now cover more than 90 percent of all persons in paid jobs; 85 percent of the population age 65 and over are drawing benefits. The hospital insurance program covers about 20 million people age 65 or over. Unemployment insurance covered about 60 million persons in 1970, or four-fifths of the total number of wage and salary earners. About 5 million will be added in 1972 when coverage is extended to small firms and nonprofit organizations.

When the social security program was enacted in 1935, considerable emphasis was placed on its resemblance to private insurance: "contributions" are paid by the worker and the employer into a trust fund, interest is credited on trust fund balances, and benefits are formally based on the worker's previous earnings. This emphasis promoted public acceptance of the system as a permanent government institution.

However, the insurance analogy no longer applies to the system as it has developed. Present beneficiaries as a group receive far larger benefits than those to which the taxes they have paid would entitle them, and this situation will continue indefinitely as long as Congress keeps benefits in line with higher current wage levels. Although the trust fund balances have been growing in recent years, they remained unchanged between 1957 and 1967, so that the payroll taxes paid by workers have not been stored up or invested but have been paid out currently as benefits. When the benefits promised to people now working become due, they will be paid from the tax revenues of that future date. Thus, social security is really a compact between the working and nonworking generations that is continually renewed and strengthened by every amendment to the basic program.

In this concept of social security, payroll taxes are not insurance premiums but rather a financing mechanism for a large, essential government program. Payroll taxes should therefore be evaluated like any other major tax of the federal government; increases in benefits and expansion of the social security program should not be financed automatically by higher payroll taxes as they have been in the past, but by the best tax source or sources available to the federal government.

Features of Payroll Taxes

As the second largest source of federal revenue, payroll taxes have a significant effect on the distribution of tax burdens and may also have a substantial impact on the economy. From the standpoint of tax analysis their important features are their regressivity; their built-in flexibility; their effect on prices, employment, and wages; and their effect on personal and public saving.

Regressivity

The effective OASDHI tax rates seem to be progressive with respect to income up to $7,000 or $8,000 of money income, and regressive thereafter (Figure 7-2). This pattern of tax incidence reflects the changing importance of covered earnings as incomes rise. In the lower part of the income scale, the ratio of covered earnings to total income increases; the ratio begins to fall at higher levels because the payroll taxes apply only up to $7,800 and because property income, which is not subject to these taxes, becomes increasingly important as incomes rise above this point.

FIGURE 7-2. Effective Tax Rates, by Income Level, of a 5 Percent Payroll Tax[a] on Employers and Employees and of Alternative Methods of Raising the Same Revenue

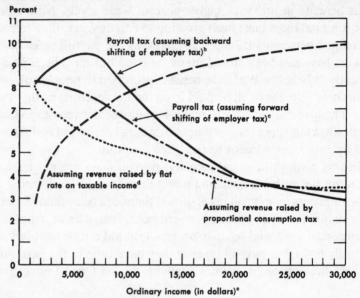

Source: Joseph A. Pechman, Henry J. Aaron, and Michael K. Taussig, *Social Security: Perspectives for Reform* (Brookings Institution, 1968), Chart VIII-2 and Appendix E. The calculations are based on a sample of approximately 100,000 federal individual income tax returns for the year 1964.

[a] Tax is 7 percent for the self-employed. Maximum earnings subject to tax are $7,800, as specified in the 1967 amendments to the Social Security Act.

[b] Employer and employee taxes are assumed to be borne by the employee; self-employment tax is assumed to be borne by the self-employed.

[c] Employer tax is distributed in proportion to consumption by income class; employee tax and self-employment tax are assumed to be borne by the employee or the self-employed.

[d] The tax is applied to taxable income as defined in the Internal Revenue Code for 1965.

[e] Ordinary income is adjusted gross income exclusive of capital gains and losses, plus excluded sick pay and dividends.

On the basis of 1964 data, the 1970 OASDHI taxes are more progressive than a proportional tax on consumption yielding the same amount of revenue would be. The income tax is much more progressive. These conclusions are the same whether the employer and employee OASDHI taxes are assumed to be borne entirely by the wage earners or whether it is assumed that only the employee tax is borne by wage earners and the employer tax is shifted to consumers.

The increases in payroll taxes that are scheduled will have a significant impact on the tax payments of the lowest income groups. When they are fully effective in 1987, the employee contribution for social security, disability, and hospital care will reach 5.9 percent of wages up to $7,800, or a maximum of $460.20 (Table 7-2). This will exceed the 1971 income tax liabilities for single persons with incomes of $4,500, married persons with incomes of $5,410, and married persons with two children and incomes of $6,710. In 1971, the federal payroll tax for OASDHI purposes will be the highest tax paid by at least half of the nation's income recipients (assuming backward shifting of the employer tax), and $1.5 billion will be paid by persons officially classified as living below poverty levels.

Built-in Flexibility

Payroll taxes are much less sensitive to fluctuations in national income and employment than is the federal individual income tax. Since payroll taxes are regressive through a substantial portion of the income scale, their yield (assuming constant tax rates) fluctuates proportionately less over a business cycle than does personal income. Automatic increases in tax rates that are enacted many years ahead have occasionally aggravated this effect. OASDI tax increases went into effect when the country was in the midst of the 1953–54 recession, and only a few months before the onset of recessions in 1957 and 1960. However, benefits have generally been raised along with or shortly after tax increases, thus offsetting their deflationary impact.

Pressures for increasing payroll tax rates at inappropriate times in the business cycle have also been experienced in state unemploy-

TABLE 7-2. Maximum Combined Employer-Employee Taxes and Maximum Tax on Self-Employed under the OASDI and Hospital Insurance Programs, 1969 and Later Years

(In dollars)

Year	Maximum employer-employee tax			Maximum tax on self-employed		
	OASDI	Hospital insurance	Total	OASDI	Hospital insurance	Total
1969	655.20	93.60	748.80	491.40	46.80	538.20
1970	655.20	93.60	748.80	491.40	46.80	538.20
1971–72	717.60	93.60	811.20	538.20	46.80	585.00
1973–75	780.00	101.40	881.40	546.00	50.70	596.70
1976–79	780.00	109.20	889.20	546.00	54.60	600.60
1980–86	780.00	124.80	904.80	546.00	62.40	608.40
1987 and after	780.00	140.40	920.40	546.00	70.20	616.20

Source: Social Security Amendments of 1967.

ment compensation programs. When the trust funds are threatened by a lack of reserves, the states are forced to raise tax rates regardless of the level of economic activity. Moreover, almost all states have adopted the "experience rating" system, which reduces tax rates for firms with stable employment. As a result, state unemployment taxes may fluctuate *inversely* with national income and employment levels.

By contrast, the expenditure side of the social insurance trust accounts has been extremely effective in promoting economic stability. Unemployment insurance benefits increase automatically as demand slackens and unemployment increases; they decline automatically as employment picks up. This automatic effect is supplemented during periods of high national or state unemployment by the payment of thirteen additional weeks of benefits to workers who have exhausted their benefits under the regular state programs. In addition, older workers can fall back on old-age insurance when they cannot find employment during slack periods.

On balance, despite the regressivity of the taxes and the inappropriate timing of tax rate increases, the social insurance system has contributed notably to the nation's economic stability during the postwar period.

Effect on Prices, Employment, and Wages

It is popularly assumed that the employee share of the payroll taxes is borne by wage earners and that the employer share is shifted forward to the consumer in the form of higher prices. But economists believe that there is no difference in the incidence of the payroll taxes legally levied on employers and employees.

The OASDHI tax is a proportional tax on wages and salaries up to $7,800. Although a few categories of workers are excluded, the tax may be regarded as virtually universal. Since it is paid in every occupation and industry, employees have no incentive to move elsewhere to avoid it. Thus, like the personal income tax, the payroll tax is not shifted.

In the short run, producers treat the payroll tax like any other production cost and try to recover it through higher prices. At the higher prices they do not sell as much as they did at pre-tax prices, and output and employment tend to decline. This effect can be offset if the government maintains real demand at the old level (through a combination of monetary and fiscal policies), but relative prices and output will be altered in any event. If money demand does not expand sufficiently, output and employment will fall.

In the long run, the impact of the payroll tax depends on the reaction of wage earners to reduced wages. Business firms aim at using just the right combination of labor and capital to produce at lowest cost. A payroll tax does not make labor any more productive, so employers have no reason to pay higher total compensation after the tax is imposed unless some wage earners react to their reduced earnings by withdrawing from the labor force (that is, unless the supply of labor is less than completely inelastic with respect to wages). If some wage earners do withdraw, employers will have to offer higher wages to attract additional employees or to keep those that remain; wages will rise as a result of the tax (though not necessarily by the exact amount of the tax), and less labor will be employed.

However, it is generally agreed that the supply of labor is inelastic with respect to wages: lower wages will not induce wage earners to withdraw from the labor force. In these circumstances, the same number of workers will be seeking the same number of jobs, wages will be lower by the amount of the tax, and the workers will bear the full burden. Although wages may not actually fall under these circumstances, they will increase less rapidly than they would without the payroll tax, thereby shifting the burden of the tax to the wage earner in the long run.

It is also possible that workers will bear the tax even if the supply of labor is not completely inelastic with respect to wages. Employees may be willing to accept a lower wage after the tax is imposed if they regard the benefits to be financed by the tax as an adequate quid pro quo. If this were the prevailing attitude, the tax would be similar to a user charge, the supply of labor would not be altered, earnings would fall by the amount of the tax, and the full burden would be borne by the wage earners.

The conclusion that the burden of payroll taxes falls on the wage earner must be qualified in one respect. The economic model upon which the analysis is based assumes rational behavior in labor markets and takes no account of the possible effect on wages of collective bargaining agreements between large firms and labor unions. Labor unions will resist any cut in the wages of their members and may succeed in inducing management to raise gross wages by an amount sufficient to offset the effect of the payroll tax. In such circumstances, part or all of the employer and employee taxes may be transferred to the consumer. Critics of this view argue that, if such market power existed, labor and management could have exercised it to raise wages and prices before the tax was imposed. Nevertheless, one cannot dismiss the possibility that the adoption of a new payroll tax, or an increase in the old one, may be the occasion when labor and management choose to exercise this power.

Personal and Public Saving

National social insurance provides protection against loss of income due to retirement, death, unemployment, permanent disability, and illness. Before these government programs were enacted, individual savings were the only protection against these hazards. It is sometimes suggested that social insurance encourages individuals to set aside a smaller amount of personal saving on the ground that a major reason for saving has now been removed. On the other hand, the availability of social insurance may well provide an incentive for individuals to save more; with major needs already covered, other savings goals may appear to be within reach.

The available evidence suggests that, over the long run, individuals covered by government and industrial pension plans tend to save more than those who are not covered. But nothing is known about the effect on saving of unemployment and disability insurance. At any given time, those who are contributing to social insurance have higher incomes than those who are receiving benefits, so that there is a current redistribution of income from high to low savers. There is no basis for judging how these opposing tendencies have affected total personal saving on balance. While personal saving rose from 5.0 to 6.0 percent of disposable income between 1929 and 1969, many other factors have had a significant influence on the saving ratio.

The effect of the social security programs on *government* saving is also unclear. As of June 30, 1970, the trust fund accumulations were over $58 billion, three-fifths of which occurred prior to 1957 (Appendix Table C-20). Had these balances not been accumulated, other taxes might have been raised to yield approximately the same revenue, expenditures might have been reduced, or additional debt might have been issued to the public. Since the administrative budget, which was used by the federal government throughout this period, excluded trust fund saving, federal saving was probably larger (or dissaving smaller) as a result of the existence of the trust funds. This may well have been a factor in slowing economic growth during the late 1950s.

The unified budget, which is now used for federal budget purposes, takes trust fund balances into account. Presumably this implies that other taxes might have been higher had the payroll taxes been lower. But it is still uncertain whether the philosophy behind the unified budget has been completely accepted by Congress. The trust fund balances rose by $22.5 billion between mid-1966 and mid-1970, when prices and wages were rising sharply. The existence of large surpluses in the trust funds probably made it easier to achieve an overall budget surplus, which was needed to help contain the inflation. In view of the great difficulties faced by the Johnson and Nixon administrations in enacting and extending the Vietnam war surtax on individual and corporation income taxes, other taxes probably could not have been raised even more to provide the additional saving that was obtained from the trust funds during this period. However, with continued emphasis on the unified budget by federal policymakers, the trust funds may have a smaller impact on fiscal policies and hence on national saving in future years.

Financing Social Security

In view of the multiple objectives of the social security (OASDHI) program, it is not surprising to find disagreement over financing methods. Some advocate recourse to the general revenues to finance future increases in benefits; others prefer continued use of payroll taxes; still others prefer a combination of the two.

The Contributory System

Financing of social security through contributory—and often regressive—taxes is well established in most countries. Receipts are earmarked to make workers feel that they are receiving benefits as a right rather than as a gift from the government. The earmarked taxes emphasize the statutory nature of the benefit and may discourage reductions in benefits when the budget is tight. Moreover, increases in benefits are believed to be easier to obtain if they are financed by the contributions of future beneficiaries rather than from general tax revenues.

Those who oppose financing social security through the contributory system point out that benefits are not tied very closely to the tax payments. There are both minima and maxima to the level of benefits. Congress has been lenient in extending eligibility to persons with minimum periods of covered employment. Under the circumstances, the benefit payments can hardly be said to approximate contributions even in a loose sense of the word. The regressivity of the taxes adds to dissatisfaction with the contributory system.

In practice, the financing of OASDHI in the United States is a compromise between these conflicting points of view. Although the taxes are regressive, the social security system does give to the lowest-paid workers the largest benefits relative to their contributions. The existence of balances in the reserve fund gives assurance to the millions of covered workers that their rights to benefits are protected. It would be possible to administer the present OASDHI system without the reserve fund device; nevertheless, every impartial commission that has ever examined this question has arrived at the conclusion that the reserve fund should be continued. However, the appropriate size of the reserve remains an issue.

A significant departure from the precedent of relying entirely on payroll taxes to finance social security benefits occurred in 1965, when Congress added medical and hospital insurance to the OASDI system. Hospital care for the insured aged was funded by payroll tax contributions from employers and employees; the general fund pays for those not insured. Medical insurance was made available to aged persons who voluntarily paid a fee of $3 a month; an equal amount was transferred to a new trust fund by appropriation from the general fund. The premium rate for medical insurance was subject to change after 1967, depending on actual experience, but the general fund continues to match the individual's payment, which rose to $5.30 a month beginning July 1, 1970.

Another departure from payroll tax financing was made in 1966, when all individuals reaching the age of 72 before 1968 were granted a pension of $35 a month ($52.50 where a husband and wife both qualify). The pension is reduced by an amount equal to the benefits of any other federal, state, or local retirement program for which the individual is qualified. The cost of this extension of coverage is paid out of the general fund.

Proposals for Reform

Suggestions for changing the method of financing social security fall into three categories, which are not mutually exclusive.

REDUCE REGRESSIVITY. The simplest way to reduce regressivity would be to raise the amount of earnings subject to tax and eventually to remove the limit entirely. The taxes would then become proportional taxes on payrolls, which would still be regressive with respect to total income but much less so than under present law. Increases in the earnings base have financed higher benefits in recent years and will doubtless continue to be used in the future.

INTEGRATE THE PAYROLL AND INCOME TAXES. A more straightforward way to remove regressivity would be to incorporate the employee contribution into the individual income tax, either directly or through a credit for payroll tax payments against the individual income tax. Financing through the income tax would make it possible to eliminate social security contributions by income recipients who are below the exemption or poverty levels, though this final step is not essential for payroll-income tax integration. In the case of the credit, cash refunds could be paid to those whose payroll taxes exceeded the income tax due.

With coverage now available to more than 90 percent of workers (in the case of OASDHI), the income tax population for any given generation of workers is not very different from the payroll tax population. The differences that do exist between the two taxes—the exemptions, personal deductions, and broader income concept—argue in favor of use of the income tax rather than the payroll tax. The psychological advantage of having a special earmarked tax to finance the social security programs can be duplicated by the credit device, or by allocating some percentage of the income tax receipts or a given number of percentage points of the income tax rates to the reserve funds.

The decision to integrate the employee tax with the individual income tax does not necessarily require a change in the employer tax, although the two would undoubtedly be considered together. One method might be to replace the employer tax by adding the necessary number of percentage points to the individual and corporation income

taxes. For example, the OASDHI tax paid by employers on 1967 payrolls was equivalent to a 3 percentage-point increase in all individual
and corporation income tax rates.

USE THE GENERAL FUND. As already indicated, precedent exists for
using general fund receipts to finance social insurance. With the combined employer-employee OASDHI tax scheduled to exceed 10 percent by 1971, use of the general fund would be preferable to rate
increases when additional funds are required to finance benefits. Since
the general fund relies primarily on progressive taxes, this would automatically improve the equity of the overall tax system.

Financing Unemployment Insurance

Two major financial features of the unemployment insurance system have been subject to criticism in recent years: (1) the variation of
tax rates by firms in accordance with their employment experience,
and (2) the inadequacy of trust funds in states suffering heavy and
prolonged unemployment.

The experience rating principle was adopted to induce employers
to stabilize their employment and also to avoid the criticism that
firms with stable employment would be subsidizing those with irregular employment records. Although experience rating has survived for
three decades, it has been subjected to almost continuous criticism.
The major argument has been that individual firms have little control
over unemployment, particularly of the cyclical variety. Moreover,
the payroll tax savings are negligible in comparison with the costs of
retaining workers when they are not producing, so that little employment stabilization can be expected. It has also been suggested that,
since contribution rates vary among firms, only those employers paying the lowest rates are able to shift the tax to consumers or wage
earners. This may well account for the resistance of employers to increases in coverage and benefits. Despite these objections, there is
considerable hesitancy to abandon experience rating, partly because
it provides an incentive for individual employers to prevent abuse of
the system by their employees, and partly because there is strong
objection to the redistribution of tax burdens among firms.

The uneven concentration of unemployment in particular industries and regions has had a very uneven effect on the state trust funds.

The extension by the federal government of coverage for workers who had exhausted their benefit rights in the 1958 and 1961 recessions was made in response to the need of many states for assistance. The 1958 legislation advanced funds to states that elected to participate, while the 1961 legislation financed the extension through a temporary increase in the federal unemployment compensation tax.

In 1970, Congress enacted permanent legislation to finance the automatic extension of benefits when unemployment becomes serious. Benefits of up to thirteen additional weeks will be paid when the national unemployment rate reaches 4.5 percent for three months, or in a state when unemployment in that state increases by 20 percent over the average of the preceding two years and is at least 4 percent. Benefits have not kept pace with the rise in wages; their liberalization will require either an increase in the earnings base from the $4,200 level now scheduled for 1972 or general fund contributions.

In addition, the federal government now finances retraining or readjustment allowances under the Manpower Development and Training Act of 1962, the Trade Expansion Act of 1962, and the Economic Development Act of 1965. The multiplicity of programs points to the need for a thorough review and realignment of methods used to ease the financial strain on unemployed workers seeking employment or undergoing training. Viewed in this perspective, use of the general fund for at least partial financing of benefits is both logical and equitable.

Summary

Payroll taxes paved the way for the enactment of a comprehensive system of social security and unemployment compensation that protects workers against income losses due to retirement, unemployment, and disability. Legislation passed in 1965 also provided protection for retired workers against the high costs of hospitalization and medical care. Although these programs were originally described as "social insurance," they have developed into a large (and essential) tax-transfer system. The payroll taxes that are now used to finance them should therefore be evaluated like any other major federal tax. These taxes lack the built-in flexibility of the individual income tax and are regressive. In the long run, payroll taxes are probably paid by the worker; it makes no difference whether the law imposes the tax on the employee or on the employer.

Although the trust fund device was introduced simultaneously with the payroll taxes, the two are separable issues. Money for the trust funds could be raised from other earmarked tax sources or from the general fund. On the other hand, payroll taxes could be continued as the basic method of obtaining employee and employer contributions without a trust fund. In the past, the accumulation of reserves has probably been deflationary, but there is no reason why federal fiscal policies should disregard the effect of the trust funds on stability and growth. Increasing use of the unified budget should help in this respect.

Given the present importance of the payroll taxes and the increases in tax rates already scheduled, the effects of these taxes on the distribution of income can no longer be ignored. Removal of the ceilings on the payroll tax bases, integration of the payroll and income taxes, or use of the general fund for financing increased social security benefits would improve the equity of these taxes.

CHAPTER EIGHT

Estate and Gift Taxes

TAXES ON PROPERTY left by an individual to his heirs are among the oldest forms of taxation. In societies in which property is privately owned, the state protects the rights of the individual in his property and supervises its transfer from one generation to the next. Consequently, the state has always regarded property transfers as appropriate objects of taxation.

Transfer taxation can take several forms, depending on when the transfers are made and how the tax base is figured. The federal government imposes an *estate* tax on the privilege of transferring property at death, while most of the states impose *inheritance* taxes on the privilege of receiving property from the dead. Both taxes are usually graduated, the former on the basis of the size of the entire estate and the latter on the basis of the size of individual shares in the estate. Usually the inheritance tax is also graduated on the basis of the relationship of the heir to the decedent, the rate being lowest for the closest relative.

Taxes at death could be avoided simply by transferring property by gift *inter vivos* (between living persons). Accordingly, the federal estate tax is associated with a *gift* tax, which is imposed on the donor. (However, only thirteen of the forty-nine states with death taxes levy a gift tax.)

Role of Estate and Gift Taxes

Opinions about death taxes vary greatly in a society relying heavily on private incentives for economic growth. Some believe that these taxes hurt economic incentives, reduce saving, and undermine the economic system. On the other hand, there is general agreement that death taxes have less adverse effects on incentives than do income taxes of equal yield. Income taxes reduce the return from effort and risk-taking as income is earned, whereas death taxes are paid only after a lifetime of work and accumulation and are likely to be given much less weight in decisions to work, save, and invest.

It is interesting that death taxes have been supported by people in all income classes. One of their strongest supporters was Andrew Carnegie, who had doubts about the institution of inheritance and felt that wealthy persons are morally obligated to use their fortunes for social purposes. In his *Gospel of Wealth*, Carnegie wrote that "the parent who leaves his son enormous wealth generally deadens the talents and energies of the son, and tempts him to lead a less useful and less worthy life than he otherwise would." He applauded the growing acceptance of estate taxes and said: "Of all forms of taxation this seems the wisest." According to Carnegie, it is the duty of a wealthy man to live unostentatiously, ". . . to provide moderately for the legitimate wants of those dependent upon him, and, after doing so, to consider all surplus revenues which come to him simply as trust funds . . . to administer in the manner . . . best calculated to produce the most beneficial results for the community."

Bequests and gifts, like income from work or investments, are a source of ability to pay. In theory, therefore, they should be taxable as income when received. However, bequests and gifts are taxed separately from income, partly because death taxes antedate the income taxes and partly because it would be unfair to tax these transfers at the full graduated income tax rates in the year of receipt. Of course, the impact of income tax rate graduation could be moderated by averaging, but this approach to transfer taxation has never been seriously considered in this country. (It is interesting to note, however, that the income tax levied in 1894, which was held unconstitutional, included in the definition of income "money and the value of all personal property acquired by gift or inheritance.") In 1966, the Royal

Commission on Taxation (the Carter Commission) in Canada recommended that the Canadian estate and gift taxes be repealed and that gifts and inheritances be included in the recipient's taxable income. Although this forced many people to think seriously about this alternative method of taxing transfers, the Canadian government has indicated that it does not intend to follow the commission's recommendation.

Despite the appeal of estate and gift taxes on social, moral, and economic grounds, taxes on property transfers have never provided significant revenues in this country. The federal government used an inheritance tax briefly for emergency purposes from 1862 to 1870, and an estate tax from 1898 to 1902; the present tax was enacted in 1916. The gift tax was first levied for two years in 1924 and 1925 and then was enacted permanently in 1932. During and after World War II, income and excise tax rates were increased substantially; but the estate and gift tax rates and exemptions have remained unchanged since 1942, and structural changes made in the postwar period have greatly reduced their importance in the federal revenue system. Estate and gift taxes accounted for 4.4 percent of cash receipts in fiscal year 1941, 2 percent in 1948, and 1.2 percent in 1953. They have risen to approximately 2 percent of federal budget receipts in recent years as a result of the increase in the value of corporate stock and other property (Appendix Table C-3).

One can only guess why the estate and gift taxes have not been more successful. A possible explanation is that equalization of the distribution of wealth by taxation is not yet accepted in the United States. In some countries, economic classes tend to be fairly stable, with little crossing-over by succeeding generations. In the American economy, membership in economic classes is fluid. The average family in the United States still aspires to improved economic and social status, and the estate and gift taxes are erroneously regarded as especially burdensome to the family that is beginning to prosper through hard work and saving.

Moreover, property transfer taxes are not considered equitable by many people. A surprising number resent even the relatively low taxes now imposed on small estates. This attitude may be due to the fact that the base of the property transfer taxes in certain respects includes more than what the public considers to be "wealth" properly subject to tax. The family home, the family car, Series E bonds, savings bank deposits, and similar property are not regarded as appropriate objects of taxation. The public generally is not aware that the major part of the estate tax base consists of stocks, bonds, and real estate, and that most people are not subject to estate taxes.

Characteristics of the Two Taxes

The calculation of the estate and gift taxes follows the pattern established by the income taxes. The total amount of property transferred is reported, deductions and exemptions are subtracted, and the graduated rates are applied to the remainder. But there are many complications.

The Estate Tax

The *gross estate* consists of all property owned by a decedent at the time of death, including stocks, bonds, real estate, mortgages, and any other property that technically belonged to him. (The property is valued either on the date of death, or an alternate valuation date, generally one year later, at the option of the estate's executor.) The gross estate also includes gifts made in contemplation of death, the value of any trusts created during life that could be revoked by the decedent at any time, and insurance owned by the decedent. Deductions are allowed for funeral expenses and expenses of settling the estate, debts, legal fees, charitable bequests, and for a bequest to a surviving spouse up to one-half the estate (the marital deduction). A specific exemption of $60,000 is also subtracted to obtain the taxable estate. Estate tax rates begin at 3 percent on the first $5,000 of the taxable estate and rise to 77 percent on the amount of the taxable estate in excess of $10,000,000 (Appendix Table A-8).

For example, assume that a married individual owning $1,000,000 in securities bequeathed half of his wealth to his wife and half to his children. Assume also that the expenses of settling the estate amounted to $25,000 and that the decedent owed $75,000 in debts at the time of his death. If this decedent had been single or had not left anything to his spouse, the net estate before the exemption would be $900,000, and the taxable estate after the exemption would be $840,000. However, the marital deduction would reduce the net estate to $450,000 and the taxable estate to $390,000.

The estate tax rates would produce a tax of $110,500 on a taxable

FRANZ

estate of $390,000. However, credit is allowed for any death taxes paid to the state of residence up to 80 percent of the 1926 federal tax. This amounts to $8,400. Thus, the net tax payable to the federal government would in this case be $102,100 ($110,500 minus $8,400).

The Gift Tax

The gift tax is calculated in much the same way, except that the exemptions are more complicated and the tax is computed on the basis of total accumulated gifts after 1932. The tax due in any particular year is the additional tax resulting from the gifts made in that year. The marital deduction is also available for gifts made to a spouse. In addition, for married persons, a gift can be treated as if half is given by the husband and half by the wife. The gift tax rates are nominally three-fourths of the estate tax rates, but in fact are less than that because the property given to the government in payment of tax is excluded from the gift tax base, but not from the estate tax base. In higher rate brackets, this makes the gift tax rates considerably lower than the estate tax rates.

Suppose a married man with an estate of $1,000,000 decides to distribute it to his two children systematically over a period of ten years. The law gives both him and his wife a lifetime tax exemption of $30,000 each, and an annual exclusion for each child of $3,000. The total lifetime exemption for the couple is $60,000, and the annual exclusions amount to $6,000 a year for each child, or another $120,-000. Thus, the taxable gifts amount to $820,000, and the amount of gift tax paid is $175,350:

	Husband	Wife	Total
Total gifts	$500,000	$500,000	$1,000,000
Deduct:			
Lifetime exemption	30,000	30,000	60,000
Annual exclusions			
($3,000 per child per year)	60,000	60,000	120,000
Total taxable gifts	410,000	410,000	820,000
Total tax	87,675	87,675	175,350

By contrast, if the same amounts had been subject to the higher estate tax rates, each spouse would have paid an estate tax of $126,500, or a total of $253,000. Disposition of the estate through gifts would save $77,650, or almost 31 percent.

The Tax Base

Estate and gift taxes are levied on only a small proportion of privately owned property in the United States. Less than one-fourth of the total wealth owned by those who die in any one year—and only about 4 percent of their estates by number—are subject to estate or gift taxes (Appendix Table B-10). The relatively small size of the tax base is explained in part by the generous exemptions, which exclude a large proportion of the wealth transfers, and also by defects in the taxes that permit substantial amounts of property to be transferred free of tax.

The total number of estate tax returns filed in 1966 for citizen and resident alien decedents was 97,339 (Appendix Table C-21); of these, 67,404 were taxable. The value of the gross estates reported on taxable returns was $19.2 billion. Exemptions and deductions reduced this amount by more than 50 percent, leaving an estate tax base of $9.1 billion. The estate tax amounted to $2.4 billion, or 26 percent of the taxable base (Appendix Table B-11).

Two-thirds of the taxable returns reported total estates of less than $200,000, but these accounted for only 9 percent of the total tax liability. Returns on estates of $1,000,000 or more, on the other hand, accounted for 50 percent of the total tax and only 3 percent of the number of taxable returns. The tax liability (before state tax credit) ranged from 4 percent of total estates in total estate classes below $200,000 to 23 percent above $20,000,000.

Gifts reported for the year 1966 amounted to $4.0 billion, of which $2.4 billion were reported on 29,547 taxable returns. Taxable gifts totaled $1,455 million, and gift tax paid amounted to $413 million, or 17 percent of the total gifts on taxable returns and 28 percent of the taxable gifts (Appendix Table C-22).

Structural Problems

Structural defects greatly impair the effectiveness of the present estate and gift taxes. These defects have unequal impact, depending on how and when dispositions of property are made. Such disparities are hard to justify, because many people—for personal or business reasons or because of early death—cannot avail themselves of the opportunity to minimize the taxes on their estates. Rate increases or exemption reductions would aggravate these inequalities. Because property can be transferred in many different ways, it is difficult to devise one solution that will be equitable in all cases. The major problems are: (1) the treatment of transfers of husband and wife, (2) separate taxation of gifts and estates, (3) the use of trusts to escape taxation for one or more generations, (4) charitable foundations, and (5) tax payments by small businesses.

Transfers by Husbands and Wives

Transfers by married couples present a difficult problem because it is hard to decide whether they should be taxed as if their property is separate property or part of one estate. Since the estate and gift taxes are excises on transfers of property, the concept of legal ownership plays an important part in determining the amount of tax to be paid. The distinction between community and noncommunity property is crucial in this respect.

COMMUNITY AND NONCOMMUNITY PROPERTY. Under the community property system, which prevails in eight states, all property acquired during marriage by a husband and wife (except for property acquired by gift or inheritance) belongs equally to each spouse. The community property states vary as to whether the income from property owned before marriage or acquired during marriage by gift or inheritance belongs to both spouses equally or to the original owner or recipient alone. In noncommunity property states, each spouse retains ownership of all property acquired or accumulated out of his separate earnings or inheritance even after marriage.

Prior to 1942, federal estate and gift taxes recognized the community property system: only half of the community property transferred between spouses was taxable under the estate tax, and gifts to third parties were treated as if half were made by each spouse. In noncommunity property states the entire amount of property accumulated by a spouse was taxable to him.

To equalize estate and gift taxes as between residents of community and noncommunity property states, the Revenue Act of 1942 provided that transfers of community property were taxable to the spouse who earned it. In effect, the 1942 law treated community property as if it were noncommunity property.

The Revenue Act of 1948 attempted to achieve equalization by moving in the opposite direction. In the spirit of income splitting for income tax purposes, transfers of community property were made taxable under the pre-1942 rules, while in the case of noncommunity property, a deduction was allowed for the amount of the property transferred to the surviving spouse, up to half the estate. In the case of a gift of noncommunity property by one spouse to another, only half of the gift was made taxable. Gifts to third persons were to be treated as though half were made by each spouse. These rules are still in effect today.

The marital deduction greatly increased the amount of property that married persons might transfer free of tax. Interspousal transfers up to half the value of estates and half of all gifts made by married persons were eliminated from the bases of the estate and gift taxes. As a result, the estate tax exemption for married persons was in effect doubled from $60,000 to $120,000, provided that the decedent transferred at least $60,000 to the surviving spouse. Gift splitting also in effect doubled the annual exclusion from $3,000 to $6,000 and the lifetime gift tax exemption from $30,000 to $60,000.

Transfers between spouses are, of course, subject to tax at the death of the recipient or when the recipient makes gifts, but the total tax on the couple was nevertheless substantially reduced by the marital deduction. For example, an estate of $10 million left by a married person was subject to a tax of over $6 million under the 1942 law. Under the 1948 law, assuming that half the estate is left to the surviving spouse, the tax was reduced to $2.43 million. Even if the $5 million received by the spouse is later taxed in full under the estate tax, the subsequent tax is $2.43 million, and the total tax on the original $10 million is $4.86 million, a tax decrease of over $1 million, or 20 percent below the liability under the 1942 law (Table 8-1).

These large tax differences might be tolerable—despite the large reduction in estate and gift tax revenues—if the 1948 amendments had accomplished their objective of equalizing the tax in community and noncommunity property situations. In fact, they did so in some, but not in others. Suppose a married man who accumulated a $1,000,000 estate through his own efforts bequeaths all the property to his wife and he dies first. Under the 1948 amendments, only half the estate will be taxable whether he lives in a community property state or in a noncommunity property state. (In the noncommunity property state he is allowed a marital deduction of 50 percent; in the community

TABLE 8-1. Estate Taxes Paid by a Married Couple, by Net Estate Levels[a]

Net estate before exemption (dollars)	Tax on husband (assuming he leaves no bequest to wife) (dollars) (1)	Tax on husband (assuming he leaves half of estate to wife)		Tax on husband and wife (assuming bequest from husband is taxed in full at wife's death)	
		Amount (dollars) (2)	Percentage of column (1) (3)	Amount (dollars) (4)	Percentage of column (1) (5)
100,000	4,800	0	0	0	0
120,000	9,500	0	0	0	0
150,000	17,900	1,050	5.9	2,100	11.7
200,000	32,700	4,800	14.7	9,600	29.4
500,000	126,500	47,700	37.7	95,400	75.4
750,000	212,200	86,500	40.8	173,000	81.5
1,000,000	303,500	126,500	41.7	253,000	83.4
2,000,000	726,200	303,500	41.8	607,000	83.6
5,000,000	2,430,400	968,800	39.9	1,937,600	79.7
10,000,000	6,042,600	2,430,400	40.2	4,860,800	80.4
20,000,000	13,742,000	6,042,600	44.0	12,085,200	87.9

Note: Effective rates are before the credit for state death taxes.
a Assumes that the husband dies first.

property state, his wife automatically owns half his estate, and he is taxable on only his half.) However, if the wife predeceases him and leaves her property to the children, she is taxable on half of the property accumulated by the husband in a community property state, and he is later taxable on the second half when he dies. In the noncommunity property state, the husband is taxable on the entire estate when he dies, and because the rates are graduated, he pays more than the couple in the community property state. On the other hand, a couple in a community property state will pay a higher tax if the wife dies first and leaves her share of the community property to the husband.

INTERSPOUSAL EXEMPTIONS. If it is assumed that Congress will not restore the 1942 law, the problem can be solved by extending the marital deduction to include all transfers between husband and wife. This would permit transfers of noncommunity property between husband and wife to be made tax free. A man who gave as much as half his estate to his wife would be taxable on only his half, whether he dies first or last, as in community property states.

Complete exemption of transfers between husband and wife suggests that the husband and wife are a single unit. It would follow that their combined estates should be cumulated for estate tax purposes. The initial installment on the combined tax would be collected on the death of one spouse, and the remainder (figured on the basis of the cumulated estates) would be collected on the death of the second spouse. The attractive feature of this proposal is that it would equalize the taxes paid by married couples in all states regardless of the order in which they disposed of the estate, without ultimately weakening the estate tax base.

However, estate cumulation may produce inequitable results where the wealth of the husband or wife was separately inherited or accumulated. For example, a woman married to a wealthy man for a relatively short period might be taxed at the maximum estate tax rates even though the amount of property she owned was small. This objection could be met by cumulating only as much of the property transferred by the wife (during life or at death) as was originally acquired from the husband. Tracing difficulties could be avoided by cumulating transfers of the wife only up to the dollar amount of property received from the husband. However, such a compromise would fail to take into account any increase in the value of the property taking place after the interspousal transfer. Estate cumulation would also require the solution of some intricate problems involving the treatment of gifts made before marriage and the taxation of transfers by widowed or divorced persons who had married again.

A second approach would be to provide a 100 percent exemption for all interspousal transfers without cumulating the estates of the husband and wife. The advantage of this approach is that owners of noncommunity property could arrange their affairs in the same way as owners of community property. The disadvantage is that it would substantially reduce the yield of the estate tax at least in the short run. While it is conceivable that the revenue loss could be offset by rate adjustments, it is hardly likely that the adjustment, if any, would be precise, and the benefits would go mainly to very wealthy individuals.

Still a third approach would be to give married couples the privilege of making an irrevocable choice between (a) exemption of interspousal transfers and cumulation of transfers to third parties, and (b) waiver of the marital deduction and elimination of the automatic splitting of community property, combined with noncumulation of transfers to third parties. The major difficulty with this approach is that many complexities would arise out of the instability of the family unit. Divorce, as well as remarriage after the death of one spouse, might provide avenues of escape from the cumulation of transfers that would otherwise be required. Moreover, it is probably unwise as a matter of policy to permit taxpayers to make such a decision irrevocably, since later changes in circumstances might create inequities and considerable dissatisfaction.

Separate Taxation of Estates and Gifts

A wealthy individual is well advised to transfer a substantial part of his property by gift during his lifetime rather than by bequest, for four reasons. First, the estate is split between the estate and gift tax brackets, thus moderating the full impact of estate tax graduation. Second, the gift tax rates are 25 percent lower than the estate tax rates. Third, the lifetime exemption of $30,000 and the annual per donee exclusion of $3,000 under the gift tax permit additional tax-free transfers over and above the $60,000 estate tax exemption. Fourth, the amount paid as gift tax does not enter into the gift tax base, whereas the estate tax is computed on the basis of the decedent's entire property, including that part used to pay the tax.

Figure 8-1 illustrates the estate and gift taxes paid on various combinations of bequests and gifts made by one individual to his wife and children. To minimize tax liability, he would have to take into account the large tax differences shown in the figure, as well as any tax that might be due on the death of his wife. Although there are many uncertainties, it is clear that a carefully drawn plan of wealth distribution during the life of a wealthy person can pay handsome dividends in lower tax burdens.

USE OF GIFTS. Information on the distributions of wealth during life and at death has been collected by the Treasury Department on the basis of the estate and matched gift tax returns of the wealthiest decedents for whom estate tax returns were filed in 1945, 1951, 1957, and 1959. Information on gifts made before 1932 was available from the 1945 and 1951 estate tax returns. Thus, it was possible to build up an aggregate figure for the property distributed by each decedent during life and at death for the two earlier years, and a total, excluding gifts prior to 1932, for the two later years.

FIGURE 8-1. Estate or Gift Taxes for Alternative Property Transfers During Life and at Death

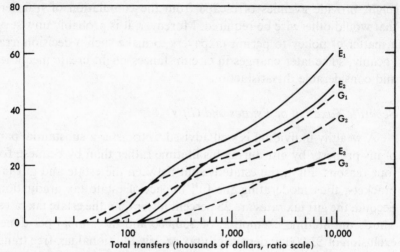

Effective rates (percent)

Total transfers (thousands of dollars, ratio scale)

Note: Effective rates are before credit for state taxes.
E_1—bequest not eligible for marital deduction
E_2—bequest by husband with full marital deduction; wife's half subject in full to estate tax rates
E_3—bequest with full marital deduction; no tax on wife's estate
G_1—gift in one year, one donee, no marital deduction
G_2—gift in one year, one donee, full marital deduction
G_3—equal gifts in ten-year period, two donees, full marital deduction

The figures (Table 8-2) show clearly that wealthy individuals prefer to retain the bulk of their property until death and fail to use gifts to maximum tax-saving advantage. The small proportion of gifts is due to a number of reasons. First, there is a natural reluctance on the part of most people to contemplate death. Uncertainty regarding time of death encourages delay in making estate plans even by individuals with considerable wealth. Second, many wish to retain control over their businesses. Disposal of stock or real estate frequently means loss of control over substantial enterprises. Third, donors may wish to delay transfers of property until their children have had an opportunity to make their own careers. Fourth, many people—even those who are wealthy—do not know the law and often do not take the advice of their tax lawyers on such personal matters.

Whatever the reason, the present use of gifts has resulted in much less erosion of the tax base than might have taken place. The major criticism of the law is that it discriminates against those who, for

TABLE 8-2. Frequency of Gifts and Percentage of Wealth Transferred by Gift during Life among Millionaire Decedents, 1945, 1951, 1957, and 1959

Total wealth transferred during life and at death (millions of dollars)	Percentage of decedents with gifts during life				Percentage of wealth transferred by gift			
	1945	1951	1957	1959	1945	1951	1957	1959
1.00– 1.25	77	74	52	56	14	12	5	5
1.25– 1.50	76	65	57	58	17	7	6	8
1.50– 1.75	83	74	55	67	21	12	7	8
1.75– 2.00	89	70	67	71	28	10	6	8
2.00– 3.00	84	88	65	68	20	14	6	8
3.00– 5.00	88	84	69	84	20	14	7	11
5.00–10.00	100	95	75	84	20	18	10	11
10.00 and over	91	100	92	100	38	25	15	17
Total	83	77	60	66	24	16	9	10

Source: Special tabulations by the Treasury Department.
Note: Includes only returns with total transfers before tax during life and at death of $1,000,000 or more. Data for 1945 and 1951 include gifts prior to 1932; those for 1957 and 1959 exclude such gifts.

business or personal reasons, do not dispose of a substantial portion of their wealth during their lives.

UNIFICATION OF ESTATE AND GIFT TAXES. The remedy for the inequalities resulting from the separate taxation of gifts and estates is to integrate them into one tax. Bequests would be added to gifts during life to determine total wealth for transfer tax purposes. Tax would be paid on gifts on a cumulated basis (as under present law), and bequests would be regarded as final transfers or "gifts." As a substitute for separate exemptions, a unified system would have a single exemption, which would be used by the taxpayer first against his lifetime gifts and then against the estate for the remainder, if any. Since there are now separate exemptions of $60,000 and $30,000 for the estate and gift taxes, respectively, the exemption under a unified system would presumably be between $60,000 and $90,000. The exclusion for lifetime gifts could be retained at the present $3,000 per donee per year.

Unification is opposed by those who believe that gifts should be encouraged through the incentive of lower tax rates. It is argued, in fact, that the lower gift tax rates tend to reduce the concentration of wealth by encouraging transfers in small amounts to a relatively large number of donees.

However, incentives could be built into the structure of a unified transfer tax to encourage people to distribute property by gift. Lower rates of tax could be charged on lifetime transfers than on transfers at death, for example, by setting the rates of tax on gifts 10, 20, or 30 percent lower than the rates of tax on bequests. The amount of the rate discount could even vary with the total amount of gifts that a donor made.

If the tax on lifetime transfers were excluded from the unified transfer tax base, as the gift tax is excluded from its base now, just such an incentive would be incorporated into the tax structure. But there are powerful arguments against this method of computing tax on lifetime transfers. The marginal savings to a donor from making additional gifts would grow in size, both absolutely and as a percentage of the corresponding tax on bequests, as he made more and more gifts. This might not be the kind of graduation that would focus tax savings where they would do the most good. More important, if the tax on lifetime transfers were not included in the tax base, it would also have to be excluded from the cumulative base, on top of which later transfers would be taxed. As a result, wealthy persons would be rewarded with larger tax savings than less wealthy persons for making the same total of lifetime transfers.

A unified system would eliminate the need for special estate tax provisions dealing with gifts in contemplation of death. When there is a separate estate tax, gifts made just before death to escape the estate tax are usually included in the estate tax base. But it is almost impossible to determine objectively whether a gift was in fact made in contemplation of death. The federal law now presumes that gifts made within three years before death are in contemplation of death, but this presumption is rebuttable if there is evidence that the decedent did not expect to die. In practice, plaintiffs have usually had little trouble convincing the courts that thoughts of death were furthest from the decedent's mind when he made his gift, and so the presumption is rarely used now. Despite its ineffectiveness, the provision is a chronic irritant in relations between government and taxpayer—the one continually gathering into each decedent's estate as many gifts as it can discover, the other continually searching for evidence to prove that the decedent had never contemplated the possibility of his own death. Court dockets are crowded with cases in which the disagreements that result are litigated to conclusion. The British remove uncertainty by including all gifts made within four years of death in the estate tax base and an increasingly smaller percentage of gifts between four and seven years. Such provisions would be unnecessary under a unified estate and gift tax that made no distinction between gifts and bequests.

Generation-Skipping through Trusts

The most intractable problem in estate and gift taxation results from the existence of the *trust*, a legal institution used to administer funds on behalf of individuals or organizations. Suppose A wants his wife to have the income from his estate as long as she lives. He may place his property in a trust, the income of which would go to her for life; the trust might be dissolved at her death and the property distributed to the children. The trust is administered by a *trustee*—usually an old friend or associate, the family lawyer, or a bank—who is the legal owner. He is required by law to manage the trust strictly in accordance with the terms of the trust instrument.

Legal terms are used as shorthand in trust language for the various beneficiaries of a trust. In the above example, A's wife, who is entitled to receive the income from the trust, is the *life tenant*. Any number of life tenants may be designated, and they need not be confined to members of the same generation. The creator of the trust may designate his wife and children as joint or successive life tenants and prescribe the proportions in which the income is to be distributed among them. When the trust is terminated, the trust property is legally transferred to the *remainderman*, who then owns the property outright. More often than not, children are the remaindermen of family trusts; but grandchildren or other relatives as well as unrelated individuals may also be remaindermen. In some cases, the trust is created with the wife and children as life tenants, and the remainder is distributed, after the last one dies, to one or more charities. In all but a few states, all noncharitable interests in a trust must vest not later than at the death of the last survivor among a reasonably small number of persons specified in advance, and alive when the trust was created (*lives in being*), plus twenty-one years. This rule has the effect of restricting noncharitable trusts to lives of less than a century.

The trust has a profound influence on the taxation of property transfers. Trust property is not subject to estate tax when one life tenant is succeeded by another or when the trust property is received by the remainderman. An estate or gift tax is paid when the trust is created, but tax is not paid again until the remainderman transfers the property. Given these characteristics, the trust is frequently used by wealthy individuals to avoid estate and gift taxes for at least one generation and sometimes more. In extreme cases, trusts may be set up to last for the lives of the children and grandchildren, with the remainder to go to the great-grandchildren, thereby skipping two estate and gift tax generations.

USE OF TRUSTS. The trust device is used frequently by wealthy individuals to transfer property to later generations. The data from the Treasury studies of 1945, 1951, 1957, and 1959 returns indicate the following patterns:

1. Since World War II, more than three of every five millionaires have transferred at least some of their property in trust. Transfers in trust accounted for at least one-third of noncharitable transfers by millionaires in this period (Table 8-3). The data also indicate that trusts are used primarily by wealthy people. Individuals with smaller estates give much more of their property outright.

TABLE 8-3. Frequency of Noncharitable Transfers in Trust and Percentage of Wealth Transferred in Trust by Millionaire Decedents, 1945, 1951, 1957, and 1959

Total wealth transferred during life and at death (millions of dollars)	Percentage of decedents with noncharitable transfers in trust				Percentage of noncharitable transfers made in trust			
	1945	1951	1957	1959	1945	1951	1957	1959
1.00– 1.25	75	72	57	56	44	39	28	26
1.25– 1.50	75	78	53	61	48	44	25	29
1.50– 1.75	80	77	53	62	38	44	24	30
1.75– 2.00	71	80	63	69	37	49	37	31
2.00– 3.00	89	69	61	64	55	39	34	34
3.00– 5.00	84	87	63	70	42	51	32	35
5.00–10.00	87	74	77	67	44	44	43	30
10.00 and over	91	100	73	92	58	59	33	30
Total	80	76	59	63	47	46	32	31

Source: Special tabulations by the Treasury Department.
Note: Includes only returns with total transfers before tax during life and at death of $1 million or more. Data for 1945 and 1951 include gifts made prior to 1932; those for 1957 and 1959 exclude such gifts.

2. There is little difference in the eventual disposition of property transferred outright and property transferred in trust. Outright transfers are received in the first instance largely by the wife and children; these properties are in turn transferred to grandchildren and great-grandchildren. In the case of trust transfers, wives, children, and grandchildren frequently receive only life interests, and so the grandchildren and great-grandchildren receive the property undiminished by estate or gift taxes. As Table 8-4 indicates, about half of the trust property of wealthy decedents escapes estate and gift taxes until the death of the grandchildren or great-grandchildren. Only a very small proportion of the property transferred outright escapes tax for a similar period.

ALTERNATIVE SOLUTIONS. There are legitimate reasons for trusts, and it would be unwise to abolish them altogether. On the other hand, some economists have pointed out that it would also be unwise to encourage excessive use of the trust device, thus reducing the supply of capital available for risky investments, since trust property is managed more conservatively than property owned outright. Moreover, since trust transfers go to the same people as outright transfers, there does not seem to be a good equity reason for imposing lower taxes on trust transfers. Equity suggests that the two types of transfers should be treated equally.

Several methods have been devised to remove or reduce the tax advantage of trust transfers. The most direct method would be to treat life estates as if the property generating their income were owned by the income beneficiaries, a procedure now followed in Great Britain. Under this method, the capital from which the life estate is supported would be included in the life tenant's gross estate, and the tax would be apportioned between the trust property and the life tenant's own property.

Although this method is consistent with the principles underlying the present estate tax, several objections have been raised against its use. First, while a life tenant enjoys the income from a trust, he does not always possess the other attributes of ownership (though he may often enjoy broad powers to invade the trust principal at his discretion, and he may have the power to name the remainderman). Second, the inclusion of trust property in the estate of a life tenant would increase the rate of tax applying to the property he owns outright. Third,

TABLE 8-4. Timing of Next Estate Taxes on Outright and Trust Transfers of Millionaire Decedents, 1945, 1951, 1957, and 1959

Person at whose death the next estate tax falls due	Outright transfers		Trust transfers[a]	
	Amount (millions of dollars)	Percentage of total	Amount (millions of dollars)	Percentage of total
1945				
Spouse	77	24		
Children	154	48		
Grandchildren	9	3		
Great-grandchildren	b	b		
Other	80	25		
Total	320	100		
1951				
Spouse	164	41	2	1
Children	137	34	95	28
Grandchildren	11	3	124	37
Great-grandchildren	b	b	20	6
Other	89	22	96	28
Total	400	100	337	100
1957				
Spouse	405	39	2	c
Children	362	35	90	18
Grandchildren	56	5	209	43
Great-grandchildren	b	b	24	5
Other	212	21	162	33
Total	1,034	100	487	100
1959				
Spouse	468	42	4	1
Children	366	33	91	18
Grandchildren	68	6	208	42
Great-grandchildren	b	b	37	7
Other	214	19	160	32
Total	1,117	100	500	100

Source: Special tabulations by the Treasury Department. Figures are rounded and do not necessarily add to totals.

a Data not available for 1945.

b Outright transfers to great-grandchildren were not tabulated separately, but the amount is negligible and is included in transfers to "other."

c Less than 0.5 percent.

the method assumes that the alternative to a trust transfer is necessarily an outright transfer of the same property to the life tenant. In the absence of life estates, owners of wealth might divide it between those who are now designated as life tenants and remaindermen. A more moderate tax would be appropriate under such circumstances. Finally, the tax on the trust property may be avoided in a number of ways. For example, the trustee might be given full discretion over the disposition of the trust, and the life tenant would have no legal share on which a tax could be imposed. Lawyers generally believe that it would be difficult to prevent such practices.

An alternative to the British approach would be to impose a separate tax on the entire value of the property in which a decedent has a life interest. This method would not eliminate the full advantage of transferring property in trust, since it would still be advantageous to fragment the estate tax base by a combination of trust transfers and outright transfers.

A third possibility would be to impose a separate tax on the remainderman when the trust dissolves. This method would be more practical than the others, but it would be a substantial departure from the estate tax principle of taxing wealth at the point of transfer rather than at the point of receipt. Furthermore, it would permit the skipping of death taxes over the lives of the life tenants. There would also be the problem of deciding what tax rate should be applied.

As a fourth alternative, a separate tax could be imposed when the property was placed in trust. It would be in addition to the usual estate or gift tax that would be imposed no matter how the property was transferred. The additional tax would be a substitute for the taxes that ought to be imposed whenever one tenant succeeds another and when the remainderman receives the property. Ideally the tax should be graduated with respect to the circumstances of these later beneficiaries; in practice it would be impossible to foretell what their circumstances would be, and so the tax would have to be imposed at a flat rate or at some fraction of the ordinary transfer tax rate, perhaps modified to reflect the number of generations represented among the beneficiaries.

In brief, the trust presents a troublesome problem, for which there is no easy solution. If a departure is to be made from the present liberal treatment, it is likely to be a compromise among conflicting points of view.

Generation-Skipping through Outright Transfers

Transfers in trust and outright transfers are to some degree substitutes for one another. If they are subject to taxes of unequal size, many persons will avoid the more heavily taxed kind of transfer and will make the one that is taxed more lightly. It is just such an inequality in tax burdens that has caused many wealthy people to tie up property in trust for one or two generations rather than have it taxed each time it passes from one generation to the next. If an additional tax were imposed on generation-skipping transfers in trust, it is likely that many people who would otherwise create such trusts would instead make generation-skipping outright transfers, unless those also were subject to an additional tax. Instead of establishing a trust and naming his child as life tenant and his grandchild as remainderman, a donor could transfer property outright to them in amounts equal to the present value of the interests in trust that they would otherwise receive. The gift of property to the grandchild is the generation-skipping component of the outright transfers. The substantial similarity between the outright transfer and the single transfer in trust has led some to argue that if an additional tax is imposed on generation-skipping trusts, it ought to be accompanied by an equivalent tax on generation-skipping outright transfers, in order to preserve fairness in the tax system and to prevent tax avoidance.

It is easier to design an additional tax to reach generation-skipping outright transfers than one to reach generation-skipping transfers in trust, because property given outright can ordinarily be valued exactly at the time it is transferred, whereas interests in trusts are often impossible to value at the time they are created. Many state inheritance taxes already incorporate some form of relationship discrimination in their rate schedules, and the same principle could be used in designing a generation-skipping tax on outright transfers under the federal estate tax. Arbitrary rules based on the age relationship of the transferor and the recipient could take care of transfers to persons outside the transferor's direct line of descent. The tax rate could be set in any one of a number of ways. It might be set at some fraction of the transferor's average tax rate on all of his other transfers. Or the transfer might be taxed according to a separate rate schedule, whose rates were graduated according to the total of all generation-skipping transfers that the transferor had ever made. Whatever method was adopted, the additional tax clearly would add features of the inheritance tax form of death taxation to the federal estate tax.

Charitable Foundations

Unlike the deductions allowed under income taxes, charitable bequests and gifts are deductible without limit from the estate or gift tax bases. (Contributions are deductible up to 50 percent of income in the case of the individual income tax and up to 5 percent in the case of the corporation income tax.) The charitable deduction has stimulated only a minority of individuals to allocate substantial portions of their estates to charity. Slightly over half the estate tax returns of millionaire decedents in 1957 and 1959 reported no contributions above the annual exclusion during life or at death, and only about 15 percent of the total transfers by this group was given to charitable organizations. Nevertheless, the total amounts deducted are significant; they rose from $254 million on all 1945 estate and gift tax returns to $1.8 billion on 1966 returns.

Concern has been expressed about the charitable deduction in recent years as a result of the large growth of private foundations, some of which have been suspected of abusing the tax exemption privilege. Owners of closely held corporations may avoid the impact of the estate tax by dividing the stock into voting stock, which is retained in the family, and nonvoting stock, which is transferred to a foundation. In this way, the family continues to control the assets without being subject to the full estate and gift tax rates when control passes from one generation to the next. In many cases, the economic power of the family grows rapidly as the enterprise continues to expand; the estate tax does not encroach on the property because the property belongs to the foundation and has been permanently removed from the estate tax base. This type of transfer amounts to giving up the income from the property rather than the property itself, yet the transfer is treated as if control of the property has also been relinquished by the donor.

Private foundations were not even required to file statements regarding their financial operations until 1950, when the tax law was amended to require public information returns on their assets, earnings, and expenditures. These reports did not completely eliminate shady dealings on the part of a minority of donors and foundation officials. Investigations by congressional committees revealed abuses ranging from excessive salaries for foundation officials to use of loans from foundation funds for personal investment purposes.

The large majority of foundations operate in the public interest. However, by 1969 there was substantial agreement that their affairs should be subject to stricter public controls. As a result, the Tax Reform Act of 1969 included prohibitions against loans to contributors, officers, and directors; rules to prevent the use of foundation funds to influence legislation and to prevent accumulation of income; and requirements to broaden the foundation's management so as to avoid indefinite control by one family. The legislation also included a 4 percent tax on the investment income of private foundations. These measures will go a long way toward curbing the abuses of the relatively few foundations that had misused the exemption privilege before the 1969 legislation was enacted.

Small Business and the Estate Tax

A perennial problem in estate taxation is its effect on small business. Small businessmen have always felt that the estate tax is especially burdensome. Often there is little more than the business in their estates. Heavy taxation or a rule requiring payment of taxes immediately after the death of the owner-manager would necessitate liquidation of the enterprise and loss of the business by the family.

As the previous discussion has indicated, a little advance estate planning would be sufficient to prevent or mitigate most of these problems. Nevertheless, payment difficulties may arise even in carefully planned situations. The law contains two provisions to help in these cases:

First, tax payments on estates of which a small business is a large proportion may be made in installments over a period of ten years (with interest of 4 percent on the unpaid balance—an attractive rate for small enterprises). This option, which is exercised by the executor, is available if the value of the business exceeds 35 percent of the gross estate or 50 percent of the taxable estate. Installment payments are limited to the portion of the entire estate tax accounted for by the business.

The option to pay the estate tax in installments is rarely exercised because the executor is personally liable for all future payments even if the estate loses its value. This could easily be corrected by limiting the executor's liability to the value of the estate on the due date of the installment.

Second, liberal provision has been made for redemption of stock in closely held corporations to pay the estate tax and other costs of the estate. Such stock redemptions are, of course, indistinguishable from ordinary distributions of profits by private corporations, which are subject to tax. Since 1951, however, they have not been subject to the individual income tax.

Farm Property and the Estate Tax

In recent years increasing attention has been given to the problems that arise when farmland enters decedents' estates. Spokesmen for farm interests allege that farmland is often assessed for estate tax purposes at values that are far in excess of its value in agricultural production. As a result, heirs to the property who frequently want to keep it in family hands and continue to farm it are forced to sell in order to pay the tax.

In the absence of any studies of this subject, it is hard to estimate how often this situation arises, to know how far the difficulties described are attributable to an estate tax squeeze, and to know what ought to be done to help the heirs. Prices of farmland have been rising rapidly, and the increase must be due in some cases to increasing demand for the land for nonagricultural uses, particularly when it is located on the fringes of metropolitan areas. If the principle is adhered to that decedents' assets are to be included in their estates at fair market value, it must be expected that the estate taxes on such property often force its sale to people who will put the property to more profitable use. Not even a generous liberalization of payment provisions would keep the property in farm use if too little income could be earned to pay the tax and a competitive return on invested capital.

The problem, if there is one, that confronts the tax policymaker is to decide how far government funds should be used to subsidize farming in general, and family farming in particular. Until the question is studied from this point of view, it would be unwise to rush toward such a solution as offering executors the option of valuing farmland either at its fair market value or at its value in agricultural use, whichever is lower, as has been suggested by some farm spokesmen. A provision in the United Kingdom that abates estate duty on agricultural property has reportedly caused much mischief by encouraging wealthy persons to shift into such assets to reduce their death duties.

Alternatives to the Estate Tax

Extensive reforms would be required to make the estate and gift taxes more equitable. Some have argued that it would be better to abandon the present transfer tax structure and start afresh. The alternatives most often recommended are based on the inheritance or accessions tax principle.

Although widely used by the states, the inheritance tax is rarely considered for use at the federal level. Its most serious deficiency in its unmodified form is that each receipt of a gift or inheritance is taxed separately. Thus, two individuals would pay the same tax on equal inheritances received in the same year. However, if one received his inheritance in a lump sum and the other received his from several decedents, they would pay different taxes.

This deficiency would be remedied by the modern modification of the inheritance tax principle—the *accessions tax*. This is a progressive, cumulative tax on the total lifetime acquisitions of an individual through inheritances and gifts. The tax in any one year would be computed by subtracting the tax paid on earlier acquisitions from the tax on total acquisitions received. There would be small annual exclusions and a lifetime exemption. Although tax rates could be varied on the basis of the relationship of donor and donee, there is little support for such differentiation under an accessions tax.

The accessions tax has appeal for those who advocate a more equal distribution of wealth than the present estate tax provides. It would also be more equitable than the estate tax since it would be graduated on the basis of the total wealth received by any one individual. It is probably true that the accessions tax would encourage individuals to distribute their property among a larger number of heirs, but the result would not necessarily be a more equal distribution of wealth, since property is ordinarily kept in the immediate family. Moreover, in practice, only the wealthiest persons could afford to divert property from wife and children to more distant relatives to benefit from the tax savings offered by an accessions tax. Thus, to the extent that the accessions tax did encourage a more equal distribution of estates, it might do so by shifting some of the burden of the wealthiest estates to the smaller estates.

The accessions tax offers some practical advantages. For one thing, it would equalize the taxes on transfers during life and at death, thus overcoming one major fault of the existing tax system. Second, it would eliminate the problem of handling gifts in contemplation of death. Some of the proponents of the accessions tax also claim that it would facilitate the inclusion of property settled in trust in the tax base. For example, receipt of trust property by remaindermen would automatically be subject to accessions tax, while it is not subject to estate tax. On the other hand, the estate tax collected when the trust is created would not automatically be recovered by the accessions tax. To include such transfers in the accessions tax base, the benefits received by the life tenant would have to be valued—a problem that has not been solved satisfactorily even after years of experience with the estate tax.

The most difficult problem in accessions taxation is the opportunity it creates for avoidance of the tax through discretionary trusts. With a discretionary trust, a family fortune could be tied up for as long as permitted by the rule against perpetuities, with the accessions tax being levied only on those amounts that are actually distributed to the beneficiaries.

A practical argument against the accessions tax is that it would probably not raise as much revenue as do the estate and gift taxes. To obtain a given yield, accessions tax rates would need to be much higher and exemptions much lower than under the present transfer taxes. Given the long experience with the current estate tax rates and exemptions, the drastic revisions necessary to preserve the revenue yield would be difficult to obtain. It follows that, unless the pattern of property distribution is altered radically, the accessions tax would be a less effective wealth equalizer than the estate tax.

Summary

In theory, estate and gift taxes are among the better taxes devised by man; in practice, their yield is disappointing, and they have little effect on the distribution of wealth. Tax rates are high, but there are ways to escape them. The major avenues are the marital deduction, distribution of estates by gifts during lifetime, generation-skipping through trusts and outright transfers, and use of the tax-free charitable foundation to maintain control without paying tax on the bulk of the estate. These problems can be solved, but the solutions are technical, and some would regard them as unnecessarily harsh and inconsistent with the principles of property law.

Although tax theorists almost unanimously agree that estate and gift taxation should play a larger role in the revenue system, they have not been successful in convincing Congress. The public does not appear to accept the desirability of a vigorous estate and gift taxation system. The major obstacles to the improvement of these taxes are public apathy and the difficulty of understanding their major features and how they apply in individual circumstances. The merits of property transfer taxes will have to be more widely understood and accepted before they can become effective revenue sources.

CHAPTER NINE

State and Local Taxes

THE STATE-LOCAL SEGMENT of the national revenue system is its most dynamic element. State and local expenditures have grown rapidly in recent years and will continue to grow in the foreseeable future. These governments spent more than $116 billion in fiscal year 1969, almost 75 percent of federal expenditures and almost three times as much as total federal nondefense expenditures (Figure 9-1). Whereas the federal government income tax rates are at their lowest levels in more than two decades, state and local tax rates continue to increase steadily and sharply.

The growth in expenditures and taxes reflects a persistently increasing demand for state and local services. State and local governments had a large backlog of unmet needs at the end of World War II; and population growth added to their problems. The age groups requiring the costliest government services and contributing the least to the tax base increased the fastest: between 1949 and 1969, when the total population increased by 36 percent, public school enrollment rose by 89 percent, and the number of persons over 65 rose by 63 percent. The mobility of the people accentuated the problems of population growth. Entire new communities had to be developed, with schools, roads, sewers, police and fire protection, and other public services. Since the Korean war ended in 1953, employment in state and local governments has increased at a faster rate than employment in private industry or in the federal government.

211

FIGURE 9-1. Federal and State-Local Expenditures, Fiscal Years 1948–69

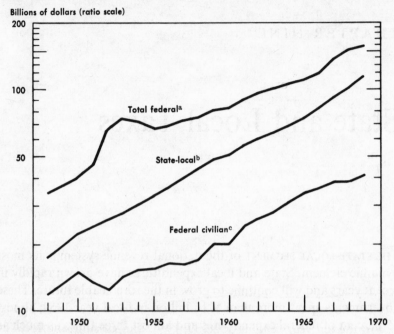

Billions of dollars (ratio scale)

Sources: 1948–55: U.S. Bureau of the Census, *Census of Governments: 1962,* Vol. 6, No. 4, *Historical Statistics on Governmental Finances and Employment* (1964), pp. 35–36, 38–39; 1956–65: *Census of Governments: 1967,* Vol. 6, No. 5, *Historical Statistics on Governmental Finances and Employment* (1969), pp. 36–37, 39–40; 1966–69: U.S. Bureau of the Census, *Governmental Finances in 1968–69* (1970), pp. 17, 18.
a Excludes insurance trust expenditures.
b Excludes insurance trust, utility, and liquor stores expenditures.
c Total expenditures as defined in note a, minus expenditures for national defense and international relations, interest on the general debt, and grants-in-aid and other payments to state and local governments.

The major characteristics of the state-local tax system are its regressivity and sluggish response to income growth. The states rely heavily on consumption taxes and local governments on property taxes—revenue sources that are particularly burdensome for the poor. Fear of driving out commerce and industry and discouraging the entry of new business restrains the use of most taxes; this is true particularly of the income tax, which is the most equitable and most responsive to growth. At constant tax rates, state and local tax receipts rise barely in proportion to the gross national product, while the rate of growth of expenditures is at least one-third faster than the GNP growth rate.

In these circumstances, the federal government has filled a major part of the gap. Federal grants-in-aid to state and local governments have risen from $6.4 billion in 1959 to $19.2 billion in 1969 and will reach $25 billion in 1971. Most of these grants help to finance needed expenditures for education, health, welfare, and roads. Furthermore, revenue sharing has been proposed by the Nixon administration to link the states more directly to the superior tax resources of the federal government.

The pressure for larger revenues has generated a great deal of fiscal activity throughout the country. Tax systems are being examined by official and unofficial commissions, legislative committees, and experts in order to increase revenues, achieve greater equity, improve administration, and reduce the cost of compliance by taxpayers. Many states have adopted new taxes, increased rates on old taxes, introduced withholding for income tax payments, and reformed their tax administrative machinery. Under pressure from the states, local governments have improved property tax administration. Some large cities in a few states have adopted municipal income and sales taxes. But much remains to be done to satisfy state and local financial needs.

The State-Local Tax Structure

In the ten years ending June 30, 1969, annual state and local expenditures for general purposes (all activities other than public utilities, liquor stores, and insurance trust funds) rose from $48.9 billion to $116.7 billion, an increase of $67.8 billion. In the same period, state and local revenues rose from $45.3 billion to $114.6 billion, an increase of $69.3 billion. Only 18 percent of the revenue increase came from federal grants; 82 percent came from state and local sources. Although the rise in receipts slightly exceeded the rise in expenditures for the entire period, expenditures were larger than receipts in every year except 1966, and state-local debt rose from $64.1 billion to $133.5 billion (Appendix Tables C-23, C-24, and C-25).

The state and local governments relied on all their major sources to produce the additional revenue: 28 percent came from property taxes, 28 percent from consumption taxes, 16 percent from income taxes, and the remaining 28 percent from user charges and other miscellaneous taxes (Figure 9-2).

While state and local tax sources are often considered together, the two levels of government have very different tax systems. The state

FIGURE 9-2. Sources of Growth of State-Local Revenue, 1959–69

Billions of dollars

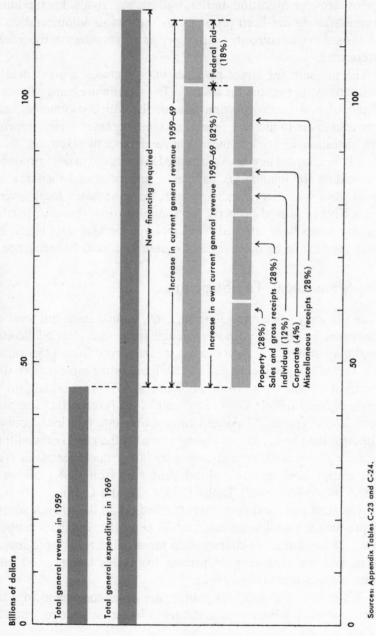

Total general revenue in 1959

Total general expenditure in 1969

New financing required

Increase in current general revenue 1959–69

Federal aid→ (18%)

Increase in own current general revenue 1959–69 (82%)

Property (28%)
Sales and gross receipts (28%)
Individual (12%)
Corporate (4%)
Miscellaneous receipts (28%)

Sources: Appendix Tables C-23 and C-24.

governments rely heavily on consumption and income taxes; local governments are dependent largely on the property tax.

State Taxes

State tax structures have changed dramatically since the turn of the century. In 1902, almost half of state revenue came from property taxes and the rest from selective excise taxes. Today, the general sales tax is the largest single source of state revenue, with automotive and income taxes next. Most states have relinquished the general property tax to their local governments; only Wyoming and Arizona raise more than 10 percent of their revenues from this tax.

SALES AND EXCISE TAXES. State legislatures have been irresistibly attracted to the productivity and stability of revenues from consumption taxes. Selective excise taxes on gasoline, cigarettes, and liquor are now in extensive use throughout the country. These taxes have been supplemented increasingly by the retail sales tax in the past thirty-five years.

The retail sales tax emerged as a major source of state revenue in the 1930s. It is now in use in forty-five states, at rates ranging from 2 to 6 percent. To moderate its regressivity, fifteen states exempt food, and twenty-four exempt medicine. A recent development, which is likely to spread, is a credit against state personal income tax for sales tax paid. For example, Indiana provides an $8 tax credit (equivalent to its 2 percent tax on $400 of purchases) against the personal income tax for the taxpayer and each of his dependents. Colorado, Nebraska, Idaho, Vermont, Hawaii, and Massachusetts have followed suit. (Wisconsin, Minnesota, and Vermont provide a similar income tax credit to the aged for property tax payments. Minnesota provides a credit for renters.) Cash refunds are paid to individuals and families who do not pay enough income tax to recover the entire credit. (In Idaho the rebate is paid only to taxpayers 65 and over.)

INCOME TAXES. State individual and corporation income taxes in their modern form began in Wisconsin in 1911. (Hawaii had adopted both taxes in 1901, but this experience apparently had had no influence on the states.) General individual income taxes are now in force in thirty-seven states and the corporation income tax in forty-three states. State tax rates are much lower than the federal rates, and personal exemptions are generally higher. Tax brackets used for the individual income tax are narrower, and graduation is steeper but terminates at a much lower level, usually between $5,000 and $25,000. The maximum individual income tax rates are levied in Alaska, where the top rate is 14.6 percent. Minnesota has the highest corporate income taxes, with a rate of 11.3 percent.

The nominal tax rates overstate the *net* impact of the state income taxes because these tax payments are deductible from taxable income in computing federal taxes. In addition, many states permit the deduction of federal taxes in computing taxable income for state tax purposes. In most cases the net effect of deductibility is to make the burden imposed by state individual income taxes considerably heavier on the lower and middle income classes than on the higher income classes. Of the thirty-seven state income taxes, twenty-one place a higher net burden on those in the lowest federal tax bracket (taxable incomes of $0 to $500) than on those in the highest bracket (taxable incomes over $100,000), and thirty of the states place the highest net burden on a bracket below $12,000. After allowing for deductions, the maximum net burden is found in New York, where those with taxable incomes between $23,000 and $26,000 pay a net additional rate of 7 percent. The corporate income tax burden is highest in Alaska, where the net additional rate is 4.9 percent (Appendix Table C-27).

State income taxes are generally patterned after the federal taxes, and in recent years there has been a movement toward uniformity with federal definitions. All but two of the personal income tax states have an optional standard deduction. Over half modify the adjusted gross income concept by (1) subtracting interest on federal securities and (2) adding state income taxes and interest on out-of-state state-local bonds. Withholding for individual income tax purposes was introduced by Oregon in 1948, and all the states except California and North Dakota now withhold on wages and salaries. Most of these states complement withholding by requiring declarations of estimated tax for incomes on which tax is not withheld.

DEATH AND GIFT TAXES. Death taxes were levied by states long before the federal government enacted an estate tax in 1916. Pennsylvania taxed inheritances as early as 1825, and Wisconsin set the modern pattern by adopting a progressive inheritance tax in 1903. Only Nevada does not tax bequests. The gift tax is levied in thirteen states.

For the United States as a whole, estate and gift taxes amount to less than 3 percent of total state tax collections.

Local Taxes

Municipal and county governments are limited in the tax sources they are able to use. They have always relied heavily on the property tax, and, despite persistent efforts to diversify their sources of funds, the majority of local governments assign nonproperty taxes a relatively unimportant place in their finances.

PROPERTY TAX. The property tax provides two-thirds of the revenue from all local sources (seven-eighths of the tax revenue). Dependence on this tax reflects the reluctance of many state governments to give localities authority to levy other taxes. It also reflects local fears of inducing migration or purchases in neighboring communities. Taxation of real property may have significant effects on the price and use of land, but not on its location.

Although critics have long predicted the demise of the property tax, it has performed creditably in the postwar period. State and local property tax collections rose from about $6 billion in 1948 to $30.7 billion in 1969, an annual rate of growth of 8 percent during a period when the gross national product (in current dollars) grew at a rate of 6.3 percent. Average effective property tax rates are 3 percent or less in all states; in 1966, the median effective state rate was 1.1 percent, and only five states had average rates in excess of 2 percent.

NONPROPERTY TAXES. Some large cities in a limited number of states have successfully diversified their revenue sources. Sales taxes are the most productive nonproperty taxes, with taxes on earnings or income next. Local general sales taxes are now used in twenty-three states by over 3,500 local governments, mainly in Alabama, California, Illinois, Texas, and Utah. Local income taxes are levied in ten states, but are widespread only in Kentucky, Maryland, Ohio, and Pennsylvania.

NONTAX REVENUES. Nontax revenues are most important at the local level. In 1969, they accounted for 24 percent of local revenues from their own sources and for only 15 percent of comparable state revenues. Such nontax revenue sources include charges for water, electric power, and gas, special assessments, license and other fees, and user charges for transportation, medical care, and housing. Payments for most government services that yield measurable benefits are substantially below marginal cost, primarily because it is feared that user charges will hurt low-income families.

State-Local Fiscal Performance, Capacity, and Effort

The fiscal performance and tax capacity of the fifty states during fiscal year 1969 are summarized in Figure 9-3. *Performance* is measured by per capita revenue collected from state-local sources; *capacity* is measured by personal income per capita; and *revenue effort* is the ratio of performance to capacity, or the ratio of revenue collected to personal income.

When the states are arrayed by size of per capita personal income, the per capita revenue obtained from state-local sources increases

FIGURE 9-3. Per Capita State-Local Revenue and Revenue Effort, by States, by Quintiles of State Personal Income Per Capita, Fiscal Year 1969[a]

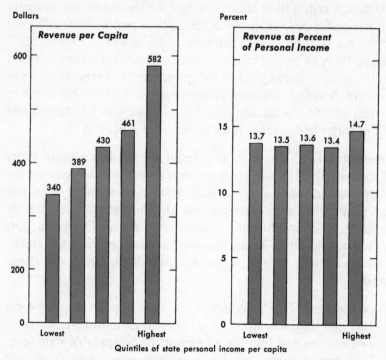

Quintiles of state personal income per capita

Source: U.S. Bureau of the Census, *Governmental Finances in 1968–69*, pp. 31–33, 52.
[a] State-local revenue excludes federal grants.

from low- to high-income states. In 1969, the poorest ten states raised only $340 per capita, whereas the richest ten states raised $582 per capita. This pattern of performance cannot be attributed to a lack of effort on the part of the poorest states. In fact, the average revenue effort in the poorest one-fifth of the states is greater than the average effort made in the next three-fifths. Even if the poorest states increased their revenue effort from their 13.7 percent in 1968–69 to the 14.7 percent of the highest one-fifth, they would raise only $365 per capita —still far below the amount raised by other states. These figures indicate that the poorest states will not be able to provide adequate levels of public services just by increasing their revenue effort.

Major Issues

The state and local tax systems are now in transition. Larger expenditures require higher taxes, which create equity and economic problems. Most of these problems are not new, but they have become acute as tax burdens have increased.

Income Taxes versus Sales Taxes

The relative merits of an individual income tax and a sales tax for state use continue to provoke emotional responses in many areas of the country. The debate is primarily over equity, but other considerations enter.

The major argument in favor of the income tax is its progressivity. Proponents of the income tax believe that state as well as federal taxes should be based on ability to pay. Moreover, the deductibility of state income taxes in calculating the federal income tax greatly moderates the impact of the top state rates on high-income taxpayers (see discussion on deductibility below). The income tax is also much more responsive to economic growth than is the sales tax.

Proponents of the sales tax believe that it is undesirable to pile a state income tax on top of the high federal tax. Even with deductibility, they fear that high-income taxpayers will migrate to avoid the state income tax. They feel that tax progressivity is not essential at all levels of government, provided the entire federal-state-local tax system is progressive on balance.

Both the income and sales taxes can be productive revenue sources for state governments if they are levied on a broad base. Most states levying both sales and income taxes derive more revenue from the sales tax. While it is possible to devise an income tax with a yield equal to that of almost any sales tax, sales taxes of 3 to 5 percent are generally more productive than income taxes with rates graduated up to 10 percent. These are the ranges currently used in most states. The balance, of course, swings toward the income tax as incomes increase.

Whether an income tax would drive wealthy residents to sales tax states is difficult to determine. For example, in 1967, the Michigan sales tax and the New York income tax yielded approximately the same dollar amounts per capita. Table 9-1 compares the combined federal-state tax burdens of individuals with different incomes, after taking into account the effect of the deductibility of state taxes in computing the federal income tax. A married person with two children who is subject to the New York income tax would have paid $69 less tax on an income of $6,000, but $835 more tax on an income of $25,000. Reactions to such differentials depend heavily on individual attitudes toward equity, the need for state revenues, and the benefits of improved public services. In any case, the opposition to state income taxes is often vocal and influential and may prevent use of income

TABLE 9-1. Combined Federal and State Tax Liabilities for a Married Couple with Two Dependents in an Income and in a Sales Tax State, 1967

(In dollars)

	Federal income tax plus		
Adjusted gross income	New York income tax[a]	Michigan sales tax[a, b]	Difference (Income tax less sales tax)
3,000	0	95	− 95
4,000	140	235	− 95
5,000	311	396	− 85
6,000	496	565	− 69
8,000	875	902	− 27
10,000	1,288	1,262	26
15,000	2,596	2,351	245
20,000	4,156	3,620	536
25,000	5,909	5,074	835

[a] After taking into account deductibility of the state income or sales tax in computing the federal income tax. All other deductions were assumed to be equal to the federal standard deduction.

[b] Sales tax as estimated by the Internal Revenue Service for purposes of federal deductibility (see instructions to 1967 Form 1040).

taxation regardless of its effect on location decisions. It may be noted that Michigan finally enacted an income tax in 1967, after a long struggle.

There is little to choose between income and sales taxes on administrative and compliance grounds. Costs of administration are somewhat lower for the income tax than for the sales tax. Compliance is more difficult for the taxpayer in the case of the income tax, while the sales tax imposes a burden on retailers. Some support the sales tax because its revenues come partly from tourists and other visitors who use the facilities of the state temporarily. On the other hand, income taxes can be, and generally are, imposed on employees who live outside the state and work within the state. These differences may be significant in a few places where interstate travel and commuting are important.

In recent years, the need for revenue has tended to soften attitudes on both sides of the controversy. At one time most states had either an income tax or a sales tax, but the number of states with both has been increasing. On July 1, 1970, thirty-three states had both, twelve had only a sales tax, four had only an income tax, and one (New Hampshire) had neither (Table C-26). Credits for sales taxes against state individual income taxes, adopted in seven states, make it possible to eliminate the regressive feature of the sales tax. There are few remaining objections on equity grounds to the use by states of either type of tax, or both, if such credits are allowed.

Deductibility

The discussion in Chapter 4 of the deductibility of state taxes in calculating the federal income tax base implied that simultaneous use of the same tax source by two (or even three) levels of government is acceptable, provided the combined rates are not excessive. Deduction from the federal tax base of income, sales, and property taxes paid to state and local governments is considered desirable to encourage state and local use of these taxes and to narrow interstate and intercommunity net tax differentials.

Most states with income taxes have borrowed the deductibility features of the federal law. While practices vary, state and local sales and excise taxes are deductible in arriving at taxable income in most states. In addition, sixteen of the thirty-seven individual income tax states permit deduction of federal individual income tax (two on a limited basis), and eight permit deduction of the state individual income tax itself; approximately one-fourth of the forty-three corporation income tax states permit deduction of the federal corporation income tax, and about the same proportion allow deduction of the state corporation income tax.

Deductibility of any tax from the base of another (or from its own base) has two effects: first, the extra burden on the taxpayer of the deducted tax is reduced by the marginal rate of the tax against which it is deductible; and second, the net yield of the tax with the deductible feature is reduced, requiring higher nominal rates to obtain any given amount of revenue. The net marginal burdens of state taxes with federal and federal plus state deductibility are illustrated in Table 9-2. For example:

1. A proportional 2 percent state income tax is converted to a regressive tax by the deductibility feature of the federal income tax. Such a tax would impose a net burden of 1.72 percentage points on

TABLE 9-2. Marginal Burden of State Income Taxes under (a) Federal Deductibility[a] **and (b) Federal and State Deductibility,**[b] **at Illustrative Marginal Rates**

(In percentages)

Marginal federal tax rate	Type of deductibility	Marginal state tax rate				
		2	3	5	7	10
14	Federal only	1.72	2.58	4.30	6.02	8.60
	Federal and state	1.48	2.23	3.72	5.23	7.50
20	Federal only	1.60	2.40	4.00	5.60	8.00
	Federal and state	1.29	1.93	3.23	4.54	6.53
30	Federal only	1.40	2.10	3.50	4.90	7.00
	Federal and state	0.99	1.48	2.49	3.50	5.05
40	Federal only	1.20	1.80	3.00	4.20	6.00
	Federal and state	0.73	1.09	1.84	2.59	3.75
50	Federal only	1.00	1.50	2.50	3.50	5.00
	Federal and state	0.51	0.76	1.28	1.81	2.63
60	Federal only	0.80	1.20	2.00	2.80	4.00
	Federal and state	0.32	0.49	0.82	1.17	1.70
70	Federal only	0.60	0.90	1.50	2.10	3.00
	Federal and state	0.18	0.28	0.47	0.66	0.97

[a] State income taxes paid are deducted in computing federal income taxes.
[b] Same as note a; in addition, federal income taxes paid are deducted in computing state income taxes.

a taxpayer subject to the lowest federal rate of 14 percent, 1 point on a taxpayer subject to a 50 percent federal rate, and only 0.6 point on a taxpayer subject to the top federal rate of 70 percent. If the state allowed its income tax to be deducted from its own income tax base, the regressivity would be even greater.

2. Federal deductibility of state income taxes already greatly reduces the burden of the top state income tax rates; as the following table shows, state deductibility accomplishes little more for the taxpayer at a substantial cost to the state. With federal deductibility of the state tax, a top state rate of 10 percent imposes a net additional burden of only 3 percentage points on a taxpayer subject to a federal rate of 70 percent. With state deductibility of the federal tax, the net additional burden of the same 10 percent state tax is only 0.97 of a point. The 2.03 points net reduction in the taxpayer's total burden costs the state 6.77 points, or more than three times the taxpayer's saving.

Tax collected as a percentage of income
(70 percent federal rate, 10 percent state rate)

Level of government	Federal deduct- ibility only	Federal and state deductibility	Difference
Federal	63.00%	67.74%	+4.74%
State	10.00	3.23	−6.77
Total	73.00	70.97	−2.03

3. Federal deductibility reduces the progressivity of the state tax and may actually convert it to a regressive tax. Adding state deductibility of the federal tax aggravates matters. For example, if the state rates are paired with the federal rates along the diagonal in Table 9-2, the net impact of the state tax on an additional $1 of income is as follows:

Marginal federal rate	Marginal state rate	Net impact of the state tax		
		Federal deduct- ibility only	Federal and state deductibility	Difference
14%	2%	1.72%	1.48%	−0.24%
20	3	2.40	1.93	−0.47
30	5	3.50	2.49	−1.01
40	7	4.20	2.59	−1.61
50	10	5.00	2.63	−2.37
60	10	4.00	1.70	−2.30
70	10	3.00	0.97	−2.03

If the federal income tax allows deductibility of the state tax, the state tax adds 1.72 percentage points to the federal tax in the lowest federal bracket, rising to 5 points in the 50 percent bracket. If, further, the state permits federal income tax to be deducted against its own tax, the additional tax reaches a maximum of only 2.63 points.

Although the income tax rates in the top brackets raise only a fraction of their nominal values in many states, very high rates at the high income levels act as a psychological barrier to further use of the income tax for needed revenues. Since deductibility of the state tax in computing the federal tax already protects taxpayers against excessive rates, removal of the deductibility of the federal tax against the state tax would provide some additional revenue for the states and improve and simplify state income taxes.

The Property Tax

In spite of widespread and occasionally vehement criticism, the property tax continues to be the major revenue source for local governments. Its survival is due largely to the impressive growth of revenue already noted. Its poor performance on equity and efficiency grounds, however, argues for a reevaluation of the property tax as the mainstay of the local tax system.

Although the property tax was at one time intended to be a tax on all wealth, it no longer is general in coverage. While practices vary from community to community, the tax falls chiefly on real estate, business equipment, and inventories. The tax rate is determined as a residual. Local governments assess the value of property subject to the tax, estimate the revenue needed from this source, and calculate the tax rate required to obtain the predetermined result. The property tax is more adaptable to local government needs than are income or sales taxes, whose rates vary only with legislative action, and the ease of raising rates has probably contributed to its durability.

ADMINISTRATION. Administration of the property tax has been subject to universal criticism. Because the value of the tax base for any particular property is not determined by a market transaction, property assessments are often arbitrary and can result in an erratic distribution of the tax burden. Two-thirds of the states require full valuation, but substantial underassessment is the rule rather than the exception. In 1956, 1961, and 1966, for example, property was assessed at an average of less than 20 percent of its market value in eighteen states (Table 9-3). Moreover, there is great variability in assessments of properties of equal value, creating irritating inequities among tax-payers and among different communities within the same state. Since local shares of state grants and property tax limitations are often based on assessed valuations, underassessment impairs the ability of local governments to finance their needs.

The poor quality of assessments is due partly to the spotty evidence on property values available to the assessor. Either the information is nonexistent, or the taxing jurisdiction lacks the staff and resources to take advantage of it. The Advisory Commission on Intergovernmental Relations (ACIR)—a permanent commission created by act of Congress to make recommendations on intergovernmental relations—has recommended centralization of property assessment in one state agency, to take advantage of the states' superior technical resources. The commission also recommends that assessors be appointed rather than elected, in order to remove the process from political influence.

ALLOCATION EFFECTS AND INCIDENCE. The property tax has a reputation for distorting allocative effects, as well as for being erratically administered. The tax burden on business property varies substantially among industries. After allowing for differences in local rates

TABLE 9-3. Distribution of States by Percentage Ratios of Assessed Value to Sales Price of Real Property, 1956, 1961, and 1966

Assessed value as percentage of sales price[a]	Number of states		
	1956	1961	1966
0– 9.9	2	3	1
10.0–19.9	16	15	17
20.0–29.9	16	13	10
30.0–39.9	4	6	7
40.0–49.9	7	10	5
50.0–59.9	2	2	6
60.0–69.9	1	1	2
70.0–79.9	0	0	0
80.0–89.9	0	0	2
Total	48	50	50
Average assessment	30%	29.5%	32.5%

Sources: James A. Maxwell, *Financing State and Local Governments* (Brookings Institution, 1965), p. 139, and revised ed. (1969), p. 139 (citing the 1957, 1962, and 1967 *Census of Governments*), supplemented with data from U.S. Bureau of the Census, *Census of Governments, 1967*, Vol. 2, *Taxable Property Values* (1968), Table 9.

[a] These are the simple sales-based average percentages derived by dividing the total assessed value of all properties sold that are included in the Census samples by the aggregate of their sales prices.

and coverage, taxes are generally higher in capital-intensive industries or in those that use large amounts of real estate (since personal property usually escapes taxation). This encourages the substitution of other inputs for real property and, if such substitutions cannot be made, may divert resources to other firms and industries. The property tax also affects land use. Heavy taxation of improvements discourages rebuilding in urban areas, especially when tax rates are lower in the surrounding suburbs.

Residential property is one of the major sources of property tax revenue. The high taxes on housing might be expected to discourage demand for housing. For many households, however, the income tax advantages of home ownership and the benefits financed by the property tax often offset its deterrent effects.

Since the supply of bare land is fixed, owners bear the burden of taxes on the value of sites when they are first levied or increased. The incidence of property taxes on improvements and on business property is in dispute. Some believe that they are shifted forward in the form of higher prices to business customers and to housing occupants, because the taxes tend to discourage investments in business and housing property. On the other hand, if the total supply of saving is not responsive to the return on investment, a partial or general property tax is shifted backward to the owners of capital in general in the form of lower rates of return. (See Chapter 5 for this analysis as it applies to the corporation income tax.)

On the traditional assumption that the property tax on improvements is shifted forward, the distribution of the property tax burden is regressive in the lowest income classes, but roughly proportional at higher levels if the federal income tax offset is considered. But the tax is probably progressive if total saving is not responsive to rates of return on investment. The benefits financed by the tax heavily favor the poor, and thus it improves "vertical equity" on balance, even if the tax itself is regressive. Because of the inequalities in assessments, the tax scores low on "horizontal equity."

ALTERNATIVES. Other forms of real estate taxation have been proposed as alternatives to the general property tax. One is the use of annual rather than capital values as a base, often advocated by those who wish to "tax the profits out of the slums," where high-rent, low-capital-value housing prevails. Such a system would favor properties in low-return uses and, like the present tax, would discourage improvements to increase annual income from properties.

A second alternative is site-value taxation: taxing the value of the sites themselves while exempting the value of improvements. Site-value taxation has merit on equity grounds; since the value of land is enhanced by population growth and general improvements financed by the community at large, the community has the right to tax this "unearned increment." Site-value taxation would also discourage the hoarding of land for speculative purposes and encourage more efficient use of land in and around the nation's cities. Shifting from the present system to a site-value tax, however, would pose problems for present property holders who had paid the full current value, or close to it, for their land and who therefore have not received large unearned increments.

A third proposal, with similar equity and economic advantages, is to tax land-value increments. This would avoid the transitional problems of the site-value tax, but would yield much less revenue than the property tax if it were levied at moderate rates only at the time of transfers of ownership.

A different approach to property taxation is that of a user charge. It is argued that the distribution of taxes based on property values has little relation to the distribution of services to property provided by local governments. A series of user charges would be more clearly linked to the benefits received. For some services, like fire protection, the appropriate benefit charge would be easy to determine because the area of service is well defined; others, like transportation, would be more difficult to allocate. This proposal, however, would not deal with the bulk of current tax revenues that finance services to persons rather than to property.

It is possible to devise better methods of financing local government than with the property tax, but the alternatives would not yield comparable revenues at reasonable rates. This fact will probably preserve the property tax as a major source of local government revenue, making the need for improved administration especially urgent.

Tax Coordination

Tax overlapping among different levels of government was at one time considered a major drawback of the national tax system, but attempts to divide revenue sources have had little success. The state and local governments failed to pick up the electrical energy tax, which was repealed by Congress in 1951, although they had urged the federal government to relinquish this tax for their use. The same was true of reductions in the federal admissions tax during the 1950s. In 1958–59, the Joint Federal-State Action Committee (consisting of state governors appointed by the chairman of the Governors' Conference and representatives of the federal government appointed by the President) could not reach agreement on a proposal to eliminate some federal grants in return for relinquishment of the local telephone tax by the federal government.

Such attempts fail because it is difficult to devise a plan that all states regard as equitable and because the state and local governments are likely to view the specific federal taxes relinquished with the same reservations that motivated Congress to give them up as revenue sources in the first place. Tax overlapping was moderated slightly by the 1965 federal excise tax reductions, but these cuts were made for other reasons. Experience to date suggests that the major cases of duplication—in income, estate and gift, and selective excise taxes—will persist.

The situation is by no means as serious as it appears, however. In recent years, new methods of administrative cooperation between federal and state governments have been developed. State income taxes resemble the federal taxes in major respects; many in fact start with the federal definition of adjusted gross income for individuals and taxable income for corporations. Several states have simplified their tax returns. Most experts now accept some tax overlapping as inevitable, and even desirable, if the taxes used in common are good taxes. The approach now being taken is to relieve major taxpayer compliance problems, remove inequities resulting from tax overlapping, and extend the area of intergovernmental administrative cooperation as much as possible.

ESTATE AND GIFT TAX COORDINATION. The administrative and compliance problems raised by overlapping estate and gift taxation are out of all proportion to their revenue yield. Most of the states use inheritance taxes, but they have a wide variety of exclusions, deductions, and exemptions. The federal credit for state death taxes (enacted in 1924 and enlarged in 1926) placed a floor under state taxes, but did not produce uniformity. The states left their own taxes unchanged and later added special levies to pick up the difference between these taxes and the maximum allowable credit. Today, thirty-seven states have inheritance taxes, forty-three have pick-up taxes (thirty-three have both), and ten have estate taxes (six with inheritance or pick-up taxes as well and one with all three). Only Nevada levies no state death tax.

The states have long felt that estate and gift taxes should be left to them, but would not have the credit arrangement repealed. They recognize that, without the protection of the federal credit, interstate competition for wealthy taxpayers would quickly destroy most state death taxes. The credit ensures that any state can tax up to the amount of the credit without running the risk of losing its taxpayers to other states, but in its present form the credit provides no incentive for states to adopt uniform definitions of the tax base.

The Advisory Commission on Intergovernmental Relations has recommended the substitution of a two-bracket graduated credit for the present estate tax credit, which was originally computed as a flat percentage of the 1926 tax. The ACIR proposal would make available to the states a larger share of the tax on smaller estates, on two conditions: first, that they increase their death taxes by at least the amount of the increase in the credit; second, that they enact estate taxes. The first condition was considered necessary because existing state death taxes generally exceed the federal credit; without a revenue maintenance provision, the higher credit might result in a net reduction rather than in an increase in state revenues. The second condition was intended to encourage the states to follow the pattern of the federal law, although it did not require uniformity in other respects.

The states had also asked for a federal credit for their gift taxes. The ACIR rejected a gift tax credit because it would force gift taxes on all the states, even though the revenue involved for the states is negligible and the states do not need gift taxes to safeguard their death taxes (the federal gift tax already serves this purpose). In any event, the increased federal estate tax credit could be made generous enough to compensate the states for not having gift taxes.

Action on the commission's recommendations for a higher estate tax credit was deferred until estate and gift tax revision could be considered in its entirety. However, the recommendations stimulated little interest in Congress or in the executive branch, partly because the degree of coordination they might achieve would not seem to justify the federal revenue loss. The federal government might be more receptive to the loss of revenue if the recommendations were modified to require greater uniformity.

STATE TAXATION AND INTERSTATE COMMERCE. For years the states have been reaching out to exact taxes from activities that cross state lines. On the whole, their claims have been sustained by the Supreme Court. In 1959, when the court upheld a corporation income tax on a firm whose activities consisted solely of the solicitation of sales within a state, interstate business interests promptly appealed to the federal government for relief. Congress responded by enacting stop-gap legislation under its power to regulate interstate commerce. This halted further expansion of state income tax jurisdiction pending the outcome of a congressional study to determine what legislation, if any, was needed.

After many years of study, the Subcommittee on State Taxation of Interstate Commerce of the House Judiciary Committee recommended legislation affecting corporate income, sales, use, gross receipts, and capital stock taxes. These recommendations were the basis for a bill passed by the House in 1968 and approved again in identical form in 1969, after the Senate failed to act on the 1968 bill. The legislation deals primarily with three issues: (1) the type of business activities within a state that should give rise to taxing jurisdiction; (2) rules to divide the income of multistate firms among the states; and (3) requirements for the collection of use taxes by firms shipping into a state.

1. Because state laws are ordinarily couched in broad terms and vary by type of tax, business firms are uncertain of their tax status if they have minimal activity in a particular state. The judicial process, limited as it is to case treatment, has not always produced solutions conducive to the free flow of commerce. States themselves have difficulty in achieving voluntary compliance from firms unless there is a physical presence in the state.

The proposed legislation would restrict states' taxing jurisdiction to firms earning less than $1 million on an average of federal taxable income, which own or rent property within the state, have at least one employee in the state, or regularly keep an inventory for sale in the state. This provision is intended to promote certainty and improved voluntary compliance and is consistent with the view that a taxpayer's obligations are to his "home" state.

The opposing view—which is supported by most state officials—is that the states' power to tax should extend to all business activities, including sales activities, within their borders. State officials are generally resigned to accepting the P.L. 86-272 standard—the permanent establishment concept—for income tax purposes, but they strongly oppose making it the basis for use tax collection. They feel that, as applied to sales, it would discriminate in favor of the multistate operator, who would enjoy tax immunity, and against the local firm. Also involved is the attitude toward state "tax sovereignty." Spokesmen for the states contend that the states' power to tax gives them the right and obligation to balance a variety of considerations. According to this view, Congress should interfere with state taxation only on a clear showing that the taxes involved constitute a significant burden on interstate commerce.

2. The forty-three states with a corporation income tax have various formulas to compute the allocation for state tax purposes of profits of multistate firms. While twenty-five states have adopted uniform laws for allocation purposes (patterned after the proposal of the National Conference of Commissioners on Uniform State Laws), the others give varying weights to property, payroll, and sales. This diversity produces anomalous results: some interstate corporations are taxed lightly; others claim that they pay state taxes on an aggregate tax base that exceeds their net income. Reporting for state income tax allocation is time-consuming and costly, especially for small and medium-sized businesses with small accounting and legal staffs. Agreement is widespread that states should adopt uniform rules, but there is disagreement on who should prescribe and administer the rules and what factors should be considered.

Under the proposed legislation, businesses subject to taxation would have the option of computing their state income tax liability under the existing state formulas (based on payroll, property, and sales) or under an optional federal tax apportionment formula based on payroll and property. No business would be obligated to pay a state tax greater than that calculated under the two-factor federal formula. The theory of the two-factor approach is that income should be apportioned according to the factors used in producing it, and sales should be taken into account only to the extent that they involve the use of company facilities or labor in a particular state.

The opposing view is that there is no realization of income without sales. Sales reflect the relative importance of each state as a market for the output of any particular company and should therefore be given recognition in the division of income rules. The opposition also holds that the elimination of the sales factor would create a competitive environment that discriminates against local firms.

Support for the two-factor formula reflects the interest of many small firms whose accounting and legal staffs are not prepared to cope with the current diversity in state apportionment formulas. The opposition to the formula mirrors the reluctance of the states to make the Treasury responsible for administrative interpretations that have traditionally been within the purview of state tax officials.

The overall revenue consequences for the states of either approach are small: the two- and three-factor formulas would change tax revenues by as much as 1 percent in only two states, and in a majority by less than one-half of 1 percent. Nonetheless, shifts in tax burden from out-of-state to home-state firms in states with relatively high corporate income tax rates could be significant. This gives rise to concern about a state's competitive position for location of industry.

3. A further recommendation of the subcommittee, not included in the House bill, deals with state requirements that firms shipping into a state collect "use" taxes for the state. All forty-five sales tax states levy use taxes on out-of-state purchases to supplement their sales taxes. This tax is imposed on the buyer for the privilege of using the commodity in the state. States cannot enforce such taxes by collecting them from the purchasers except for registered automobile owners and business purchasers who are registered vendors.

To eliminate tax avoidance in connection with out-of-state purchases, states began to require out-of-state sellers to collect the use tax for them. In 1941, the Supreme Court permitted Iowa to require a mail order house with retail stores in Iowa to collect a use tax on mail order sales sent to its out-of-state customers; and in 1960, it upheld Florida's right to require use tax collections by a Georgia corporation that had representatives in Florida but no office or place of business there.

Although the volume of interstate sales in relation to local sales is small, sales across state lines create some of the most troublesome problems in sales taxation. Interstate sellers object to the requirement that they collect use taxes. The tax base is not uniform from state to state, and interstate sellers sometimes find compliance with use tax collection requirements more burdensome than compliance with state corporation income tax laws. Not only are sales and use tax regulations complicated, they are changed frequently. As more states place increasing reliance on these taxes and as rates rise, state tax officials feel an increasing obligation to protect local firms from competition by enforcing the use tax on out-of-state sellers.

The problem could be solved if the states agreed to tax sales at the point where they originate (the "origin" principle). But the states could not tax on this basis without congressional authorization; moreover, they would be reluctant to enact a principle of taxation that would increase the costs of firms within their borders that ship across state lines. Insistence on the "destination" basis concept stems from the view that, except in the case of business purchases, the sales or use tax is borne by the consumer and that the consumer's state (destination) is the appropriate one to impose such a tax. The destination principle is now the common rule.

The subcommittee recommended a somewhat restricted state jurisdictional rule for the use tax. It also recommended an optional approach that would maintain the status quo or permit the states to join in a cooperative federal-state sales tax administration under a uniform sales and use tax law to collect use taxes on interstate shipments. The only way to avoid the coercion of federal legislation is for the states to cooperate in the collection and mutual enforcement of each other's taxes. The bill proposed by the House subcommittee, as well as a similar bill introduced in the Senate, would authorize such cooperation through interstate sales tax agreements.

Resolution of these issues involves a balancing of the values of state sovereignty in taxation against the advantages of, and constitutional requirement for, the free flow of commerce across state lines. With the increasing interdependence of all regions of the country, a higher degree of uniformity and certainty in state taxation of interstate activities is both desirable and inevitable, but the process of accommodation to economic realities by the states is painful.

While no further legislation has been enacted by Congress, the subcommittee's studies and recommendations have not been without effect. Most of the states have amended their laws or regulations to eliminate practices that were criticized—for example, failing to allow the taxpayer a credit for a sales tax previously paid to another state; charging the taxpayer the cost of sending a tax auditor to an out-of-

state headquarters; denying a trade-in allowance on out-of-state purchases but allowing it on local sales; and failing to provide a standard
method for apportioning income tax liability on multistate business
operations. The states have also asked Congress to consent to a
multistate tax compact that would prohibit these practices. The compact would also provide for a multistate tax commission, composed
of representatives of the member states, which would promote the
acceptance of uniform laws, regulations, and procedures, conduct
audits of a taxpayer on behalf of a number of states, and provide for
the settlement of disputes that involve a single taxpayer and two or
more states by an arbitration procedure. Twenty states have enacted
legislation adopting this compact although Congress has as yet taken
no action on the consent bills.

STATE TAXATION OF NONRESIDENTS. Rules regarding the allocation of
personal income for state income tax purposes vary greatly. The states
assert their right to tax all the income of their residents, whether it is
earned in the state or not. They also claim the right to tax income
originating in the state and going to nonresidents. Most states have
eliminated discrimination by allowing credits for income taxes paid
by their residents to other states, provided the other states grant
reciprocal credits. In addition to the resident credit, a number of
states grant credits to nonresidents for income taxes they pay to their
home states, provided those states reciprocate. The nonresident credit
unnecessarily complicates state personal income taxes and has encouraged at least two non-income tax states to impose selective taxes
on residents of other states who work in these states—solely for the
purpose of diverting its neighbor's tax dollars to its own treasury.
However, the likelihood that an individual will owe tax to two states
on the same income is now small.

Situations of multiple taxation do arise, nonetheless, when two
states claim the same person as a resident, because their definitions of
residence vary. An amendment to the House legislation mentioned
above would prevent this problem by allowing states to tax individual
income (1) earned during periods when the individual lives outside
the state only if the income is earned within the state, or (2) earned
outside the state by individuals living in the state only to the extent
that the tax exceeds the tax paid to the state where the income is
earned.

The problem is more acute where residents of a state without a personal income tax work in a state having such a tax. In these cases, the employees pay income tax to the state in which they are employed, but receive no credit in their home states, where their principal tax payments are in sales or property taxes. This problem would be solved, of course, if all states taxed personal incomes, as has been recommended by the ACIR. This group has also recommended the elimination of the nonresident credit and the adoption of a uniform definition of residence. Adoption of a uniform definition might be required as a condition for continuing the deductibility feature of the federal income tax, or for the enactment of a federal credit in lieu of, or as a supplement to, deductibility (see the discussion of federal assistance below).

COOPERATIVE TAX ADMINISTRATION. Formal federal-state cooperative tax administration dates back to the Revenue Act of 1926. The earliest form of cooperation involved examination of federal income tax returns by state tax officials; in 1950, a plan for coordinated federal-state use of income tax audits was developed. While the states benefited from these arrangements, the federal government received little in return.

In 1957, a new series of agreements on the coordination of tax administration was launched to extend cooperation to other taxes and activities. These agreements, which had been negotiated with forty-six states by late 1970, provide for examination of federal tax returns by state officials and of state returns by federal officials, including the exchange of automatic data processing tapes and information disclosed by federal and state audits. In addition, special enabling legislation permitted the Internal Revenue Service to perform statistical services for state agencies on a reimbursable basis and to enroll state enforcement officers in its training programs. In 1952, a Treasury Department regulation permitted federal agencies to withhold income taxes for state governments. Legislation to permit federal agencies to extend similar help to cities has so far failed to make headway although it has the support of the Treasury Department.

These evidences of federal-state cooperation suggest that federal, state, and local tax officials are willing to coordinate their activities in the interest of greater efficiency. The ACIR has recommended that Congress authorize the federal government to enter into agreements with the states for federal collection of state income taxes. Given the proper attitudes, there is no reason why most of the administrative and compliance benefits of unitary administration (including the same or similar tax returns for all units of government for any one tax, joint audits, and joint collection of taxes other than income taxes) could not be achieved by agreement between the federal and state governments rather than through federal coercion.

State-Local Fiscal Relations

Most public services enjoyed directly by a resident of the United States—education, health, sanitation, and sewerage facilities, welfare aid, and police and fire protection—are provided by local governments. Yet local governments derive all their powers, including fiscal powers, from their parent state governments. Fortunately, the states are increasingly recognizing that local governments cannot be left to their own devices to finance an adequate level of public services.

PROPERTY TAX ADMINISTRATION. Many state governments have taken the initiative to improve local property tax administration; as a result, seven states have raised their average assessment ratios above 50 percent since 1961, and many have reduced the variability of assessments significantly. The reforms initiated involve more state participation in the administration of the tax, greater reliance on professional personnel, and reorganization of local assessment districts into larger and more efficient units. Most states collect comparative statistics on assessment ratios, which reveal the diversity in assessment practices and permit state officials to locate the major areas of administrative weakness. The states are also beginning to take an active part in supervising local assessment practices, training assessment personnel, and providing technical assistance where needed. The ACIR has also recommended publication of the value of property that is exempt from local property taxes by state action, and elimination of unnecessary and inequitable property tax limitations.

With the growing sophistication of assessment techniques, it should be possible to reduce further the major inequities in the administration of this basic tax. Participation in the administrative process by state governments, with their superior financial and technical resources, should accelerate the adoption of the latest techniques, to the fiscal advantage of the local governments.

INCREASING LOCAL TAX CAPACITY. There are limits to the freedom that can be given to local governments in the field of taxation. Unless they were restrained by the state governments, they might soon find themselves with a maze of complicated, burdensome, and inefficient taxes that would impair economic growth. However, several techniques permit local governments to take advantage of the revenue productivity and growth potential of the major nonproperty taxes—sales and personal income taxes—within limits set by the state governments for purposes of control. These include:

Tax supplements. Under this arrangement, the local rate is added to the state rate, the state collects the two taxes and then remits the local shares. The tax supplement has the advantages of simplicity, elimination of duplicate administrative costs, and ease of compliance for the taxpayer. It also retains the local governments' freedom of choice in selecting revenue sources. Local tax supplements on sales taxes are now used in eighteen states.

Maryland *requires* its local governments to add their own income tax to the state tax, with a minimum of 25 percent of the state tax and a maximum of 50 percent. Practically all local governments were close to the maximum within three years of the enactment of the legislation. The principal result has been that local property tax increases have been modest as compared to increases in other states.

Tax sharing. Most state governments earmark one or more taxes for partial or total distribution to the local governments. The state government decides the tax to be shared, the rate to be imposed, and the formula for allocating receipts. Taxes are frequently returned to the communities where they were collected, but other methods of distribution are also used. Tax sharing imposes statewide uniformity in tax rates and automatically eliminates intercommunity competition. Like the tax supplement, it eliminates duplicate tax administration and relieves local governments of unnecessary administrative costs. The device is widely used in the case of automotive taxes, but it may be applied to the entire gamut of state taxes, including income, sales, and cigarette taxes, and other excises and fees.

Tax credits. This is a little-used device to force local governments to use a particular tax. The state levies a statewide tax, but gives a credit to the taxpayer for a specified portion of the tax (sometimes as much as 100 percent) that is paid to a local government. Credits for taxes paid to the state are given by the federal government under its estate and unemployment insurance taxes. In California and Utah tax credits are used to divide the sales tax revenues between counties and cities. The states require the counties to credit sales taxes levied by the cities within their jurisdictions. Florida credits municipal cigarette taxes, and Virginia credits municipal taxes on bank shares against the corresponding state taxes. The tax credit is similar to the shared tax, except that local governments may exceed the credit if the state permits. On the other hand, the tax credit perpetuates duplicate tax administration although local governments often benefit from the spillover of experience under the state tax.

There is no a priori basis for judging which of these three devices is most appropriate in given circumstances, although each has advantages for particular objectives. In states where a specific tax is already in widespread use among the local governments, the tax supplement may be the best alternative. Tax sharing will be more acceptable where local taxes tend to be uniform or where the tax to be shared is not widely used at the local level. The tax credit provides the least coordination at the state-local level, but it may be the only alternative in states where the diverse interests of the local governments are difficult to reconcile.

STATE GRANTS-IN-AID. Grants are similar in many respects to shared taxes. However, instead of distributing funds on the basis of the local tax base, grants provide financial aid to local governments on the basis of some predetermined formula. The source of the revenue may be specified in the legislation, but the grants are often appropriated from general funds. Distribution formulas give weight to such factors as population, number of school children, income, property tax base, miles of paved streets, and so on. The grants are usually for specified purposes (such as schools, roads, and health services), but in some cases they are given on an unconditional basis for general local use.

State assistance to local governments is not a new phenomenon. It amounted to 6 percent of local general revenue in 1902 and rose to 23 percent in 1934; since World War II, it has accounted for about 30 percent of local general revenue. In the past thirty-five years, state transfers to local governments have amounted to more than one-third of all state expenditures (Figure 9-4).

Most state grant systems have grown without systematic planning. They are often complicated and inequitable, and may even defeat the purposes for which they were designed. Distribution formulas remain

FIGURE 9-4. Federal Aid to State-Local Governments, and State Aid to Local Governments, Selected Years, 1902–50; Annually, 1952–69

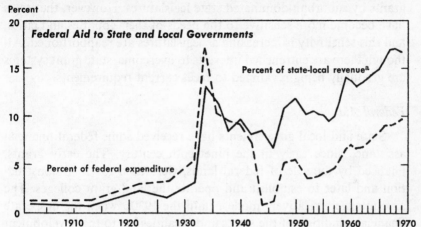

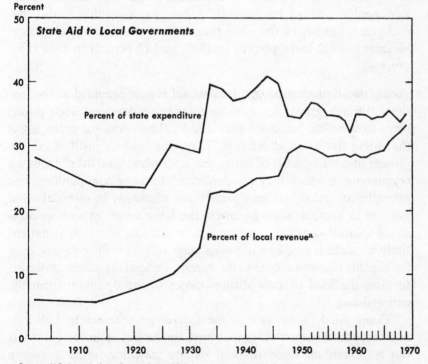

Sources: U.S. Bureau of the Census, *Census of Governments: 1962*, Vol. 6, No. 4, *Historical Statistics on Governmental Finances and Employment* (1964); *Census of Governments: 1967*, Vol. 6, No. 5, *Historical Statistics on Governmental Finances and Employment* (1969); *Governmental Finances in 1967–68*; *Governmental Finances in 1968–69*.
a Including intergovernmental revenue and excluding utility, liquor store, and insurance trust revenue.

unchanged for decades, despite huge population shifts. Many of the nation's largest cities are denied their appropriate shares of state grants by suburban-dominated state legislatures. However, the states have become more sensitive to the needs of their counties and cities, and this sensitivity is increasing as legislatures are reapportioned. Although there are entrenched interests to overcome, state grant systems are gradually being revamped to meet current requirements.

Federal Aid

State and local governments have received some federal financial assistance since early in the nineteenth century. The early grants, financed by the sale of federal lands, were used for road construction and later to establish and operate the land grant colleges. The amounts were relatively modest until the 1930s, when the desperate financial condition of the states and localities led to the development of a great variety of grants to help finance their programs in education, health, welfare, transportation, housing, and other fields. Federal grants have risen from less than 1 percent of state-local general revenue in 1902 to 11 percent in 1948, and 17 percent in 1969 (Figure 9-4).

CONDITIONAL GRANTS-IN-AID. Federal aid is now provided almost entirely through grants for specific government services. Such grants serve to stimulate increased state and local action in particular areas that serve the national interest. They may also be justified on the ground that the benefits of many public services "spill over" from the community in which they are performed to other communities. For example, an individual may receive his education in one state and migrate to another when he enters the labor force. In such circumstances, investment in education will be too low if it is financed entirely by state funds, because each state will be willing to pay only for benefits likely to accrue to its citizens. Federal assistance is needed to raise the level of expenditures closer to the optimum from the national standpoint.

Conditional grants permit the federal government to tailor its assistance to those activities that have the largest spillover effects. It can set minimum standards and require matching funds to ensure state or local government support and participation. It can also allocate funds to states and communities where the need for a particular program is greatest or where fiscal capacity is least.

Conditional grants improve state-local services without transferring their operation to the federal government. However, the recent proliferation of grants makes them increasingly subject to criticism. Congress has under consideration legislation to consolidate related grant-in-aid programs in order to reduce the administrative complexity that now exists. Critics also charge that existing grants involve excessive federal direction and interference with state-local prerogatives, divert large sums from other urgently needed state-local programs, and tend to be perpetuated long after their original objectives are met. On the other hand, the ability to control the use of funds and to require state-local financial participation is a feature that is appealing to Congress. On the basis of recent experience, it seems clear that conditional grants will remain the basic means for providing federal assistance to state and local governments.

GENERAL PURPOSE GRANTS. The federal government appropriated funds to the states for any state-local purpose in 1836, when federal surplus revenues were large enough—partly as a result of receipts from the sale of public lands—to retire the entire national debt and to accumulate a Treasury balance besides. Beginning January 1, 1837, the funds were distributed quarterly on the basis of the number of congressmen and senators from each state, which was very nearly the same as a per capita distribution. The federal surplus disappeared before the end of 1837, a recession year, and the grants were terminated after three installments. Since then, all federal grants have been conditional.

General purpose grants are justified on two grounds. First, all states do not have equal capacity to pay for public services. Even though the poorer states make a larger relative revenue effort (Figure 9-3), they are unable to match the revenue-raising ability of the richer states. While on balance conditional grants (excluding transportation grants) have an equalizing effect (Figure 9-5), the assistance they provide is inadequate relative to total needs in the poorer states. Within states, conditional grants have widened fiscal disparities slightly among metropolitan areas, rather than narrowing them. Second, federal use of the best tax sources leaves a substantial gap between state-local need and state-local fiscal capacity. Moreover, no state can push its tax rates much higher than those in neighboring states for fear of placing its citizens and business enterprises at a disadvantage. On this line of reasoning, all states need some federal

FIGURE 9-5. State-Local General Revenue from Own Sources and from Federal Grants, Other Than Transportation, by States, by Quintiles of Personal Income Per Capita, Fiscal Year 1969

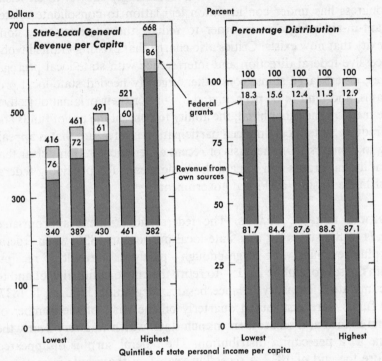

Quintiles of state personal income per capita

Sources: U.S. Bureau of the Census, *Governmental Finances in 1968–69*, pp. 31–33, 52; U.S. Department of the Treasury, Bureau of Accounts, Division of Government Financial Operations, *Federal Aid to States, Fiscal Year 1969* (1970), pp. 16, 19, 20.

assistance even for purely state-local activities, with the poorer states needing relatively more help because of their low fiscal capacity.

As federal revenues have increased in recent years, considerable support has developed for some way to use part of the increasing federal receipts for general purpose grants. Several proposals have been considered in Congress, including one by the Nixon administration. Although they differ in detail, the proposals have a number of features in common:

1. A certain percentage of a growing base—for example, total federal revenues, total income tax collections, or the individual income tax base—would be automatically set aside in a special federal fund.

2. Disbursements from the fund would be made primarily on a per capita basis, a method that helps the poorer states relatively more than the richer states. More equalization could be provided by using a small part of the fund (perhaps up to 10 percent) for the poorest states only, or by varying the per capita amounts inversely with state tax capacity. Tax effort might also be given some weight in the formula to give the states an incentive to maintain or increase tax collections out of their own sources.

3. The funds would be turned over to the states, with the understanding that a major share would go to the local governments. The percentage could be stipulated in advance or left to the state legislatures under procedures ensuring participation by local officials in the decision. The Nixon administration's proposal, for example, would allocate funds among the subdivisions of each state according to the ratio of each subdivision's local general revenues to the sum of state and local revenues in that state. Under a formula proposed by the National Commission on Urban Problems in 1968, and since endorsed by the Advisory Commission on Intergovernmental Relations, the local government share would be allocated only to municipalities or urban counties with a population over 50,000. The grants would depend on the ratio of local to total state and local revenues and on population, with the larger cities receiving a relatively larger share.

4. Various constraints on the use of the funds are visualized, but these would be much less detailed than those that apply to conditional grants. They could be treated as "block grants" to be used in such general areas as health, education, and welfare; or they might be made available for any expenditures not otherwise prohibited by the legislation.

5. An audit of the actual use of the funds would be required. Some proposals also call for certification by appropriate state and local officials that all applicable federal laws, such as the Civil Rights Act, have been complied with in the activities financed by the grant.

Reaction to proposals for general purpose grants depends largely on attitudes toward the relations between the federal and state governments. They are opposed by those who wish to control the use of federal funds in great detail, who have little faith in the willingness or ability of state governments to use the funds wisely and who believe that general purpose grants will weaken the role of conditional grants. They are supported by those who wish to strengthen the role of the state governments and to limit federal control over state-local spending, and who believe that conditional grants are already overworked in the federal system. Some oppose the expansion of federal assistance, in the form of either conditional or general purpose grants, on the ground that separation of the expenditure and financing functions will lead to excessive and wasteful expenditures.

However, categorical grants and general purpose grants have very different functions. Categorical grants insure that the states do not neglect areas where the "spillover" effects are clearly in the national interest. General purpose grants, on the other hand, link the states and localities to the superior revenue resources of the federal government and help the poorer states provide services of the same scope and quality as those of the wealthier ones without putting far heavier tax burdens on their citizens. In light of the well-known principle that two objectives cannot be satisfied by using only one instrument, general purpose grants are needed to supplement, not to replace, categorical grants.

OTHER METHODS OF FEDERAL ASSISTANCE. Other alternatives for accomplishing the objectives of federal grants involve the reduction of federal revenues. These include: (1) reducing federal taxes or relinquishing specific types of federal taxes; (2) sharing federal tax collections with the states; and (3) granting credits for state and local taxes against federal taxes. These are the same methods that state governments use to provide assistance to local governments. Such measures would help state and local governments in varying degrees, but they would not achieve the broad objectives sought through the grant device.

The response of the state and local governments to federal tax reduction or relinquishment is bound to be spotty because it depends on action by many individual executive and legislative bodies. State and local revenues would rise mainly through the indirect effect of the increased national income resulting from federal tax reduction, but this would amount to only a small fraction of the released federal revenues. To the extent that state and local tax rates increased, the richer states would benefit most.

As has already been indicated, tax sharing is a common arrangement at the state-local level, but not at the federal-state level. Now that the federal government has been left almost exclusively with income and estate and gift taxes, the tax sharing alternative would not be logical unless the states were willing to give up these taxes.

Tax credits would not automatically increase state-local revenues: state and local governments already imposing the taxes that could be credited would have to raise their rates. Since this could be done without raising the total taxes paid by their citizens, they might be encouraged to do so, but there would be strong opposition from the groups that would prefer to enjoy the tax reduction provided by the credit. If the credit applied to income taxes, the thirteen states without individual income taxes would benefit only after they imposed such a tax. However, this might be regarded as federal coercion and, in some states, would face constitutional barriers. The earlier discussion of the estate tax credit indicated that the tax credit can be an effective coordinating device, but it would not redistribute resources to the neediest states. At best, the credit diverts federal revenues to the states where they originate.

Summary

Despite the sluggish response of their taxes to economic growth, the state and local governments have made a good record in the postwar period. But they will continue to be hard-pressed in the foreseeable future as their financial needs continue to grow at a faster rate than the national income.

Most of the additional revenue needed must be raised by the state and local governments themselves. At the state level, the trend is toward the use of moderate income and sales taxes. In some states, there are longstanding traditions against one or the other of these two major taxes, but historical precedents are breaking down. The adoption in seven states of a credit against the income tax for sales taxes paid suggests that the objection to sales taxes on equity grounds can be dealt with effectively. The fact that the federal income tax permits deductions of state income taxes should make income taxation at the state level more acceptable. However, states that permit the deduction of federal income taxes from their own income tax bases should recognize that they lose much more revenue than their taxpayers save, and reduce the equity of their income taxes.

At the local level, there is need for immediate strengthening of property tax administration. This tax will continue to be the main revenue source of local governments; state governments should take a strong hand in promoting improvements in the professional quality of assessment personnel and assessment procedures. In addition, the states should seriously consider expanding their use of the tax sharing device. They should also consider the feasibility of permitting local governments to supplement the overworked property tax with revenues from income or sales taxes. There are serious dangers in permitting local governments to levy such taxes, but unnecessary complications and inefficiencies can be avoided if local income and sales taxes are levied in the form of supplements to the corresponding state taxes.

Even if they make a substantial effort of their own, the state and local governments will be unable to meet their growing needs without substantial federal assistance. Part of this assistance will come from conditional grants, which will help finance activities in which the federal government has a strong interest. But the state and local governments will also need financial help for other state-local programs. As the nation faces up to the enormous tasks of improving education, providing welfare and health facilities, and reconstructing the blighted areas of its cities, a new program of supplementary federal grants for general purposes becomes an increasingly urgent need.

Historical Summary of Major Federal Taxes

THE FEDERAL TAX SYSTEM as we know it today is of relatively recent origin. From 1789 to 1909, the federal government relied almost exclusively on excise taxes and customs. An income tax was used for emergency purposes during the Civil War, and rudimentary death taxes were levied in the years 1797–1802, 1862–70, and 1898–1902. The corporation and individual income taxes—now the backbone of the federal revenue system—were enacted in 1909 and 1913, respectively. The modern estate tax was first levied in 1916 and the gift tax in 1924. Payroll taxation was first introduced by the Social Security Act of 1935.

The Individual Income Tax

The Civil War tax on individual incomes was in effect from 1862 through 1871. The tax contained a flat $600 exemption with no allowance for children, was graduated up to 10 percent (in 1865 and 1866), and was collected at the source on wages, salaries, interest, and dividends. Total revenues under this tax amounted to $376 million. At its peak in 1866, it accounted for almost 25 percent of internal revenue collections. The tax was allowed to lapse in 1872, when the urgent need for revenue disappeared.

For almost twenty years after the expiration of the Civil War tax, there was only isolated support for the reenactment of an income tax. As the country grew and prospered, great industries and fortunes were established, and inequalities in the distribution of income became more disturbing. The income tax was reenacted in 1894, when the country was in a mood for reform against the evils of monopolies and trusts. However, this tax was declared unconstitutional by the Supreme Court in 1895.

The high court held that the portion of the personal income tax that fell on income from land was a "direct" tax, which was required by the Constitution to be apportioned among the states according to population. The decision was assailed by many groups, and agitation for a change in the Constitution continued until the Sixteenth Amendment was ratified in 1913. This amendment provided that "Congress shall have power to lay and collect taxes on incomes, from whatever source derived, without apportionment among the several States, and without regard to any census or enumeration."

The 1913 tax, which was enacted shortly after the Sixteenth Amendment was ratified, applied to wages, salaries, interest, dividends, rents, entrepreneurial incomes, and capital gains. It allowed deductions for personal interest and tax payments, as well as for business expenses. The tax exempted federal, state, and local government bond interest and salaries of state and local government employees; it also exempted dividends from the normal tax, but not from the surtax. Taxes were collected at the source on wages and salaries, interest, rents, and annuities, with an exemption of $3,000 for single persons and $4,000 for married couples. A normal tax of 1 percent was applied to income above the exempted amounts, with a surtax of 1 to 6 percent.

The following are the most significant changes made since the original 1913 act: a credit for dependents and a deduction for charitable contributions were introduced in 1917; collection at source was eliminated in 1916 and was reenacted for wages and salaries only in 1943; preferential rates on long-term capital gains were adopted in 1921; in 1939, the exemption of salaries of state and local government employees was eliminated, and the sale of tax-exempt federal bonds was discontinued in 1941; the standard deduction was adopted in 1944; "income splitting" for married couples was enacted in 1948; an averaging system and a minimum standard deduction were introduced in 1964; and in the 1969 act, the minimum standard deduction was replaced by a low-income allowance, and a minimum tax on selected preference incomes and a top marginal rate on earned income of 50 percent were adopted.

Rates and exemptions have changed frequently (Tables A-1 and A-2). Maximum marginal rates reached 77 percent during World War I, 94 percent during World War II, and 92 percent during the Korean war. They declined to 24 percent in the 1920s and rose to 79 percent in the 1930s; in the late 1950s and early 1960s, the maximum rate was 91 percent. At present, the maximum rate is 70 percent. A special Vietnam war surcharge was in effect at 7.5 percent of tax in 1968, 10 percent in 1969, and 2.5 percent in

1970. Exemptions showed a downward trend during the first three decades of income taxation in this country, reaching a low of $500 per taxpayer during World War II, and then rose to $600 for each personal exemption in 1948, $625 in 1970, $650 in 1971, $700 in 1972, and $750 in 1973.

The Corporation Income Tax

The corporation income tax rate began at 1 percent in 1909, reached 12 percent during World War I, 13.5 percent in the late 1920s, 40 percent during World War II, and 52 percent during the Korean war. The Revenue Act of 1964 reduced the rate to 50 percent for 1964 and 48 percent for later years (Table A-3). The Vietnam war surcharge also applied to corporations at 10 percent of tax in 1968 and 1969 and 2.5 percent in 1970.

Between 1909 and 1935, the tax was levied at a proportional rate on taxable income. A small exemption was allowed in computing taxable income for sporadic periods: $5,000 in the years 1909–13; $2,000 in 1918–27; and $3,000 in 1928–31. Graduation was introduced for the first time in 1936, with rates ranging from 8 percent on the first $2,000 of taxable income to 15 percent on income over $40,000.

Beginning in 1938, graduation was limited to corporations with incomes of $25,000 or less. Above this point, a flat rate applied to the entire taxable income of the corporation, on the theory that rate graduation in the corporation income tax cannot be defended on equity grounds as in the case of individuals. The limited graduation was intended as a concession to small business. This rationale produced a peculiar rate schedule, which persisted until the end of 1949. For example, between 1942 and 1945, the rates began at 25 percent on the first $5,000 of taxable income and rose to 53 percent for taxable incomes between $25,000 and $50,000 (Table A-4); beginning at $50,000, the rate was a flat 40 percent on total taxable income. The 53 percent rate—called the "notch" rate—was just enough to raise the corporate rate to 40 percent at $50,000 and thus avoided a discontinuity in effective rates at that point.

While it produced the desired result, the notch rate was regarded as a penalty on small business. After considerable agitation, the 1950 act removed the notch rate and restored a simple two bracket system of graduation. This was accomplished by enacting a normal tax applying to all corporation profits and a surtax applying to profits in excess of $25,000. For the years 1952–63, the combined rates were 30 percent on the first $25,000 and 52 percent on the amount in excess of $25,000. In 1964, they were reduced to 22 percent and 50 percent, respectively, and, from 1965 through 1967, were 22 percent and 48 percent. Including the Vietnam war surcharge, the rates were 24.2 percent and 52.8 percent for 1968 and 1969, and 22.55 percent and 49.2 percent for 1970. They returned to 22 percent and 48 percent in 1971.

Dividends distributed by corporations were excluded from the individual *normal* tax before 1936 and were subject to the *surtax* (which was the progressive element of the individual income tax). In 1936, this exclusion was removed, and a tax on undistributed profits was imposed at the corporate level. This tax was intended to force corporations to distribute most of their earnings as dividends. The tax was vigorously attacked as a deterrent to corporate growth and was repealed after being in operation for only two years.

Between 1939 and 1954, the individual and corporation income taxes were levied without any attempt at integration of the two taxes as they applied to dividends. In 1954, individuals were allowed to exclude the first $50 of dividends from their taxable income ($100 for joint returns) and to subtract as a credit from the tax 4 percent of the dividends received in excess of the exclusion. After several years of debate, Congress reduced the credit to 2 percent in 1964 and eliminated it entirely beginning in 1965; at the same time, the exclusion was increased to $100 ($200 for joint returns).

The corporation income tax has been supplemented by an excess profits tax during World War I, World War II, and the Korean war. The method adopted was to tax at a very heavy rate (as high as 95 percent in World War II) the excess of a corporation's profits over a prewar base period or over a "normal" rate of return (specified in the statute) on invested capital. For example, the base period for the World War II excess profits tax was 1936–39. The excess profits tax creates difficult economic, equity, and administrative problems; taxation of even a portion of a corporation's net profits at rates close to 100 percent tends to be unfair. To relieve the most glaring inequities, the law provided alternative methods of computing excess profits and also permitted adjustments for hardship cases. But such provisions made a complicated law even more difficult to administer. The experience to date indicates that excess profits taxation is appropriate only for wartime use.

Excise Taxes

Immediately after the ratification of the Constitution, the new government introduced a fairly elaborate system of excise taxes, including taxes on carriages, liquor, snuff, sugar, and auction sales. Even at that time, these taxes were considered unfair and burdensome on the poor. The Whisky Rebellion of 1794 was a revolt by farmers against the federal tax, which ran up to 30 cents per gallon. Except for the tax on salt, the early excises were abolished by the Jefferson administration in 1802, revived during the

War of 1812, and then terminated again in 1817, not to reappear until the Civil War.

The Civil War excise tax system foreshadowed what was to happen during every major war thereafter. Liquor and tobacco taxes, which remained as permanent parts of the federal revenue system after the war, were supplemented by taxes on manufactured goods, gross receipts of transportation companies, advertising, licenses, legal documents, and financial transactions. During World War I, the list was again expanded, this time to include special occupational taxes and taxes on theater admissions, telephone calls, and retail sales of jewelry, toilet preparations, and luggage. Following the war, tobacco and stamp taxes remained as the major excise taxes. The liquor taxes remained in effect throughout the prohibition era.

A break with peacetime precedent was made during the early 1930s, when Congress enacted a series of manufacturers' excise taxes on such items as automobiles, trucks, buses, appliances, and other consumer durables; also taxed were long distance telephone calls. These taxes were to be continued at varying rates and with varying degrees of comprehensiveness until 1965. The depression taxes were enacted after an attempt to introduce a general manufacturers' sales tax was defeated in Congress. During World War II, the rates of most of the then existing excise taxes were increased; and new excise taxes on retail sales of furs, jewelry, luggage, and toilet preparations, on local telephone service, and on passenger and freight transportation were introduced.

A bill to reduce the excise taxes was passed by the House just as the Korean war began. These changes were quickly eliminated from the Revenue Act of 1950, which was enacted within three months after the beginning of hostilities. In the following year, the excise taxes on liquor, tobacco, gasoline, automobiles, consumer durables, and other products were increased, and new taxes on wagering and diesel fuel were adopted.

A major innovation in excise taxation was introduced in 1956, when a number of excise taxes were earmarked for a specially created highway trust fund to finance the construction of the 41,000-mile federal highway system. The earmarked taxes included the old taxes (with increased rates) on gasoline, diesel, and special motor fuels, trucks, and tires, and new taxes on tread rubber and the use of heavy trucks and buses on the highways. An airport and airway user trust fund was set up along similar lines in 1970 to finance construction of airports and improvements in the airway system. The taxes earmarked for this fund included those on passenger tickets, airfreight, gasoline used by general aviation aircraft, tires and tubes used on aircraft, a special $3 tax on international air trips, and an annual aircraft user tax.

The Korean war excise tax structure was dismantled, beginning in 1954; the process took more than a decade. The original Korean war tax increases had been enacted for a period of three years, but most of them were extended each year as revenue requirements forced continued postponements of their repeal. The first significant break came in 1954, when all excise tax rates in excess of 10 percent were reduced to 10 percent, with the exception of the 20 percent cabaret tax. The freight tax was repealed in 1958; the cabaret tax was reduced to 10 percent in 1960; and in 1962, the railroad and bus passenger tax was eliminated, and the air transportation tax was reduced from 10 percent to 5 percent. The interest equalization tax was enacted in 1963 for balance-of-payments reasons.

The present excise tax system was enacted in 1965, when Congress scaled down the Korean war excises to all but a few major taxes levied for sumptuary and regulatory reasons and as user charges (Table A-5). The reduction, which amounted to almost $5 billion, was to be made in two major steps, on July 1, 1965, and January 1, 1966, and in smaller steps on January 1 of the succeeding three years. The reductions to be made on January 1, 1966, 1967, and 1968, were postponed several times during the Vietnam war. When the full reductions become effective, excises will be confined to four general categories: (1) alcohol and tobacco taxes; (2) highway and airway user taxes; (3) a tax on truck parts and accessories of 5 percent of manufacturers' prices, and a 10 percent tax on fishing equipment and firearms; and (4) regulatory taxes on narcotics, phosphorous matches, and wagering.

Payroll Taxes

The Social Security Act of 1935 imposed payroll taxes to finance the old-age insurance system and unemployment compensation benefits. Later the tax was used to finance survivor, disability, and health insurance. Railroad employees are covered under a separate system of taxation, which is similar to, but not identical with, the general social insurance system.

The OASI Tax

The 1935 act established the principle that the retirement system would be financed by equal taxes on employers and employees. Under the original act, the tax was 1 percent each for employer and employee on covered wages up to $3,000 per employee. The act also provided a schedule of rate increases for subsequent years, reaching a maximum of 3 percent for 1949 and later years. However, the original increases were deferred when the social security trust fund accumulated substantial reserves. Later, as benefits were raised, both the tax and earnings covered were increased repeatedly. The 1967 amendments raised the base to the first $7,800 of earnings of employees, beginning January 1, 1968. They also provided for a maximum rate of tax of 5.9 percent each on employers and employees, beginning in 1987 (Table A-6).

The original act exempted agricultural and domestic labor, members of the professions, public employees, a few other classes of employees, and the self-employed. The coverage has been gradually expanded to include all employed persons except for federal civilian employees (who are covered by their own retirement system), self-employed persons who have self-employment income of less than $400 a year, and domestic and farm workers earning less than specified amounts from a single employer. The self-employed began to be covered in 1951 at a rate equal to one and one-half times the corresponding rate for employees (rounded to the nearest 0.1 percent beginning in 1962).

Unemployment Insurance Tax

The unemployment insurance tax was originally imposed in 1936 on employers of eight or more persons at a rate of 1 percent of payrolls, with automatic increases to 2 percent in 1937 and 3 percent in 1938 and later years. The coverage was expanded to employers of four or more in 1956, and the rate was increased to 3.1 percent in 1961. The rate was raised temporarily to 3.5 percent in 1962 and 3.35 in 1963, but was restored to 3.1 percent beginning in 1964. Legislation in 1970 expanded coverage to employers of one or more, effective in 1972, and increased the rate to 3.2 percent beginning in 1970. The tax was originally applicable to all wages, has been limited to $3,000 of wages since 1939, and is scheduled to increase to $4,200 of wages in 1972 (see Table A-7).

The federal government allows a credit against its tax for amounts contributed to state unemployment insurance programs, up to 2.7 percent of covered wages. The remainder of the federal tax is used to pay the administrative costs of the state programs.

State unemployment taxes are levied at the standard rate of 2.7 percent to use up the federal credit. In three states the tax is levied on employers and employees; in the others it is levied only on employers. In almost all states, employers are taxed according to an experience rating that may result in a larger or smaller tax than the standard 2.7 percent. This device permits states to lower the tax rates on firms with stable employment and to increase it on those with unstable employment. However, the full 2.7 percent credit is allowed against the federal tax where the tax rate has been reduced by a good experience rating. As a result of these provisions, tax rates differ greatly from one state to another as well as within a single state.

Railroad Taxes

Payroll tax rates have always been higher in the railroad industry than in other industries. The retirement tax for railroad employees dates back to 1937, when the rate was 2.75 percent each on employers and employees, and the maximum monthly wage subject to the tax was $300. Since 1937, the rates and wages subject to tax have been changed frequently. Under the 1967 amendments, the tax on both employers and employees will reach 10.65 percent on earnings of up to $650 a month in 1987 (Table A-6).

The railroad unemployment insurance program is supported by a tax on wages of up to $400 per month per employee paid by the employers. Prior to 1948, the tax rate was 3 percent. It was reduced to 0.5–3 percent in 1948–59, depending on the financial condition of the trust fund, and was raised to 1.5–3.75 percent on June 1, 1959, and 1.5–4 percent beginning in 1962 (Table A-7).

Estate and Gift Taxes

The 1916 estate tax was levied at rates ranging from 1 percent to 10 percent, with an exemption of $50,000. During World War I, the rates ranged from 2 percent to 25 percent. In 1926, the top rate was reduced to 20 percent, and the exemption was increased to $100,000.

One of the major developments during the 1920s was the enactment of a credit for state death taxes against the federal tax. Some of the states requested that the federal government abandon the death tax field entirely, but the credit was enacted instead. It was first limited to 25 percent of the federal tax in 1924 and was then raised to 80 percent in 1926. The same credit (based on the 1926 rates) exists today, even though the federal tax has been increased (Table A-8).

Substantial changes in rates and exemptions were made during the 1930s. The exemption was reduced to $50,000 in 1932 and to $40,000 in 1935, and then was raised to $60,000 in 1942, when a special $40,000 exclusion for life insurance (enacted in 1918) was repealed. The top rates were increased in several steps from 45 percent in 1932 to the present 77 percent in 1940 (Table A-9).

The gift tax was first levied for two years in 1924 and 1925, but was repealed on the ground that it was too complicated for the revenue it yielded. It was reenacted in 1932, when the estate tax rates were greatly increased, to limit avoidance of the estate and income taxes.

Gift tax rates have always been set at 75 percent of estate tax rates. A lifetime gift tax exemption of $50,000 was adopted in 1932, when the present gift tax was enacted. This exemption was reduced to $40,000 in 1935 and to $30,000 in 1942. In addition to the lifetime exemption, taxpayers were allowed an annual exclusion of $5,000 for each donee under the 1932 act. This exclusion was reduced to $4,000 in 1938 and to $3,000 in 1942. The lifetime gift tax exemption of $30,000 and the annual per donee exclusion of $3,000 are still in effect (Table A-10).

TABLE A-1. History of Federal Individual Income Tax Exemptions and First and Top Bracket Rates

| | Personal exemptions[a] | | | Tax rates[b] | | | |
| | | | | First bracket | | Top bracket | |
Income year	Single persons	Married couples	Depen- dents	Rate (percent- ages)	Income up to	Rate (percent- ages)	Income over
1913–15	$3,000	$4,000	—	1	$20,000	7	$ 500,000
1916	3,000	4,000	—	2	20,000	15	2,000,000
1917	1,000	2,000	$200	2	2,000	67	2,000,000
1918	1,000	2,000	200	6	4,000	77	1,000,000
1919–20	1,000	2,000	200	4	4,000	73	1,000,000
1921	1,000	2,500[c]	400	4	4,000	73	1,000,000
1922	1,000	2,500[c]	400	4	4,000	56	200,000
1923	1,000	2,500[c]	400	3	4,000	56	200,000
1924	1,000	2,500	400	1½[d]	4,000	46	500,000
1925–28	1,500	3,500	400	1⅛[d]	4,000	25	100,000
1929	1,500	3,500	400	⅜[d]	4,000	24	100,000
1930–31	1,500	3,500	400	1⅛[d]	4,000	25	100,000
1932–33	1,000	2,500	400	4	4,000	63	1,000,000
1934–35	1,000	2,500	400	4[e]	4,000	63	1,000,000
1936–39	1,000	2,500	400	4[e]	4,000	79	5,000,000
1940	800	2,000	400	4.4[e]	4,000	81.1	5,000,000
1941	750	1,500	400	10[e]	2,000	81	5,000,000
1942–43[f]	500	1,200	350	19[e]	2,000	88	200,000
1944–45[g]	500	1,000	500	23	2,000	94[h]	200,000
1946–47	500	1,000	500	19	2,000	86.45[h]	200,000
1948–49	600	1,200	600	16.6	2,000	82.13[h]	200,000
1950	600	1,200	600	17.4	2,000	91[h]	200,000
1951	600	1,200	600	20.4	2,000	91[h]	200,000
1952–53	600	1,200	600	22.2	2,000	92[h]	200,000
1954–63	600	1,200	600	20	2,000	91[h]	200,000
1964	600	1,200	600	16	500	77	200,000
1965–67	600	1,200	600	14	500	70	100,000
1968	600	1,200	600	14	500	75.25[i]	100,000
1969	600	1,200	600	14	500	77[i]	100,000
1970	625	1,250	625	14	500	71.75[i, j]	100,000
1971	650	1,300	650	14	500	70[j, k]	100,000
1972	700	1,400	700	14	500	70[j, k]	100,000
1973 and later	750	1,500	750	14	500	70[j, k]	100,000

Sources: Adapted from *The Federal Tax System: Facts and Problems, 1964*, Materials Assembled by the Committee Staff for the Joint Economic Committee, 88 Cong. 2 sess. (1964); and relevant public laws.

[a] Beginning in 1948, additional exemptions are allowed to taxpayers and their spouses on account of blindness and/or age over 65.

[b] Beginning in 1922, lower rates apply to long-term capital gains. See text, pp. 96–99.

[c] If net income exceeded $5,000, married person's exemption was $2,000.

[d] After earned income credit equal to 25 percent of tax on earned income.

[e] Before earned income credit allowed as a deduction equal to 10 percent of earned net income.

[f] Exclusive of Victory tax.

[g] Exemptions shown were for surtax only. Normal tax exemption was $500 per tax return plus earned income of wife up to $500 on joint returns.

[h] Subject to the following maximum effective rate limitations:

Year	Maximum effective rate	Year	Maximum effective rate
1944–45	90.0%	1951	87.2%
1946–47	85.5	1952–53	88.0
1948–49	77.0	1954–63	87.0
1950	87.0		

[i] Included surcharge of 7.5 percent in 1968, 10 percent in 1969, and 2.5 percent in 1970.

[j] Does not include 10 percent tax on tax preference items beginning in 1970.

[k] Earned income subject to maximum marginal rates of 60 percent in 1971 and 50 percent beginning in 1972.

TABLE A-2. Federal Individual Income Tax Rate Schedules under the Revenue Acts of 1944, 1945, 1948, 1950, 1951, 1964, 1968, and 1969

(In percentages)

Taxable income (in dollars)	1944 Act Calendar years 1944–45	1945 Act Calendar years 1946–47	1948 Act Calendar years 1948–49	1950 Act Calendar year 1950	Calendar year 1951	1951 Act Calendar years 1952–53	1951 Act Calendar years 1954–63
0 to 2,000	23	19.00	16.60	17.40	20.4	22.2	20
2,000 to 4,000	25	20.90	19.36	20.02	22.4	24.6	22
4,000 to 6,000	29	24.70	22.88	23.66	27.0	29.0	26
6,000 to 8,000	33	28.50	26.40	27.30	30.0	34.0	30
8,000 to 10,000	37	32.30	29.92	30.94	35.0	38.0	34
10,000 to 12,000	41	36.10	33.44	34.58	39.0	42.0	38
12,000 to 14,000	46	40.85	37.84	39.13	43.0	48.0	43
14,000 to 16,000	50	44.65	41.36	42.77	48.0	53.0	47
16,000 to 18,000	53	47.50	44.00	45.50	51.0	56.0	50
18,000 to 20,000	56	50.35	46.64	48.23	54.0	59.0	53
20,000 to 22,000	59	53.20	49.28	50.96	57.0	62.0	56
22,000 to 26,000	62	56.05	51.92	53.69	60.0	66.0	59
26,000 to 32,000	65	58.90	54.56	56.42	63.0	67.0	62
32,000 to 38,000	68	61.75	57.20	59.15	66.0	68.0	65
38,000 to 44,000	72	65.55	60.72	62.79	69.0	72.0	69
44,000 to 50,000	75	68.40	63.36	65.52	73.0	75.0	72
50,000 to 60,000	78	71.25	66.00	68.25	75.0	77.0	75
60,000 to 70,000	81	74.10	68.64	70.98	78.0	80.0	78
70,000 to 80,000	84	76.95	71.28	73.71	82.0	83.0	81
80,000 to 90,000	87	79.80	73.92	76.44	84.0	85.0	84
90,000 to 100,000	90	82.65	76.56	79.17	87.0	88.0	87
100,000 to 136,719.10 } 136,719.10 to 150,000 }	92	84.55	{ 78.32 { 80.3225	80.99 } 82.503 }	89.0	90.0	89
150,000 to 200,000	93	85.50	81.2250	83.43	90.0	91.0	90
200,000 and over[d]	94	86.45	82.1275	84.357	91.0	92.0	91

Sources: Same as Table A-1.

Note: Beginning in 1948, married couples are allowed to split their income for tax purposes. A separate rate schedule was adopted in 1955 for heads of households to give them approximately half the advantage of income splitting. Under the 1969 act a separate schedule for single persons who are not heads of households was provided to limit the tax paid by single persons to no more than 20 percent more than the tax paid by married couples with the same taxable income.

TABLE A-2. continued.

Taxable income (in dollars)	1964 Act Calendar year 1964	1964 Act Calendar years 1965–67	1968 Act Calendar year 1968[a]	1968 Act Calendar year 1969[a]	1969 Act Calendar year 1970[a,b]	1969 Act Calendar year 1971 and later years[b,c]
0 to 500	16.0	14	14	14	14	14
500 to 1,000	16.5	15	15	15	15	15
1,000 to 1,500	17.5	16	17.2	17.6	16.4	16
1,500 to 2,000	18.0	17	18.275	18.7	17.425	17
2,000 to 4,000	20.0	19	20.425	20.9	19.475	19
4,000 to 6,000	23.5	22	23.650	24.2	22.55	22
6,000 to 8,000	27.0	25	26.875	27.5	25.625	25
8,000 to 10,000	30.5	28	30.1	30.8	28.7	28
10,000 to 12,000	34.0	32	34.4	35.2	32.8	32
12,000 to 14,000	37.5	36	38.7	39.6	36.9	36
14,000 to 16,000	41.0	39	41.925	42.9	39.975	39
16,000 to 18,000	44.5	42	45.15	46.2	43.05	42
18,000 to 20,000	47.5	45	48.375	49.5	46.125	45
20,000 to 22,000	50.5	48	51.6	52.8	49.2	48
22,000 to 26,000	53.5	50	53.75	55.0	51.25	50
26,000 to 32,000	56.0	53	56.975	58.3	54.325	53
32,000 to 38,000	58.5	55	59.125	60.5	56.375	55
38,000 to 44,000	61.0	58	62.35	63.8	59.45	58
44,000 to 50,000	63.5	60	64.5	66.0	61.5	60
50,000 to 60,000	66.0	62	66.65	68.2	63.55	62
60,000 to 70,000	68.5	64	68.8	70.4	65.6	64
70,000 to 80,000	71.0	66	70.95	72.6	67.65	66
80,000 to 90,000	73.5	68	73.1	74.8	69.7	68
90,000 to 100,000	75.0	69	74.175	75.9	70.725	69
100,000 to 200,000	76.5	70	75.25	77.0	71.75	70
200,000 and over	77.0	70	75.25	77.0	71.75	70

[a] Includes surcharge of 7.5 percent in 1968, 10 percent in 1969, and 2.5 percent in 1970, beginning with the $1,000–$1,500 bracket. A partial surcharge exemption, based on a graduated scale, applied to this and the next higher bracket. Therefore the marginal rates in these brackets varied slightly from those shown here.

[b] A 10 percent minimum tax on certain tax preference items was imposed by the 1969 act for 1970 and later years.

[c] Earned income subject to maximum marginal rates of 60 percent in 1971 and 50 percent beginning in 1972.

[d] Subject to the following maximum effective rate limitations:

Year	Maximum effective rate	Year	Maximum effective rate
1944–45	90%	1951	87.2%
1946–47	85.5	1952–53	88
1948–49	77	1954–63	87
1950	87		

TABLE A-3. History of Federal Corporation Income Tax Exemptions and Rates

Year	Exemptions, brackets, or type of tax	Rate (percentages)
1909–13	$5,000 exemption	1
1913–15	None after March 1, 1913	1
1916	None	2
1917	None	6
1918	$2,000 exemption	12
1919–21	$2,000 exemption	10
1922–24	$2,000 exemption	12.5
1925	$2,000 exemption	13
1926–27	$2,000 exemption	13.5
1928	$3,000 exemption	12
1929	$3,000 exemption	11
1930–31	$3,000 exemption	12
1932–35	None	13.75
1936–37	Range of graduated normal tax	
	First $2,000	8
	Over $40,000	15
	Range of graduated surtax on undistributed profits	7–27
1938–39	First $25,000	12.5–16
	Over $25,000	19[a]
1940	First $25,000	14.85–18.7
	$25,000 to $31,964.30	38.3
	$31,964.30 to $38,565.89	36.9
	Over $38,565.89	24
1941	First $25,000	21–25
	$25,000 to $38,461.54	44
	Over $38,461.54	31
1942–45	First $25,000	25–29
	$25,000 to $50,000	53
	Over $50,000	40
1946–49	First $25,000	21–25
	$25,000 to $50,000	53
	Over $50,000	38
1950	Normal tax	23
	Surtax[b]	19
	Total	42
1951	Normal tax	28.75
	Surtax[b]	22
	Total	50.75
1952–63	Normal tax	30
	Surtax[b]	22
	Total	52

TABLE A-3. continued.

Year	Exemptions, brackets, or type of tax	Rate (percentages)
1964	Normal tax..	22
	Surtax[b]..	28
	Total..	50
1965–67	Normal tax..	22
	Surtax[b]..	26
	Total..	48
1968–69[c]	Normal tax..	24.2
	Surtax[b]..	28.6
	Total..	52.8
1970[a]	Normal tax..	22.55
	Surtax[b]..	26.65
	Total..	49.2
1971 and after	Normal tax..	22
	Surtax[b]..	26
	Total..	48

Sources: Same as Table A-1.
[a] Less adjustments: 14.025 percent of dividends received and 2.5 percent of dividends paid.
[b] The first $25,000 of corporate net income is exempt from the surtax.
[c] Includes surcharge of 10 percent in 1968 and 1969 and 2.5 percent in 1970.

TABLE A-4. Marginal Rates of the Federal Corporation Income Tax Since 1942

(In percentages)

Years	Under $5,000	$5,000–20,000	$20,000–25,000	$25,000–50,000	Over $50,000
1942–45	25	27	29	53	40
1946–49	21	23	25	53	38
1950		23		42	
1951		28.75		50.75	
1952–63		30		52	
1964		22		50	
1965–67		22		48	
1968–69[a]		24.2		52.8	
1970[a]		22.55		49.2	
1971 and later years		22		48	

Sources: Same as Table A-1.
[a] Includes surcharge of 10 percent in 1968 and 1969 and 2.5 percent in 1970.

TABLE A-5. Federal Excise Tax Rates on Selected Items as of December 31, Selected Years, 1913–70

(In dollars, except where percentages are indicated)

Tax	1913	1919	1928	1932	1944	1952	1954	1963	1970
Liquor taxes									
Distilled spirits (per proof or wine gallon)	1.10	2.20	1.10	1.10	9	10.50	10.50	10.50	10.50
Still wines (per wine gallon)									
Not over 14 percent alcohol	—	0.16	0.04	0.04	0.15	0.17	0.17	0.17	0.17
14 percent to 21 percent alcohol	—	0.40	0.10	0.10	0.60	0.67	0.67	0.67	0.67
21 percent to 24 percent alcohol	—	1	0.25	0.25	2	2.25	2.25	2.25	2.25
Beer (per barrel)	1	6	6	6	8	9	9	9	9
Tobacco taxes									
Cigars, large (per thousand)	3	4–15	2–13.50	2–13.50	2.50–20	2.50–20	2.50–20	2.50–20	2.50–20
Cigarettes (per thousand, 3 pounds or less)	1.25	3	3	3	3.50	4	4	4	4
Tobacco and snuff (per pound)	0.08	0.18	0.18	0.18	0.18	0.10	0.10	0.10	—
Documentary, etc., stamp taxes									
Conveyances (per $500, or fraction thereof, if value is over $100)	—	0.50	—	0.50	0.55	0.55	0.55	0.55	—
Bond and stock issues (per $100, respectively)	—	0.05	0.05	0.10	0.11	0.11	0.11	0.11, 0.10	—
Playing cards (per package of not more than 54)	0.02	0.08	0.10	0.10	0.13	0.13	0.13	0.13	—
Manufacturers' excise taxes									
Lubricating oils (per gallon)	—	—	—	0.04	0.06	0.06	0.06	0.06	0.06
Matches, white, phosphorous (per hundred)	0.02	0.02	0.02	0.02	0.02	0.02	0.02	0.02	0.02
Matches, in general (per thousand)	—	—	—	0.02	0.02	0.02	0.02	0.02	—
Gasoline (per gallon)	—	—	—	0.01	0.015	—	0.02	0.04	0.04
Electrical energy (percent of sale price)	—	—	—	3	$3\frac{1}{3}$	—	—	—	—
Tires (percent of sale price 1919, per pound 1932 and after)	—	5	—	0.0225	0.05	0.05	0.05	0.10	0.10
Inner tubes (percent of sale price 1919, per pound 1932 and after)	—	5	—	0.04	0.09	0.09	0.09	0.10	0.10
Tread rubber (per pound)	—	—	—	—	—	—	—	0.05	0.05
Trucks (percent of sale price)	—	3	—	2	5	8	8	10	10
Automobiles (percent of sale price)	—	5	—	3	7	10	10	10	7
Truck accessories (percent of sale price)	—	5	—	2	5	8	8	8	8
Automobile accessories (percent of sale price)	—	5	—	2	5	8	8	8	8
Radios and accessories (percent of sale price)	—	—	—	5	10	10	10	10	—

260

Refrigerators, mechanical, household (percent of sale price)	—	—	—	5	10	10	5	5	—
Firearms, shells, cartridges (percent of sale price)	—	10	10	10	11	11	11	11	11
Pistols and revolvers (percent of sale price)	—	10	10	10	11	11	10	10	10
Sporting goods other than fishing equipment (percent of sale price)	—	10	—	10	10	15	10	10	—
Fishing equipment (percent of sale price)	—	10	—	10	10	15	10	10	10
Musical instruments and phonographs (percent of sale price)	—	5	—	—	10	10	10	10	—
Records (percent of sale price)	—	5	—	5	10	10	10	10	—
Electric, gas, and oil appliances (percent of sale price)	—	—	—	—	10	10	5	5	—
Business and store machines (percent of sale price)	—	—	—	—	10	10	10	10	—
Cameras and photographic apparatus (percent of sale price)	—	10	—	10	25	20	10	10	—
Photographic film (percent of sale price)	—	5	—	—	15	20	10	10	—
Mixed flour (per barrel containing 99–196 pounds)	0.04	0.04	0.04	0.04	—	—	—	—	—
Automatic slot vending and vending weighing machines (percent of sale price, respectively)	—	5, 10; 5	—	—	—	—	—	—	—
Candy (percent of sale price)	—	—	—	2	—	—	—	—	—
Retailers' excise taxes									
Jewelry (percent of sale price)	—	5	—	10[a]	20	20	10	10	—
Furs (percent of sale price)	—	10[a]	—	10[a]	20	20	10	10	—
Toilet preparations (per 25¢ or fraction, 1919; percent of sale price thereafter)	—	0.01; 10	—	10[a]	20	20	10	10	—
Luggage (percent of sale price)	—	10	—	—	20	20	10	10	—
Gasoline used in noncommercial aviation (per gallon)	—	—	—	—	—	—	—	—	0.03
Fuels other than gasoline used in noncommercial aviation (per gallon)	—	—	—	—	—	—	—	—	0.07
Diesel (beginning 1951) and special motor fuels for highway vehicles (per gallon)	—	—	0.01[a]	0.015[a]	0.02[a]	0.02[a]	0.02	0.04	0.04
Miscellaneous excise taxes									
General telephone service (percent of amount paid)	—	—	—	—	15	15	10	10	10

TABLE A-5. continued.

Tax	1913	1919	1928	1932	1944	1952	1954	1963	1970
Miscellaneous excise taxes (continued)									
Toll telephone service (percent of amount paid; prior to 1944, per message)	—	0.05–0.10	—	0.10–0.20	25	25	10	10	10
Cable and radio messages, domestic (percent of amount paid; prior to 1944, per message)	—	0.10	—	0.10	25	15	10	10	—
Telegraph messages, domestic (percent of amount paid; 1919, per message)	—	0.10	—	5	25	15	10	10	—
Leased wires, or teletypewriter and wire mileage service (percent of amount paid)	—	10	—	5	25	25	10	10	10[b]
Wire and equipment service (percent of amount paid)	—	—	—	—	8	8	8	8	—
Transportation of oil by pipeline (percent of amount paid)	—	8	—	4	4.5	4.5	4.5	—	—
Bowling alleys, pool tables (per unit, per year)	—	10	—	—	20	20	20	20	—
Transportation of persons other than by air (percent of amount paid)	—	8	—	—	15	15	10	—	—
Transportation of persons, air (percent of amount paid)	—	—	—	—	15	15	10	5	8
International flight (per person)	—	—	—	—	—	—	—	—	3
Transportation of property (percent of amount paid)	—	3	—	—	3	3	3	—	5
Airfreight (percent of amount paid)	—	—	—	—	—	—	—	—	5
Aircraft registration (annually, per civil aircraft)	—	—	—	—	—	—	—	—	25
Aircraft poundage fees, takeoff weight above 2,500 pounds									
Propeller-driven aircraft (per pound)	—	—	—	—	—	—	—	—	0.02
Turbine-powered aircraft (per pound)	—	—	—	—	—	—	—	—	0.035
Use tax on highway vehicles weighing over 26,000 pounds (per 1,000 lbs. per year)	—	—	—	—	—	—	—	3	3
Lease of safe deposit boxes (percent of amount collected)	—	—	—	10	20	20	10	10	—
Admissions (for every 10¢ or fraction, 1919–43, 1954–63; 5¢ or major fraction, 1944–53)[c]	—	0.01	0.01	0.01	0.01	0.01	0.01	0.01	—
Leases of boxes or seats (percent of amount for which similar accommodations are sold)	—	10	10	10	20	20	10	10	—

Cabarets, roof gardens, etc. (for every 10¢ [or fraction] of 20 percent of total charge, 1919–40; percent of amount paid, 1941–63)	—	—	0.015	0.015	0.015	20	20	20
Wagers (percent of amount of wager)	—	—	—	—	—	10	10	10
Occupation of accepting wagers (per year)	—	—	—	—	—	50	50	50
Dues and initiation fees (percent of amount paid)	—	10	10	10	10	10	10	10
Domestic oleomargarine (per pound)								
Uncolored	0.0025	0.0025	0.0025	0.0025	0.0025	0.0025	—	—
Colored	0.10	0.10	0.10	0.10	0.10	0.10	—	—
Butter (per pound)								
Processed	0.0025	0.0025	0.0025	0.0025	0.0025	0.0025	0.0025	0.0025
Adulterated	0.10	0.10	0.10	0.10	0.10	0.10	0.10	0.10
Filled cheese (per pound)								
Domestic	0.01	0.01	0.01	0.01	0.01	0.01	0.01	0.01
Imported	0.08	0.08	0.08	0.08	0.08	0.08	0.08	0.08
Use of boats (per foot, according to size, 1919; per boat, according to size or type, 1932; length, 1944)	1–4	10–200	10–200	10–200	5–200	—	—	—
Coin-operated devices (per unit, per year)								
Amusement	—	—	—	10	10	10	10	10
Gambling	—	—	—	100	250	250	250	250
Narcotics								
Opium sold (per ounce)	0.01	0.01	0.01	0.01	0.01	0.01	0.01	0.01
Opium for smoking (per pound)	300	300	300	300	300	300	300	300
Importers of opium (per year)	24	24	24	24	24	24	24	24
Marihuana (per ounce)[d]	—	—	1	1	1	1	1	1
Marihuana, authorized users (per year)	—	—	24	24	24	24	24	24
Interest equalization tax								
Stock (percent of actual value)	—	—	—	—	—	15	15	11.25
Bonds and loans with maturity of 1 year or longer (percent of actual value according to period remaining to maturity)	—	—	—	—	—	—	2.75–15[e]	0.79–11.25

Sources: 1913–63: Tax Foundation, *Federal Non-Income Taxes, an Examination of Selected Revenue Sources* (New York, 1965), pp. 23–26, supplemented by data from U.S. Treasury Department, *Annual Report of the Secretary of the Treasury,* 1940, pp. 484–511; 1950, pp. 260–67; and 1962, pp. 380–88, and relevant public laws; 1960: relevant public laws enacted, 1963–70.

a Tax levied at manufacturers' level.

b Tax levied on teletypewriter service only.

c Admission charges below specified amounts, which changed over the years, were usually exempt from the tax.

d This tax applies to persons who have already paid the required taxes on importers, users, or producers of marihuana. A tax of $100 per ounce applies to other persons selling marihuana.

e Applied to loans after Feb. 10, 1965.

TABLE A-6. History of Social Security and Railroad Retirement Tax Rates

Year	Maximum taxable wages[a] (dollars)	Tax rate (percentages) Employer	Employee	Self-employed
	Old-Age, Survivors, Disability, and Health Insurance			
1937–49	3,000	1.0	1.0	b
1950	3,000	1.5	1.5	b
1951–53	3,600	1.5	1.5	2.25
1954	3,600	2.0	2.0	3.0
1955–56	4,200	2.0	2.0	3.0
1957–58	4,200	2.25	2.25	3.375
1959	4,800	2.5	2.5	3.75
1960–61	4,800	3.0	3.0	4.5
1962	4,800	3.125	3.125	4.7
1963–65	4,800	3.625	3.625	5.4
1966	6,600	4.2	4.2	6.15
1967	6,600	4.4	4.4	6.4
1968	7,800	4.4	4.4	6.4
1969–70	7,800	4.8	4.8	6.9
1971–72	7,800	5.2	5.2	7.5
1973–75	7,800	5.65	5.65	7.65
1976–79	7,800	5.7	5.7	7.7
1980–86	7,800	5.8	5.8	7.8
1987 and after	7,800	5.9	5.9	7.9
	Railroad Retirement, Survivors, Disability, and Health Insurance			
1937–39	300	2.75	2.75	—
1940–42	300	3.00	3.00	—
1943–45	300	3.25	3.25	—
1946	300	3.50	3.50	—
1947–48	300	5.75	5.75	—
1949–51	300	6.00	6.00	—
1952–June 30, 1954	300	6.25	6.25	—
July 1, 1954–May 31, 1959	350	6.25	6.25	—
June 1, 1959–1961	400	6.75	6.75	—
1962–Oct. 31, 1963	400	7.25	7.25	—
Nov. 1, 1963–1964	450	7.25	7.25	—
1965–Sept. 30, 1965	450	8.125	8.125	—
Oct. 1, 1965–Dec. 31, 1965	450	7.125	7.125	—
1966	550	7.95	7.95	—
1967	550	8.65	8.65	—
1968	650	8.90	8.90	—
1969–70	650	9.55	9.55	—
1971–72	650	9.95	9.95	—
1973–75	650	10.40	10.40	—
1976–79	650	10.45	10.45	—
1980–86	650	10.55	10.55	—
1987 and after	650	10.65	10.65	—

Sources: OASDHI: Robert J. Myers, "Old-Age, Survivors, Disability, and Health Insurance Provisions: Legislative History, 1935–67" (leaflet, U.S. Department of Health, Education, and Welfare, Social Security Administration, January 1968). RRSDHI: 1937–65, Marice C. Hart, "Railroad Retirement Act as Amended in 1965," Social Security Bulletin, Vol. 29 (February 1966), pp. 27–28; 1966 and after, Railroad Retirement Board.

a Maximum taxable wage is in dollars per year for OASDHI and in dollars per month for RRSDHI.

b Not covered by the program until Jan. 1, 1951.

TABLE A-7. History of Unemployment Insurance Tax Rates

Year	Covered wages[a] (dollars)	Statutory range of rates[b] (percentages)	Actual rate paid[c] (percentages)
Federal Unemployment Insurance[d]			
1936	All wages	—	1.0
1937	" "	—	2.0
1938	" "	—	3.0
1939–60	3,000	—	3.0
1961	3,000	—	3.1
1962	3,000	—	3.5
1963	3,000	—	3.35
1964–69	3,000	—	3.1
1970–71	3,000	—	3.2
1972 and after	4,200	—	3.2
Railroad Unemployment Insurance			
July 1, 1939–47	300	3.0	3.0
1948–June 30, 1954	300	0.5–3.0	0.5
July 1, 1954–Dec. 31, 1955	350	0.5–3.0	0.5
1956	350	0.5–3.0	1.5
1957	350	0.5–3.0	2.0
1958	350	0.5–3.0	2.5
Jan. 1, 1959–May 31, 1959	350	0.5–3.0	3.0
June 1, 1959–Dec. 31, 1961	400	1.5–3.75	3.75
1962 and after	400	1.5–4.0	4.0

Sources: Same as Table A-1, supplemented with data from *Annual Report of the Secretary of the Treasury on the State of the Finances for the Fiscal Year Ended June 30, 1940*, pp. 522–23; *1950*, pp. 270–71; and *1962*, pp. 392–93, and from the Railroad Retirement Board and the U.S. Treasury Department.

[a] Covered wages are in dollars per year for federal unemployment insurance and dollars per month for railroad unemployment insurance.

[b] For federal unemployment insurance, employers are taxed by the states on the basis of an experience rating determined by past unemployment records. All employers are permitted to take the maximum credit allowed against the federal unemployment tax, even though they may, in fact, pay a lower rate because of a good experience rating. In 1969, the effective tax rate on covered wages ranged from 0.4 percent in Texas and Illinois to 2.9 percent in Alaska. *Unemployment Compensation*, Hearings before the House Committee on Ways and Means, 91 Cong. 1 sess. (1969), p. 183.

For railroad unemployment insurance, the rate paid each year is determined by a sliding scale and is fixed annually in accordance with the balance in the railroad unemployment insurance account on September 30 of the preceding year.

[c] For federal unemployment insurance, credit up to 90 percent of the tax is allowed for contributions paid into a state unemployment fund. Beginning in 1961, credits up to 90 percent are computed as if the tax rate were 3 percent.

[d] Applicable to employers of 8 persons or more between 1936 and 1956, to employers of 4 persons or more from 1956 through 1971, and to employers of one person or more in 1972 and later years.

TABLE A-8. Federal Estate Tax Rates and Rates of the State Tax Credit, 1942 to Date (1970)

Rates before credit for state taxes		Rates for computing state tax credit	
Taxable estate (dollars)	Rate (percentages)	Taxable estate (dollars)	Rate (percentages)
0– 5,000	3	0– 40,000	0
5,000– 10,000	7	40,000– 90,000	0.8
10,000– 20,000	11	90,000– 140,000	1.6
20,000– 30,000	14	140,000– 240,000	2.4
30,000– 40,000	18	240,000– 440,000	3.2
40,000– 50,000	22	440,000– 640,000	4.0
50,000– 60,000	25	640,000– 840,000	4.8
60,000– 100,000	28	840,000– 1,040,000	5.6
100,000– 250,000	30	1,040,000– 1,540,000	6.4
250,000– 500,000	32	1,540,000– 2,040,000	7.2
500,000– 750,000	35	2,040,000– 2,540,000	8.0
750,000– 1,000,000	37	2,540,000– 3,040,000	8.8
1,000,000– 1,250,000	39	3,040,000– 3,540,000	9.6
1,250,000– 1,500,000	42	3,540,000– 4,040,000	10.4
1,500,000– 2,000,000	45	4,040,000– 5,040,000	11.2
2,000,000– 2,500,000	49	5,040,000– 6,040,000	12.0
2,500,000– 3,000,000	53	6,040,000– 7,040,000	12.8
3,000,000– 3,500,000	56	7,040,000– 8,040,000	13.6
3,500,000– 4,000,000	59	8,040,000– 9,040,000	14.4
4,000,000– 5,000,000	63	9,040,000–10,040,000	15.2
5,000,000– 6,000,000	67	10,040,000 and over	16.0
6,000,000– 7,000,000	70		
7,000,000– 8,000,000	73		
8,000,000–10,000,000	76		
10,000,000 and over	77		

Source: Revenue Act of 1941.

TABLE A-9. History of Estate and Gift Tax Rates

Revenue Act	Date of death	Tax rates (percentages) Estates	Tax rates (percentages) Gifts	Minimum rate (thousands of dollars)	Maximum rate (thousands of dollars)
				Bracket subject to:	
1916	Sept. 9, 1916, to Mar. 2, 1917	1.0–10.0	—	0–50	5,000 and over
1917[a]	Mar. 3, 1917, to Oct. 3, 1917	1.5–15.0	—	0–50	5,000 and over
1917[b]	Oct. 4, 1917, to Feb. 23, 1919	2.0–25.0	—	0–50	10,000 and over
1918	Feb. 24, 1919, to Feb. 25, 1926	1.0–25.0	1.0–25.0[c]	0–50	10,000 and over
1926	Feb. 26, 1926, to June 5, 1932	1.0–20.0	—	0–50	10,000 and over
1932	June 6, 1932, to May 10, 1934	1.0–45.0	0.75–33.5	0–10	10,000 and over
1934	May 11, 1934, to July 29, 1935	1.0–60.0	0.75–45.0	0–10	10,000 and over
1935	July 30, 1935, to June 24, 1940	2.0–70.0	1.55–52.5	0–10	50,000 and over
1940	June 25, 1940, to Sept. 19, 1941	2.2–77.0[d]	1.65–57.75[d]	0–10	50,000 and over
1941	Sept. 20, 1941, to date	3.0–77.0	2.25–57.75	0– 5	10,000 and over

Source: Same as Table A-1.
[a] Revenue Act of 1917.
[b] War Revenue Act of 1917.
[c] In effect June 2, 1924, to Dec. 31, 1925.
[d] Includes defense tax equal to 10 percent of tax liability.

TABLE A-10. History of Estate and Gift Tax Exemptions and Exclusions
(In dollars)

Revenue Act	Estate tax Specific exemption[a]	Estate tax Insurance exclusion	Gift tax Specific exemption[b]	Gift tax Annual exclusion per donee
1916	50,000	—	c	c
1918	50,000	40,000	c	c
1924	50,000	40,000	50,000	500
1926	100,000	40,000	c	c
1932	50,000	40,000	50,000	5,000
1935	40,000	40,000	40,000	5,000
1938	40,000	40,000	40,000	4,000
1942	60,000	—	30,000	3,000

Source: Same as Table A-1.
[a] Specific exemption granted to estates of nonresident citizens dying after May 11, 1934, on the same basis as resident decedents. No exemptions granted to estates of resident aliens until Oct. 21, 1942, when a $2,000 exemption was made available.
[b] Under the Revenue Act of 1924, exemption allowed each calendar year. Under the 1932 and later acts, specific exemption allowed only once.
[c] No gift tax.

Tax Bases of the Major Federal Taxes

THE CONCEPTS OF TAXABLE INCOME for both the individual and the corporation income taxes as defined by the Internal Revenue Code differ substantially from the national income aggregates, which are widely used for purposes of economic analysis. This appendix derives the tax bases of the two income taxes and compares them with the official estimates of personal income and corporate profits incorporated in the national income accounts. It also presents the latest distributions by rate brackets of the tax bases of the income and estate and gift taxes.

The Individual Income Tax

Among the various tax concepts, *adjusted gross income* most nearly resembles personal income. Total personal income exceeds the aggregate of adjusted gross incomes reported on tax returns by substantial amounts each year. However, a large portion of the disparity can be explained by differences in definition. The individual income tax base is derived below in two steps: (1) aggregate adjusted gross income of all persons in the United States is estimated from personal income; (2) personal exemptions and deductions are subtracted from adjusted gross income to obtain taxable income.

Relation between Personal Income and Adjusted Gross Income

Table B-1 summarizes the conceptual differences between personal income and adjusted gross income for calendar year 1968, the latest year for which income tax statistics are available. The differences are: (a) items of income that are included in personal income but not in adjusted gross income (for example, transfer payments, practically all incomes in kind, tax-exempt interest), amounting to $137.7 billion; and (b) incomes that are included in adjusted gross income but not in personal income (primarily the social security taxes paid by employees and capital gains), amounting to $48.7 billion. When these differences are taken into account, the 1968 personal income of $688.7 billion corresponded to an adjusted gross income of $599.7 billion.

The relationship between personal income and adjusted gross income has been fairly stable in recent years. Since World War II, when a substantial portion of personal income was received by members of the armed forces in the form of nontaxable pay and allowances, the difference between personal income and adjusted gross income has been on the order of 11 to 14 percent of personal income (Table B-2). Since 1964, the difference has been about 13 percent of personal income.

If all income recipients were required to file returns and everybody reported his income accurately, the total adjusted gross income on tax returns would correspond closely to the amounts shown in Table B-2. Since neither of these conditions holds, adjusted gross incomes reported on tax returns are lower than the aggregate for all recipients. As Table B-3 indicates, this gap has been declining as a percentage of total adjusted gross income; by 1968, the figure was down to 7.6 percent. The decline was very sharp during World War II years, when exemptions and filing requirements were lowered drastically, but it has continued—although at a much slower rate and with some interruptions—throughout the 1950s and 1960s as the rise in incomes pushed more and more people above the filing requirement levels.

In 1968, the gross difference between personal income and adjusted gross income reported on tax returns was $134.3 billion (see Tables B-2 and B-3). About 66 percent of this difference—or $89.0 billion—is explained by conceptual differences, and only $45.3 billion did not appear on tax returns. But this $45.3 billion cannot be regarded as a measure of underreporting. Included in this figure is the income received by persons with incomes below $600 annually, who were not required to file returns, the exact amount of which is unknown. Moreover, a large number of nontaxable individuals in such low paid occupations as domestic service and farming do not bother to file even though the law requires them to do so. Considering the large magnitudes involved, the portion of the gap between personal income and adjusted gross income that remains unexplained is relatively small. Even if as much as two-thirds of the $45.3 billion was due to underreporting, the degree of underreporting was only about 5 percent.

The Individual Income Tax Base

The steps in the derivation of the individual tax base for the years 1947 through 1968 are shown in Table B-4. In 1968, as was previously indicated, adjusted gross incomes totaled $599.7 billion, and of this amount $554.4 billion was reported on individual income tax returns. Nontaxable individuals reported $16.1 billion, while those who were taxable reported $538.3 billion. The personal exemptions of taxable individuals amounted to $102.7 billion, and their deductions amounted to $83.7 billion. Subtracting these two items from adjusted gross income leaves a taxable income of $351.9 billion. To this must be added the small amount of taxable income— about $800 million—of individuals whose tax liabilities were wiped out by the retirement income and other credits. Thus, the tax base amounted to $352.7 billion in 1968.

Table B-5 compares the tax base with personal income since the beginning of World War II. From 9.9 percent of personal income in 1939, taxable income rose to 39.7 percent in 1953 and reached 51.2 percent in 1968.

Distribution of Taxable Individual Income

An estimated distribution of taxable income by rate brackets is shown in Table B-6 for calendar year 1967. Only a small proportion of taxable income is subject to the very high rates. Of the total taxable income of $302.7 billion, $153.9 billion, or 51 percent, was subject to the first four bracket rates of 14–17 percent.

The Corporation Income Tax

Table B-7 gives a detailed reconciliation for calendar year 1967 among three concepts of corporate profits: (1) *profits before taxes* as defined in the national income accounts; (2) *net profits* of all corporations as tabulated from federal corporate income tax returns; and (3) *taxable income* of corporations.

Relation between Profits before Tax and Taxable Income

The major differences between the national income definition of profits before tax and net profits reported on tax returns are accounted for by differences in coverage and in definition of income. For example, profits before taxes include the income of government financial institutions and adjustments of the profits of insurance carriers and mutual financial intermediaries for national income purposes; on the other hand, they exclude dividends received from corporations and net capital gains, include estimated profits resulting from audit, and do not allow for the deductions for depletion, state corporation income taxes, and adjustment for bad debts. In 1967, corporate profits under the national income definition were $79.8 billion, while net profits reported on tax returns amounted to $79.3 billion.

As is shown in Table B-7, differences in coverage amounted to $1.1 billion, while differences resulting from different definitions of income amounted to −$1.7 billion.

To arrive at taxable income, the losses of deficit corporations must be added back to reported net profits, and the nontaxable components of reported net profits must be eliminated. After these and other minor adjustments, corporate taxable income in 1967 was $74.8 billion, or $4.5 billion lower than reported net profits.

A comparison of the three income concepts for the years 1958–67 is given in Table B-8.

Distribution of Taxable Corporate Income

Unlike the individual income tax, most of the corporation income tax base is concentrated in the top rate bracket. This reflects the great importance of large corporations in the corporate sector. For calendar year 1966, taxable corporate income amounted to $77.1 billion, of which $3.1 billion was subject to the alternative tax of 25 percent on long-term capital gains, leaving $74.0 billion subject to the normal tax and surtax rates. Only $3.8 billion, or 5 percent, of the latter amount was subject to the 22 percent rate, and the remaining $70.2 billion, or 95 percent, was subject to the 48 percent rate (Table B-9).

Estate and Gift Taxes

In 1966, 67,404 taxable estate tax returns and 29,547 taxable gift tax returns were filed. The total amount of wealth subject to tax amounted to $10.6 billion—$9.14 billion under the estate tax, and $1.46 billion under the gift tax.

The decedents represented on the 1966 taxable estate tax returns were 3.9 percent of all adult decedents in that year (Table B-10). These returns showed gross estates of $19.2 billion; debts and mortgages amounted to $1.25 billion, leaving *economic* estates of $18.0 billion. The $9.1 billion of taxable estates thus accounted for about half of the wealth left by decedents subject to estate tax (Table B-11). Most of the tax base is concentrated in the lower rate brackets. In 1963, 40 percent was subject to rates below 30 percent; 53 percent was subject to rates between 30 percent and 50 percent; and only 7 percent was subject to rates of 50 percent or more (Table B-12).

Total gifts on taxable returns in 1966 amounted to $2.4 billion. After allowing for deductions and exclusions, only $1.5 billion—or 61 percent—was taxable (Table B-13). About 80 percent of the 1963 gift tax base was subject to rates below 30 percent; 15 percent was subject to rates of 30 to 50 percent; and 5 percent was subject to rates of 50 percent or more (Table B-14).

TABLE B-1. Derivation of Adjusted Gross Income from Personal Income, 1968

(In billions of dollars)

Income and adjustment items		Amount
1. Personal income		688.7
2. Portion of personal income not included in adjusted gross income	137.7	
a. Transfer payments (except military retirement pay)	57.0	
b. Other labor income (except fees and military reservists' pay)	23.2	
c. Imputed income	37.1	
d. Other income received by nonindividuals	5.4	
(1) Property income retained by fiduciaries	3.8	
(2) Property income received by nonprofit institutions	1.6	
e. Differences in accounting treatment	4.2	
(1) Gain on sale of livestock, timber, and real estate	1.2	
(2) Accrued interest on U.S. government bonds	0.7	
(3) Noncorporate nonfarm inventory valuation adjustment	−0.7	
(4) Depletion and oil well drilling adjustment	0.7	
(5) Bad debt adjustment	0.3	
(6) Change in farm inventories (in excess of tax return data)	0.1	
(7) Excess of residential and farm tax depreciation over Office of Business Economics depreciation	1.9	
f. Other excluded or exempt income	10.8	
(1) Excluded business expenses	5.3	
(2) Excluded sick pay	ᵃ	
(3) Excluded moving expenses	ᵃ	
(4) Excluded contributions to retirement plans by self-employed	ᵃ	
(5) Excluded dividends	1.1	
(6) Tax-exempt military pay and allowances	3.3	
(7) Tax-exempt interest income	0.9	
(8) Tax-exempt dividend distributions	0.2	
3. Portion of adjusted gross income not included in personal income	48.7	
a. Personal contributions for social insurance	22.8	
b. Net gain from sale of capital assets	17.8	
c. Annuities and pensions reported on tax returns	6.0	
d. "Other income" from Form 1040A	2.1	
4. Total adjustment for conceptual differences (line 2 minus line 3)		89.0
5. Estimated adjusted gross income of taxable and nontaxable individuals (line 1 minus line 4)		599.7

Source: Worksheets of U.S. Department of Commerce, Office of Business Economics.
ᵃ Less than $0.05 billion.

272

TABLE B-2. Comparison of Personal Income and Total Adjusted Gross Income, 1947–68

(Dollar amounts in billions)

Year	Personal income	Total adjusted gross income	Difference Amount	Difference Percentage of personal income
1947	$191.3	$171.8	$19.5	10.2
1948	210.2	185.2	25.0	11.9
1949	207.2	183.2	24.0	11.6
1950	227.6	201.5	26.1	11.5
1951	255.6	227.8	27.8	10.9
1952	272.5	240.9	31.6	11.6
1953	288.2	255.0	33.2	11.5
1954	290.1	252.9	37.2	12.8
1955	310.9	273.4	37.5	12.1
1956	333.0	293.9	39.1	11.7
1957	351.1	306.5	44.6	12.7
1958	361.2	310.9	50.3	13.9
1959	383.5	333.3	50.2	13.1
1960	401.0	346.0	55.0	13.7
1961	416.8	359.3	57.5	13.8
1962	442.6	380.1	62.5	14.1
1963	465.5	400.2	65.3	14.0
1964	497.5	431.5	66.0	13.3
1965	538.9	467.0	71.9	13.3
1966	587.2	511.2	76.0	12.9
1967	629.3	545.5	83.8	13.3
1968	688.7	599.7	89.0	12.9

Sources: 1947–66, *Survey of Current Business*, Vol. 50 (May 1970), p. 21; 1967–68, Worksheets of the U.S. Department of Commerce, Office of Business Economics.

273

TABLE B-3. Comparison of Total Adjusted Gross Income and Adjusted Gross Income Reported on Tax Returns, 1947–68

(Dollar amounts in billions)

Year	Adjusted gross income		Difference	
	Total U.S.	Reported on tax returns	Amount	Percentage of total U.S.
1947	$171.8	$149.7	$22.1	12.9
1948	185.2	163.6	21.6	11.7
1949	183.2	160.6	22.6	12.3
1950	201.5	179.1	22.4	11.1
1951	227.8	202.4	25.4	11.2
1952	240.9	215.3	25.6	10.6
1953	255.0	228.7	26.3	10.3
1954	252.9	229.2	23.7	9.4
1955	273.4	248.5	24.9	9.1
1956	293.9	267.8	26.1	8.9
1957	306.5	280.4	26.1	8.5
1958	310.9	281.2	29.7	9.6
1959	333.3	305.1	28.2	8.5
1960	346.0	315.5	30.5	8.8
1961	359.3	329.9	29.4	8.2
1962	380.1	348.7	31.4	8.3
1963	400.2	368.8	31.4	7.8
1964	431.5	396.7	34.8	8.1
1965	467.0	429.2	37.8	8.1
1966	511.2	468.5	42.7	8.4
1967	545.5	504.8	40.7	7.5
1968	599.7	554.4	45.3	7.6

Sources: Total adjusted gross income: Table B-2; adjusted gross income reported on tax returns: *Survey of Current Business*, Vol. 50 (May 1970), p. 21.

(In billions of dollars)

Year	Total adjusted gross income	Deduct: nonreported adjusted gross income	Equals: adjusted gross income reported on individual returns	Deduct: adjusted gross income reported on nontaxable returns	Equals: adjusted gross income reported on taxable returns	Deduct: exemptions on taxable returns	Deduct: deductions on taxable returns	Equals: taxable income on taxable returns	Add: taxable income on nontaxable returns[b]	Equals: total taxable income of individuals
1947	171.8	22.1	149.7	14.4	135.3	44.3	15.6	75.4	—	75.4
1948	185.2	21.6	163.6	21.5	142.1	50.9	16.4	74.8	—	74.8
1949	183.2	22.6	160.6	22.0	138.6	50.1	16.8	71.7	—	71.7
1950	201.5	22.4	179.1	20.6	158.5	55.2	19.0	84.3	—	84.3
1951	227.8	25.4	202.4	19.2	183.2	61.4	22.6	99.2	—	99.2
1952	240.9	25.6	215.3	18.7	196.6	64.5	24.9	107.2	—	107.2
1953	255.0	26.3	228.7	18.2	210.5	68.9	27.3	114.3	—	114.3
1954	252.9	23.7	229.2	19.5	209.7	67.0	27.5	115.2	0.1	115.3
1955	273.4	24.9	248.5	18.9	229.6	71.2	30.5	127.9	0.1	128.0
1956	293.9	26.1	267.8	18.2	249.6	74.6	33.6	141.4	0.1	141.5
1957	306.5	26.1	280.4	18.2	262.2	76.8	36.2	149.2	0.2	149.4
1958	310.9	29.7	281.2	19.0	262.2	75.8	37.2	149.2	0.2	149.3
1959	333.3	28.2	305.1	17.3	287.8	79.7	41.7	166.4	0.2	166.5
1960	346.0	30.5	315.5	18.3	297.2	81.2	44.5	171.5	0.2	171.6
1961	359.3	29.4	329.9	18.6	311.3	82.5	47.2	181.6	0.1	181.8
1962	380.1	31.4	348.7	18.1	330.6	85.1	50.5	195.0	0.4	195.3
1963	400.2	31.4	368.8	18.4	350.4	87.4	54.5	208.6	0.5	209.1
1964	431.5	34.8	396.7	20.7	376.0	88.3	58.4	229.3	0.6	229.9
1965	467.0	37.8	429.2	19.9	409.3	91.9	63.1	254.3	0.7	255.1
1966	511.2	42.7	468.5	18.3	450.2	96.2	68.4	285.5	0.8	286.3
1967	545.5	40.7	504.8	17.4	487.4	99.1	74.0	314.3	0.8	315.1
1968	599.7	45.3	554.4	16.1	538.3	102.7	83.7	351.9	0.8	352.7

Sources: Taxable income on nontaxable returns and total taxable income: Statistics of Income, Individual Income Tax Returns. Other data: Same as Table B-2. Figures are rounded and do not necessarily add to totals.
[a] Excludes taxable income of fiduciaries.
[b] Taxable income of persons whose tax liability was completely offset by tax credits.

275

TABLE B-5. Comparison of Personal Income, Taxable Income, and Individual Income Tax, 1939–68

(Dollar amounts in billions)

Year	Personal income	Taxable income Amount	Taxable income Percentage of personal income	Individual income tax Amount	Individual income tax Percentage of Personal income	Individual income tax Percentage of Taxable income
1939	$ 72.8	$ 7.2	9.9	n.a.	—	—
1940	78.3	10.7	13.7	n.a.	—	—
1941	96.0	22.7	23.6	n.a.	—	—
1942	122.9	36.1	29.4	n.a.	—	—
1943	151.3	50.1	33.1	n.a.	—	—
1944	165.3	55.3	33.5	16.2	9.8	29.3
1945	171.1	57.1	33.4	17.1	10.0	29.9
1946	178.7	65.3	36.5	16.1	9.0	24.7
1947	191.3	75.4	39.4	18.1	9.5	24.0
1948	210.2	74.8	35.6	15.4	7.3	20.6
1949	207.2	71.7	34.6	14.5	7.0	20.2
1950	227.6	84.3	37.0	18.4	8.1	21.8
1951	255.6	99.2	38.8	24.2	9.5	24.4
1952	272.5	107.2	39.3	27.8	10.2	25.9
1953	288.2	114.3	39.7	29.4	10.2	25.7
1954	290.1	115.3	39.7	26.7	9.2	23.2
1955	310.9	128.0	41.2	29.6	9.5	23.1
1956	333.0	141.5	42.5	32.7	9.8	23.1
1957	351.1	149.4	42.6	34.4	9.8	23.0
1958	361.2	149.3	41.3	34.3	9.5	23.0
1959	383.5	166.5	43.4	38.6	10.1	23.2
1960	401.0	171.6	42.8	39.5	9.9	23.0
1961	416.8	181.8	43.6	42.2	10.1	23.2
1962	442.6	195.3	44.1	44.9	10.1	23.0
1963	465.5	209.1	44.9	48.2	10.4	23.1
1964	497.5	229.9	46.2	47.2	9.5	20.5
1965	538.9	255.1	47.3	49.5	9.2	19.4
1966	587.2	286.3	48.8	56.1	9.6	19.6
1967	629.3	315.1	50.1	62.9	10.0	20.0
1968	688.7	352.7	51.2	76.6	11.1	21.7

Sources: Personal income: *Survey of Current Business*, Vol. 50 (July 1970), p. 50. Taxable income: 1939–45, author's estimates; 1946, worksheets of the U.S. Department of Commerce, Office of Business Economics; 1947–68, Table B-4. Income tax: *Statistics of Income, Individual Income Tax Returns*.
n.a. Not available.

TABLE B-6. Distribution of Taxable Income and Individual Income Tax, by Rate Brackets, 1967

(Dollar amounts in millions)

Rate (percentages)	Amounts		Percentage distribution	
	Taxable income	Tax	Taxable income	Tax
14	$46,193	$6,467	15.26	10.78
15	40,098	6,015	13.25	10.02
16	36,959	5,913	12.21	9.85
17	30,628	5,207	10.12	8.68
18	1,928	347	0.64	0.58
19	75,354	14,317	24.90	23.86
20	872	174	0.29	0.29
22	29,399	6,468	9.71	10.78
25	12,077	3,019	3.99	5.03
27	118	32	0.04	0.05
28	6,189	1,733	2.04	2.89
31	79	24	0.03	0.04
32	3,978	1,273	1.31	2.12
35	41	14	0.01	0.02
36	2,784	1,002	0.92	1.67
39	2,037	794	0.67	1.32
40	26	10	0.01	0.02
41	22	9	0.01	0.01
42	1,566	658	0.52	1.10
43	19	8	0.01	0.01
45	1,243	559	0.41	0.93
46	27	13	0.01	0.02
48	998	479	0.33	0.80
50	1,415	707	0.47	1.18
52	7	4	a	0.01
53	1,252	663	0.41	1.11
55	752	413	0.25	0.69
56	4	2	a	a
58	491	285	0.16	0.47
59	5	3	a	0.01
60	326	196	0.11	0.33
61	4	3	a	a
62	361	224	0.12	0.37
63	4	2	a	a
64	236	151	0.08	0.25
66	165	109	0.05	0.18
67	4	2	a	a
68	120	82	0.04	0.14
69	92	64	0.03	0.11
70	784	549	0.26	0.91
Subtotal	298,659	57,997	98.67	96.65
50b	4,021	2,010	1.33	3.35
Total	302,679	60,008	100.00	100.00

Source: U.S. Department of the Treasury, Internal Revenue Service, *Statistics of Income—1967, Individual Income Tax Returns* (1969), p. 85. Totals and percentages are derived from unrounded data.
a Less than 0.005 percent.
b Alternative capital gains tax rate.

277

TABLE B-7. Reconciliation of Corporation Profits before Taxes, Net Profits Reported on Tax Returns, and Taxable Income, 1967

(In billions of dollars)

Income and adjustment items		Amount
Profits before taxes, national income definition		79.8
Differences in coverage:		
Income of Federal Reserve banks, federal home loan banks, and federal land banks	−2.1	
Adjustment for insurance carriers and mutual financial intermediaries	−0.2	
Corporate income from equities in foreign corporations and branches	7.0	
Total income received from equities in foreign corporations (including individuals), net of corresponding outflows	−3.6	
Subtotal		1.1
Differences in definition:		
Dividends received from domestic corporations	4.4	
Net capital gains from sales of property	7.8	
Costs of trading or issuing corporate securities	1.0	
Income disclosed by audit	−5.7	
Depletion, drilling costs in excess of depreciation, and oil-well bonus payments written off	−4.4	
State corporation income taxes	−2.4	
Bad debt adjustment	−2.4	
Subtotal		−1.7
Equals: Net profits reported on tax returns, all corporations[a]		79.3
Adjustments to compute taxable income:[p]		
Losses of corporations with no net income	8.3	
Constructive taxable income from related foreign corporations	1.1	
Wholly tax exempt interest	−2.0	
Dividends received deduction	−2.7	
Net operating loss deduction	−2.5	
Western hemisphere trade deduction	−0.4	
Taxable income of Subchapter S corporations	−2.5	
Regulated investment company income	−3.9	
Subtotal		−4.5
Equals: Taxable income		74.8

[p] Preliminary data.

Sources: *Survey of Current Business,* Vol. 50 (July 1970), p. 46; 1967 Source Book of *Statistics of Income, Corporation Income Tax Returns.* Figures are rounded and do not necessarily add to totals.

[a] Designated as "receipts less deductions" in *Statistics of Income.*

TABLE B-8. Comparison of Corporation Profits before Taxes, Net Profits, and Taxable Income, 1939–67

(In billions of dollars)

Year	Profits before taxes, national income definition	Net profits reported on tax returns[a]	Taxable income
1939	7.0	7.2	n.a.
1940	10.0	9.3	n.a.
1941	17.7	16.7	n.a.
1942	21.5	23.4	n.a.
1943	25.1	28.1	n.a.
1944	24.1	26.5	n.a.
1945	19.7	21.3	n.a.
1946	24.6	25.4	n.a.
1947	31.5	31.6	n.a.
1948	35.2	34.6	n.a.
1949	28.9	28.4	n.a.
1950	42.6	42.8	n.a.
1951	43.9	43.8	n.a.
1952	38.9	38.7	n.a.
1953	40.6	39.8	n.a.
1954	38.3	36.7	n.a.
1955	48.6	47.9	n.a.
1956	48.8	47.4	n.a.
1957	47.2	45.1	n.a.
1958	41.4	39.2	39.3
1959	52.1	47.7	47.6
1960	49.7	44.5	47.2
1961	50.3	47.0	47.9
1962	55.4	50.8	51.7
1963	59.4	55.7	54.3
1964	66.8	63.1	60.4
1965	77.8	74.7	70.8
1966	84.2	81.3	77.1
1967	79.8	79.3[p]	74.8[p]

n.a. Not available.

[p] Preliminary.

Sources: Profits before taxes: *Survey of Current Business*, Vol. 50 (July 1970), p. 50. Reported net profits and taxable income: *Statistics of Income, Corporation Income Tax Returns;* the data for 1967 are from the 1967 Source Book of *Statistics of Income.*

[a] Includes corporations with and without net income. Beginning in 1963, reported net profits are designated "receipts less deductions" in *Statistics of Income.*

TABLE B-9. Distribution of Corporation Taxable Income, by Rate Brackets, 1966

(Dollar amounts in millions)

Taxable income brackets	Tax rate (percent)	Number of corporations	Taxable income	Tax
Amount				
Normal tax and surtax				
Under $25,000..........................	22[a]	547,214	$3,769	$ 859[b]
$25,000 and over.....................	48[a]	159,632	70,229	32,814[b]
Subtotal............................	45.5[c]	706,846	73,998	33,673
Add: Long-term capital gains subject to alternative tax............................	25[a]	—	3,102	776
Totals before credits....................	—	—	77,100	34,449
Less: Foreign tax credit...................	—	—	—	2,861
Less: Investment credit...................	—	—	—	2,006
Totals after credits.....................	38.4[c]	706,846	77,100	29,581
Percentage distribution				
Normal tax and surtax				
Under $25,000..........................	—	77	5	3
$25,000 and over.....................	—	23	95	97
Total...............................	—	100	100	100

Source: *Statistics of Income—1966, Corporation Income Tax Returns*, pp. 128–29. Figures are rounded and do not necessarily add to totals.

[a] Statutory rate.

[b] These amounts are not exactly equal to the product of taxable income and the statutory rate because the classification by taxable income brackets does not take into account the investment credit and foreign tax credit.

[c] Computed effective rate on taxable income.

280

TABLE B-10. Number of Taxable Estate Tax Returns Filed as a Percentage of Adult Deaths, Selected Years, 1939–66

| | | Taxable estate tax returns filed | |
| | | | |
Year	Adult deaths[a]	Number[b]	Percentage of adult deaths
1939	1,204,080	12,720	1.06
1940	1,235,484	12,907	1.04
1941	1,215,627	13,336	1.10
1942	1,209,661	13,493	1.12
1943	1,275,400	12,726	1.00
1944	1,237,508	12,154	0.98
1945	1,238,360	13,869	1.12
1947	1,277,852	18,232	1.43
1948	1,284,535	19,742	1.54
1949	1,284,196	17,469	1.36
1950	1,303,171	17,411	1.34
1951	1,328,809	18,941	1.43
1954	1,331,498	24,997	1.88
1955	1,378,588	25,143	1.82
1957	1,475,320	32,131	2.18
1959	1,498,549	38,515	2.57
1961	1,548,061	45,439	2.94
1963	1,663,115	55,207	3.32
1966	1,727,240	67,404[c]	3.90

Sources: 1939–61: *The Federal Tax System,* p. 280 (see Table A-1). Adult deaths in 1963 and 1966: U.S. Department of Health, Education, and Welfare, Division of Vital Statistics. Taxable estate returns in 1963 and 1966: *Statistics of Income, Fiduciary, Gift, and Estate Tax Returns, 1965,* p. 87.

[a] Age 20 and over.

[b] Citizens and resident aliens.

[c] Not strictly comparable with prior years. For 1966, estate tax after credits was the basis for determining taxable returns. For prior years, the basis was estate tax before credits.

TABLE B-11. Number of Taxable Estate Tax Returns, Gross and Economic Estate, and Estate Tax before and after Credits, Selected Years, 1939–66

(Dollar amounts in millions)

Year[a]	Number of taxable returns	Gross estate on taxable returns	Economic estate[b] on taxable returns	Taxable estate[c]	Estate tax Before credits	Estate tax After credits
1939	12,720	$2,564	$2,390	$1,538	$330	$277
1940	12,907	2,448	2,295	1,479	296	250
1941	13,336	2,578	2,410	1,561	346	292
1942	13,493	2,550	2,373	1,525	354	308
1943	12,726	2,452	2,284	1,397	398	362
1944	12,154	2,720	2,551	1,509	452	405
1945	13,869	3,246	3,081	1,900	596	531
1947	18,232	3,993	3,804	2,319	694	622
1948	19,742	4,445	4,224	2,585	799	715
1949	17,469	4,272	4,059	2,107	635	567
1950	17,411	4,126	3,919	1,917	534	484
1951	18,941	4,656	n.a.	2,189	644	577
1954	24,997	6,288	6,007	2,969	869	779
1955	25,143	6,387	6,109	2,991	872	778
1957	32,131	8,904	n.a.	4,342	1,353	1,177
1959	38,515	9,996	9,540	4,651	1,346	1,186
1961	45,439	12,733	12,213	6,014	1,847	1,619
1963	55,207	14,714	14,059	7,071	2,087	1,841
1966	67,404[d]	19,227[d]	17,974[d]	9,143	2,752	2,414

n.a. Not available.

Sources: 1939–51: *Statistics of Income, Part 1;* 1954–66: *Statistics of Income, Fiduciary, Gift, and Estate Tax Returns.* Data are for estate tax returns of citizens and resident aliens.

[a] Returns are classified by year in which they were filed.

[b] Economic estate is gross estate reduced by the amount of debt (including mortgages).

[c] Prior to 1953, "Taxable Estate" was labeled "Net Estate" in *Statistics of Income.*

[d] Not strictly comparable with prior years. For 1966, estate tax after credits was the basis for determining taxable returns. For prior years, the basis was estate tax before credits.

TABLE B-12. Distribution of Taxable Estates, by Rate Brackets, 1963

Estate tax rate (percentages)	Amount (millions of dollars)		Percentage distribution	
	Taxable estate	Tax[a]	Taxable estate	Tax
3	264	8	3.7	0.4
7	240	17	3.4	0.8
11	421	46	6.0	2.2
14	358	50	5.1	2.4
18	308	56	4.4	2.7
22	268	59	3.8	2.8
25	237	59	3.4	2.8
28	731	205	10.3	9.8
30	1,392	418	19.7	20.0
32	938	300	13.3	14.4
35	464	162	6.6	7.8
37	293	108	4.1	5.2
39	201	79	2.8	3.8
42	144	61	2.0	2.9
45	201	91	2.8	4.4
49	129	63	1.8	3.0
53	90	48	1.3	2.3
56	68	38	1.0	1.8
59	52	31	0.7	1.5
63	70	44	1.0	2.1
67	44	29	0.6	1.4
70	30	21	0.4	1.0
73	20	14	0.3	0.7
76	25	19	0.4	0.9
77	80	61	1.1	2.9
Total	7,071	2,088	100.0	100.0

Source: *Statistics of Income, Fiduciary, Gift, and Estate Tax Returns, 1962.* Figures are rounded and do not necessarily add to totals.
[a] Tax before credits.

283

TABLE B-13. Number of Taxable Gift Tax Returns, Total Gifts, Taxable Gifts, and Gift Tax, Selected Years, 1939–66

(Dollar amounts in millions)

Year[a]	Number of taxable returns	Total gifts on taxable returns	Taxable gifts (current year)	Gift tax (current year)
1939	3,929	$220	$132	$19
1940	4,930	347	226	34
1941	8,940	714	484	70
1942	4,380	222	121	25
1943	4,656	209	124	30
1944	4,979	276	148	38
1945	5,540	289	170	37
1946	6,808	426	265	62
1947	6,822	439	257	64
1948	6,559	391	209	45
1949	6,114	340	178	36
1950	8,366	596	338	78
1951	8,360	516	304	67
1953	8,464	489	258	56
1957	14,736	923	518	113
1959	15,793	928	478	105
1961	17,936	1,219	657	158
1963	20,598	1,402	790	183
1966	29,547	2,373	1,455	413

Sources: 1939–53: *Statistics of Income, Part 1*; 1957–66: *Statistics of Income, Fiduciary, Gift, and Estate Tax Returns*.

[a] Returns are classified by year in which they were filed.

Table B-14. Distribution of Taxable Gifts, by Rate Brackets, 1963

Rate (percentages)	Amount (thousands of dollars) Taxable gifts	Tax	Percentage distribution Taxable gifts	Tax
2¼	39,386	887	5.0	0.5
5¼	31,671	1,664	4.0	0.9
8¼	50,371	4,155	6.4	2.3
10½	38,513	4,044	4.9	2.2
13½	31,136	4,203	3.9	2.3
16½	26,129	4,311	3.3	2.4
18¾	22,415	4,203	2.8	2.3
21	65,366	13,727	8.3	7.5
22½	122,698	27,607	15.5	15.1
24	91,880	22,051	11.6	12.0
26¼	51,861	13,614	6.6	7.4
27¾	33,964	9,425	4.3	5.1
29¼	25,701	7,518	3.3	4.1
31½	22,590	7,116	2.9	3.9
33¾	32,195	10,866	4.1	5.9
36¾	19,780	7,269	2.5	4.0
39¾	15,015	5,968	1.9	3.3
42	10,072	4,230	1.3	2.3
44¼	6,641	2,939	0.8	1.6
47¼	14,671	6,932	1.9	3.8
50¼	11,510	5,784	1.5	3.2
52½	8,479	4,452	1.1	2.4
54¾	4,703	2,575	0.6	1.4
57	2,939	1,675	0.4	0.9
57¾	10,623	6,135	1.3	3.3
Total	790,311	183,351	100.0	100.0

Source: *Statistics of Income, Fiduciary, Gift, and Estate Tax Returns, 1962.* Figures are rounded and do not necessarily add to totals.

Statistical Tables

TABLE C-1. Federal Receipts, Expenditures, Surpluses or Deficits, under the Official and National Income Accounts Budget Concepts, Fiscal Years 1954–70

(In billions of dollars)

Fiscal year	Official (unified) federal budget[a]			National income accounts budget[a]		
	Receipts	Expenditures	Surplus (+) or deficit (−)	Receipts	Expenditures	Surplus (+) or deficit (−)
1954	69.7	70.9	− 1.2	65.8	74.2	− 8.5
1955	65.5	68.5	− 3.0	67.2	67.3	− 0.1
1956	74.5	70.5	+ 4.1	75.8	69.8	+ 6.0
1957	80.0	76.7	+ 3.2	80.7	76.0	+ 4.7
1958	79.6	82.6	− 2.9	77.9	83.1	− 5.1
1959	79.2	92.1	−12.9	85.4	90.9	− 5.5
1960	92.5	92.2	+ 0.3	94.8	91.3	+ 3.5
1961	94.4	97.8	− 3.4	95.3	98.0	− 2.7
1962	99.7	106.8	− 7.1	104.2	106.4	− 2.1
1963	106.6	111.3	− 4.8	110.2	111.4	− 1.2
1964	112.7	118.6	− 5.9	115.5	116.9	− 1.4
1965	116.8	118.4	− 1.6	120.5	118.5	+ 2.0
1966	130.9	134.7	− 3.8	132.8	131.9	+ 0.9
1967	149.6	158.3	− 8.7	147.3	154.6	− 7.2
1968	153.7	178.8	−25.2	160.9	172.4	−11.5
1969	187.8	184.6	+ 3.2	192.7	186.7	+ 6.0
1970p	193.8	196.8	− 2.9	198.8	199.2	− 0.4

p Preliminary.

Sources: Official federal budget, 1954–69, and national income accounts budget, 1960–69: *The Budget of the United States Government, Fiscal Year 1971*, pp. 594, 592, respectively. National income accounts budget, 1954–59: *The Budget of the United States Government, Fiscal Year 1969*, p. 543. National income accounts budget, 1970: *Survey of Current Business*, Vol. 50 (September 1970), p. 14. Official federal budget, 1970: "Preliminary Statement of Receipts and Expenditures of the United States Government for the period from July 1, 1969, through June 30, 1970," p. 1. Figures are rounded and do not necessarily add to totals.

a For an explanation of the differences between the two budget concepts, see p. 16.

TABLE C-2. Relationship of Federal, State, and Local Government Receipts to Gross National Product, 1929–69[a]

(National income accounts basis)

| | | Receipts of federal, state, and local governments | | | | | |
| | | Amount (billions of dollars) | | | Percentage of gross national product | | |
Year	Gross national product (billions of dollars)	Total	Federal	State and local[b]	Total	Federal	State and local[b]
1929	103.1	11.3	3.8	7.5	11.0	3.7	7.3
1930	90.4	10.7	3.0	7.7	11.8	3.3	8.5
1931	75.8	9.4	2.0	7.4	12.4	2.6	9.8
1932	58.0	8.9	1.7	7.2	15.3	2.9	12.4
1933	55.6	9.4	2.7	6.7	16.9	4.9	12.1
1934	65.1	10.4	3.5	6.9	16.0	5.4	10.6
1935	72.2	11.4	4.0	7.4	15.8	5.5	10.2
1936	82.5	12.9	5.0	7.9	15.6	6.1	9.6
1937	90.4	15.3	7.0	8.3	16.9	7.7	9.2
1938	84.7	15.0	6.5	8.5	17.7	7.7	10.0
1939	90.5	15.4	6.7	8.7	17.0	7.4	9.6
1940	99.7	17.7	8.6	9.1	17.8	8.6	9.1
1941	124.5	25.0	15.4	9.6	20.1	12.4	7.7
1942	157.9	32.6	22.9	9.7	20.6	14.5	6.1
1943	191.6	49.2	39.3	9.9	25.7	20.5	5.2
1944	210.1	51.2	41.0	10.2	24.4	19.5	4.9
1945	211.9	53.2	42.5	10.7	25.1	20.1	5.0
1946	208.5	50.9	39.1	11.8	24.4	18.8	5.7
1947	231.3	56.8	43.2	13.6	24.6	18.7	5.9
1948	257.6	58.9	43.3	15.6	22.9	16.8	6.1
1949	256.5	56.0	38.9	17.1	21.8	15.2	6.7
1950	284.8	68.7	49.9	18.8	24.1	17.5	6.6
1951	328.4	84.8	64.0	20.8	25.8	19.5	6.3
1952	345.5	89.8	67.2	22.6	26.0	19.5	6.5
1953	364.6	94.3	70.0	24.3	25.9	19.2	6.7
1954	364.8	89.7	63.8	25.9	24.6	17.5	7.1
1955	398.0	100.4	72.1	28.3	25.2	18.1	7.1
1956	419.2	109.0	77.6	31.4	26.0	18.5	7.5
1957	441.1	115.5	81.6	33.9	26.2	18.5	7.7
1958	447.3	114.7	78.7	36.0	25.6	17.6	8.0
1959	483.7	128.9	89.7	39.2	26.7	18.5	8.1
1960	503.7	139.8	96.5	43.3	27.8	19.2	8.6
1961	520.1	144.6	98.3	46.4	27.8	18.9	8.9
1962	560.3	157.0	106.4	50.6	28.0	19.0	9.0
1963	590.5	168.8	114.5	54.2	28.6	19.4	9.2
1964	632.4	174.1	115.0	59.0	27.5	18.2	9.3
1965	684.9	189.1	124.7	64.3	27.6	18.2	9.4
1966	749.9	213.3	142.5	70.8	28.4	19.0	9.4
1967	793.9	228.9	151.2	77.7	28.8	19.0	9.8
1968	865.0	263.3	175.4	87.9	30.4	20.3	10.2
1969	931.4	298.7	200.6	98.1	32.1	21.5	10.5

Sources: 1929–63: U.S. Department of Commerce, Office of Business Economics, *The National Income and Product Accounts of the United States, 1929–1965: Statistical Tables* (1966), pp. 2–3, 52–55; 1964–65: *Survey of Current Business* (July 1968), pp. 19, 31, 32; 1966–69: *Survey of Current Business* (July 1970), pp. 17, 29, 30. Figures are rounded and do not necessarily add to totals.

a The receipts in this table are on the national income accounts basis of the Department of Commerce and therefore differ from the official unified budget receipts as defined in the budget message. In this table, receipts of trust funds and taxes other than corporation taxes are on a cash basis, but unlike the unified budget, corporation taxes are on an accrual basis.

b State and local receipts have been adjusted to exclude federal grants-in-aid.

TABLE C-3. Federal Budget Receipts, by Source, Fiscal Years 1954–70[a]

Fiscal year	Total				Taxes				
		Individual	Corporation	Excises	Estate and gift	Employment[b]	Customs	Other[c]
				Amount (millions of dollars)				
1954	69,719	29,545	21,103	9,946	934	7,210	542	438
1955	65,469	28,749	17,862	9,131	924	7,866	585	352
1956	74,547	32,190	20,881	9,930	1,161	9,323	682	381
1957	79,990	35,656	21,167	10,534	1,365	9,997	735	536
1958	79,636	34,737	20,074	10,638	1,393	11,239	782	773
1959	79,249	36,776	17,309	10,578	1,333	11,722	925	605
1960	92,492	40,741	21,494	11,676	1,606	14,683	1,105	1,187
1961	94,389	41,338	20,954	11,860	1,896	16,438	982	919
1962	99,676	45,571	20,523	12,534	2,016	17,046	1,142	843
1963	106,560	47,588	21,579	13,194	2,167	19,804	1,205	1,023
1964	112,662	48,697	23,493	13,731	2,394	22,012	1,252	1,084
1965	116,833	48,792	25,461	14,570	2,716	22,258	1,442	1,594
1966	130,856	55,446	30,073	13,062	3,066	25,567	1,767	1,875
1967	149,552	61,526	33,971	13,719	2,978	33,349	1,901	2,108
1968	153,671	68,726	28,665	14,079	3,051	34,622	2,038	2,491
1969	187,792	87,249	36,678	15,222	3,491	39,918	2,319	2,916
1970[p]	193,844	90,371	32,829	15,711	3,620	45,296	2,420	3,587

288

Percentage of total

Year								
1954	100	42.4	30.3	14.3	1.3	10.3	0.8	0.6
1955	100	43.9	27.3	13.9	1.4	12.0	0.9	0.5
1956	100	43.2	28.0	13.3	1.6	12.5	0.9	0.5
1957	100	44.6	26.5	13.2	1.7	12.5	0.9	0.7
1958	100	43.6	25.2	13.4	1.7	14.1	1.0	1.0
1959	100	46.4	21.8	13.3	1.7	14.8	1.2	0.8
1960	100	44.0	23.2	12.6	1.7	15.9	1.2	1.3
1961	100	43.8	22.2	12.6	2.0	17.4	1.0	1.0
1962	100	45.7	20.6	12.6	2.0	17.1	1.1	0.8
1963	100	44.7	20.3	12.4	2.0	18.6	1.1	1.0
1964	100	43.2	20.9	12.2	2.1	19.5	1.1	1.0
1965	100	41.8	21.8	12.5	2.3	19.1	1.2	1.4
1966	100	42.4	23.0	10.0	2.3	19.5	1.4	1.4
1967	100	41.1	22.7	9.2	2.0	22.3	1.3	1.4
1968	100	44.7	18.7	9.2	2.0	22.5	1.3	1.6
1969	100	46.5	19.5	8.1	1.9	21.3	1.2	1.6
1970p	100	46.6	16.9	8.1	1.9	23.4	1.2	1.9

p Preliminary.

Sources: 1954–60: Statistical Appendix to Annual Report of the Secretary of the Treasury on the State of the Finances for the Fiscal Year Ended June 30, 1969, pp. 14, 17; 1961–70: Treasury Bulletin (August 1970), pp. 2–3.

ᵃ Receipts in this table are on the official unified budget basis, and are net after refunds. For 1954–56, breakdowns for tax refunds for individual, corporation, excise, and estate and gift taxes are based on data from the consolidated cash budget statement in The Budget of the United States Government for the Fiscal Year Ending June 30, 1965, p. 462.

ᵇ Includes payroll taxes for social security and unemployment insurance, employee contributions for federal retirement, and contributions for supplementary medical insurance.

ᶜ Includes deposits of earnings by Federal Reserve banks and miscellaneous receipts.

TABLE C-4. Relationship of Direct and Indirect Taxes and Other Revenue in Fifteen Countries to Gross National Product and to Total General Government Revenue, 1966

Source of revenue	United States	Canada	Japan	Austria	Belgium	Denmark	France	Germany	Italy	Netherlands	Norway	Spain	Sweden	Switzerland	United Kingdom
Percentage of gross national product															
Direct taxes on households															
Social security	5.0	3.2	3.8	7.8	8.9	1.9	14.4	10.2	9.9	12.1	7.2	1.6	6.5	4.7	4.8
Other (including income)	9.7	6.7	4.3	10.6	7.2	13.6	4.6	8.3	6.6	10.7	11.8	3.8	18.4	7.6	9.7
Direct taxes on corporations	4.6	3.8	3.6	2.0	1.9	1.1	1.9	2.3		2.6	1.6	2.8	2.1	2.3	2.0
Indirect taxes	8.9	14.6	7.6	15.6	13.2	15.0	17.7	14.2	12.6	10.4	15.2	8.4	14.1	7.1	14.9
Income from property and entrepreneurship	—	3.0	0.8	0.7	0.3	1.5	0.5	1.8	2.1	2.1	1.7	1.1	3.5	2.4	2.6
Other	a	0.8	1.2	0.2	a	0.5	0.1	0.3	0.6	0.7	1.6	a	1.7	1.3	0.3
Total current revenue	28.2	31.9	21.2	36.9	31.5	33.5	39.3	36.9	31.9	38.4	39.1	17.6	46.3	25.4	34.1
Percentage of total revenue															
Direct taxes on households															
Social security	17.9	9.9	17.7	21.0	28.2	5.6	36.7	27.5	31.0	31.4	18.4	8.9	14.0	18.6	14.0
Other (including income)	34.4	20.9	20.4	28.6	22.7	40.7	11.6	22.4	20.8	27.8	30.2	21.5	39.7	30.0	28.4
Direct taxes on corporations	16.2	12.0	16.7	5.4	6.2	3.2	4.9	6.1		6.7	4.0	15.7	4.5	9.0	5.7
Indirect taxes	31.5	45.6	35.9	42.4	41.8	44.7	45.1	38.4	39.5	27.0	39.0	47.8	30.6	28.0	43.6
Income from property and entrepreneurship	—	9.3	3.7	2.0	1.1	4.5	1.3	5.0	6.7	5.4	4.4	6.1	7.7	9.3	7.5
Other	a	2.4	5.6	0.5	0.1	1.4	0.3	0.7	2.0	1.7	4.0	0.1	3.6	5.1	0.8
Total current revenue	100.0	100.0	100.0	100.0	100.0	100.0	100.0	100.0	100.0	100.0	100.0	100.0	100.0	100.0	100.0

Source: Organisation for Economic Co-operation and Development, *National Accounts Statistics, 1957–1966.* Figures are rounded and do not necessarily add to totals.
a Less than 0.05 percent.

TABLE C-5. Distribution of Taxes and Other Revenues[a] by Major Source and Level of Government, Selected Fiscal Years, 1902–69

Fiscal year	Income	Consumption	Property	Payroll	Other	Total
Amount (millions of dollars)						
Federal						
1902	—	244	—	—	287	531
1927	2,138	503	—	25	1,072	3,738
1938	2,610	1,678	—	572	1,578	6,438
1948	30,276	7,337	—	3,878	1,456	42,947
1958	52,793	10,535	—	10,955	2,502	76,785
1969	124,906	15,156	—	44,227	7,021	191,310
State and local						
1902	—	28	706	—	245	979
1927	162	470	4,730	—	1,793	7,155
1938	383	1,794	4,440	—	1,811	8,428
1948	1,174	3,861	5,838	—	3,361	14,234
1958	2,719	8,671	13,499	—	8,174	33,063
1969	12,237	23,848	30,708	—	19,242	86,035
All levels						
1902	—	272	706	—	532	1,510
1927	2,300	973	4,730	25	2,865	10,893
1938	2,993	3,472	4,440	572	3,389	14,866
1948	31,450	11,198	5,838	3,878	4,817	57,181
1958	55,512	19,206	13,499	10,955	10,676	109,848
1969	137,143	39,004	30,708	44,227	26,263	277,345
Percentage distribution						
Federal						
1902	—	46.0	—	—	54.0	100
1927	57.2	13.5	—	0.7	28.7	100
1938	40.5	26.1	—	8.9	24.5	100
1948	70.5	17.1	—	9.0	3.4	100
1958	68.8	13.7	—	14.3	3.3	100
1969	65.3	7.9	—	23.1	3.7	100
State and local						
1902	—	2.9	72.1	—	25.0	100
1927	2.3	6.6	66.1	—	25.1	100
1938	4.5	21.3	52.7	—	21.5	100
1948	8.2	27.1	41.0	—	23.6	100
1958	8.2	26.2	40.8	—	24.7	100
1969	14.2	27.7	35.7	—	22.4	100
All levels						
1902	—	18.0	46.8	—	35.2	100
1927	21.1	8.9	43.4	0.2	26.3	100
1938	20.1	23.4	29.9	3.8	22.8	100
1948	55.0	19.6	10.2	6.8	8.4	100
1958	50.5	17.5	12.3	10.0	9.7	100
1969	49.4	14.1	11.1	15.9	9.5	100

Sources: 1902, 1927, and 1938: U.S. Bureau of the Census, *Historical Statistics of the United States, Colonial Times to 1957* (1960), pp. 724–26; 1948, 1958, and 1969: Worksheets of the U.S. Department of Commerce, Office of Business Economics. Figures are rounded and do not necessarily add to totals.

[a] Revenues are defined as receipts in the national income accounts, less contributions for social insurance other than federal payroll taxes.

TABLE C-6. Number and Amount of Standard and Itemized Deductions, Taxable and Nontaxable Federal Individual Income Tax Returns, 1944–68

Year	Total number of returns (millions)	Standard deduction Number[a] (millions)	Standard deduction Amount (billions of dollars)	Itemized deductions Number[a] (millions)	Itemized deductions Amount (billions of dollars)	Total deductions Amount (billions of dollars)	Total deductions Percentage of adjusted gross income
1944	47.1	38.7	8.0	8.4	4.8	12.8	11.0
1945	49.9	41.5	8.1	8.5	5.5	13.6	11.3
1946	52.8	44.1	8.9	8.8	6.3	15.2	11.3
1947	55.1	44.7	9.8	10.4	7.8	17.6	11.8
1948	52.1	43.2	11.5	8.8	7.9	19.4	11.9
1949	51.8	42.1	11.1	9.7	8.8	19.9	12.4
1950	53.1	42.7	12.0	10.3	9.9	21.9	12.2
1951	55.4	43.9	13.3	11.6	11.9	25.2	12.5
1952	56.5	43.7	13.7	12.8	13.6	27.3	12.7
1953	57.8	43.4	14.2	14.4	15.6	29.8	13.0
1954	56.7	41.0	13.3	15.7	17.4	30.7	13.4
1955	58.3	41.4	13.6	16.9	20.0	33.6	13.5
1956	59.2	40.7	13.8	18.5	22.6	36.4	13.6
1957	59.8	39.7	13.8	20.2	25.7	39.5	14.1
1958	59.1	38.3	13.2	20.8	27.5	40.7	14.5
1959	60.3	37.8	13.4	22.5	32.0	45.4	14.9
1960	61.0	36.9	13.1	24.1	35.3	48.4	15.3
1961	61.5	36.2	12.9	25.3	38.4	51.3	15.6
1962	62.7	36.3	13.1	26.5	41.7	54.8	15.7
1963	63.9	35.8	13.1	28.2	46.1	59.2	16.1
1964	65.4	38.5	20.2	26.9	46.8	67.0	16.9
1965	67.6	39.7	20.6	27.9	50.7	71.4	16.6
1966	70.2	41.6	21.8	28.6	54.6	76.4	16.3
1967	71.7	41.9	22.1	29.8	59.6	81.7	16.2
1968	73.7	41.7	22.1	32.1	69.2	91.3	16.5

Sources: *Statistics of Income, Individual Income Tax Returns;* amount of standard deduction for 1944–57 estimated by author on the basis of the distributions of the number of tax returns by income classes and marital status in *Statistics of Income,* and for 1958–61 obtained directly from *Statistics of Income.* Figures are rounded and do not necessarily add to totals.

a Returns with standard deduction, 1955–68, include a small number with no adjusted gross income and no deductions. For 1944–54, returns with no adjusted gross income are included in the number of returns with itemized deductions.

292

TABLE C-7. Federal Individual Income Tax Liabilities, Prepayments, Final Balances of Tax Due and Overpayments, 1944–68

(In billions of dollars)

| Year | Tax liabilities | | | Prepayments | | Final balances | |
	Total	Income tax	Self-employment tax	With-holding	Declaration payments	Tax due	Over-payments
1944	16.2	16.2	—	9.6	5.5	2.4	1.4
1945	17.1	17.1	—	10.5	6.0	2.4	1.8
1946	16.1	16.1	—	9.2	6.0	2.7	1.9
1947	18.1	18.1	—	11.2	5.8	3.0	2.0
1948	15.4	15.4	—	10.6	5.3	2.2	2.7
1949	14.5	14.5	—	9.6	4.7	2.1	2.0
1950	18.4	18.4	—	11.8	5.6	3.1	2.1
1951	24.4	24.2	0.2	16.6	6.6	3.7	2.5
1952	28.0	27.8	0.2	20.3	7.1	3.6	2.9
1953	29.7	29.4	0.2	22.6	7.0	3.4	3.3
1954	27.0	26.7	0.3	20.5	7.2	3.0	3.7
1955	30.1	29.6	0.5	22.7	7.2	3.8	3.6
1956	33.3	32.7	0.5	25.2	7.9	4.1	4.0
1957	35.0	34.4	0.6	27.4	8.2	3.9	4.5
1958	34.9	34.3	0.6	27.6	8.0	4.1	4.8
1959	39.3	38.6	0.7	30.8	8.6	5.1	5.1
1960	40.3	39.5	0.8	32.7	8.6	4.7	5.7
1961	43.1	42.2	0.8	34.4	9.0	5.7	6.0
1962	45.8	44.9	0.9	37.4	9.3	5.6	6.6
1963	49.2	48.2	1.0	40.2	9.7	6.3	6.9
1964	48.2	47.2	1.0	36.9	10.1	7.1	5.9
1965	50.6	49.5	1.1	39.3	10.7	7.5	6.8
1966	57.6	56.1	1.5	46.6	11.6	7.6	8.6
1967	64.5	62.9	1.6	52.8	13.0	8.4	10.2
1968	78.3	76.6	1.7	62.7	15.8	10.4	11.0

Source: *Statistics of Income, Individual Income Tax Returns.* Figures are rounded and do not necessarily add to totals.

TABLE C-8. Number of Federal Individual Income Tax Returns by Type of Final Settlement, 1944–68

(In millions)

Year	Total number of returns	Returns with		No over-payments or balances due
		Tax due	Overpayments	
1944	47.1	22.6	22.9	1.6
1945	49.9	14.5	33.5	1.9
1946	52.8	13.6	34.4	4.8
1947	55.1	15.3	33.0	6.7
1948	52.1	8.1	38.4	5.6
1949	51.8	13.8	30.2	7.9
1950	53.1	14.3	32.0	6.8
1951	55.4	18.6	31.0	5.8
1952	56.5	19.3	32.1	5.1
1953	57.8	19.0	32.7	6.2
1954	56.7	16.6	35.2	5.0
1955	58.3	18.7	35.4	4.2
1956	59.2	19.4	36.1	3.7
1957	59.8	18.6	37.6	3.6
1958	59.1	18.1	37.4	3.6
1959	60.3	19.1	38.4	2.8
1960	61.0	18.1	39.4	3.5
1961	61.5	18.6	40.0	2.9
1962	62.7	18.7	40.9	3.1
1963	63.9	19.3	41.4	3.3
1964	65.4	22.5	39.3	3.5
1965	67.6	20.0	44.3	3.2
1966	70.2	17.8	49.4	3.0
1967	71.7	17.5	51.2	3.0
1968	73.7	20.3	50.6	2.8

Source: *Statistics of Income, Individual Income Tax Returns.* Figures are rounded and do not necessarily add to totals.

TABLE C-9. Distribution of Taxable Federal Individual Income Tax Returns and Tax Liabilities, 1941 and 1968

Income class[a] (dollars)	Taxable returns		Tax liabilities	
	Number (thousands)	Percentage of total	Amount (millions of dollars)	Percentage of total
1941[b]				
Under 3,000	14,473	82.3	781	20.0
3,000– 5,000	2,165	12.3	409	10.5
5,000– 10,000	637	3.6	406	10.4
10,000– 25,000	243	1.4	683	17.5
25,000– 50,000	50	0.3	574	14.7
50,000–100,000	15	0.1	463	11.8
100,000 and over	5	c	591	15.1
Total	17,588	100.0	3,908	100.0
1968				
Under 3,000	10,200	16.6	1,246	1.6
3,000– 5,000	9,727	15.9	3,489	4.6
5,000– 10,000	22,975	37.5	17,933	23.4
10,000– 25,000	16,800	27.4	31,988	41.8
25,000– 50,000	1,233	2.0	8,740	11.4
50,000–100,000	300	0.5	6,182	8.1
100,000 and over	82	0.1	7,002	9.1
Total	61,315	100.0	76,579	100.0

Source: *Statistics of Income, Individual Income Tax Returns.* Figures are rounded and do not necessarily add to totals.

[a] For 1941, data are classified on a net income basis; for 1968, on an adjusted gross income basis.

[b] Includes taxable fiduciary returns.

[c] Less than 0.05 percent.

TABLE C-10. Federal Individual Income Tax Liabilities and Tax Saving for Single Persons, Heads of Households, and Married Couples Filing Joint Returns, Compared with Basic Rate Schedule (Married, Separate Returns), by Taxable Income, Selected Amounts, $500 to $1 Million, 1971 Rates

Taxable income	Tax liabilities				Tax savings over basic rates			Tax savings as percentage of basic rates		
	Basic (married, separate returns)	Single	Head of household	Married, joint returns	Single	Head of household	Married, joint returns	Single	Head of household	Married, joint returns
$ 500	$ 70	$ 70	$ 70	$ 70	$ 0	$ 0	$ 0	0	0	0
1,000	145	145	140	140	0	5	5	0	3.5	3.5
1,500	225	225	220	215	0	5	10	0	2.2	4.4
2,000	310	310	300	290	0	10	20	0	3.2	6.5
3,000	500	500	480	450	0	20	50	0	4.0	10.0
4,000	690	690	660	620	0	30	70	0	4.4	10.1
6,000	1,130	1,110	1,040	1,000	20	90	130	1.8	8.0	11.5
8,000	1,630	1,590	1,480	1,380	40	150	250	2.5	9.2	15.3
10,000	2,190	2,090	1,940	1,820	100	250	370	4.6	11.4	16.9
12,000	2,830	2,630	2,440	2,260	200	390	570	7.1	13.8	20.1
14,000	3,550	3,210	2,980	2,760	340	570	790	9.6	16.1	22.3
16,000	4,330	3,830	3,540	3,260	500	790	1,070	11.5	18.2	24.7
18,000	5,170	4,510	4,160	3,820	660	1,010	1,350	12.8	19.5	26.1
20,000	6,070	5,230	4,800	4,380	840	1,270	1,690	13.8	20.9	27.8
22,000	7,030	5,990	5,500	5,020	1,040	1,530	2,010	14.8	21.8	28.6
24,000	8,030	6,790	6,220	5,660	1,240	1,810	2,370	15.4	22.5	29.5
26,000	9,030	7,590	6,980	6,380	1,440	2,050	2,650	15.9	22.7	29.3
28,000	10,090	8,490	7,800	7,100	1,600	2,290	2,990	15.9	22.7	29.6

32,000	12,210	10,290	9,480	8,660	1,920	2,730	3,550	15.7	22.4	29.1
36,000	14,410	12,290	11,280	10,340	2,120	3,130	4,070	14.7	21.7	28.2
38,000	15,510	13,290	12,240	11,240	2,220	3,270	4,270	14.3	21.1	27.5
40,000	16,670	14,390	13,260	12,140	2,280	3,410	4,530	13.7	20.5	27.2
44,000	18,990	16,590	15,340	14,060	2,400	3,650	4,930	12.6	19.2	26.0
50,000	22,590	20,190	18,640	17,060	2,400	3,950	5,530	10.6	17.5	24.5
52,000	23,830	21,430	19,760	18,060	2,400	4,070	5,770	10.1	17.1	24.2
60,000	28,790	26,390	24,400	22,300	2,400	4,390	6,490	8.3	15.2	22.5
64,000	31,350	28,950	26,720	24,420	2,400	4,630	6,930	7.7	14.8	22.1
70,000	35,190	32,790	30,260	27,720	2,400	4,930	7,470	6.8	14.0	21.2
76,000	39,150	36,750	33,920	31,020	2,400	5,230	8,130	6.1	13.4	20.8
80,000	41,790	39,390	36,400	33,340	2,400	5,390	8,450	5.7	12.9	20.2
88,000	47,230	44,830	41,440	37,980	2,400	5,790	9,250	5.1	12.3	19.6
90,000	48,590	46,190	42,720	39,180	2,400	5,870	9,410	4.9	12.1	19.4
100,000	55,490	53,090	49,120	45,180	2,400	6,370	10,310	4.3	11.5	18.6
120,000	69,490	67,090	62,320	57,580	2,400	7,170	11,910	3.5	10.3	17.1
140,000	83,490	81,090	75,720	70,380	2,400	7,770	13,110	2.9	9.3	15.7
150,000	90,490	88,090	82,520	76,980	2,400	7,970	13,510	2.7	8.8	14.9
160,000	97,490	95,090	89,320	83,580	2,400	8,170	13,910	2.5	8.4	14.3
180,000	111,490	109,090	103,120	97,180	2,400	8,370	14,310	2.2	7.5	12.8
200,000	125,490	123,090	117,120	110,980	2,400	8,370	14,510	1.9	6.7	11.6
300,000	195,490	193,090	187,120	180,980	2,400	8,370	14,510	1.2	4.3	7.4
400,000	265,490	263,090	257,120	250,980	2,400	8,370	14,510	0.9	3.2	5.5
1,000,000	685,490	683,090	677,120	670,980	2,400	8,370	14,510	0.4	1.2	2.1

Source: Computed from Table 4-2.

TABLE C-11. Influence of Various Provisions on Effective Rates of Federal Individual Income Tax, 1969 Act

(In percentages)

Total income[a] class (dollars)	Nominal tax rate[b]	Reduction due to						Actual tax rate[g]
		Personal exemptions	Deductions[c]	Tax preference items[d]	Capital gains[e]	Maximum tax[f]	Income splitting	
0– 600	14.0	13.9	—	—	—	—	—	0
600– 1,000	14.4	13.2	1.0	—	—	—	—	0
1,000– 1,500	14.8	11.1	3.6	—	—	—	—	0
1,500– 2,000	15.3	10.1	4.7	—	—	—	—	0.3
2,000– 2,500	15.9	9.8	4.3	—	—	—	—	1.5
2,500– 3,000	16.4	9.5	4.2	—	—	—	—	2.5
3,000– 3,500	16.8	9.2	4.0	—	—	—	.	3.3
3,500– 4,000	17.1	8.5	4.1	—	—	—	—	4.2
4,000– 4,500	17.5	8.3	3.9	—	0.1	—	—	5.0
4,500– 5,000	18.0	8.3	3.8	—	—	—	0.1	5.5
5,000– 6,000	18.5	8.1	3.8	—	0.1	—	0.2	6.2
6,000– 7,000	19.3	7.9	3.7	—	0.1	—	0.4	7.1
7,000– 8,000	20.0	8.1	3.8	—	0.1	—	0.6	7.3
8,000– 9,000	20.8	7.7	4.0	—	0.1	—	0.8	8.1
9,000–10,000	21.5	7.7	4.3	—	0.1	—	0.9	8.5

Income classes								
10,000– 11,000	22.3	7.2	4.5	—	0.2	—	1.2	9.2
11,000– 12,000	23.1	7.2	4.7	—	0.2	—	1.4	9.6
12,000– 13,000	24.0	7.0	5.0	—	0.2	—	1.6	10.1
13,000– 15,000	25.2	6.7	5.3	—	0.3	—	2.0	10.9
15,000– 20,000	27.9	6.4	6.2	0.1	0.5	—	2.7	11.9
20,000– 25,000	31.9	5.9	7.1	0.2	1.0	—	4.0	13.6
25,000– 50,000	38.8	4.6	8.1	0.6	2.2	—	6.3	16.8
50,000– 75,000	47.6	3.1	8.5	0.7	4.3	0.3	7.2	23.5
75,000– 100,000	52.8	2.2	9.0	1.0	6.8	0.5	6.4	26.7
100,000– 150,000	57.5	1.6	9.7	1.5	9.6	0.5	5.6	28.7
150,000– 200,000	61.2	1.2	9.8	1.6	13.4	0.4	4.8	29.8
200,000– 500,000	64.8	0.7	10.1	1.7	16.6	0.3	3.4	31.8
500,000–1,000,000	67.8	0.3	9.5	2.0	21.1	0.1	1.5	33.1
1,000,000 and over	69.3	0.1	8.4	3.1	23.0	h	0.5	34.0
All income classes	25.4	7.1	5.1	0.2	1.1	—	1.7	10.1

Source: Special tabulation based on a file of about 87,000 federal individual income tax returns for 1966. Calculations are based on rates, exemptions, and other provisions of the Tax Reform Act of 1969 scheduled to apply to calendar year 1973 incomes.

a Total income is the sum of adjusted gross income, excludable sick pay, excludable dividends, excludable moving expenses, and tax preference items as defined in the Tax Reform Act of 1969, including excluded net long-term capital gains. Preference items were estimated on the basis of diverse sources.

b Rate schedule for married persons filing separate returns applied to total income.

c Standard and itemized deductions plus dividend, sick pay, and moving expense exclusions.

d Special calculation for tax preference items, except excluded net long-term capital gains. The net effect of this category was calculated by eliminating the minimum tax on preference items and including these items in total income to be taxed at the regular rates.

e Combined effect of the alternative tax calculation for taxpayers with capital gains and excluded net long-term capital gains.

f Effect of maximum marginal tax rate of 50 percent on earned taxable income.

g Includes reductions due to retirement and foreign tax credits, which are not shown separately.

h Less than 0.05 percent.

TABLE C-12. Itemized Deductions as a Percentage of Adjusted Gross Income, by Adjusted Gross Income Classes, Federal Individual Income Tax Returns with Itemized Deductions, 1968

Adjusted gross income class (dollars)	Total	Contributions	Interest	Taxes	Medical	Other
Nontaxable returns						
Under 1,000[a]	103.8	13.8	18.8	30.0	31.3	7.5
1,000– 3,000	60.3	7.3	8.7	15.5	24.8	3.5
3,000– 5,000	49.1	5.8	11.3	11.9	15.7	3.7
5,000 and over	58.8	10.2	14.5	8.7	16.5	7.1
All nontaxable	56.9	8.1	12.0	11.8	18.7	5.1
Taxable returns						
600– 1,000	12.5	b	0	b	b	c
1,000– 3,000	28.5	5.2	3.0	8.0	9.1	3.0
3,000– 5,000	24.5	4.0	4.1	7.3	6.2	2.7
5,000– 10,000	20.6	2.9	5.6	6.6	3.3	2.0
10,000– 20,000	17.4	2.5	5.3	6.5	1.6	1.5
20,000– 50,000	15.6	2.7	3.9	6.6	1.1	1.3
50,000–100,000	15.4	3.4	3.4	6.4	0.6	1.6
100,000 and over	18.8	6.7	3.7	6.1	0.3	2.1
All taxable	18.1	2.9	4.9	6.5	2.0	1.7
All returns	18.8	3.0	5.0	6.6	2.3	1.7

Source: *Statistics of Income, 1968 Preliminary, Individual Income Tax Returns*, p. 31. Figures do not add to totals because the total column includes small amounts for which the type of deduction was not specified.
a Excludes returns with no adjusted gross income or deficit.
b Not shown separately because of high sampling variability, but included in total.
c Less than 0.05 percent.

... from Capital Gains and Income Taxation, 1948–68

(Dollar amounts in billions)

Calendar year of liability	Individuals and fiduciaries			Corporations			Individuals, fiduciaries, and corporations		
	Total income taxes after credits	Estimated tax on capital gains and losses		Total income and excess profits taxes before credits	Estimated tax on capital gains and losses		Total income and excess profits taxes	Estimated tax on capital gains and losses	
		Amount	Percentage of total tax		Amount	Percentage of total tax		Amount	Percentage of total tax
1948	$15.6	$0.6	3.8	$11.9	$0.2	1.7	$27.5	$0.8	2.9
1949	14.7	0.4	2.7	9.8	0.2	2.0	24.5	0.6	2.4
1950	18.5	0.9	4.9	17.3	0.3	1.7	35.9	1.2	3.3
1951	24.4	0.9	3.7	22.1	0.3	1.4	46.5	1.2	2.6
1952	28.0	0.8	2.9	19.1	0.3	1.6	47.2	1.1	2.3
1953	29.7	0.7	2.4	19.9	0.3	1.5	49.6	1.0	2.0
1954	26.9	1.1	4.1	16.9	0.5	3.0	43.8	1.6	3.7
1955	29.9	1.6	5.4	21.7	0.5	2.3	51.6	2.1	4.1
1956	33.1	1.5	4.5	21.4	0.5	2.3	54.5	2.0	3.7
1957	34.8	1.2	3.4	20.6	0.4	1.9	55.4	1.6	2.9
1958	34.6	1.4	4.0	18.8	0.6	3.2	53.5	2.0	3.7
1959	39.0	2.3	5.9	22.5	0.4	1.8	61.5	2.7	4.4
1960	39.8	1.9	4.8	21.9	0.6	2.7	61.7	2.5	4.1
1961	42.6	2.9	6.8	22.2	0.8	3.6	64.8	3.7	5.7
1962	45.3	2.1	4.6	23.9	0.7	2.9	69.3	2.8	4.0
1963	48.7	2.3	4.7	26.3	0.7	2.7	74.9	3.0	4.0
1964	47.8	2.7	5.6	27.9	0.7	2.5	75.6	3.4	4.5
1965	50.2	3.4	6.8	31.7	0.8	2.5	81.9	4.2	5.1
1966	56.8	3.4	6.0	34.4	0.9	2.6	91.3	4.3	4.7
1967	63.8	5.0	7.8	33.3	1.0	3.0	97.1	6.0	6.2
1968	77.6	7.2	9.3	n.a.	n.a.	n.a.	n.a.	n.a.	n.a.

n.a. Not available.
Source: Office of the Secretary of the Treasury, Office of Tax Analysis. The actual revenue figures are as reported in *Statistics of Income*, annual issues. Percentages are derived from rounded data.

TABLE C-14. Estimated Federal "Tax Expenditures,"[a] by Budget Function, Fiscal Years 1968 and 1969

(In millions of dollars)

Budget function and tax provision	Amount of tax expenditure	
	1968	1969
National defense		
Exclusion of benefits and allowances to armed forces personnel	500	550
International affairs and finance		
Exemption of certain income earned abroad by U.S. citizens	40	45
Western hemisphere trade corporations	50	55
Exclusion of gross-up on dividends of less-developed country corporations	50	55
Exclusion of controlled foreign subsidiaries	150	165
Exclusion of income earned in U.S. possessions	80	90
Total	370	410
Agriculture and rural development		
Farming: expensing and capital gains treatment	800	860
Timber: capital gains treatment for certain income	130	140
Total	930	1,000
Natural resources		
Expensing of exploration and development costs	300	330
Excess of percentage over cost depletion	1,300	1,430
Capital gains treatment of royalties on coal and iron ore	5	5
Total	1,605	1,765
Commerce and transportation		
Investment credit	2,300	3,000
Excess depreciation on buildings (other than rental housing)	500	550
Dividend exclusion	225	260
Capital gains: individuals	7,000[b]	7,000[c]
Capital gains: corporations (other than agriculture and natural resources)	500	525
Excess bad debt reserves of financial institutions	600	660
Exemption of credit unions	40	45
Deductibility of interest on consumer credit	1,300	1,600
Expensing of research and development expenditures	500	550
$25,000 surtax exemption	1,800	2,000
Deferral of tax on shipping companies	10	10
Total	14,775	16,200
Community development and housing		
Deductibility of interest on mortgages on owner-occupied homes	1,900	2,200
Deductibility of property taxes on owner-occupied homes	1,800	2,350
Excess depreciation on rental housing	250	250
Total	3,950	4,800

302

TABLE C-14. continued.

	Amount of tax expenditure	
Budget function and tax provision	1968	1969
Education and manpower		
Education expense deduction	—	40
Additional personal exemption for students	500	500
Deductibility of contributions to educational institutions	170	200
Exclusion of scholarships and fellowships	50	60
Total	720	800
Health		
Deductibility of medical expenses	1,500	1,600
Exclusion of medical insurance premiums and medical care	1,100	1,400
Total	2,600	3,000
Income security		
Disability insurance benefits	—	100
Provisions relating to aged, blind, and disabled[d]	2,300	2,700
Additional exemption for blind	10	10
Sick pay exclusion	85	95
Exclusion of unemployment insurance benefits	300	325
Exclusion of workmen's compensation benefits	150	180
Exclusion of public assistance benefits	50	50
Treatment of pension plans		
Plans for employees	3,000	4,000
Plans for self-employed persons	60	135
Exclusion of other employee benefits		
Premiums on group term life insurance	400	400
Deductibility of accident and death benefits	25	25
Privately financed supplementary unemployment benefits	25	15
Meals and lodging	150	165
Exclusion of interest on life insurance savings	900	1,000
Deductibility of charitable contributions (other than education)	2,200	3,000
Deductibility of child and dependent care expenses	25	25
Deductibility of casualty losses	70	80
Standard deduction	3,200	3,600
Total	12,950	15,905
Veterans' benefits and services		
Exclusion of certain benefits	550	600
Aid to state and local governments		
Exemption of interest on state and local debt	1,800	2,000
Deductibility of nonbusiness state and local taxes (other than on owner-occupied homes)	2,800	4,150
Total	4,600	6,150
Total, all tax expenditures[e]	43,550	51,180

Sources: All data except capital gains for individuals are from the statement of Murray L. Weidenbaum, "How to Make Decisions on Priorities," in *Changing National Priorities,* Hearings before the Subcommittee on Economy in Government of the Joint Economic Committee, 91 Cong. 2 sess. (1970), Pt. 1, pp. 56–57. Capital gains for individuals is from *Annual Report of the Secretary of the Treasury on the State of the Finances for the Fiscal Year Ended June 30, 1968,* p. 340.

[a] See Table C-15, note a, for definition of tax expenditures.
[b] Midpoint of estimated range of $5,500–$8,500.
[c] Estimate for 1968 carried over to 1969.
[d] Additional exemption for aged, retirement income credit, and exclusion of social security payments, combined.
[e] See Table C-15, note d.

TABLE C-15. Federal Budget Outlays, Estimated "Tax Expenditures,"[a] and Tax Expenditures as a Percentage of Outlays, by Budget Function, Fiscal Years 1968 and 1969

(Dollar amounts in millions)

Budget function	Total budget outlays[b]		Tax expenditures		Tax expenditures as percentage of budget outlays	
	1968	1969	1968	1969	1968	1969
National defense	$ 80,516	$ 81,240	$ 500	$ 550	0.6	0.7
International affairs and finance	4,619	3,785	370	410	8.0	10.8
Space research and technology	4,721	4,247	0	0	—	—
Agriculture and rural development	5,944	6,221	930	1,000	15.6	16.1
Natural resources	1,702	2,129	1,605	1,765	94.3	82.9
Commerce and transportation	8,076	7,873	14,775	16,200	182.9	205.8
Community development and housing	4,076	1,961	3,950	4,800	96.9	244.8
Education and manpower	7,012	6,825	720	800	10.3	11.7
Health	{ 43,508	11,696	2,600	3,000	{ 35.7	25.6
Income security		37,399	12,950	15,905		42.5
Veterans' benefits and services	6,882	7,640	550	600	8.0	7.9
Interest	13,744	15,791	0	0	—	—
General government	2,632	2,866	0	0	—	—
Aid to state and local governments	n.a.	n.a.	4,600	6,150	n.a.	n.a.
Total	$178,862[c]	$184,556[c]	$43,550[d]	$51,180[d]	24.3[d]	27.7[d]

n.a. Not applicable since this is not a budget function.

Sources: Budget outlays: *The Budget of the United States Government, Fiscal Year 1970*, p. 69; *The Budget of the United States Government, Fiscal Year 1971*, p. 75. Tax expenditures: Table C-14.

a. "Tax expenditures" are tax revenues that the federal government does not collect because income subject to tax is reduced by special tax provisions in the tax system. They are called tax expenditures to call attention to the fact that they would be included in the budget totals if the same activity or objective were financed by direct outlays.

b. Excludes net lending.

c. The individual functions include certain undistributed intragovernmental payments which are not separately available but are deducted in arriving at the budget total.

d. The true revenue cost of all the provisions taken together would be greater because the absence of any one provision would put a taxpayer into a higher rate bracket and thus cause the other provisions to have higher revenue effects. An effort to take this interaction into account in estimating separate items would require arbitrary decisions on which provisions to take into account ahead of other provisions.

TABLE C-16. Schedule of Transition to the Current Payment System for Corporations

(Percentage of tax liability due in each installment)

Income year	Income year April	June	September	December	Following year March	June	September	December	Total
1949	—	—	—	—	25	25	25	25	100
1950	—	—	—	—	30	30	20	20	100
1951	—	—	—	—	35	35	15	15	100
1952	—	—	—	—	40	40	10	10	100
1953	—	—	—	—	45	45	5	5	100
1954	—	—	—	—	50	50	—	—	100
1955[a]	—	—	5	5	45	45	—	—	100
1956[a]	—	—	10	10	40	40	—	—	100
1957[a]	—	—	15	15	35	35	—	—	100
1958[a]	—	—	20	20	30	30	—	—	100
1959[a]	—	—	25	25	25	25	—	—	100
1960[a]	—	—	25	25	25	25	—	—	100
1961[a]	—	—	25	25	25	25	—	—	100
1962[a]	—	—	25	25	25	25	—	—	100
1963[a]	—	—	25	25	25	25	—	—	100
1964[a]	1	1	25	25	24	24	—	—	100
1965[a]	4	4	25	25	21	21	—	—	100
1966[a]	12	12	25	25	13	13	—	—	100
1967[a] and later years[b]	25	25	25	25	—	—	—	—	100

Source: Same as Table A-1.

[a] Applicable only to tax liability in excess of $100,000. The first $100,000 of a corporation's tax liability was paid in equal installments in March and June of the following year.

[b] Beginning in 1968, the $100,000 exclusion was reduced to $5,500. A transitional exemption was provided for 1968–71 (80 percent in 1968, 60 percent in 1969, 40 percent in 1970, and 20 percent in 1971). A second transitional period begins in 1972 that places corporations on a completely current basis by 1977.

TABLE C-17. Selected Ratios Relating to the Corporate Sector, 1929–69

Year	National income originating in corporate business as percentage of income originating in business (1)	Corporate gross product as percentage of business gross product (2)	Corporate gross saving as percentage of gross national product (3)	Property income as percentage of corporate gross product less indirect taxes[a, b] (4)	Dividends as percentage of corporate cash flow (nonfinancial corporations)[b, c] (5)
1929	58.2	n.a.	7.3	n.a.	n.a.
1930	58.1	n.a.	5.5	n.a.	n.a.
1931	55.6	n.a.	2.4	n.a.	n.a.
1932	53.4	n.a.	−0.3	n.a.	n.a.
1933	53.6	n.a.	0.1	n.a.	n.a.
1934	57.8	n.a.	3.1	n.a.	n.a.
1935	56.6	n.a.	4.4	n.a.	n.a.
1936	59.6	n.a.	4.0	n.a.	n.a.
1937	59.8	n.a.	4.7	n.a.	n.a.
1938	57.9	n.a.	5.2	n.a.	n.a.
1939	59.4	n.a.	5.4	n.a.	n.a.
1940	61.4	n.a.	6.8	n.a.	n.a.
1941	62.5	n.a.	6.0	n.a.	n.a.
1942	62.1	n.a.	6.1	n.a.	n.a.
1943	62.9	n.a.	6.0	n.a.	n.a.
1944	62.2	n.a.	5.8	n.a.	n.a.
1945	58.7	n.a.	4.8	n.a.	n.a.
1946	56.5	56.5	4.5	24.9	28.3
1947	60.4	59.4	6.0	27.0	24.6
1948	61.2	60.8	8.0	29.7	24.3
1949	61.7	60.4	8.2	29.4	28.0
1950	63.1	61.4	7.0	31.0	26.0
1951	63.8	61.7	6.7	30.6	27.7
1952	63.6	61.8	6.8	28.4	28.7
1953	64.7	62.6	6.5	27.2	27.3
1954	64.0	62.0	7.1	27.5	26.5
1955	65.7	63.8	8.1	29.6	23.9
1956	66.2	64.9	7.7	27.8	24.9
1957	66.2	64.8	7.6	27.3	25.2
1958	64.5	63.1	7.3	26.7	26.2
1959	66.5	64.9	8.0	28.3	24.0
1960	66.6	65.0	7.6	27.1	25.8
1961	66.0	64.7	7.6	27.2	25.2
1962	66.6	65.1	8.3	28.1	24.1
1963	66.8	65.3	8.1	28.4	25.0
1964	67.4	65.9	8.5	29.0	23.3
1965	67.6	66.3	9.0	30.0	23.0
1966	68.1	66.5	8.9	29.9	22.9
1967	67.8	66.1	8.4	28.8	23.7
1968	68.3	66.6	7.9	28.8	24.5
1969	68.3	66.8	7.3	27.5	24.8

n.a. Not available.

Sources: Cols. (1) and (3), 1929–62: U.S. Department of Commerce, Office of Business Economics, *The National Income and Product Accounts of the United States, 1929–1965: Statistical Tables* (1966), Tables 1.13, and 1.1, 5.1, respectively; 1963–69, *Survey of Current Business*, July 1967, 1968, 1969, 1970, Tables 1.13 and 1.1, 5.1, respectively; cols. (2), (4), (5), 1946–62: *National Income and Product Accounts*, Tables 1.7, 1.13, 1.14; 1963–69, *Survey of Current Business*, July 1967, 1968, 1969, 1970, Tables 1.7, 1.14, and 1.13, 1.14, 5.1, and 1.14, respectively.

[a] Property income includes corporate profits before tax and inventory valuation adjustment, net interest, and corporate capital consumption allowances.

[b] Excludes amounts originating in the rest of the world.

[c] Cash flow is net corporate profits after taxes plus corporate capital consumption allowances.

TABLE C-18. Rates of Return before and after Federal Income Tax, Manufacturing Corporations, 1927–41, 1948–61, and 1964–67

(In percentages)

Year	Rates of return				Debt-capital ratio[c]	General corporation income tax rate
	On equity capital[a]		On total capital[b]			
	Before tax	After tax	Before tax	After tax		
1927	7.5	6.5	7.6	6.7	15.1	13.5
1928	9.1	8.0	9.0	8.0	15.6	12.0
1929	9.9	8.8	9.6	8.7	14.9	11.0
1930	2.1	1.5	2.9	2.4	15.3	12.0
1931	−1.6	−2.0	−0.4	−0.6	15.4	12.0
1932	−3.9	−4.2	−2.3	−2.5	15.5	13.75
1933	0.5	0.0	1.3	0.9	15.5	13.75
1934	2.4	1.8	2.8	2.3	13.7	13.75
1935	4.8	3.9	4.9	4.1	14.9	13.75
1936	9.5	8.0	8.8	7.5	14.2	15.0
1937	9.2	7.6	8.6	7.3	15.4	15.0
1938	3.9	3.0	3.9	3.2	15.4	19.0
1939	8.5	7.0	7.9	6.6	14.9	19.0
1940	12.2	8.7	11.1	8.1	14.4	24.0
1941	22.3	11.7	19.6	10.6	14.9	31.0
1948	22.4	14.0	19.5	12.4	15.7	38.0
1949	16.4	10.1	14.5	9.2	14.7	38.0
1950	25.4	14.0	22.2	12.5	14.8	42.0
1951	24.5	10.5	21.2	9.5	17.3	50.75
1952	18.9	8.3	16.2	7.5	19.2	52.0
1953	19.1	8.3	16.2	7.5	19.1	52.0
1954	15.6	7.6	13.4	6.9	18.9	52.0
1955	20.6	10.3	17.5	9.2	18.2	52.0
1956	18.1	9.1	15.5	8.2	20.0	52.0
1957	15.9	7.9	13.6	7.2	20.5	52.0
1958	12.2	6.0	10.7	5.7	20.4	52.0
1959	15.8	7.9	13.6	7.3	20.4	52.0
1960	13.4	6.5	11.7	6.2	20.6	52.0
1961	13.0	6.4	11.4	6.1	20.6	52.0
1964	16.3	8.6	14.0	8.0	22.3	50.0
1965	18.9	10.2	15.8	9.2	23.9	48.0
1966	19.5	10.7	16.1	9.5	26.6	48.0
1967[p]	16.5	8.9	13.7	8.1	27.7	48.0

[p] Preliminary.

Sources: 1935–58: Marian Krzyzaniak and Richard A. Musgrave, *The Shifting of the Corporation Income Tax* (Johns Hopkins Press, 1963), p. 73; other years: *Statistics of Income, Corporation Income Tax Returns;* 1967 data are from the *1967 Source Book of Statistics of Income.*

[a] Equity capital is average of book value of stock and undistributed surplus at the beginning and end of the year.
[b] Profits plus interest paid as percentage of average equity capital plus debt capital at the beginning and end of the year.
[c] End of year.

TABLE C-19. Sources and Uses of Funds, Nonfarm Nonfinancial Corporate Business, 1960–69

(In billions of dollars)

Source or use of funds	1960	1961	1962	1963	1964	1965	1966	1967	1968	1969
Internal sources	34.4	35.6	41.8	43.9	50.5	56.6	61.2	61.5	62.5	62.5
Undistributed profits	10.0	10.2	12.4	13.6	18.3	23.1	24.7	21.1	20.9	19.9
Corporate inventory valuation adjustment	0.2	−0.1	0.3	−0.5	−0.5	−1.7	−1.8	−1.1	−3.3	−5.4
Capital consumption allowances	24.2	25.4	29.2	30.8	32.8	35.2	38.2	41.5	44.9	48.0
External sources	13.7	21.0	23.1	23.2	21.3	36.5	39.4	33.0	47.3	56.0
Stocks	1.6	2.5	0.6	−0.3	1.4	0	1.2	2.3	−0.8	4.3
Bonds	3.5	4.6	4.6	3.9	4.0	5.4	10.2	14.7	12.9	12.1
Mortgages	2.5	3.9	4.5	4.9	3.6	3.9	4.2	4.5	5.8	4.3
Bank loans[a]	1.9	0.7	3.0	3.7	3.8	10.6	8.4	6.4	9.6	10.9
Other loans	1.9	0.6	0	0.2	0.9	0.6	1.4	1.4	3.6	6.2
Trade debt	0.6	5.4	4.6	5.3	3.6	9.1	7.3	2.6	5.7	10.9
Profits tax liability	−2.2	1.4	0.6	1.9	0.5	2.2	0.2	−4.1	3.7	0.8
Other liabilities	4.0	1.7	5.2	3.7	3.5	4.6	6.5	5.2	6.9	6.5
Sources, total	48.1	56.6	64.9	67.1	71.8	93.1	100.6	94.4	109.8	118.4

Purchases of physical assets	39.0	36.7	44.0	45.6	52.1	62.8	77.1	72.0	76.9	87.0
Nonresidential fixed investment	34.9	33.2	37.0	38.6	44.1	52.8	61.6	62.5	67.5	76.9
Residential structures	1.1	1.9	2.3	2.6	2.1	2.0	1.1	2.3	2.4	2.9
Change in business inventories	3.0	1.5	4.7	4.3	5.9	7.9	14.4	7.3	7.0	7.2
Increase in financial assets	4.7	15.6	16.0	17.7	12.8	23.1	15.5	13.5	26.6	24.2
Liquid assets	-3.2	3.7	3.5	4.7	1.2	1.7	1.9	0	10.1	2.3
Demand deposits and currency	-0.5	1.7	-0.9	-0.8	-2.3	-1.5	0.7	-2.2	1.3	0.5
Time deposits	1.3	1.9	3.7	3.9	3.2	3.9	-0.7	4.1	2.2	-7.8
U.S. government securities	-5.4	-0.2	0.5	0.5	-1.5	-1.6	-1.2	-3.1	1.8	-1.4
Open-market paper	1.7	0.4	0.6	0.9	1.6	0.5	2.0	1.5	4.5	8.7
State and local obligations	-0.2	0	-0.3	0.2	0.2	0.5	1.0	-0.4	0.4	2.3
Consumer credit	0.4	0.2	0.7	1.0	1.3	1.2	1.2	0.9	1.7	1.3
Trade credit	5.3	9.5	8.5	8.1	8.1	15.1	11.3	8.8	14.8	17.3
Other financial assets	2.2	2.1	3.2	3.9	2.2	5.1	1.0	3.8	0.1	3.4
Uses, total	43.7	52.2	60.0	63.2	64.9	85.8	92.5	85.5	103.5	111.2
Discrepancy (sources less uses)	4.3	4.3	5.0	3.8	6.9	7.2	8.0	9.0	6.3	7.2

Source: Board of Governors of the Federal Reserve System.
a Not elsewhere classified.

TABLE C-20. Assets of Selected Federal Trust Funds, Fiscal Years 1937–70

(In billions of dollars)

June 30	Old-age and survivors insurance	Disability insurance	Hospital insurance	Supplementary medical insurance	Unemployment insurance	Railroad retirement
1937	0.3				0.3	ᵃ
1938	0.8				0.9	0.1
1939	1.2				1.3	0.1
1940	1.7				1.7	0.1
1941	2.4				2.3	0.1
1942	3.2				3.2	0.1
1943	4.3				4.4	0.2
1944	5.4				5.9	0.3
1945	6.6				7.3	0.5
1946	7.6				7.4	0.7
1947	8.8				7.9	0.8
1948	10.0				8.3	1.4
1949	11.3				8.2	1.8
1950	12.9				7.4	2.2
1951	14.7				8.1	2.5
1952	16.6				8.7	2.9
1953	18.4				9.2	3.2
1954	20.0				9.0	3.4
1955	21.1				8.5	3.5
1956	22.6				8.8	3.7
1957	23.0	0.3			9.1	3.7
1958	22.8	1.1			7.8	3.7
1959	21.5	1.7			6.7	3.6
1960	20.8	2.2			6.7	3.9
1961	20.9	2.5			5.8	3.8
1962	19.7	2.5			5.8	3.8
1963	19.0	2.4			6.3	3.8
1964	19.7	2.3			6.9	3.9
1965	20.2	2.0			7.9	4.0
1966	19.9	1.7	0.9		9.3	4.2
1967	23.5	2.0	1.3	0.5	10.6	4.5
1968	25.5	2.6	1.4	0.3	11.6	4.6
1969	28.2	3.7	2.0	0.4	12.7	4.7
1970ᵖ	32.7	5.1	2.7	0.1	13.1	4.9

ᵖ Preliminary.
Sources: U.S. Treasury Department, *Treasury Bulletin* (August 1944, 1952, 1961, 1970).
ᵃ Less than $50 million.

TABLE C-21. Number of Estate Tax Returns, Value of Estates, and Amount of Tax, by Size of Economic Estate, 1966[a]

(Size classes in dollars; other dollar amounts in millions)

Size of economic estate	Number of returns	Total estate[b]	Economic estate[c]	Estate tax before state tax credit	State death tax credit	Estate tax after credit
Deficit estate	139	$ 25	$ −38	[d]	[d]	[e]
$ 1– 60,000	3,836	264	180	$ 3	[e]	$ 3
60,000– 100,000	37,950	3,134	2,967	25	[e]	25
100,000– 150,000	23,033	2,940	2,792	95	$ 2	93
150,000– 200,000	10,463	1,902	1,806	121	3	118
200,000– 300,000	9,304	2,357	2,254	230	10	221
300,000– 400,000	4,152	1,495	1,430	190	11	179
400,000– 500,000	2,256	1,052	1,005	152	10	142
500,000– 1,000,000	3,959	2,815	2,697	478	41	437
1,000,000– 2,000,000	1,498	2,132	2,029	434	50	384
2,000,000– 3,000,000	359	905	868	214	29	185
3,000,000– 4,000,000	149	534	512	135	20	116
4,000,000– 5,000,000	78	373	350	109	17	92
5,000,000–10,000,000	115	824	795	241	40	202
10,000,000–20,000,000	33	487	446	150	27	123
20,000,000 and over	15	518	512	116	22	94
Total	97,339	$21,757	$20,606	$2,695	$280	$2,414

Source: U.S. Internal Revenue Service, *Statistics of Income, Fiduciary, Gift, and Estate Tax Returns, 1965* (1967), pp. 68, 80. Figures are rounded and do not necessarily add to totals.

[a] Returns are classified by year in which they were filed.

[b] Total estate is gross estate plus life insurance policy loans and minus lifetime transfers.

[c] Economic estate is total estate less debts (including mortgages) and less life insurance policy loans

[d] Not separately available; the data are included in totals.

[e] Less than $500,000.

TABLE C-22. Number of Gift Tax Returns, and Amounts of Gifts and Gift Tax, by Size of Total Gifts before Splitting, 1966[a]

(Size classes in dollars; other dollar amounts in millions)

Size of total gifts before splitting	Number of returns	Total gifts[b]	Taxable gifts Current year	Taxable gifts Prior years	Taxable gifts All years	Gift tax, current year
Taxable returns						
No total gifts before splitting[c]	4,615	—	$ 198	$ 287	$ 485	$ 47
Under $10,000	3,199	$ 19	21	171	192	4
$ 10,000– 20,000	3,897	57	45	264	309	15
20,000– 30,000	2,970	73	27	157	184	3
30,000– 40,000	2,870	100	34	134	168	5
40,000– 50,000	2,394	106	34	100	134	4
50,000– 100,000	5,613	393	147	304	451	20
100,000– 500,000	3,462	638	365	649	1,014	79
500,000– 1,000,000	291	202	126	227	353	34
1,000,000– 2,000,000	144	198	120	173	293	36
2,000,000– 3,000,000	40	95	51	89	140	18
3,000,000– 5,000,000	25	98	48	64	112	18
5,000,000–10,000,000	16	103	50	28	78	20
10,000,000 and over	10	292	189	301	490	109
Total	29,547	2,373	1,455	2,949	4,404	413
Nontaxable returns	83,249	1,589	—	1,026[d]	1,026[d]	—
Total, all returns	112,796	$3,962	$1,455	$3,975	$5,430	$413

Source: *Statistics of Income, Fiduciary, Gift, and Estate Tax Returns, 1965*, pp. 41, 50–51. Figures are rounded and do not necessarily add to totals.

[a] Returns are classified by year in which they were filed.

[b] Total gifts are before splitting provision for gifts by and between husband and wife.

[c] Taxed on spouse's gifts, under gift splitting provisions.

[d] Returns were nontaxable for current year gifts, but taxable for prior year gifts.

TABLE C-23. General Expenditure of State and Local Governments, by Major Function, Fiscal Years 1959 and 1969

(Dollar amounts in millions)

				Increase 1959–69	
	Amount			Percentage distribution of	Percentage
Function	1959	1969	Amount	increase	increase
Total state and local					
Total general expenditure[a]	$48,887	$116,727	$67,840	100.0	138.8
Education	17,283	47,238	29,955	44.2	173.3
Highways	9,592	15,417	5,825	8.6	60.7
Public welfare	4,136	12,110	7,974	11.8	192.8
Health and hospitals	3,724	8,520	4,796	7.1	128.8
Police and fire	2,624	5,694	3,070	4.5	117.0
Natural resources	1,076	2,552	1,476	2.2	137.2
Sewerage and other sanitation	1,609	2,969	1,360	2.0	84.5
Housing and urban renewal	615	1,902	1,287	1.9	209.3
General control and financial administration	2,003	4,105	2,102	3.1	104.9
Interest on debt	1,416	3,732	2,316	3.4	163.6
Other	4,810	12,489	7,679	11.3	159.6
State					
Total general expenditure[a,b]	17,318	43,244	25,926	100.0	149.7
Education	3,093	12,304	9,211	35.5	297.8
Highways	6,414	10,414	4,000	15.4	62.4
Public welfare	2,124	6,464	4,340	16.7	204.3
Health and hospitals	1,850	4,257	2,407	9.3	130.1
Police	228	585	357	1.4	156.6
Natural resources	813	2,035	1,222	4.7	150.3
Housing and urban renewal	3	15	12	c	400.0
General control and financial administration	619	1,496	877	3.4	141.7
Interest on debt	453	1,275	822	3.2	181.5
Other	1,722	4,400	2,678	10.3	155.5
Local					
Total general expenditure[a,b]	31,570	73,483	41,913	100.0	132.8
Education	14,190	34,934	20,744	49.5	146.2
Highways	3,178	5,003	1,825	4.4	57.4
Public welfare	2,012	5,646	3,634	8.7	180.6
Health and hospitals	1,874	4,262	2,388	5.7	127.4
Police and fire	2,396	5,109	2,713	6.5	113.2
Natural resources	263	517	254	0.6	96.6
Sewerage and other sanitation	1,609	2,969	1,360	3.2	84.5
Housing and urban renewal	612	1,887	1,275	3.0	208.3
General control and financial administration	1,384	2,609	1,225	2.9	88.5
Interest on debt	963	2,457	1,494	3.6	155.1
Other	3,089	8,089	5,000	11.9	161.9

Sources: 1959: U.S. Bureau of the Census, *Census of Governments, 1967,* Vol. 6, No. 5, *Historical Statistics on Governmental Finances and Employment* (1969), pp. 39, 42, 45; 1969: U.S. Bureau of the Census, *Governmental Finances in 1968–69* (1970), p. 23. Figures are rounded and do not necessarily add to totals.

a Excludes insurance trust, utility, and liquor store expenditures. Includes federal grants-in-aid.

b Grants-in-aid are shown according to final spending level.

c Less than 0.05 percent.

TABLE C-24. General Revenue of State and Local Governments, by Source, Fiscal Years 1959 and 1969

(Dollar amounts in millions)

Source	Amount 1959	Amount 1969	Increase 1959–69 Amount	Increase 1959–69 Percentage distribution of total increase	Increase 1959–69 Percentage distribution of revenue from own sources
Total state and local					
General revenue[a]	$45,306	$114,550	$69,244	100.0	
Revenue from federal government[b]	6,377	19,153	12,776	18.5	
General revenue from own sources	38,929	95,397	56,468	81.5	100.0
Taxes	32,379	76,712	44,333	64.0	78.5
Property	14,983	30,673	15,690	22.7	27.8
Sales and gross receipts	10,437	26,519	16,082	23.2	28.5
Individual income	1,994	8,908	6,914	10.0	12.2
Corporation income	1,001	3,180	2,179	3.1	3.9
Other	3,966	7,431	3,465	5.0	6.1
Charges and miscellaneous	6,550	18,686	12,136	17.5	21.5
State					
General revenue[c]	24,448	67,312	42,864	100.0	
Revenue from federal government[b]	5,888	16,907	11,019	25.7	
Revenue from local governments	364	868	504	1.2	
General revenue from own sources	18,196	49,537	31,341	73.1	100.0
Taxes	15,848	41,931	26,083	60.9	83.2
Property	566	981	415	1.0	1.3
Sales and gross receipts	9,287	24,050	14,763	34.4	47.1
Individual income	1,764	7,527	5,763	13.4	18.4
Corporation income	1,001	3,180	2,179	5.1	7.0
Other	3,232	6,193	2,961	6.9	9.4
Charges and miscellaneous	2,348	7,606	5,258	12.3	16.8
Local					
General revenue[d]	29,621	71,943	42,322	100.0	
Revenue from federal government[b]	489	2,245	1,756	4.1	
Revenue from state governments	8,399	23,837	15,438	36.5	
General revenue from own sources	20,733	45,861	25,128	59.4	100.0
Taxes	16,531	34,781	18,250	43.1	72.6
Property	14,417	29,692	15,275	36.1	60.8
Sales and gross receipts	1,150	2,470	1,320	3.1	5.3
Individual income	230	1,381	1,151	2.7	4.6
Other	734	1,239	505	1.2	2.0
Charges and miscellaneous	4,202	11,080	6,878	16.3	27.4

Source: Same as Table C-23 (for 1969, the data are on p. 20 of the source). Figures are rounded and do not necessarily add to totals.

[a] Excludes insurance trust, utility, and liquor store revenue. Total state and local general revenue does not equal the sum of state general revenue and local general revenue because duplicative transactions between state and local governments are excluded.

[b] Includes grants-in-aid, shared taxes, payments for services performed on a reimbursement or cost-sharing basis, and payments in lieu of taxes. Excludes loans and commodities or other aids in kind.

[c] Excludes insurance trust and liquor store revenue.

[d] Excludes insurance trust, liquor store, and utility revenue.

TABLE C-25. State and Local Government Debt, Fiscal Years 1959–69

End of fiscal year	Debt outstanding	
	Amount (millions of dollars)	Index 1959 = 100
1959	64,110	100.0
1960	69,955	109.1
1961	75,023	117.0
1962	81,278	126.8
1963	85,056	132.7
1964	92,222	143.8
1965	99,512	155.2
1966	107,051	167.0
1967	113,659	177.3
1968	121,158	189.0
1969	133,548	208.3

Sources: 1959–64: U.S. Bureau of the Census, *Census of Governments, 1967,* Vol. 6, No. 5, *Historical Statistics on Governmental Finances and Employment,* p. 58; 1965–69: Bureau of the Census, *Governmental Finances in 1968–69,* p. 19.

TABLE C-26. Use of Major Tax Sources by the States, July 1, 1970

State	Tax sources					
	Sales	Individual income	Corporation income	Motor fuel	Cigarette	Alcoholic beverages
Alabama	x	x	x	x	x	x
Alaska	—	x	x	x	x	x
Arizona	x	x	x	x	x	x
Arkansas	x	x	x	x	x	x
California	x	x	x	x	x	x
Colorado	x	x	x	x	x	x
Connecticut	x	—	x	x	x	x
Delaware	—	x	x	x	x	x
Florida	x	—	—	x	x	x
Georgia	x	x	x	x	x	x
Hawaii	x	x	x	x	x	x
Idaho	x	x	x	x	x	x
Illinois	x	x	x	x	x	x
Indiana	x	x	x	x	x	x
Iowa	x	x	x	x	x	x
Kansas	x	x	x	x	x	x
Kentucky	x	x	x	x	x	x
Louisiana	x	x	x	x	x	x
Maine	x	x	x	x	x	x
Maryland	x	x	x	x	x	x

TABLE C-26. continued.

State	Sales	Individual income	Corporation income	Motor fuel	Cigarette	Alcoholic beverages
			Tax sources			
Massachusetts	x	x	x	x	x	x
Michigan	x	x	x	x	x	x
Minnesota	x	x	x	x	x	x
Mississippi	x	x	x	x	x	x
Missouri	x	x	x	x	x	x
Montana	–	x	x	x	x	x
Nebraska	x	x	x	x	x	x
Nevada	x	–	–	x	x	x
New Hampshire	–	–	x	x	x	x
New Jersey	x	–	x	x	x	x
New Mexico	x	x	x	x	x	x
New York	x	x	x	x	x	x
North Carolina	x	x	x	x	x	x
North Dakota	x	x	x	x	x	x
Ohio	x	–	–	x	x	x
Oklahoma	x	x	x	x	x	x
Oregon	–	x	x	x	x	x
Pennsylvania	x	–	x	x	x	x
Rhode Island	x	–	x	x	x	x
South Carolina	x	x	x	x	x	x
South Dakota	x	–	–	x	x	x
Tennessee	x	–	x	x	x	x
Texas	x	–	–	x	x	x
Utah	x	x	x	x	x	x
Vermont	x	x	x	x	x	x
Virginia	x	x	x	x	x	x
Washington	x	–	–	x	x	x
West Virginia	x	x	x	x	x	x
Wisconsin	x	x	x	x	x	x
Wyoming	x	–	–	x	x	x
Total	**45**	**37**	**43**	**50**	**50**	**50**

Source: Advisory Commission on Intergovernmental Relations.

TABLE C-27. The Marginal Burden of State Individual and Corporation Income Taxes before and after Allowing for Federal and State Deductibility, July 1, 1970

(In percentages, except income classes, which are in thousands of dollars)

State	Individual income tax						Corporation income tax	
	Range of state's nominal rates	Highest marginal state tax burden[a]		Marginal burden of state tax in:			State's highest nominal rate	Marginal burden of state tax in highest federal tax bracket
		Adjusted gross income class	As a percentage of adjusted gross income	Lowest federal tax bracket	Highest federal tax bracket			
Alabama[b]	1.5 – 5.0	$5– 6	3.1	1.1	0.5		5.0	1.4
Alaska[c]	3.2 –14.56[d]	18–38	4.7	2.8	4.4[e]		9.36	4.9
Arizona[f]	2.0 – 8.0	6– 8	4.2	1.5	0.7		8.0	2.1
Arkansas[c]	1.0 – 5.0	11–12	2.7	0.9	1.5		6.0	3.1
California[c]	1.0 –10.0	14–16	6.1	0.9	3.0		7.0	3.6
Colorado[b]	3.0 – 8.0	9–10	4.0	2.2	0.8		5.0	2.6[e]
Connecticut[g]	—		—	—	—		8.0	3.9
Delaware[c, h]	1.5 –11.0	8–10	5.8	1.3	3.3		6.0	3.1
Georgia[c]	1.0 – 6.0	10–12	4.1	0.9	1.8		6.0	3.1
Hawaii[g]	2.25–11.0	5– 6	6.1	1.9	3.0		6.435	3.4
Idaho[b]	2.5 – 9.0	5– 6	5.6	1.9	0.9		6.0	3.1[c]
Illinois[c]	2.5	0– 2	2.1	2.1	0.7		4.0	2.1
Indiana[c]	2.0	0– 2	1.7	1.7	0.6		2.0	1.0
Iowa[b]	0.75– 5.25	9–10	2.8	0.6	0.5		8.0	2.3
Kansas[b]	2.0 – 6.5	7– 8	3.7	1.5	0.6		4.6	1.3
Kentucky[b]	2.0 – 6.0	8–10	3.2	1.5	0.6		7.0	2.0
Louisiana[c]	2.0 – 6.0	10–12	2.7	1.7	1.8		4.0	2.1

317

TABLE C-27. continued.

| | Individual income tax | | | | | Corporation income tax | |
| | | Highest marginal state tax burden[a] | | Marginal burden of state tax in: | | | Marginal burden of |
State	Range of state's nominal rates	Adjusted gross income class	As a percentage of adjusted gross income	Lowest federal tax bracket	Highest federal tax bracket	State's highest nominal rate	state tax in highest federal tax bracket
Maine[e]	1.0 – 6.0	10–12	2.7	0.9	1.8	4.0	2.1
Maryland[c]	2.0 – 5.0	3– 4	4.1	1.7	1.5	7.0	3.6
Massachusetts[g]	4.0[i]	0– 1	3.3	3.3	1.2	7.5	3.6
Michigan[c]	2.6	0– 2	2.2	2.2	0.8	5.6	2.9
Minnesota[b]	1.5 –12.0	9–10	5.3	1.1	1.2	11.33	3.2
Mississippi[c]	3.0 – 4.0	5– 6	3.1	2.6	1.2	4.0	2.1
Missouri[b]	1.0 – 4.0	9–10	2.1	0.7	0.4	2.0	0.6
Montana[b]	2.2 –12.1	10–12	4.2	1.6	1.2	6.25	3.3[c]
Nebraska[g]	1.82– 9.1[j]	20–26	3.1	1.5	2.5	2.6	1.3
New Hampshire[c]	—	—	—	—	—	6.0	3.1
New Jersey[c]	—	—	—	—	—	4.25	2.2
New Mexico[g]	1.0 – 9.0	12–14	4.5	0.9	2.5	5.0	2.5
New York[c]	2.0 –14.0	23–26	7.0	1.7	4.2	7.0	3.6
North Carolina[c]	3.0 – 7.0	10–12	4.8[k]	2.6	2.1	6.0	3.1
North Dakota[b]	1.0 –11.0	8–10	5.3	0.7	1.1	6.0	1.7
Oklahoma[f]	1.0 – 6.0	7.5– 8	3.2	0.7	0.5	4.0	1.1
Oregon[b]	4.0 –10.0	5– 6	6.2	3.0	1.0	6.0	3.1[c]
Pennsylvania[g]	—	—	—	—	—	7.5	3.6

Rhode Island[c]	—	—	8.0	—	—	—	4.2
South Carolina[c,1]	2.0 – 7.0	10–12	6.0	4.8	1.7	2.1	3.1
Tennessee[g]	—	—	5.0	—	—	—	2.6
Utah[b]	2.0 – 6.5	5– 6	6.0	4.0	1.5	0.6	1.7
Vermont[g]	3.5 – 4.5[m]	2– 4	6.0	3.5	2.9	1.3	3.1
Virginia[c]	2.0 – 5.0	5– 6	5.0	3.9	1.7	1.5	2.6
West Virginia[c]	1.7 – 7.6	14–60	6.0	2.4	1.5	2.3[e]	3.1
Wisconsin[g]	2.7 –10.0	13–14	7.0	5.7	2.3	2.7	3.4[n]

Sources: Basic data are from Advisory Commission on Intergovernmental Relations, *State and Local Finances, Significant Features, 1967 to 1970* (1969), Tables 40, 42, and 46, supplemented by data from *Tax Administrators News*, Vol. 34 (June 1970), and the ACIR office.

a The marginal state tax burden is defined as the percent of an additional dollar of income that is taken in taxes as a result of the state income tax, using basic rates (married, filing separate returns).

b State tax deductible against federal tax and federal tax deductible against state tax.

c State tax deductible against federal tax.

d Alaska's individual income tax is 16 percent of the federal income tax liability as payable at rates in effect on Dec. 31, 1963.

e The state tax involves several rates within the highest federal tax bracket. This number is for the highest state bracket.

f State tax deductible against federal tax, federal tax deductible against state tax, and state tax deductible against state tax.

g State tax deductible against federal tax and state tax deductible against state tax.

h Federal deductibility is limited to $300 for single persons and $600 for married couples. This table assumes that federal tax is not deductible.

i The tax is on earned income and business income. Interest, dividends, and capital gains on intangibles are taxed at 8 percent, annuities at 2 percent.

j Nebraska's individual income tax is 13 percent of federal tax liabilities.

k This rate is applicable only to single persons. Since North Carolina does not allow joint returns, marginal rates for couples reach a maximum of 5.5 percent in the $5,000–$6,000 adjusted gross income class.

l Federal deductibility is limited to $500 per taxpayer. This table assumes that federal tax is not deductible.

m Vermont's individual income tax is equal to 25 percent of federal income tax liabilities, but is limited to 4.5 percent of adjusted gross income. A temporary 15 percent surcharge beginning in 1969 is not included.

n Wisconsin limits the deductibility of federal corporation income taxes to 10 percent of corporate net income before federal tax. The marginal rate shown assumes that federal tax is not deductible; inclusion of the 10 percent deduction lowers the marginal burden in the highest bracket to 3.1 percent.

APPENDIX D

Bibliographical Notes

Chapter 1.   Introduction

Among standard textbooks in public finance devoting considerable space to federal taxation are the following: James M. Buchanan, *The Public Finances*, 3rd ed., Richard D. Irwin, 1970; John F. Due, *Government Finance*, 4th ed., Richard D. Irwin, 1968; Harold M. Groves, *Financing Government*, 6th ed., Holt, Rinehart & Winston, 1964; and Earl R. Rolph and George F. Break, *Public Finance*, Ronald Press, 1961.

A concise treatment may be found in Otto Eckstein, *Public Finance*, 2nd ed., Prentice-Hall, 1967. The most authoritative advanced treatises are by Richard A. Musgrave, *The Theory of Public Finance*, McGraw-Hill, 1959, and Carl S. Shoup, *Public Finance*, Aldine, 1969.

Outstanding articles in the history of taxation are reprinted in Richard A. Musgrave and Alan T. Peacock, eds., *Classics in the Theory of Public Finance*, Macmillan, 1958; and in Richard A. Musgrave and Carl S. Shoup, eds., *Readings in the Economics of Taxation*, Richard D. Irwin, 1959.

The articles on "Taxation," in the *International Encyclopedia of the Social Sciences*, Macmillan and Free Press, 1968, Vol. 15, pp. 521–60, give a general overview of the objectives of taxation and analyses of the major taxes now in use in the United States and other countries. Peter Mieszkowski provides an excellent review of the literature on the incidence of taxation in "Tax Incidence Theory: The Effects of Taxes on the Distribution of Income," *Journal of Economic Literature*, Vol. 7, December 1969, pp. 1103–24. For a competent and imaginative analysis of the requirements of a modern tax system, see the Canadian *Report of the Royal Commission on Taxation* (Carter Commission), 6 vols., and the accompanying *Studies of the Royal Commission on Taxation*, 30 vols., Ottawa: Queen's Printer, 1966 and 1967.

Chapter 2. Taxes and Economic Policy

The role of taxation in economic policy is discussed in David J. Ott and Attiat F. Ott, *Federal Budget Policy*, rev. ed., Brookings Institution, 1969, Chaps. 4, 5, and 6. Wilfred Lewis, Jr., in *Federal Fiscal Policy in the Postwar Recessions*, Brookings Institution, 1962, measures the quantitative impact of the automatic stabilizers and discretionary actions taken during the post-World War II recessions and recoveries.

The various budget concepts in use by the federal government and a proposed revision of the budget, which was later adopted as the official unified budget, are discussed in *Report of the President's Commission on Budget Concepts* and *Staff Papers and Other Materials Reviewed by the President's Commission*, U.S. Government Printing Office, 1967. The economic implications of various budget concepts are analyzed in Wilfred Lewis, Jr., ed., *Budget Concepts for Economic Analysis*, Brookings Institution, 1968.

The concept of the full employment surplus and current economic thinking on the role of tax policy in economic decisions are lucidly presented in *Economic Report of the President, January 1962*, pp. 70–84. The concept is integrated into the analysis of saving and investment in *Economic Report of the President, January 1966*, pp. 42–44. For an able defense of the full employment surplus and an analysis of the problems of interpretation during inflationary periods, see Arthur M. Okun and Nancy H. Teeters, "The Full Employment Surplus Revisited," in Arthur M. Okun and George L. Perry, eds., *Brookings Papers on Economic Activity* (1:1970), pp. 77–110. Also worth reading are: the rationale for the 1964 tax cut in *Economic Report of the President, January 1963*, pp. 66–83, and Walter W. Heller, *New Dimensions of Political Economy*, Harvard University Press, 1966; and the discussion of the Employment Act on its twentieth anniversary in *Economic Report of the President, January 1966*, pp. 170–86.

The budget policy of the Committee for Economic Development was first presented in *Taxes and the Budget: A Program for Prosperity in a Free Economy*, A Statement on National Policy by the Research and Policy Committee, CED, 1947. A shorter version of the policy is given in CED's pamphlet, *The Stabilizing Budget Policy: What It Is and How It Works*, CED, 1950. For a discussion and critique of this policy, see Walter W. Heller, "CED's Stabilizing Budget Policy After Ten Years," *American Economic Review*, Vol. 47, September 1957, pp. 634–51 (reprinted in *Readings in Business Cycles*, Richard D. Irwin, 1965, pp. 696–712).

The most recent estimates of the built-in flexibility of the federal tax system and its components were prepared by William H. Waldorf, "Long-Run Federal Tax Functions: A Statistical Analysis," Office of Business Economics, U.S. Department of Commerce, Staff Working Paper in Economics and Statistics, No. 15, 1968.

The literature on fiscal policy and its impact on economic growth and stability is very large. For a sample of the best in this literature, see Paul A. Samuelson, "Principles and Rules in Modern Fiscal Policy: A Neo-Classical Reformulation," *Money, Trade, and Economic Growth: Essays in Honor of John Henry Williams*, Macmillan, 1951, pp. 157–76; Herbert Stein and Edward F. Denison, "High Employment and Growth in the American Economy," *Goals for Americans: The Report of the President's Commission on National Goals*, Prentice-Hall, 1960, pp. 163–90; *Foreign Tax Policies and Economic Growth*, A Conference Report of the National Bureau of Economic Research and the Brookings Institution, Columbia University Press, 1966; Albert Ando, E. Cary Brown, and Ann F. Friedlaender, *Studies in Economic Stabilization*, Brookings Institution, 1968; Walter W. Heller and others, *Fiscal Policy for a Balanced Economy*, Organisation for Economic Co-operation and Development, 1968; Arthur M. Okun, *The Political Economy of Prosperity*, Brookings Institution, 1970; and Milton Friedman and Walter W. Heller, *Monetary vs. Fiscal Policy*, Norton, 1969.

The issues raised by wage-price or incomes policies to help reconcile full employment with price stability are presented in George P. Shultz and Robert Z. Aliber, eds., *Guidelines, Informal Controls, and the Market Place*, University of Chicago Press, 1966, and John Sheahan, *The Wage-Price Guideposts*, Brookings Institution, 1967. The basic empirical work on the relation between unemployment, wages, and prices in the United States was done by George L. Perry, *Unemployment, Money Wage Rates, and Inflation*, MIT Press, 1966. For an excellent analysis of the costs of inflation and of slowing it down, see Arthur M. Okun, "Inflation: The Problems and Prospects Before Us," in Arthur M. Okun and others, *Inflation: The Problems It Creates and the Policies It Requires*, New York University Press, 1970, pp. 1–53 (reprinted as Brookings Reprint 182).

For a discussion of national debt policy, see Marshall A. Robinson, *The National Debt Ceiling*, Brookings Institution, 1959. The latest thinking on the "burden" of the national debt is summarized in James M. Ferguson, ed., *Public Debt and Future Generations*, University of North Carolina Press, 1964.

Criteria for evaluating government expenditures are discussed in Francis M. Bator, *The Question of Government Spending*, Harper, 1960; Jesse Burkhead, *Government Budgeting*, John Wiley, 1956; Robert Dorfman, ed., *Measuring Benefits of Government Investments*, Brookings Institution,

1965; and Samuel B. Chase, Jr., ed., *Problems in Public Expenditure Analysis*, Brookings Institution, 1968. The methods of evaluating government are discussed critically in Charles L. Schultze, *The Politics and Economics of Public Spending*, Brookings Institution, 1968; and Peter O. Steiner, *Public Expenditure Budgeting*, Brookings Institution, 1969.

Chapter 3.   The Tax Legislative Process

The standard work on the tax legislative process is Roy Blough, *The Federal Taxing Process*, Prentice-Hall, 1952. In addition to the discussion of legislative procedures, this book examines in detail the interest and pressure groups involved in tax legislation and also reviews the considerations relating to the level and distribution of taxes. The political cross-currents that influence the tax decision-making process are analyzed in Edward S. Flash, Jr., *Economic Advice and Presidential Leadership: The Council of Economic Advisers*, Columbia University Press, 1965, Chap. 5; John F. Manley, *The Politics of Finance: The House Committee on Ways and Means*, Little, Brown, 1970; and Ira Sharkansky, *The Politics of Taxing and Spending*, Bobbs-Merrill, 1969.

The reader will obtain a good insight into the intricacies of the legislative process by reviewing the tax messages, hearings, and committee reports relating to any one of the major tax bills enumerated in Table 3-1. The Tax Reform Act of 1969 left the most voluminous official history, including the following U.S. Congress publications: (1) *Tax Reform Studies and Proposals, U.S. Treasury Department*, Joint Publication of the House Ways and Means Committee and Senate Finance Committee, 91 Cong. 1 sess. (1969), Parts 1, 2, 3, and 4; (2) *Tax Reform, 1969*, Hearings before the House Ways and Means Committee, 91 Cong. 1 sess. (1969), 15 parts; (3) *Tax Reform Act of 1969*, House Committee on Ways and Means, House Report 91-413, 91 Cong. 1 sess. (1969), Parts 1 and 2; (4) *Tax Reform Act of 1969*, Hearings before the Senate Finance Committee, 91 Cong. 1 sess. (1969), 7 parts; (5) *Tax Reform Act of 1969*, Senate Finance Committee, Senate Report 91-552, 91 Cong. 1 sess. (1969); (6) *Tax Reform Act of 1969*, Conference Report, House Report 91-782, 91 Cong. 1 sess. (1969); (7) *Summary of Senate Amendments to H.R. 13270, Tax Reform Act of 1969*, Prepared by the Joint Committee on Internal Revenue Taxation, 91 Cong. 1 sess. (1969), Parts 1 and 2; (8) Public Law 91-172, 83 Stat. 487; (9) *Revenue Estimates Relating to the House, Senate, and Conference Versions of H.R. 13270, Tax Reform Act of 1969*, Prepared by the staff of the Joint Committee on Internal Revenue Taxation (1969).

The congressional method of conducting responsible and thorough reviews of federal tax issues is best illustrated by the 1955 inquiry of the

Joint Committee on the Economic Report and the 1959 inquiry of the House Ways and Means Committee. In each case, a set of papers by leading experts was first published, and hearings or discussions on these papers were later held to permit the committee members to interrogate the experts. See the U.S. Congress publications: Joint Committee on the Economic Report, *Federal Tax Policy for Economic Growth and Stability*, 84 Cong. 1 sess. (1955), 2 vols. (Papers and Hearings); and House Ways and Means Committee, *Tax Revision Compendium*, Compendium of Papers on Broadening the Tax Base (1959), Vols. 1–3, and *Income Tax Revision*, Panel Discussions, 86 Cong. 1 sess. (1960). Federal excise taxes were evaluated in a series of papers by some of the nation's leading tax experts in House Ways and Means Committee, *Excise Tax Compendium* (1964); panel discussions on June 15 and 16, 1964, were published in *Federal Excise Tax Structure*, 88 Cong. 2 sess. (1964), Part 2, and subsequent hearings were published in Parts 3–6. These papers and hearings were very influential in the preparations for the Excise Tax Reduction Act of 1965.

Chapter 4.   The Individual Income Tax

The most authoritative treatise on this tax is Richard Goode, *The Individual Income Tax*, Brookings Institution, 1964. A scholarly analysis of the arguments for and against progression will be found in Walter J. Blum and Harry Kalven, Jr., *The Uneasy Case for Progressive Taxation*, University of Chicago Press, 1953; a recent review of the issues is given in Charles O. Galvin and Boris I. Bittker, *The Income Tax: How Progressive Should It Be?*, American Enterprise Institute for Public Policy Research, 1969. The reader will also wish to consult the following classics: Henry C. Simons, *Personal Income Taxation*, University of Chicago Press, 1938; and William Vickrey, *Agenda for Progressive Taxation*, Ronald Press, 1947.

The best empirical analyses of the impact of income taxation on economic incentives, based on interviews with individual taxpayers, are J. Keith Butters, Lawrence E. Thompson, and Lynn L. Bollinger, *Effects of Taxation: Investments by Individuals*, Graduate School of Business Administration, Harvard University, 1953; George F. Break, "Income Taxes and Incentives to Work: An Empirical Study," *American Economic Review*, Vol. 47, September 1957, pp. 529–49; and Robin Barlow, Harvey E. Brazer, and James N. Morgan, *Economic Behavior of the Affluent*, Brookings Institution, 1966.

Estimates of the built-in flexibility of the individual income tax are given by William H. Waldorf, "The Responsiveness of Federal Personal Income Taxes to Income Change," *Survey of Current Business*, December 1967, pp. 32–45.

The usefulness of the concept of a comprehensive income tax is discussed in detail by Boris I. Bittker, Charles O. Galvin, R. A. Musgrave, and Joseph A. Pechman in *A Comprehensive Income Tax Base? A Debate*, Federal Tax Press, 1968. Quantitative measures of the erosion of the individual income tax base are provided by Joseph A. Pechman, "What Would a Comprehensive Individual Income Tax Yield?" *Tax Revision Compendium* (1959), pp. 251–81, cited above, and by the official estimates of "tax expenditures" prepared by the Treasury Department, the most recent of which are given in the statement by Murray L. Weidenbaum, "How to Make Decisions on Priorities," in *Changing National Priorities*, Hearings before the Joint Economic Committee, Subcommittee on Economy in Government, 91 Cong. 2 sess. (1970), Part 1, pp. 51–58. (See Appendix Tables C–14 and C–15.) Two interesting books for the general reader on income tax erosion are Louis Eisenstein, *The Ideologies of Taxation*, Ronald Press, 1961; and Philip M. Stern, *The Great Treasury Raid*, Random House, 1962.

The major structural features of the individual income tax are discussed in detail in the following sources: Michael E. Levy, *Income Tax Exemptions*, Amsterdam: North-Holland, 1960; Harold M. Groves, *Federal Tax Treatment of the Family*, Brookings Institution, 1963; C. Harry Kahn, *Personal Deductions in the Federal Income Tax*, Princeton University Press for the National Bureau of Economic Research, 1960, and *Employee Compensation Under the Income Tax*, Columbia University Press, 1968; Lawrence H. Seltzer, *The Nature and Tax Treatment of Capital Gains and Losses*, National Bureau of Economic Research, 1951, and *The Personal Exemptions in the Income Tax*, Columbia University Press for the National Bureau of Economic Research, 1968; David J. Ott and Allan H. Meltzer, *Federal Tax Treatment of State and Local Securities*, Brookings Institution, 1963; Martin David, *Alternative Approaches to Capital Gains Taxation*, Brookings Institution, 1968; and Arnold C. Harberger and Martin J. Bailey, eds., *The Taxation of Income from Capital*, Brookings Institution, 1969.

Negative taxation in the form suggested in the text was first discussed by Milton Friedman in *Capitalism and Freedom*, University of Chicago Press, 1962, pp. 191–94. The philosophy and mechanics of negative taxation are analyzed in detail in Christopher Green, *Negative Taxes and the Poverty Problem*, Brookings Institution, 1967, and James Tobin, Joseph A. Pechman, and Peter M. Mieszkowski, "Is A Negative Income Tax Practical?" *Yale Law Journal*, Vol. 77, November 1967 (reprinted as Brookings Reprint 142). The President's Commission on Income Maintenance Programs recommended a negative income tax for the United States in its report, *Poverty Amid Plenty, The American Paradox*, U.S. Government Printing Office, 1969; background materials prepared for the Commission are assembled in *Background Papers*, U.S. Government Printing Office, 1970, and *Technical Studies*, U.S. Government Printing Office, 1970. President Nixon's family assistance plan is described in detail in Senate Finance Committee, *H.R. 16311, The Family Assistance Act of 1970*, Revised and Resubmitted to the Senate Committee on Finance by the Administration, 91 Cong. 2 sess. (1970).

Chapter 5.   The Corporation Income Tax

Richard Goode's classic, *The Corporation Income Tax*, John Wiley, 1951, provides a thorough analysis and appraisal of the role of the corporation income tax. A discussion of the merits of the corporation income tax in comparison with other taxes is given in a symposium volume of the Tax Institute of America, *Alternatives to Present Federal Taxes*, the Institute, 1964.

For a sample of the differing viewpoints on the incidence of the corporation income tax, see Marian Krzyzaniak and Richard A. Musgrave, *The Shifting of the Corporation Income Tax*, Johns Hopkins Press, 1963; Challis A. Hall, Jr., "Direct Shifting of the Corporation Income Tax in Manufacturing," *American Economic Review*, Vol. 54, May 1964, pp. 258–71; Arnold C. Harberger, "The Incidence of the Corporation Income Tax," *Journal of Political Economy*, Vol. 70, June 1962, pp. 215–40; Marian Krzyzaniak, ed., *Effects of Corporation Income Tax*, Wayne State University Press, 1966; Robert J. Gordon, "The Incidence of the Corporation Income Tax in U.S. Manufacturing, 1925–62," *American Economic Review*, Vol. 57, September 1967, pp. 731–58; and Peter Mieszkowski, "Tax Incidence Theory: The Effects of Taxes on the Distribution of Income," cited above for Chapter 1.

The treatment of dividends under the income taxes has been investigated thoroughly in two books by Daniel M. Holland, *The Income-Tax Burden on Stockholders*, Princeton University Press for the National Bureau of Economic Research, 1958, and *Dividends Under the Income Tax*, Princeton University Press for NBER, 1962. The influence of federal taxation on corporate financial policy is appraised in Dan Throop Smith, *Effects of Taxation: Corporate Financial Policy*, Graduate School of Business Administration, Harvard University, 1952. John A. Brittain in *Corporate Dividend Policy*, Brookings Institution, 1966, measures the impact of the income taxes on the dividend payout policy of corporations.

The basic article on the incentive effects of depreciation is by E. Cary Brown, "Business-Income Taxation and Investment Incentives," in Lloyd A. Metzler and others, *Income, Employment and Public Policy: Essays in Honor of Alvin H. Hansen*, W. W. Norton, 1948. Another useful article on investment incentives is Sam B. Chase, Jr., "Tax Credits for Investment Spending," *National Tax Journal*, Vol. 15, March 1962, pp. 32–52. The need for liberalized depreciation policies in taxation (before the adoption of these policies in recent years) was ably presented by George W. Terborgh in *Realistic Depreciation Policy*, Machinery and Allied Products Institute (MAPI), 1954. Terborgh has also provided a succinct summary of the effects of the investment credit and depreciation changes in 1962 on rates of return in *Incentive Value of the Investment Credit, The Guideline Depreciation System, and the Corporate Rate Reduction*, MAPI, 1964. Measures of the impact on investment of accelerated depreciation and the investment credit are provided by Gary Fromm, ed., *Tax Incentives and Capital Spending*, Brookings Institution, 1971.

Other structural features of the corporation income tax are discussed in Stephen L. McDonald, *Federal Tax Treatment of Income from Oil and Gas*, Brookings Institution, 1963; Lawrence B. Krause and Kenneth W. Dam, *Federal Tax Treatment of Foreign Income*, Brookings Institution, 1964, and Peggy B. Musgrave, *United States Taxation of Foreign Investment Income*, Harvard Law School, International Tax Program, 1969; *Treasury Department Report on Private Foundations, February 2, 1965*, Senate Finance Committee Print, 89 Cong. 1 sess. (1965); Richard E. Slitor, *The Federal Income Tax in Relation to Housing*, prepared for the National Commission on Urban Problems, Research Report No. 5, U.S. Government Printing Office, 1968. The effect of the corporation income tax on export prices is analyzed by Robert Z. Aliber and Herbert Stein in "The Price of U.S. Exports and the Mix of U.S. Direct and Indirect Taxes," *American Economic Review*, Vol. 54, September 1964, pp. 703–10. A report of the National Bureau of Economic Research and the Brookings Institution, *The Role of Direct and Indirect Taxes in the Federal Revenue System*, Princeton University Press, 1964, discusses the effect of various taxes on the balance of payments.

Chapter 6.   Consumption Taxes

There are excellent treatises on the major general consumption taxes. John F. Due in *Sales Taxation*, University of Illinois Press, 1957, discusses the role of consumption taxes in the tax structure and evaluates the different forms and features of sales and value added taxes, taking the experience of various countries into account. A brilliant defense of, and plea for, the adoption of a graduated expenditure tax may be found in Nicholas Kaldor, *An Expenditure Tax*, London: George Allen & Unwin, 1955. The value added tax is explored by Clara K. Sullivan in *The Tax on Value Added*, Columbia University Press, 1965. Daniel C. Morgan, Jr., appraises the retail sales tax in the light of recent developments in economic analysis in *Retail Sales Tax: An Appraisal of New Issues*, University of Wisconsin Press, 1964.

The relative merits of income and consumption taxes are examined in detail in *The Role of Direct and Indirect Taxes in the Federal Revenue System*, cited above for Chapter 5. For an evaluation of the federal excise tax structure, see the *Excise Tax Compendium*, cited above for Chapter 3.

Chapter 7.   Payroll Taxes

The literature on payroll taxes is an outgrowth of the discussions of financing the social security system. One of the earliest analyses of payroll taxation is contained in Seymour E. Harris, *Economics of Social Security*, McGraw-Hill, 1941; Part II of this volume is devoted to the incidence of payroll taxes. For a recent analysis, see Joseph A. Pechman, Henry J. Aaron, and Michael K. Taussig, *Social Security: Perspectives for Reform*, Brookings Institution, 1968, Chap. VIII. For a comprehensive analysis of the economic and distributional effects of payroll taxes, see the forthcoming Brookings Institution volume by John A. Brittain, *Payroll Taxes for Social Security*.

The reader will also wish to refer to Margaret S. Gordon, *The Economics of Welfare Policies*, Columbia University Press, 1963; John J. Carroll, *Alternative Methods of Financing Old-Age, Survivors, and Disability Insurance*, Institute of Public Administration, University of Michigan, 1960; Richard A. Lester, *The Economics of Unemployment Compensation*, Industrial Relations Section, Princeton University, 1962; William Haber and Merrill G. Murray, *Unemployment Insurance in the American Economy*, Richard D. Irwin, 1966; and *The American System of Social Insurance: Its Philosophy, Impact, and Future Development*, edited by William G. Bowen, Frederick H. Harbison, Richard A. Lester, and Herman M. Somers, McGraw-Hill, 1968. Questions of financing are discussed in the reports of the Advisory Council on Social Security.

A comprehensive survey of social security systems in other countries is summarized in U.S. Department of Health, Education, and Welfare, Social Security Administration, Office of Research and Statistics, *Social Security Programs Throughout the World, 1969*, U.S. Government Printing Office, 1970.

Chapter 8.   Estate and Gift Taxes

Although it is out of date now as a statement of current law, the classic account of the development of the federal estate and gift taxes in this country is still Randolph E. Paul, *Federal Estate and Gift Taxation*, 2 vols., Little, Brown, 1942, and *1946 Supplement*, Little, Brown, 1946. A later historical review and analysis of these taxes is Louis Eisenstein, "The Rise and Decline of the Estate Tax," *Federal Tax Policy for Economic Growth and Stability*, Papers Submitted to the Joint Committee on the Economic Report, 1955, cited above, pp. 819–47 (reprinted with minor changes in *Tax Law Review*, Vol. 11, March 1956, pp. 223–59). The most recent volume on wealth taxation is by Alan A. Tait, *The Taxation of Personal Wealth*, University of Illinois Press, 1967.

Robert J. Lampman provides estimates of the size distribution of wealth in the United States in *The Share of Top Wealth-Holders in National Wealth, 1922–56*, Princeton University Press for the National Bureau of Economic Research, 1962, based largely on data from federal estate tax returns. His estimates were updated in U.S. Internal Revenue Service, *Statistics of Income—1962, Personal Wealth Estimated from Estate Tax Returns*, 1967.

The first estimates of the amount of gift and trust transfers were made on the basis of 1945 estate tax returns and prior gift tax returns of the same decedents. These estimates were presented by Secretary of the Treasury John W. Snyder in Exhibit 5 of his statement before the House Ways and Means Committee on February 3, 1950, and published in Vol. 1 of the Hearings, *Revenue Revision of 1950*, 81 Cong. 2 sess. (1950), pp. 75–89. More recent data on gift and trust transfers and a thorough analysis of the major structural problems in estate and gift taxation may be found in Carl S. Shoup, *Federal Estate and Gift Taxes*, Brookings Institution, 1966. The use of trusts and the methods of taxing them under the transfer taxes are explored in detail in Gerald R. Jantscher, *Trusts and Estate Taxation*, Brookings Institution, 1967.

G. S. A. Wheatcroft, ed., *Estate and Gift Taxation, A Comparative Study*, London: Sweet & Maxwell, 1965, provides a comparative analysis of the transfer taxes in Great Britain, Australia, Canada, and the United States.

The recommendations of the American Law Institute estate and gift tax project are contained in *Federal Estate and Gift Taxation: Recommendations Adopted by the American Law Institute and Reporters' Studies*, American Law Institute, 1969. The proposals of the Carter Commission in Canada appear in Vol. 3, Chap. 17, and Vol. 4, Chap. 21, of the *Report of the Royal Commission on Taxation*, cited above for Chapter 1. A model accessions tax was worked out in detail under the direction of the American Law Institute estate and gift tax project and appears in their report cited above. A briefer description is contained in William D. Andrews, "The Accessions Tax Proposal," *Tax Law Review*, Vol. 22 (May 1967), pp. 589–633.

Chapter 9.   State and Local Taxes

The best general sources on the state-local tax structure and the major issues in this area are: L. L. Ecker-Racz, *The Politics and Economics of State-Local Finance*, Prentice-Hall, 1970; James A. Maxwell, *Financing State and Local Governments*, Brookings Institution, rev. ed., 1969; Dick Netzer, *State-Local Finance and Intergovernmental Fiscal Relations*, Brookings Institution, 1969; and Advisory Commission on Intergovernmental Relations, *Tax Overlapping in the United States, 1964*, U.S. Government Printing Office, 1964, and *State and Local Finances: Significant Features, 1967 to 1970*, U.S. Government Printing Office, 1969.

The literature on the property tax is very large. Jens P. Jensen, *Property Taxation in the United States*, University of Chicago Press, 1931, provides an evaluation of this tax from the vantage point of the late 1920s and early 1930s. Dick Netzer, *Economics of the Property Tax*, Brookings Institution, 1966, is the most recent authoritative analysis of the economic impact of the tax and of its role in the U.S. tax system. Recent developments in property tax administration are summarized in the Advisory Commission on Intergovernmental Relations staff information report, *The Role of the States in Strengthening the Property Tax*, U.S. Government Printing Office, 1963, 2 vols. Problems of land value taxation are discussed in *Building the American City*, Report of the National Commission on Urban Problems, House Document 91-34, U.S. Government Printing Office, 1969, Part 4, Chap. 6. Increases in the value of real estate are estimated by Allen D. Manvel, "Trends in the Value of Real Estate and Land, 1956 to 1966," in *Three Land Research Studies*, Prepared for the National Commission on Urban Problems, Research Report No. 12, U.S. Government Printing Office, 1968.

Federal-state-local fiscal relations may be studied by referring to ACIR, *Measures of State and Local Fiscal Capacity and Tax Effort*, the Commission, 1962; ACIR, *Fiscal Balance in the American Federal System* (2 vols.), U.S. Government Printing Office, 1967; James A. Maxwell, *Tax Credits and Intergovernmental Fiscal Relations*, Brookings Institution, 1962; ACIR, *The Role of Equalization in Federal Grants*, the Commission, 1964; Richard A. Musgrave, ed., *Essays in Fiscal Federalism*, Brookings Institution, 1965; George F. Break, *Intergovernmental Fiscal Relations in the United States*, Brookings Institution, 1967.

The literature on revenue sharing is summarized in *Revenue Sharing and Its Alternatives: What Future for Fiscal Federalism?* Hearings before the Subcommittee on Fiscal Policy of the Joint Economic Committee, 90 Cong. 1 sess. (1967). The pros and cons of revenue sharing are discussed in Walter W. Heller and others, *Revenue Sharing and the City*, Harvey S. Perloff and Richard P. Nathan, eds., Johns Hopkins Press, 1968, and *Financing State and Local Governments*, Federal Reserve Bank of Boston, 1970. President Nixon's revenue-sharing plan is compared with a number of other variants in Murray L. Weidenbaum and Robert L. Joss, "Alternative Approaches to Revenue Sharing: A Description and Framework for Evaluation," *National Tax Journal*, Vol. 23, March 1970, pp. 2–22.

For more specific aspects of intergovernmental relations, see *Coordination of State and Federal Inheritance, Estate, and Gift Taxes*, ACIR, 1961; *Federal-State Coordination of Personal Income Taxes*, ACIR, 1965; and Report of the Special Subcommittee on State Taxation of Interstate Commerce of the House Committee on the Judiciary, *State Taxation of Interstate Commerce*, Vols. 1 and 2, House Report 1480, 88 Cong. 2 sess. (1964), and Vols. 3 and 4, House Reports 565 and 952, 89 Cong. 1 sess. (1965).

Numerous official state and city tax commission reports provide excellent sources of information and analyses on state-local tax problems. Among the best are *Report of the Governor's Minnesota Tax Study Committee, 1956*, Colwell Press, 1956; *Michigan Tax Study Staff Papers*, Lansing, Michigan, 1958; University of Wisconsin Tax Study Committee, *Wisconsin's State and Local Tax Burden: Impact, Incidence and Tax Revision Alternatives*, University of Wisconsin, 1959; University of Maryland, College of Business and Public Administration, *Maryland Tax Study*, the University, 1965; City of New York, Temporary Commission on City Finances, *Toward Fiscal Strength: Overcoming New York City's Financial Dilemma*, Second Interim Report, New York City, November 1965 (available from Municipal Reference Library); and *Report of Governor's Revenue Study Committee, 1968–69*, State of Illinois, 1969. The intergovernmental problems of urban communities and methods of increasing the fiscal resources of the nation's cities are discussed in ACIR, *Urban America and the Federal System*, U.S. Government Printing Office, 1969.

Appendix A.   Historical Notes

Edwin R. A. Seligman in "Income Tax," *Encyclopaedia of the Social Sciences*, Macmillan, 1932, Vol. 7, pp. 626–39, traces income taxation in Europe and the United States up to the early 1930s. The reader may also wish to refer to the history of the development of progression in the British income tax in F. Shehab, *Progressive Taxation*, Oxford University Press, 1953. A history of taxation in this country through 1951 is provided in Randolph Paul, *Taxation in the United States*, Little, Brown, 1954. Lewis H. Kimmel analyzes the changes in American attitudes toward government taxing, spending, and borrowing in *Federal Budget and Fiscal Policy, 1789–*

1958, Brookings Institution, 1959. Herbert Stein traces the changes in attitudes toward federal budget deficits by government officials, economists, and businessmen in *The Fiscal Revolution in America*, University of Chicago Press, 1969.

The *Annual Reports of the Secretary of the Treasury on the State of the Finances* summarize the major features of tax legislation enacted each year in a section entitled "Taxation Developments." Comprehensive summaries of tax rates are provided for the period 1913–40 in the 1940 Report (pp. 466–534); 1940–50 in the 1950 Report (pp. 251–80); and 1950–62 in the 1962 Report (pp. 370–402).

Index*

* References to tables and charts are in italics.

333